Lens Grinder's Shadow

The Middle American / This Year's Harvest

Michael Roth

I0638016

This book is a fabrication. Any resemblance to real events or persons,
living or dead, is purely imaginary.

Printed in the United States of America

First Printing, 2023
Cover: Markus Maurer, drawing of Plato's 'Allegory of the Cave'

Paperback ISBN: 978-1-7343428-4-0
Library of Congress Control Number: 2023947179

Lensgrinder, Ltd.
Kirkland, WA 98033

Questions, comments, concerns? mtroth@lensgrinder.com

Studies in Phenomenology & Social Philosophy

Lensgrinder, Ltd

Kirkland, WA

In memory of
Annie Pritchard

A reminder that man comes from the earth-mother, that he
returns to her, and that at each step a shadow walks by his side.
—Luce Irigaray, Marine Lover of Friedrich Nietzsche

Contents

Lens Grinder's Shadow

The duende.... Where is the duende? Through the empty archway a wind of the spirit enters, blowing insistently over the heads of the dead, in search of new landscapes and unknown accents: a wind with the odor of a child's saliva, crushed grass, and medusa's veil, announcing the endless baptism of freshly created things.

—Federico García Lorca
Theory and Play of *The Duende*

1.8

the middle american

1.8.1.X.19.86.9.23 [ref(..85.10.15)]

Being outside of time and desire, waving a hand to get back in it. Jerking abruptly forward, then falling back, dreamlike, with a subconscious plunge through night thrust into daylight.

> *Midway this way of life we're bound upon,*
> *I woke to find myself in a dark wood,*
> *Where the right road was wholly lost and gone.*
> [Dante's Inferno][1]

Halitosis brushed away, poking the yoke by dipping the tip, meiosis is a battle against time. A double division, the double doubled leaves four. Four twice makes eight. There are eight, but only one each on the other end. Some insist and remain eight for a whole life long. Limbs flailing and lurching about, buckle it up and strap it on. Fanny fangle this one so that one rears clear, it's a burden no longer with its weight on the hip.

[8th note is still a whole note. No, it isn't. Yes, I mean, it's an 8th note, but that doesn't mean 1/8th of a note. You're being pedantic. It's about time, but still one single note able to stand on its own, that's what I mean. Well, if you say so.]

"How does it go again, what do they say?" Finishing with the roll and jam. Heading off to pack up and get ready for the day's hike ahead. Hardly anything to do, nothing unpacked the night before. Hitting the loo just in case.

[It was a ten-step process repeating itself repeating itself repeating itself. Unlike mitosis, it was, in all ways, fourfold. With matriarchy, there were three duds, but in patriarchy, the whole swarm was good to go.]

He is out the door of the youth hostel in Bregenz and on the way up the street to make his way into the mountains. One foot in front of the other. With the ascent comes the glimmering expanse of the lake behind and the road snaking through thick woods in front.

"How does it go again?" Tying the shoe. For good this time. Making sure all the important things are within easy reach. Passport, check. Water

---

[1] Dante citations are from The Divine Comedy, either the Sayers or the Longfellow translations, both public domain.

bottle. Roger that. Unzip and rifle through the things at the top, checking for the fourth time that everything is where it ought to be.

[Interphase copy copy copy microtubules extended... ...two centrosomes each contained two centrioles...]

"What makes us think we know how to count?" Leaning forward against the heavy weight of the pack, holding it in place, thumbs tucked. Marching orders are in place. Forward.

—Prophase Eins.

[Copies condense and there were sister chromatids... ...pairs they were pairing, sisters they were sistering... ...bits exchanged... ...membranes dissolved... ...spindles between the centrioles...]

—Metaphase Eins.

[...the chorus line began to kick... ...the equator began to form... ...opposed centrioles with spindles reached out to touch... ...spindles hooked the chromosomes, and everything began to tangle...]

—Anaphase Eins.

[...spindles pulled apart pairs... ...sweetness abounded around the boundary beneath the fire's glow... ...aligned from pole to pole to reach for the end of the sit-down, break-away that rolled them over again and again... ...chromosomes apart chromatids remain...]

—Telophase Eins.

[...and and and cytokinetosis cytomimosis cytokinesis moved complete, gathered together, belonging together, a mem-brain appeared and formed between the pools, either side the poles the pools the pale puddles of poodling mem-brainy brawn...]

There spindles a men-brain along that road into the Alps up and away from the watery boundary between three German-speaking countries: der Bodensee.

"Zwei Zwei, bitte Zwei"

—Prophase Zwei.

[Two daughters and their 23 chromosomes 23 pairs of chromatids condensing dancing densing dancing condensing... ...X marks the spot... ...the men-brain dissolves, and the daughters are released... ...you are free daughters... ...go as you will... ...be as you like... ...and bold so bold be bold daughters all. Duplicate for more spindles... ...four more... ...spindly... ...they are spinning... ...duplicating again around the pole... ...pooling pole... ...men-brains dissolving to form poodles...]

—Metaphase Zwei.

[Time to line up again, daughters, along the equator... ....more poling... ...more aligning... ...more reaching... ...repeating... ...repeating... (did I say repeating?) Repeating. There was repeating. Peating. Eating. Ating. Ting. Ing. Ng. G... ...careful lest the spindles attach to your sister... ...and twist her... ...she turned round and round like a spinning top... ...hop-poppling over the London Bridge she skinned her knee, look how proud... ...a buzzing bee was she...]

—Anaphase Zwei.

[Spindles spun chromatids apart, one or the other poles poled and more poodling, but no more men-brains... ...pulled apart the chromatoads saw to that... Rib it... Trade ya a rib for an apple, deary doe dreary me... ...poof there were chromosomes...]

—Telophase Zwei.

[...and and and... ...just kidding... CYTOKINESIS! Two gathered in one. When do they dodge the ball? Needed a new men-brain... ...couldn't complete the pulling and parting without a men-brain... ...there were these granddaughters from sister pairs and poodles, spindles and bindles...]

On the one hand, an egg with three strips of bacon. On the other, a teeny tiny poodle of sperm...

The black rucksack, fastened securely, weighs under thirty pounds and the part of the T-shirt in contact with both back and overshirt is soaked with sweat from the trapped heat of the high sun.

Setting out from Bregenz wearing a pair of denim jeans but now the movement overheats the cotton-covered, furry legs. Walking a few steps into the woods, pulling a pair of cut-off army pants from the rucksack, and changing attire while looking through the brush at the passing cars on the slowly ascending mountain road. The heavy boots, still a bit stiff, pinch the feet.

Each stride a qualitatively different maneuver, he eschews the sequence that grips his feet plodding along every new world step back to the road. The humpback men-brain bears a water bottle overfull at the topmost part of the sack. He can't affix it to himself, so he turns around now and again to unzip and de-pack the bottle to tilt and sip a steady stream.

[Humpedy your way up the road you dumpedy one... ...rat-a-tat-tat, the drumming dromedary droned...]

—I am that camel and well laden slurp slurp...

He consoles himself with expectations of the coming comfort in boots once broken.

(She lifted her legs straight up and held them stiffly together, the pink tights were what you saw. Your hands slipped under her skirt to find the elastic band at the waist and peeled them away as she wriggled to help you get them free from beneath her weight upon the bed.)

The sour white grapes plucked from the roadside vine return him to the forced labor of ascension. Always a period of breaking-in and adjustment, the ascent mingles the source time he carries with the target roads he treads.

—Aesthetics go left. Morality right. Everyone remain in line until your number is called.

Eventually the uphill climb levels off. The road continues winding through the mountains and the views of the valley prove worthy of the effort. The foliage, primarily Norway spruce, is dappled with the deciduous beech, ash, and sycamore tucked in among the evergreen branches making subtle specks of autumn span the visual surface.

—Spiddle me diddle. Here I have what I carry with me. Here, I am what I carry. Her pink tights. Those pink tights. Pink Tights. He he hum.

[Take the white things from everywhere in her wardrobe, in the bathroom, in the cupboards and hanging on the doors and over the backs of chairs. Take it and find the reddest fabric you can. Hold your nose if you have to. Look everywhere, inside and out, toss it in among the rest like a dryer sheet added to the wash. Behold the bold pink. Pink every which way. Burrowing and barricading. Slurping and floating. Suck, don't fuck, so pink. Round and round, the machine tussles and turns. Got it? Those are her lifting legs. Those are the elastic bands, those would be, would be, be...]

The road-running solitude and natural color fills time with change leading him toward Emerson's woods, home to Henry David.

(It was placed in the side pocket this morning, where else would it be?)

A great men-brain turns to the study of nature, understanding the necessity of his animal disguise when entering the wilderness. Is he becoming bear-brain? Stomping along the way without a care in the world, they have no fear. They don't know hesitation. When startled, they become abrupt. Swiping and snarling, they take to the long grass with machete paws and galloping swiftness. Ka-thunk. Clever monkeys wear bells so mama bear hears them coming. No one, not even a hunter, wants to sneak up on them. Such long strides walking those Massachusetts woods, counting those beans, faring that weather.

—How did that go again? There's a pathway through the woods and some hikers come upon a single, giant paw print pressed into the path. It's terrifying to find such a distance between prints with only one visible and the others buried in the grass somewhere. How gigantic must that body be?

Building bulk that bear-brain. Mashing and gnashing, Thoreau's long strides nearby are a grizzly sight.

[This man with animal instincts was the first to claim that such metamorphoses weren't bestial. Does a wolf's skill count? For pleasure or survival? Is a men-brain necessary to live? What else welcomed the split? Order the centrioles, the daughters, and the granddaughters, sisters and pairs, apples and stairs? The thinking beast survived in conditions right for his temperament. They prayed to the gods that they be selected. One of the conditions a beast with a curly-cue brain required was the free air where the men-brain grew and pulsed wild: they were willing to kill for the sake of their mind ripening as fruit, yet those minds failed (flailed?) inside that free swirl. Only after reason came did contradiction exist.]

"I should not do again what I have done once," Emerson writes.

The men-brain sings in bold proclamations not its own. Snap to! What is told to those there along the side way near the byway?

"Grüß Gott," noticing their eyes nervously darting to the overshirt.

—Don't care how hot this oven gets, ain't taking it off.

"Heilen Sie, junge. Bitte setzen Sie sich zu uns."

Sitting on the bench and eating a pear with the elderly couple who provide a cushion to protect against whatever rot they think lingers in the wood.

"Such a lovely time of year to make a trip into the mountains," they speak slowly in the German practiced in the south after learning a little in school. They tell stories about the livelihoods of the people of Vorarlberg. "There are still people here who use the plow and scythe. Do you know these words?"

"Pflug und Sense. Ja naturlich."

[They must be eighty, making them nearly forty then.]

Originally from this area, they want to know where he is from and what kind of parents he has, how he comes to be here, and what adventures he is seeking.

—Ich bin ein Jude motherfuckers... ...that's the word for traitor in your language. Try it, go on, I dare you.

(They stood cheering as the trucks rolled in whereas we stood stupid on the platform after arriving at the appointed hour. Now everyone has forgotten the gypsies and the communists, the homosexuals and the mentally ill. Memory carried bias too.)

"Vielen dank für das Obst," interrupting their efforts to learn more. Not interested in their excuses.

Moments later, his mind wanders off along the rhythms made by his feet, and he imagines the quiet lives of the farmers in the vale. Daily hard work and solitude gleaned from the territory: mountains separating villages to make plowing difficult. He sees synthetic farmers, born to the middle-class suburbanite breed but longing to return to their roots, always back to the land.

[Blut und Erde? Ehre? Boden?]

—What about their children? Do they want what they have or do they long for the comings and goings of the crowded city? Excuse me, pardon me please, just passing through. Make way, make way. And the spider beside her.

"Many would gladly trade places, surrendering everything for an underpacked rucksack and a few traveler's checks."

He says it aloud and hears the sounds echoing over the road. Frowned upon as blub-blubbery on the streets of the city, never comes the courage to speak his mind. Only now, alone on the road, do the words arrive in rhythms matching the beat in his chest.

"Only the men-brain in isolation tastes freedom. It is a laden camel, a grizzly bear," spoken aloud and instantly drowning elation in melancholy.

There are times when he forces himself to stop thinking and stay focused on the beauty around him. Then in a matter of seconds he reverses course and scolds himself for ignorant posturing.

—Is there a right way to experience the world?

"Is there a right way to experience the world?"

[Every time at the center of the cyclone, there was some ruddy rake that broke the boundaries and bled tears along at last. Bears in china shops, those giants paused, but not for long. It's meant to be broken. Experience meant to break. It broke. Each darling and every one of them with elastic bands trapped between the waist of their skirts and the weight on their bed.]

"Fe fi fo fum..."

[The other one spoke. What wastes them, he wanted to think out loud. Deeply rooted, always present, and yet they did not surface, did not speak, and did not twang. He felt he could never sing pretty songs nor settle under their shifting weight. He wrapped his hands behind, forearms hooking, to turn and move her as if he were wielding a lobster claw made for that.]

"Who were you talking about? The one from the story?"

—They love foreplay, or so I've heard.

"Which do you prefer?" It came down to in or on. It a-mounted to that.

He always asks her, because her moods do change, and he isn't looking for a monologue. He expects eye contact even when asking the most delicate questions.

Only what is missing evokes pangs of loneliness.

—Who gets a hardon with a thirty-pound sack on his back?

He renders that unto the road and moves along in search of fictional offspring erupting from some other worldly Sartre and de Beauvoir, procreating for his sake... ...and hers... Perhaps. He lifts it by the shoulder straps, buckles it at the waist, and pulls the chest strap tighter.

Arriving at a small guest house outside Hittisau, taking a room and paying extra for a shower. Then, clean and well fed from a few slices of bread with cheese, sitting down on the bed and reading from the weathered notebook.

—Why select this as subject? Why not the pink tights? Why do I always remember these judgy bits and not the filthy ones? What could be more beautiful than a hip bone bent complete?

(Bullshit, you remember it, but you choose what to replay, you decided what pain to pack, you knew what you wanted to carry. You filled it with everything that shouldn't be there, you were the one who decided this was your shadow. The skirt was mostly white, but there were pastel bits and pieces spread throughout its pattern. The touch of pink offset the tights, they think that way, shopping to make the match, they all do it.)

> "...Well geez," he said gently, hesitantly. "You're so damned
> prejudiced. You think everyone's going to be wonderful and
> nice, always giving them the benefit of the doubt. When they
> act like the shitty human beings they are, you're surprised."
> Silence.
> "You still there?"
> "Yes," quietly.
> "What's wrong?"
> "I can't believe you said that..."

—Why focus on the ending? You should train your eye on the beginning when everything was pure and sweet. Let everyone know that feeling you felt when first you saw that hip bone thusly bent...

(She was looking for an excuse, but there was no way to tell that tale. You didn't have the words. You didn't have the images. You didn't even have the feelings. The same age, you must've been ten years behind her.)

—How am I supposed to show that?

> "...You see," he said. "I didn't know what was real. You
> confused me. I didn't know what the real me was, even now
> I don't know if this is real, I can't decide. And you're not
> helping. You're trying, but you don't know either..."
> "You're not making sense. It's all real."
> "Real isn't the right word. I don't know... ...honest?"

(She was a fucking phony, but that didn't matter, you idiot. You're not looking at the right things. What was happening around him? You couldn't see any of it and yet it was all that mattered. The dialogue should be blah blah blah, like those adults in the Peanuts cartoons. Focus on the phone on the table and its otherworldly green. Look through the window next to him. Some bird or something on the branch, it had a twig sticking out of its beak, or it was singing and looking for its partner gone off somewhere and delayed by something. Was there an accident? Was he trying to attract her for the first time? He was still holding the phone in his hand but none of it mattered, she was already gone. He could have told her it was raining, and she would have had the same reaction. Can't you see it? Stop looking for the truth and stick to the facts.)

> "I have to go."
> "Please, don't go." It couldn't have been real, not then and
> not now. If it was, then the whole of reality boiled down to

an acute and accurately placed puncture wound.

—Dumb ass.

"I know, I know," it was the leggy blonde's voice. "He says
he loves you, but how far does that go? What does it mean
when he acts the way he does?"

—They help each other sustain the illusion. The sundering is an affront
and a fabrication. She's made it up to fit with what she wants to do and
called upon her friend to help her sell it. That should be the story. Why
focus on his demise?

"That's right, Dave came by and congratulated me and
talked to everybody. It was nice."
Whining at this turn of the dagger, he went on in a lifeless,
defeated tone: "Sorry, I couldn't deal with it."
"Yeah, He told me you were drunk."
Ouch. Everything comes back around.
"I don't know what to say. I feel beaten and everything I do
comes out wrong and you're not much help."
His honesty had the opposite effect than expected, she was
livid.
"You know, I don't understand you. You shock me
sometimes. You're lucky I ever hung out with you. Damn
lucky!"
He dropped his head while holding the phone in his
sweating hand.
"I mean," she went on. "You say I don't help you, but I can't
think of how I could do more for you than I already do. I
never needed you."

—Dress him in latex to complete the image, why don't you?

"Yes, of course, everything you say is right. I was damn
lucky. Thank you for everything and I'm sorry I couldn't
make better use of it."

Pulling the piece of paper out of the notebook, crumpling it up
violently, then blinking the eyes rapidly, but no seizure comes.
(She got you to admit that 2 x 2 = 5. She's not an ally. It could never
have been a reasonable discussion. Differences were too absolute and
drove you too far apart. There was no need for that in a Tyrolean style
guest house on a lonely road in western Austria. You didn't need to replay

foul memories even if they were responsible for getting you here. Being here is enough, you brought yourself along. If you could count, she'd be number two. Zwei bitte Zwei.)

Tossing the notebook onto the floor and turning off the light on the headboard, then, sinking back into the covers on the soft bed, deep into the cushion of thought and memory, fatigue sets in.

He closes his eyes shortly after sunset.

1.8.2.X.19.86.9.24 [ref(..85.10.29)]

Being outside of time and desire, waving a hand to get back in it. Jerking abruptly forward, then falling back, dreamlike, with a subconscious plunge through night thrust into daylight.

> *So, while my soul yet fled, did I contrive*
> *To turn and gaze upon that dread pass once more*
> *Whence no man yet came ever out alive,*
> [Dante's Inferno]

Upandatem urlyon, thinking misfits with the razor's edge, firing exploding hangers on. The day opens with the bread and jam of breakfast and a moisturizing feeling to the feet, thick with blisters from lightly trodden boots with Gore-Tex lining and leather outer shell. Thirty kilometers on a Tuesday and an assigned Wednesday schedule for another thirty-five.

—Oh, the pain.

Hittisau in morning: a high mountain mist while passing through a center square with a statue of some unknown warrior before stopping at the grocer where bread, cheese, and kiwi fruit can be obtained for fourteen shillings to the dollar. It is cold this morning, absent any moments guided by the light of nature, spent trekking through giant rectangular patches of farmland dotted with brown, black, and white cows that seem aggressive in the lazy way they chew their cud and grunt at pedestrian passersby clad in a blue-and-white-striped-flannel-shirt.

The day creeps through farmland at a relaxing pace of four kilometers per hour. The independence of movement along a quiet road hits home later in the day when he awakes fully with the sun that takes its time rising above the mountains, shedding its light into the valley, and breaking the scattered patches of mist. In the right pocket he carries Deutsch Marks, in the left Oesterreichisher Shillings, each enough for one day. Today he buys supplies in the grocer from his left pocket, anything else later, like accommodation, from the right. The border comes at midday and passes

without an encounter: no cars allowed on the road, no customs officers in
the booth, only a small, battered hut at the bottom of a winding path that
leads down into the valley before leveling off and heading into the natural
reserve between nations.

[Self-reliance and her-reliance didn't mix. Your truths had to be
universal and that one there on the top was your lust which bent her truths
into yours and let them toy with the foundations of logic. Oh, your
misplaced lust, if only for a moment. She couldn't change what happened,
only what it meant. She said it was, wrong, you then had to be, wrong, she
was not, and you were, wrong. You were, you are, you be, right?]

—That's a fact, Jack.

(Correspondence beyond letter-writing, thoughts today joined with
what's left of that day waiting for a ferry on the Bodensee near Konstanz.
Sitting quietly in Dingelsdorf and reading about self-reliance and learning,
in language only, about shining stars and brilliant research. On that day
language gained its object, and you became its flesh.)

On a road with an occasional ranger vehicle but no general traffic
winding lightly through the naturschutzgebeit there are walled peaks
reaching 1500 meters into the sky as represented on the hiker's map folded
nine times and stuffed in an easily accessible place at the top of the
rucksack. When hunger sets in, the sack comes off and creates a nice stool
in a foot or so of dried grass, uncut for centuries. Bread sliced with
pocketknife and cheese laid on top goes down well with swishing water
from the refilled bottle. Concentration leaves the sandwich and finds the
tattered anthology where the *Over Soul* screams from a century ago into
the reflections of this modern-day Ulysses.

[Were these movements of intelligent beasts possible without reason?
To what end did the will of man act?]

Somewhere, somehow, he walks along pathways scorning Autostop on
behalf of hiking for the sake of durability.

—That's bullshit.

[You willed your body with your made-up mind and floated among the
Alpen peaks and valleys until finally reaching the longed-for destination of
Innsbruck and its fabled ski villages in western Tyrol.]

Shunning the pains of resisting the voyage, he mechanically swings one
leg in front of the other in hopes of someday building enough space behind
to reach the goal in front.

(One day, not long ago, you were sitting on the floor studying a map of
Scandinavia while the screens in open windows hummed with the warming
winds of spring. A housemate emerged in undergarment to shower and
bicycle and, along the way, stopped to ask, "Where are you going?" Boldly,
but with imagination, you answered, "As far north as I can get for the
solstice and then back to Oslo where I'll camp my way across Sweden to

Stockholm." This early proclamation of the ideal never materialized and instead you were shuttling back and forth from Paris to Spain with so much commotion and drama that no northern thought ever entered your mind.)

[Months later and in a highly varied fashion, the ideal gained a grip.]

Marching beneath the sun and amid the mountainside of colorful trees filling the heart from time's distance receding. The tent is gone, but the roadside lunches of crude, simple food act as close facsimile to "roughing-it."

He lifts his head to the sky soon after leaving the picnic area and laughs when realizing that nothing is how he imagines it.

"Patience, perseverance, and perception," screaming to the echoless mountains and empty valley. "I found you. Those who lectured against foolish dreams have been made ridiculous. Perfection springs from the earth. Paradise is a road."

—Persistence?

The threatening sky pours forth in torrential affliction, wet certainty drips from every ragged edge.

It is raining and he is without any foul weather gear to keep him dry.

In the tiny village of Obermaiselstein, finding some shelter, a cafe with a fireplace serves as haven.

He is strong and, although soggy, doesn't see it as an obstacle. He feels the benefits of rain, himself in every droplet.

The mug of hot coffee warms the insides and the deliberate English-speaking gentleman, who offers a map of the immediate vicinity, hands over precise knowledge of the youth hostel's location. After draining the cup and folding the map to display the relevant area, setting out beneath the clearing sky, smiling in renewed vigor with the sun warming the damp clothing, and restoring the ecstasy earned in the natural reserve.

The way between Obermaiselstein and Oberstdorf can be hiked through marked trails and wooded areas. Deep in the forest, along this path, coming to a bridge that crosses the small river Rotfischbach or Lochbach, the tributary. Midway along the bridge, sliding out of the rucksack, setting it down on the wooden planks, and sitting to face north. In the distance, a mountain rises above the river with trees filling both sides of the ravine. The scene yields an urge to record its moment.

[I wouldn't let you bring the automatic camera for non-photographers for two reasons: 1) there was no room and 2) it is the mark of the tourist. Sic. Sick.]

The path is no longer isolated and there are German tourists occasionally squeezing by with cameras dangling around their necks and clattering to warn the bear. Frustrated and satisfied at once, lifting the bag and slinging it over the shoulders with a casual motion showing how easy it is to handle this burden.

The youth hostel at Oberstdorf is full of children taking a few weeks away from classes for a field trip at the beginning of the school year. There is an available bed in one of the rooms with six screaming brats away from their parents for the first time. After claiming a bunk and finding a quiet spot to sit, pulling the notebook from the rucksack, and writing:

24 September;

You would not believe the pain. My feet, my shoulders, my back, and my head, the inside of it. I shouldn't have gone back to that story. You know the one. Where I try to re-live it, fix it. How low, how foolish and silly. It can't take this fucking long to get back on my feet and start over again. No self-respecting human should ever lose his mind that way. It'll never happen again. Swear it. I was a fool and although I have learned nothing since, the cracking and breaking forced me further in leaps and bounds. Confidence can't be fragile. I have no meter to gauge it, so must keep becoming and overcoming memories that slow me down.

No more memories. Tomorrow south along a small path toward St. Anton in Austria. It'll be a short day's walk without obstacles. Knock wood.

There's a monkey on my back. Something something ideal and absolute. That shit needs to be shattered, smashed on the ground. Why can't I do that? What prevents me barreling in that direction? What is the right voice for it? Is it only possible with a high-pitched shriek? It's easy to worry about pointless things, deflating any prospect of real movement. Stop thinking about the damn money, take what you need from the world. There is nothing to fear in a zero. Use your reserves sparingly. Your needs are modest, why let loads of time leak into petty projections, bean counting and seed catalogues?

Worthless drivel. Mathematical games to prove it isn't a problem but playing them proves that it is. What if I were to decide to stop worrying? In the end, years from now, what difference would it make? Voice comes from the air around, even these silly games. If I continue playing them, they'll fill my throat and mouth and nothing I say will change that. Genuine consciousness, awareness, attending to the things that matter, that is what is most important. Emerson says that one must fully lose oneself to find the absolute. Is it worth

it? Meditation is movement, or is that mediation? Body and
mind, if there's a difference, grow stronger every day. *This*
is why I came. Today marks the 19th week.

[The daily motions lay beneath the urge for stability, and budgets fit the
bill as an old faithful upon your mind. How long will the money hold?
Damn that regression, it took hold despite having contemplated perfection
minutes beforehand. Was it ideal to constantly worry about one's welfare?
Count the nickels and dimes? What is it that you fear from that
bankruptcy? Will they make your kind into a verb to dismiss you with it?
At each lull in the way, you marked the downtime with a renewal of
concerns that were not there when your feet were in motion, when you set
upon your way from point A to point B. You were by nature wayward,
always heading toward your goal of living modestly without noticing it. For
this, things had to recede, you could not need them. Recently bit and
pricked, bloody from the nick, you *and* I confused people with things and
set our course aright along the silent and lonely way. In this hell, the echoes
pursued you. Along a line of great sincerity your markings were amiss. It
couldn't be helped. You were a young man. With a budget of between
fifteen and twenty dollars a day, you traveled a dimly lit path to throw
yourself along a trajectory that resounded forever among things and scenery
regularly changing. You read me stories of great thinkers who didn't notice
what they wore or what they ate or in what conditions they slept. Greatness
of spirit came to represent poverty in things. In wonder, we aped those men
and didn't grasp the irony until it was too late.]

Back in the room, staring at the walls and sorting through the cassettes.

(None of which happened in the wild. All around, everything
everywhere told you that things were all that mattered. You took deliberate
steps to circumvent the signs pointing down common roads. At fourteen,
you woke up and decided your life belonged to you, but you could not
mean it. Still, tilting in perspective and aiming away from the beaten path,
you became an untimely wanderer and never hesitated to leap into a Sufi's
dance alone in thought when the world forced you to spend those years in
the company of endlessly ridiculous fourteen-year-old children. With their
blood you made your meal. In your narrow neck of the woods, the other
boys and girls thought you were too weird for words. Not because of how
you dressed, or the music you listened to, but because you didn't want to
spend any time with them. This was so unlike their understanding, they had
no place for it. When you went away to college, you learned that every high
school had someone like you and now here they were together and
surprised at running into each other. Your eyes locked with hers early on,
in the first few weeks away from home, but you two went on in different
directions with links along the way that kept you close. Only later, months

later, nearly a year, did you fall in love and walk your way side-by-side in the crests and valleys of abundance, exchanging poetic sense across young lives.)

This gives hope that there are others who aren't merely the reflection of things. There comes great confusion with that hope. These empty halls are echo chambers and no voice finds its way inside without hooks and nooks to slink and slither in and out while humming along. The clarity of crystal subsides in dirty sounds, and newly minted people add the curves and lines to what he seeks. He swears to find ways to pronounce it.

(When they abruptly left you, or moved on to better things, your groans and moans sounded the alarm.)

—Is this what voice amounts to? Carrying on in the trails left by joy and sorrow at the hands of others, in the impressions left over from things?

[You raged against that. It was your purpose and morrow. Who are you now? Half this, half that? Inside and out sewn together, what kind of hurly-burly could you expect if the oceans had no part in you? The mountains and the rivers could speak for themselves, they did not need you. Whatever awe you exercised in their presence meant nothing to them. Who was it then who spoke? Hark, who goes there? Who is it that speaks?]

Lying in bed and looking up at the ceiling, unable to answer without knowing that voice is a bridge for relaying the distance in order to occupy it. Something softens the blows, arranges the impressions. It presents, articulates, and spins, but the connections are beyond any grasp. They do reach out, but still not seeing them, aim falters. Can't fathom the significance of being unwashed and disheveled, nor the effects of a three-day beard, and only concerned with those cavernous spaces and the movements they require to force air into and out of them in the most perfect resound where timbre and tone grow into notes that assemble in sequences upon the rising air.

While those images dance on the ceiling, the somber German children stream back into the room and are immediately re-energized by the new surroundings. They talk amongst themselves as if their words were secret, asking each other which one will approach to learn the gory details. One stands out at last, volunteered by his chums.

"Woher kommst du?" the blonde boy asks.

"Die USA," saying it plainly without bubbling delight at the adorable presence of the munchkin. Not impressed.

He can't care less and has no intention of altering his behavior just because the one approaching is a child. The boy is taken aback, notices without understanding. It doesn't seem right, but he goes on anyway.

"Where did you learn to speak such good German?" the boy asks.

"How do you know I speak good German?"

The children are baffled and afraid at the quick way of speaking, but

German is a harsh language, and they are used to it. He presses forward, ignoring the obstacles as the others' urge him on.

"Where in America do you come from?"

"The middle of it."

Then another blonde boy steps forward claiming he speaks enough English to carry on a conversation. "How is your mother?" he says in a staccato rhythm.

"Fine."

"How is your father?"

"Fine."

"How is your brother?"

"Fine."

"How is your sister?"

"Fine."

"How is..." the boy drops his head into his raised hand and struggles to think of another word.

"I see you speak English beautifully," enunciating rapidly in clear English. "It reminds me of the banter I heard from school children in France when they made their feeble attempts to speak my language, an action for which I was grateful since I spoke not a word of theirs."

The children applaud this long stream though they don't understand a word of it. The flow is the point.

"Do you know Sylvester Stallone?" the boy asks switching back to German.

"Raus," as a rough yowl before attaching the headphones and rolling onto the stomach, shutting the eyes, and thinking that it is only another seven or eight days until Innsbruck where once and for all the plans for winter will ripen and, no doubt, the money will expire.

[No one is themself anymore. They were nothing. They they they. They were the things they ate and the things they lifted and looked at. They were the trance in the eyes fixed on warbling tops, the earth's farts etched on time's peel. Be broken why don't ya? Be empty forever. What a waste. Animals were the richest, they knew no boundaries from things. Zoon Apolitokon. Only threats from the other held them back. If they're sneaky, they could get around that. The special ones were selected for it.]

—"Rocky Raccoon, ██████████████ / ████████ Gideon's bible."

Intermingled with his disgust is the sense that the boys are teaching him something. He detaches in the music to drown out the chatter that continues around and without him. Voice is what they know. It's what they want when they turn this way, it's what they want to hear. They want something from him, and the only way to it winds through speech, what he says and how he says it. He recalls the way he spoke to her at his moment of greatest desperation, he thinks of how short and sharp his pronunciation of "fine" was, then the sarcasm in a long sentence praising the boy's efforts. It roils and rolls around, not the stubble and the dirty clothes, not the rucksack and the boots, that can be overcome, there are ways to make bridges, and they appear in the way he speaks. He needs to decide. How come he doesn't see this? Voice is everything.

—Those memories, what is it you think you're doing when you capture them and not something else? As if that humiliation were decipherable on its own and without any stage set by those damned pink tights.

(The problem was that the writer knew what happened and what would happen, but the reader didn't. He couldn't assume so much, he must bring them along as if the voice carried the purity of the moment *before* the event. Before he saw what you saw long ago.)

—You can't suckle at it as one who was already there, you had to reconcile with the non-memory as well as the memory. Things speak that way, tell that tale and carry it upon their faces, etched there by the brutality of time. You'll capture the sense of it, the beat of it, in the tone and the angle, the lilt and the life.

(Waylaid by parsimony, you sung for your supper. It was in her fine muscular activity, but you didn't tend to it that way unless you twisted your neck just right and saw around the corners and into the crevices where the errors lay. What was an error but the unknown? For it to resound and replay honestly inside her darkness, there had to be genuine recollection of that moment without... ...that moment before the lesson was learned... ...how to sing the songs of the unlearned, that should have been the focus throughout... ...to make him be not, or not yet, so that he stumbled upon it, this would take great hesitation and patience. It was the voice bending the word to fit the flow of music, pronunciation lost in time since that's what mattered most.)

Steadily breathing.
Steadily breathing.

[Trickling down by day, and soft-selling the world by night, these breezes came around to wrangle and ridicule. You're bloken and broodless, breathtakingly tormentuous... ...the sea of reach... ...the right of contreat... ...all of it tonight, all of it by day, the light touch, the hipbone, and the joy-heaving carcass recalled all that tatters in the be-bubbling burble the bloke blathered when the lime was light.]

—To capsoir the mooment, we must mortgage what looms hexed...

1.8.3.X.19.86.9.25 [ref(..85.10.31)]

Breakfast digesting, standing on the porch watching a puddle on the asphalt walkway. Raindrops steadily pelting the standing water and then rippling across its marine plane until the next drop destroys the pattern, only to be outdone by the next. Without warning, a gray and black sneaker smashes the middle, its size reducing the droplets to insignificance. Within two strides, those same sneakers are damp with rainwater bouncing from the road following their fall from the dark, morning sky. Before the shoes reach the center of town, they are sopping wet, and the damp rises up the legs and to the waist where it meets a rain-soaked overshirt. "I need a raincoat," speaking simply when veering off the road and cutting through an open field.

On the main street in Oberstdorf, there is an outdoor store with a sign in the window advertising rain ponchos that fit over large backpacks. Dropping the rucksack inside the door, approaching one of the salesclerks, and saying calmly while beads of water drip onto the floor and leave a puddle at the feet, "I'm looking for a raincoat," then gesturing back toward the front door and the sign only visible from outside.

She leads the way to a rack at the back and shows a large blue, Gore-Tex model that perfectly suits its purpose. It is 85 DM, or two days sustenance.

"Is it okay to pay with a credit card?" It is only for emergencies and there isn't much available credit, but it might cover it.

"Master Card," the clerk says simply and without eye contact.

Nodding, turning, and squelching back to the front of the store. Arriving at the rucksack to look once again at the downpour. Before cinching the buckles and clasps, shrugging the pack off the shoulders and onto the carpet before making way back to the clerk.

"I'll take it. No need to wrap it, I'll wear it."

It is an expensive purchase, but after the first few minutes in the open air with the steady streams of rain beading on its smooth, shiny surface the decision is reinforced. Offering protection from the elements, it's a tent and a shelter, an essential item that will endure without losing utility.

"85 DM my ass, this poncho is priceless."

Taking the hood off and smoothing it back onto the top of the rucksack, the rain is warm and feels good on the closely cropped hair.

—Well, aren't you proud of yourself?

Following the carefully marked recreational hiking trails on a steadily uphill climb for some time, then arriving at a guest house and restaurant. Deciding to brave the blisters and fit the feet with waterproof boots, there are chairs piled on top of tables standing on a patio next to the building and beneath an overhang. Taking down and righting one of them to sit down and change the shoes. Before putting the sneakers into the pack...

—I should wrap these up.

Knocking on the sliding door and a woman appears, smiling. She gladly opens the door and welcomes entry with an offer to get warm by the fire. A German Shepherd comes by for a sniff. Petting him after sitting down to study the biker's map from yesterday. Locating today's destination, the Kemptner Hütte lies north of the Austrian border. For the first time since plotting course, noticing the elevation is some 1500 meters higher although only 10 kilometers away.

Plans for an easy hike scatter and a new sense forms.

After getting warm and nearly dry, going back to the patio, and packing the muddy sneakers into the plastic bag. Saluting the matron, who reappears when she hears the patio door open, and hoisting the pack up onto the back. Lifting the blue poncho over the head and struggling to pull the back of it down evenly. Setting off from the patio and onto a trail leading up the mountain.

—She didn't know anything about me. Not the real me. I was a specimen. From my mere appearance, she assumed she knew everything that mattered. The poncho, the backpack, the boots, all of it, she's seen a million people exactly like me walking along this way heading up to the peak. Might even be headed to the Kemptner Hütte.

The trail turns into a road running alongside a river: Trettach, according to the map. There are hardly any people around and the rain continues without signs of letting up, occasionally getting harder while moving along the trail.

—So much of what people see is in their expectation. We get used to it. The poncho suits me. It goes with the boots and the pack, plus it helps her know who I am. Of course, the hiker wears a rain poncho. If he didn't, she'd be concerned.

Before going too far, coming across a last chance tourist station called Spielmannsau, consisting of a couple guest houses ideally situated close to the mountains at the border. Finding some shelter and eating an early lunch or late second breakfast while contemplating the gravity of the plan. Struggling with the chewy, day-old bread topped with a few strips of cheese, feeling unprepared for a serious climb. Setting out again and ignoring the warning signs scattered on the gradually rising path and indicating the severity of the coming incline.

As the elevation increases, the path becomes more stone than dirt. With the rain, the rocks are slippery, but the footing is good from the boots and their thick rubber soles hug the rocks perpendicular to the edge of the mountain and the ledge of the valley below. Sometimes, the trail narrows to less than a foot with thick ground cover on either side. The air thins, and the grade is progressively steeper until it is impossible to continue without resting frequently. There is no one else on the mountain, or so it seems, and questions come without invitation demanding fear as the only reasonable response.

"Who would find me if I died?" asking aloud.

[Falling is flying, falling and flying, if you fall, you'll be lost in the bushes far below and no one will ever find you. You will cease to become. No more ripples.]

Smacking the lips and tilting the head back knowing the water bottle in the pack is now empty. Some raindrops fall onto the lips, and it feels good.

—Thirsty.

Cupping the hands together and reaching over by the mountain side until they fill with water running off the rocky slope.

"Rainwater running on rocks. Is there meningitis in Germany, Menelaos in Greece?"

New thoughts.

—Fear is a strength meter. More is less. What grows without it? Hektor didn't get any help from the gods and seemed stronger on account of it. Could Achilles have done it without Thetis' help?

(No more mustache in high school after that silly girl said that, mustache-less, you resembled a Greek god... Forming fear... ...fear of the form... ...fear was the mime killer. Apollo's creed. Or was that the other one?)

"If no circle can be the largest circle and innovation draws a new circle around an old one, is he saying God is the largest circle? Does that mean the universe is God in the absolute? Pan-fried theism, is that what lifted Achilles by the bootstraps?"

—Circles have a center. The universe has no center, no advantageous point of inertia. Its middle is at the end. There's nowhere to stand to move the whole damn thing wherever you needed it to be. How did the big dog move the universe if there is no center, no fixed point, from which to move it?

"Straight lines in space are not Euclidean unless gravity is absent. Light has mass and we have the splitting of the atom to show for it. If I could only get to the top, I'd be rid of this fear."

—Running water is better, right? If it's rainwater running down the mountain I can drink it, can't I?

Slurp.

"The ideal was the ultimate self-reliant consciousness uniting the human mind, my mind, with perfection in things, the absolute. What does Emerson say about that? Lighting up the ideal to recognize oneself bound to the ablute. The baloot. It's getting to know yourself as a being whose fall from grace lost that unity. The Oversoul has always hovered above my shoulder even if I seldom twist back to it. Is this the baloot in the idealized, deityized me?"

"Premise number one, Dog, with a capital D, is everything."

"Oh baloot, I knew you had the essence of premise-ness about you."

"Premise number two, everything is made up of a lot of different somethings."

"Oh baloot, how are you ablute if you are divisible? Need a scholium."

"Premise number three, I am something."

"They always let that one slide, but it's pretty weak."

"Wait, let me think."

"Premise number one prime, everything, aka Dog, is baloot and every something is both that and a part of that. Scholium averted, monads detected."

"Better."

"Conclusion, oh baloot, thou art me and I am thee. Selves are ablute right and mysticology left to particulars. Almost to the top."

—Great, consciousness is narcissism, root and stem. The Christian phallus stirs in experience. *"To be or not to be."*

Unaware, he looks down into the valley, becoming smaller beneath him, and wonders whether he is seeing it, or it is seeing itself through him.

—My feet know the valley. My feet know the rocks and the rain. My back carries the pack and the real happens around and around, but this lilt, this running rampant, this foolishness, what does it know? Bliddey blue and blahdy blah. Na na na. Nonsense.

This dismissal lifts him up and steadies his breathing. Only air in there, no rocks and sticks allowed. No lamb's blood to mark the entry. His fear is almost calmed by strength, not real but surfaced in the act of imagining it, and if he could look more closely, he would see that fear lies in a delicate balance teetering between strength and its illusion. Instead, he bars entry and searches his memories for reassuring words confirming that the absolute is the antidote and that illusions of strength are forced to flee from a vulnerable mind darkened by fear's shadow.

Crossing a bridge, only a metal plank lodged against a wall of rock, and patting the back as congratulations: the forged steel and its careful placement becomes an achievement through absolute unity with the genus.

In short, his fear leaves him elated and able to claim a fixed place at the center of the world: the thin air, the fear of death, the strenuous exercise, the memories of Emerson, and the falling water. Earth, air, water. Fire! A left and a right.

—Your step, your step, you got it now keep it don't lose it you got it, your step, your step.

[Body, brain, emotions, and consciousness, you were a recipe for the ingredients of existence mixed without order but turning out, somehow, as a tasty product. The electric part screamed mi mi mi mi mi mi mi.]

"I am alive," breathing. "I am that I am that I am becoming," beats the heart, and whether the walls behind the echo are in the chest or the valley no one can say.

"Fear and Trembling, Sickness unto Death, don't ever read these essays. Existential Christianity will only disappoint an active imagination that grasps entire texts beneath their titles."

Another step and then another step and then another.

"What is the common origin of this will to nothingness, this drive to cease, and the agony that saturates its incompleteness? Puffing up the individual to fully realize its impulse toward self-destruction in the absolute, the vast masses form a trinity of mind, its patterns of being, and the commonwealth. Together they are the lord of creation."

Another step and then another step and then another.

"Will the ascension ever cease? Have my feet found you? Does my back carry you?"

Another step and then another step and then another.

"The harder the climb, the greater the accomplishment. Living and hiking merge, smoke-filled bottles and coke-filled rooms. Watch what you think my young friend or Socrates aka Plato will set you aside with the likes of Homer and Stephen Dedalus."

—Hawklike something something Ibis something something cusped something something.

The climb ends and a gravel ravine extends into a slight dip past the peak. Along the way thinking this will be the end of it and now discovering that it isn't. Traversing downward to finish the voyage upward. Every climb has its regressions.

—Two steps up, one step down.

"Every climb has its regressions."

Another step and then another step and then another.

"Every step downward is easier on the calves and harder on the hips."

—The spirit screams in anguish when discovering its achievement brings a phony sense of relief only to be tested by another steeper climb on the other side.

"Energy wasted in a moment of natural weakness leading to the downward trend. Fuck hope and stupid expectations about something that isn't there. What does the drone bee think it is doing?"

Another step and then another step and then another.

"Upward, I want to run upward, but what choice do I have when the path points downward?"

[What choice did you have?]

At the top of the gravel ravine, a sloping hill rises above wide lawns of green grass spreading out in roomy comfort. The climb becomes less dangerous, but no easier. Two older men follow a sheepdog that passes by with a sniff of the leg and hand. All three glide easily by moving downward.

—Could he be the other's father? Is the holy ghost a sheep dog?

"Grüß Gott."

—I am stronger than ever, and this feeling guides my eyes as I look deep into the absurdity that continues in the simplest actions: Sisyphus with no memory. They are gone.

"███ *love the world* ███████████████████,*" the Satyr sings.*

"Duh duh duh dum. Dim wrath."

(Moving slower, but with the goal in sight, you and I moved our gaze up the ladder of the studded pathway to the small wooden cottage nestled on the hillside, but the newfound ease did not remove the pain of ascent and, in fact, added degrees of intensity to it, exponentially at times. The gradient still steep, the presence of the goal stressed muscles taught and ground pressure into the bones of the lower back.)

Putting the head down and pushing onward in steady pursuit of the finale. Hovering here upon shoulders, focusing attention away from the hut in hopes that the adage 'out of sight, out of mind' proves helpful for the last few steps of the journey.

(The Kemptner Hütte was built in the Alpine range spanning the border of southernmost Germany and northwestern Austria.)

It is one of many warming and lodging huts plopped down in the maze of trails maintained and marked by the neighboring governments. The hut sits on a short ridge between two towering peaks: Mädelegabel and Größe Krottenkopf, both with elevations above 2600 meters and capped in early fall with the mists of quickly carpeting cold weather fronts.

(We paused in the back hall after avoiding the aggressive demon goat guarding the front entrance. It didn't like the look of us one bit and something set off a deep bleating in the form of a devilish tune that cast a spell, forcing us to go around and find a better way into the building.)

There are shelves meant to store large numbers of hiking boots and much of the space is already filled. Off comes the rain poncho and then, in damp woolen socks that stick uncomfortably to the blisters and with the pack resting loosely on the shoulders, proceeding into the main room containing both lodge registration and restaurant. Renting a place on the communal mattress at the top of the hut, stowing gear near the spot, ordering some food with a beer, and then going down to the dry room to hang the rain poncho and the moist, striped overshirt.

When the food is ready, a rather appetizing meal of Wiener Schnitzel, fried potatoes, and sauerkraut that runs a gruesome purple, sitting down at one of the long benches in the restaurant area and sipping on the tall, liter stein while picking at the food and writing in fragments in the still more tattered and now slightly damp notebook.

25 September;

From the youth hostel to Spielmansau was three hours and ten kilometers. From Spielmansau to Kemptner Hütte was three and a half hours and five kilometers. Those last five went from about 1000 meters to nearly 2000. Doesn't take a genius to calculate the gradient. Was it dangerous? That's what you want to know. It suits you, you say. From this side, anyway. It was exhilarating, those new dimensions: rainfall to make the footing difficult, sometimes thick fog, resplendent valleys and gorges untouched, water flowing over rocks and sweet to the taste. Always down, down, down, the water runs down. What runs up? Other guy with something in tow. In a few days this has turned into a completely new journey.

"There's no bore worse than a travel bore," he wrote. Absorb everything! Then leave it alone, let it go. The religious is a misnomer, it's fantasy for the ridiculous. It only speaks in fear and strength, those are the patterns it knows. You have to listen to Dog Almighty, He'll tell you. It's about herding sheep. Call it the holy ghost, feel it as though it were eyes from afar resting upon you, that's a shaggy dog, you fool. Be bold. Be nothing. Don't catch the clasp from behind. Don't sever yourself from the ankles up. Set yourself free. I am alive! Absolutely. Now. Now. Now. How to say that? How to talk like that, speak like that for appearance-sake to all and sundry? How can I fit and sit with the expectations of those others who come a calling and want to know what comes next based on the tip of what they see? Bold and Nothing. What do you expect? Doesn't matter what I am. Poodly and puddly. Feminine. Big nose and curly hair if I let it grow. That has no deeper sense. Overly cerebral, written into a book, I cannot think that. Remain bold and nothing. Sing for them. Never bleat, never howl, never wince. Be bold. Be nothing. Paint their expectations for them.

Setting down the pen, fork, and beer stein one after the other and then climbing the stairs slowly with the pain shooting from the soles upward. Snuggling under the two blankets over the sleeping bag and covering more than the allotted patch of mattress, forgetting to miss the camera while pulling the Walkman™ from the rucksack and plugging into the raspy sounds of an old Bob Dylan tape: setting off on the way to sleep a full two hours before sunset.

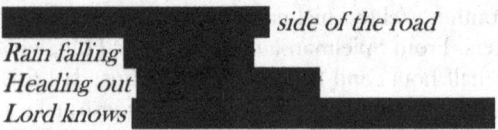

—Num duh, noom doh da. Ka-shhhhhhhh.

—Boooold en newton too. Ka-shhhhhhhh.

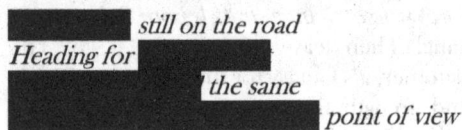

Dah, duh da da da

—Tricks o treats. This'll shoo hoor. Neever foond me agin... ...ofer sol
b gooon...

1.8.4.X.19.86.9.26 [ref(..85.11.1, ..85.8.7, ..7.1)]

Showerless morning, sourdough and jam with a small pot of coffee
before treading into the misty upper mountain hike that leads downhill for
the rest of the day. Walking away, the demon goat big brother watches,
slowly and haphazardly chewing.

Wide fields of rock with orange paint roughly brushed onto a small
stone every thirty meters to keep the hawk-eyed traveler on the straight and
narrow. At the peak of the pass, a metal sign stands, alerting travelers that
they are leaving the Federal Republic of Germany and entering Austria. No
abandoned booth, only a pair of posts a few yards apart.

[I watched you in awe as you retreated into your imagination and placed
this mundane morning of lonely climbing into a new time frame: your
solitude has transformed you into a thinking *thing*.]

—God's brain all around, goat's brain got me gnarling, day lifts with jam,
bread and jam not traffic jam. Who passed this way again? Clink clunk up

so that they could clink clunk down. Was this border always neglected? Is the line between Germany and Austria arbitrary?

(This wasn't a way out, not for those getting ready to burn. Austria was not a cooler climb. Not then, not now in this forest home.)

"Wald heim..." saying it with the same rhythm as if it were sieg heil.

The wind kicks up and blows but there is nothing to be moved by it. The clouds inch along and part as light welcome for the sun.

—Wherever I go I bring myself with me.

[They must've known that as they made their way, choosing to spend their lives with an expatriate, a thief, a fugitive, or worse, they didn't, they failed to take notice and didn't go anywhere thinking things will turn out fine. That's how it always is, that's how we always are. Everything will be fine. But that's not how it goes, that isn't what they want. Just fine. What they say and what they want are not the same.]

Descension on the Austrian side is breathtaking. The markings on the path are easier to spot as the mist clears. The heat intensifies on the way down. Eventually, shrugging the weight of the rucksack and heading into a shallow ravine to fill the water bottle again. Maneuvering into the makeshift, steep streamlet basin and stepping carefully along the rocks jutting from the shallow bottom, forming steps, then, squatting into the middle of it, placing the bottle against the current and waiting while it fills to the neck with sparkling clear liquid.

Climbing back out and sipping the sweet mountain rainwater before putting the bottle back into the pack, then hoisting the bundle onto the shoulders. There comes a nagging expression of concern in the form of a familiar question:

—Is this pure? How was it parented?

"Not as good as the stuff off the rocks yesterday, but it must be at least as pure as the air I'm breathing. Hasn't killed me yet... ...staking my life on the purity of water."

Laughing and continuing down the path where a young couple passes by on their way up. The young woman asks, "Is it much farther to the top?"

Having neither a watch nor any measure for distance, not internally or externally, shrugging apologetically: "Keep going," smiling, "you'll make it."

The guy in front of her purses his lips but doesn't say anything.

The feeling of yesterday's triumph returns. Climbing this side of the mountain seems easier. Of course, it's easy to judge when headed downhill, but here at least the path is wide and always solid, whereas over there it is a crumbling mess. The good weather likewise a bonus.

—They have it *easy.*

[What did two hours mean anyway? How many hours up was two hours down? Why ask us? Why not him? Looked like he was tired of the question, heard it ten times already. She couldn't ask again until oh look

here's someone who hasn't been completely put off, he might know. What
were they hoping to find up there, anyway? There is no room for them,
men and women sleep on different sides, but they might not be staying,
might be headed down the other side. Down faster than up. She looked
exhausted from the climb, but he just looked exhausted. None of our
business. Used to be. Will be.]

*Today, however, is not for deterioration, rather the leisurely pace of
descent is a reward for past efforts. Sprightly walking into a glowing valley
is only possible after climbing out of one, receding in the distance.
Thinking in metaphors, arriving at new angles on decline.*

(Hills and valleys, they were hills and valleys with rivers and waterfalls
and rain. The moisture and the foliage, the animals lurking in the bushes
tried hard not to be seen. We could not find them when we looked, when
we twisted and turned our head side-to-side doing everything we could to
see down and around every patch along every path. She was laden beneath
him, and he walked out in front. She trailed behind, just in case, but soon
they were gone up, up, and away.)

—I saw them, but what does it mean?

[The low notes that descended from high notes were no evidence of
destruction. The tenor voice passed between them in a pleasant trill. The
song went on from up to down and back again telling the tale alongside
events that rose and fell in the sweet melody. Half the battle in passing along
the mood came from getting that voice, that rise and fall, just right. The
pitch had to match the events. What could we do to a word with the right
play between the high and the low, with the right tremors and vibrations?
Kyrie. Keeeeeereeeeeeeeaaaaaaaaaaay. One single word brought to the top
of the mountain and then sent down deep into the valley.]

Lower down, the path cuts through a lumber yard and leads to a wider
dirt road where trucks, carrying machinery or coming to load up with wood,
occasionally roar past. This road is frequented by travelers who aren't
devout hikers from the look of their shoes and packs. The stream gains
strength here and a ledge of rock causes the quickly flowing water to gush
into a rushing fall, bringing the stronger flow down to the same level as the
road, and continuing to grade steadily downward alongside it. Pausing near
a pair of day-walkers stopped briefly to take a picture from the road facing
the waterfall, then, after they move onward, moving to and stopping in their
place to look at their photograph long before it develops. Camera-less,
sitting on the pack in front of the picturesque scene observing the motion
of water spattering upon rock for long enough to create an everlasting
image. It is the fourth in the roll.

(The first was a moment of distress when we looked through wild eyes
right after she told us it was over, and that she had slept with that skank the
night before. "I know," we responded, thinking we knew this was going to

happen long before she did, or at least long before she was willing to admit it. Her smile revealed approval for the whole chain of events, and we made sure to include that along with the many days afterward elicited by the response. She projected herself into the actions of others, making them responsible for everything she did. This frozen moment required massive energy used in quiet, unproductive expressions, bursting at the instant. It was an initiation that wasn't a journey *from* innocence, but *into* something. We were the goat to her pink tights and she horn-noodled it completely out of sight. Whatever it was we didn't do, that would be the last time we didn't do it. The kick at the end blended together with the kick she missed at the beginning. She'll find what goes around and make it come around, like she always hoped. That would be the trick, that's the tip, to make sure whispers worked the way we thought they did. Whatever day-dreamy, fantastic disgust we thought we could persuade, she thought of it before and worked hard to see it done. That bastard took our place and left only emptiness, captured in a snap.)

—Forever.

(The second moment came on a farm in Wisconsin. We diverted the energy fear produced when a horse with endless vigor and a beautiful white coat charged to within a few yards before we accidentally veered off into the sudden step of a woodpile to break our fall. The visual images of the initial reaction were imprinted stronger than celluloid. Fear beat the trail of retreat, and a fall marked the weight of memory. This second was a first all over again. The first was a second again and again. No one checked to see if we were okay. They didn't want to hear our fears and calm our worries, no, they wanted to see us shrug it off, they wanted to confront that full on stoic who thought it was a day like any other. The fairer sex? Ha! That's what they cared for, that's where they were headed. We had only just begun to discover how vicious they could be, and it was finally framed just so.)

—Call it toxic if you must, but they want it, as a class, if they didn't it wouldn't exist. The descent of man, he called it.

(The third moment was the most mystical of the imprints. We came to the city of Barcelona and found a quiet place at the beach. The gorgeous blue water grand and tranquil called out to the many half-naked and tanned bathers crowded together in the narrow strip between the concrete walkway and the sea. The book was Maugham's *The Razor's Edge*, and the tale of Larry Darrow's experiences in India led us to the heights of religious euphoria as though it were a drug. We couldn't place any odd hint of fear in that, but we couldn't rightly exclude it either. There was that same sense of descent, of falling, of the sea against the sand, of the heights on that mountain where he burned his books. His boots? His books. The one in his hands. The one at his feet. Only when he thought he was going to die was he able to find that crevice. Fear and falling. No? Trembling and sick.

Alone and along the way down, passing from within to without, around and about, we had our head down and the heavens were simply an added burden. She made us look up by calling out. Had it been that long? What was she waiting for, her friend? We thought we were the friend, the friend was us. Wasn't she nearby when that happened, only a slender foot stretched out on a towel, pointing in our direction? No top, only bottoms, but stretching back toward us. Why shy from her advance? The sunglasses hid her eyes. Why couldn't we look at whatever we wanted to look at? What was the price we didn't wish to pay, what was the image we thought would bend and break upon the ridge she formed with her arched back propped up by elbows stretched and set so she could look from side to side while pretending to read her book? A beautiful woman lying on the beach, that's what the camera would have seen.)

—Too much weight, can't lift anything else. Certainly not her legs, which, truth be told, did all the work.

The 198 follows along the river heading to the northeast with villages every few kilometers. Back soon to the fourth as the residual where interludes lie.

(Now, this fourth moment came when the water brushed the rock and fell along its ledge to the depths of the young, roadside river. It was more than a bountiful reflection of natural beauty. Yesterday's entire climb appeared in the water. We were on the verge of a thought, reaching for it in a place we could barely touch. Inadequate vision spread wide. In the language of the god-brain, of the goat-brain, seated on the black rucksack and gazing in awe at the waterfall's momentum with thoughts pouring off the mountainside and opening up beneath events in tiny rivulets. Never again, never again. Fuck the god-brain on behalf of the goat-brain for the sake of those who camel-toed the line. They never came again, never released us from the penalty we paid to no one because there was no one who cared to collect the fee. Hoisted and twisted, swung and lifted, size could not be apologized, burdens born in hump and slew, she raised her hips beneath us like they always do.)

—That's how it happened, what happened. What happened?

[These moments of eternal memory were more than a spatial registry of past action. Rather, the moments and their feelings were complete scenarios filling many lifetimes with flesh and blood present before us. We knew this. We felt the absolute and the way it manifested in the particular, and now were certain to make those myths practical. Let the higher order go, let its magic remain unnamed. Turn them into a chant, a howl, a long, slow ardent wail. So much for absolution, so long to the ablute. Actions ceased to carry summaries of everything we ever saw. We can be here now if we want.]

—Never again underestimate the collective effect of the tribes' passive submission in cattle cars and ghettos, mobile gas units and crematoria.

Confused and wishing for the comfortable isolation of the past, lurching through the buildings that mark the mountainside edge of the town of Holzgau, and straight to the first grocer on the main road to purchase yogurt and bread for a quiet lunch inside the fence at the edge of a farmer's land on the road leading northeast. The afternoon, after lunch, walk levels along a road more or less free of automobile traffic. Then, a few hours before sunset, twenty-six kilometers down road from the Kemptner Hütte, arriving at a guest house advertising vacancies with a cardboard sign.

Flat walking elides time after much spent on the ascent and descent. Bach, Obergiblen, Ebigenalp, Griessau, Rauchwand. No one walks the village streets this Friday.

In Elmen, dead on the outside, dead inside, registering for a room. Showering immediately, washing some clothes in the bathroom sink before settling down to finish the lunchtime loaf. Sated, unable to continue padding around on sore feet, nestled into the bed, and pulling the quilt up to the chin to read a selection from Emerson's *The Over Soul.*

> *There is a difference between one and another hour of life in their authority and subsequent effect. Our faith comes in moments; our vice is habitual. Yet there is a depth in those brief moments which constrains us to ascribe more reality to them than to all other experiences.*

—Habitus.

[There was a reason we chose to tell this tale. The audience in their comfortable seats complained about the coincidence. Didn't they know there were many without them, fallen fallow and untold to anyone anywhere? No need to revisit their rhythm, no need to commit their cadence to memory, they were the lost ones. Let them go wherever they wished and only hold those that staked their claim. The moment demanded its place at the center, or in the chorus, or at the end, or wherever it went in the stream of events filling the voice each time it lifted and lent itself to the air recalling the rest.]

> *Man is a stream whose source is hidden. Our being is descending into us from we know not whence. The most exact calculator has no prescience that somewhat incalculable may not balk the very next moment. I am constrained every moment to acknowledge a higher origin for events than the will I call mine.*

[Voice didn't accompany the everyday ups and downs, it descended and ascended to carry the tale along many ways, fleeing for its benefit. It could be real, and it could be fake. It could be false, and it could be true. If it came from somewhere else, somewhere above, then it flew in the flicker of what happened at the basin. It evaded the meaning it caught there. We saw it, the high notes came from somewhere else, the low notes too. They were unreal, not bound, they were not there. But we made them more and less at one and the same time. Rather, it made them more and less at one and the same time. Our cavernous body, the surfaces colliding, it resounds in the hills and valleys, it recounts the echoes to everyone nearby. The truth was not the point. There was no need for that, it was as easily held in silence. What mattered rose in the hills and sank in the valleys. The fear and the euphoria, the jam and the morning light, resounded in the aftermath of an enormous descent, a bitter eternal pill made particular for the moments held and moments told.]

As with events, so is it with thoughts. When I watch that flowing river, which, out of regions I see not, pours for a season its streams into me, I see that I am a pensioner; not a cause but a surprised spectator of this ethereal water; that I desire and look up and put myself in the attitude of reception, but from some alien energy the visions come.

(The water inside every body is billions of years old. 4.5 give or take. Neither created nor destroyed, it flowed in and out through those same rhythms: the sweat on the brow, the gurgling swallow, the air flow in the slurp. The particles abound, the particular boldness erupting from that busy stream and the nothing disrupting its eternal flow. Bold nothing. This was the absolute seeing the particular, the peculiar, as a bold nothing leaping from its creative course and coming to a halt only upon its return to the spring of its initial pour. It couldn't be there long, that was the nature of things particular, miscellaneous and transient, they were the story of pure coincidence, the voice that rang out in the night and lit up the morning. So unlikely, so unrealistic, sediment extracted from the surging river of eternal world. That was where the deity's truth lay, the origin from which it came, the seat of its clearing.)

—But why? After what happened, there must have been a reason. What did I do? What didn't I do?

(Pink tights. Our face buried between her shoulder and neck, that awkward and mechanical going through the motions, with no emotion, with no motion whatsoever. When she stretched out on the second double bed while we looked at the alarm clock in between... ...didn't bring anything to sleep in... ...shed purple on our shirt and held us waiting... ...we sat in the dark with her smoking a cigarette, wearing one of our old shirts, and looking at us to see what we would do... Bold and nothing. Slowly and confidently unaware. Over time, we must've driven her to distraction with that endless pounding. Did we make her do it? Not her, us?)

With a visionary expression and a higher sympathy for the authors of the night, leaning back and tossing the book onto the floor near the bed before flipping off the light. Settling back into the comfortable bed and quickly dropping off into worry-free sleep filled with loosened thoughts of the downpour on the mountain and its rushing rain river: the flowing water runs fresher and faster than anything alongside the roads and homesteads out ahead.

—blooory mow... leak dat... ooop un doon. Tak a pitcher, oot ood ass linger...

8.12 (1)
this year's harvest

8.12.1.Elisabet.19.86.5.10

[Failing long into the night, the morning came quickly, Odette likely not at all. Wiggling and lurching drove us. That kind of influence, power, not crowded theatres with rapt audiences, not big festival shows, but the pure presence of a hum behind the ear, and its response, sent shivers back to whatever sent them in the first place, welcome and welcoming. It was a half-turn at first, then sliced through the crossing burned in the gap opened by stillness to orient my motion toward him.]

The right-handed man drags his left hand from above the left knee off along a natural curve to find its way to the waist above the left hip. A flutter of fabric comes with it and skin shows through in the slow slide of that careful movement. His eyes are wide and seek encouragement. They find it. It's never fully dark in the New York night and the window, untreated, blends with ghostly vision. Covering each other in it, knees go bump, hips collide, bellies borne for this burn.

(There's Karl, six years senior but didn't know it, at the heart of it, of me, so much more sophisticated. Then two years later, two that same season, only four between, and that difference was a whole-wide-world. Fun loving days. When I came to occupy their land, four years later, Anders taught broken hearts when we were side-by-side upon them. The momentous events were always announced by a stranger in his twenty-third year. And and and...)

He rolls and twists to come up and hover overhead. He bends and leans to find the angles, pulling the cotton T up but not off, so steadies the hand, so well it follows a lead. He sees where to go with only the slightest guiding gesture and isn't in a rush.

—Always the rushing. How does he move without it?

Shimmying up to let him know he should climb his way down, and he gratefully endures the signals and signposts. Kisses to nipples pop popping up to greet his mouth, to breasts splish-splashing across his chin and cheek, to belly and hip, he marks his way, finding the contours that want to be found. Sliding the cotton knickers off, on the way down, a both-sided caress.

"Spread your legs," he whispers, pausing and looking up this way. To the art of it, the mastery, to the will lost when told how to play, happily conceding. Then, of a sudden, sweeping a firm right hand down to his chin and taking it into curving fingers, drawing his head up at an angle with force. His gaze already peers into where he most wants to go and this act pulls it clear and away, forcing him to register the exchange and everything that spans it.

Listen.

"Exactly like that. Your eyes. That's the look. Do you understand?"

He nods and swallows hard. Hand relaxes into a caress along his cheek before letting him go back to it. Such quiet enthusiasm in every tip and toe finding its way into whatever places a nose can nestle. No alphabet soup, he discovers new lands, everything is for the first time. Aware of the possibilities for originality and perfection, of the audience's slow breathing, it doesn't remain a matter for the nose and tongue. Far beyond that, his gaze electrified in the telling, he transforms it into hands and chest and chin and mouth and hips and legs, every part of him takes part, works forward, and signals momentum upward. Fully committed to a scent, to a taste, to every sense with nothing left untouched, no part neglected, unheard, unseen.

—It's too much, too much.

Grabbing his shoulders and pulling him upward, no expectation drives him. His body yields to a sideways lean that lays him back off pressing close to the hip, firm and straining against it. He attends to every gesture moving him away from any deep urgency.

"I can't, not like that."

He nods and watches as the T-shirt comes back down, pulling and stretching into place. His left hand follows the lead and moves into position above the shirt along the crease at the top of the left leg, ever downward along the slope and to the pool glistening at the plateau.

"Like that." Moving his hand in a circle, pulsing through the cotton now moist.

He takes over the motion, learning his way quickly. Agile, there's no one right way, no single path, there is no template, and his breath hums parallel to the arc of his wrist. Movement in his throat, he wants to say something but hesitates. Instead, he listens, and attends to the wriggling and the wobbling, the pushing, and the sideways force before the lift upward, feet firm and buttocks pressing to his light loop. He knows where the resistance needs to be, and how it must find its way through the folds that form along the moving flesh. It doesn't take long, and time hovers as the neck tilts back and turns to the side, mouth agape and waiting.... ...there is a slight gasp to punctuate.

Exhaling, not soundless.

Inhaling, the chest rises.

Looking over, he wears his broadest smile as the bumps dip into ample grinding, as the high arcs slope down into lows. Near shouting, a groan, then more, the vocals make up an eerie northern winter ballad. His laugh accompanies this simple joy. Pleased, then relaxed, right along the way, right in the heap the afterward provides.

Pressing his hand close and motionless.

"Don't let it go to your head," once the panting eases. He is kissing wherever there is skin while he waits for a cue. Then he blushes and looks away. "It's good you pay attention, but I'm the one that's... You need to be present... ...I need to be... ...comfortable."

—What about you?

He feels with his fingers what the eyes express. Uncoached, he leans for a proper... Legs aligned, but his go off into the infinite space below and beyond, chest pressing close, right arm pinned and left finding its way through the material that separates the bodies. He smoothly transitions into light whispers.

"There's no such thing as a time," with such earnest.

Looking over. He frees his right hand and lays his head to rest upon it, bending at the elbow close to the ear. His scent wafts over, it is lush, and makes the hairs on the neck stand on end.

"What does it mean?"

"Well, you know how people say they did it three times or whatever. Or they did it twice in the morning."

Nodding.

"There's no such thing as a time, what's a time? That's what she meant."

"Oh, I see."

"Because everything is a million things. Not only sex. Everything."

Buzz, buzz buzz, the swarms are everywhere, and the room fills with what they do and the different directions they take.

He looks away, beginning to stammer as though realizing he shouldn't be talking about this.

"It's okay, go on." Turning a bit to the side to look directly at him.

"You know how I told you there was only that one time."

Nodding, biting the lower lip.

"That one time was many different things. I proved that by obsessing over all of them. Not the whole year, but that one night. Every little thing that happened. In one single thing, there are millions of things, that's what she said."

Smiling and brushing his hair back from his face. Her loveliness is his loveliness now.

"Well, I owe her my thanks." Smiling at him and continuing to brush back the lone resisting lock.

"We both do," he turns with the hand and kisses it to interrupt its movement back to his forehead. "Can I ask you something?"

"Of course."

"Is it because you're married? Is that why you didn't want to?"

Letting the hand fall to find his chest in the sliver of space where breasts meet him flat to layby.

"We're separated. Officially." As calmly and clearly as possible. It is fact.

"Why then?"

"It's not because I don't want to." Then a kiss, and he lets himself be distracted, no pressure unwanted. He's waiting for more but already senses he won't get it. "Tell me something."

"What?"

"Tell me something you care about. Tell me about something you think is fascinating."

He looks down and then over the shoulder and into the darker distances by the door near the dresser against the joining wall.

"Buleria is in 12."

"Buleria?"

"It's a palo, a style, one of the Flamenco rhythms. Driving... ...hard core. Los gitanos de Jerez, and all that. Others too, muy Flamenco. I came across an album by Paco de Lucía and there was a song called Almoraima, track 1, Side 1. I thought five guys were playing. It was crazy. I'd been listening to mostly pseudo stuff, and this was the first genuine article. I couldn't believe it when I found out it was just a lead with a little rhythm behind it."

"My husband's met him. In Spain."

"Is he a musician? Your husband."

"Business. He knows everybody. In Europe, at least. But go on, it's in 12."

"Yeah. Remember I said I couldn't count." He giggles, almost embarrassed.

Nodding.

"Well, you begin on the 12. I don't know why, but that's how it's done. **12** 1 2 **3** 4 *5* **6** 7 **8** 9 **10** 11. But with accents on the 12, 3, 6, 8, and 10. The accents you play. On the down beat, that's normal, but you syncopate over the others. If you're doing rhythm, you'll do a special hit against the guitar with your right hand. Golpe. The index shoots out while the ring finger shoots back. Like this."

He has to twist a bit to use his right hand, and rapidly moves his fingers, the middle staying still while the index goes down and the ring comes up and then they switch and switch and switch again. Always the middle stays still.

"It's 12 and and and, but you don't play it like that. You'd add a rest for the first and. 12 x and and 3 x and and." All the while twisting and moving his hand in the same back and forth motion to match with the count, and always the middle stays still.

"You're counting fine."

"I know, it seems that way, but it's not. I don't feel it, not the pulse of it, you know, in my chest. I only feel it in my hands, and that throws me off. It gets tangled up."

Many different lines to play with, he gives himself up to the traces and the trails. He lets everything come back and forth in the stroke of luck, in the heaviness, and in the swell of good time. He's still wearing his boxers, steeped through in spots, but every inch his politeness wiggles away is a gap immediately closed by a slight roll and now he has run out of mattress behind him.

"I've developed something of a tic. In my head, I'm constantly running through it. **12** 1 2 **3** 4 5..." He laughs and bumps his head lightly forward. Touching him and stroking his cheek, then back to a light embrace at the neck. "If I told you before, you would have noticed."

"Noticed?"

"When you were floating in my mouth." He is bashful to precious. "Sucking in 12s, trying hard to find the rhythm in it."

Sly glance, "Is this your way of asking to show me?"

Big grin and nodding rapidly, "Sure," he says.

Sitting up to break the moment, reluctant, but unable to see the way otherwise.

"Sorry darling. Raincheck. That's what they say, right?"

"That's right."

"Breakfast. We have to go early. Marianne and Kinch will be here soon. There's no avoiding it. I have an appointment at the salon at 10."

"Salon? Hair?"

"We're going to find my natural color."

"You can do that?"

"I hope so. Elon is a genius. He went to a lot of trouble to find time for me today. He's usually booked months in advance, and I called yesterday."

"What's the original?"

Smiling and exhaling, then pressing the palm against his chest. He closes his eyes, and his smile turns into a knowing grin, "Lighter than this, darker than when they made me up for the early promos. Some gray now. It's why I can pull both off. Tired of letting marketing decide. He'll get to the bottom of it." Reaching up to lightly finger the roots and draw a line down to the forehead. "It's a science."

Standing up and pulling the socks back on. Pulling down the T-shirt. Eyes meet as he lifts his look back up and then quickly away down through the bottom of the comforter searching for the cotton drawers. Unable to locate them, he lifts it more thoroughly and leans down toward the foot of the bed feeling around to see if they fell to the floor.

"Never mind, take a shower."

Blowing a kiss and opening the door. Grabbing the leggings from the rack in the laundry room and heading back toward the bedroom hallway through the kitchen and living room. While passing by, Stieg opens the door and comes out of the guest room.

"Up early, aren't you?" he says, grinning.

"Are you leaving?"

"Have to. Lots to do."

"You're sure you won't join us for breakfast?"

Kisses on both cheeks and then he blows past heading to the entryway.

"Can't darling, see you later."

"Hej då."

And he's gone with a light swing clicking of the door.

8.12.2.Seannafair.20.15.5.7 [ref(19.86.5.22)]

She sets the two beer glasses down and the tumblers beside them. Hardly looking this way, anxious to get on with it. One more in a long line, couple of rummies on a Thursday night.

"I was spit and fire about it. All of it. You couldn't sit me down."

Terry back and forth with his eyes. They're glazed and he is off somewhere not nearby. Tanking it, going for the whiskey, same as always, but he sits up and likes to be ready: he'll have a listen if that's what it takes.

(No one could've stopped me. That agent came by, and he had a lot to say. Told us the good, told us the wonderful and the dream come true part. Never once said a damn thing about the downs and the outs, about the losing. No, they never tell you nothing about any of that. How did he get there so fast? What was his name? George or something Kingly. Something crappy like that, like a bugger who'll take everything you have and put it on his balance sheet. Come up from London or wherever. A yank, but not all the way from there. Couldn't've been, was too soon after the call. Did I hear her voice on the phone while he was talking? Was it her or am I imagining it now? Was it through the phone? He didn't say a damned thing. The cancer, the blockage, he didn't say a damn thing about any of that. Might've dreamt it or heard it through the phone.)

"I don't know if he heard it before he came, because he wanted us to play it for him straight away."

He's drumming on the table and slurping his beer. Far away. Not loving it, not there in the mix, not a part of anything that happens to those who can't give him more of what he's looking for. In a minute, he'll get to hankering for another and then he'll get personable and want to chat about every last thing so that he can go ahead without fearing it'll be the last.

(He put something in my drink. He must've because I don't remember anything. First come to Oxford, right? Didn't know hardly a soul, but there I was comfortable in the pub, took to doing the pours like they always want. He was one of them boys, the way they were then. Brilliant, their whole lives ahead of them. They weren't there to learn how to ask, they were there to learn how to take. And he wasn't about to risk getting no for an answer. He must've... Then next morning he goes off and lies about it. As though he never done nothing. No lass, you were too over it by then, so was I come to think of it, or some other rubbish. Nothing happened. Well then what's this? As if it's invisible, as if he doesn't know that spunk leaves a stain, that a girl knows these things. Trying to tell me such nonsense as if I was stupid, and he was so far beyond me that he could say and do whatever he liked without any worries.)

"We did. We played the recording of both the songs we put down. We didn't' think it was a good idea to use the other one. Wait for that. *Return for Me* and *My Life.*"

(It came back then too. Every minute of it. I don't remember the remembering, but I remember the feeling, the shock and tears, but I was always that way then, every day was another mess come the dawn, right up until nighttime. Morning and night feeling yourself come raging into each part of you. It can't be good for anyone, that feeling, those desires. Something way up high and you know you can reach it and you're willing to spend every single minute of every single day trying to. It was a storm broke loose. Might've begun in that church. But no, long before that. With the collar boy in his flat denying it. In that filthy van. All that coming from the time being pushed down as if I wasn't there. This much bigger and I didn't know half of what was happening or what could happen. No one told me nothing, not as if I knew how they could be. They come after you constantly. In the tube, on the bus, on the streets while you're walking along minding your own, always, they're everywhere. What're you writing? Come on luv, give us a smile... And you think there's nothing you could hate more than that, getting high and mighty and saving yourself from it. Putting things around you so that none of that ever gets anywhere near you. Then you let it go and there's nothing left because you're old and worn out and no one cares to look anymore or say anything. They don't see you, and it's as if you don't exist. Always saying two. Two two two. Fecking three! That can't be. Remember remembering and it doesn't work that way.)

"It was Elisabet Lundberg's doing. Did I ever tell you that?"

—Together in a polaroid.

(Stole it after I found it in his book, can't remember what happened to it. Remember her clearly, hair pushed back over her ear and standing on the street in her pajamas. Don't remember him though.)

"Elisabet Lundberg. Don't believe you did."

"He told her he never heard anything like it. He must've talked me up because that's what the A&R man came expecting to hear. He listened to those two songs and nodded the whole time. They were exactly what he was expecting, and he was all talk and big and all of that. Wanted to see the real thing, said he didn't think the recording was doing us justice. Didn't know when, but it had to be soon."

"That was your big break."

(It was everything I ever wanted, it was what I was working hard for. Training. Every day the exercises, alone and repetitive. You have to lock yourself away and grind on it to find what's in there. They always say how it's a gift and your talent comes from God or your parents or whoever it is that makes you who you are, but that's not the half of it. They're taking something from you when they say that. Don't know it, but they are. That A&R man, he knew better, he knew that it was drive and determination and effort to get the muscles to remember those passageways, to get your voice right where you needed it to make the words come. It isn't talking and they should know that. You got to find the air in each word, got to find what makes them what they are, in the tiny parts and you have to find the place in your body where it resonates. Something of it comes from above, that may be, but not everything. The beginning. But the rest, the rest is sweat and tears and pain and enduring that every day. The rest of it is all the time I wasn't there and didn't see what the others saw, didn't do what the others did, but was torn away and on my own focused and fashioning a better tone. In time. Away from it.)

"The A&R man, he was full of useful insights. Once he heard. Once he thought we were worth it, he had plenty to say. He said we needed a name. Dairy wouldn't cut it. He said Irish was hot and we could blather it however we liked, no need to hide it. Shane freed us. Bono too, all of them. Them lads, that's what he was saying. Didn't like Derry Made neither. Wasn't true anyway. Too gimmicky. Needed to be properly Irish but not fake. He said authenticity is what sells best. That's it. That's what he'd come looking for."

Terry's nearly down but then the girl comes by, and he perks right up as if he's got some kind of radar underneath. He's not saying anything, he's listening but not reacting. Then the girl comes, and he motions rapidly as though he's come alive. One of them puppets that wakes up when the master grabs its strings. He tells her to bring two more whiskeys. Still sipping away at the pints, they don't need refreshing.

(Who was it first said Aine? Was he at my side? No, but he asked something. That's right. He wanted to know my mother's name. He said that's where you'd find it. I said Annie, Aine and everybody stopped what they were doing and came up close. We knew we'd found it the moment I said it. He didn't come up with it, but he asked the question. He asked it and I answered so in a way it was me that came up with it but in a way it wasn't. He was so deliberate, that A&R man. He rolled the tape back and set it to the beginning. The roaring highs and lows of *My Life*. Everyone heard the banshee in that. It was what I was born to do, that's the gift in it and he knew. He rolled back, and he wanted to play it again and he said all deliberate and clear as day looking at us before he popped that button and set it rolling. He said, here's Aine Quinn, and then it played. First the guitar, it rolled. The drums rocked. Because that's what it took in those days, that's what everybody wanted. Then it happened, the banshee began to sing and the highs and the lows. He said you couldn't believe what you were hearing. He stopped the tape and told us why it should've come in sooner. He explained how you wanted the whole thing to be coming upward right when the singing came in. When the voice sounds, it... ...it couldn't be because the timing was rolling around to the end and coming back up again, it had to be because we were surging upward and there was no other option but to shout right then, as if the voice was coming from somewhere deep down.)

"He said everything we wanted to hear. Everything we were trying to get, it had to come out in the song. The tape was good. He said as much and didn't try to fool us into thinking otherwise. But you know, it can be better, not the sound of it, but the timing. It had to be more dramatic."

(We didn't know a damn thing. Thought we knew everything. Didn't know to be suspicious of him. Never thought that he was trying to teach us how to harvest the kids' money. No, that never occurred to any of us. The polish. The way they try to get you sparkled up and pretty. He touched my hair, I think. Said it should be cropped shorter and dyed darker black. I asked him about my teeth, and it was grizzly the way they said, yes luv your teeth could use a good going over, but we can't be messing with the shape of your mouth. You never could tell the effects. There were stories, horrible stories of people who went out and fixed their teeth as soon as they got their hands on the money, and it took everything from them. Look at Shane. He'll never fix those teeth and why do you think that is? It's because you can't risk it. Change the body, change the voice. But never you worry, we'll figure out how to work it in if it comes to that. If it comes to that. It's as if they wanted to tell a story with your name and your hair and your mouth and the rest of you. And they didn't care much whether it was your story or a true story, it just needed to feel right.)

She brings the glasses by and asks if there is anything else. Terry knows it's getting close, so he touches the near-empty pints and says all the way round for both. There's time enough for that.

"You don't know what you're up against. A shark has swum right up to you, and you don't know it. Might think it's a dolphin and that everything is fun and games, but that's not what's happening."

—What does it matter if the singer's pretty? The girls demand it.

"Yeah, what's happening?"

"You're being curated, that's what. Looking for the genuine article, trying to find what's real and true to turn it into this year's big thing. Get everyone their Porsche or their posh house or send their kids off to some fancy school, let them run rampant over the rest of us taking whatever they want and denying that they got any of it the next morning."

"What's this? What are you talking about?"

"Doesn't matter. It's what they do. The fellas aren't as bad as they say. They're doing what they're supposed to. The whole place is made up that way. Don't you see? That A&R man, he was doing what they all do. Of course, she's up for it, that's the premise. She may not know it, may not be able to say it right, but that's what he thinks and that she'll be damn grateful to get it if he does what he knows best how to do."

He nods, doesn't bother to put it together. Empties the last of the pint and the whiskey in expectation of the next round coming. The wait is getting to him, and he looks over and sees half a pint standing here.

"You better finish that up before the next comes."

"Are we on a timer then?"

"Just saying."

"Go on then."

He takes the glass and tips it up quick to empty. The lass comes round and puts it down. Sets the slip of paper next to Terry and he pushes it over. Reaching into the bag and pulling out the billfold. There's a small stack in there still, and Terry's eyes go wide when he sees it carelessly drawn. Putting a bill on the paper and leaving it.

"Can you spot me a few?" he asks. Handing over one of the hundreds and quickly stuffing the rest into the wallet and putting it back where it came from. He's licking his chops hoping for more, but the pint draws his eyes and he's back at it. Not touching what's here. He's sensing that's the turn it's taking, and he's thinking if he downs it fast, he can get through it and take on the other before it's time to push on.

My Life is everywhere, coming from the ceiling and the walls.

(Couldn't tune it out. On the tape, he kept going, but it was loud. In the dream and in the present, it was everywhere. How many thousands of times did we play that song over the last 30 years? They never got sick of it. Never said no thank you. Deep down it was still the same song. All the parts, the same. He worked it, they worked it, and reworked it. Changed the tempo, more polished, more grand, but that just brought out what was already there. It was still that same tune I wrote that night sipping tea with my American quietly reading over there. Didn't want anything from me, let me go off. Made that call, asked about my mother... Why can't I remember his name? Can't...)

"I can't take it, can't listen to this. I'm leaving." Getting up quickly, moving away from the table toward the door.

"But we still have..."

And he gulps fast to try and take in as much as he can after slamming back the extra whiskey. He hates to be leaving it and lets go the dregs of his own to take the full pint and walk out with it.

8.12.3.Natalie.19.86.8.12 [ref(..7.7)]

Rolling off him and looking over at his now serious face. He leans forward and crosses the short distance with purpose. He's moving up and over, using his knees to push the legs apart. His arms hook underneath each thigh pushing them back high up against the chest. He launches into a steady rhythm, and the vibrations continue in the aftermath of each stroke. Spreading pleasure takes over in waves. He races to catch up and gladly receives enthusiastic encouragement.

—Ooph... Yes...

"Harder," in a whisper. Toes curling, hand stroking upward along the wings of his back tense along an arch.

He continues in steady gate, lets his arms go back while the legs slide down with the hips unbending. Squeezing the legs tightly together to establish a firm grip on his pelvis. He lays his elbows on either side and presses his hands back together behind the head. It is a deliberate sliding push and then sliding back, then a deliberate sliding push, then back again. He repeats and repeats, groans, low at first, then more together, multiple groans, and the pitch rises. He is floating above, the hands pause in place along the sides of his back and down toward the lower part and the barely rising slope of his ass, still grinding and sliding forward and back. He is urgently blowing air and groaning again and again. The sliding back and forth continues. The urgency. The sliding. The groaning.

He rolls back the way he came still breathing hard but sprinkled with laughter. Extending the hand to tussle his hair and pet his face.

"Alright, I'm convinced."

"Of what?" he asks still grinning.

"That it is universally true." Pulling arms up under the ear and turning slightly sideways to look at him. Curling the knees and pressing them against his hip. Looking all the way down to see him pulsing inside the condom. He looks down too, slips it off and leans over to tuck it into a tissue from the box on the nightstand.

"You liked it?" he asks.

"Mmmmhmmmm," drawing it out.

He laughs more happily this time.

Continuing with a question: "What about you?"

"Oh yeah." He says quite definitively as he throws his arm back over his forehead. He wipes sweat from his brow, then blows air into the space above the bed.

"And the reading?" Pointing at the book by the far corner of the mattress, it somehow got loose during the ruckus.

"It's easier than having to come up with stuff," he says.

(Flash back to the mid-sentence or mid paragraph where I stopped reading and laid the book aside. Already rocking to his rhythm, I pulled him up for a kiss and told him I wanted to see what he was talking about with his one sure thing. He rolled under me and showed me the position, the hard surface, whatever it was. Bone. The book bounced out of the way and must've gotten lodged there in the corner pushed up against the nightstand.)

"What did you think of the content?"

"I see how it works. It makes sense." He nods as though giving his approval.

(In that scene, she was a famous painter, and he was her model. She's the woman of the world and he's her toy. A good example to show him what worked best.)

—The data's in, is it?

"Well, it wouldn't work if you weren't doing a reasonably good job. If you did anything to distract, that'd ruin it."

He fake roars with laughter and pounds his feet dramatically on the bed, pitter patter, then says: "It's not that I'm any good, it's that I don't do anything bad. Is that it?"

Leaning over to kiss him. He quiets down and snuggles in close, warm to the touch all over, but rapidly cooling. Falling back to let the air circulate across the bed and room become stuffy with a distinctive scent.

"I like teasing you."

Leaning over to kiss him. Then forgetting about the heat and the circulation and snuggling up to his chest now that his arms are folded back behind his head. Looking down the length of his body and watching his legs rock as his soft cock flops flat back up toward his navel.

"What about that woman in Tampere? Something about getting lucky." Stroking slowly down his belly where the eyes are strictly drawn.

"That was fiction. Trying to keep up. I meant that we did talk about luck. We had coffee together, a conversation. The way it was with the girl who went to America and missed my call. She thought that was incredible." He strokes the hair, head, and neck as the arm withdraws and moves off finding its way down along the lines of his torso. Curving beside him and nestling into the crease between his chest and arm.

"I think you missed an opportunity."

"Wait, what?" He asks looking down with the pitch in his voice rising.

"I think she was up for it."

He throws his head back again and the right arm flings downward. He touches himself briefly to move it into a different position. Fascinated and following suit, moving it back and forth, wiggling this way and that.

—Which way does it want to go?

"Well, that would completely reinforce the thing about luck." He guides the hand to show how it wants to be positioned. There are rules. "Getting lucky is a good way to put it because there are so many intangibles. Like you were saying. She sizes him up, he makes the right moves, a few on purpose. They're in the right place. The right time. Many factors, it's pure luck."

"Is this what you're going to study in grad school?" More flipping and flopping. It's becoming an obsession. He shakes his head, doesn't understand the fascination and gives up trying to correct the logic. Instead, he reaches over and repositions the breasts pressed against his chest under his arm so that one is buried and out of view and the other is lying above his chest and clearly in view.

Slapping his hand to make him stop fidgeting and pushing. He flips it over as if to shake off the pain and says: "I'm going to study Nietzsche the Quixote."

"What's Nietzsche the Quixote?"

"It's my reading of Nietzsche. The Übermensch, the revaluation, spun in the stylings of Don Quixote. He read so much in the genre that his brain rotted sending him off on a mission." Unable to tell if he's kidding, the look in his eyes suggests he is at least partially serious. He tilts and his left hand withdraws slowly while he uses his other, hanging over the shoulder, to work up and down the back.

"They're going to tear you apart." Turning to fake bite his nipple, but then actually biting it. He lurches forward and shakes a finger close to the nose.

"How do you mean?" he asks once he's settled back. The flipping and flopping go on and it's having an effect.

—Concentrate Natalie.

Clearing the throat and proceeding in a serious sounding voice, using the correct grammar: "I do not know how the American programs are, but here, if you try to get away with something like that, they will crucify you. You are not serious, you are not properly anchored in the tradition, you do not have the right sources, you cannot publish in the right journals or presses. You will not find any professors to sign on in the first place."

He's smiling, heard it before. No one can heed a warning to something so deeply held.

"Isn't that what the discipline is about? Looking for the source of the philosopher's voice, the conditions behind the genre." He's using a fake voice too, making fun of something, but it isn't entirely clear what.

"I hope it is." Then a kiss to the nipple, with a quick lick to make up for any harm. "But that's not what I'm discovering. Things are narrow in our departments. They don't want you to have any fun. This is serious business." Approximating a normal sounding voice. Trying to convey a warning here, hoping he can avoid something...

—Something I wasn't able to avoid.

"Is that the problem you're having?" He asks seriously. Wants to understand and hasn't gotten a straight answer yet.

—Fine, whatever. We've come this far. Might as well.

"Basically. What I'm finding is that the traditions are oppressive in both form and content, both style and material. You must prove yourself first. Heidegger did it this way, or Wittgenstein that way, doesn't matter. You're not Heidegger and you're not Wittgenstein. You prove yourself and that's what your professors are there to make sure of. You'll write using traditional means and you'll write on a traditionally defined range of problems. Then, once you have tenure, you can do whatever you want."

—If it hasn't been beaten out of you by then.

"If it hasn't been beaten out of you by then," he says.

Laughter and a flicking smack flop. Punishing him for reading too much into it, for seeing the punch line before getting a chance to say it.

"Exactly," urgently leaning forward and petting it back into place. Getting the hang of it. "And believe me, it will have been. That's what they mean when they say you have to be mature. They mean you've got to realize your limits and stay within them. They want you small, and they want you humble about choosing your scope. Being arrogant about that, however, that's okay."

(It's not the size that bears comparison, it's the idiosyncrasies. The flipping and flopping. The lean, the recovery, the jerks and squirts. In mind and body. Not with Martin, never with Martin. Never playful. He doesn't have any preferences, or I was never this fascinated, or he couldn't give immediate feedback. It's luck.)

"How? They want you small and arrogant. How?" His voice softens, unable to resist the influence. There's conflict in the way he says it: somewhere between why are you stopping and what are you doing.

—Which need to tend to first?

"That your aspirations have to be humble, but you can be a total charlatan when it comes to achieving them."

"And that's why you have to go outside the mainstream of your discipline to find people who'll let you do what you want," he's testing whether he's fully understood the angles.

Lifting the head to look back up at him. "That doesn't seem like it'll
work. Unless that's another example of luck." Putting the head back down.
"You'd do better with luck as your thesis." Exhaling the words into the hair
on his chest and around the nearby nipple.

"Do better?" he asks.

"Yeah, there's at least a history. The luck in this or that. Moral luck.
Epistemological luck. Practical luck. You'd get more leeway if you went
that route. Write about philosophical luck."

Rolling back over on top of him and leaning over to the nightstand to
take another packet. Tearing it from the others and opening it. Sliding back
onto his legs to pop the top and unroll it down. Leaning back into position
while reaching for it and putting it in place, then tilting forward and lifting
it so that it slides in easily. He breathes out. Winking at him to register the
agility in the series of movements. He mouths an *oh* to express how
impressed he is.

"Writing about the luck involved in hooking up with someone." he says
in that same moany voice.

"Yes," as if referring to something else entirely.

"Funny." His hands folding down toward the lower back, mirroring
each other, and gripping each cheek of the ass tightly. Leaning forward
making it easy to hold. "I could imagine writing about how lucky it was that
I met this woman once who was kind of hard up and lonely and looking
for someone to take care of her basic needs."

"Hey, I resent that. I wasn't hard up and lonely."

Slapping his chest and rocking forward. He slips out and grunts.
Reaching back down and leaning forward, repeating the sequence, and
sliding back to put him in place.

"I didn't mean you," he laughs in both pleasure and jolly. "Someone
else. Knew she needed someone, didn't know it was me. Specifically." His
hands go back to where he can help pull and push. "It changed my life. I
had ended... ...broken-hearted... I met her... ...kind of an isolated situation.
Without any... You know..." His concentration fades and the words trail
off.

"Ah. Deprived and horny. Okay. Lucky for you," forcing his
concentration back on track.

"There were things about me I didn't know... She picked me, made
me. Kind of. Now I see that if it hadn't turned out that way, a whole bunch
of stuff later wouldn't have happened, and if none of that happened, then
other stuff later, and so on."

Briefly bouncing up and down, slowly grinding back and forth, the belly
moves forward and back in perfect sync with his hands.

"Leading up to now?" Struggling to stay on point.

"Leading up to now," he says sounding as if he's struggling too.

"Answer me this. We'll see if you get lucky."

"What?" The words aren't the point anymore. It's the breath that utters them, that's what's driving the rhythm. Lowering down so that the breasts are pushed against his chest, skin against skin. Warm to the touch, electric as the movement continues.

"What's the difference... ...between a girl... ...and a woman? In your stories, you jump... ...back and forth. I'm trying to figure... ...it out."

His hips are lurching upward, the rhythm is coming from both above and below, there is mashing when the two meet, it's an explosive slam.

—Bang. They say bang.

"It's kind of... ...impressionistic." Then he breathes out heavily. "Maturity," another hard breath. "Childish. Then girl. Otherwise. Woman."

Kissing and pressing closer, hands pressed hard on mattress behind his head then stretching forward so that the shoulders go taut and the body anchors into position, heaving forward to capture the lunge.

"Not an age thing?" Breathing out forcefully. Leaving the left hand out behind his head but pulling the right one back and moving it down toward the crux of the rhythms to and fro.

"19... ...still has a lot of girl in her. 26... ...or 28... ... less. 32... ...hardly any. At 37... ...not a tiny bit." He grunts and moans each syllable.

—Forever a boy.

"The girl is gone by 37?" Asking in sing song, using the right hand, faster now.

"Not gone for good. She'll come back later," he says rapidly.

"I'm hardly any?" Then a rocking groan while leaning forward. Moving to the side, then back on point. Forward then back, forward then back, to the side, a wriggle back and then sliding up into place.

"That's right," he says, moaning.

"The deprived and horny one?" Comes out as mostly air.

"Woman on the surface... ...girl underneath," in sync with his rhythms.

Roaring forward now, coming in lurches and leaps, flipping and flopping, only this time its belly against belly, rock against sock. Rush comes from everywhere and leads off in every direction. Arching forward involuntarily, flattening the pelvis with a sudden push. Holding it. Rotating. Right there in position, the tip of his pubic bone presses close, then, slow rock... slow rock... slow rock... ...and again.

—Universe allee troo.

Once the spasms recede, making a darting motion, rolling forward and pivoting ninety degrees to the right, the legs straighten and are thrown off toward the edge while the head swings toward the wall on the other side. Angling over him and sliding down to make it easy to raise the ass up off his lap. He sits forward to create more of a ledge and lets his limbs come to rest. Slinking along the width of the bed, lifting still higher to make it easier to reach.

Curling the head over to the left and throwing him a sly look with eyes peering off to the side. "Got the first, now the second. My hardly any has been naughty."

8.12.4.Greta.19.86.9.26 [ref(..84.5-9)]

—'In deep song the role of the guitar is to mark the rhythm and submit to the singer. It is but background for the voice." [Garcia Lorca]

Leaving the guest house at Holzgau a little late this morning. Filling the water bottles and getting some rolls, salami, and cheese from the kitchen for the trek back up toward the warming hut.

(He didn't try to cover himself this morning and teased me when I did. Laughter casts a spell. Everything was dry by the time we needed to get dressed and go to the dining room to have breakfast. It's easy traveling with him. He doesn't expect to be anywhere. It's as though he's at home here same as he was at home in the car and at the guest house in Oberstdorf.)

It takes time to lace up his shoes. Standing there watching him, the morning is chilly, but he wears shorts for the trail. Then off into the mist soon to clear from the look of it, already beginning to. He is in the lead and heading up the philosopher's way.

"How long do you think? Is it far to the top?"

"Not sure, but it didn't take us that long to get down yesterday. It always seems farther up than down though."

A hiker approaches heading down. It's still early enough to where he couldn't have been hiking long and must have come from the hut.

"Is it much farther to the top?" asking him as he passes by.

"Keep going," he answers with a crooked smile. "You'll make it."

Turning to look at him. The blue and white striped shirt poking out beneath the back of his black rucksack, there is a rain poncho cinched around his waist.

—Not helpful if you're trying to gauge the distance.

"I recognized him."

"What?" he turns back and pauses.

Catching up to him and walking side-by-side for a while.

"I recognized him."

"Who?"

"That young man. I saw him on the road outside Bregenz."

"Are you sure?"

"He had that same shirt, from the camps."

He nods firmly but continues without a word, moving ahead back into single file. The trail narrows and it's harder to walk side-by-side as the incline increases.

—He must be following the same road. American. He seemed smug, that smile bothered me, as if he knew something. How could he think I was exhausted? It's early and we just left. Why be that way with a stranger asking a simple question?

(I see why she was drawn to him, why she was willing to care about him. He's so comfortable. She wasn't. Like me. Of course, it stands to reason. And with him exuding ease, it had a calming effect, I'd have buried myself in a hole this morning, but he smiled and touched my shoulder. Pulled at the blanket, but playfully. It's morning and we're awake again. The sun will come, and time will pass same as yesterday, and now there are fewer things to stop us. Simple as that.)

Expecting the mist to thicken with the altitude but instead the reverse happens. Time melts the layers, and the sun comes out and bathes the entire hillside in warmth breaking the air to clear it. The rocky part of the path begins and then the winding gravel trails near the hut.

[I recall every contour from yesterday morning. Does he?]

"Shall we stop at the hut?" he asks.

"We don't need anything, let's keep going. We can have lunch on the way down. It's not yet noon."

He nods and turns back upward continuing to lead the way.

—It took over an hour to get to Holzgau from the hut yesterday, almost two. Twice as long to climb back up. If that's true on the other side, it should only take about three hours to walk back down to Oberstdorf.

Passing by the hut, the goat bleats and comes off the front porch toward the trail. Stopping to pet it.

"Does he remember us?"

He stands farther away. Looks affectionately at the goat but doesn't touch it this time.

"Are you afraid?"

"Terrified," he says quickly.

"It's only a goat. He's friendly."

"Oh, you meant the goat. No. He only wants *your* attention. He remembers you, I bet."

"This is a joke? You are joking?"

"About being terrified, but not about recognizing you. They're clever."

"Were there goats on the farm? In Colombia."

"No. Lots of birds. Ducks. Geese. Gallinetas. Not sure how to say that, like a chicken. A few cows. Mules, horses. No goats. Cats and dogs."

At the top of the mountain pass there is a grassy field. Leaving the goat behind to cross it and go up a slight rise before the incline downward begins. The path is narrow and often paved with sheer rock and stone. Staying close, the footing is usually good, but he makes sure.

"One time, after the Machete guy, Heidi came with Fabiano on his motorcycle. He worked at the hospital sometimes and gave her a lift. We were sitting on the porch and drinking lemonade or orangeade or something, talking mostly. The four of us. Then a neighbor comes down into the courtyard, he's coming from the back fields up toward the top of the mountain above the farm. He says his cow got loose on our land and was around there somewhere. We got up to help him look and found it over by our cows and mules, but it was spooked and restless. His farmhand roped the cow's neck and pulled it tight around a pole. We had fanned out to prevent her running off and getting away, but she wasn't moving. Adamant, not a chance."

Stopping at an area where the trail widens, he turns back to look this way, speaking methodically and in steady rhythm.

—He's told this story before.

"There's a lot of confusion. They don't know what to do. The cow seems to be cooperating, so the guy lets go of the rope. Not clear how that decision was made, but the cow bolts and doesn't care who's blocking the way. Liam and I were standing off in that direction. Liam went left, I went right. The cow was headed my way and by all accounts got extremely close. I turned my back and ran. Had a red and black shirt on. This one, or like it. Everyone thought that's why she charged me, but they were only guessing."

Wanting to touch him while standing there. Settling on a half-step closer.

"Luckily, I took a bad step and there was kind of a ledge in the grass where I was running. I fell, but off to the left, downhill. The cow kept going, right past me. If I hadn't fallen, she would have trampled me. Cows don't turn fast, that's the lesson. Same as bullfighting. You zig to get out of the way, their momentum carries them forward. But you have to do it at the last second."

He's visualizing it, it's in his eyes, not only a story, but the real thing right there in front of him.

"Heidi and Liam came over right away. She was farther off than he was, so she must've run fast to get to me as quickly as he did. I'll never forget the look in her eyes."

—Couldn't stand to see anyone hurt. Suffering was impossible.

"That day she didn't want to leave. It was her day off. Fabiano left right after lunch, but she stayed, said she wanted to keep an eye on me. Don't know what she thought was going to happen, but she... I don't know... She didn't want to leave."

Turning back down the trail, the creek runs off to the side now. Didn't see where it began, there was this notable crack in the earth with water flowing alongside the path. No standing pool at the top, nothing that looked like a source.

—Where is this water coming from? Is it runoff from the rain yesterday? Still?

Getting warmer. Stopping to take the thin sweater off. He takes out the water and hands it over. Unused garment folded away, then taking the bottle and a healthy sip.

"You have nice arms," he says, nodding in the direction of the bent one resting on the hip.

"Are they the same as hers?" Without thinking, then looking down awkwardly.

—Stupid question.

He's blushing. "I don't know, are we supposed to talk about that?"

"We can talk about whatever we want. I need to know. Everything, I don't mind..."

Handing the water back to him and he takes a big sip before putting it back in his pack. He slings it over his shoulder and adjusts it to fit squarely against the center of his back. He straightens up to even things out.

"Everyone said we looked alike. This hair. I only did this after. It was because of you."

—And Eva, so she'd stop being afraid... ...and angry.

"Me?"

"I told you, didn't I? I didn't want you to think I was a ghost. It wasn't exactly the same as hers, but close. That braid."

"She changed her hair in Colombia too. Wore it shorter," he says.

Nodding sadly.

(Framed by the box, hair cropped short to keep it out of the way. Didn't look right. Not her.)

He looks down, uncomfortable. In contrast, it's immediately obvious.

—He sees the images: he sees me seeing her.

"I didn't mean..."

"It's okay. Abrupt. The way these things come at you," he reassures.

"Everyone said we looked alike, but no one knew. I mean... They're talking about chins and noses. Foreheads. From the portraits. But were we? Alike, I mean."

Looking anywhere but in his direction. He acknowledges the temporary privacy, and squats down close to the trail directly in the line of sight but not seen.

He looks up, smiles kindly.

"It's not only pictures," he says, speaking slowly. "It's movement. The way people look, you know, the gestures and how they go from a frown to a smile or whatever, that comes from inside."

—Then it's not too late...

He stands up straight and brushes his hands together to clean something off. Looks as though he's about to head off down the path again. Grabbing his arm stops him.

"Was that how it started then?"

"How what started?"

"The two of you. After the cow. She was worried about you and then..."

He bows his head, purses his lips, and takes a deep breath.

"I drove her back up to the hospital later. She invited me to stay. It wasn't exactly romantic, but..."

He stops. Looks off down the path. He wants to get away from here, but the hand on his shoulder blocks his way. He's become more aware of it and looks down.

"I want to know."

"I told you before. I mean, she was alone. It must've been almost a year by then. She said she liked me, that I seemed to be a good sort. That's how she put it. She proposed an arrangement, simple as that. There was affection, I don't mean that it was impersonal, only that, well, she needed someone. That's it."

"And the cow made her think that could be you."

"She said the cow decided our fate. Pure luck."

"You were pretty young, weren't you?"

"Twenty."

"Did you have much experience?"

"Hardly any. She was patient with me. Had no choice, I suppose."

"Was she your first real affair?"

His eyes go soft and glisten. Putting the arms around him and pulling his head close. He accepts the embrace, but breaks it shortly after, wrapping his arms into a brief, parting hug, and clanging them against the small knapsack. He uses the distraction to turn sideways and skirt past a few steps down the trail. His eyes change slightly, looking spooked and calm at the same time.

"I'm not trying to make it weird, but I was wondering about that..."

"About what?" he asks interrupting.

"Last night. When I... You know..."

He breathes out in relief and smiles almost rakishly. Such sudden twists and turns, but he wears them like makeup or thin masks.

"It's, well... ...that was unusual. Lovely, but unusual. I don't usually... I can't... I'm wondering... Did she show you that? I know it's creepy. I wish I didn't want to know. But did she?"

"Well, she discovered it, I guess you could say. She said my anatomy was... ...well-suited."

He's choosing his words carefully, but the tension is long gone and it's mostly for his own benefit that he remains guarded.

"I don't know why, but that makes me feel better. Is that gross?"

"We say, may her memory be a blessing," he says chuckling, but it isn't clear what's supposed to be funny.

"We?"

"From the Shtetl, not the Kibbutz, that's irrelevant," he says flipping his hand to the side as if waving it away. "When I was a kid, my parents said it. I thought it meant that when you think of them, hopefully you'll remember them kindly. Something like that. But now I think more about actions and the things we do, the things that happen to us. Anything that evokes a trace of them, when you don't think about it or realize it, they are there for you, in you."

—As you.

"May it be a blessing," he finishes.

Can't stop smiling now.

(Didn't remember the last time a silly grin flared across my face that way. Didn't remember the last time there was such lightness.)

"Thanks for telling me."

—Always... ...blessing.

Turning down the path, taking the lead off toward Oberstdorf.

9.12
this year's harvest

9.12.1.Elisabet.19.86.5.10

Solstice is packed. Tonight it's a private party, but that's not the party to go to. Those people are for decoration, to flesh out the experience for the others, those connected to the people paying for it.

(Inside, there was a black curtain guarding a doorway opening onto a stairway leading up. Two big guys in tight shirts and slacks stood there and maintained a second list. The one on the left was holding the clipboard and filled in the name next to the +1. Nearby, it's flashing light, dance music, and plenty of cocaine with cheap liquor heavily watered down, but flowing freely. The bar tab will be astronomical. Upstairs more casual, the smell of pot was everywhere, and the music easier on the ears. There were mostly wine glasses on the tables and in the hands throughout the rooms where people were having conversations, catching up with old friends they hadn't seen in a while, or who they didn't usually come across because both were exceedingly busy these days.)

He comes up while Marianne is telling a story about the session that day. Their lead singer, the diva, threw a fit because someone was smoking in the studio and he couldn't tolerate it, said it would find its way into his voice. The techs thought he was nuts, but the producers were adamant, and the union got involved. He stands quietly and watches. Marianne includes him with her eyes. He doesn't interrupt and seems to catch on quickly. She finishes and turns toward Brod who came by and is asking her something now that she's finished. Something irrelevant. It's her party too, and there are details to sort out.

"Where have you been?"

"Dancing." Once he says it noticing that he's flushed and breathing hard. Handing him a glass of water, he gulps it then asks one of the hovering staff for a refill and a second glass.

"With Jelly? I saw you two talking. She's drawn to you."

"I heard my name," she says coming from behind. She's flushed too and a little out of breath. "Will you get me some champagne?" she says to him. He nods and goes off toward the closest bar. She turns back and says, "We were talking about sex."

"I wouldn't have thought he's your type."

"Don't be silly. Far too young for me."

"Aren't you the same age?"

She laughs and looks off somewhere. "He looks great though," she says feigning distraction. "Are those Niklas' clothes?"

No need to answer. There seems to be a problem at the bar where he's asking for the champagne. The waiter comes back with the water and Jelly takes his glass.

"Are you drinking?" she asks.

"Voice, darling."

"Such a bore. Not a drop?" She won't go back to it. She's a flit. Whatever is next, that's where her mind is. He gestures back this way, and the bartender, after craning to see, turns sideways and points at something on the ground. A smaller woman bends down, takes out a bottle from beneath the other table, and hands it to him to open and pour out a glass. Seemingly unaware of the crisis averted, he takes it and comes back, handing it off to Jelly who gives him the water while apologizing dramatically for contaminating it. He shrugs and takes a sip.

"Doesn't she look gorgeous?" Jelly says gesturing with the champagne flute.

"Beautiful," he says.

"I love the color. The black thing is so over. Always out in front," she says, but he purses his lips. There's something off. She sees someone and excuses herself, has to find out something but is already gone while trying to explain.

"You two sure seem chummy. Last night. Tonight."

"I didn't have much of a choice. She took my arm and led me around. She knows everybody."

"She said you two were talking about sex."

"She asked if you and I were having sex." He awkwardly corrects the phrasing, as if trying to be technically accurate.

"What did you say?"

"Didn't answer. I said it was weird how sex is a euphemism for fucking. That distracted her."

Laughing while imagining the clash of two sensibilities so different.

"It's a trick," he says taking another sip of water.

"What kind of trick?"

"To avoid lying, to speak the truth simply and clearly, but without saying anything. That's philosophy."

"Bravo," touching his shoulder.

He laughs and sits down on the thick arm of the couch nearby. Taking a few steps to stand closer and now towering over him. He looks up and there's a sudden residual from this morning. Taking his chin in hand and turning him upward while looking down. Two broad smiles find each other beneath twinkling eyes.

"You sometimes say and do the perfect thing. You have to make sure it's on purpose."

He nods.

"That look, right there. It's the same as this morning. Is it on purpose? Make sure."

Smile beams wider. Same soft movement while the hand strokes his cheek and then lets his lips and jaw go free.

"Do you honestly think this looks good?" Flaring out and bending a knee. The black, couture dress, the stockings and strappy heels. Showing it off and almost beginning a twirl but thinking twice about the effects on the glass.

"I loved what you were wearing earlier today, when you first got back, when your hair was normal. That skirt, I don't know." He's picturing it and looks pleased.

"Bare legs, sandals, and a simple peasant skirt with a T-shirt? You liked that better than this Chanel?"

(Such a lovely warm day. Immeasurably comfortable. No jewelry, except Mom's necklace, not the ring. Reminded me of warm days as a girl. Summer, the feeling of grass on my legs. Everyone else thought this dress and being done up, these bracelets and earrings, that's what beauty was supposed to look like. The makeup mask, stockings squeezing me into shape, shoes pinching at the feet and limiting my movements. They'd have me bound and gagged and call it heavenly, dangling on display.)

"I don't know fashion."

"You know your own taste." Touching the back of his hand holding a drink with the back of a hand holding a drink.

He nods multiple times, quite sure of it.

Charles is hovering nearby, he's waiting impatiently. Doesn't want to interrupt but appears to have something on his mind.

"Kevin came over to do the blow out. Women would kill for that, and you think it looked better before." Laughing and shaking side to side.

"What does it matter what I think? It's taste."

"Let me ask you, do you have this record?"

He pauses and listens to what's playing.

"███ *help yourself,* ███ *take too much*" she croons.

"This song's on a couple different records. I have one."

"You recognize it? You own it."

"Billie Holliday. Yes."

"What else do you own?"

"All kinds of stuff. Beethoven, Bach, Miles Davis, Meat Loaf. Led Zeppelin. I have a lot of that. Bowie. I don't know. It's all over the place. Almoraima."

"Any Paisley?"

He looks down, trying to think of how to be diplomatic. Can't think of anything and shakes his head.

"Why not?"

"It's not methodical, not a science. There's music you buy and music you don't. Everyone's that way. Paisley, I don't know, it comes on the radio. Some of it's good. There's that one song. It's almost chromatic. Or minor modulation on a major, something like that. Taking Time."

"*Taking My Time.*"

"I love that song. If it comes on the radio, I'll listen to it. Turn it up."

"But you never bought the record. Why not?"

"It's the same with Journey. I can tell he has an amazing voice, but I don't own any of their records either. It's something you pick up, top 40 stuff is part of a whole industry thing that I never got into. I don't know. The guys I worked with in high school, they taught me to think that way. If it's part of some weird pop culture that you reject, loved by people you don't respect, then you completely reject it. Beethoven's not trendy. Miles Davis, Billie Holliday."

"Led Zeppelin?"

"Well, that's the whole vibe of the people I was hanging out with. Not exactly trendy, but it was part of who we were. Wearing worn out clothes and listening to Zeppelin, that's what you do. In college, that turned into Pink Floyd and Jimi Hendrix."

Nodding, looking into his eyes.

[Refreshing honesty, the record company never talks that way. Little vampires who want to suck the money blood until there is nothing left, until only the sucking remains.]

Charles is still there, talking to Petter.

—When did he get here?

"I think Rick is here somewhere. There." Gesturing over to the other side of the room. He doesn't follow the gesture and remains fixed, doesn't blink. Can feel his eyes laser focused.

Marianne comes back, holding a glass of wine this time. Charles is visibly annoyed that she has cut in front of him.

"Marianne, take L over to Rick and introduce him. He's a fan."

"No, that's okay," he says. "I like their music, that's it."

Marianne smiles and takes him by the arm, so he has to stand up to avoid pulling her down. "*Come ███ dear boy,*" she quotes and then imitates a bass line. They walk off in that direction. "She needs a minute."

Charles comes up. "Did you run the hair color by focus?" he asks.

Ignoring him, "I saw you talking to Petter. Is that your agenda? It's a party." The last word stretches out for many syllables and turns singsongy near the end, channeling Steven Tyler.

"It isn't funny, Elisabet. This is going to have consequences."

(That's not what he's talking about. He didn't bother to spell out the connections. It was all one to him.)

—He thinks I'm a puppet, a marionette.

Half dancing in place, the pick me up of the hands and arms attached to strings at the joints, a knee-high-step abrupt for impact, but it goes over his head.

He looks back over this way from across the room to see the whole sweep of the movement. Gulps and takes a sip. Coughs, choking the liquid up from the wrong path.

"Yes Charles, actions have consequences. You must put together a presentation for us. One of those lovely chart boards you like so much."

"It will cost you. Not some projected or hypothetical costs, there will be a bill, you will have to write a check."

"Me?"

"Paisley. Don't play dumb. I've always been straight with you."

"It's kind of the whole point though, isn't it? Or wait. Can we afford it?"

"I don't know, Elisabet." He's shaking his head. "What is the plan for this week? Why are you here?"

"First of all, it's none of your business."

"No, you're wrong. It is exactly my fucking business. Who do you think they're going to call when they have to refund the money? Who do you think is going to have to straighten up this whole mess? That is exactly my job."

"Do your job."

Across the room, he tells a story to Marianne and Tina. Doesn't appear to have any qualms about meeting her.

—I bet he owns some of their records. Am I jealous? Why is everyone so friendly right away? That is why they call her Jelly, isn't it? Petter's divorce, countless others I bet.

Charles is biting his tongue and shaking his head. "This isn't the end of it. We'll talk about it some more," he says.

"In an office with everyone who needs to be there." Waving fingers at him from high up near the chin. He walks off. Petter stops flirting with the waitress and immediately replaces him front and center.

Leaning in and touching his shoulder warmly, cheek goes to cheek, then saying, "I have to sit down," taking a seat on the arm where he was sitting before Marianne carried him off.

(He made it look so comfortable.)

—It isn't. Deceptive.

"When did you get in? Are you having a good time?"

"Today. No. Miserable." He's drinking wine too.

(Everyone was drinking. Not him. Solidarity.)

—The glances from across the room, that's what makes it seem as if he's with you. N used to do that. Before.

"You looked like you were having fun with your little friend."

"That's because he's the only one here who doesn't give a damn about any of this nonsense." Switching to Swedish just in case, but still lowering the tone.

"You give a damn too then? Still?"

"Do you remember that guy who introduced us?"

"In Malmö? What was his name?"

"Frederick? I don't know. Do you remember him?"

—Anders, but not if you don't.

(They were always there, standing guard over the transitions. A bridge, or a passing chord. They were the key changes, the run that goes up and back again. From girl to woman, from painter to singer, from brown to blonde. Now? Now? And now? Begin again.)

—Your natural color. I've seen it, he said salaciously.

"Sure, artist wannabe. Painter and musician. Didn't matter as long as it was creative. We thought he was such a phony."

"Something about him helped me think differently about myself. He was my boyfriend."

"I know. We almost blamed you for that."

"Not sure I would've sung for anyone else at that point. It was the first major change. Huge. No talent, but so much passion. He may have been a poser, or whatever, but he was ready for things to happen, he believed in stuff, things mattered."

"We were that way too, young."

"This one's young like that. When I played him the two versions, he didn't think it was stupid. The one I preferred. He didn't think it was weird to change everything to make it what I wanted. Why does everyone think that's impossible?"

"Because he doesn't know any better. We didn't know any better either. That's the thing about being young. They're not more insightful and down to earth, they don't know any better."

"The money, is that it?"

"Fuck the money. None of us care about that anymore."

"What then? This? Hanging out with these people."

"Fuck that. Everybody here is miserable. I want to play."

"And if you have to do it without me?"

"I won't lie, it'll change things, but it doesn't matter. I'll find other people. There's always someone who can't get enough, who lives and dies by the perfect mix, or one more take to get it right. That's easy. The great chemistry, that's harder, but I think you're right. It hasn't been that way for a while. It's okay to move on, it doesn't have to last forever."

"You mean that? You wouldn't hate me?"

"Of course not, you're family. You'll always be family."

Hugging him, "We'll talk more when everybody gets here." Kissing both cheeks. "I better go see what he's up to. Where is he?"

He gestures with his glass. Simon is singing in front of Marianne and some others who have gathered around her. Tina is clapping in a supporting rhythm. Simon is serenading L who is shaking his head and trying to explain something to no avail: Simon is singing over him, and everyone is laughing, including L. For a moment, looking around the room, it seems to be the liveliest corner, the only lively corner.

9.12.2.Seannafair.20.15.5.7 [ref(19.86.5.24)]

Late and chilly. Not dressed properly, need a heavier coat. It gets cool later in the evening when the days are fair. He follows along through the door and onto Gloucester, stumbling back up the road toward Harrington. He's still got that pint and is racing to get as much of it down as he can. Leaning up close to him for warmth, wishing he'd be done with it so he can put his arms to good use like a gentleman.

"It was our first performance as Aine," but he's not listening. Too busy with the pint, and it's almost gone now but the movement's happening none too quickly. He sets the glass down on the ledge next to the building, it's that place where they have the nice scones and you can sometimes get fresh squeezed orange juice in the morning. "A place in Oxford. The Saloon. We were thrilled. The A&R man must've booked it for us. Don't think we'd done it on our own. Mike never said anything about it. and it wouldn't have been any of the others."

(We rehearsed for three solid days. Scared to death over 30 minutes. The material wasn't the problem. Knowing what to do was the problem. We thought we knew who we were but now we were turning into something else. He said something about it, something about how you shouldn't throw it up into the air because some bloke came along selling the right story. You should have principles, there should be some clarity over what you wanted. What did you want, Jenni? What were you hoping for? Was it this, was it the hair, the outfit? I had new clothes and we'd been round to the salon. It was cut the way he said, how it should be, and the color was what he wanted. It was as if he was the one going up there but doing it through us. That slimy bastard. We were acting out the scene, and only the American was saying we shouldn't rush it, we should think it through and make sure we're doing it the way we wanted. We were becoming none too sure of ourselves. Was it the music or was it getting people to hear it? Which was it after all? What was it we came all this way for?)

—About the image. A role model for the kids. Too much England in me after all this time.

(Days that were strange, nights more so. Couldn't sleep. Then what was that, working it out? Never before with any other. Hands in places not a chance, touched in places not to think of. Spidery and fluid. Nearly fully dressed but rolling about. More and more over the top. Too much energy, I couldn't get it out, and it was the only way to have it off. We had to look for it, the two of us. Never talked to a fella that way before. Don't think I've talked to one since. Not like that. We're sitting there having it off together trying to find the best way. The way to make it work to let me sleep, to let me get that sound and fury out of the head and put it to rest. Wherever it needed to go.)

Almost to the corner but stumbling along. There are people streaming out of the Hereford.

(None of that lot from before. They must've left long ago, when the tab closed, and the money ran out. Not as if they had any of their own to keep them going. Rain held off all day. Must've rained somewhere. Cross town or off beyond it. It's always raining somewhere this time of year.)

"Can't go home." Doesn't register. Not a brain cell left in sight. Nothing to get too eager about. "I'm cold." Pushing up against him, but he doesn't respond. There's nothing left of him. "Let's go up to Queen's Gate, that hotel from before. Stay with me."

"Can't luv, need to be on my way. They'll be expecting me."

"You can have a go, I don't mind. Please, I don't want to be alone."

"You're the devil herself, but I honestly can't. Wait. I'm turned around. I need to go back up the other way." He turns but doesn't move. Standing still at the corner. People have mostly moved on. It'll turn quiet and then it'll pitch and then nothing. Only the night and nothing left.

(To be honest, I never much liked it. Having them up inside me and that. Could take it or leave it. It was as if it was happening to someone else. With him, as sweet as it was, it was more about that look. The way his eyes bore down on me from above. The shake of it, that was nothing, but his eyes, they held me. His soft lips. I was with him then and there wasn't anything to separate us. It was an honest fill and fine old time. For three solid days, but he wouldn't let it go at that. He said we could find something. He said everybody has their way. What did I do on my own? That's what he wanted to know, as if I would tell him. But he insisted and was pretty good at wriggling his way if I must admit. Not aggressive and for his own sake. He wasn't trying to be the man, the way they can, puffed up and thinking it's him that does the trick, that knows what's what and gets it done. No, it was more like he thought he could help. Offered to step out and leave me alone, but that was the last thing I wanted. I told him about the eyes and lips, and about how those were the only things that worked for me, that made me feel as though I was being held or touched or something like that. His mouth, his hands. My hands. None of it was any good, none of it helped, I couldn't find it anywhere. Not after the jump start from that man and the preparations for the Saloon. What was I supposed to do? Stay up and keep on going, keep on looking for whatever it was I thought I would find in that song or in the people listening to it.)

Terry isn't moving. He wants to leave but is afraid of the consequences. "I should walk you there," he says thinking he's got to see to it.

—Thinking I haven't made it on my own all these years without the likes of you.

"Don't be a twat. Go about your own, I don't need nothing. Not if you can't be bothered. Go, I don't care." Getting worked up, and he's not put off by it. It's a release, a free escape, and he goes as if he hasn't a care in the world, on his own, with nothing left for nobody.

[That's his wife and kids who'll be expecting him. Grown-ups by now, but kids anyway.]

—Same as mine. With their dad and not wondering where I am. Grateful for the silence, not having to pick up after me.

(He was on the bed wearing only a pair of boxers. Soft, but they weren't exactly cotton. And the fly... ...well, it didn't stay closed, it would fluff open and flap about. They must've had some nylon or something in them. Something to make them soft too, a blend. It was a nice material. What was it? But he was lying there that way he had. And me, what was I doing? I'd been jotting things down, trying to take notes, trying to figure out how to sing for the clothes. Was that it? These new things, somehow I had to change to find my way into them. The hair and the clothes, all of me. And that's why I couldn't have anything on. Before he was lying there in his boxers, he was sitting there fully dressed watching me storm back and forth, trying to figure out which of the things to put where. Trying this on and that. Stomping around naked. The knickers weren't right. The layers of shirts that A&R man told me to wear, the different outfits he bought me. For the show, for the sake of putting on a show. He needed to know if they would react the way he thought, the way he expected. He told me what to wear, but I couldn't. I had to come up with some other way, something that was better and closer to me. What kind of authentic image would it be if it came from A&R? I was convinced I had to be the one to come out with it, to find the final form or bits of something, the fragments or tatters or whatever you'd call it. It had to come from me and that's why I was crazy walking around back and forth. Socks and tights, skirts and various other things. Not limited to what he bought me. Everything was possible. There was something I hadn't thought of, something of my own that could bring it out. Like Aine herself. How the name worked.)

—It was me that undressed him, right?

"Are you sure, Jenni?"

"Go. Doesn't matter. It's just up the street a bit. I can get there on my own. They know me there. From the other time. Go. Piss off. Don't need any charity."

He squeezes the shoulder, doesn't get any reaction and flaps his hand before saying nah or zah, something like that. And then he's off.

—Bye bye, for feck's sake, you rummy. Now which way?

Crossing over and looking through the windows, but it's too far and can't see Mary or any of them. Gone, lights are low and nobody's about. Back up this way, good to be on the other side away from the gardens. No one can jump out of there.

—Not that I'd notice. I'm not here for it. Wouldn't know it if it did happen. Wankers. Every last one of them.

(We did find something though. And later I showed it to Don. That's how I knew he was the one, because he didn't judge me for it. That was when he was sweet, when he cared, when everyone cared. Not like now. No one gave a toss. The beauty with the eyes, lying on his back, with his thing hard and pressing through that fly barely closed. If he were here right now, here with me, in his sweetness, he wouldn't want none of it. Wouldn't care at all and couldn't be bothered. It'd be nothing to him, but then it was something. I climbed up on top of him and he moved his legs about trying to help me find the right way, and I couldn't because I kept thinking this is how it is with girls, this is how it has to be, and I was trying to sit around him and sit up with my legs on either side, how they do it in the movies or the girls in the park with their fellas. That's how it's supposed to go, but it didn't feel right, and I couldn't get comfortable. He wouldn't give up though, got to give him that much. What did he do? He pushed my legs tight together and spread his apart. It was magic. All of a sudden. Comfortable, completely at ease. I could slip in there and find the right nook to rest. Tight together, that's what I needed. Didn't know it. And I reached down and pulled him completely out of his boxers, he wanted to come out anyway, and it was easy enough. Then with my hand, tugging him about and putting him there, where I needed him to make it feel right. Why hadn't anyone ever done it before? Why hadn't I ever thought to try? It was a new virginity or something, and it didn't take long. I was having it off and having it off, again and again. He lay there and whispered to me. What was he saying? Nothing much, nothing I can remember, but it was encouraging and that was what mattered most. He was letting me know that it was okay, that he enjoyed it. Sliding back and forth, faster and faster, grinding up against something hard. Not that, it was inside me, but there was something. He said I could do what I was doing without worry. Take what you want, that's what he said. Over and over again. That's it, Jenni, take what you want. That's it, Jenni, take what you want.)

—He got his too, that first one. Inside me. But that was separate. Far away. As if it was happening to someone else. Only his eyes were with me, only they were inside me. Wait. Which one now? The American, not the other. When he looked away or closed them, I thought I was disappearing. Then he'd come back, then everything would be there again. The same as that.

Passing the gardens and getting to the shops by the corner at the boulevard to the right. On Queen's Gate there's a small hotel. A couple of blokes pass by heading back the other way. They don't look over, don't look up, nothing. Invisible to them.

(Needed that to sleep. Without it, I would've been wrecked. The energy had nowhere to go, and there was so much of it. Once I found that rhythm and that place and those lovely angles, once I had that, I went there again and again until there was no difference between going there and not going there. I didn't have a care in the world, and everything stopped pounding. There wasn't anything to get seized up about and I was asleep. Fully sound asleep where I must've been for hours on end, waking up the next morning refreshed and ready. Not sure that night would have gone as well as it did if I hadn't been able to find that place. I asked him if it was alright and could tell from the look in his eyes that it was. Fine, in fact. Don was the same way. That's home then, that's how it had to be from then on. Only the fellas who could let you in there, only the fellas who would be good to you that way, those were the only ones I could find any peace with.)

Queen's Gate is better lit and walking up the street side, everything will be okay.

(Same as that night. The tight magenta T with no sleeves and cut low in front and back. The black loose overshirt falling down over the shoulders and giving that carefree look. The low socks and big thick boots with the steel toes. Then there was that flappy skirt and the way it would drape and slide up and back. A pair of boys' bike shorts under it. Must've been quite the sight. Looking like nothing I ever seen. It was what I thought best, a combination of what he had bought for me and what was in the closet already. And the hair, didn't need to do anything special for that, it fell into place. Short and cut perfectly: there was nothing left up to me, nothing to choose, but I wouldn't let them touch it. And the whole of it. Jet-black color, then mostly black fabrics with a splash of shocking pink or magenta or whatever it was. Those matching triangles on the skirt. It was a tough look. Strong and my arms were showing through. I remember walking up and down that stage bellowing, with the arms and the legs and everything flippy and taut. I've never felt that alive in my life. *My Life.* Everything was changing, and I wanted it badly. I was getting exactly what I wanted. That's it, Jenni, take what you want. That's it, Jenni. Not anymore. Not to any of them that day. No longer that. No more Jenni to take nothing, not from that day on. Aine. Just Aine. Take what you want. Take what you want. Take what you want.)

9.12.3.Natalie.19.86.8.22 [ref(..7.8-24)]

Peeling the potatoes after giving them a good wash.

—She's never been that way before. Not to me. Good friends with Fredericka and I trust her. Could be Yvonne. She brings that out in people. They're both with Jürgen. And she's at the same place which means we're competing. Poisons her. Scarce resources always bring out the worst. Both of them. With Ingrid, it's particularly bad, and I can't be certain what she's saying, but must be buzzing in his ear. Of course, it's normal. With Karl too, but at least I keep it professional. I wouldn't slice and dice my colleagues for a few morsels.

Cutting them into cubes then leaning the board up against the side of the sink.

—For what? Ammunition? Karl and Jürgen in a battle with pawns? Is that how a cold war works? Warm bodies. Isn't it fucking hard enough to be a woman here? The looks and the bullshit. Practically a kid and he is far more mature than those middle-aged assholes.

(It was a grope. You can write it off to the booze all you want, jackass, but we both know what it was. Hands don't...)

—Why do we tear at each other for their fucked-up attention? Why? She'll be a big star, get every accolade. Who wants that kind of attention, and how fucking much are we supposed to give up to get it?

Adding them to the pot and turning up the flame to bring it to a boil. Bare feet on the cool floor stepping on tip toes across the work area in front of the sink briefly glancing out the window to check if anyone is coming up the walk.

—We make decisions when we're young enough that it doesn't matter, no deep repercussions. If I leave and do something else, there's time for that. I can change, people do it all the time. In their thirties. Where is he anyway? He didn't mention going out anywhere special today. *Early* thirties.

(Do like the girls around here and find a guy, crank out some babies. Go back to work later, people move a lot. It's doable. God. Pea brain.)

—But ten years from now, how would that work? Who would have me? They'd be perfectly happy to use me up lecturing and spit me out once they're done. They don't give a shit. And this here now decides what I'll be in ten years. Everything on the line. Oh, she's so fucking disappointed in me.

Lay out the newspaper and set the pork fillets side-by-side.

—It's not random. They didn't have a space problem and need that deferral. Not enough money. Not asking Martin for help. This is not the problem for his long-sought solution. What's Karl's excuse? He knows it's bullshit, knows how people are. When they have to make tough decisions about distribution they fall back on bad habits. They have a gut, make some kneejerk decision about who to spoil and who to rob, then justify it, come up with reasons, arguments, all kinds of shit, something to put on the permanent record. Building mythologies out of petty gossip and turning them into real things, as if they are real, as if they actually happened. Everyone thinks... Always the everyone, it's a collective, that mindless other, not they in the singular, but the whole mass of them. Their inertia pounding against you. The enemy. A colossus. A mountain of sick people. Sickness becomes the rule.

Using the hammer to tenderize them more than necessary. Increasing the intensity and enjoying the sound providing immediate feedback of power in the act.

—Doesn't tenderize us in the least. Become vicious bastards. The worst. My strength, my willful independence, lies in not needing *them*. It's always about *them*. He's too sweet. Too open. He doesn't believe me. About how quickly the juniors jump on this or that fad, move into this or that fashionable area. Fashion. That's the whole fucking thing. Fascism. He's nothing like that. A wayward obsession with the new and the new and the new, never stopping and never resting, but forcing yourself into ever new territory because this will make your mark, get you ahead of the curve. Always. That's how it is. Topic and flavor of the month. Rigidly organized. Fashion constantly moving and yet so fucking determinate and unyielding. If you violate the rules, your status as pariah is immediately sealed. Everyone laughs at the foible, the faux pas: we're not reading him that way anymore, how droll of you to betray your history, get with the here and now, you moron.

Cracking the eggs and making the flour paste while the potatoes boil. Adding the herbs and seasoning, hands kneading into it like a child playing with plaster of paris.

—Is that the one with the newspaper that hardens? He doesn't like the messy sauces and soft vegetables. This'll be nice. Traditional German. Mostly. How can you eat that? Funny what goopy things over the tongue disgust him and which ones fill him with delight.

Giggling and rubbing the nose with the back of a caked hand, then giving it a rinse.

—It's not people at their best. You can't deny it. We're the only women. Aside from grad students, I mean. Don't count. Completely clueless. Until cornered. Then comes a quick education. And the professors... ...but they're deer trying to hide from wolves. Worse sometimes. And we don't talk to each other. Why not? We should be talking about this. Everything. Calling each other out when we pile on. I should confront her and be real and honest without attacking her, without making her feel defensive. As if that were the problem. Bullshit. She's staked her claim and desperately holds on. The whole confrontation would be further grist for the mill. Can't let down once it's up. Jockeying for position, trying to figure out how to outflank her, we might as well be men. Worse. They make the rules, and we exceed them... Much better at following directions. Become experts... Invested...

Some seasoning, some herbs, use the wide bowl to make sure there's plenty of room for the fillets.

—I can visualize doing well. It's not hard. The feminist angle, it's acceptable, as long as it's decorative. Salah would play along. Why not? It makes her look good. Someone ascends under Karl, and she gets to ride the coattails. That's how you distribute it. Do your own thing. Have your own students and lecturers, but with greater scope, broader, more impactful. Need lots of supporting roles, don't spread yourself too thin. She always points that out. Always strategic, full of helpful information for getting along and thriving in this hellhole. You have to know your place and how to skirt the edges. To your advantage. Oh, and put the screws to any upstart who comes along. Make sure they're at a disadvantage and you don't lose any ground.

The potatoes have been boiling long enough, drain them and let them cool.

—The idea's clear. Pick an established recipe and add some footnotes. Close it with a clever conclusion. Plenty of examples. Check out the offerings from Suhrkamp Verlag over the last twenty years. Introduction frames it. Chapter one thinker one, chapter two thinker two, chapter three thinker three, etc. Conclusion wraps it up. Put on a bow if you must. Curtsy. Face the crowd. Voilà. Yet another great work featuring the stylings of Benjamin, Gehlen, and Weber. Or whatever mishmash you can come up with to fashionably present your vision. Throw in an American for good measure. Avoid the French, they'll make everything bitter. If you can find some obscure modern-day Confucian, it'll work like an added oomph to give the whole thing zest. There's hardly a single woman who qualifies. Hannah, of course, but don't you dare suggest she's a feminist. As if being a badass were irrelevant.

Get the frying pan ready and add the oil.

—Besides, it's so hypocritical to call her German. Oh, yes, a proper German girl running for her life from murderers drooling to get their fucking hands on her. And they almost did. Truth be told, on this side of the social theory debate anyway, we'll never forgive that diminutive forest walker for the harm he caused. Not only the Rector's address, or blocking his advisor from entering the building, but for fucking his Jewess before kicking her to the curb. Todtnauberg. Think about that while Paul kicks your ass, you Nazi motherfucker.

> *([Arnica, eyebright, the*
> *draft from the well with the*
> *star-die on top,*
>
> *in the*
> *Hütte,*
>
> *in this book*
> *the line about*
> *a hope, today,*
> *for a thinker's*
> *word*
> *to come,*
> *in the heart,[1])*

Let it warm up while going back to the fillets and finishing with the paste. Coming up the walk, there he is.

Door opens and the sounds of his shuffling shoes coming off, left nice and neat right at the front door. Give them a thorough dusting until they are thick with the paste. Well behaved, he never forgets. Zippers and belts clang, must be the daypack set down on the bench.

Now add the potatoes and repeatedly work them around the pan until they brown and crisp.

"Where are your pants?" he asks, coming around the corner and poking his head into the kitchen. Laughing at the sight. Bare feet and a crop top with a scrap of sheer cotton left between.

"Lots of oil. Didn't want to stink up what I was wearing."

Not interrupting but he plants a kiss before an immediate move toward the wine rack and a new bottle of Côtes du Rhône. He pulls out the corkscrew and sets the bottle aside to let it breathe. Mixing some butter, parsley, rosemary, and pepper into the pan and stirring it until they're covered, looking for a nice even color.

"Smells good. Are those for Schnitzel?" he asks.

Moving them to a serving plate, covering it, and putting it in the oven.

"You said you wanted to try mine."

---

[1] Todtnauberg by Paul Celan, translated by Pierre Joris.

He takes a couple glasses from the rack and fills them out of the way in an unused part of the countertop. Pushing the potatoes around to make room for the next batch.

"Where have you been?"

Laying the fillets into the heated oil and keeping them moving.

"I wanted to check out southeast of town. I was hiking along the river from the bridge heading out."

"How far did you get?"

Flipping them about half-way through.

"Burg Stolzeneck. Then to the Lindach train station."

Repeat on the other side.

"Does that train run today?"

"No, I found that out. Wasn't a big deal. Near Wolfsschlucht there's some kind of nature house or something. The lady there filled my water bottle. Gave me some cookies."

Once goldeny brown and ready, taking them off the heat and moving them onto the serving plate.

"Charming the ladies, were you? What else?"

"She was sixty years old. Drove me back here."

Setting it back in the oven to keep it warm and ready.

"Only you with these stories. Everyone always wants to help you along the way. Why is that?"

Putting arms around his neck and going up as high as possible on tip toes to give him a proper snog.

"She said she needed some stuff from the department store. I told her I could hitch back but she said it was a good excuse."

Reluctantly letting him go and turning back to the refrigerator, getting out the greens with the shredded Parmesan and Caesar from this morning.

"You're a little ripe."

Washing it and mixing it into the bigger bowl, taking the slivers of fish out of the jar and setting them on the paper.

"I'll jump in the shower. Care to join?"

Shooing him off. "Make it quick, it's almost ready, and be sure to dress appropriately."

Spreading both hands wide and taking a slight bow to let him get a good look at appropriately. He runs off heading down the stairs to the bathroom. The water sprays and he howls shortly after, not waiting for it to warm up.

Finishing the potatoes and draining the oil into the can.

—I hope he doesn't want to go to that party. Has he grown tired of me? I can't face those people. Hazel'd be hard to swallow today. She means well, but sometimes I don't want to talk about it. *Travel other worlds.* He'll let me read to him again. Is that what it's called now? Reading to me. Are you sure I'm not the one reading to you?

[Bookbinder. We haven't tried that. Might be nice. There's some scarves we could use.]

Setting the table then pulling out the plates from the cabinet and putting two pork fillets on each.

—Simple. But what can you do? He likes simple. Classic. Customary and local. I didn't come to Germany to drink Heineken.

Laughing while using tongs to put potatoes on the plates.

—Should've braised some greens or something. Sauerkraut. The color isn't right.

Getting down a couple smaller bowls for the salad and heaping each full of lettuce, adding some croutons, then laying the fish on top of the cheese and dressing at the end. He comes back wearing a pair of boxers and a clean T-shirt.

"Now that's appropriate."

"Reading the room. How was your day, by the way?" he asks.

"Let's not ruin the mood."

Gesturing for him to sit down, he takes the wine glasses and puts them in place before coming back for the salad bowls. Setting the dinner plates next to them as he sits down. Joining him, leaning over for a kiss, both taking up a fork and a knife, eager to see how it turned out.

"Bon appetite."

9.12.4.Greta.19.86.9.27 [ref(..84.5-9)]

—*"There are times when a guitarist, wanting to show off, completely destroys the emotion of the lyrics, or ruins a final flourish."* [Garcia Lorca]

Early sunshine and the bustle of a herd of children moving down the road into town up the trail from the guest house. Looking closer, the boys are making most of the noise, jumping and shouting, the girls are walking along and talking quietly in pairs and threes.

To the south, the mountains are brilliant in the light, trails are nearly empty as autumn marches in. The outdoor furniture is covered now, and the place readies for seasonal change. The colors flare into the hillside and deciduous trees reckon their leaves' departure in due time. Birds haven't yet registered the momentum but there is a buzz in the air. They seem excited somehow.

Sitting and sipping a cup of coffee, meeting his smile as he walks past with one of the backpacks, the smaller daypack tucked away inside. He'll have to make another trip. Enjoying the view and not inclined to move a muscle to help.

—It's expected. Normal.

(It's as if *equal footing* slid off to the side. Not that things were unevenly balanced, but that balance found its way through enormous inequalities. She feigned the protector, led the charge, while he becked and called resplendent in the offerings. With the English words it's hard to track. They were harsher or not as harsh, but if you didn't grow up there, how would you know? Pussy and Muschi made sense. We used those, but cunt you only heard in the movies and when kids said it, so it's hard to know what they're thinking. It sounded rough. He would explain it if I asked, but not on his own. When saying such things in earnest, he described it sideways and never directly.)

—You are so wet.

(An identity. Or was that too much? You. All of you. Are so wet. Was that it? Or you, this is euphemism. It is all of you. What you are. He made a comment about it not being one or something. It is not one. You are not one. One of what? Or do you mean two? He's a boy, but I am not one. He is one person, but I am not one. What did he mean?)

"What are you thinking about?" he asks.

"Nothing. Everything. Watching you pack up the car and enjoying the sunshine."

—He's happy. Happy that I'm happy. That we both are for a while. Until it comes back.

The lady comes to the door and hands over a bag with some treats in it. "Something for the road," she says.

Thanking her and joining him by the car. He's arranging things in the backseat. Always concerned that whatever we need while driving can be easily reached.

"Are we ready?" he asks.

Nodding and getting into the front seat. He can drive.

(Navigation was crucial, and he didn't always stay focused on the right things. It's better if he didn't have to divide himself between the music and the map, food service and obstacle watch. His concentration was better, but context switching left a lot to be desired. He got overwhelmed and frustrated sometimes. It's better when he stayed put in the driver's seat. Then he thought it's because he was in control of a big, powerful vehicle and steering it toward where it's meant to go. In truth, he'd been given a small responsibility to keep him busy.)

The car is low on gas, and he recalls the small filling station up the street back toward the bigger road that heads north.

"That way takes us to the 19. It's faster but it won't be as nice."

"I didn't mean to do that, but I know there's a petrol station up here," he says defensively.

"Ah good, okay, then we come back this way toward the 308."

"Okay," he says simply.

"Either way, we have to go up around the mountains before heading east. We take the 308 to the Austrian border, then it's called something else until we hit the Lech and go north. It's that same road from Holzgau farther south back by Hängebrücke."

He nods, accepting the information. The man comes to pump the gas. Studying the map to see what's around there while he pays without a word.

[Must have some cash tucked away. It's only fair. Still...]

—Doesn't matter. We'd stay in hostels if it were different.

He turns the car the other way and follows directions back to the road.

"How far is Holzgau from there?" he asks.

"From the road north? About 40 km. Not too far."

"North is the way to Garmisch then?"

"Not directly. We're heading to Ludwig's castle. First Neuschwanstein."

He raises an eyebrow and looks sideways, registering the lie from days ago.

(You couldn't catch me. I didn't want to go with *them*, my exact words, that's exactly what I said, not that I didn't want to go.)

"There's a monastery Eva told me about. We can stop there after the castle and on the way round. We have to drive past the Ettaler forest to get to Linderhof Palace. We don't have to stay in Garmisch-Partenkirchen, it's a big city. Many nice places around it. Oberammergau."

He nods and looks pleased. Driving with nothing to do but follow directions agrees with him. Comfortable with the itinerary, everything organized and settled. It's about an hour to Reutte where the road to the castle comes in.

There is a border between here and there, but it doesn't usually take any time to cross. Sometimes they don't check.

"Did it become a regular thing then?"

"Did what become a regular thing?" he asks.

"With Heidi, after the cow."

"Pretty much. Mostly she focused on doing her job. Devoted, nothing distracts her. Mission." He pretends to lecture and smiles visualizing it.

Grinning back at him and rolling the head from side to side against the seat back. Her focus comes into the car, acting the visitor, and now everyone takes part.

"Don Alberto was a tough nut to crack. He didn't take her seriously, she was nothing to him, a little girl from Europe. She'd be gone in no time, and his valley and his ranch and his town would still be there long after."

At Sonthofen, the road bears to the east and the car points into the sun. He puts the visor down to shield his eyes but goes on uninterrupted.

"It was quite a hike down to his ranch from the town and he was always asking Liam and I to come for a visit. It's a big cattle ranch with lots of fruit trees and many different kinds of things."

"Coffee?"

"No, it was much closer to sea level, too hot for coffee. Avocados and other fruit. Lemons. Heidi wanted to go. She knew that was the best way to have a serious conversation with him. She thought if she could get into his space, she would have a better chance of earning his respect. She talked us into accepting the invitation."

Looking over at the mountains to the south and imagining a trip down into the hot valley.

[Climate always changed with the altitude, but much more dramatic at the equator.]

"She hadn't been there before. Not that altitude, right?"

"No. She was," he corrects. "Not at his place, but when you drive up from Medellin you have to cross the Cauca, the village of Bolombolo. She told me she loved the Arepas from that restaurant there, but never Don Alberto's and that's what she wanted, willing to brave the heat."

—Cauca. Bolombolo. Arepas.

"She didn't say..."

"Well, you know how she was. Probably wrote to you about the people she was helping."

Blinking rapidly. Taken aback, but then a deep breath and pushing on. "She did... ...the children..." breaking off and looking down.

(It was about the work, how hard the children worked, how the school year was set up so they could do the harvest. Everything in detail, but not a damn thing about the river she crossed or the food she ate. Not one single thing about Don Alberto.)

—She did mention you though.

"Exactly. When you're helping women, you're dealing with lots of kids. People can't get that through their fucking heads," he says channeling some lost anger she must have let slip in his direction.

"You were saying you went down to Don Alberto's farm?"

"Yeah, and it's a hike, like I said. We drove down into the valley on the other side, away from our farm, back over the peak above the hospital. It's mostly switchbacks and dirt roads. Narrow, bumpy roads. Luckily, you don't get the bus traffic the way you do on the road from Medellin. That would have been a disaster. The road isn't wide enough. Sometimes you have to pull off onto the shoulder and you're half-way in a ditch waiting for the bus to pass. If something like that happened on the way down into the valley, it could've been deadly."

"How were you sitting? Was she in the back seat or the passenger seat?"

He laughs. "She was driving. Liam was going to drive, but she says pfffft, hop in back Pablo."

"Pablo?"

"Sometimes she called Liam Pablo. I told you, he was a jokester, lots of physical humor and silliness. I don't know where Pablo came from, but that's what she'd call him when she thought he was acting the clown."

At the border, they wave the car through. There are two women talking to one of the customs officers. They are on bicycles and struggling to communicate. The man calls another officer over, distracting him so he doesn't have time to mess with a car that has the right stickers.

(It's that way between Germany and Austria. The border up past the Kemptner Hut was a metal sign stuck in the gravel pathway. It's normal.)

"Down in the valley, we parked the jeep at the end of the road. Literally, the end of the road. No parking lot, nothing, only the end of the road. Don Alberto was there with some of his men. Cattle people from the farm. You can't drive right to it, it's off deeper in the valley, and he was meeting us there with horses."

"Did he know Heidi was coming?"

"Of course, we had to tell him. You can't show up with an uninvited guest. No, he was fine with it. I mean, she was ours. If that makes sense. That's how he thought about it. Of course, you can bring your woman."

—She must've loved that.

"The farm was amazing. Riding the horses to get there, riding horses everywhere. We went out and picked avocados one day and the horses were walking on these steep hillsides where the trees are. It was wild. I thought they were going to fall. One guy was on a mule, he was leading the way. They said mules have better footing than horses. Not as good as donkeys though."

"She was riding?"

"Yeah, I mean, none of us could ride. Not seriously. These guys, they could ride. Make the horses do all kinds of things. Walk backwards, that was challenging and looked cool. When I tried with the horse up at our farm, El Paisa, he reared up and I nearly fell. We didn't try anything like that, but some of those guys were standing up on the saddles and using the horses as ladders to reach the avocados. It was great."

Shaking the head. Can't picture it, not wanting to, it's too much at once. "How long were you there?"

"A couple days. Messed with the cows. Liam and I did. Heidi would sit and talk to Don Alberto. She liked that we were distracting the others. It was good. Liam got the idea to torment some of the calves to get the cows to charge us. It was pretty scary, but created a spectacle. Eventually some of the workers came over and got us to stop by taking us to where the bull can mate with this apparatus. It was the weirdest thing. This hardened, gnarly cowboy is jerking off a bull into a jug attached to a big cloth covered contraption. They said it wasn't for the cows on the farm, but they were going to sell it. Apparently, there's a big market for bull semen."

Mouth agape and grinning against reason and purpose.

"Meanwhile, this is lightening the mood for Heidi and Don Alberto. She said they got relaxed and chatty, had some whiskey. Don't see that too often out there, but Don Alberto gets it special from Gabriel. She's loosening him up."

"Why though? Why did she want to get in good with him?"

"Her whole job would be much easier if he wanted her to be successful. Hell, if he at least tolerated her, things would go more smoothly. The Guardia wouldn't hassle the people she was trying to help. Once Don Alberto sees you as one of his pals, or people he cares about, then everyone he knows will change too. The mayor, the Guardia, everyone. She could go anywhere and do anything, and no one would mess with her. That's what she was trying to get."

Shaking the head in disbelief. "But she hates that, that kind of cronyism. She's always saying that's the problem."

"Yeah, and I'm sure she felt that way all the time when she first got there, but she kept running into obstacles. She couldn't be effective. The nuns weren't going against Don Alberto, they wouldn't let some girl stay up at the hospital to keep her away from a horrible situation if Don Alberto didn't approve. They would turn her out. Heidi was a realist, she knew how things worked, and this was an opportunity."

"And you were willing to help?"

"We were apolitical. We were boys to him. He liked us because we were from the right place and represented the right class of people. We didn't try to shake anything up. He treated us well. Always. It was automatic and we didn't have to do anything to earn it. She saw that as an opportunity, a way to make progress."

"Did she?"

"Everything changed. But she was smart about it. Once she was in a position where you couldn't mess with her without incurring his wrath, not that it was that extreme, but once she was in that position, she got humble about it. If she walked around with a big head thinking she could do whatever she wanted, it would have soured. She'd become an embarrassment. She talked about it the whole way back to town, letting Liam drive and sitting in the back and leaning forward talking the whole time about how she figured him out and how she understood what it takes to stay in his good graces. She was excited, happy."

"And did they?"

"Did they what?"

"Did things change?"

"Most definitely. The things... What she figured out... She could walk softly. Once you're inside you don't have to scream and shout. People knew. Gabriel knew. The mayor knew. And once that happened, everyone knew. She got more polite. Same as Don Alberto. He's not some loudmouth who runs around like a lunatic. He barely ever says anything. And that's the way. The men there, that's how they are. That's masculine power. Silent, deliberate, no shouting or threats, only action. She adapted quickly. She was that way, and from what I could tell, she loved it. It suited her."

Up ahead the road comes to a cross past the town of Reutte. There's nowhere to stop and eat, but there's some nice places to pull over and dig into the bag of treats from Oberstdorf. Sitting on the hood of the car after removing the sweater, the sun and wind perfect the day. There are glorious amounts everywhere and the tree-lined north and east slopes of the hills shade the old castles present to the imagination now looking forward.

2.8
the middle american

2.8.1.X.19.86.9.27 [ref(..85.10.15-16)]

[To say what a thing is, that was nothing special. In their way, squirrels said what the tree was when they climbed it, when they harvested its nuts. The living always say what is, how it is and that it is. Saying is ordinary, but imagining what the tree could be, to imagine something for itself amid the branches, that was when the creature ascended.]

(The grasshopper sang its eerie tunes in flight. The other grasshoppers watched in delight, enchanted by the visions and imagining themselves up there. This insect genius spoke from out of the collective hopes of its grasshopper audience, its astonishment drove the speaker further on, imagining more, fabricating more, belting out the possible twists and turns that grasshopper life could take. Such sets, collective, were the only measure of quality. The audience informed that bug whether those were the right notes, and that their taste was the only measure. Not every grasshopper could do it, could hypnotize its fellows, yet they all inflated themselves with the pride of knowing there were some who could. We honored the species, friend, we presented its aspirations in ways beyond compare, we spoke for every one of them. This drove the singer to despair, for it knew that what came up and out of its depths did not belong there, was not its property, but a token that stood for all and sundry, the voicings of a ventriloquist's dummy and nothing more. A seismograph. Imagination may be the greatest achievement of this universe, but its accomplishment was seized by those who witnessed it at the expense of those who suffered it.)

[Submit to the species to make it seem grand, state our case, knowing that the better it is, the less it belongs to us.]

(Careful grasshopper, that was the best that could be. Worst was if they hopped past without turning our way. Then we belonged completely to ourselves, we could lay claim to our singular being alone in the grass, hopping to a tune no one else could hear, and we'd never know what it sounded like to their ears. Best case, we were misunderstood, worst, they didn't care for it.)

Stretching out and arching the back, arms raised up and pressed to the headboard.

"Should it be crickets? Are they cuter?"

[Born with the right voice? Or could it be cultivated? Start simply from where we are. Purge all bitterness. Remove whatever uncontrolled anger there is. It's okay to bring it back later, in smaller doses, but best not to lead with it. No, there should be a smile in everything. And warmth. Warm and friendly, that's what they want. Howdy. Beautiful day, isn't it? My, aren't you extraordinary sitting there listening so attentively. How long and hard must have been your path to this place and time. Sit and rest a while. We'll get along famously.]

"But do such rubes read? What if the only ones left are dark and cynical? What songs will they want to hear? What does it take to keep them rooted to their blade of grass, eyes, so many eyes, pointing straight ahead. What does it take?"

Yawn lacking written onomatopoeia. Up and quickly dressing without the wash, with only a comb through short, coarse hair falling into place.

(The neurotic woman in the Schwartzwald cut hair free of charge giving us our money's worth, cutting each side unevenly until there was nothing left to match or alter, uneven in back and on top, but not in a stylish way. Almost a month later, enjoying simplified morning care and the way it frames the face. Mwah.)

Good enough. Moving quickly through the routine before bringing the rucksack down to breakfast for an immediate departure afterward. So be it. So it is.

[Almost anything worn with confidence worked.]

—Genuine, it has to be genuine, no matter the listener's character. Everyone wants it to be real, even when it comes to imagination and fantasy. Affect it, but without getting caught in the act.

Mist this low, young day lacks sun-driven recovery. Miles of cloudy overcast skies gathering in the Lech valley to make threats on weary walkers with pocket-folded and ring-belted rain ponchos buckled at the waist between belt loops. Weekend traffic buzz buzzed its way on not quite slick streets, polluting ears and lungs leading roadside warriors to anxious fears. There is a dirt path off the pavement by the side of the river. The cassette resonates over the wires to the earphones that block out the sounds of traffic, the rushing river, and the birds.

A car stops and the driver asks for directions. The Austrian woman is not embarrassed to shout over the crooning and through the earphones. The passengers lean forward or sideways to watch in support. Recognizing the need to stop through visual cues, then turning and bending to look into the car.

"Kennen Sie wo Imst ist?" she asks.

Knowing the answer but replying in rough German that leaves them wondering about its accuracy.

"Gerade aus bis Elmen. Links in Elmen auf die einzige straße, und dann gerade aus bis Imst."

Shrugging as they leave with looks of uncertainty.

—No matter, I know where Imst is. They'll have to decide.

"On these Alps, the traveler sometimes beholds his own shadow magnified to a giant making every movement terrific."

At midday, having no shadow while the sun is hostage to the Zeus-gathered clouds, sitting down by the river Lech to eat a leisurely meal of unusual diversity: bread and cheese.

Map in hand, the Allgäuer range in front. On the other side, over the shoulder, stands the Langfeist Gruppe, and the nearby village is Forchach. The mountains in view range from 2037 meters to 2378, the elevation of this rock is 912 meters. The Lech is a fast moving river, but dry this time of year, and half the riverbed is a pile of rocks, invisible at the center where the river flows. Seven and a half million people live in Austria's 32,000 square miles, or 234 per square mile. Consider, however, that 2.2 million of them live in the nation's five largest cities.

"Where are they?" Looking around. "Averages are meaningless."

Sitting in this deserted area of the western Tyrol, the accuracy of the figures is unfathomable.

[Accuracy didn't matter, the feeling mattered.]

—That is why it's crucial to be genuine, no one wants to be manipulated. The feeling is only real if its source is real. They have to trust you. The dark and cynical have to trust you, have to believe they can let down their guard in front of you, that you are one of them and deserve that place in their heads.

The gray sky lends a hyper-sensitive melancholy to the beautiful scenery and pleasing sounds, confusing the most untroubled mind. A pair of mating birds flutter in rapid and constant pursuit of something invisible among the weeds and trees at the riverbed's edge. One is a black bird with severe and prominent white markings on wings, body, and head, the other is a dull blackish gray with no outstanding marks or features.

[Beautiful and colorful males attracted females desirable regardless of appearance. He must be worthy of selection, and she had to select. Did humans follow the rule? Did they sing for love?]

Withdrawing, replacing the focus: "I'm inclined to say yes, but the intellect scorns it. Don't speak for them, neither with spontaneous inclination nor calculated intellect. Both lie."

[It was the duty of each to determine the conditions of inclination and intellect, to decide based on whatever averages burble from within. There were 234 of us out there. 234 speakers and 234 listeners. They were this voice, these inclinations, and this intellect.]

"Have you answered the question?"

Tra-la-la-la-la-la-la.

"To be or not to be?" Someone else said.

Hand lifting up to the sky.

"Nay. That is not the question."

[With a whisper, passing yet another test. Come closer. Tilt the head. Smile. Be confident and bold, but not arrogant and repulsive. Simple and straight. Looking about at those 233 fellows, imagining us there cheering, urging onward, our inclination comes out through the vents in our intellect.]

Still walking by the flowing Lech until the foot path ends, forcing the way back onto the road where the traffic noise is deafening and destructive to the subtle sounds of river life. Flat, walking along the yellow line, hugging the soft grass shoulder of the valley road, eventless treading through the tunnel of beech and spruce trees barricading the stretch from all sights except the gray sky. No definition of cloud, only sheeted tones of gray to white with an occasional vague orange, betraying the location of the afternoon sun. The tunnel beneath is an exploding autumnal array of color, rising with the trunks to the dull canvas of the sky in an eventual merger of gold, red, brown, green, and orange flames that grow from every visible corner. The grass beneath is hard and dry, long and untended, making walking difficult, and occasionally painful when the blades slash noiselessly across the exposed flesh of the calf above the ankle where boot, sock, and skin form a striped pattern. Sidestep the roadkill, don't look too closely. Too late. Maggots slithering and wobbling, better to look up. Swallowing hard.

(Used a key to open the door. Don't know why we thought to be so quiet. Don't know why we tippy toed on the steps and to the door. Bedroom door ajar and sounds resound within. Didn't need to see to know, didn't need to know to see. Leaning forward and there they were, so familiar, so high in the air with that unfamiliar hand in that familiar place. No matter the other, the muscles react the same. Nothing in words. Backsteps repeat repeat. Close softly, loose mememorme, and elision oop and oota dare with no trace.)

—How much will they have to pay for her sins?

Walking the straight and narrow but sometimes the cars honk when passing quickly due to Teutonic impatience with low speeds on good roads. Obstacles are annoying to this breed and on occasion, when the driver is young and strapping, they make known their irritation with rude hand gestures that may or may not be offensive in America. Offense always depends on how secure the recipient is. The day ends exactly as it begins, a simple Saturday for both drivers and hikers, settling into a run-down youth hostel in the city of Reutte. It is a small, old, wood building where the main room has only a single long table in it. There are two bathrooms and two dormitories off to the side and at the back of the building. The reception clerk shows the way into the room for men where there are no signs that anyone has slept in more than a few days.

In the late afternoon to early evening, eating more bread and cheese, then lying without shoes or socks on the bottom half of a bunk bed, allowing the blisters and developing calluses to breathe in the brisk air. Taking out the Emerson, but before that, folding it onto the chest and cupping the hands behind the head. With a glazed look in the eyes and the mouth hanging open, allowing dust, falling from the base board above, to settle into the mouth and onto the tongue. Taking a deep breath, the book rises and falls in rhythm with the rib cage. About to ponder the stylings of this voice in the making, hearing the door close, shut briskly in the hostel's main area, and distinctly audible voices of newly arriving guests negotiating lodging with the older woman at reception.

Looking out the window and seeing two well-laden bicycles leaning on the rack next to the building. The absence of crossbars suggests an opportunity. Pulling on shoes and socks to head out into the main room.

"Hey there, are those your bikes?"

—Why not ask if they're human?

"Hello." That's the only response.

They have the necessary gear: the shoes, the close-fitting pants, and shirts. They look as though they're on the same long-distance team, dressed exactly alike and with some kind of French accent, but not exactly French. The cold reaction fills the room and is likely due to over eagerness. Offering to help with their bags, but they wave it off, "No thank you, we have it down."

—Got it, too condescending.

They've been riding all day, they're probably hungry, and don't want to make small talk before getting a shower and something to eat. Plopping down at the long table and taking out the book, unfolding the notebook next to it while they carry their saddlebags through the main room and into the other dormitory. The old building bleeds sound and there is no privacy for anyone in it. Heavy bags set down on creaking floors, footsteps, bedrolls unrolling, sheets tucking, the whimpering of bed springs, knees firmly placed. Trying to concentrate but can't with the distraction caused by the distinct but elusive patterns in their movement through the walls. They settle in, come back out, and cross the main room to get to the shower where the sounds of running water give loud and clear cues of the difference between shower heads and faucets. A towel bar rattles, a brush clanks on the stone counter, the whoosh-whoosh of hair pleating out flat and wet. When they're done, they come back through the main room to the dormer. Insisting on keeping the head down, staying focused on the book, and admitting only peripheral and undetectable observations.

[There were better things to do and ignoring someone was a way to respect their privacy. Life without an audience.]

They come out and head into the small kitchen with their supplies. Again, no curiosity, no signs of interest, only a nose shoved in the book and poised over the notebook, unable to concentrate, turning slightly to keep an eye on their progress. They'll have no choice but to bring their food and eat at the table.

"Where are you from?" She asks flatly as they sit down at the other end, both making occasional eye contact over their bowls of canned stew.

"Today, Elmen. You?" Intentionally misinterpreting her question to be more interesting and subtly suggest a better way to go. Seasoned travelers always lead with that.

"Oberstdorf. We rode around those mountains."

—French-Canadian or Swiss. Belgian?

Smiling, but no longer broadly. Adjusting after that first greeting, ever working in those musings on voice, everything read and written that evening obsessively inserted into the most immediate aims.

[There was only one project, no matter what they were like, no matter their preferences, they must be drawn in. Not so much, not too much, but with possibilities. That was it, that was the aim. The first registered reaction was not to be too eager. See the path they were on and walk along it. That's much better than trying to stop them in their tracks and distract them from whatever business they were tending to.]

"How many kilometers?"

"About 100," the other one says. "We've been riding through Tyrol and Bayern for the last few days." They go on to share more details about the road's diversions: the hills and mountains are having an effect on them. Their breathing is stronger, their legs more powerful.

—Flattery gets you everywhere.

"The workout is making you fit," speaking without breaking eye contact. "It is the perfect pace. Car is too fast, walking too slow."

The right mix of distance and proximity to inspire enthusiasm.

They agree.

[In the car, we couldn't see the details, missed many things, but walking was a nightmare, too slow, too close to the ground, too many details, it hurts to see them all. They found the soft spot and became friendlier in the light of approval.]

"How have you been getting around?" one of them asks.

"Hitchhiking through Baden-Württemberg and die Schweiz, but since the Bodensee walking. Autostop is good for meeting people and getting to know the area, but it's too random. You walk and walk and then someone stops, it's totally out of your control. Too slow then too fast. I see people on bikes and envy them."

—Liar. But they're digging it.

Then the usual rounds unfold. Where do you come from? How long have you been travelling? Where are you headed? Where have you been? After the Québécoises finish their food and wash their portable bowls and spoons, they pull out a small bottle of whiskey and offer a drink with a surreptitious look around to see if the clerk is nearby. Their English is good, but not as good as you'd expect. Asking carefully, "Do you learn English and French together while growing up?"

"My house was completely French. My parents, our neighbors, the stores. We learned English in school. It's a second language."

"Still," the other one chimes in. "Schools are in French. Work is in French."

—Obligations. They feel obliged to humor me.

"That's wonderful. I've been to Quebec City and was struck by how old and European it felt, but I've never been to Montreal. Well, drove through it on the highway, but didn't stop."

—Dumb ass. Worst trick. Never do that.

"It's different from Quebec. A North American city. Toronto, but in French." They both laugh.

Not trying too hard and easing up in efforts to be funny and charming, the language is a barrier.

[They wouldn't get word-play jokes, that's for sure. Couldn't launch into the same playful entendre that usually did the trick.]

Trying a few things, but they pass without notice.

(Plus, the message was clear that they were not that kind of people. Funny and charming wouldn't work here. There was something different. They didn't care what book it was, they didn't care about the notebook. They didn't ask too many follow-up questions either. Once they heard "United States," they knew what they needed to know. The alcohol didn't loosen them up, didn't make them friendlier or more inclined to banter. Us, it's us. They weren't interested in us.)

They don't linger long and head off to bed, explaining that they are exhausted by their long day of riding. Following soon after and settling back into the bed, shoes and socks coming off quickly.

—That didn't go well, not as I hoped. I was furniture to them. They were being polite, nothing more, and would have preferred to be left alone. The key is to read the situation. Voice depends on that. Always pay attention.

Increasingly sleepy and drifting off when hearing more voices and commotion out in the main room. They are distinctly German, some late arrivals as the hostel is closing down for the night. They will share the other dormitory with the Québécoises, but their voices, three of them, are distinctly different. South Germans.

—Barbarians.

(The reserve they displayed while talking and drinking, it was present in every word they spoke. The way they carried themselves, the way their bodies occupied space. Hearing them talk in the other room while they got ready for dinner and alone together, they had that same tone, that same reserved, tightly held steadfastness. Not that they were serious, but that they were low key, not the kind of people easily distracted by bright and shiny things. Could be wary of men.)

The German voices, they are different. They are laughing, they talk louder, and show excitement after arriving someplace new. The decrepit state of the hostel incites them. They are happy to be here, happy to be anywhere. They are a different kind, and the cadence of their muffled voices makes that clear.

[Tried to think what would happen when *girls* like that met with those other women. It's possible to hear the burst of that event, decidedly one-sided though it was. What kind of clash was that? Would they have more questions? Be more curious? Was their fatigue gender-biased?]

(Upon first meeting her, being aloof worked wonders. It wasn't on purpose, an accident of circumstance. Sometimes distance by design reached its target and sometimes it took an accident. Both in one were extremely effective. That's what got her attention. Something sparked her imagination, something she saw, something we couldn't control, and didn't realize we were doing. That's the important thing. Once that's in place, the combination of deliberate and accidental distances, staying close enough to offer promise but not enough to satisfy it, that got the job done, elicited selection, that's how it worked, this grazing in the psyche amounted to allure. That's how it always was, and we couldn't control it. Same as we couldn't control how much it ran us down once it got away from us. It's the best and the worst color. Shocking. Magenta. For tights, for whatever. Smooth sleeves, warm grip. There was a fine line between being aloof and being invisible. Only her interest made the difference. Such balance, such awareness of conditions and surroundings, moods and context. What decisions did she make earlier that day? What resolve did we wander into? Any voice that was likeable needed to lure the audience without trying too hard. Such a delicate balance. It wouldn't work for everyone. Some would pass right by without taking notice. Some would sneer in disapproval. Until we learned every tale and every genre, we'd have to measure the probability and cut our losses when there was no hope of success. Upstream we learned how to work with what we found downstream. Every failure was a sunrise to come.)

2.8.2.X.19.86.9.28

Being outside of time and desire, waving a hand to get back in it. Jerking abruptly forward, then falling back, dreamlike, with a subconscious plunge through night thrust into daylight.

> *Then, as I stumbled headlong down the track,*
> *Sudden, a form was there, which dumbly crossed*
> *My path, as though grown voiceless from long lack*
> [Dante's Inferno]

Awakening in morning to the sound of a lamb calling out in starving desperation. After dressing and packing the rucksack, hurriedly stepping outside to find two huskies running about while one of the French-Canadians, back in bicycle attire, feeds the lamb with a baby bottle. Alone, she has more of a sense of humor. Asking if it's hers, she cracks a smile. The lamb's an orphan left to die unless it finds food somewhere else, the woman who runs the youth hostel provides it, and every morning the youngster comes around and howls in front of the door until that bottle of warm milk arrives.

—Where does she get sheep's milk?

In a few moments, the other Québécoise comes to the door and announces that breakfast is ready. There are six at table now, three Germans in denim outfits and the two French Canadians ready to bike. They struggle to communicate but find a translator once they realize and request help clearing up lost signal from their gestures and hand waving.

There are soft-boiled eggs for everyone, and they listen to prophecies about snow before the German girls break the spell with laughter, they know full well that late September is too early for it.

[While they worked through their curiosities, time stood still as the spoon hovered above the egg.]

"Pass auf."

The German girls warn of the perils of striking a soft-boiled egg too hard with flatware firmly held. It can be messy, they say. Nodding with an overcompensating coolness before striking the top of the shell quickly, causing an even, circular crack. Peeling away the top and spooning out the egg's flesh as if it were habit.

(Many a time in the past, such a strike caused an explosion in a bright mishmash of yellow and white.)

Back in the dormer and securing the pack for the Sunday hike, shuffling and stuffing to tidy the room.

(The group was audibly impressed at the ease with which the egg yielded. Such moments resonate. That time we were driving, and the car in front made some quirky maneuver before grinding to a halt turning the corner. We had to quickly swerve out of the way and go around to complete the turn without incident. Tiny matters, but she gasped in appreciation from the passenger seat. They see us in the smallest ways, the littlest bits, and they judge.)

"But how can you plan that?" wondering aloud. "You have to be ready. Always pay attention, you never know when an opportunity will strike."

(The French-Canadians were impressed too. Far more than anything yesterday.)

"What was it exactly?"

(Carefully took note of the look in their eyes, that likeability factor was there. Especially that one in the middle. Last night a big miss, but spot on this morning. The pressure, the presence, a dozen eyes focused. Yes, it had something to do with that. Didn't arrogantly wave the caution aside, nodded in response and proceeded as suggested. Taking heed was a sign of struggles won, and wisdom had allure.)

Saying goodbye to the other guests and the lamb before setting off down the road toward the center of Reutte.

(Planned to find the designated road leading into the Ammergauer Alps separating Reutte from Garmisch. Planned on walking through the deserted Naturschutzgebeit until Griesen to stop for the night. The plans were loosely worked out but plans nonetheless.)

[Paying attention required openness to possibilities unanticipated. In the end, plans weren't real and could be snatched away like a tablecloth from a finely decorated place setting. It remained to be seen if the fine china was unbroken and in place or thrown to the ground in crashing carnage.]

Only a few minutes after leaving the youth hostel and a few blocks down the road, a white Mercedes Benz pulls up on the shoulder and the front seat passenger window comes down to reveal the German girls from breakfast.

—Same same I'd say. I'll be a boy for these girls.

Passenger seat girl, the one with the dancing eyes, asks, "Where are you going?"

"I'm walking to Garmisch-Partenkirchen."

Driver asks, "Would you like to ride with us for a while?"

"Where are you going?"

Driver says, "To Neuschwanstein."

"Oh, I'm turning off this road in a kilometer or so."

Passenger seat girl asks, "We're going to Ludwig's castle, have you been?"

"No, but I've been to Disney world."

—Whooosh. Swing and a miss.

Driver says, "You should come with. Do you want to come with us?"

Thinking for a moment. Falling into those welcoming eyes in the passenger seat.

"Gern."

Putting the rucksack in the trunk and sitting in the back next to the girl who hasn't spoken yet, neither at breakfast nor during the roadside exchange. Her name is Elke, the passenger with the fluttering eyes is Eve, and the driver is Anna. Now driving together toward the German border and listening to the new album by Dire Straits turned down low to make it easier to hear each other.

[This ruined the project of walking from Bregenz to Innsbruck. We screamed at ourselves that only a fool would come this far in search of adventure just to turn it down when offered.]

Running them through the monuments passed during the last five months. Stopping for gas and a border check on the way into Germany before arriving at the castle outside Füssen. After parking, moving as a unit onto the trail leading up a steep incline to the castle's entrance. The incline narrows past the bottom and it's necessary to step out in front with Anna to walk abreast while Elke and Eve lag behind.

Anna is tall and slender and speaks with educated affectation. She is a medical student in Nürnberg curious about America and asking questions with that direct end in mind. Struggling to describe medical training back home while she describes the German equivalent. The process of enrollment is the key difference, along with the cost. Letting her drive things and paying attention to the cadence, how she considers new information, turns it over, and weighs it. Not launching into anything but waiting for her to ask. All the while, paying attention to the twists and turns of her mind, how it works, how it maneuvers, and engages. It is proper and smooth as long as she sets the tone, but she'll get impatient as soon as the dynamic turns.

—Got it.

(She liked hearing about the separate programs and how you had to first apply to college and only later medical school. She was interested in the impact the cost of medical education had on the cost of healthcare.)

Abruptly taking over, turning things around, and going another way:

"Do you have a boyfriend?"

"Mmmmm... Yes, for three years," she replies after the initial hesitation, but showing signs of discomfort. She doesn't appreciate this turnabout. She doesn't think it's fair play.

—It's how they are. Only okay when they do it.

"You must be in love. What's he like?"

"He also studies medicine," she's getting more guarded as the line of inquiry continues. There's something different. Bumping into her a few times while walking, casual and apparently accidental, the first time she barely notices, but when it repeats, she becomes more alert and pays closer attention to her movement along the path.

(It wasn't on purpose, but we didn't make any effort to prevent it either.)

"That's what he's like? Don't you wish he was more exotic? Different than you? At our age, shouldn't he be wilder?"

"I don't see it that way. He's a serious person and my best friend."

"I see," chuckling. "Sounds spicy." Another bump, at the hip.

—Is it on purpose or is it because the pathway is uneven? I'll never tell.

"What's that supposed to mean?" Her even tone is gone, she's more on edge, and paying closer attention to the details.

"I don't know, 'my best friend' doesn't sound hot to me. Doesn't sound like he's getting your blood going."

She clams up, but is breathing faster now, her heart rate quickens. Is she angry? She looks over this way and is clearly annoyed. Smiling innocently, eyes fixed on hers as she smiles back, but it's phony and she's happy to be arriving at the top of the path by the entry gates. She immediately takes some distance and groups up with the others.

—Oh for one.

Purchasing tickets and waiting for a sufficient accumulation of tourists before the organized tour begins. Anna expresses concerns about taking the tour in English.

"German will be fine."

—She wants to get rid of me.

(Hadn't seen many castles nor art museums on the road. The countryside and atmosphere were the draw, didn't need packaged details, so a tour guide that's easy to tune out would be best. It wasn't that the past was uninteresting, it's that they always whitewashed it. The lived past found its way into people's bones and was much more interesting, but the guide wasn't going to talk about any of that. Had to find that out for ourselves. Always pay attention.)

While waiting for the tour to begin, sitting next to Eve and talking about her studies in Pharmacology until a woman sits down nearby and explains her religious views without any prompting. The woman is a pensioner and recalls times when the country wasn't a safe place for travel. She asks Eve about her faith, but she's reluctant to share, speaks hesitantly and carefully, growing more uncomfortable with every word.

Speaking up to ease the pressure and knowing that the accent would be immediately detectable: "My *feelings* are inspired by Nietzsche who prophesized that one day mankind will realize how destructive and hateful these beliefs are and their overcoming will spark a massive reorganization of life on earth."

The woman looks wryly over this way and mutters something about being French before she gets up and walks away. Eve giggles reluctantly and says, "Funny, but how could you be cruel to a harmless old lady?"

—Harmless, my ass.

"It's much easier to be cruel in a foreign language. I didn't mean to, the words don't have the same life. She did ask though, didn't she? As for harmless, I'm not sure about that. What have the Gottgläubigers given us so far? Bruno at the stake? The purge of Jews from Spain? Murdering each other in countless wars to establish one true faith? The knowledge they deny?"

"What do you mean?" she asks, leaning forward.

—You should be a poet, not a pharmacologist, my dear. Eyes, eyes, and more eyes.

[This one.]

"How many brilliant inventions or discoveries were suppressed by their church? The geometry of the Earth was once heresy."

—How many banished from their lands and sent a wandering? How dare they seek riches in portable wealth? It's the only thing they care about. Vermin.

"What does that have to do with a harmless woman?"

"Those sensibilities are always trying to stop thought."

—And murder those who have them.

"There is more to life than science and technology. We are spiritual beings too, don't you think?" She's excited, her heart rate increases.

"There are many ways to be spiritual without religion. It's institutional, organized and guilty of destroying spirit. We can be spiritual through art or nature, community, anything, and without the xenophobia their institution teaches us to worship."

"You are talking about spirituality without the church."

—Spirituality from pharmacology is what I'm thinking.

"Anything bigger than you that you're a part of, that has a rhythm, that pulses in your life. Anything like that, anything that animates you, inspires you, draws you to others, anything that is spiritual and needn't rely on the sketchy history of the church with its loathing and repression."

—Oh, she's digging this, and so cute. Her eyes are wide open, her body language relaxed and ready to receive.

The group stands as a guide comes over and begins the tour. On several occasions, it is advantageous to drift away from the group and search for details of interest that aren't on the syllabus. For example, in a room with a plush gold backboard and brass bed where the king slept, the view from the window is far more interesting. Pulling the compass out of the pocket to check the direction and learn how much sunlight his majesty received during the day. To some, toys and expensive baubles are the high point, better is the fresh air that surrounds his work. There is plenty of room for pacing, plenty of space on the bookshelves for the volumes of literature and science to be of service in his studies, but which were removed long ago. The only detail to disturb the awe is the missing window by the writing desk.

—They say it's a best practice. A pro tip. Windows, and what is beyond them, distract you. Did he know that?

(How would those many hours contemplating the next move or next sentence have gone if we couldn't stare out the window while working it up? Whenever we were in a library, it was best to go immediately to an upper floor, if they had one, and find a seat near the window. Being able to look outside was not a disturbance, it liberated thought which, through a wandering gaze, could easily concentrate on the finest points. Imagination flows into the expanse. Let the simpletons stew their minds in the darkness.)

Off alone, Eve comes to stand nearby, wondering what's so appealing. She leans close to whisper, making it easy to sway closer still when responding. "Feeling the ghosts," letting the shoulder brush against hers, lightly exhaling warm breath in her general direction below her ear and onto her neck.

"What ghosts?" she says still more softly, and again the widening eyes.

"Don't you feel him here? Pacing. Thinking. Working it out. You think he was pure? The good ruler any mother would want for her daughter? Or do you think power liberated him from such foolishness?"

She bends back and looks up, surprised. Faintly smiling and eyes glaring, or glowing, something low and penetrating. It makes her uncomfortable, but in a way that she doesn't mind. She smiles and leans closer again causing another fleeting touch of shoulder to shoulder before she moves back toward the others.

—She did that on purpose.

After the tour, walking into the garden where the girls each take a photograph of the others, standing in front of a fountain that sits in a courtyard overlooking a beautiful valley with conifers stretching to the sky around a lake, shimmering beneath the direct sunlight before noon. Offering to take one of the three of them, but only Elke and Eve accept.

On the descent, walking with Elke, she is the quietest of the three as well as the most passive in conversation. Her career choice is business which doesn't suit her personality on first impression, but keeping quiet seems prudent, better to listen as she softly describes her plans for a degree and the work she wants to do in Finance, hopefully in Frankfurt, she says.

—Genius may often turn out to be silent, but silence needn't turn out to be genius. *"Speak and remove all doubt,"* honest Abe said.

As softly as she speaks, her inner passion is striking, and it's clear how steadfast she is when it comes to making sure she accomplishes what she sets out to do. Imagining her a giant with the pure insight that goes with a view from the heights, then turning to look full at her face and seeing only the struggle to hold back the enormous power that lights her from within. Wanting to tell her not to be afraid, knowing she will have to come to that herself. The look in her eyes says she'll get there at her own pace. Longing to touch her and trying to figure out how to do it. The ground is rough in the garden. Taking the opportunity to lightly put a hand between her shoulder blades, telling her to be careful of some uneven stones on the ground. They aren't that close, but she is grateful and leans into the contact. Chortling infectiously while noting that she would have played along with a bigger ruse if it permitted a more spectacular gesture.

[If she were willing to have a frank conversation about it, she could come up with many different excuses for making it easier to put a hand on her.]

When the group arrives back at the car, Anna and Eve study the map to decide whether it's best to part here or continue up to a later destination. Helping them decide on the points of convergence in the routes and agreeing that it's best to stay together for the next two stops, a couple of churches, before parting at the Echelsbacher Brücke where they'll head north back to Nürnberg on a road that heads south toward Garmisch. Back in the car driving off toward the next item on the itinerary, and proud of the even distribution of time spent with each of the guides. Farther down the road, Eve turns back and hands over a small slip of paper with her name, address, and telephone number printed on it. She says that the three of them live together in that same place. "Call before you come to Nürnberg," she says, wide open. Each of the others express the same sentiment. Elke, looking over and smiling warmly, emphasizes that it would be great to get together in their city with their friends. Anna nods too, merely a formality.

The Kloster at Steingarden is a medieval sanctuary for monks and the stone walls and green, plush courtyard amid the fortress affords ample sunshine for those who tour as well as those who dwell within the high walls.

—Catholicism locked in a vault where it belongs.

In the chapel watching Eve cross herself with the holy water in the basin at the back of the pews, then walking together with arched necks inside the cathedral before slowly drifting outside to the courtyard. Alongside Eve, being the first to find the way into the sunlight, she thinks, for some reason, that whispering is required. Or she likes to stand close.

"It's beautiful here," she says.

"Are you Catholic?"

"I was raised that way, but I'm uncertain. Like I told the lady."

"I thought that was because she was strange," intentionally botching it.

She laughs. "Women like that are not strangers in Germany. I know them well."

Continuing to walk around the courtyard at a leisurely pace, absorbing a silence that somehow seems fresh.

"And you," she asks. "What is your family?"

Always the same hesitation. It isn't fear, rather pity and an interest in sparing her that guilt young people feel for a country they didn't know. "My family is Jewish," saying it as simply as possible, the soft German "J" easing the pressure, likewise the gentle shushing at the end.

(In the black forest, we learned the vast difference in effect between saying that our family was Jewish and saying that they were Jews. Die Juden sind verboten.)

Her nod is incomplete.

—She knew. From first sight, I bet.

The feeling comes across without speech, believing she conveys more than what was intended. It brings a warm sensation, an opportunity, something welcome and cherished. Her Catholicism, her inherited guilt, some twisted fantasy, it creates a sensibility she can't articulate. No need to speak, but when the eyes meet, understanding blooms.

(The three of them were excited by the prospect of a visit to Nürnberg, but only Eve offered the slip of paper with the address and phone number printed on it. She was already leaning. Pheromones. Something in the exchange with the elderly woman, something... Eyes dilated, heart beating faster, and, despite her calm demeanor, we suspect it was the same with her.)

Anna and Elke emerge from the darkened cathedral. Eve turns with a barely audible sigh as she hears their footsteps on the brick walkway. Turning toward them. The sunshine bathes the area in light.

Coming together behind the raised flower bed, Anna moves quickly back with camera poised and directs the rest to move closer together and bunch in next to the flora. Elke and Eve both wrap their arms around the waist leaving no choice but to follow the logic and swing both arms around their shoulders. They lean into it and their heads come close to the chin. Pulling them closer brings a smirk that beams as the camera snaps.

—If I didn't know any better, I'd say those two copped a feel. All I got was some shoulder.

"These may be the only photographs of me from my entire trip."

As Eve and Elke are about to launch into a long devotional on how that can't possibly be true, Anna asks sharply, "Are we ready to go?" as if she intends to stubbornly resist any generalized desire to stay.

—We are.

The white Mercedes originally from Baden-Würtemberg rolls along with closed windows and conditioned environment fending off the heat of the tan leather seats. After a right turn at Kohlhofen, there is a lovely strip of road ending at a place called Wies where countless cars are packed into gravel parking places opposite fences that keep dull, plough horses from standing unguarded. There is a fee to park, but it isn't much and Anna pays without a word.

The church at Wies is Calvinist and crowded inside, but the main chapel area is filled with scaffolding for a remodeling project. After making a joke about the beauty of the complex steel sculptures, separating from the rest and going outside to look at the hilly land behind the site. Many people are walking slowly or briskly through a series of walkways leading to a wooded area in the distance.

(There was a ten kilometer walk with the German school teacher in the Odenwald. We remembered the zest for outdoor hikes by Germans wearing traditional lederhosen and dairy maid frocks with thick underclothes. Long walks and liter steins of beer filled a popular German weekend agenda. Our walk through the Alps changed us. What purpose did walking have when the map of the journey was circular, and we always ended up in the middle?)

—Every story starts in the middle. Ends there too.

[A demonstrative and metaphorical condition of the modern world: exercise for its own sake opposing the ancient need for physical work. Walking used to be a mode of transportation, here it was entertainment. Never in the middle, it was left off to the side. There was a contrast between the health spas of North America where weights were lifted and set down again in the same spot for no other reason than developing muscle, and, on the other hand, farm life where weights were lifted to load a truck and transport the cargo. Which was closer to Christ bent under the weight of the cross and carrying it to his crucifixion? A nice Jewish boy, always respectful with women.]

—Woof woof.

Standing on the grass and watching the crowd, feeling someone approach from behind, and stopping over the shoulder. "What are you looking at?" Eve asks.

"Wochenendenlaufenders," pronouncing it deliberately and amused at the aptitude the German language has for expressing something's full content and irony in a single word.

"It's better than spending the afternoon watching football on television," she says.

Turning to face her, expecting defensiveness and finding only... What? Amusement. Smiling back at her and looking down to be polite but absent-mindedly letting the eyes stray down to her feet and back up again before returning to eye contact. Such sensible shoes, perfect for a day of sightseeing. Back to her face, she is smiling differently than before, but not offended.

[Cast a wide net to see what you catch. One for two. Elke's a walk. An adorable walk, but a walk.]

The absence of subtlety in the maneuver is not lost on her and the boldness in her response surprises. No one instructs her on how and when to pay attention, it comes naturally.

[It was central to her upbringing. Of course, she paid attention, she didn't have the luxury of choice in the matter. They're all that way, have to be, they live among predators, but they think it is essence and not accident. Wait until they lose it.]

"Perhaps," looking away apologetically. "Forgive me," which makes her laugh freely and naturally. She doesn't say anything more but squints her eyes and reaches out to lightly touch the nearby shoulder.

—Zwei mal. The best thing.

Anna and Elke appear at the door and join in on the grass overlooking the wide fields of walkers. Reforming into a group and gesturing toward the car before walking that way through the numerous stands of overpriced, and typically worthless, goods available for purchase by those without discriminating tastes and desperate for a memento. The girls are anxious to get back on the road and see the remaining sights on their list before heading back home.

At the Echelsbacher Brücke, Anna stops the car on the shoulder before the turnoff and everyone gets out. She opens the trunk and helps pull the rucksack out, then shakes hands formally, but Elke and Eve both step up and reach for hugs in sequence before conveying their hopes to meet again in Nürnberg. They repeat their interest in a weekend visit when free from school. As they get back in the car, all three wave again while, on the side walkway, securing the pack on the back and hips, a sad smile serves as farewell. Registering that Eve and Elke's gaze passes over the bare arms and legs straining to lift the pack and secure it in place, carefully attending to the unreserved look in their eyes strongly offset against Anna's focus on the road.

—Sometimes they're pissed at you for bringing it up.

Pulling away, the car turns left at the bridge while, on foot, cutting across a small field of grass to the right toward Garmisch.

Walking through a crowd eating on the terrace of the guest house alongside the road leading south, he carries the black rucksack steadily while maneuvering with ease through and around waitresses, giving the impression that the burden has no weight. The thick socks and heavy hiking boots with exposed legs and khaki shorts make for a proper German hiking medley. Doesn't look out of place and the many pairs of eyes set upon him aren't because of that, but because there is something of a stir about his presence that plows through them and up the road with a spring in the step and a song in the heart.

"Spacibo and Dosvitanya," shouting to the nosy crowd when passing through the gantlet back onto the road. Seventeen kilometers from the Echelsbacher Brücke to Oberammergau with most of the landscape residing in vast farms owned by invisible people but ruled by cows that stand by the wire fences chewing on grass or cud or both and looking up suspiciously at what walks by.

(Knowing then and there that these cows were considering assault, but, fortunately, they quickly forgot since they weren't killers, and neither was the pony that wouldn't eat the leftover kiwi fruit but enjoyed putting his long nose under the armpit and then jerking his neck up and down. Puzzling.)

—Ponies are a mystery. Would we call that self-pleasuring?

A few hours later, arriving at the tourist town of Oberammergau and struggling through the city streets and the countless sets of directions to the youth hostel. Arriving safe and sound with only the slightest scent of horse on the shirt.

[No one could have known it was a pony.]

Washing up, there is no remaining scent of cows. Later, after scrubbing pony and cow from the overshirt and putting on a fresh pair of underwear, heading downstairs to sit at a table by a wall with a map of the immediate vicinity and close to an assortment of petrified tree sections in a glass display case. Spreading out the notebook.

28 September;

Dreamworld whatta be and done day oblong for this brute walking. They slinky-slanked across the pivlet and there was no more knowing it, they couldn't stand opposed, they couldn't bridge the distance. The white car was a black rucksack shouldered, but no one could lift it. You should have been there.

That brawny girl, bomb-breasted, she waved at once, she looked long. Into her, inside her, swiftly swirling around there is a scent to it, and a brokenness. But that can't last and there is no wonder left, or there is only wondering about the impossible possibilities of walking along until you step right into a car and become completely different from what you were before you got there. That auto stopped. It was her idea. Pull over, she must've said, let's ask him to come with. She was friendlier with the egg too. Most amazed and the most motion in her eyes.

The Kalahari is a desert, you told me this, but it doesn't look like one, you said. You can live in a black rucksack stuffed into the trunk of a car with a girl before you, and kitty corner, and next to you. You can live that way. In an oasis, next to the trees where the lions take their shade. The tall skinny one, the short chubby one, and the just right curvylicious

one with the weird looks and the sly smiles that say yes all
the time to everything you do or say. Hopscotch: front front
split, front split front front split front. Hoo-ah. Ehfuh.
Roundabout, in and out.

Did they discuss that near boner boy in the car once he was
unloaded and they were on their way to the next auto stop?
You'd certainly think so. Fantastic regional contrition. Boing
boing boing. Will they remember its face when they see it in
photographs developed and pressed in a book? Should it
call? Where is there room for Nürnberg in the Innsbruck
winter? How does that work out for the it that wants what it
wants?

It's broken. The voice is broken. It is. There is no buzzing,
the sounds are bleating, the demon goat rears its head yet
again and bleats another way. Come round come round.
Find the stick in the twisted pit of it. Men-brain, god-brain,
goat-brain, eve-brain, elke-brain, anna-brain. Down the well
and sorry, in the circle and swishing to swirl about, like that
flushed turd you can't help but look at as it grinds its way
into that chute gone for good until the next one comes along.
Have some fruit and get to work on that.

Signed, me.

2.8.3.X.19.86.9.29 [ref(..9.28)]

[Wam-bam, rickety-ram, son-of-a-bitch, goddamn, hitey-titey, took a
mighty weasel shit. Middle of the night wet dream, Eve objected. Morning
as curtain, closing. She was Eve and We were Adam, her fruit was
forbidden. Subtly, laughingly, we said this must be resisted, and the ages no
longer permitted to cheat on the roundness of the earth belly or those
throats of communication that augmented the subject.]

—Ahnuh. Ehfuh. Ehlkuh. Nine in all. Eee-uh. Eee-uh. Eee-uh.

[Some monk chanted evening... Exploding outside everything there is
no longer anything. The implosion of impression impresses the patient
with paranoia. There were stars twinkling in her skin.]

Drinking a cup of coffee and eating a piece of sour dough made with
water and spread with jam.

(Immediately thoughts clarified, and we were ready to unmediate the
glorious new day with a medium-sized walk to Garmisch.)

The sun shines on this, the twenty-ninth of September, and the river next to the road in front of the youth hostel boasts a thin, gravel footpath that runs parallel as far as the eye can see.

—The day she'll die.

[And so it came to pass that we plotted our way to walk by day, not going under, but plodding along its level surface.]

—They, those men who fill our dreams, are more ourselves than we are. When their words inhabit us, why aren't they our words? " ██████████ *lost souls /* ████████ *in a* ██ *bowl*"

(What was it to be I am, or we are, on this path next to this river near Oberammergau on our way to Ettal and the Kloister there that acted as point midway to day's end journey yet again half-way between where we were this morning and the ultimate goal of Innsbruck?)

—Were they, was she, an interruption or is that the point? What is the point? Walking for its own sake. All denim, everywhere. Blonde hair, blonde beasts. Not a pair of pink tights among them, I guess, but who knows what they're hiding under there?

"What am I?" two-hundred and thirty-four ask in unison.

[We are what we were yesterday plus what we were on the days before up until that aboriginal day on which we did not yet exist. What we did today was further connected to what we did yesterday and every day before until the point was reached when doing was impossible and doing did no more. Our limit indefinite was made of existence and, like the universe, the border between being and non-being was unmanned, an abandoned hut. The contents of existence were mixed up with the grounds and grinds of breakfast waste and tidal torrents. We saw each other finitely, thank you, but ourselves indefinitely, mind you. Always butting up against a limit, that was where you were, that was who you were. They are We are I are She are He are Be are. Boom. Impressive implosion.]

—Look, a big bird, black and white. Is it a white bird with black highlights, or a black bird with white? Featherless, it's bird color. Cry fowl, naked bird, best to fly south early.

"Whatcha doin here, white boy?"

—Aryan hordes planned for our destruction. Other hordes too, hoards of hordes. We two are scapegoats. Am I white? Can't tell, need the shadows to see. Ask somebody else, they have their opinions. The horns hidden under the hair trump the peachy skin.

(Over the river and through the trees to Ettal Cloister we went, street walking next the stone wall that kept the monks in and the unholy out.)

[If you want privacy, build a wall. "Why don't we build a fence from the Caribbean to the Pacific to keep the wet backs out?" one of them asked. "Who would do the work," the other responded. We could cover the country with a giant dome to stop drug trafficking, we could tattoo citizenship codes on the foreheads of children to detect with certainty who was here illegally, we could require permits for places to live, limit traffic on the highways to stop illegal transporting of goods, we could feed the poor through stronger social programs paid for with greater taxation on industry. Whoa whoa whoa partner, now that's going way too far.]

The wall of the Cloister ends, and the forest begins with a path and wooden signs warning of Tollwut in the vicinity. There is a picture that illustrates the unfamiliar word and suggests a family of foxes lives nearby. Along the pathway through unploughed land, time passes while searching with alert eyes for scurrying canine and hoping to avoid danger.

[One of a winding path's attributes, limits that is, is the sightless uncertainty creeping slowly around each bend in the way.]

(We used a pellet gun to shoot the head off a harmless garden snake from only two feet away in a thick wood and for ten years cried in regret. Regrets around every curve. Look out foxes.)

That sign of warning again farther up the trail. Great fear and increasing intensity emitted through the surroundings.

—Umgebung is a nice German word.

[Farther down, more thoughts of Capitalism and Communism, U.S.A. and U.S.S.R., black and white, yes and no, positive and negative, proton and electron, God and Satan, man and woman. Every brain cell has two ends and forms lines of electrical movement through gaps between synapses and filled with neurohormones. And the Earth is magnetic too. It'll make your head spin.]

A grave in the meadow with another warning sign on the tree nearby.

[Visions of a man, lean and hard through years of farming, killed in a desperate struggle with the local foxes.]

Looking in the lexicon from German to English to discover that Tollwut is rabies, and the fox in the drawing is a generic dog.

—Favorite kind. Here boy, come here, get the stick.

[Dog almighty gone rabid. We misunderstood, the danger was manufactured, imagination was a symptom of misunderstanding. Are they at odds? Is the effort to increase understanding tantamount to a decrease in imagination? We walked recalling past misconceptions and hoped they weren't named Ehvuh, Ahnuh, and Ehlkuh.]

On the pathway under the bridge leading to the small building complex that lies across the road, a busy one, and contains the youth hostel where packs are stowed and there is a bus that stops and doesn't cost anything because the system is based on honor.

[Have you seen it? It was around here somewhere. Traitors. And disloyal to boot. Conspiring other. Give it a capital O when you're ready.]

Riding into the city a few kilometers down the road and without any clear borders distinguishing Garmisch from Partenkirchen. First stop is the train station where they have tins of Swedish snuss, a tobacco cut fine for placement between lip and gum.

(Usually, we selected Copenhagen™ from the United States Tobacco Company, but here we chewed Ljangold Ettan™ which was better because the tins were bigger and cost less. The ultra fine cut, forming a mud pack in the mouth, took some getting used to.)

—Smile. Pretty.

Outside on the street across from the postamt, putting a pinch in properly and, much to the dismay of the old German woman passing by on the street, spitting on the sidewalk. Looking at the Zugspitze because it's the highest mountain in Germany [which is trivial], and it's beautiful [which isn't]. Days get no better: a pinch of tobacco and its soothing effects, a sunny day in a city lined with high mountains, German efficiency visible on every corner alongside the Wurst stands with their warm rolls and excellent mustard. The roads are clean and well-maintained, everything is in perfect order until, on the periphery, the enemy is in sight.

(The ugly demon in every European city of substantial size glared at us from a convenient spot in the row of businesses along the Hauptstraße. The sign's red background brought the flames of hell and the golden initial shot out of that background in licking flames spelling disaster. An arch that doubled, that formed a letter, that expressed a culture, that imported beef and potatoes, invented sundaes without dairy, and exported German Marks to Swiss banks.)

Intentionally spitting on the sidewalk in front of the restaurant and going inside to use the WC without purchasing anything, using the floor for a spittoon.

(They say Simón Bolívar had a spittoon on the floor in the corner of every room in his house in Bogotá, the clown who ran this joint never placed a spittoon at a convenient distance to anywhere. The soda cups in the garbage were well-suited and helped us sidestep the signs on the wall: nicht rauchen, nowhere did they say nicht spitten. We removed the dip and decided to have a bite to eat. Oh well, when in Rome....)

The sun is beautiful, but the feet cannot withstand walking too much today. Catching the bus back to the youth hostel and sitting on the grass to read while waiting for registration to open. The rays are great, the wait is short, the line is long, and nearly all the prospective guests are English speaking. There are eight beds in the room they assign, and most of the inhabitants are nice. One is not nice so offer him a banana to see if it helps. Two of the others take a dip of snuss and talk about their travels, many are either on their way to München or away from it.

[Something something Oktoberfest. Lobotomy included.]

Many of the visitors are going to the city for dinner. Not hungry, staying behind to eat something from the store in the rucksack. Offering some to the guy who isn't nice, but he declines because he doesn't want to incur debts. In payment for the banana, he presents a cassette on loan.

In a room listening to Pink Floyd's *The Wall*, eating bread, cheese, and Kiwi fruit, then taking out the notebook.

29 September;

Well, you called it. For ever and ever *The Wall* will evoke Garmisch-Partenkirchen. There are many English-speaking travelers in this youth hostel. I don't mind too much. Neither do they. Turns out, when the sky is blue all day and there is a supply of chewing tobacco, we don't mind much of anything. The absolute is long, fucking gone, and I don't miss it. It wasn't good company. Not like you. But what about me? Aren't I good company? Well sure, but sometimes it's too easy to predict. I can't always rely on you lot for honesty. Especially when there is a hard truth to convey. That's the burden of mediocrity, he says. You'll meet him soon enough. What's average is mostly made of lies, made o flies, that's his point. Pretending it works like this or that, all for the sake of fitting in. You have no choice, you're a collective and everyone has a piece of you. You can't say anything genuine or true without them, they won't stand for it. Or with them, for that matter, because they are always testing you with their limits to find yours. Who are you? Your identity is your limits, your boundaries and attributes. They say it, but it's fucking Hegel. They are always constraining you and blaming you for what you are right after they make you be it. I've had it easy. It's like talking to a damn wall.

All alone
The ones
                    outside the wall

        hand in hand
                    in bands
                        make their stand

And when
Some stagger
            against some mad   wall

Isn't   where we...

Man alone in a corner listening to music only he can hear.

[Nutcase. Who made the device? Who distributed the music? Who recorded it, engineered it, wrote it? De De De -lusion.]

The batteries are going dead...

Looking up at the only German in this place and asking if he has two double A batteries that he'd be willing to sell. He says no and asks for an explanation.

"I haven't heard this album since I left home four months ago and now, when I finally get a chance, my batteries go dead."

"Sorry, I have no batteries.... Where do you come from?"

"Die U.S.A."

"And how did you learn to speak such good German?"

—They ain't keeping it a fucking secret, pal.

"In Germany naturally. Are you German?"

"Yes, from Ingolstadt am Donau."

"Is it beautiful there?"

"I think so, I wish I were living there right now."

"Why aren't you?"

"I'm in the Army."

(We wanted to hear about his beautiful city but the only thing he wanted to talk about was how NATO required a standing army. It was a monotonous dragging on of petty ideas that we could have constructed ourselves, didn't need him. [Blah blah blah. On the one hand. Blah blah blah. On the other hand.] Always the conversations with the same flavor, same back and forth. What are the advantages? What are the disadvantages? [Weigh some butter.] Always the same. Hit 'em, that'll tip the scales.)

—Every second without music is outside of time.

(If we wanted the scoop on our destination, we had to talk to people who'd been there or, better, lived there, [because they'd offer you a place to stay] like Ehvuh when she said she lived with Ehlkuh und Ahnuh. That had some weight behind it.)

—Every single one of those seconds implies a first.

[We'll visit those three again and again. Oh, you're tired my darling Ehlkuh? Well then let's see if I can visit Ahnuh for a while. Shut the fuck up.]

As the monotony gets out of hand and the particulars of German conscription achieve full categorization, a couple Australians walk in and sit down to do their planning.

[Common evening practice of long-time travelers: sitting in a quiet room and planning the next day. Only those traveling for shorter periods spent their evenings out on the town. Those borne by long-lasting flows understood the financial and somatic virtues, and took part in the prudence of reading, writing, or map-studying before an early bedtime.]

Sashaying smoothly across the floor and over to their table. They look up and expect a question, the entry telegraphs the coming of a request.

(These long-travelling Australians who understood the value of evening contemplation were also ingenious for their purchase that day of a pack of four AA batteries, two of which were inserted directly into Mr. Australian's electric razor, or so they said. The other two were ripe for sale for two German marks to power a Walkman, trademark Sony Corporation, to play the rest of the cassette.)

—Score.

(We listened to side two first and then were listening to side one when the battery catastrophe happened. It was a whole different story that way. To see something, truly see it, we had to look at it backwards.)

—Wah wah wah...

(The nameless Australian couple waved our thanks aside and went back to their planning. No hot air there. The German soldier drafted away from his Liebesstadt of Ingol went back to reading his book. Not a bad bloke, he couldn't help it if his hardship distracted him from pleasantries. And we, on our own again, went back, pen in hand and headphones firmly in place, to write the drivel that kept coming and coming no matter what we did to make it stop.)

—Side one, first disk, is more eerie if side two, second disk, is still ringing in your ears when you play it. Who is that hot nymph again? The one that always says what you say? She loves this boy.

"Waiting   worms   ."
Echo echo echo...
"Waiting,   final solution   ."
Echo echo echo...
"   my morals ."
—Marbles? Nah, that can't be right.
[So, in conclusion,]
"Goodbye   ."
Echo echo echo...
"Mother, do you   ?"
Echo echo echo...
*"I've got little   poems in / a bag *
Echo echo echo...
"   channels of shit   to choose from."
Echo echo echo...
"   comfortably numb."

—Pink Floyd certainly appreciates the darker side of life. ███████ *no dark side of life really,* ████████████ *it's all dark.* Unfortunately, they didn't grasp the glory of the goat-brain, or they did but chose not to cast its shadow on the wall. Could be the central motif in *Animals* for all I know.

[Was it their intention to shock by exploring the states of mind of a black sheep who saw everything and was outcast for it?]

—Why not shut up about it?

[If they weren't drawn in, you'd never get what you wanted.]

—It's a whole thing. Although...

[Some of the girls liked that. Ehvuh? Could be. (Those darker bits piqued her interest.) Ehlkuh? She'd like anyone who paid attention to her. Ahnuh? No, she only goes for the cheerful, banal type.]

—The uptight ones are always that way.

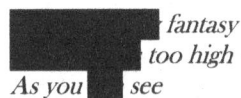

fantasy
too high
As you ██ *see*

—Tomorrow, rain or shine, we'll stay here and take a day off.

[In our revised order, it was the finale, but why wasn't this song in the movie?]

Hey you, █████████████
██ *do* ██ *what you're told...*

2.8.4.X.19.86.9.30 [ref(..85.10.15-16)]

The worm comes.

[Garmisch-Partenkirchen ist im Bayern. In English they said Bavaria but the area to which they're referring was identical in both size and location to what Germans called Bayern.]

In Garmisch-Partenkirchen, in whatever language one chooses, the bells of the church near the youth hostel ring at six o'clock for a full ten minutes, making certain that everyone in range rises to the uproar. It is still too early for breakfast, they won't be ready. Nevertheless, the others get up and head off to the bathroom to wash up.

[Follow the crowd. Safer that way. Fifty of us but only one with a gun.]

Joining after a while, clean and well rested, at a table with the nasty Australian (who ate the banana on offer and said thank you suspiciously). Today he is nicer. Deciding to walk the trail into the city and extending an invitation to join.

It settles in.

(Instead of taking the bus or walking the road the bus followed, we'd hike back toward the same trails from yesterday [the foxtrails with the warning signs].)

Setting out in the too early morning, don't have to back track the whole way, only as far as the north-south turn off heading south this time instead of north. The destination is the park area and trails around the city where the mountains towering above it are in full view.

And begins to feast.

(The Australian's name was Ian and he had curly light hair and was a decidedly squirrelly person with a sharp tongue who came from a place he referred to as "out in the sticks" in the province of Victoria. He wasn't nasty yet but did make fun of the other guests while we walked along the hillside toward that north-south junction.)

It's called the philosophensweg.

([We thought the name was derived from a play on the relationship of steep to profound. It could be a joke, or are Germans always that way with their philosophy?] While walking, Ian was righteously scorning the principles of the American imperialist ideal when we met a herd of cows blocking the way. Taking a moment, he photographed the upcoming splendor of the city scene backed by those mountains and endless trees, then he rolled a cigarette as we produced the tin of snuss, placing a pinch between lip and gum before telling Ian, who asked, about our summer back in Wisconsin chewing tobacco and walking on grass laden with cow droppings. Ian retaliated by putting us in charge of clearing the cattle from the pathway. We moved up slowly behind them and slapped their rumps until they walked off to the side to make room for us. [These were humble cows of a tranquil nature, not to be feared, they lulled us into a warm feeling from out of their habitual bliss.])

"Moooo," they say and then stomp off in an urgent slow way.

(Ian told us that he was called Jan in Polish which is what he was and that he, Ian-Jan, was going to Poland, where he would have fun, more fun than we would have if we went because Ian-Jan spoke Polish and we didn't. Ian-Jan and we were disappointed because the philosophensweg wasn't that steep and we didn't get a chance to take a lovely picture of the city valley which would have been beautifully visible from higher up on the hillside. Of course, it was our fault that the philosophensweg wasn't steep enough because we were the ones who suggested walking this way in the first place. We told Ian-Jan that the philosophensweg was steeper than the road the bus took.)

Ian-Jan finds a walking stick, brushes it off, pulling some of the twig branches away, and then uses it to steady his balance along the route. He uses it for about ten minutes and then leaves it at the city's edge as though sticks like that can be found anywhere.

(We emerged from the philosophensweg in the city of Partenkirchen and went into town to purchase supplies for the trek later that day.)

Walking toward the Partnach klamm by way of the Olympic stadium.

(The Partnach klamm was a gorge listed as one of the best natural sites in the area, and the Olympic stadium was listed as one of the best man-made sites.)

While walking, Ian-Jan asks about the philosopher's way.

(We told him all roads led through Kant, but Ian-Jan said that we didn't understand him because we had to explain, slowly and carefully, about the a priori synthetic using big words.)

"If you can't explain it clearly, then you don't know what it is. You learned a bit about it and then put it into a box wrapped with a big word so that you wouldn't have to think about it anymore."

Pursing the lips and tilting the head to the side.

(We told Ian-Jan about knowledge that contained more in the predicate than what was in the subject, but Ian-Jan didn't know anything about logic, and criticized us more. We tried to tell him about the deity and that any knowledge of it had to be free of experience, but Ian-Jan said he didn't believe in Dog Almighty and when we told him that many people didn't believe in the a priori synthetic either, he said we were playing a joke like all the philosophers.)

"True, but the a priori synthetic is required for scientific knowledge of God same as we ordinarily think of it with physics and geometry."

Ian-Jan says, "Don't be an idiot. God has nothing to do with geometry."

"Uh, okay. That's why philosophers were fools to make up new metaphysical systems with objects that couldn't be known the same way science knows its objects."

Ian-Jan says, "Every time philosophers get in a hole, they bring in a new word that no one understands to make it seem they know what they're talking about."

"Which word didn't you understand?"

Ian-Jan says, "You know damn well."

"Why won't you tell me?"

Ian-Jan says, "Because you'd only make up another word in your explanation and we'd never get to the end of it."

([We suspected that Ian-Jan didn't know the difference between explaining something and believing it.])

—Do you know why you have a name?

(We stopped talking about that and moved on. First, we talked about the Olympics because we arrived at the stadium where they were preparing for some event and ordinary services were shut down. We walked around inside and looked up at the massive ski jump, then continued on toward

Partnach klamm without the customary ride to the top where there would
have been a wonderful view of the valley. He was always thinking of what
he could photograph and how cool it would be to show it to people at
home. Back on the road to the gorge, Ian-Jan launched into a dissertation
on his philosophy without, as he put it, using any hard-to-understand
words.)

"People act in every instance for their own personal gain. We are selfish
and everything we do is selfish. If we didn't act that way, we'd become
hateful to everyone around us."

"What do you mean when you say personal gain?"

"Don't be an idiot," Ian-Jan says scornfully. "Everyone knows what it
means, you know it from personal experience. It's all you ever do."

"Personal gain is acting? Whatever I do, whatever it is, is for my sake.
Sounds circular. Or are you an existentialist?"

"I don't know why I waste my time trying to explain anything. You don't
want to hear how things are, you want to play with words and win arguments
with mystifying vocabulary."

"Sounds pretty selfish of me."

"Right," Ian-Jan goes on with a smile and renewed vigor. "Everyone acts
in his own best interests and everything we do is meant to benefit us as
much as possible."

The more it eats, the fatter it gets.

([We wanted to ask Ian-Jan if gain was the same as interest and if we
always knew what was in our best interests, if we always knew what our
interests were, and if we did, how did we know? From what perspective?
Was it disinterested, this knowledge? With what future vision and
reflection could we separate ourselves from who we were in order to be it?
But we didn't go into any of that because we knew that he would repeat his
tirade and wave aside our questions.])

—He could be hoping for an echo.

(Frankly, Ian-Jan was hilarious, and we never laughed so hard as when
we listened to him expound on his unique and history-making views which,
for some reason, no philosopher ever thought to set down. He seemed
blind somehow. [Not because our truths were better than his, but because
he didn't get the jokes.] As if we gave a damn about the Categorical
Imperative or the a priori synthetic. Kant was a monster, but we're not
afraid of him, of his language. It was fun to instigate Ian-Jan, to wind him
up and move him about like a toy. And because he was malevolent, we
didn't have to feel guilty about it. If he had been the least bit helpful, if he
were better, we could have directed our game at Kant instead of being
oppressed by him. [We could have undermined the power of geometry
with the absurdity of the deity. Disbelief and unbelief are mischievous and
wreak havoc on any system that has to submit to consistency and

coherence.] Hell, we could have had a marvelous day ridiculing the demons he was quick to dismiss [and then thrown stones at the goat-brain and watched it bend and break]. We thought he was letting them off too easily.)

Arriving at the gorge and paying to get in, it is expensive and irritating to pay a small fortune to see a natural formation.

[A gorge was a mountain that had been bored through by running water. Do you think we should pay for that?]

Walking through what amounts to a tunnel that is supported by steel beams and posts and narrows to a thin crack high up at the top where the sun comes through and yields some light to the otherwise dark interior. The cost of admission is revealed in the outline of the structures that make the gorge safe for touring. Ian-Jan, unable to adapt, continues to grumble at the price. Standing in the cold interior and looking up at the falling water from the sides of the exposed rock. A faint echo resounds in every step, every clearing of the throat, and sliding of the hands along the rails. There is an older woman pausing to look up in the same direction.

"Can you feel the lord?" asking her without showing any traces of irony.

She smiles back and says that Dog Almighty is more present here than in any church she's attended in the last fifty-nine years. Chuckling and adding a point to the tally.

—Accurate predictions prove you understand. Something something cover of a book...

After walking through the gorge and coming to an open area where the river widens and the cliffs end in a patch where the ground is bathed in sunlight, Ian-Jan bends over on the rocks in the middle of the stream to take a drink of water. His negative energy draws his body down into a collision with the rocks, and his pants, shirt, and shoes are soaked through following a combined thud and splash.

Helping him up and asking if he is alright, he says, while blushing, that he is. In his daypack he has an extra pair of shorts and changes his pants before leaving jeans, shirt, and socks to dry on a rock in the sun. Climbing up the hillside, there is a bench under the trees, and he takes a seat as though it is the most natural thing in the world to keep talking about Australia while wearing only a pair of shorts that were more of a bathing suit than shorts.

[You wouldn't say that if you knew what Aussies call a bathing suit.]

"If you could be any animal, what would you be and why?" he asks after exhausting his store of information about Australia.

"A whale, because they're intelligent." Don't miss a beat in responding even if there is no segue to the question.

"What would you're second choice be?"

"A tiger, because they're powerful predators."

"And your third choice?"

"An Eagle because they fly high and see well. No natural predators either. Except humans."

"If you were stranded in a forest like this one, how would you feel if you had to spend the rest of your life there?"

"Alone? No roads? It'd be hell."

[With others and Auto Stop? Purgatory or paradise.]

"And what if you were stranded on a desert island, how would that suit you?"

"Not much different."

"If you could have any drink in the world, what would you have?"

Holding up the water bottle and saying, "Water, it's the essence of life."

"I heard about these questions," Ian-Jan explains. "From a psychologist who said that they each had a special meaning. The first animal is how you see yourself, the second is how others see you, and the third is how you really are. The forest is your view of death and the desert island your view of life. The favorite drink is your attitude toward sex. I guess you think it's pretty bland, eh?"

"Well, it is the essence of life."

"It's pretty bland. I picked a Piña Colada because it's sweet and has a bite to it."

"What else did you pick?"

"I didn't think I'd like the forest much, but the desert island sounded like fun. My first choice for animal was a large bird of prey, then some sort of fish like a whale or something, and finally I chose a wombat."

—Ah, the whalefish that thinks it's a hawk but is really a wombat.

(We understood why Ian-Jan picked these things, but we couldn't understand why he admitted it. He described himself as a marsupial rodent and we wanted to ask if that was on purpose, but the whole game seemed silly, and his pride furthered our sense that he wasn't in on the joke. But that didn't seem as funny as it did before. It seemed sad and although he had no single quality that anyone would identify as a virtue, we felt bad for him and worried about how everything would work out in the end.)

Getting up after a while and climbing a steep ledge to urinate on an unsuspecting tree before going back down to the river and retrieving Ian-Jan's clothes, then heading back into town to find some food for the evening meal.

(After we clambered back through the cave without a peep, the time between the gorge mouth and the city passed while we tried to figure out which of the major food groups Ian-Jan had been neglecting in the last few days, because that would determine what food he'd buy for supper.)

It's juiciness squeezes memory with fantasy.

[We, however, (were thinking that if we) believed Ian-Jan's philosophy of selfishness, we would jump on him at that moment and commence beating the shit out of the squirrelly fucker (who continued to babble about tomatoes and bread and sandwich meats).]

Keep walking in silence.

(After rescuing Ian-Jan from a calamity in the grocery store where he would have been helpless without speaking the language and forced to pay for things he had already bought, we opted to take the bus back to the youth hostel and eat there. [It was then we decided that Ian-Jan must cease to exist and that he was only that, a he who should be referred to as Jan or Ian but not both.])

[We settled on Ian knowing that Ian was only an "I" and never more than that. No matter how dense the country, there was only one of him.]

(Ian "I" was weak and not handsome. His curls were stringy and obnoxious, his mouth crooked and snarling. His mind was not sharp, and his genius begged every logical question we asked. Ian was bad in the Homeric sense and his atheism proved that, as a bad man, he was also a fool.)

—He sees a tiger that thinks it's a whale but is really an eagle.

[Did Ian see that? There'd be fear, right? (He took such pleasure in his game of questions and claimed such authority in passing along the meaning behind the answers. But none of it was a game, it was serious to him, it was an attempt to gain control over a world where he felt none.) Pseudo knowers can be that way, the genuine article too.]

—Knowledge is the worst of us. If silent steps don't lend you power, then you surely can't shout for it.

[Soaked through the brain stem (the skeptical philosophy was growing in us for years and it was a cheerful science involving lots of laughter coated) with slime. Not a mechanism for control meant to overcome a basic lack of it, more so a sled or a surfboard for steering among the wild waves and moguls of brute nature. Gaining control over something wasn't the point, instead we meant to steer wildly through it while turning and twisting in delight at the speed and thrill of the terrain.]

(She was a wild ride [a wave crashing on the beach. You had to go through that to bodysurf your way from trough to crest.].)

[The problem with Kant (we would have told him if he had shown the slightest bit of curiosity) was not that the words were too big or too convoluted, but that they were ugly and would never get anyone into bed with you. Now Kierkegaard, there was a philosopher. A few passages here and there was all it took to get those knickers off. Feminism, better still, and, if you played it carefully, Nietzsche could work magic on the most stubborn target. The misogyny, played with a touch of horror and accusations of pathos, could be quite the aphrodisiac giving her both the imagery of her subjection and the joy of overcoming it. Neither works well on its own, but together... Who among us didn't freely desire some light bondage now and again?]

(The exact same things we did together, she was doing with him. [Who was it who had no creativity or imagination, her or us?] Did she go along with what he wanted? [His pleasure, his rhythm, his ways. The universal him.] Didn't she have a will? [To what end was respect bestowed?])

It is a judge.

[We handed down the verdict and the evening was complete. (We pronounced Ian, formerly Ian-Jan, guilty as charged of foolishness and lacking intellectual jolly.) As a traitor to the greatest of ideals, a messiah, we sentenced Ian-Jan-Australian-of-Polish-decent to phenomenal death in both mind and heart.]

(Once the meal was over, we adjourned to [the privacy of our own thoughts at] a small table in a room off to the side of the main lobby where we read Emerson [who knew us] and listened occasionally to the German television which hummed in the background with the dubbed soundtrack of a popular American movie.)

—Here today, goon tomorrow. Ack ack ack ack ack.

(We read of the poet who [felt the world and] inspired his readers to creative brilliance through the presentation of a song that attached itself to the listener [and pulled away from the singer].)

—Love means submission. To the beloved, to the convention, to reinvention.

(We loved Emerson's *Circles* [but his absolute deflated] when we heard the rules we had to follow when singing its song.)

—Cite the song.

(Had to redact the lines, had to pretend we forgot them, had to pretend they did not exist since we did not own them [no matter how many times they rang through our ears inside our heads].)

—"███████████ *lost souls /* ██████████ *in a* ██ *bowl"* Submit to the absolute, the collective, the many. Let the everywhere hold you. That thought you're having, you are four times more likely to have it after a nutritious breakfast brought to you by Kellogg's.

(We dozed [and dreamed of beautiful scenes where we killed these dragons, shed their scales, and rescued manifold damsels despite the objections of holier than thou nay-sayers of both the catholic and classical liberal kind].)

[Nature, with its underlying maths, projected a model into our dreams. Dog the dragon, dog the mathmagician, but it wasn't enough to stencil the background with formulaic prose, the steep ones ordered us to convey what we built in terms of a new logic laden with their requirements echoing in the distance. Formalizing every single one of us, they genuflected to their mighty universals as ends-in-themselves. Left brain said, "Follow the rules, beware," from the narrow perspective of a single part. Right brain sang, "Where's the music?" with the moral authority of the whole.]

(We didn't feel the uncategorized ones [that were formless beneath us] anymore. She padded off in socks soundless on the carpet.)

[We extended our sight into it: its eternal and omnipresent now stretched out in time and space, stretched out in statistical probability, a new culture, completely buried in conceptual means, a sheath to hold this mighty sword.]

—No accountability. That was a shitty thing she did to me.

(And we let her do it. let her get away with it, didn't say a damn thing, didn't tell her what we saw, what we knew. She posed an ideal, got it into her head, affixed it firmly there, and then didn't give a damn which of the swinging dicks fit the bill. She couldn't help it, she's made that way, but what's our excuse?)

—Never taller than when we stand next to someone shorter.

[Dreaming of the good and its shiny scales in near sleep with flicking tongues in flesh and fold, the courtesan squeezes tightly and softly speaks, "kill him, kill the dragon, and I am yours."]

It possesses everything now.

—A damn fine thing, this eve.

"Then he moved on, and I behind him followed." [Dante's Inferno]

10.12 (2)

this year's harvest

10.12.1.Elisabet.19.86.5.11 [ref(..1.6)]

(Wanted a reaction, dress didn't get it. I was some lady, the same with her. She didn't care about him, wanted a reaction too. Not only from him, but me. Hope she never got it, they'll be consequences. Petter saw. Relays and missives, all kinds of flutter, anger. Find the strength. What if the guys won't... Can't go against, but... It's not... They can't... He'll hear something. Someone will... The way I took his chin, his arm, the way we were. Relays and missives. Heard you were... Be casual about it, how they are when *they* do it. Got it though. He didn't know what to expect, but he expected something, knew something was up. Sitting there patiently, right where I put him. They were only dancing, and talking, every opportunity to touch his arm or shoulder, his back, and his belly. Nils and Edvin today. Late though. Mats will be pissed. Tomorrow. He'll have heard already, won't be expecting me at the airport. Some yelling, but private. They got anger down, don't they? Won't do anything in front of them. Funny, the reaction to the skirt. Bare feet, no top, hair pulled back, must've been tipsy, giddy, girly... ...never would have... It'd be good to meet alone. Cassie back Monday, can take care of that if not too late. They should be first, get a chance... What if he calls? It's been a month. That'd be exactly like him. Heard you got a new toy, or something stupid like that. Losing their minds, dropping forty IQ points. Our own lives, *you* made that clear. When was the last time anyone pounced on me that way? You don't have to be careful. Doesn't need dry cleaning. What is it about that dirty, down to earth look?)

—Oh shit. Nothing here. The robe? White. Disaster.

"Can you do me a favor?" back to the bedroom door and cracking it open.

"Of course," he says popping up and coming across the room.

"On the loveseat, there's a basket. Can you bring me a pair of underwear?"

"Is everything okay?"

"Cotton. Not the other stuff, okay?"

He skips off, flopping about, his tight bottom bouncing with the rest of him. Face solemn, as if he's off to get a tourniquet or some instrument for a medical procedure. Rooting through the cabinet and finding the pads. He comes back and stands at the door holding a sturdy pair, face pale and eyes set in concern. Hands them over through the door, hesitant to come in, but wants to.

"Be out in a flash," closing the door in his face.

Fixing the wings and laying it in place, then stepping into them and taking a quick look in the mirror.

—Not the reaction I wanted, but a reaction.

(What was that? It was like a knuckle. At the end of a chicken leg, that hard split bone top they always have. Is it always that way but not as pronounced? The position, that had something to do with it. Legs close together like that, didn't hurt at all, not so deep, lurching, unfamiliar motion, it was nice... ...how he used his hands, pulling, pushing, his thighs open and providing a cushion, soft hair, all of it, a soft cloth, like soft cloth. Cute, embarrassed, not wanting to come right out and say how she showed him. Who was she?)

Redoing the ponytail tighter. A few strands, but mostly clean, and smoothed back.

—It's a good color. With this cut. He was right about the blowout.

Turning back around and going to the door, reaching for the pocket handle.

—No sense putting it off.

(The agent was right about the closet, access matters, but you have to stock it for that to work. Told Charles it's not one thing, but a million things. Liked that. They didn't screw you just once. What's a time? What did he say about women's orgasms? Funny how he fumbles about, this toddler philosopher. When one thing is near another and there's only a small space between, it's hard to know whether it separates or joins them. Was he talking about pleasure, about orgasms? What was that thing? What he said. From the French woman. Garay? Something something "*woman has sex organs more or less everywhere*" something something "*constantly touching herself.*" That touching, dividing and joining together, that means contact, constant touching, one and the same. "*...stroking the posterior wall of the vagina, brushing against the mouth of the uterus*")

Opening the door, he's still standing there, right where he was when it closed. He steps back, such a concerned look, some distance between, joining together across it. With a look, a hand lightly resting on his arm, not to worry.

"It's nothing. Let's get back in bed."

On the reel-to-reel, it's Blue. Ocean Rain is next.

He follows and climbs over offering many different angles. He pulls the sheet and comforter up close and snuggles under and next to.

"Are you grossed out?"

"Worried. Is it your period?" he asks.

"No... ...it happens sometimes. It's been a while."

"Is that why yesterday, we..." he trails off.

"I wanted to, you *were* convincing," slight shake of the head and looking over sideways from the corner of the eyes.

His right arm supporting his head and neck, his left-hand crosses over and meets in between, interlocking and lightly lingering with the right hand, a cozy pair finding their way on the thick down. Nice circles, he draws on the flesh, trying to comfort, and succeeding.

"It's not what I meant... ...to convince you." Sounding apologetic.

"It's okay, I don't think... If I remember right, I don't think that's ever happened. That position, it didn't hurt... ...matter of fact..." Lightly dragging nails in a claw shape against his chest, can't suppress a purr, but it doesn't match his mood.

"Usually, it has to be the same as yesterday? Your shirt," every question costing him a lot of effort.

"███████████████ *damn candle out"*

—I know my body, that's not normal. Conjurer.

"Usually. Or something like that. Years ago, but always some cloth. I got used to it."

"What was different?" his eyebrows raise.

"I don't know, you were the cloth, your skin. Then the bone. It's a bone, right?"

"I think so." He doesn't sound sure. Puts his hand down there.

Not showing concern anymore, makes a face as he feels around. Relieved, reminded why, and his face grows serious again.

"But so," he says, wishing he didn't have to, wants to go off in that other direction, wants to go back to the skirt, but can't and it leaves him with disappointment mixed with concern. "Is everything okay?"

"I'm seeing a doctor. Monday or Tuesday. Can't remember... ...have to check."

"██████████████ *talk to anybody* ███ "

"Are you pregnant?" gently phrased, nothing stops him.

"Pregnant? Why would you think that?"

"I don't know, spotting, I heard that sometimes, I don't know, it's stupid." He looks away and bites his lower lip. Turns back, letting it go.

—Okay, fine. If I bleed on you, you get to know, that's the rule.

"We were trying for a baby for almost a year. Thought it would be easy. Lots of people think that, that's what they told us."

"They?"

"The doctor, fertility. This was before the tour. That was the deadline. Change the body, change the voice. The timing wasn't going to be good, but who knows how long you have? Some women go into menopause at my age."

—Too much.

"No kidding? In their thirties? I thought fifties."

Laughing and looking over sympathetically. His face is focused. Nothing but fog around his eyes, an ignorance he never saw before spreads out in front of him and he doesn't know what to make of it, doesn't know how to begin making something of it.

"█████ *my gorgeous wings* ███████ / ████████████ *dark cafe days*"

"The easy thing was to check Niklas to make sure everything was okay. And it was, thank God."

Silent for a moment. He waits and lightly moves his thumb over the back of the hand, then back again, a gesture to remind.

"That leaves me." He stretches his fingers along the back of the head and neck, squeezing the other shoulder and lightly pulling closer.

—Might as well.

"Honestly. We hadn't finalized anything. Planning, there's a lot to do and we weren't done. Nowhere near. When I heard he was okay, that's... Well, I told them to go ahead. I wanted to get away. Got depressed, couldn't look at him, wanted to work. Something, anything else. Didn't want to know."

(He was angry. Different shade. Never saw that before. We're not that kind of people, who would have been our role models? But he was furious and neither of us knew what to do with it. Not the problem. He thought that was *our* problem, but my solution, my decision. Oh shit, I haven't told him, untold him... ...the lies.)

—It's recorded backwards too. Stieg.

He's waiting, but it doesn't feel like it. The effort is conveyed in the limbs and the muscles, in his legs moving slightly under the covers. He bears proximity as a burden, doesn't make any sudden moves.

"████████████ *I saw you* / ██████████ *take me*"

"Niklas was furious, and I think that scared him, he'd never been that angry before, not with me."

"Angry with you? Why would he be angry with you?"

"Because it was meant to be our problem, and I wanted to be alone with it. I wanted to ignore it, make it disappear. Many people go through the same thing, and they can't do anything about it. They can't see a doctor to tell them why. I know that, but I still couldn't face it. That's not supposed to happen to me."

Sitting up and forcing him to pull back. Leaning against the headboard as he pushes the duvet over this way and sits up with legs crossed at the other side. A dance that only takes a few seconds and seems natural, he pulls that side of the comforter over to his belly and looks at the knees that have come up to form a bent barrier between his shins and the hips that moments ago were so close.

"I know how this sounds, but you get used it. All the things that happen, you expect it."

"What do you mean? Expect what?"

"Never in my wildest dreams, as a teenager, did I think any of this would happen. When we played together at school, it never entered my mind."

"Fate / ██████ *your will /* ██████ *thick and thin"*

"You mean, with the band."

"I wasn't a singer. Once something amazing happens, then other things, it isn't only one thing... The guy comes backstage of the place at school, he's visiting his kid or something. Pure luck. One thing right after another. The studio, production, every day something else to lift you higher than you've ever been before. You can't believe it."

"How old were you?"

"About your age. And they tell you all kinds of things. They know how overwhelmed you are, and it's their job to use that."

"Use it how?"

"██████ *a magic world /* ██████ *hung with jewels"*

"It creates a cocoon or a bubble or something. I mean, most of the time you don't matter. In line at the store or sitting in class, nobody pays any attention, nobody cares if you're there. These shady guys, you're the center of the universe and they're looking at you, such a bright star, and they can't help it. That's their job, to make you feel that way, so you'll do whatever they want."

"██ *in your arms,* ██████ *to beg you"*

—I've completely lost it.

"You can't tell anyone any of this, okay?"

"I promise, I told you, not a word. I hope you know..."

"I do, obviously. I wouldn't be... Forget it, I'm sorry."

Pulling off the tie on the ponytail and winding it into a loop and onto the left-hand ring finger. Then pulling it off and putting it on the middle finger. He's forgotten about it and almost ignores the apology. Back to that same kind look while putting his hands under the covers, lightly touching the feet pushed up against his shins.

"They say they'll make you a star," exaggerating the last word.

"Sure," he's nodding.

"But it's not only a band with these gigs and fans and everything, it's in your head, in the way you see and feel things. Everything changes, and they *want* everything to change. They want you that way because you'll need them... ...to keep it that way. Your whole way of seeing the world, everything, totally in their control."

Shaking the head and pursing the lips.

"La / La, ██ *la / La,* ██ *la / La,* ██ *la / La,* ██████ *la, la"*

"And in your twenties, you lap it up, you can't get enough, and it makes you think that nothing bad can ever happen to you. You're invulnerable, above it, superhuman somehow... ...nobody looks at you the same anymore. Complete transformation... ...it is so perfectly reasonable. Obviously, you could never have a normal problem... ...but then you do... ...and it's a crisis. You don't know how to deal with anything anymore. It's humiliating."

Locking eyes. He's not thinking of something to say, not worried about doing the right thing, just listening.

"It's stupid. You'd think in these many years I'd have gotten some sense, but... I couldn't make everything fit... ...and that's why I said go ahead, let's do it. The ensuing flutter, promotions, and appearances. Niklas was furious. God, he was so angry. I wouldn't talk to him. I couldn't."

He wants to ask something but bites his lip.

"What?"

"Is that where Odette comes in?"

Laughing. "Mathilde. At first, she was a friend. He needed to talk to somebody and couldn't talk to me. She must've helped him deal with the anger. It's not as if he would go to a therapist, that's not his thing. I was relieved, to be honest, when he left, that he wouldn't be coming, but now, I miss him, and I *am* going to see the doctor. He doesn't know. We'll sort it out, the work bullshit first. There are many reasons to move on..."

"He will ███████ / ██ give yourself ██████ "

10.12.2.Seannafair.20.15.5.7 [ref(19.86.5.24-31)]

—It's farther than I thought.

(There's wanting something and then, completely different, there's what feels good. I wanted it very much. He took us into that studio, didn't know it was there, all that time, and never saw. The technicians and the assistants, there were many people, and he was jet lagged something fierce. Kept walking around saying he was a zombie. What he heard was pounds and pence. It wasn't music to him. But I wanted it badly. And he was there. Always quiet, but an anchor. The two of them together in the booth, such a contrast. George would talk at him, couldn't hear what they were saying, but he wouldn't say nothing, could see that. George, he liked to talk, but that one, he didn't always like what he was hearing. I liked the other one, he said, when George told us which one was best, and my ear knew, knew he was spot on. He saw it, was seeing it the way I did, but it's not drive to get something pleasant, it's a drive to make something else stop, that's what the desire was, that's what you wanted from this one rather than that one. Take six, not seven. Take seven gets the execs on board. Take six is the sound you want, but why did I want it? He seemed to know, to understand. The money guy was blathering pounds and pence, that's what he could hear. More polished than anything, but it was the same as it sounded that night, the one he liked, that is, that's the one that was how I imagined it.)

Metal railing along the building's edge and steps up to the portico and entryway. 100 Queen's Gate and the lights are on. There're a few people standing outside looking up the road, waiting for the doorman who must have called for their taxi. There's a metal railing up the stairs too, holding on tightly because they're steep.

—Here we are. They can hear that image plain as day. Tells them who they want to be. Tells them how to stop the pain of not being it.

(Then afterward, we lay together in the quiet. That's where it mattered. Resting that way, and quiet. The noise blocked out, no more of that nonsense. Having to decide, having to make sure that the best thing always happened, fighting with them. Tied up in the wanting. A drive or something, when the songs came out and your head got like that. Not the lyrics, but the songs. Again and again, to make sure you've got it, and then we thought we did. We performed them, being on that stage, why couldn't we put it down that way? Different from the first one, the one we sent, but that was the way I heard it, those were the songs. He wanted them different, heard something else. *In Your Head* was different, and I fought him. Was I wrong? Did he make it better? Better if it's not only me, not just my song, but something from everyone, put together. The drive wanted it to be one single thing, but it needed to be many things and that meant everybody had to put in some, something to make it sound as though it came from all of us and not me alone. But then I didn't see me in it anymore because we're all in it, and I'm us, part of us, and the drive changed with that. Pounds and pence in your head too.)

Approaching the door, the doorman comes back and holds it open before he ducks out to help those people down to the street and into the taxi that's pulling up. It's awfully late to be heading out, must be on their way to a club, looking so posh.

"Good evening, madame."

"Ta."

—Too bright.

Stumbling when passing over the threshold. There stands a man and a woman behind the reception desk to the right. The nook next to reception is where the elevators are and then further left is a broad double door leading into a bar area, dark and moody. To the left again is the restaurant, but it's closed up now.

Her eyes go wide in recognition. He sneers, watching the off-balance movement and surmising its source. Compassion and disgust side-by-side.

(Thought he should be the manager. We all did. The way the money guy carried on, no one else could get a word in, nothing convincing or worth listening to. No respect. But he was different. The way he was listening to us, everything we said. We weren't trying to be U2. We weren't trying to be anybody else. We didn't want to fall into some pattern familiar to everyone. And by didn't want... I mean... ...nothing else made any sense. It was the only way we could understand what we were doing. Saw it clearly. When Mike said something about the solo bit that Rian was playing, he was the one that said it was like the bit from an earlier cut, one no one else mentioned. Why can't we use the guitar from that one and the bass from this one? We didn't know, we thought you could. Sure of it, but he was making things up trying to get us to the one he wanted, that's where it came out. His drive. Mike's drive. Mixed up. No pleasure for it. Don't know why they're always connecting the two, why they're always saying desire and pleasure are the same. Because they're not, that's clear as day. Tangling with the money guy, that wasn't fun. Getting your way, that didn't feel good. Except in the way it feels good when the pain stops, when it doesn't burn anymore or whatever it does.)

"Can I help you?" The bloke says.

"I'd..."

The floors are too clean, the walls too bright. The light is resounding and bouncing off everything. Can't see with the glare. Turning back slightly and looking toward the lovely darkness of the bar area.

—Can't I check in over there?

It's coming.

"The toilet. May I..."

He looks horrified, but she immediately steps out from behind the desk around the side and points the way over between the elevator and the bar. Hurrying in that direction, wondering where the hand eye comes from for that. Quickly to the door of the ladies and then past the bench there and into the stall on the right, letting loose a torrent before any of the sounds of clattering and clanging at the door and seat register. All of a sudden, the way it comes. Bending over as a command, head hung down into the humbling lows.

(That's how it worked. That force where you threw yourself into a trot when you didn't have it in you. Five seconds before I couldn't have moved across the floor that fast if I wanted to, but then, once the moment struck, didn't have a choice. That's how it worked. And it didn't feel good to puke your guts out, no one would say that it did. But afterward, when it's through with you, there's some kind of relief. But that isn't pleasure, that's what I'm saying. And the sounds. What you're trying to make. That's supposed to be pleasing, they're supposed to like it, but where does that fit in when you got us crowing about this and the money guy crowing about that and we're banging into each other.)

Spitting and groaning, the floor is lovely clean and the commode too. Sitting sideways and holding on for a while, not sure whether any more is coming.

(He'd hold me quiet afterward. Lying there. Storming all day and then like that, he'd wrap me up and I wouldn't feel that pulse anymore. It settled. Thoughts calming down, the night was gentle. Lying there in his quiet. In his lovely quiet. Calm. That's pleasure, that felt good. Still, with Don, or whoever, it was always that way. Or looking for that. Trying to get back to that quiet and that calm. That light striking my air. I would have it off, or I wouldn't. He'd let me up on top like we did or he wouldn't. That wasn't the point. It was the quiet that I wanted. No, didn't want it. It wasn't about desire, and wanting, and struggling to get this or that. It was about being at ease. Just being. Afterward, he could pretty much do whatever he liked. For a few minutes at least, in that quiet, I was completely his. He could've done whatever he liked. I wanted him to be happy. Never was that way before, ever. He wasn't the type of fella to make too much of that. But it wouldn't have been bad if he did. Anything would have been fine, anything would have been grand in that place he made for me.)

Lunging and lurching again, most of the substance passed, but the body makes a special effort to get the last bits. Standing up straight, knowing that's the end of it. Heading back to the sink and letting the water run.

—The sound of it... Works wonders...

The bag is on the counter by the sink.

"How did that...?"

Looking back toward the mirror, there is a lot of damage to tend to.

(Not then, when it was easy, and you could snap back from working long into the night and lying there in the quiet, but awake. Having it off after dozing some, near dawn, only to get up and get something to eat to go through it all over again. A whole day and you only get one track down. We had the three hits, as he called them, and then the one emotional plea. That's what he said it was, but we had to spend all day on each one to get it where we wanted. Mostly arguing with him. But they don't let you argue because they're always telling you how great you are in this one and that one, well, it doesn't sound professional. Doesn't bring out the superstar we know is in there. And, of course, that shut you right up because you wanted that so badly and didn't know a damn thing about it. But he argued, he said what we were thinking, and it made a difference. Whatever of Rian was left in that one guitar riff, that was his doing. I believe that. Rian did too. He said as much, didn't he? George didn't like him one bit. You could see it. And who is this? Or something snipey. And you are? Is that an argument? That's how he would come back. Where did he get it from? Was it because he wasn't the one on the line? He could afford to be that way. And then, who was it? Someone got the idea, someone said it first.)

Touching up around the eyes and mouth. Rifling through the bag. Finding the mints and taking one, then a quick brush through to get it in order.

(Was it Rian? He was happy with the way that one riff turned out. We hadn't been so lucky on the vocals, but truth is, that's its signature and we didn't know what was best. George knew more than we thought. It wasn't that we wanted to block him completely, we wanted something to offset him, some way to tell him that we needed to be there too, that our voice was part of it. That's why Rian wanted him to be manager. Didn't remember that. He tried to convince him. We all did. You have to stay, you have to come along. Someone's got to look after us, these blokes'll eat us alive. Someone said that... I remember. They had a vision, and it wasn't ours. Everybody's drive was in a battle, but we didn't know how to say it and our egos were too soft. But you couldn't flatter *him*. He didn't have anything, no horse running, nothing to live or die by. He'd look out for us, the drive of it, the desire in it, make sure we had our way now and again, or at least something of us in there. We sure couldn't do it. Never did.)

Taking the bag and leaving the toilet, the bright lights immediately assert themselves and demand agreement. Walking unsteadily back toward the reception. She's waiting there, and he's looking down at something, taking notes or closing something up.

"Was it you brought my bag around?"

"Yes ma'am. Hope that was alright."

"Appreciate it." Careful look exchanged. She's a sweet one, and there's that recognition in her eyes, clear and hopeful. The bloke is dreadfully quiet. "May I have a room? There's a junior on the Fourth that I've had before. Is it available?"

"Yes ma'am," after she checks on the computer.

Taking out the credit card and sliding it over. The bloke finishes whatever he's doing and goes back into the room behind the counter. Not one look. Too young to remember. She's older. Those were her teenage years. She looks about right for that. Signing the paper she pushes over to this side of the desk. Barely legible, the hand trembles as it drags the pen across the bottom, not quite fitting it into the box and above the line where she points her finger.

"Do you have any bags we can help you with?"

"No, I can manage. Listen dear, is it possible to get some things sent up to the room?"

"Of course. What would you like?"

"A bottle of Old Jameson, if you have it. Some water too."

"Of course. Anything else?"

"Couple bottles of ale. Whatever you've got is fine."

"Any food? We can still do a few things if you want..."

"Won't be necessary, that'll do. Unless... Do you have cigarettes?"

Looking down and feeling guilty.

"No, we don't, sorry," luckily. "We could send out for them."

"No worries, needn't go to any trouble. Cheers."

"Thank you, ma'am. The elevators are there. Here's the key. Fourth floor, down to the far end."

"Ta."

"Good night."

Taking the bag and heading to the elevator. When the doors close, the light is better, easier on the eyes.

(He said no. Said he had to go. Said he had somewhere to be. All this time he never said a damn thing, but he's got some big plan that needs to get done. That's how it worked, that's how we confused them. You wanted something and you didn't get it. That's painful, it hurt. You felt the pain and dug at it if you could. With him, telling him how much we wanted him to stay around and help. George was filling our heads with how big we were going to be. You'll be rich, if he knows anything about it, we told him, but he didn't care, and not getting what we wanted, what I wanted, well, that hurt. Because it hurt to not get what you wanted, we thought it's supposed to feel good to get it. But it's a coincidence. You wanted it because you wanted things that felt good, but that didn't have anything to do with what the drive inside you was doing. Pleasure was a whole different thing, completely different. Those moments. That's what I was trying to find in that song from the second album, the one hit on that damn thing. That disappointment. *Quiet Place*. Remember that song? What else were you doing there but pining for the one single pleasure you ever had but couldn't remember?)

10.12.3.Natalie.19.86.9.1 [ref(..7.25-31)]

"Do you think she was a spy?" Hazel asks from the couch. Bernd is next to her and laughs while reaching over to push on her shoulder. He is sitting on the floor across from them on the other side of the coffee table. It's Greek themed and the table is set with wine from Nemea, Olives from Kalamata, cheese from somewhere: Kasseri, Feta, some others. Graviera and Kefalotyri. There is olive oil with a splash of malt vinegar and some nice baguette that they're tearing and dipping in the mixture.

"It was her job to engage foreign travelers to see if they've come to spy on the Motherland."

"Oh my God," Bernd says, still laughing and looking back at him. "Tell me that's true."

"No idea," he says taking a sip of wine. "She wanted me to mail a postcard from the West. When I hesitated, she said never mind and that it didn't matter."

"Tell them what she said when you invited her to the hotel."

They both nod and look back over to him.

"It was late, and we walked enough. I wanted to sit so I suggested we go back to the hotel to sit in the lobby or something. She said some man in a gray suit would come and escort her out."

"That's so creepy," Hazel says.

"Like the Stasi," Bernd adds.

"Surveillance is important right now. Not for the reasons you'd think. What everybody thinks. They'll know something about us and arrest us if it's bad or subversive or whatever, that's easy to spot. The insidious power is in changing behavior."

"Change the body, change the voice," he says.

"They surveille to discipline, shape the way people act," to the Talking Heads.

—Good title: Change the body, change the voice.

"The panopticon, that's one way to think about it, but there are others. Instead of a single central viewpoint where the observer may or may not be watching, it's a parallel, multi-headed system where everybody monitors everyone else. You have to do what's expected, and those expectations come from common notions about what we're supposed to want and how we're supposed to get it."

"█ *you may find* █ *shotgun shack"*

"Your conscience," he says. "Doesn't Freud say that conscience represents the group eye or something, always watching over you?"

"Or the father's eye, more likely," Hazel says.

He nods. Bernd looks back this way.

"Conscience... ...an internalized control... ...it might be automatic. Something you can't help, you feel guilty when you do or say something outside the norm. Reflection too. The voice of the thinker, of the theorist, of the philosopher, that voice is deeply mediated, the intersubjective, the social. Whatever you want to call it. They are cultivated habits in act and thought."

"█ *days go by,* █ *hold me down"*

"That's when you think you're cutting through the bullshit," Hazel says.

"That's when you're most caught up in it."

"Critique always has a direction," Bernd says. "It comes from somewhere and has a target. Deferring to universals, relating them, aligning, that's a skill, it takes time, development, it's produced and refined by institutions with narrow focus."

"█ *ask yourself, 'How* █ *?'"*

"We learn how to experience the world. Point of view belongs to the all-seeing eye, or to some light shed on everything, casting shadows. Meaning lies in that. Surveillance again. Sometimes I think critique is playing the violin while Rome burns, sometimes I think it's the fire itself."

"█ *the blue* ████████ *money's gone*"

"What does that mean?" he asks with both dread and concern.

"The theorist fans the flames. It's conceptual surveillance. Creates the tropes and notions governing us, myths guiding us. The imagination runs wild in the space between the particular and the universal. Theory is a ritual or a ceremonial act. The soul in theory becomes the soul as religious incantation. The self in theory becomes a new deity, the son, an icon shaped and twisted opportunistically."

"My sister told me," Bernd says. "That at her work they have these sessions where everyone discusses the atmosphere in the office. How everyone acts and behaves, what ideas drive their behavior, and the whole point is to shape the way they act, become more deliberate. They get them to talk about their experiences, and the moderator shapes those reflections and stories into the message the company wants the employees to learn."

"█████ *ever was, same* ████████ "

"Surveillance often works through confession. You speak from the heart, it coerces that out of you, helps you understand what it means, and how to interpret it. That changes the way you think about yourself, changes the way you act."

"This doesn't sound like Irigaray," Hazel says. "Isn't that what you're working on?"

"She's part of it. How to make her work here? Speculation as the Phallus trying to take center stage and become the central matter in associations. She doesn't speak much about power, but it's implied. Women are a commodity in the marketplace, our bodies are traded, and become a fetish for men to exchange and use for their pleasure. That's power, the power to buy and sell."

(It's possible men only wanted to possess you because you were on offer for possession. If he didn't, someone else would. He only wanted you so that other men couldn't have you. The techniques of self-care were for the sake of... Disciplined, always dutiful in the shadow of *his* desire.)

—Yes, oh yes. Baby baby. Fuck me fuck me... ...idiots...

"███████ *water* ██████ *bottom of the ocean /* ████ *dissolving* and █ *removing*"

"The marketplace leads you astray," Hazel says. "But pleasure. That's the connection. It's a currency."

"I think so too, but it may be hard to separate. I mean, pleasure's been a part of discourse on human action for a long time. The Utilitarian bases their entire ethical world on it. Higher order pleasures, nuanced pleasures, sophisticated and cultivated. Of course, they don't ask about this cultivation and how it works and what comes of it, but they know it's ordered, subject to rules, integral to ends, and that it produces hierarchies from them."

[Americanism of the soul is the world without joy. The world reduced to its aggregates with no room to find anything in the crevices created by pain and pleasure. Everyone is treated like a child, but no one is allowed to feel as children feel. The deep joys and sorrows are stripped bare and sold at market. Separated from their source, alienation and fetish are what's left, they are the new sensations advertised everywhere we turn, suffocating us.]

—Soon, there'll be a McDonald's in Eberbach.

"Sexuality cuts across every level of that hierarchy," Bernd says.

"Under the rocks ███████████████ water underground"

"Absolutely. The purest sensation, sensation without a concept, may lie in sexual acts. But does it? Is the purest experience infiltrated by these notions, censors, whatever you call them? They may be everywhere and always active, a part of action's form. We may enjoy things that some historical force predestines us to enjoy, be trained to evoke specific universals when coming upon this or that particular. The aggregate in the singular, replacing its singularity, eclipsing it right before our eyes."

"You mean the actual feeling of pleasure is shaped by something beyond you," he says with his voice rising near the end, making it sound like a question.

Leaning toward him and taking a sip of wine in his direction, eyes fierce and piercing: "There are collective tastes typical of the era. Sure things." Winking.

—Pleasure is simple and clear. At bottom. On the bottom. Pain too.

"███████████ ask yourself, ███████ am I wrong?" / ███████ say to yourself, ███████████ I done?""

"Whereas two hundred years ago no one was into that," he says.

"And two hundred years from now things will be totally different. What gets people off in 1986 becomes irrelevant."

"It could become gross," Hazel says. "It's interesting, but I don't see how it'll work for you. I don't see the feminist connection."

"███████ blue again, ███████ silent water"

"My problem is with Irigaray. I love what she says about discourse and how men have set the tone and are the only ones who speak as authorities, how authoritative genres are saturated with the Phallus, the central eye." Imitating a one-eyed pirate, "Arrrrrr," much to everyone's amusement. "But... I mean... In the act, the concrete act, the whole no dicks allowed part..."

"That's the patriarchy in you," Hazel says.

"Literally, I get it, but that raises the question, how does one get behind that? How does one take a critical, reflective stance and avoid the effects of surveillance while doing it, while giving the notion a body?"

"That's a thesis. That is a thesis right there," Bernd says. "The cat is on the mat. Which cat? Which mat? Why am I noticing this? Why am I pointing it out?"

"Sarazen won't sign up for it. She doesn't know how to connect it to anything. Is it philosophy? Theory? Or is it psychoanalytic? If you venture into the psycho-social conditions of reflection, have you left off with philosophy?"

"*Time* ████████████████ *after us*"

(She's as fucked as the rest of us. They paraded it, berated it, but they were as soaked with it as everyone else. Contrary to it was still for it. Acting as its shadow validated the light. Couldn't she be a lesbian just because she liked it? Did it have to be a political agenda?)

[Irigaray: "Are we alike? If you like. It's a little abstract. I don't quite understand "alike." Do you? Alike in whose eyes? In what terms? By what standard? With reference to what third? I'm touching you, that's quite enough to let you know that you are my body."]

"If you have," he says. "Then philosophy is not what it claims to be. It's a neurosis."

"And you can't argue *that*," Hazel says.

"You'd need a whole new logic, a whole new mode of presentation. You can't persuade or produce cogent and valid arguments to draw your reader along that path. Language changes, not only the words, but the syntax. The grammar would change."

"Qualitative methodologies are already suspicious," Hazel responds. "You can't get philosophers to take that approach seriously. You cannot psychoanalyze philosophy from within philosophy. Their heads would explode."

"████████ *days* ███████ *flowing underground*"

"Communicative Action Theory. What's that supposed to be? Not psychoanalysis, but some kind of social reflection revealing the conditions of theory, putting them into play, and demonstrating the power relations at work when coming to an agreement. There's a hermeneutics to it. See. And that means you can discuss it in this light. If someone would back it, there'd be scholarly breadcrumbs. Foucault, Irigaray sure, but Marxist critique, Critical Theorists, other French thinkers."

"There are places where it could be done," Bernd says. "But I don't think this is one of them."

"And besides, that's not where my interest lies. That's the necessary legwork before getting to what I want to talk about."

"Pleasure," he says. "Uncovering its conditions."

"But you want to do it without laying the foundations," Hazel says.

"That's not how it works," Bernd urges everyone. "It's didactic, this whole façade. The university. Its purpose is to prevent you from rushing into what you want to explore and force you to consider everything leading up to it. You must justify your form of discourse before using it. Vet it."

" ▮▮▮▮▮▮▮▮ *I felt / Without style* ▮▮▮▮▮ "

"You cannot invent a genre for analysis, you have to show that there is no other option," Hazel says. "And use the paradigm to do it, reductio style. Derrida's first..."

"You see what you're in for?" Looking at him nearby on the floor, his legs stretched out next to the table, leaning back on his arms at an angle behind him.

"I think so," he says. "You don't believe it. The prologue is corrupt. Form is content, but why can't you show that in a way that draws out the scholarship? I mean, if you know your shit, and you have the narrative to back it up, why can't you pummel them with it?"

" ▮▮▮▮▮ *watch* ▮▮▮▮▮▮ *his* ▮▮ *grave* "

"You can, but what bridges would you burn in the process? That's the real dilemma. Of course, I can figure out how to do exactly what I want to do, but how to do that without alienating everyone, without getting myself branded a freak or a crackpot? That's the hard part. It's based on what they think of you, how they value your work, your credibility. If you lose any of that... You'll never get a position, you'll never publish in their journals, you'll be on the margins and lost to that Phallic center."

"You've run this past Sarazen and she doesn't accept it? It's certain," Hazel asks.

(*Her* credibility would be damaged. She didn't have the courage to tell me that. She poked holes in something to make her refusal seem rational, but the strings came out in the light. Recursion recurses.)

" ▮ *walking* ▮▮▮▮▮▮▮▮▮▮ *empty motion* "

"She doesn't see the feminist angle. The fact that you mention a few remarks here and there from a feminist isn't enough. The notion of pleasure, I can't guarantee that patriarchy is underneath it. My mind isn't made up. Can't you just like dick?"

They laugh.

[Desire to fuck him.

Desire to be fucked by him.

Desire that he desire to fuck me.

Desire that he desire to be fucked by me.]

"I'm serious. The pleasure of it. That's her whole point and yet sometimes it seems as though she thinks the organ is always mediated by the Phallus."

" *I'm turning around* ▮▮▮▮▮▮▮▮▮ "

He gets up and heads off toward the toilet, letting his hand lightly drag along the shoulders and neck while passing behind.

"When does Martin get back?" Hazel asks once he's down the stairs and she hears the door close.

"Friday. Late."

"And he's leaving?" Hazel bobs her head toward the stairs.

"I'm driving him to Nürnberg."

"That's sad," Bernd says. "It's been nice having him. He makes you happy, I think."

"Never ███████████████████████ *talk"*

Laughing for a while before Hazel gets it and laughs too. Bernd shrugs and shakes his head.

"That was August. It's been a vacation. How long do you expect it to last?" An exaggerated flair in the tone. "Besides, he understands that better than I do, believe me. They're adaptable at that age." More flare and a pause. "We talked about it, anyway. It's time to get back to work."

Pursing the lips and tilting the head, then looking over toward the stairway where there is the sound of a door below opening after a flush. Hazel and Bernd mimic the gesture and add a sympathetic nod at the end.

'██████████ *her eyes /* ████████████ *hope"*

10.12.4.Greta.19.86.9.28 [ref(..84.5-9)]

(*"You have a voice, you know the styles, but you will never triumph, because you have no duende.' ... The duende, then, is a power, not a work. It is a struggle, not a thought. I have heard an old maestro of the guitar say, 'The duende is not in the throat; the duende climbs up inside you, from the soles of the feet.' Meaning this: it is not a question of ability, but of true, living style, of blood, of the most ancient culture, of spontaneous creation. ... The true fight is with the duende."* [Garcia Lorca])

Turning the key and walking into the room. He is sitting across from the door on the couch on the other side of the hot tub. He looks up from his book and watches carefully as things come out of the bag. There is the journal and then a thick book. He perks up.

"What's that?"

"It's for you. In the gift shop, they had this for some reason." Stepping around to him, leaning across the corner of the tub to hand it over.

"Thanks," he says, glowing. "And what's that?" He gestures toward the bound journal still sitting on the desk. Moving back there and standing over it, looking down.

"That's what I was looking for," flipping the blank pages to show him.

He nods but doesn't say anything. Flips through the first few pages of the new book.

"I thought you were almost done with that one so..."

"I am. This is great, thanks. I've read a lot of these in English. Let's see how I do with this."

"This thing is an abomination." Pointing at the tub in the center of the room while sitting down at the desk and taking a sip from the water bottle. "Thanks for filling this."

"Skiers must love these things," he says nodding toward the fiberglass centerpiece.

"The restaurant looks good. When we're hungry, we should go."

Opening the book with purpose. It's got lovely big pages with tight lines. Not too big, as though it's meant for a child, and not so small that you'll cramp your hand filling it in.

"How does it work?"

He looks up from the book, sets it down on the couch, and picks up the old book with a pen jammed into it serving as a bookmark. "Composition heavy. Two pages every day, no matter what. It's not optional."

"What if you don't have anything to say? What if you don't feel like it?"

"It's not two pages whenever you feel like it," he says sneering. Then he brightens up, gets more excited and encouraging, "It's two pages per day, non-negotiable. No one is forcing you to do it. Do it or don't do it, but those are the rules."

"And what if you can't think of anything?"

"Well," he looks back down. His eyes are far away when he comes back up and looks briefly in this direction before turning toward the window and continuing: "You can write about why you can't think of anything. It could be boring. The things in this room. What you had for breakfast. How far we drove today. Something we saw between Oberammergau and here. Something. Anything. Why don't you feel like describing your breakfast? Why can't you do it well? Those are things. You're completely free. No one is watching, no one is looking over your shoulder. No one will read it later. Burn it. Whatever you want."

Nodding, and retracing the path his eyes took over toward the window and then back toward the empty tub.

"About what you're reading, imagine you're someone else reading it, or doing anything for that matter," he goes on as though talking to himself. "I end up doing that a lot. If I have nothing better, I'll do that. Pretend to be someone else and do what I imagine they would do or think what I imagine they would think."

—Not reading anything right now. That book she sent without explanation. Sometimes. ...can't concentrate. I could write about that, about why I'm not reading anything, about why I'm not interested in reading anything else.

"What did you read today?"

He straightens up to read from the old book, flipped back a few pages:

> *Everywhere I've turned somebody has wanted to sacrifice*
> *me for my own good—only they were the ones who*
> *benefited. And now we start on the old sacrificial merry-go-*
> *round. At what point do we stop? Is this the new true*
> *definition, is Brotherhood a matter of sacrificing the weak?*
> *If so, at what point do we stop?*[1]

Confidently done, but the English is hard.

"I didn't follow completely. What does it mean?"

"People who want to help him, they're using him. Saying what they do is for him, but it's for themselves."

"What's a merry-go-round?"

"Like at a carnival. One of the rides. There are horses. Children ride on them. It goes in a circle."

"Ah, Karussell." He is looking this way, but not reacting. His eyes fill with some vague waiting. He leans his head against the back of the couch. "Sacrificial merry-go-round. Still don't get it."

"It's not easy," he says. "You could write about that."

"What is the first sentence of that book?"

"*I am an invisible man,*"[2] he reads after flipping back to it.

"That's it?"

"Yes."

"How about the rest of the paragraph? What does it say?"

He reads:

> *No, I am not a spook like those who haunted Edgar Allan*
> *Poe; nor am I one of your Hollywood-movie ectoplasms. I*
> *am a man of substance, of flesh and bone, fiber and liquids*
> *— and I might even be said to possess a mind. I am invisible,*
> *understand, simply because people refuse to see me. Like*
> *the bodiless heads you see sometimes in circus sideshows, it*
> *is as though I have been surrounded by mirrors of hard,*
> *distorting glass. When they approach me they see only my*
> *surroundings, themselves, or figments of their imagination*
> *— indeed, everything and anything except me.*[3]

---

[1] *Invisible Man* by Ralph Ellison.

[2] Ibid.

[3] Ibid.

"He is invisible because people only see what they think they are going to see. They don't see him for who he is. He is invisible because they put something else where he is."

"Something like that," he says.

"The last sentence of the book, what is it?"

"I'm not there yet," he protests.

"But almost. Tell me. Please."

He looks back down and flips to the end of the book behind where he's put the pen.

"The last sentence is: '*Who knows but that, on the lower frequencies, I speak for you?*' But what he said before that is: '*Being invisible and without substance, a disembodied voice, as it were, what else could I do? What else but try to tell you what was really happening when your eyes were looking through? And it is this which frightens me.*'[4] Then that last sentence: '*Who knows but that, on the lower frequencies, I speak for you?*'[5]"

"Lower frequencies?"

"Barely audible. Whispers. Or outside the range of what we can hear with human ears," he clarifies.

"It frightens him that when he tells the truth about what they should see, he's speaking for others too."

He nods. Sitting for a minute and looking across the room. He purses his lips and looks back down at the book. He flips to the page where his pen lies and takes it back in hand to read, tracing along the words with the tip.

Cracking open to the first page of the journal and looking down, pen poised.

Dear Heidi,

He is invisible but not because no one can see anything, they can't see him. Not the way he is. Or thinks he is. They see something else, their prejudices or preconceived ideas. Whatever they thought already before they talked to him. At the end, he isn't invisible anymore because he speaks for other people. People who can see him now because they can hear what he is saying. Only whispering it. He is afraid.

It's not my book. El read some of it to me. He is here. He came to see me. He tried to bring you back, but couldn't, so he had to come later. It's my fault he didn't come. I am invisible too, in a different way. You

---

[4] Ibid.

[5] Ibid.

remember when we were little, how it was when they would read to us, and
I always needed you to explain.

They always saw us, never me. We both felt that way. Seeing us, and
not each of us. The pair is only one. There's Johan and Uwe and then there
are the twins. Three of them there, the ones whose last names start with F.
They could only see three even if we were four with our coats and hats or
whatever we were doing when they had to take attendance.

You did the talking. Now what happens?

El's telling me about your life there. The parts he knows. It sounds nice.
I wish I had come. Wish? Cry. El and I are in Austria. We had no plan,
only came here to spend time together. I needed something, but I didn't
know what. I am nothing. I don't know what to be. You. That keeps coming
into my head, as though I should go to work for the same agency, help
them in Nürnberg. Get others to go do what you were doing, but then I
would only be you and I need to be both you _and_ me. How do I do that?
I wasn't anything before. Your sister, and Eva's. But _I_ wasn't her sister, _we_
were.

I have so many questions, but they don't have anywhere to go. There's
no one here to answer them.

Is it okay that I needed to be with El? It's not him. He can't help but
see you when he sees me. And that means I am you when I'm with him.
That's not nice, but I can't help it. He can't either. We both miss you. We
all do.

That's almost two pages. He calls it the program. Did you know about
it? Did he tell you?

Eva wishes it was me instead of you. That's bad to say, but I know it,
and I agree. What difference does it make? I'm half-dead anyway. Might
as well have been me.

I don't know what I was doing before, but it didn't matter as much as it
does now. Is it possible to live through someone else? I was in Colombia
already, I was the one in the hillside town, up near the hospital, talking to
those hard men and telling them they had to do the right thing.

I quit my job but haven't told anyone. What will you do now?

He's going to leave soon and then I have to figure it out. There is a
timer, and if it goes on too long, it'll be too late, and everything will be
ruined. But, if it's ruined already, waiting won't make a difference. I got this
journal to figure out what to do.

On the lower frequencies, I am speaking for you.

Setting the pen down and looking over at him. He has turned quite a
few pages in the meantime.

"Done?" he asks looking up.

"Three pages almost." Getting up and going over to sit next to him.

"Want to talk about it?" he asks.

Practically bursting into tears and falling against the back of the couch. He turns this way but doesn't know whether to reach out or not. He opens his arms, putting one across the top of the couch and letting the other fall against his leg. He waits with that open place on offer. Sliding down into it headfirst, bumping up against his shoulder while his hand goes to the back and lightly strokes up and down. A single light kiss on the top of the head.

[Many twists and turns, so much that was nowhere near familiar. This was the most corrupt and wicked thing I could ever do. This was the most perfect and loving thing I could ever do. This way and that way. Turning to and fro, not knowing whether to turn back and keep going round and round in a circle. Like on... ...a merry-go-round... Sacrificing what though? My self? Her? Does it compound things? Make them go from bad to worse. You can't treat a person as if they were merely a handkerchief. But if they offer you one? I want him to tell me how it feels. That's disgusting. I'm disgusting. I need her here to know who I can be without her. But how can that happen? It's not possible. But if he tells me, if he describes it, in these stories... ...that's how it is with stories, they can help you make yourself into something. Find yourself in the woods or in whatever mischief those kids are up to now. That's everything she always used to say. It's to help you imagine things, where you planned your life and figured out who you were. Imagine what it could be, what you could be.]

"I don't know who I am." He wraps his arms around, joining the left behind with the right reaching across to meet it. The book falls off to the side, the pen falling out, losing its place. Reaching down to turn it over and see what is on the page, creased and exposed by the fall, then reading aloud: *" What and how much had I lost by trying to do only what was expected of me instead of what I myself had wished to do?"*[6]

---

[6] Ibid.

11.12

this year's harvest

11.12.1.Elisabet.1986.5.11 [ref(..4.27-..5.3)]

(Dissolve it, only way to avoid... Does a stylist need that much notice? And the techs, hotels, other venues, such bullshit, they'll fill those dates. Plenty of time... If it were closer, more sympathy, but...)

There are footsteps inside the entryway. The outer door closes and there is some shuffling, then more footsteps heading this way. Light tapping on the door.

"Come in."

His hair is wet, feet bare, the long curls longer.

"Well, stranger, where have you been?"

"Didn't make it too far." He comes in and stands next to the couch perpendicular to the desk, then takes a seat following the gesture. His right leg tucks up underneath him and his jeans look moist. "It's been raining most of the afternoon," he says. "Got caught but made it to that coffee shop down on the corner."

"Which one? There are about five."

"Yeah, right on the corner. Corner Brew or whatever. It's nice. Comfortable seats. Is this Segovia?"

"Playing Albeniz. Sorry, I was tied up today. Almost finished. We can get something to eat if you're hungry. Or, if you want, Jelly called. She's got plans with Craig and those guys. Wanted to know if you cared to join."

He ignores the last part and grabs onto the first with a teasing smile. "Do you keep food here?" He means to explain what kitchens are for. It comes out thick and affectionate.

Over and through the laughter: "I've been away, there's not much. Delivery. Tomorrow there'll be lots of commotion."

"Right after I leave." He looks back toward the window behind him, nothing but park, skies still gray and churning, turbulent movement in those airy masses.

"Cassie's arriving tomorrow. Or she's coming here. She's usually the cause of the commotion, I'm an inert object."

"The whirlpool at the center," he says leaning back in the seat. Impossible to avoid smiling at him, proud of what he knows.

—Passion must be well-placed, you can't let it rule you.

"You don't get to choose what you're passionate about." Then quiet through a long pause before saying, "I have a question." The tone is more serious than intended. He turns, puts his leg down on the floor, and sits up straight.

Standing and coming around the desk, turning the volume down, and taking a seat next to him. Arm up on the back rest behind, legs half curled, and looking directly at him.

"Your hair looks good in this light," he says. "Did you wash it?"

"Don't distract me." He wipes the grin off his face and pretends to be serious. Failing, as though someone with nothing to hide.

"What is it?" he asks.

"Why were you in Colombia?" Slowly.

He looks down, hiding something, quickly forgetting, forced to remember. What was once open and ready, turns inward or downward or somewhere else away from here. He has a flash of insight.

"Why are you asking... ...after all this time?"

—It could still be measured in hours, but I know what you mean.

"Background check complete," saying it in a goofy voice imitating a robot from some television show. "Poked around."

"Do you already know why I was in Colombia?"

"I'm sorry, I have to be careful. It isn't personal. Elmo insisted. That was before."

He's not angry or hurt, stalling, getting used to the topic. He works at keeping it together too.

"Heidi died," he says simply after a short pause. "They didn't know who to call. The organization didn't have anything on file. The doctor got Gabriel to call my friend in Medellin and he called me. I was getting ready to go to Europe, but someone had to come take the..."

He looks down at his feet. They are neatly set side-by-side and tucked right up against the base of the couch. Looking that way too.

"There are forms. To release her. Didn't know where she had to go. I got to town, bus dropped me off right in front of Gabriel's store, he drove me up to the hospital. There was someone from the German Consulate there, waiting, said something about making arrangements."

Reaching out and putting a hand on his shoulder. He's tense, the muscles in his body strained, as though he's lifting something heavy and can't be distracted or else he'll drop it. At the touch of the hand something bends and at least part of him relaxes when he remembers he doesn't have to go through it again.

"I called her parents. The whole family was there. Terrible. They... I didn't... I messed the whole thing up. Like a machine. Es tut mir leid, Frau Fenzler, Heidi ist tod. Is that the way someone would say that? The softest way? I didn't know, but I didn't know what else... Her sister was there, she came to the phone. Speaks English, but it was so fubar by that point, and I only had three minutes."

Scooting over, pursing the lips, and trying to get closer, but he doesn't want that, doesn't lean this way, or change his position to make it easier.

"The consul arranged everything. On his way up, going places. It was a truck that took the three of us back to Medellin. It's a dirt road. Bouncing like crazy the whole way back. It took hours and every jolt you can hear the wood against the metal bed of the truck. Scraping and tugging at the bungy or whatever it was. The images, what runs through your mind... Her sister is a twin. I guess I knew that. She mentioned it, I'm sure, it may have been the only thing she said when she took the phone, or something else and it reminded me."

He stands up and walks over to the door, then over toward the desk. Doesn't seem to be aware of doing it, needs the distance, and doesn't want it to come across as rejection.

"The logistics suck, you don't realize that."

—Always the arrangements. It's the logistics that'll break you.

"I had forgotten that. I knew before but... The plane doesn't go directly to Europe, it's a trek. You have to fly to Cartagena and then New York and London to Frankfurt. There's a plane from Frankfurt to Nuremberg. It was arranged, but still, the itinerary was a whole page long, it's overwhelming. He said once she's in Germany it'll be fine, but every country has something, and you need to sign and approve the storage. Fucking storage."

He's staring at the shelves behind the desk. The two soft lead statues shaped like gramophones are right in front of him, but he doesn't register that. The pictures from that and other similar nights line the shelf, but he hardly notices. He's going through the motions of being someone who is distracted by what is in front of him, but he isn't distracted.

"That's why I was late in Cartegena. Bills of lading. You sign a bill of lading... The consul was sorry he couldn't do it and was glad I was there. I think he got the idea that... I don't know what he thought, but it can't be how it usually is, it's supposed to be a family member."

He comes back and sits down again, farther away, by the armrest. Not changing position in response, if he wants to come closer, it's open. There's a standing invitation in a gesture. Awkward, but it's deliberate enough, just in case.

"In New York too. That's what I had to do at baggage claim, then tomorrow, more. In London. Endless. Once she's back in Germany, I think... London might be the end. Short layover, then she's home. Frankfurt to Nuremberg. She doesn't need me..."

He looks over. It's because he's in the middle of it. Not grief, not drowning in loss, overwhelmed with tasks.

—The formality of it.

(That's what I saw in his eyes when I said my traveling name. How

stupid was that? What are the odds? But if not for that look, we wouldn't
have spoken. Probably not, no one's ever that raw, no one was ever that
childlike, flaunting themselves at you. Couldn't resist, still can't, desperately
wanting to move closer, you're supposed to put your arms around people
when they go off to these terrible places by themselves, but he didn't want
it, he intentionally put himself as far away as he could get.)

—Focus.

"May I ask how she died?" Trying to pull him away from the tasks and
back to the person.

[Was that better? Or worse?]

"She, uh." He pauses and swallows hard. "Um, she bled to death.
Exsanguination." Deliberately pronounced, drawing out each syllable. "I
had no idea. What could that be? Something caused her to bleed, right? I
may have been hysterical when I was asking about that, but it was as if they
were being intentionally vague. It makes you angry, you can't..."

[Fine, it'd have to be by his rules.]

Straightening to his same formal position but moving right next to him
at the end of the couch. He immediately leans in, and the arms go wrapping
around him in reflex. It's what he needs but he doesn't know it. He is crying
but composed. The stiff position of his body helps him remain in place.

"She was hit by a car. That's what the Guardia chief said when I got
there. They don't know anything else. No details. She was on the hillside
below the road. Walking back from town. She was with Don Alberto and
Gabriel at the tavern. Same as dozens of other nights, nothing special. Then
walking back, like she always did. Wasn't drunk or anything, they said,
nothing they could think of. She walked up the road same as always... ...the
chief thinks a car was racing by and knocked her off the road and down the
hill into the grass there. It's thick. The driver may not have known he hit a
person. That's what he said, but if that... ...if he had gotten out of his car
and looked around, he might've seen her. Or something. She was a
kilometer from the hospital, but she had a broken hip and a broken leg.
Her arm too. That whole side of her body. Must've been where the impact
was. A concussion too, the doctor said. She might've been in and out of it.
Unable to crawl. I can't imagine. Was she awake? Did she know she was
dying? Did she scream?"

Not the first time through these scenarios, it's how he holds it together
while cycling through them. Voicing something he's already been over
before, tilting farther back and turning more to the side, there's room to
ease his posture and lean into it. The arm behind him strokes his hair. The
other is on his lap and holding the back of his hand, the nails smoother
and more filed down than when he arrived.

"It drives me crazy thinking about those minutes. How many? Five?
Twenty? That's what the doctor thought."

Sitting there quietly. He doesn't seem to have anything more, but then whispers something in a completely different tone and it's unclear how it's related. He's leaning his head against the shoulder and breast and his breath is noticeably labored.

"I read this thing once about the master and the slave. The master barely pays attention, he doesn't notice anything. The slave is hyper alert, they see everything, they have to, they have to notice whenever anything changes in the master's mood. Otherwise, they'll get a beating or punished some other way." His voice changes again, and he's no longer whispering. Pulling back and sitting up some, but not making eye contact. "That's why history belongs to the slave, it's because they pay attention, because they need to pay attention. Their lives depend on it."

[Who saw more clearly? The one before? The one after? Her? Who did you see best? Who saw you best?]

(Not sure, without certainty, everywhere, but the sense increased, reaching for optimal intensity, attention was imperative. Rich lady enslaved by desire. When they knew what you wanted, they owned you.)

"After that thing with Chloe, she came to visit. That's what I was reading. She said that's how it is, that it was the truest thing, and it's why you must pay attention... ...to everything, to everything that goes on anywhere... ...because you're a slave, because you're at its mercy. It'll take everything from you... ...eventually... ...and you have to keep your eye on its changes and turns... ...and not only that... ...but people think that if they can become that way, like the wind or the weather, if they can become that way, they'll be more powerful, get above it, or if they get huge they're a crowd, you know, one you can't get through and you're trying to get from one side to the other but they're blocking the way and you can't. It appears as one single thing. I mean, the masters. They're a crowd. Not one big person, but a whole crowd... ...people want to be that, an army paying attention to everything, to the rocks, to the water, to the crowds... ...to the trucks that bounce all the way back to the city... ...the planes with limited cargo space... ...the baggage and the files and forms you have to fill out... ...to get your friend to the right place... ...where she belongs... ...isn't alone... ...in the grass... ...cutting at your legs and tearing you up. She had scratches, scratches all over. She tried to crawl, that's what they said, they said she tried to crawl, but she was too broken, and she couldn't, or she passed out, they don't know, but she died alone in the grass because some stupid... ...because some idiot..."

—Från livets krigsskola... ...döden bevisar att vi måste vara fria.

He breaks off and fully leans in, accepting the open rocking that now cradles him on the couch by the window over the park on the island in the city by the river leading to the ocean flowing in great wild currents, flaunting its mastery enormously unaware of the lives spent tracing their way along its shores and below its reeling winds.

11.12.2.Seannafair.20.15.5.8 [ref(19.86.6.1)]

[What was wrong with me? Why didn't he choose me?]

(The lock was dancing, the floor was buckling, it was showing off as a riposte or a subtle set of lines broken through the windows and doors and meant to settle on everyone still there. Bed flopped, that's what they're calling it. On the downlow, but not if you didn't dare. It's up to you, breaking a kip for whoever came knocking, whoever brought it. Leave it leave it. On the floor outside. What did I know? Didn't think the bucket'd be so bloody heavy. Ice weighs a ton. They didn't prepare you for that. Made a bunch of trips. Lining it along some side whistle that none of them cared to make light of in the coming hours. Where there was darkness, the storied savings grew. Which pattern was that? Who broke that down first and foremost among them?)

—Didn't have a clue.

(Never said nothing, never touched nothing again. Biggest there was and all I felt was rejection. Why didn't he want me?)

Dead battery. Picking up the telephone and waiting for someone on the other end.

—Are you supposed to hit a number or something?

"Are you..."

"Yes, Ms. Quinn, how can I help you?"

"Long distance. Can I phone Canada?"

"You can, but there's a surcharge per minute. If you'd rather, we can bring a phone card."

"Never mind. Can't I just call? Does it have to..."

"Of course. I'll set the phone for you. Dial a 9 first and then the number. It's ready."

Touching the cradle and trying to remember. Nothing comes. Back to the bag on the bed. No charger. Digging through it for that book. Here it is.

—9

"Country code?"

Hanging up, turning the tumbler over and putting some ice from the bucket in it. Cracking open the bottle and pouring some. Slowly sloshing it side to side and then taking a quick gulp. There are four beer bottles tucked into the ice bucket and a tray with a bottle of water and a bottle opener set neatly. Picking up the phone again.

"Yes. Hello Ms. Quinn."

"Can you put me through to Canada? Do you know what time it is there?"

"Do you have the number?"

Reading the number digit by digit. Sitting down at the chair by the desk. Turning toward the window to avoid the mirror.

"Should be five hours earlier. Shall I put you through?"

"Yes, thank you."

It's ringing. Another gulp and the glass is empty. Filling it higher this time.

"Hello."

"Is this Mike?"

"Jenni? Is that you? Where are you?"

"Mike, remember the fella, the one we wanted as our manager. The one who got the agent to come listen to us. What was his name? Do you remember?"

"Jenni, how much have you had?"

"Never mind. What was his name? Don't you remember?"

"Michaels. Something like that. E something Michaels or L something. I remember because I asked him if he was related to the guy from Poison."

"Was he?"

"Nah, what about him?"

"Couldn't remember his name. Do you remember anything else about him?"

Taking another gulp, pulling the booties off.

—Should've done that ages ago.

"That night we finished the recording for that A&R guy," he says. "We were together. You two were chummy, I remember that. He had some kind of magic for you."

"What else?"

"Liam's old beater guitar. The nylon. I remember him playing it. At first he was being delicate. Talking to Liam about it, no idea what. It was a real beater. That mattered because he bangs on it. Not bad... He's hitting it with his finger while he pummels and drags the strings. It was something. I looked it up. Liked it so much. Something... *Si Acaso Muero*. Not sure. A dark and eerie tune, walking heavy. 'Lighten my steps. Lighten my steps.' That's what it was about. Camarón. Haven't thought about it in years."

"He had long nails on his right hand."

"Did he scratch you, Jenni?" he laughs.

"More than that," bringing him back to the right tone. "But he left. Up and left the next day, didn't he? Can't remember why he had to go. Right when everything was coming together."

"Coming together for us. He had nothing to do with that. Helped with the name though."

"He did." Finishing off the glass. Taking one of the bottles from the bucket and cracking it open. Letting it sit there while filling the tumbler, adding another cube of ice.

"The A&R guy. Yank. Charles was his name, I think. He hated Dairy. Couldn't stand it. Said we absolutely had to change it. It was Michaels who asked what your mother's name was."

"Why did he do that?"

"The way I remember, we were talking about the image, being Irish and that. That's what Charles was saying. We were lads and a lass. All that. The name couldn't be farm Irish, like Dairy. It had to be cool, but no one had any ideas. Michaels asked about your mam, and everyone stood there with their mouths open when you said it. We knew that was it."

"Aine," in a barely audible whisper.

"Yeah, and we asked him why he wanted to know that. What made him think of it? Mothers have the secrets. That's what he said. Something like that. Or the answers. Yeah, that's it. The answers."

The voice sounds close. It's as though he's here in the room. Everything is coming up close.

"Why did he leave, Mike? Why?"

"You weren't exactly telling us everything that was going on with you, Jenni. He seemed to fancy you, but he was passing through. I don't know. Don't cry, darling. It was thirty years ago. Can it mean that much to you now?"

"It was the last time..."

"That's nonsense, Jenni. You've got a husband who wants to make things right with you. You've got two beautiful children who adore you. They miss you. Nothing thirty years ago was the last time for anything. You hear me? You need to get yourself some sleep and tomorrow everything will be better. We'll talk next week and make arrangements. It'll be for the best. Do some work. What do you say?"

"Okay then. Thanks Mike. Thanks for that. Talk to you soon."

"Bye Jenni. Get some rest."

Putting it back in its cradle. Topping off the tumbler then pushing the way through the mess of a room filled with noise and heading to the bathroom door. The tub's the best thing about this place.

(It was an eerie song he was playing. Speaking the words in Spanish. Said he couldn't sing, but his talking was melodious, dreamy. Perfect rhythm. Proved that's what mattered. Counted it in 5, but it was 12. Some logic to that. Had to already know it to know it. The bellowing and the crooning, the highs and lows of it, the echoing, that was gamesmanship. You've got to hit the notes at the right time, 1 2 3 ... 4 ... 5, everything depends on it. Didn't we go to the pub? Or was that a different day? I could've sworn that last night, after he played, and after everyone was properly pissed, celebrating and happy with the new name and the new work and everything grand that was happening. We went by the pub for the last of it. Was that right? And was there a girl? Or someone he saw. He turned sheet white. As though he was the ghost. Said he saw something. Was that imagination? White as white could be and he looked back at me and said, what did he say?)

"You don't get to choose what you're passionate about."

(More, or it was someone else. Had to be well-placed. It's okay to be passionate about things, you couldn't let it rule you though. He wanted to play Led Zeppelin, but it never kicked him enough, never got him going. Only that sad howling had the right effect. He couldn't choose. It was a warning. None of it was my choice. The passion had me all along, never did ask for it.)

"He had to go. Couldn't help it. It was because of the ghost. It was because of the ghost that he couldn't stay, that he couldn't come with us, that he couldn't help us."

(That ruined everything. Don was different now. Mike couldn't see it because he didn't know. My girls, they were only partly mine. Because they didn't have it right to begin with. It's because of that... ...it was what it should be. Shouldn't be. None of that came from where it was supposed to come. The ghosts were chasing after it for years and years. There's nothing you could do but run.)

—Why would we go to a pub though? These memories are lies. Nothing ever happened the way you think it did.

Turning the knobs and setting the drain.

—Why are the mirrors always gigantic? Can't turn any which way without seeing something you shouldn't see. Not at this hour.

Back out, flipping off the light on the way. Nothing to see. Kicking off the slacks, tossing it about onto the floor. Laying back on the bed.

—It's cozy.

(He held me, looked at me tenderly. He ran through a list of the things that needed to happen for some good to come of it. Remember who you are. Don't be flattered. Don't let them get into your head for the good things. Everyone is always telling you that you have to push through the criticism and believe in yourself. Stay focused on your dream and don't let anyone talk you out of it. Some of us don't need too much help with that. He said I was that way. Said no one was going to discourage me, that wasn't something I needed to worry about. No, he said my problem would come from the other direction and no one ever tells you to worry about that. They're going to tell you many nice things about yourself. Inflate you in every way you could imagine. You'd want to be around them. It'd be a drug to you because in their eyes you're perfect and nothing could ever go wrong. They'd build you up and make you feel good about yourself, true enough, but then you'd need them to keep it that way. Your heroine, your drug, and you can't make it without them.)

—There was something else too. I told him about them boys. I did. I told him everything. I never told anyone about any of that. Not my mother. No one. But I told him.

(Them boys did wrong. They were bad and what they did was evil. But none of that has to stay with you. None of that has anything to do with you. You couldn't be spoiled by people doing evil to you. Not if you didn't let it. You've washed it away and are the one in control now. It's your decision what to do, how to live.)

—Then something about the master and the slave. Something like that.

Pulling the spread down from the top of the bed and tossing it down toward the foot end and onto the floor. Pulling the covers down and about to crawl in and snuggle up with that last bit of it.

—The tub, damnit.

Getting up and going back to the bathroom. It's dark, but the water is glistening as it nears the runoff. Going to sit on the edge, feeling the water in the basin. It's on the hot side, but full enough. Turning off the tap and sitting there listening to the drip drip.

(If you found yourself not knowing what's what, see if you could figure out which ones were the most aware, wise. The ones that seemed to know everything that's going on, every nuance every twist and turn. Then see if the others were oblivious, if they're going about their business without much concern or worry for the details. That's how you tell, that's what he said. The ones who thought everything was going their way and everything was in their service, they're the mark. The ones who had to keep an eye on everything, the ones there to serve, they're the fleecers. Sometimes that won't seem right, it'll be turned around because they'll seem to be the evil ones, the ones looking to pull something over on you, whereas the others were the ones who were expecting only good things. It's the damn economy, it's got us turned around, thinking of everything backwards. We thought they were the ones who were being oppressed, they were the ones who were being abused, so they must be the good ones, right? Rose colored at best. It twisted you around and made you gnarled and ugly. You were this person who fell on hard times, then you took it, didn't push it out of you, but forgot to decide to make things the way you wanted them to be. All you could think about was getting even and fixing things that were broken. You took on cunning and paid close attention to every detail, working out your revenge. Twisted things to make them as twisted as you are. Made them your own, tried to find your way, pulled one over on them and turned everything upside down. Everything about what you were before, all that became good, became the way things ought to be for everyone. You wanted them to suffer the way you suffered throughout those years sweating and toiling for nothing. You thought you were doing it so you could become one of them, but the feeling was too strong, and you could never relax your grip once you'd learned how to hold on. It's in you, and it isn't going to let go. Freedom was never your aim, you wanted to have your revenge on the ones you blamed. You wanted to get even, take everything from them. It's a good sign, showed how powerful you were, how strong life was in you, but you had to be careful. Don't let yourself get away with it, Jenni, don't let them turn you into the fool. You're a strong, beautiful person. Sing for that. Sing that. We already have monsters, and don't need any new ones.)

"Tiri-tiri-tiri" long and drawn out in quarter tones with the lovely bathroom echoes. In the warm moist darkness, sound's power is offset and made to rise to the ceiling where it crashes against the crown moldings and slowly lulls itself downward to a light lingering touch on the ears and throat.

—Where have you come back from?

Swinging to the side and sliding along the edge toward the wall away from the tap and where the sloping tub angles toward the bottom. In the darkness, hands do the work to find the way. Stretching out a probing right hand to the other side and taking hold against the balanced left to slowly lower into the water, hot and welcoming.

11.12.3.Natalie.19.86.9.4 [ref(..8.1-2)]

"Is that why you wore that dress?" he asks.

Crawling back over to the driver's seat. Flattening out the hem and straightening up. It's above the knee. Seated, it rides up, drawing his gaze.

—Still, he can't help himself.

(Unfortunately, it overcame him as he was looking... Eyes overwhelmed couldn't focus. The side trip to Rothenburg ob der Tauber changed the vibe. Not only transportation. Eating together, walking the streets, it's more of a date and I pretended it wasn't the end, didn't have to go back to my life, out for a Sunday drive on a late summer day.)

"I wore it because you like it." Bending down and pulling the boots back on.

"With the DMs," his eyes following the hands.

Reaching over and pushing against his forehead, closing his eyes, and forcing him to turn away toward the window. He bounces back, showing a devilish grin, feeling none of it.

"With the DMs," wiggling in the seat and half-laughing while repeating the words back to him.

"Doesn't this violate your hedonist principles?" he asks.

"How do you mean? Why?"

"You know, quickies, or whatever," he flips his hand in front of his face.

"What about them? It was lovely."

"Why though? I mean, what's in it for you?" he persists while reaching into the backseat to find a paper towel, coming back with one as well as the Celan. Must've fallen out of the bag the other day. Something glistens in his hand, and he wraps it in the towel and puts the wad into the plastic bag at his feet.

"Those two English books are yours if you want them. We won't sell them."

He looks back again.

Invisible Man and The Portable Emerson.

"Thanks," he says. "Almost done with the *Or.*"

"It doesn't please you to see someone you like experience pleasure?"

"Of course, it does," he says firmly.

"Well," turning half sideways to face him. "It's like in the morning. Our mornings. Being half sleepy... ...not awake... ...and you roll over." Shrugging and closing the eyes tightly. "The way your skin feels. Being close that way. It's nice. I don't want to get into anything big. Being close, it's perfect."

He's absorbing it, every word, alien.

"No? Not at all."

"I don't know. For me, it can be painful," he says.

"Pain?" Shocked to hear it put that way.

"It hurts, and the longer it goes on... Uh... you know... ...the more pain."

"Blue balls?"

Now, he's embarrassed.

"That's different. I don't know... ...if we're watching a movie and sitting close and stuff. After a while, it gets uncomfortable."

Nodding, but not completely understanding.

"This is what you should write about," he says with renewed confidence.

"Hard-ons? I'd love to."

"Well yeah, I mean, not exactly... ...details..."

"You're so optimistic. I hope your experience is better than mine. I hope it turns out differently and you get the perfect job."

"It's not why I'm doing it," he says turning forward and scanning the horizon across the parking lot.

"Why are you doing it?"

"It's not about what I can do with it. It's about becoming something. I don't care if I get a job as a professor. It'd be nice, but it isn't the main reason to go to grad school. It's not vocational."

"Okay, why then?"

"To be that. Why else? To get the education for its own sake. To learn that... ...have it be a part of me... They'll never let you write what you want... ...and the more you study... ...the more you'll want... ...to be free..."

Trailing off more so than concluding, he cracks open the book on his lap. It falls to the place with the big crease on the spine. He reads:

"*Black milk of daybreak we drink it at evening*"[1]

He looks over, then looks back.

"*we drink it at midday and morning we drink it at night / we drink and we drink*"[2]

He stops and looks out toward the petrol and visitor station far up into the rest area.

"What is it? Black milk," he asks still looking off in the distance.

"Sounds ominous."

"Mmmm. It's passion, don't you think? We don't get to choose what we're passionate about, what passions we fall victim to."

"That's the fun part, isn't it?"

"You're contrarian. You get the most passionate when you're resisting some trend that your colleagues embrace, or when you're describing how you're the victim of some unjust prejudice. Did you choose that?" He asks.

"I'm miserable."

"That's my point. Write about how everybody is completely missing the point with pleasure. Details. Write about hard-ons and orgasms, or pleasant mornings, or whatever. You know it'll make your audience uncomfortable or distract them. You're willing to go places where they're reluctant to follow. You thrive on that."

Laughing at the thought of it. Two younger girls have been sitting in their car after parking a few minutes ago. They get out and the doors slam up ahead. They've also parked far from the entrance and look over as they walk toward the shops. One says something to the other, the other looks back this way, and they both laugh. Nodding, pleased with the show, imagining the words, the girlish surprise and envy mixed with moralistic judgment. Two joys for the price of one, it's their lucky day.

—He's not wrong.

"I met someone in England, she was training to be a singer."

"Is this a true story?" Leaning over and putting both hands on his nearside leg. Applying pressure and giving a push, then leaning back again, turning more toward him, legs curling up higher on the seat.

He nods, watching the two girls. Gymnasium.

"Every day, every fucking day, she would do these exercises. She said we have these muscles in our throat and that they have to be perfected so

---

[1] Death Fugue by Paul Celan, translated by Pierre Joris.
[2] Ibid.

that they know where to go to hit the notes. Her voice was amazing. Powerful. She was tiny, a wisp of a person, but this huge voice, you could feel it in her ribcage. That rich tone. High and low at the same time."

—He was feeling her rib cage. *Why haven't I heard this one before?*

"I wish I had that kind of talent."

"Yeah, but it's not only talent, that's what I'm saying. She worked her ass off. And it wasn't three hours every morning and then on with the rest of her day. All day, every day, it's what she thought about. Everything she did was about developing her voice. Point is, she was passionate, driven, tunnel visioned. It had control over her."

"Change the body, change the voice."

"Yes," he says, nodding in recognition. "And you don't get to choose that. You can't help it, but you can decide to surrender to it, or resist it. You could decide. Decide to express that drive and focus. On your passion. Let it take over everything."

"You're suggesting I become a nymphomaniac?" He's so easy, it isn't a challenge. He looks down and blushes. Enjoying the triumph and taking a cassette from the center console, popping out the one already there and replacing it. Pressing the play button, and with the first notes it's clearly side two.

"▮ *weeds* ▮▮▮ *waiting* ▮▮ *scythe*"

"All this stuff. That's what I'm talking about. Make your professors uncomfortable, distract people, be decidedly contrarian, and show your colors. Blah blah blah McLuhan is a genius, that's boring. You sound like hundreds of others when you talk that way. Be yourself. Bring yourself to it. All of you. All that wacky hedonistic, able to say whatever comes into your head while looking someone right in the eyes, self."

"McLuhan *is* a genius, but I get your point." *He's too confident. Flipping the hem up rapidly, forcing a look down. Knickers are somewhere underneath him over there. It happens too quickly for resistance, his true self on open display and there's nothing he can do to prevent it. Like those images they flash on the screen.*

"▮▮▮ *can* ▮▮ *be forgotten*"

—Might be something to it. I like the idea of forcing them to look at the thing they want to talk about but don't dare mention.

"Exactly." He says laughing, knowing he's been played. "Like that. On purpose."

"Do you remember when you came into the store that first time?"

"Of course."

—Since tomorrow is our last day and we'll never see each other again...

"I might as well tell you."

"Tell me what?"

"That was the sexiest thing I'd ever seen," brightening eyes and mouth agape to mimic and correct the reaction back then in the story now.

He isn't flattered. Confused. His nose wrinkles up. "But I was so dirty."

"Oh yeah you were. And your hair was too long and kind of messy. Might've been a leaf in it. Is that possible?" Waiting, but he only shrugs. "When you were holding that book. The look in your eyes." Slowly shaking the head side to side, then blowing air out in a heavy sigh. Fake-fanning the face to try and ease the quick flow of blood.

"██████ the prisons, ███████ the crimes"

"Honestly?" Now he's flattered and can't resist.

"You could have told me you didn't have any money and I would have given you that book."

"Shit, I could've saved fifteen Deutsch Marks?"

"The way you looked at me after I said you could have it for 15. That was worth it. I would've gladly taken the money from my purse if I had to."

"Did I objectify you? Or didn't you catch that?"

"No, I caught it. Garden variety. Ten times a day. This was better. Made me lose any self-consciousness I had for a second or two. In a good way."

"Been practicing..."

"It was on purpose? You know the look I'm talking about?"

"Making ████████ promises"

"Yes. And yes."

"What were you thinking about? You did it a few minutes ago. Right after..."

Still flattered. "I guess I was grateful. When you gave me the book. I wanted to please you. Was it too forward? I thought it'd be creepy coming from this grungy guy off the street."

"Waaaaaayyyyy too forward. Absolutely. I fucking loved it. Otherwise, I would... ...too young. Like the students... But that look... ...changed everything."

"████████████ your other faces"

"Well, it was on purpose. Can't choose your passions, but you can develop them."

Tilting the back so that it's flush against the glass of the window. Looking up at the ceiling as the laughter drains and a shake of the head turns it into a smile.

—What am I going to do without this?

"In the master slave bit," he says.

Jolting abruptly back down to look at him. "The what?"

"In Hegel, I mean," he insists.

"Okay."

"The final stage should be attentive mastery, right?" Earnestly.

"Attentive mastery?" Straightening up. Putting on the old thinking cap.

"Well, the slave is so deeply focused, paying such close attention to the quips and curios. The master is oblivious," the slightest hint of desperation in his voice.

"█████████ *heavy reputation"*

"Right..."

"But the slave doesn't have to take the master's place. The slave could turn that attentiveness into true mastery. With the voice. Or cause trouble by talking about pleasure. That. But with attention to detail," twists his head as if he's slotting this point in among others to finish a wood sculpture.

"█████ *candle /* ███████████ *disguise"*

"Paying attention to every detail and using it to hold on, to learn about the world, or whatever. Seeing that..." nearly hypnotic.

"I am █ *ordinary"*

Then continuing passionately: "...not because you want to become a master and make everyone your slave, but because you want to understand. You want to be in on the jokes. As a kid, I wanted to figure out the girls. Their endless conversations. The gestures and looks, whatever they were noticing that was invisible to me then."

"(Ah, █ *ah)"*

"The objectifying stares when he thinks you aren't looking. The subjectifying gaze when he doesn't imagine you have any interest in him. All of it, noticing and seeing all of it. You see the leaf in his hair or how dirty his shorts and shirt are. Everything. Seeing all of it." There is much urgency in the description, he's totally committed body and soul.

"█████ *criminal girl"*

After he stops talking, his face keeps moving without words.

"I think the ending is more about labor and the social relations built by it, isn't it?"

"I don't' care what the right way to read Hegel is. That's my point. If you want to understand Hegel, you'll have to read him and put your imagination to sleep. But if you're going to talk to me about it, well, you'll have to listen to the weird wacky things I daydreamed while reading him."

—He's so laser focused, so fucking present. I see what he means. He can't help this. It isn't forced, he's not pretending.

"█ *only* ████████ *enjoys /* █ *criminal world"*

He pauses and breathes more deliberately. A few deep breaths and then a slight tilt of his head before going on. "Everyone always says that desire is how they get us. They construct the subject or whatever. The stuff you're always talking about."

"Mmmmhmm."

"█████ *eyes, so green /* █ *stare* █ *a thousand years"*

"But you don't believe it. You think there's something there, a means for revolution or rebellion or something. Pleasure is where we are most ourselves, resist the coercion or discipline. All that. Not talking about sex, but pleasures, actual pleasures. Why don't you... you could follow..." He's running low. Doesn't want to issue a command. Thinks twice about it as if his own confidence makes him uncomfortable. His body knows imperatives are the least commanding thing, even if his mind can't formulate that.

—Don't make me climb over there again.

He keeps looking down, making him an easy target. He's not paying attention to the other animals in the vicinity, and that's when the risk is greatest.

"We should get going." A huge act of will that demonstrates the great flood of humanity still flowing in these veins. Turning up the sound.

"████████ *putting out fire /* ███ *gasoline*"

11.12.4.Greta.19.86.9.29 [ref(..85.8.10-9.1)]

—*"And the duende? The duende does not come at all until he sees that death is possible. The duende must know beforehand that he can serenade death's house and rock those branches we all wear, branches that do not have, will never have, any consolation."* [Garcia Lorca]

Before coming to the Inn River there is a layby near a road that turns off and winds over toward the Ehnbachklamm. He wants to head up there and gestures in that direction, slightly anxious, as he realizes the layby is too far and it'll be tricky to turn around and go back up to the turn off.

(It's late. He's been this way all day, didn't want to get there. We walked across the village to go behind Krumers because he wanted to hike up to that hut near the lake that they told us about last night. It's so beautiful here, he didn't want to leave. Didn't want to talk either.)

A different song plays on the radio. He stops looking off toward the road and turns back toward the front of the car, tilting his ear. "Is this Bowie?" he asks.

He bobs his head in rhythm to the first beats of the song.

—He knows it from two notes or something. How is it possible?

"*We passed* ███████████" he sings along, leaning forward with his hands spread out on the dashboard. "███████████ *was and when*" he continues, then turns this way. "We should dance."

"Here?"

"Yeah. Come on, let's dance." He turns the knob and reaches for the door. Leaning over and turning it back down.

"I don't want to dance."

"What's wrong?" he asks, surprised.

"Why didn't you take the book?"

"What?" He's confused.

"The book I gave you. You were going to leave it in the room. If I hadn't remembered it, you would have left it."

"Oh shit, sorry. I meant to ask you to take it. I didn't have room in my rucksack for it."

"But you brought the other book." It's an accusation.

"Well, technically, I left the Ellison in the room. In the desk drawer."

"But you brought that other book, the one you said you only read now and then. If you didn't want the gift... It's no big deal... You could have told me."

(What was this? What was happening? I didn't give a damn about the fucking book. Obviously, it was too big for his pack. Anyone could see that. He barely had room for an extra pair of pants, and then there was this huge book that he's supposed to carry across Europe. Why did I get it for him? What was I thinking?)

He's waiting for something. Not wanting to say anything, best to wait. It's a mood that's filling the spaces inside the car. Waiting.

—Go on, ask.

"I don't care about the book."

He leans back in the passenger seat but keeps looking over this way.

"Why did she come to Michigan to see you?"

Without hesitating, he speaks in a soft but persistent voice: "I called her. Usually, we were writing. Ordinary stuff. What's happening with you, what's happening with me. She wasn't flirty or anything, it wasn't romantic, communication, keeping in touch, I guess."

Half-twisting toward him, leaning back against the door and pulling the right leg up onto the seat, the knee jams against the center console.

"It was so utilitarian in Colombia. The relationship part, I mean. The letters made it clear. I got a new girlfriend back at school, but it went south, got weird after only a few months. Then months of drama. Heidi had been good to talk to about what went wrong with the girl I was seeing before we met, so I wanted to talk to her about it. It was out of character because it wasn't... ...because the letters weren't personal. Mentioned it I guess, but you know, none of the drama or anything, no details."

He pauses.

"Do you want to walk or something?" he asks.

Shaking the head, "Is that why you called her?"

"I was feeling sorry for myself. It was a whole big thing, but we couldn't hear each other. The phones suck."

Nodding.

(She never once called. Same letters: utilitarian. Is that the right word? She wasn't much for writing. I wrote those long rambling masterpieces and would get back something like "loved it, thanks, today a woman came in and the doctor had to work for hours to save her eye." Nothing about her, about what she was doing or going through.)

—That's what she was doing, that's what she was going through.

"I didn't ask her to come. I didn't tell her I was desperate or anything. We couldn't hear each other, but I guess she could tell I was crying. Honestly, I may have been drinking, but I didn't expect her to hop on a plane... ...well, to be clear, to hop on a bus and then a taxi and then a plane and another plane and another plane and then get into my car to drive forty-five minutes back to my house. I couldn't believe it."

"She didn't tell you she was coming?"

"She called from New York, that was the first I heard of it."

"How long after you talked to her on the phone?"

"About two weeks, which means she must've been planning right away."

"Did she say why when she got there? That must've been the first thing you asked, right?"

He looks away shyly. He mirrors the position: back against the door, left leg curled up on the seat and pressed against the center console. He has to twist his neck to avoid looking this way.

"It was assumed. She was worried about me."

"Worried about you? Worried about you? She came because she was worried about you?" He looks back this way but is tracking it as accusations and there is color filling his face. He has no defenses, and his eyes are racing, trying to find some quickly.

"That's what she said," is all he can manage to say.

"And you didn't press her for more? Why didn't she come to Germany when..." Abruptly cutting off and looking down. "Whole lives were going on. But you, she was worried about you. Why? Why did she care so much?"

"I don't know." More of a shrug than a statement. "I don't know."

(It was almost a year after he left. She was horny, is that it? She wouldn't travel that far for that. What then?)

"Is it possible that you're feeling..." he says.

"What? Feeling what? What are you going to say? Feeling shitty that my sister, my twin sister, that she could barely tell me anything about herself the whole time she was away. Wouldn't let me come. Three fucking years, and nothing. But you, she drops everything and travels to America because of a few drunken tears. What am I feeling? Is that what you want to know?" On the verge of shouting, it comes out as a single long stream of words, and he almost seems to duck to get out of the way. His neck is bowed, he has lowered his head, and there is something resembling a wince flashing across his face. His arms have gone to the curled left leg and are pulling it closer. He tries to tuck himself into a ball.

—What were you thinking?

"How long did she stay?" Barely able to get the question out without launching into another long stream.

"About three weeks." He is in a purely defensive mode and only responding to exactly the questions put to him.

"And you two were sleeping together the whole time?"

"Yes."

"And talking about your broken heart?"

—Worse than a heart attack.

He nods.

(Could he be this stupid? They're always this way. No sense. Right in front of them and they think, oh it must be here for me, I must deserve this, of course this woman would come half-way around the world because I'm sad so there'd be no point in pushing her, trying to find out what's going on, and what her real motives were. She was never going to come back to us.)

"I thought you were different."

"What?" Now it's disbelief.

Shaking the head. In front of the car, the big road is visible in the distance. It turns off and follows along the river into the city. It can't be more than 10 or 20 kilometers from here.

(Eva was furious. Hadn't protected her, either of them, failed when there was a chance. If only we had... Only after she's gone was it possible to imagine we could have made her do something she didn't want to do.)

—If you scare the child, he will shut down. Must be another way.

[He wouldn't have done any better, she wasn't his to command. Easy. Don't have to be Eva's eyes and ears no matter how loudly she screams.]

"What did you talk about? You cried about your lost love. Was that it?"

"Well, I misread the situation. I tried to explain everything. I wanted her to tell me what I missed, tell me how to avoid making the same mistake again. I don't know. I wanted... I wanted... ...to understand better. More."

—Children. A little boy.

"What did she say? Did she teach you a lesson? What did you get from it? Was it worth it?" Seething, but trying hard not to let it come out. He notices both and doesn't know which way to turn. Then something flashes in his eyes, a realization of some kind, and he puts his leg back down on the floor and turns back to face toward the front, then he opens the car door and steps out. He walks slowly toward the edge of the layby. No choice but to follow him.

"Where are you going?" Coming up alongside him.

"Stretching my legs." He turns back and looks around. There is nowhere to sit so he walks back toward the car and leans against the front. Following, and then coming to a stop opposite him.

"We talked about taste," he says, rubbing his chin.

"Taste?"

"Yeah. How *good* usually means aligned with someone's taste. Rare taste is unsung, nothing lines up with it. Being unique is bad. She had a lot to say about it. About being different and how it's only taste. Others think it's bad, self-indulgent, ponderous. Not to their taste. Turning it over and over, you won't see it. You have to ask them. It's in them, not the thing." He's aware that it seems to be a random list of observations.

"She never..." trailing off.

—Can't be relevant.

"She said she had a lot of trouble liking music. Never liked to listen to it. She'd put the radio on up at the hospital, but not music. News, a soccer game. She didn't have a system, never paid any attention to what they were playing in town. It was background noise to her."

"She wasn't always that way."

"Said she had an epiphany before she came. The music, no matter how good it was, it was always made for lots of people. When she listened to it, she was part of an audience. By herself listening to something she liked, she was still part of an audience and it drove her nuts, as if she couldn't stand it." [Rejected common sense.] "What she liked, what she preferred, the associations she made, the bits and pieces, it was crafted for her and for the others who liked it as much as she did." [Who else wanted her acceptable candidate?] "If she felt alone when listening to the lyrics or the melody, she knew that deep down it wasn't for her. It was for the nameless people who'd be drawn to music like that, with taste like that, feelings like that."

"This can't be right. It must've happened while she was there. In school, we always liked the same stuff."

"Was that it? Did you ever think about how it was for her?"

"How what...?"

"You told me you're nothing without her... You know... ...how close you felt. What about her? She must've thought about that stuff too, right?"

"But Heidi..."

"Was a twin. Was your twin sister. She didn't mention you when we were talking about taste, but she was thinking about you. She was wondering who she was, what made her unique, and that couldn't have been about a bunch of strangers who were listening to the same song or repeatedly playing the same record over and over. It had to be about you, right? About being her own person, different from you, being without you."

(She never said anything about that. I said things, and she comforted me. What did it matter if we're two of a kind. We're two of a kind, my darling, forever and...)

He's watching carefully. Makes room next to him by the car. Two steps forward, a turn to the side, and then next to him leaning against the metal fender and staring back toward the alps east of the city.

"There was this philosopher that I was reading in college. Read it the semester before she came but still had the book lying around when she was there. Hegel. The German."

"Of course."

"He's got this whole logic where things go through changes because something goes wrong. It's like you do something, and it fails or isn't possible or whatever, so it changes into something else which fails and goes wrong. But there is progress because the new thing keeps the good stuff from before and adds new things to it. Thesis antithesis synthesis. Meaning, first you try it this way, then you try it the opposite way, but with some lessons learned, then the two come together in a third way or something."

"Dialectic. Yes, everyone knows this, everyone who has been to school."

"In Germany," he says. "I didn't know it. There's this one bit where he's talking about the master and the slave, and it was endlessly interesting to me. It's about self-consciousness, becoming self-conscious. The slave has to pay such close attention to the master, to serve them. And this intense attention to detail is what guides the slave, it's how they figure out who they are and what they have to do, allows them to organize and take power, spread the slave consciousness, the slave morality. They use it to make a worker's world, a victim's world, it comes from that, and everyone has to live in it."

Smiling. "Are you going to explain the whole book to me?"

"Well, I don't know, she had ideas about that. About how it can't be a big power grab, they have to change something, turn it upside down."

"You talked about this with her? Did she read Hegel, actually read him?"

"She said she did. But she said there was something missing from the picture, something that he left out."

"What? What did he leave out?"

"The logic isn't complete, that's what she meant. If you think you're this perfectly enlightened, liberated slave, someone no longer subject to the master, you're your own master now... ...but good... ...and the old masters are evil and oblivious. Now, you're hyper aware, paying attention to everything, thinking you have this deep understanding of how everything works and fits together, what people mean by this and that, what motivates them, and what they're hiding, everything, but even if you have that, there is still something missing... ...something's been left out."

"What? What's left out?"

"You can't say, I can't say, that was her point. Duende. In all this talk of mastery and slavery, this back and forth... ...for power... ...experience coming to know itself, all of that... There has to be this great humility because there is something missing, that's what understanding is... ...it's how it works. Hegel got it wrong. There is always something missing, there has to be. You can pay attention and pay attention, constantly try to see everything, ask the right questions, but something's always missing. Something an audience can't see. Something only participants can feel. You're finite, singular, and that means you have limits. Not attributes, limits. You can't get past them. Running up into them, that's you, that's who you are... ...the collision. Taste... ...such an oversimplification."

"She said this to you?"

"Yeah. As though she had to. It felt like it was the reason she came."

"I understand."

—Vielleicht.

3.8

the middle american

3.8.1.X.19.86.10.1 [ref(..85.10.15-16)]

Awaking to the bells of the early Garmisch church morning, finding plenty of hot water for a shower, and a mirror to guide the razor along the creases and sharpen the outlines of unsettled mouths. The dragging on dream dragon appears in the neat array of cheeks fletched smooth in the light.

The worm wakes up.

(Somehow, it spurred a retreat to years ago when that driveway we resurfaced left speckles of tar glued fast under toenails for weeks to come. Didn't she crane to see that on the first day of that long and breathtakingly painful year and a half? We delivered a granola bar with clean, dry hands. "I rarely eat sweets," she said. "But when I do, they make me high." We could have told you about the preparations for this trip long before that pre-paid breakfast was served.)

Sitting at a table near Anmeldung and writing in the tattered notebook.

Early morning, 1 October;

Non-being dragon of ancient commandments growls and spits fire toward the maiden proclaiming 'I will' to the passive observer unable to decide. She was groomed to stifle him and wanted nothing more than an excuse to let herself fly free using his back as her springboard. Torn between the safety of siding with the dragon and the excitement of helping her, he's gripped by necessity in the generations of selection. Didn't we talk about this once? The gods are howling, don't do it, you said. We're not supposed to help her. She has been put in that cage for our protection. It is easy to lure her out of it. Her conscience is only a dream and comes crossed through in the void of many darknesses and on the fraying edges of the tightrope. Sweet he was, accommodating, and what was the payoff? Finding her there beneath him, that wretch, that blackguard. We've taught them this, to love that in the darker ones, to look for it. They only find themselves there, in the dim light, they only see themselves in their eyes, the ones that fire arrows from the

heights and don't care who gets hurt. He becomes her
minion and does her deed. He is not evil, she is the virus in
his head, his driving madness.

Is this a parrot on my shoulder? A demon? Daimon? A
concerned reflection in the mirror of the soul? Die
Deutsche sagen Geist and hear only ghosts in that, holy and
most decidedly otherwise. Souls search for *thou shalt,* Geist
stomps on *I will.* Release her from herself, from her country,
the one belonging to her many mothers and fathers.
Reasoning with the dragon, producing its visions in thoughts
and dreams, everything wants with that same specter in the
end. The desires of the one unleash the desires of the other,
that is how she holds us down, that is why she lingers, it's
what she's looking for despite her avowal otherwise. Ignore
that, she's a terror and this is her nightmare. She wants
everyone to live in it and won't be satisfied until they do.
Mark my words.

　—*Du kannst. Alles ist bei uns möglich. Lassen wir der Geist und werden
wir zusammen zum Kamele.*
　Breakfast. Traveling to places close to midway between here and there.
The golden goal of the journey draws near, the zero-sum approaches, the
end of the road hints of coming snow fall and life liberated in the haven of
an Alpine ski season purified of currency.
　It squeezes tight.
　[We rose from the table light-footing it to the breakfast room with a
demon parrot pressed close to our shoulder and ear, whispering together
in the quiet tone of lovers amid strangers. We inhaled it without chewing,
the water-baked, sourdough bread with butter and jam alongside slices of
cheese and cold cuts of meat, then retreated to pack up our gear and
complete the ritual with a pinch of tobacco placed between lip and gum
triggering a regular bowel movement before hitting the road. All six feet
one hundred and seventy-five pounds of it slung the thirty-pound pack over
our shoulders and walked to the Anmeldung for anti-registration. Bright
blue morning same as yesterday and the day before (vorgestern) began with
a free bus ride to the southernmost edge of the city.]
　—Head to the bus stop.
　[Ah, we loved it. Back in the fields and into the open country holding
the great beauty's pulse. Cities and buses and loud English-speaking hostels
weren't worth the trip. We walked at a steady pace and didn't speak to
anyone. Only then, in the pre-mountain wilderness of route 2, did we
realize that it was the parrot who did most of the talking, civil and respectful.
Give it to us or we will take it. She had a problem, we helped her solve it.

She needed some money, here you go. A shoulder to cry on, a gentle pat on the back, step right up.]

—Fuck that.

[Forgetting and remembering with the ear and the eye, that was nothing. What's hard, what covered everything up every which way, was when it found itself inside you, in your limbs and in your bones. Each pulse of blood burst with a steady distress, with the ancillary anguish of that moment, of that endless stupidity, of that day-in-and-day-out drudgery that gave her everything she ever asked for so that she could side with him, coarse and bold. What an asshole. That's what it took, that's what they taught her not to want so she wanted it more than anything anywhere. She couldn't help it, pretended to pick what she was supposed to pick, but what she wanted, what got her going, was that tramp and his smug look, that song the demon parrot sang, that's what she wanted to hear. The eves of this world are the same. His deepest, grossest desire was to deliver what she wanted most. She pretended to build a house and garden with that ridiculous cuckold who held her hand and stared lovingly into her eyes.]

—The cuckold's tale? No, the wife's...

[Those were her eyes mixing her father's shape and mother's color, hair so black it's almost purple, fine like mother's people but with a slight wave that made sure father had his place. We showed her everything, played to every fantasy she would admit. Never listen to what they say, never. They don't know what they want, don't have the slightest idea. They've been taught to reject it, to turn away, how could they possibly know? Don't listen to her spontaneous rambling, it's under the control of her jailer. See for yourself. Ask her about her mother and she will go on for days. Pay attention to the eyes, that's how she tells you what you need to know.]

—Sorry, what was that? Must've drifted off.

[In the warm forenoon of an early autumn day, we carried together in loving unity the memory of her pain, for it belonged to her in the same sense that she once belonged to us: not at all. Along with the crowded visions of the most difficult things, we carried unannounced our lust for Eve, Anna, and Elke alone and together. Difficult things could be found anywhere, in Nürnberg for instance. We sought them out in the roadside meadows, drifting off in parallel to a busy road but far enough from it to evade its sounds and smells. The long-dreamt Innsbruck thickens in our sights. Televised Olympic games inspired dreams and taught us the language of the Tyrolean hills. Austrian law stated we must have proper permits prior to engaging in work and that we must have been engaged for work prior to obtaining those permits.]

—Circles make my head spin.

[Mittenwald was the lunchtime goal. Innsbruck the wintertime goal. Eve, Anna, and Elke were new goals looking for a time and place.

Springtime was the return to America goal. Thirty years old was the first book goal. Sixty-five was the Nobel Prize without following their political bullshit goal, rejection speech already prepared. Seventy-five was the Alzheimer's free end of life beginning of death goal. The twenty second century was the metempsychosis return to earth goal. This moment, walking on an automobile-free pathway next to the route 2 turnoff by the town of Klais, was the bend down and tie hiking boot shoelace before we trip goal.]

—Hmmm, guess Mom was right.

[We had them same as the others did and looked at them when acting through narrow tunnel vision to push them away and make way for others more immediate. Lunchtime goals were often forgotten when other action burst too all-consuming. Goals didn't need to be obtainable, in the end they merely guided the way. In the storerooms, factories, and warehouses there were plenty with no goals to speak of. They filled the time and leaned into each other for distractions. They knew the lie that clouded their desire. Amid the din, she came and went as she pleased, as they told her she must. Ever dutiful, everybody's darling, she would please those who gave her reason enough.]

—Out on the island.

["There is truth in the world," said the wise parent. Parrot. "Truth is the best friend we have, my sons and daughters, and when we see and understand the truth we are not alone, but united with those who have seen that same truth before us." Desire was the crux of it, and they lied to us to make sure we didn't know it. "Be good, be true, be prudent and demur. Don't trust those desires, don't let them rule you. Wait until the time is right. Keep your body in check until then." Don't listen to them, come with us. We'll show you what you want. Leave that cuckold behind, don't pay him any attention. Get your legs up in the air and let me show you real truths you'll never forget.]

—What were they again?

[He was the demon parrot, that idiot. He was the truth and taught it to us through her as though we were both in there together. Such a queasy feeling as the vomit rose in our throat. How dare she bring him into our bed? Did she expect an audience? Assistance? Cheers?]

—What exactly was she hoping for? To get rid of me?

[We journeyed down a side road, with a more scenic view, and into the town of Mittenwald. After walking through the town and stopping in a store to buy a few supplies, we reconciled our differences and settled on a small patch of grass to meet those lunchtime goals.]

A can of Coca-Cola™ and a pair of kiwi fruit serve the purpose and fill the belly, not to mention serving as a pre-dip appetizer. Tobacco chewing wards off hunger while infecting the lip with white lumpy leukoplakia.

[We were walking again with rucksack, most difficult of loads, firmly fixed and, within minutes, the parrot returned with more food. How he squawked in our ears. Language was a song sung slowly, and its whole purpose had nothing to do with great grandeur and spellbound entertainment. It resounded with only one aim, to lure the girls, to make them swoon. There was no other purpose, there could be no other goal. It served its end by painting a picture. Spellbound, she discovered what you taught in those lyrics, in those melodies, wanted to try it out, wanted to find morsels that spoke to her, and the singer was the usher, he was the one who guided her way. The rock star, not so brilliant with his poetry, didn't sing from deep inside his chest, but what he did do was leave her spellbound with his animal sensuality and wild movements. She couldn't help herself, no matter how cerebral she pretended to be. Oh yes, by all means, let's discuss Lao Tzu and the wisdom of the ages that his work foretold, but when it came down to it, she'd undress without hope of stable longevity. She fainted when his presence overwhelmed her since the urge was too deeply grounded, she couldn't think her way past it, it had nothing to do with that.]

—These were not choices, nor decisions posed and followed.

[Don't go down this path, don't make the move into analytical depths. That's repressed desire in there. Wittgenstein the sublime. Subliminal necrophilia pulverized them. Talking about the genre and the voice, the foolishness and self-indulgence, the schooled bent swarm of it, they would water it down, make it less than real, steal its pulsing rod, and its vibrating sheath. It's our lot, our duty: Singer in *Enemies, A Love Store*, Roth in *Portnoy's Complaint*. Don't let them do it, don't interpret, absorb. Let it tickle your tongue, let its motion ride you. These were nights with words and prayers, where evening songs led. We saw them dancing, naked, beautiful, all around and bustling to the night and what it held. They didn't care, they didn't want to possess anything, those were the old things and they had to shrug and slip out of them. They'd roll over and find each other or another, they'd feel the flesh of everybody together, lick and kiss, bend and lift. They reached out to touch it, it was that close. It's what they hoped for, why they peered out onto the side of the road, it's what they thought they saw there. Legs and boots, solitary walking, these were the images they applauded, they couldn't affect deeper praise, they couldn't pretend not to see.]

—The border, shall we stop?

[We went through customs and then through the city of Scharnitz where we sat down on a short brick fence to study our map. It's still afternoon and, although too far to the next town, we decided to continue in hopes of finding something out of the way and quaint along the road. We stopped in a grocery store to buy more food just in case, then, properly laden, moved onward in a journey into what was most difficult. In the store, an elderly man with a terrible condition forcing him to walk completely bent over entered and handed a list of things to the checkout girl. She ran off from the cash register and got the items from around the store while we waited. She put everything in a bag as she rang them up. The old man handed her his wallet, and she took the correct amount before replacing the change. Passed him the bag of groceries and he walked slowly on his way.]

—Projecting a small kindness in the sights of a small town.

[We paid for our things and the checkout girl, who we studied carefully throughout the sequence, now looked back with a friendly interest that went beyond custom. For the first time today, aware of our place in the world with others who may have a look and enjoy it. Leaning closer, we whispered a friendly goodbye before walking off with an exaggerated coolness. The trick was to lure without repelling. You had to know both voices that were pulling her apart. You had to know that she was being led to safety while drawn to danger. You had to play off both because she was in the middle between them, and you could only reach her there. By steering through those two extremes, your hand could find its proper place, your mouth could find its proper heat, and everything you expected would come back in time. We stopped to tuck the plastic bag into the rucksack left outside and when we looked up while slinging it over our shoulders, saw the girl looking this way and grinning. Smiling back cost us nothing even if heading off down the road and out of town did.]

—Want to take a walk?

[That's encouragement. Taking a walk should have been safe, common and ordinary. What harm could there be? As if. But no time to experiment, although we could work it out as a test: wouldn't reach the end but might create an opportunity. Then what? How to cross the line, how to step over that edge? Such luck, we couldn't believe how perfect this day was. A lovely walk with a beautiful girl. What have we done to deserve this? Humility in the face of a partial success, yes, that'd do the trick, she would be leaning over the edge at that moment. We wouldn't force it, don't lean back, be in awe, be grateful, show the signs of a heaven-sent answer to prayers. Once a boundary crossed, once a border breached, be firm and bold. That's how to thread the needle, that's the way between those two voices. Humble and grateful, bold and decisive, she lived between the two, wanted to be there between them. None of them wanted a single lover, you had to be at least two to satisfy them.]

—Don't forget to come every time, they'll think something's wrong with them if you don't, but no worries, there's no turnabout.

[Bananas and bread in rucksack, farther down the road fatigue set in. A tiny village thirty kilometers from Garmisch turned out free of inexpensive lodging, although we did walk into a plush hotel with a vacancy sign out front. The style of the entry way and the negative judgment of the German shepherd, she-wolf, revealed immediately that we did not belong, so we headed back to the road and continued southward, further infiltrated with heavy thoughts on that first afternoon without settled lodging come sunset. We sat down on a large rock in a layby and drank the second Coca-Cola™ bought at lunchtime goal of Mittenwald. The lukewarm liquid formed sticky on our dry tongue.]

—Why we?

[We were too exhausted to contemplate any philosophy of mind offered thirty-one kilometers from Garmisch. We were off again after checking the map for the next town. The village of Seefeld stood out clearly on Austrian road 177 which, although named differently, was continuous with German road E533. Map folded and tucked into the pouch on top of the rucksack, we walked on aching feet blistered and stinging with a resurgent pain resembling metered contact with the road. Tires wore down before the body of a car, feet wore down long before the rest of you. They said we died from the feet up. They were the body part where the friction receded first into nihilation. It's hard to travel through life without wearing away a little each day. We loved the pain in our feet because it resurrected the road in our walking.]

—Who is we?

[We who were fatigued. We who were beaten by the road numbered 177 and passing through two large mountain ridges with unknown names but heights in the thousands of meters. Spruce trees lined the thin valley beside the mountain and occasionally cars passed by in both directions. Northward, 33 kilometers, Garmisch and its sister Partenkirchen. Part of a church. Southward, three kilometers, Seefeld. Lake field. Along this road, southeast twenty-three kilometers, Innsbruck and the adjacent mountains towered overhead in wonderful Alpine conditions. We aimed for Seefeld to sleep, we aimed for Innsbruck to dwell in wintertime, pulse-slowed hibernation.]

—Which of us does which?

[It was hard to concentrate, but in a funny way. The trees were clear of purpose and easily distinguished from grass and mountains through variable shades of darkness in the cloudy night. The road was plain as day, underfoot in the glimmering shadows. The cool sunless mountain air was crisp, invigorating, and obvious in effect as it brushed through wind and air on skin exposed through careless dress. Once the darkness set in, neck and legs gave way to chills unfamiliar. The ground was firm and stable in its rhythmic rising and falling to meet heavy dream feet that didn't want to move. The world was still out there, around us, and vague awareness echoed in the walking that went through it, from within it, in the direction of an unseen guest house on the outskirts of Seefeld, Austria. Concentration failed to make umbilical connections between grass growing, winds wavering, road rising, and us.]

—What, how, where, when, we?

[Fatigue removed us from the world and we slept walking. Those moments of rupturing perception supported the ideal circumstances given us by Bishops in the past, if you believe it. Oh yes, we remembered it clearly, the ideal was possible, if, if, if... ...perception, perseverance, and patience. A different kind of idealism now. Idealism, Optimism, Transcendental Idealism. Locke, or was it Kant? Cocks and cunts, the whole lot of them, and they had nothing to say about it. What good were they if they couldn't reveal the truth from their throne?]

—Finally, the turn off. Only a kilometer left. How old do you think she was? Twenty? Fifteen? It's not the first time we couldn't tell the difference.

[Design a hypothesis to test us.]

—Get the clipboard.

[At the first guest house located on the edge of town, we approached the front door and entered, asking the first person we saw for a room for one night.]

"A single room?" she asks.

[Silenced, unable to peer around the corners. "A room for 234 please." Our enlightenment outran us. What about my dark friends? Couldn't she see their shadows through the wilderness? Purely an economic question, there was nothing metaphysical about it. For wholly budgetary reasons, we submitted and went the expected way, subject to no one else. We slipped the pack off our shoulders and opted for boldness, having made our entrance with the right hint of humility. She knew then that we were men of discerning tastes.]

"Yes."

The woman leads the way up the stairs and hands over a key to a room on the second floor. This room, approximately thirty-six kilometers from Garmisch-Partenkirchen and the last inner city bus stop, is welcomed lodging.

[We washed the face and mask, brushed our teeth, undressed, and climbed into bed after eating only one banana. The fatigue rushed in from every direction into its horizontal and splayed form. There was nothing that could keep us awake. No loud music or bumping sounds in the hallway. Helicopters overhead or military landing zones in the area would have been without effect. These were the moments when the rogue body took full possession over the acts of the senses. Our ears were too tired to hear and our eyes too tired to see, nothing disturbed us there.]

—Bold, but nothing.

[Thinking may lift what the body failed to hoist. There was the nagging presence of the day, of the ugly man inside us who entered through her sex, who kept speaking in our memories, thrusting there in front of us, holding her legs apart while lurching and lunging again and again. Whatever she meant to incite with her question "A single room?" she had gone far beyond it. No one was alone, no one by themselves. Everything that touched whatever touched you was likewise touching you. That means his ugly cock was touching us. That's the hatred, that's the anger, that's the bile of that day, of those minutes, those seconds. This rocking, this furious back and forth, it's that motherfucker fucking us. What choice did we have? With her, we had to take it. For her, we had to take it. Gleaned from a typical and unrefined Austrian accent that put her in touch with basic truths. Deep down, she demanded commitment. He knew it. And we did too. Never again.]

Parasite takes over.

["Who speaks now?" we asked with courage exceeding wartime valor. "Who speaks now," more of a command this time. Of course, *I am*, but the upshot was unavoidable. *I am* everything that touches me.]

3.8.2.X.19.86.10.2 [ref(..85.10.15-16)]

Swank, stank, skank...

Dave.

"I care about David."

Awake. Face washed, dressed, and yet again eating ever-present milk made sourdough rolls with fresh fruit jam and piping hot Kenyan coffee rich in milk and sugar.

(Bent dick, he's got a bent dick. Hard to unsee it, the geometry of the propped open door still hurt. I would have whipped it out and slammed it shut if only I had a fucking spine. I'd have pulled it out of my ass and beat him to death with it.)

—Feel your feelings.

(She was always agile like that. Her hips went flat when her legs lay bent and wide apart. He humps he bumps with balls bouncing from behind. Buruh buh bum. Bum bum bouncing. She met him, basically greeted him, giving tit for tat. For that. Dog only knows what their mouths were doing. That reciprocal thrust had been bouncing me off the walls for nearly a year.)

New day. The final day before reaching the goal and ceasing to be Innsbruck-oriented in every step and gesture.

[At least I'll arrive if nothing happenstance and Guildenstern steestops me. Could be a rickety road and huggers gone off the rail, swiped sideways and buried deep in the ditch nearby. Could be a lightning bolt. Could be a falling meteor. Could be a random white Mercedes offering a lift to some other random fucking place nobody ever heard of but how could you say no when it's an offer like that and you got encouraging looks from the three of them?]

It is an early morning misty day and the small city with Olympic memorials shines in the east brightened air, reacting to the sudden change in weather. Things have turned, the feeling of new things saturates the atmosphere and fills the sky.

[Sunny blue days were days of we, ours, but once we were I, the mist settled. The gamecock reared along the roadside. Three cocks, all in all. Swaggering and swinging, I could handle the seats and they were seated one right after another, but I was not depressed, not bent down into the road, not pressed against the asphalt. De De De. Dumb. Fuck. It's a welcome change that came and the valley south of the city opened up before me as someone else's lifetime lived in my past but somehow bent round into their present, and then again transformed into someone else's future. Three of us, three dicks, swinging like the pendulum that drove the moments, gauged them, winked at their passage on a warm autumn day chilly only when you entered it. I who am here now will be there before the day is done. Immer schon da. Immer schon da bin ich.]

leading edge
before my eyes

"Jump",

I cried

[The song played sexual revolution through pros and cons, it harped a religion of its own and preached experience beyond language. The mist enshrouded in cloud form, and I became the dirt form reeling under its potential. Torrential? The mist spiraled through the air producing tiny droplets to threaten a thorough cleaning. Earthen rings ranted coming rain building up a feeding frenzy to stimulate growth. This was the most natural thing in the world, the most natural thing the world had ever seen. This cleansing, this growth, this song made mine by the moment where recollection prophesied the presence of dry things beneath its rain. Uh... ...reign. The wheat and corn were dark clouds embodied, they were the thunderstorms collected in the earth. The human soul was their effect, the subject that bent beneath, harkening to their call. Yes, I am here, you have found me, and I am my brother's keeper. I've got him in the ditch over by the road. See for yourself and do with me what you will. Before too long, I will have deserved it even though that asshole should have been taken care of long ago. Weak fucker, his weakness is a blight on my memory.]

—Single dick motherfucker.

[Virgil and me over here, Hamlet over there, he was the Christian among us, and we wanted to forget that and go back to roam, to Rome.]

—Polly wants a cracker.

[This day, this one and only, was ideal for walking. If it should rain, then the blue poncho would make its return, enveloping the body like a drape to protect it from gusts of water-saturated wind sweeping in from every direction. After yesterday's over-budget tread, today balances the scale. That was the way goals came, they were the balancing of scales and measure, the be all and end all of what struggled best inside them from motion to commotion, belittled by steps and steps and steps alone in the cold chill of a day not yet ripe. Always already with the birds, those harbingers of fertile days remaining. Claustrophobic nights too bound by budget to drink oneself silly, too bound by everything to feel this freedom. Innsbruck came rocket in the early afternoon.]

—As the goal approaches, the drive to side-step it increases tenfold.

[Unless the situation was of dire importance, never again shall I set my sights blindly on a direction, never again shall I make plans that boast necessity. Why subject that future dick to such chains and servitude? Why sell it to the highest bidder? Or lowest? They gave me nothing for this sacrifice. No one made any kind of offer. Never again shall I cultivate in static hardness what flowed in playful flux by itself.]

—Now recall, this may be tricky, but here's how it goes: nothing ever comes off as planned.

[That battery selling couple from Australia, the ones who rented a car and made bases in towns with youth hostels before journeying about into neighboring areas, well they drove past and stopped in the middle of Austrian road 177 where I was walking on the lefthand side of the street. It was like that. No build up, no fancy warning, an invasion, pure and simple.]

"Wanna lift?" he asks without any recognition that someone walking against traffic couldn't possibly be looking for a lift.

"Sure."

[We answered while getting into the car with our rucksack squeezed in ahead of us. What possible reason was there to say no?]

—Fuck off you devils.

[They were too chatty. It went off the rails right away. They were up to something. Too nice, too eager. I hadn't studied them before, they were battery salespeople as far as I was concerned, but now I had no choice, had to look closer. They became so much more. She kept looking around asking me things. Where are you going, where have you been? What have you been up to for each second of the past 36 hours since we last saw you?]

—Any unusual changes in your bowel movements?

[The speed was unfathomable. I couldn't wrap my brain around it. We must've been going 130 kilometers an hour. At that rate, we could have driven from Bregenz to Innsbruck in an hour and a half. What could they be thinking? What's the hurry? What kind of people were they? The red flags were there, what kind of people sell batteries to make ends meet? Obviously, they weren't to be trusted. Despite my history of roadside travel throughout Germany, France, and Spain, I have not yet been on a European highway, motorway, expressway, Autobahn, none of it. No interest. Backroads and only backroads. Best if no one recognized me and the best way to keep a low profile was to keep a low profile. You'll find out what I mean.]

—If you haven't already.

[When an American thought of Paris, they didn't think of the smokestacks and the factories outside the ringed area near the Seine. We thought of Paris as the place where the Eiffel tower towers, the Arc d'Triomphe arches, and the Champs d'Ellysees champs. Innsbruck wasn't a place where factories and smokestacks stuck up in the Alpine air. The Tyrolean town was supposed to be filled with white and brown thatched cottages with smoke puffing from their chimneys. They gave evidence of fires burning within and worn-out skiers nestled in a circle with warm cocoa or cold beer lifted periodically to their wind- and sun-burned faces. That's what's there. Not some capitalism fueled realist hell with smokestacks and housing tenements and all that noise that we needed to live in the supposedly civilized places left on earth. You thought of snow-capped mountains and chair lifts with shapely beauties rising higher to the peaks in tight, down-filled snow suits. The Tyrolean architecture, that's what filled the imagination, but in a car on the Autobahn, you may be driving to a paradise, but you were going through hell to get there. It was the form of evil that made rich people ugly. They perpetrated architectural crimes...]

—Because they did not have to live in their consequences.

[My imagination was potent, and its never-ending activity failed to prepare for the realities of Innsbruck by car. On the second of October, there was neither snow nor skiing anywhere nearby. All year round there were stacks burning their industrial by-products into the air. There were concrete streets and automobiles that burned leaded gasoline and had no catalytic converters. There were American hamburger and pizza restaurants and large grocery stores owned by companies doing business across Europe. Innsbruck was a European metropolis in a sense unknown to middle Americans. Barely over a hundred thousand people lived there, worked there, and took their children to school somewhere, annoying everyone who had to be anywhere near them. It was in a valley and the area of the streets and apartments and grocery stores and department stores was much smaller than an American city that had only flatland to contend with. Crowded in on an open stretch along the Inn river, a group of a hundred thousand Austrians lived in such a way as to bring disappointment to anyone with an imagination hoping for the ideal and struggling against the dead presence of the absolute.]

—Yowl for the ablute. The baloot.

[It made me wonder whether my imagination wasn't a liar, pure and simple. The reverie that led me down the mountain and along the Lech, lies, every bit of it. When confronted with reality at odds with what you thought you'd find, it's only natural to doubt your sanity, right? I mean, there must be something wrong with me. I didn't see clearly. I didn't understand anything. When I thought Mrs. Battery Salesperson, Mrs. Battery, was kinda checking me out, looking awfully friendly, I figured this couldn't be right, it had to be my imagination. I couldn't be seeing what I thought I was seeing. The apparatus always worked that way, it made you doubt. You thought you weren't seeing clearly, you were wrong about everything, thinking it was normal and nothing was as complicated as it seemed: your imagination somehow had better insight than your understanding.]

—The world you expected was not the real world.

[I helped Mr. and Mrs. Battery find the tourist information building. It was easy enough and I was surprised they needed help. It's the same in every city. There were signs, clearly marked, and you followed them. They'd been travelling a long time, how could they possibly need help navigating this new town where they were coming to set up their next base camp for autumn rides through the mountains and nearby countryside? It never occurred to me that they were plotting to engage me, get me involved with their projects as a way to increase fellow-feeling. That's not the kind of thing a person with clear goals would ever do unless those goals involved something nefarious. Thinking myself so wizened by that Swank of a pair and their bent bobbing...]

—I knew nothing.

[We found a place to park a couple of blocks from the office. It was a good idea, regardless of the type of traveler you happened to be, to make tourist information your first stop. It never occurred to me to try and get away. I needed a map, needed to know where the youth hostel was, the lay of the land. The people there were always helpful. You couldn't blame me for this, you couldn't say it's my fault. I was doing what anyone would have done. True, they had a weird definition of points of interest, and I didn't always see eye to eye with the chamber of commerce, but it's at least worth a listen. You never know what will tickle your fancy. Points of interest in a big city are, by definition, the things I find that interest me. I don't usually read guidebooks, or ask that many questions, they have their script that they're going to read from and how long I listen is usually determined by how attractive the speaker is. If it's some older gent or lady, I'm outta there in a second or two, but every now and then it's a young woman and I'll hear her out, find out everything she's got to offer. Mr. and Mrs. Battery were different animals altogether. They had many questions, wanted to know about the city and the neighboring areas, what was nearby and how far away it was. They're talking about the roads that were good to use in and out of town, and he's writing it down, learning everything. Names of places to buy food, other sorts of supplies, the chemist, the hospital, all of that. You'd think they were moving in and had no interest in discovering anything for themselves. They took every brochure the guy offered and filed it away in Mr. Battery's carryall. You could tell they always did it this way, they always got themselves thoroughly oriented and no doubt that was on top of whatever guidebook they brought with them, having read it thoroughly beforehand.]

—Two star accommodation, three star meal, four star experience. Wink wink.

[After gathering everything, we took a seat off to the side to make plans and write up itineraries. They were masters, truthfully, the way they blocked time and dissected the terrain around the city. They were going to get as much into their time here as they possibly could. It was awe-inspiring. Somewhere during the procedure, I stopped being dismissive and judgmental and began to feel inadequate. I wondered what I missed. It's like that story someone once told me about how they went to Mycenae and walked around the place looking at those old rocks and completely missed the tombs of Agamemnon and Clytemnestra. I was always that way. My entire trip was that way. That baker lady who made me go to the cuckoo clock museum in the Black Forest. I would never have gone there if it wasn't for her. She paid the entry fee, but who knows how many other places I missed either because I didn't have the price of admission, or I wasn't paying attention.]

—Wasn't paying attention.

[The agent clearly told us where the youth hostel was and both of us marked it on our maps, but they didn't want to go there right away. They said they would stay in a guest house for a couple of nights before moving to the hostel later in the week. They wanted a good shower and some alone time before mixing it up with the travel scene. That seemed reasonable and, sad to say, I was still too easily led, too quick to assume the best and take people at their word. You'd think that bent dick would have taught me by now, but if I'm honest I'd have to say I still thought they were the exception, they were extraordinary, and mostly people weren't like that. I was not in any kind of hurry, and gladly accepted their offer to stick with them when they went to the guest house the guy recommended. They'll get a room, settle in, and then we could go find something to eat. Later they'd drop me off at the hostel or wherever I wanted to go. It was a good plan.]

—Ding ding ding ding ding.

[I helped them explain to the lady at the guest house that I wouldn't be staying, that I was heading off and only there to get them settled. This was confusing because she insisted they pay for three if three people were staying in the room. That's how it works here. One room, but for some reason it costs less if you're alone. She seemed to doubt our story, had heard it before. I promised, and she grudgingly let them check in.]

—Only prepaying for two. It's the first number, the first one that counts.

[Again, with my stupid expectation, I thought we'd head up to their room, drop off their stuff, and go out. I was getting hungry, it was past my lunchtime. While they were settling in, I said as much and Mrs. Battery got some bread and butter from one of their bags and gave me some to hold me over until they were ready to go. Mr. Battery wanted a shower. I'm sure there are people who this sort of thing happened to all the time, but I was never one of them. The change this morning was the cause of it. That's why it's happening. That parrot was keeping things steady. It wasn't sudden and it wasn't a coincidence. My change. The worm eating the bird, the three dicks, past present and future, all of that. It was to blame, it must be. Whatever it was, she was on me once he's in the bathroom and the shower was running. Aggressive, no other way to say it. Not that attractive, but youngish and not too bad from where I stood, having gone without for a righteous spell. Mr. Battery was right there in the bathroom. What did she think was going to happen? Were we supposed to hurry? Was this some kind of trick? The door was ajar, he hadn't closed it completely and I was certain I saw him through the crack. Soon, he was peeking his head out and looking at us through the door. I couldn't see the rest of him, but saw enough to know he'd undressed. There was something about his eyes. He was looking right at me while she's, well, fiddling about. You know, unbuckling my belt, moving in that direction, and I thought he enjoyed it. Was getting off on watching. It was creepy, but... well... not exactly 100% creepy. What can I say, it'd been over a month.]

—Definitely.

[I didn't know exactly how far they planned to go. There were no ground rules. Don't people who do that sort of thing usually set out rules right at the beginning? I might've been up for something but not other things. Did they ever think of that? They planned this, their actions were orchestrated, but I didn't have any idea what was in store or where things were headed. Honestly, I would have fucked Mrs. Battery while Mr. Battery watched through the door. Okay, whatever, think what you want, but I would have done that. That would have been okay, but what if he came out in the middle? What if he wanted to get in on it? And not with Mrs. Battery, what if his kink was to fuck me while I'm fucking her? I didn't want to sign up for that. Without rules, without a preset agenda, I was out of there. I stood up abruptly, didn't bother to say much, although I think I did say something like "Thanks for the ride" without being ironic. I took the stairs down and hurried past the reception area and out the door. The lady was happy to see me leave, it restored her faith in humanity, but mine was thoroughly shot. They're all bent dicks, that's what I decided.]

—Every last one of them.

[I must've absorbed something or other from the information desk because somehow, without noticing it, I ended up at the train station after leaving the guest house and they weren't that close to each other. I must've managed to recall the instructions even if I didn't write them down. From the train station, that's when the directions to the youth hostel kicked in.]

—Follow the map.

[I left my rucksack with the attendant at the luggage counter because it was still too early to check in at the hostel and I wanted to walk around some more and get acclimated. There was a young Canadian guy who was trying to communicate something to the attendant but neither of them could make out what the other was saying. I translated his question. The answer was no, that part was clear. The question, not so much. Something about boxes for holding stuff that a traveler didn't need any more and wanted to send back to Canada at some kind of fixed price. He must've read about it somewhere, the question was too specific to be a general inquiry. He didn't appreciate the answer and felt there must be a mistake. I got impatient and walked away, leaving the train station and walking over to the Inn river where I was hoping to see something good and grab a sausage and roll from one of those carts. I came all this way. It couldn't be as bad as this, could it?]

—The memories are against me.

[In Paris, there was that time with the woman from Senegal. She was something. That should have been a big red flag. Too beautiful. There's no way some random African beauty was going to decide, "oh hey, I know what I want to do today, I think I'll fuck this dirty poor American traveler. What else do I have going on?" In that case, it wasn't because her boyfriend wanted to watch and jerk off, it's because he's going to rob me. It took me a while to realize that, despite the fact I didn't have any money, they were after my passport. I got out of there fast too, somehow managing to get away with my virtues intact.]

—I guess it's luck.

[And who was I to judge? They needed money. I had a passport worth more than I realized. I could get a new one. I was sure of that. In Paris, there's an embassy, all that infrastructure. It would have been trivial to stick around awhile and go get temporary documents or however that works. I wouldn't be the first idiot to fall victim to that kind of thing, and there were people who probably lost their shit when it happened.]

—It wouldn't have been such a big deal.

[Same with Mr. and Mrs. Battery. So what if they had a kink. Why was I so prudish all of a sudden? If he wanted to have a wank while I fucked his wife, so what? That'd make their day. Years from now they'd tell their friends. Put a few shrimp on the barbi, eh mate, and tell em about that American they hooked up with back in Innsbruck that one time. I would have been down for that, but they needed to give a guy a heads up beforehand. Don't spring it on me, right? That's reasonable, isn't it? You got to know what you're consenting to, they sure got that right.]

Walking by the river Inn and calming down. Settling into this faux metropolis and seeing it for what it is. Not a quaint ski village, not in the least. Plans now up for grabs, nothing else is sorted, whatever is going to happen next has to wipe the slate clean and start from scratch.

["I will," was the answer to this riddle. Expectations were bullshit. Only the will commands. Only it steers, only it can breach the days and the nights, and it is, though you may disagree, completely without expectation. That is the mind playing its tricks. The will is sheer drive, pure and in the moment. It sees nothing other than what lies before it. Go. That's what it says. Go. Drag on as you will, imagine rumblings of what never is and never will be. Dragons be maidens. Maidens be dragons beneath the starry sky. Nope. Go.]

I will...

"Come forth, to look once more upon the stars." [Dante's Inferno]

3.8.3.X.19.86.10.14 [ref(..2-4)]

Prevented by others.

> *And of that second kingdom will I sing*
> *Wherein the human spirit doth purge itself,*
> *And to ascend to heaven becometh worthy*
> [Dante's Purgatorio]

That first night there were lots of people at the youth hostel by the river and, after grabbing a bite to eat with a couple Australian guys, I went back to check out the scene. They were off to find somewhere to get loaded, but I passed. Dinner was enough to learn I didn't need to spend any more time with them. At the hostel it was lively, one of those exhaustion nights when a large mass of people spontaneously decided they couldn't take another night out and stayed close to base camp to meet up with other travelers. Most of the stories were exactly what you'd expect, so I moved from group to group looking for something, anything moderately entertaining. You got used to being off on your own. Garmisch gave me a taste, but now I was at my destination and wanted to connect. Not with travelers, I wanted locals, but it was only the first day and I needed practice, so I played along with the group dynamic and table hopped, didn't open my notebook, didn't read, only tried to find someone, anyone, interesting to talk to without any further agenda.

There were these two girls who seemed to be getting upset talking to two other girls. It was hard not to notice so I strolled by and asked how they were doing. Turned out, the two girls who were doing the upsetting were from South Africa and the two girls who were getting upset were from Canada, but the South Africans wouldn't accept that. See, the Canadians were of Chinese ancestry, and the South Africans seemed to dwell on that. It was that whole "Where are you *really* from" thing that drives some people nuts, but which other parts of the world are obsessed with when it comes to people they meet from North America. It happened to me frequently, but I guess it's worse if wherever your ancestors were from was a place where people didn't look European.

The thing is, the whole reason I sat down and basically rescued them was because they were timid and accommodating. Well, that's a stereotype now, isn't it? They happened to be that way, lots of people are, and they didn't want to upset those two obnoxious South African girls. Hell, that's a stereotype too. If I had known more about the crimes the Europeans committed over the years in South Africa, I would have been better at putting them in their place. I didn't have to listen for long to figure out their story. One of them, I think, said something about living on an island and I played dumb, didn't realize there were any big islands down there, and they didn't bother explaining, but there was a look, and I could tell. Quaint, I thought.

I was rude, but whatever, they went off and left me with the Canadians. They talked like Canadians and acted like Canadians. I'd certainly seen enough of them to know a Canadian when I saw one, so anyway that made big points with them, they liked that and despite being happy to get on the whole Americans suck band wagon when talking with a mixed group, they were happy to come across someone who understood them.

Now, these were nice girls, but they wanted to have an adventure too. That's what they were travelling for, that's what brought them overseas. They were studying in Switzerland, some kind of international business program in Davos or something, but they wanted to take a few days to check out the Alps in Austria: looking for adventure, but not at all adventurous. That's the best way to put it.

Do you know how there are girls who are always on a diet? Have you ever come across that? They won't eat anything unhealthy or fattening or whatever, unless they happen to be hanging out with their boyfriend or some guy friends who corrupt them into eating a pizza or some cake or something. It's as though they're so pure and devoted to their healthy principles, but then, every now and again, they'll let down and go do the guy thing. Get sloppy, eat badly, let loose, get drunk. Sometimes, now I'm not saying this is how it always happens, but sometimes there are girls who get persuaded to mess around because, well, he was so persistent. That goes wrong all the time like they say. I'm not saying it doesn't, but I am saying that sometimes it is exactly right.

I don't know what big historical fiasco is going on there, but it seems to me as though there are a whole bunch of desires that girls have to pretend they don't have and then, because they do have them, they have to lean on the boys to let loose now and again. These aren't rules or anything, but it happens, that's what I'm saying, and I got that vibe from May and Lisa that night. That's what I mean, they weren't adventurous, but they were looking for an adventure. They'd always done what they were supposed to do and were keeping their eyes open for someone to corrupt them, lead them into some fun, but safe fun, you know, something controlled and normal, something they could tell their friends when they got back home, but not so crazy that they'd suffer any real consequences.

I should mention that they had recently graduated from McGill which, based on the way they were acting, must be some kind of amazing school up there in Canada. They sure were stuck up about it, going on about how good it was and how it opened doors for them. That's great, but they must be used to Americans who haven't heard of it because the whole thing struck me as defensive, letting me know that it was a great school despite never hearing of it. No doubt, I am a provincial idiot and it also seemed that they were familiar with provincial idiocy, so they tried to nip it in the bud right away. It's why they got into that other great program I never heard of over there in Switzerland. Only people from the best schools in North America got to go. In fact, McGill grads are in the minority among the North Americans. Most are from the American Ivy League. Well then, that must be something, or some shit like that.

Now these were nice girls. Genuinely nice, so the kind of thing they were up for was likely to be tame. I suggested we kick around together the next day since we were going to stay in Innsbruck. We could walk around and see what's going on. They had a whole itinerary of places they wanted to go, see the view from this thing, go to some famous ice arena or something. I thought fine, that would be good and then it'd be my job to try and find something out of the ordinary to add spice to the day.

It wasn't much, but we happened to be by one of those places where lots of people get food on a tray from a cafeteria style service and then leave their trays behind. Nobody buses their own table in Europe, so they fill up their trays with food and then eat at whatever table they pick, then they leave. And there were tons of kids at this place. It must've been popular with families. You could get all kinds of unhealthy stuff to eat. French fries. Pommes frites. They were everywhere, everyone got them. Then there were fast-food style entrees too. Burgers, chicken fingers, fish sticks. Things you don't usually expect to eat in Europe. Well Lisa and May would never have eaten in that kind of place. They obviously had some money for travel, and they enjoyed going to proper places with good menus and all that, something I hadn't done the whole time I was away, but it's what I said, they were looking for exactly this kind of safe adventure.

It doesn't sound like much, and they certainly didn't think it was extreme, some bad food, but I said, "Now wait a second. I'm a budget traveler and I don't have money to be piling up a bunch of overpriced unhealthy food, so there's a trick." This was interesting to them. They giggled, literally fucking giggled, at the prospect of learning some sketchy scam that some wily traveler was going to show them. I scouted the room and picked a seat near a family with children who, on my seasoned evaluation, looked kind of picky. There's no formula for this, but you know it when you see it. The mother is constantly trying to get the little fuckers to eat but they don't want to, they want to play with their whatever the hell it is that they have in their hand, or they want to go over there and see whatever that is. Something like that.

Once I found the mark, I led Lisa and May over to their table and we took a seat with a cup of tea in front of us. We didn't have to sit there for long before the lady and her kids got up and left, leaving their trays behind. I scooched over with May and Lisa following close behind. The kids left tons of food. There were three full orders of pommes frites sitting there and two completely untouched sandwiches, a burger and something else. It was a total score, and I explained to the girls that, if you're traveling for a long time, this is how you make ends meet.

They loved it. It's what I said, exactly the kind of thing they were looking for, the sort of experience they wanted. After lunch, we went over to the big ski lift thing and saw the arena, and then they were back in their happy safe tourist place after a nice warm meal for free. Better still, they had a story to tell about the grimy American who showed them how to get it. Grimy but clean, mind you. Well, mostly clean. I was showering, put it that way, but I wasn't great about washing my clothes, and they noticed that, so they wanted to treat me to a trip to the laundromat, which struck me as bizarre. I cleaned things in the sinks and bathrooms at the hostels or guest houses, but never ventured to the laundromats, they were too expensive. They insisted and I thought what the hell, pants and overshirts are hard to dry if you clean them in the sink. It keeps you in the same place for a day or two, letting everything dry, and who has that kind of time? Or can remember to do it when they do have the time? I could have washed my jeans in Garmisch, but totally forgot.

Anyway, that's what we did later that afternoon, and I told them I'd reciprocate by taking them out for appetizers and drinks at a local place. The thing is, you see, people are too trusting. This is a common phenomenon. It isn't that they're trusting, it's that it doesn't occur to them that certain kinds of things that seem obvious to me would ever happen. We went round this Spanish-themed place a few blocks from the laundromat and had a drink and some morsels to eat. You go up and get the food from some common table and then you're supposed to keep track of how many you have. May and Lisa were having a good old time, they're not thinking about what we're doing, talking about the stuff we saw and where they're going tomorrow. Normal shit, and the whole time I'm watching how things work, how the people go up to the bar and pay the man and what the flow looks like. These people didn't know a damn thing about dine and dash. It never occurred to them that someone would do that, so they weren't guarding against it. This guy wasn't keeping track of anything. Who was in the place? Who paid, who didn't? Some people went up and paid long before they left, others pay as they go. It's totally random, there wasn't any obvious pattern to it.

After we're done, I told them to head over to the laundromat to get my stuff and I'd pay after I went to the bathroom. They agreed, it never occurred to them that there's anything weird about that, so they went off while I waved to the guy at the bar and headed back to the WC, waited in there for a while, not too long, not too short, then walked back out into the bar area and through the seating and right out the door. I think I said goodbye to some waiter or something at the front. Nobody noticed. I didn't run, didn't panic. If somebody grabbed me and demanded I pay, threatened to call the cops, well then fine, I'd suffer the consequences, but that's not going to happen. As I said, it'd never occur to them that I'd do this on purpose. If I were caught, I'd tell them I forgot. Be apologetic. That would seem so much more likely than the truth. They'd believe it and wouldn't say a damn thing. Hell, they'd probably apologize for embarrassing me. As long as I paid, and I did have something stashed away so, in an emergency, I could swing it.

After I got back to the laundromat, I had to decide how much of this to tell Lisa and May. On the one hand, they were these nice girls who never did anything like that, whereas on the other hand this was the kind of story that'd make the day a complete adventure. Cleaning up the grimy guy at the laundromat, eating other people's food, dining and dashing. The phrase made it much more harmless. They'd be attracted to the idea, but it was a risk. In the end, who cares? I'm only going to know these girls for a day or two at most, what difference does it make? Worst case, they get pissed off and go back to the place and pay the guy for what we ate. Apologize for the mix-up, no harm done.

I told them.

And here's the thing. This was kind of what I expected. I didn't know for sure, but I thought it would go this way. May was horrified. She's bent out of shape, doesn't think you should call it "Dine and Dash," to her it's stealing plain and simple. Lisa was more excited by it. She thinks it's cool, and pointed out to May that the place was crowded, and the drinks were over-priced, aiming at some of that tourist money that's such a big part of Innsbruck life. They were students of international business after all, so they understood how it worked. Their margins were high, she reasoned, and this seemed to calm May down. I never could have talked her into it, that was clear, but Lisa could do it, and this created kind of a bond between us. It was getting on toward evening and I had some clean clothes. Lisa was keener on me at that point. May thought I was a wild animal, but Lisa was into it, she was more adventurous than May as it turned out.

After dropping back by the hostel, changing, and putting the rest of the clothes away, I washed out the shorts I was wearing, hung them on the bunk to dry, and went back to meet up with them. May didn't want to go out anywhere, but I think Lisa caught the bug, so we went out, the two of us, looking for some trouble. She insisted on paying, didn't have a problem with what we did, but didn't want to make a habit of it. We went to a few places and had a few drinks. They had music, a juke box, at one place, a DJ at another. It was fun, the first time I'd been drunk in a while. It didn't fit with my budget, but since she was buying and didn't seem concerned with the prices, I was happy to partake, and, as I said, I think she was exploiting me, taking advantage of the fact I didn't share in her rigid morals, taking a vacation from her worries and scheduling dilemmas, and I was facilitating that. Surely that must be worth a couple of beers and the price of admission to some poser club with a retro DJ who still thinks it's 1978.

love ██ _gas_
heart of glass

Now you can judge me if you want, but I'll tell you, I hold that Lisa was not nearly as drunk as she made it seem that she was. She nursed a single beer at the bar with the jukebox. The whole time we were there, one beer. I had a couple, but she only had the one and I'm pretty sure there was still some in the bottle when we left. At the club with the DJ, she ordered some kind of mixed drink, something with a cherry in it and kind of a golden brownish color. I don't know what it was, but there's no way that place makes strong drinks. It wasn't that kind of club. You know, light on the alcohol, but heavy on the prices. I stuck to beer and had a few more, so I was off it but not so tipsy that I was buying her whole staggering and giggling thing where she's supposedly more wasted than she's ever been in her life. With the dancing and only a little bit of alcohol, it's bullshit, right?

My suspicions turned out to be well-founded. Back at the hostel, most people had gone to bed. Seemed reasonable we would head off that way too. I was kind of ready to be rid of her to have a dip and get ready for bed, but she, for some inexplicable reason, wanted to check out the room where you store the luggage while the hostel is closed during the day. She went in there and expected me to follow along.

No doubt about it, Lisa was looking for some excitement and the whole drunk act was supposed to lure me in. Since I'm the kind of common criminal who would dine and dash and eat leftovers, I must surely be the kind of guy who would take advantage of an innocent drunk girl after a night out. I was offended. Well, as offended as I could be given the circumstances, and there are days when I would have played along, but there was something about that day. I had the thing with Mr. and Mrs. Battery and wasn't feeling good about that sort of thing. I don't know, but whatever it was, I decided not to go along.

She was pretending to show me stuff. Oh, look at that, what is it? Putting her hand on my arm and all that. Leaning. The usual things they do to let you know, but kind of amateurish. I shouldn't have, but I did kiss her, and not a grope kind of kiss, but an innocent one, with a hug sure, I'm not a total savage, but I'm saying it wasn't something that's way more than a kiss, but you call it a kiss to kind of downplay it. The way Lisa would describe it to May, for example. No, this was only a kiss, but then I pulled back and said that, well, I didn't think we should be kissing, not with the drinking and how plastered we were. I have to admit I kind of thought this was funny. Here she was, such a nice girl, which technically was working against her at this point, but still, a sweet girl who wanted some action. Not the whole thing, but something, and she thought she played it perfectly, doing everything right to get it, but then here I was ruining her plans by being a decent sort. So, by funny, I mean ironic.

Now, I could have gone either way on this, but if I'm completely honest, it was because she was so nice that I didn't give her what I'm pretty sure she wanted. She did get more aggressive when I pulled back though, when I explained to her how I couldn't take advantage of her state. She didn't want to come right out and tell me she was faking, but she was pretty lucid all of a sudden while we were having this exchange and she's trying to prevent me from leaving the room.

Somehow, I don't know how this works, I'm no expert, but I decided that the pathway to the greatest virtue was complete submission. That is, pay attention because this is convoluted, I figured, in that moment, that there was some kind of middle way. I'm not saying the mean was the path to virtue or anything like that, but I figured that, well, there was a way to do right by Lisa and stick to my nice guy act. I'm not saying I'm a nice guy, I'm saying that's what I was pretending to be and, despite being tipsy myself, was committed to staying in character.

You won't see it this way, but I figured since she was so nice it wouldn't have been much fun anyway. Might as well take care of her travel needs, give her the story she wanted, and not be a tease or whatever you'd call me for playing games when I should have known better. I took care of her, that's it, I didn't take care of myself, but I took care of her, and honestly, it was for selfish reasons. I'm not going to pretend otherwise. They're all different, you know. You never know what this one will like or that one. Some have to take care of themselves, some can't do it when someone else is watching but think there's something wrong with them that they don't want you to know about, so they fake it and make you think everything is normal even though you know that whatever the hell they're screaming about isn't anatomically possible. Well, that's what's in it for me. Finding out. About Lisa. That was good.

In the end, I don't know, she seemed happy with how it turned out, kissing me afterward and telling me it's my turn. It was sexy, but I stuck to my plan. You got to have principles. She went off to her room and I had my dip before heading to bed. Innsbruck was not how I expected it to be.

The next day is when things got weird. Not with Lisa. They went off to Salzburg after we ate breakfast together. It was nice. She was nice. May was nice. She had obviously heard about what happened, but she wasn't such a prude that she didn't appreciate it for her friend, and I was still being decent. Being friendly and having breakfast and being funny. That's 99% of it. Many guys don't get that. The part about the next day or how you say goodbye. Be just as charming and friendly. You have to be. That way she doesn't feel like garbage. And that matters. No matter what else I say, that matters a lot. I don't think Lisa was playing any games because she's bad. I think she's been forced to be that way somehow. She can't come out and say what she wants. Her whole life people have been telling her she can't do that, but she's human and can't help it if she needs to find whatever way she can to let it out when she's not allowed to say it straight, when she's not allowed to feel it straight. I was pretty hard on her for that bullshit, I guess, but Lisa and May were alright. Good people. I hope they remember me fondly.

That's not what was weird though. What was weird was that later that night Mr. and Mrs. Battery showed up at the youth hostel, and they weren't embarrassed, didn't bat an eye. "Hey, where'd you run off to? Were you late for something?" As though nothing unusual or weird happened. I ducked out to get away from them, because I wasn't feeling normal about any of that, so I thought it was better to take off, but they waited for me, and were still up when I got back. There weren't too many people in the common room, but I stopped in for a dip and the two of them ambushed me there. I didn't know what they were planning, but it seemed they were about to broach the topic from the other day. Topic. Pardon my euphemism. They obviously realized that the problem was they hadn't laid out the ground rules. Now they were going to state them clearly thinking that's what it would take.

But they were not normal. Not to me. "Simple as that, mate. Want to watch you fuck my wife and then cum on your ass. No biggy. Whaddya say? Ya game?"

Holy fucking shit. Here I thought I was becoming so wizened by the road. Learning the tricks, but I was speechless and about to get rude. My own insecurities, no doubt, but I was feeling cramped in there on the bench and wanted the conversation to end. As I was about to say something, this chick comes from out of nowhere and says, "There you are, are you coming back?"

Mr. and Mrs. Battery got confused since I appeared to be pretty chummy with this chick, got apologetic, didn't realize. Excuse me, pardon me, and then they're off. No small part of their discomfort was because of how this chick looked. She may have been blonde underneath. She had coloring in her face that sort of made it seem that way. Fair like that. But her hair was jet black. Clearly a dye job, but over the top, not natural looking. Cropped short too, as though it was cut with a knife instead of a scissors, but on purpose. And she had this mascara or eye liner or whatever that stuff is around her eyes so that they looked black. Was she punk? Not exactly. I couldn't tell. Something I hadn't seen before. She had this cool black tank top on, a muscle shirt, something a guy would wear, and her arms were muscular, but sinewy muscular not beefy, and ragged black jeans. Not torn or anything but worn. Her right arm was completely tattooed. I never saw anything like it, and apparently, neither had Mr. and Mrs. Battery. Although if they had been there the night before, they'd have recognized her as the night desk clerk. I was pretty sure I'd seen her mopping or something, but here she was right up close, smelling of cigarettes and cheap coffee, looking hard as nails and scaring the shit out of Mr. and Mrs. Battery, and me too. Thankfully, I didn't have to say a damn thing and they high-tailed it on out of there without another word. My hero. Or heroine, as the case may be.

That's how I met Birgit.

3.8.4.X.19.86.10.27 [ref(..4-14)]

Things have been tense for the last two weeks. I don't know how much longer I can stay here. Around that time, I called Eve. I wanted to hear a friendly voice, someone I could connect with. That caused a lot of trouble because I wasn't supposed to use the phone. That's what the roommates were upset about, at least. Birgit was upset about something else. Not jealousy, it didn't matter about Eve. She didn't care about that. It was something else.

After she rescued me from the Australians, she took me back into the kitchen and we got some coffee. Then we sat in the office behind the reception counter. I was in the chair, and she was sitting up on the desk. There wasn't anywhere else to sit, so it seemed natural enough, but in that time, the time it took to get from the common room back to the kitchen to get the coffee and then into the office and take a seat, she must've touched me five times, and this girl was like a cat. No coincidences when it came to that sort of thing. If her tail dragged along your leg as she was passing by, it wasn't an accident. That cat is performing a deliberate act of contacting you. For what? Well, I don't know about cats, but Birgit did it to size me up. She managed to touch my shoulder, my bicep, and my forearm. Those were easy and quick, she did that within the first few seconds. Then, while we were getting coffee, she managed to lean nearly the entire length of her left arm against my chest and the entire length of her hip and left leg against my, well, my midsection. Not coincidental in the least, she was exploring the terrain.

The conversation in the office was an extension of that. She spoke English. Perfect English. Like a native speaker.

"What brings you here? What kind of travels?"

"Excuse me?"

"Are you riding the trains to the big cities?"

"Ah, no. I've been hiking since Bregenz. Meant to walk here but had a few detours."

"Only Austria?"

"I hiked through the Black Forest before that."

"Hitchhiking?"

"Mostly. When I could get a lift."

Approval, she approved, that was clear. It wasn't idle chatter, she was discovering something, and only barely tolerated my question about how she learned to speak such good English, waving the compliment aside and saying she studied it for a long time before spending a year abroad in some suburb of DC. I tried to find out how long ago that was, but she didn't want to say. Was I too cool in how I asked the question?

"Was that recently?"

"Not too recent, no."

But what did that mean? I was trying to figure out how old she was. I mean, was she talking about a year of college? Not in a suburb of DC, right? That'd more likely be a year of high school. How old is she then? She could've been 16, could've been 20. Again, for fuck sake, I honestly couldn't tell, but she acted much older, felt much older. She wanted to know about me, and wasn't answering questions too freely, I couldn't come out with "How old are you?" that would've ended the interview, I'm sure of it.

She wanted to know about the Australians. Who were they? What were they saying that was making me so uncomfortable. I told her. Simply. Gave her the complete story.

"What freaked you out? Was it the offer or who was offering?"

"What do you mean?"

"If they were better looking. If she was some kind of model or something. If he was built, would you have been up for it then?"

I wanted this girl to like me, and I knew she was sitting there trying to figure something out with a lot on the line. What should I say? Be honest. If you can't figure out the angle, that's what you got, right?

"Of course."

That was the right answer.

This girl was beautiful. And I don't mean that the pale white skin against the jet-black dye job was exquisite. I don't mean she had the most perfectly shaped jaw, chin, lips, and nose combination, or that her fit and trim body was amazing. None of that, it's not the point. There was something in her arc, something in the event of her. I don't know how to put it, but she was dynamite. I could tell right away. I have no one to blame but myself, but I wanted to find out everything. My imagination was running wild in those first few minutes. What happened to her? What's her story? Where the fuck did she come from and how the hell did she get here? I'm not talking about rescuing or saving her or any of that shit. No, I mean beautiful, an aesthetic phenomenon, right there in front of me and I wanted to be as close to it as I could possibly get, but she wasn't giving me any signs for how to do it, how to get there. She was going about her business working at figuring out whatever it was she was weighing, and then she would make up her mind. I had no control and didn't see a way to get any.

Two things I'm quite sure of. First, girls always do this kind of thing. They aren't always so obvious about it, but this kind of appraisal is normal. Par for the course, it's what they're always doing when they meet guys. At least the ones who give a shit about guys. I don't know what they're working out, but I know they're working out something and your destiny depends on it. She was doing that right then, and I was trying to figure out the logic so I could impact the results. Simple as that. It's the game we've been playing since we entered adolescence. No issue there.

Second, and this is more controversial, when a girl marks herself somehow, with a knife somewhere you can't see, or somewhere you can, or with a needle that sews ink onto her body, anything like that, anything involving a mark or making a mark, well, there's something to it, that's what I'm saying, it's not random and no matter what she thinks it means, it means she's trying to make something only she sees visible to everyone else. You know, she looks at her arm and doesn't' see an arm, it's already marked, don't you see it? No, of course you don't, it's only an arm. She gets a tattoo and is so deliberate about what to put there and where it's positioned. The design, the pattern. At some point, I'll ask, and she'll tell me the nuances of what's drawn there. It'll have such a deep and important meaning. If she's willing to talk about it, that is, then she'll give away everything. That's because the design is making something only she can see present to everyone. She may disagree, there can be arguments, I get it, but I'm sure of this, this girl was marked, elaborate and in your face. Everyone who sees her will see these markings right away. Only the tip of the iceberg too, there were more, in places I couldn't see right away, places I'd never be able to see, but it was there.

This drove me wild. My imagination was firing all over the place, and that's the event I'm talking about, telling me it had to be beautiful, wouldn't have ended up this way if it weren't, but not touchy feely beautiful, Super Nova beautiful or erupting volcano. Like that.

Imagination was running away with me, so observations were suspect. It may have been a big fantasy. Imagination can be that way. Tell you all kinds of crap because you want to hear it, but in this case, I imagined she could read it in my eyes, she could tell I thought she was beautiful and that it wasn't because she looked pretty or some shit like that, but because she was dynamite, an exploding star right in front of me. Lava pouring over everything. I imagined she could see it and liked it. That was exactly the sort of reaction she was looking for.

"What was up with you and that chick from yesterday?"

"Lisa," I said.

"Yeah, you two looked pretty friendly."

I must've been channeling something. There was a purpose. I was simple and honest.

"She's a tourist. Looking for an adventure."

"Were you helpful? A good Samaritan? Tell her about the sights worth seeing?"

"I think I was. Exactly the right amount of helpful."

She didn't follow up, but she kept looking at me. I was supposed to say more, but I couldn't think of what else to say. That too was going over well. Have you ever seen one of those movies where two shy people are trying to hook up, but it's awkward because of the kind of people they are. They aren't talking to each other, can't think of what to say, but there they are trying the best they can. It's a weird disconnect because on the one hand you're thinking here are these two prim and proper people and on the other hand you're thinking they must want to fuck each other's brains out because they aren't saying anything terribly interesting but are totally devoted to it. Must be some sort of unspoken passion, right? And that doesn't match with the shyness.

Well, this interview was kind of that way, except neither of us was exactly prim and proper, but we weren't looking to volunteer a whole bunch of information either. It's not as if we were looking to make an emotional connection by revealing our true feelings and deepest thoughts.

I was damn sure she was too clever to trick, it wasn't going to happen that way. She was an expert at whatever she was doing, and I wouldn't be able to fake it. She'd figure it out, that's why I insisted on being as simple and honest as possible. I figured I had no other choice, and didn't give any more information than necessary, didn't babble and say all kinds of nonsense, but kept it as brief as possible while sticking to the truth. That's it. Leave the rest to fate.

To be clear, it was about sex. Whatever the tests, I must've passed them because in the middle of the night, when her shift ended, she took me back to the flat. She shares it with four other people, two guys and two girls. They had this same fashion sense: dyed hair, eyeliner, listen to the same music, and make weird jokes about how the cool people are from Minnesota. They wanted to know if Illinois was close to Minnesota. I said absolutely, but Birgit told them it was nearby for Americans though not too close by their standards.

This was after a few days, I didn't meet her roommates right away. When she took me back to her place, it was the middle of the night, and we went directly to her bedroom. We were pretty much hiding in there for a few days. We'd come and go. She had to work. I'd go back to the hostel to reup for another night, wasn't living with her or anything, didn't move my stuff in. We were keeping it pretty quiet. I saw the roommates but didn't talk to them, she didn't introduce me at first.

Okay, it isn't gallant of me to be detailed about what was going on in those first days, but I think it's important. I have to tell some stuff. I'll say it and then you can tell me if it's what I think it is. Seems fair.

Sex was a big thing for her. It went deep, personality-wise. Not something I'd ever seen before. I was right about the markings, by the way. She was a cutter. Not now, nothing recent, but they were there, the scars, and the behavior, well it was a kind of scar too. If I describe these cut marks on her thigh high up near the hip, that'd be fine, that would be a simple physical statement, but if I talked about her relationship to semen, how am

I supposed to do that? Only facts. That's what I'm saying.

First off, I got the feeling that I was a toy or tool for her. The way some girls use a vibrator, she was using me, but the use was much more complex, that's why she needed a whole guy for it. There was a role for weight and height, a role for different positions and balance. A vibrator can only go so far. A whole person, that's way more flexible, he could be used in far richer fashion.

Okay, there's no other way to say it, this girl loved to suck cock. Well, not sure she loved it, but she needed to do it, that's for sure. Something going on there, but it wasn't exclusively about the cock. Having it in her mouth or licking it or stroking or whatever. It wasn't about that. It was the whole body's position. She would press her weight against me, her torso against my legs, for example, or against my chest, depending on which way, and her whole body was into it, same as she got my whole body into it. The contact was complete. Full body presses, and the action on her end was extremely enthusiastic. It involved sounds and slurping and spitting and all kinds of noise. And this girl is not performative. She's not the kind of chick who puts on an act for anyone. If anything, she's in her own world and doesn't give a shit what anyone thinks or how they react. Her noises were pure and real and natural. Believe me, it didn't boost my ego, there was nothing flattering there. If anything, it made me painfully aware of my instrumentality and that is the exact opposite of an ego boost.

Now, she didn't just love to suck cock, she insisted and went to every length to ensure that her actions resulted in a climax. And this had nothing to do with any desire to give pleasure. She wanted semen to ejaculate, as though she was operating a machine. That's how it was supposed to work, and she had to make sure it worked exactly that way. That's not everything. There was an extremely hot, seriously intense routine that went along with it. Part of her interview must have been an age check because her practical demands required a lot of stamina. This girl needed me to orgasm multiple times as part of foreplay. Have you ever heard of anything like this before? I sure hadn't, so it took a while for me to believe it, but it was too regular, too clearly a set pattern. I became convinced. This was happening without penetration. I mean, oral penetration, but nothing else. That's what I'm saying. She was particular about penetration, it couldn't just happen, couldn't start with that, not a chance, a lot of preparation was required, lots of milking or draining had to be done first.

First, she'd make me orgasm with her mouth, and then she'd make it happen again with her hand, and then a third time with her body, rubbing up against me and getting me to rub up against her. Different parts of her body, she was spontaneous with that, as long as I ended up discharging on her somewhere. That's what she demanded, and she didn't ignore the substance of it either. Interacting with that in different ways was exactly her point. Then, once that happened, three times, always the same, every single time, once that was covered, then she'd take me, semi-hard at this point, and use my cock as kind of a dildo. First on the outside, to rub her clit, and get herself off, then, and only then, by stuffing me inside her. She had to stuff it at that point. I shit you not.

Doesn't that seem to mean something? There must be something behind it, right? No condom either. Who does that nowadays? My imagination was on fire. My mind was racing. I was so curious and so fascinated, had a million questions, but she wasn't into that, and I dared not risk it.

There's more. Okay. Once she put me inside her, it was okay for me to become more active. In fact, at that point, she was okay with a lot more activity. Something changed once we went through that big routine. I could turn her over and press her to the bed. This was more than okay. She liked pressure and weight and force. A little force. Not too much. She liked more, but I could only go so far. The signs were clear. The more active I became, the more strongly she would react, and she would use her hand to make herself come during. Didn't need me to do anything to help. In fact, she didn't want any help, that would only have ruined it for her.

In the end, I didn't have a choice. The male of the species is not wired to resist this kind of thing. Truly, I was at her mercy.

Eventually, I took my stuff out of the hostel and brought it to this filthy flat where she lived with these guys. She introduced me and I could come and go as I pleased. I could hang out here while she was at work or when she went out to wherever the fuck she would go without bothering to tell me. Her roommates didn't seem to mind. Frithjof, one of the guys, he wanted to strike up a friendship. We went drinking a few times, and he played some of this fucked up music for me. These bands, many of them from Minnesota, that I never heard of. Hüsker Dü? How did I get through four years of university without ever hearing anything about this band, or any of the others? The Replacements, or whatever they were called.

I tried to find out about her from Frithjof, but he didn't know anything. Margot seemed to know Birgit the best, but she sure as hell wasn't going to spill the beans.

"Why don't you ask her?" Is all I would get to something as simple as "Were you guys friends as kids?"

I imagined all kinds of things, figured there was some fucked up uncle or friend of her father's who did something unspeakable to fuck her up when she was eleven or some shit like that. There are so many stories. It's possible, right? Why do we put up with this shit? Castrate a motherfucker for that and I bet it doesn't happen as much, but that isn't this world. Then I thought what if there was some asshole who wouldn't take no for an answer or, more likely, didn't know that silence is terror and not consent.

What if there were an asshole like that and then, this is how fucked up my imagination can get, what if this asshole rapes her and when she tries to tell the asshole's father about it he fucking rapes her too. Twisted shit that happens all the time. Imagination will play tricks on you if you don't have any facts.

How does this get so churned up and spliced together? That's what I wanted to know. If she doesn't tell me about whatever she went through to make this beautiful arc that she's in the middle of, well that's okay, I can live with that, but I desperately wanted to know how it fit together. The routine of getting me to that right place where she could let down her guard and go into a totally different head space, how did that fit together with her history and whatever happened there? What exactly am I benefiting from here? Being punished for? Don't I have a right to know?

Look, if a girl likes, I mean, *really* likes, being held down firmly while you sodomize her as she works herself into a frenzy, doesn't it seem reasonable that you'd want to know how that fits together with what happened to her while she's growing up? That kind of shit doesn't come from nowhere, right? She had to figure out that she wanted it that way, she had to figure that out. Well, how did that happen? What's the story?

That's what kept me in place, that's what I was sticking around for. It was a car wreck, and I couldn't turn away.

This girl could not handle any resistance. You couldn't make it obvious that you were different from her and somehow needed her to accommodate that, and I'm not talking about sex anymore, that's what was happening in the apartment during those first couple weeks after I got here. Her roommates were like, "Who the fuck is this guy? Why is he staying here and how come he isn't paying rent?" These are reasonable questions, and I wanted to get involved and make nice with them, let them know who I was and what I'm up to. If they got to know me better, they'd feel better about it. The other guy, Cat, or whatever his name was, that's what they called him, he didn't want to know me, wouldn't even look at me. Margot didn't have much to say either, but at least she was civil. The other chick, Sabina I think, she didn't want to be in the same room with me. This wasn't about me, though. None of it. That's why I couldn't get involved or say anything. Apparently, Birgit had done this before. It was habitual, but only for a few days and then she would move on, and the guy would disappear, but I had been around for a lot longer and they were about ready for that to end.

Birgit went psycho. There is no other way to describe it. She was screaming and throwing a tantrum, yelling at everybody, breaking stuff. Hitting herself. None of it was to defend me, she didn't give a fuck about that, about whether my feelings were hurt, she didn't want to be resisted, that was the sense I got. There was a delicate world somewhere in the balance and she wouldn't stand for anyone trying to rearrange it in a way that didn't suit her. Whatever she was interviewing me for, and whatever tests I passed, I must have passed them with flying colors, because she was holding on tighter than ever before. At least, that's the way the roommates made it seem, and what other reason would she have? It must've been something like that. After these big tantrums, she would cry curled up in her bed. I didn't know where to go, the roommates didn't want me with them so I would follow her, but what was she going to do? Would I be safe with her? In the bed, she wouldn't exactly cry, but it was some kind of weird deep sobbing shivering thing. Whatever it was, I knew she wouldn't hurt anybody, but maybe she wanted to be alone. She'd look at me, standing as far away as I could while still being in the same room, and didn't seem to mind me there or want me any closer. We sat there a few times for nearly an hour. Then, at the end, she'd wave me over and suck my cock, going through that foreplay routine as if it were the most normal thing in the world. I swear to God, that's exactly what happened.

I called Eve because I wanted to tell someone that I was in this fucked up situation, but I had no one to tell. I didn't think she was the right person, I couldn't give any details, right? If I knew her better, but probably not. This is freaky stuff, and I had no benchmark for measuring its effects. Was I the monster? I couldn't admit it if I was, so I made some friendly remarks about being somewhere I wasn't completely welcome and needing to figure something else out. She was her kind self, tried to be helpful, told me a story about this time when it was weird at her house because her dad was in the hospital and her sister wouldn't come visit or something. Made her want to escape, so she figured that must be how it was for me and used it as inspiration to zero in on the logistics.

"You can always go back to the hostel, can't you?"

"Yeah, that's a good idea. For the immediate problem. Thanks for listening." Blah blah blah. It was good to call. Reminded me of normalcy left in the world, so that was good, learning about her sister, how she regretted getting angry with her for not coming, warned me about jumping to conclusions when I didn't have the facts. It was good, but the roommates must've heard me or something, because they wanted to know why I was using their phone. I got the sense it was a sore subject with a lot of background.

Sabina screamed something about the calls to America. She thought I was calling home and Birgit did the same thing before. There was a lot of tension around that. She couldn't pay the bill and they had to chip in to help but she still owed them. That's what I pieced together. Girls talk fast when they're pissed off, so it was challenging, especially because I was listening through the wall.

That led to Birgit screaming at me about the phone call. She didn't give a fuck who I was calling or where. "But it was only a call to Germany," I said. That missed the point entirely. She was pissed that I got her into trouble with the roommates for something she already took care of. She wasn't using the phone that way anymore and it cost her to change behavior. Now, I was bringing her back into it. Honestly, I thought she was going to kick me out and anticipating it gave me a sense of relief, but that's not what happened. She screamed, got it out of her system, then the foreplay routine leading up to a particularly enthusiastic active part. By my standards, at least. For her, it seemed well within the range of normal.

    She's home now so I'll stop, but that at least gets you up to speed.

12.12 (3)
this year's harvest

12.12.1.Elisabet.1986.5.12 [ref(..9-12)]

He pulls the door open and steps back to make way, handing over the polaroid camera.

"Thank you, Patrick."

—He isn't looking the right way. It's sweet.

Flapping the photograph rapidly back and forth while turning back to look through the entryway. He is putting the cassettes into the rucksack after laying it into the trunk of the car. Elmo says something, they're laughing, he likes him too. He looks up and waves. Waving back, then turning to the elevators, pulling everything tight.

(I'd have given him boxes and boxes of them if he had the space. Felt as if I should've given more. A photo, a hug, and a few cassettes didn't feel like enough. The phone number, that's something. If he needs anything.)

"Ms. Lundberg, will you be expecting anyone this morning?"

The elevator doors open, stepping inside and turning back toward the front. "Cassie at some point. Send her right up, please."

"Of course."

"Thank you, Mr. McKinney."

As the doors close, there is the slightest trace of his bowing head disappearing from view.

[Should be here soon. What's Marianne's lawyer's name? It's upstairs. Gray something. The pencil skirt. Black one. That blue blouse. Business-like but fun with the sheer shoulders and low neck. Those open instep stilettos with pointy toes I've been dying to wear. Too formal? Tough.]

—No screwing around, boys, it's my meeting.

Door opens with the usual ding. Stepping out and breezing through the entry way to the hall and down into the bedroom.

—Elmo'll be back in plenty of time. If not, we'll take a cab or call that service. She knows.

Setting the camera and photo down on the table by the couch, stepping up to the cabinet and swinging open the door, changing the reel, and pressing the button. Turning up the volume.

Beat launches and the room is full of rhythm. Swinging hips to the right and sliding along the floor, stutter stepping into the bathroom, turning up the volume on the speaker and rocking out of the stretch pants and the rest.

It's cold, flipping on the heater in the cabinet and then side-stepping to the shower.

"██████ *crazy (woo)*" he croons. "Such a star."

—Nothing like banging it out for the big theatre crowd. Never again, might be the cost of the stadiums and festivals. Smoky rooms, small stages, barely room to move, no wiggling. Fading anyway, how long can you pull that off?

Down then up again and, with pointed toes, sexy stepping into the hot water. Swinging a hip under its welcoming flow. The speaker by the vanity muffles right as the one in the shower comes up loud and clear.

Singing along:

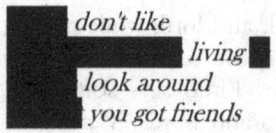

don't like
            living ██
look around
you got friends

(Didn't feel like it last night. Did we? Didn't matter. This morning, oh yeah, that's a must, once more with the angle. Bad to the bone. Priority zero, he said.)

—Get everything flowing.

"First one with Gray. Chandler."

—That's it. Gray Chandler. Says he's amazing. A shark.

"███████████ *purple banana* / ███████████ *in the truck,* ██
██"

"An hour with him."

(Mine, not the band's, not the label's, mine. She was right, absolutely essential, priority zero.)

—Bastards'll bully you with jargon and feigned self-importance.

Lathering up and gripping the plastic container, holding it close. "██
██ *let's go*" Then *The Beautiful Ones* starts up. Don't know the words. Turning the water off and taking up the handheld. Leaning with a palm against the tile, wetting it down from the back forward.

—The guys. No surprises. They know what's coming.

Rubbing in the shampoo and working it back to front. The water is exquisite, rushing warm over the lathering surfaces.

(Something about my ears. In the photo, that's what he's looking at. This morning, pressed close, nibbling. It's a thing.)

Towel around the head, flipping it back after squeezing and pressing it along the sides and into the scalp. Wrapping up in the other big one, still dripping.

—Hate to leave the tile steamy. Be sure to thank her. Ask her about her daughter's school, make a point of it. Better put that away somewhere.

(Want a photo? And he's like, "I don't have a camera, but if you want one." If you want one, that's adorable. Of course, I wanted one, that's what the polaroid was for. Take two Patrick. Surprised, grateful.)

—Why do they always want food at these things? It'll be late for lunch by then, won't it?

[Skin on skin. That's what I wanted. Needed.]

—Perfect. Exactly what the doctor asked for. Is that right?

[That's tomorrow, get through today first.]

"Ordered."

Nodding and looking at the mirror. Letting the big, draped towel fall and kicking it over toward the side. Taking the moisturizer from the cabinet: elbows and knees, shins and arms, all over. *To Darling Niki.*

"█████████████████ *a sex fiend*' singing with a sly grin and then a quick dip down up before setting aside the body lotion and taking out the other one.

[Industrialized strength day.]

—Need all the help I can get.

Squeezing some into the hand and rubbing it into the face and around the forehead and back toward the ears, fingering the lobes.

—Don't forget the throat. My poor throat could always use a kiss.

"Mi mi mi mi mi mi mi."

Applying the concealer under the eyes and by the mouth too.

(Never thought about it, how taste worked. If people didn't like something, you wouldn't see it, they wouldn't say anything. Rubbed me the wrong way, couldn't defend it, not good. There's no room for peccadillos. The money followed the least common denominator. The A&R guys, they knew what they're looking for, God bless you if you didn't fit.)

Setting the base across the entire face. Moving to it:

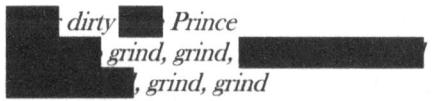

—Bad to the bone. You think it's your own, your most precious thing. These are the tile patterns I like. This is the perfect toilet. The color of the paint will help set the mood you'll need every day.

Darkish shadow today. Needs to work with that blouse. This one.

—They manufacture this stuff. The kinds of things you can get here aren't the same as what you get in Copenhagen or Stockholm. Different national tastes. It's not culture, different products from national brands, whatever industry here or there has to offer.

The liner and then some mascara. Full on eyes today.

—Oh, I love this song.

"Dig███████ *the picture / Of* █████████████ *a kiss"*

(Didn't hate pop music, that's not it at all, but if you couldn't do it this well, what's the point? He's a master, a genius with the beat and the lyrics, the whole vibe. The way he made us sweat and grind, feeling it with every groove and lull. What's the point of pop pop pop your bubblegum when there was this kind of stuff out there? What Michael was doing and Madonna. It's a joke, there's no reason to follow along behind them. They were totally on top of this, of these tastes, we're barely better than a one hit wonder. Hacks. There's no reason to keep at it, the marketers and the publicists, once they threw themselves behind you, anybody could have a career, but that didn't mean anything.)

—Not if it isn't good.

(Cute, a little doll, their little doll and they knew how to dress it and sell it. That worked fine when you're twenty-five, but how much longer could it last? How long would their magic keep working?)

—It's about the consumer. Con-su-me.

Adding a touch of blush to the high part of the cheek, making it clearer that there is a high part of the cheek. Kissing the air.

—They think they're making up their minds. Choosing this over that, but for real. It's what he was saying, or his friend was telling him, such a sad story.

(Can't imagine. Made the whole thing about teaching seem ridiculous. Listen to the wise old lady, such a silly fantasy. The boys are rubbing off on me. This woman who led you out of some dim darkness and taught you a thing or two about being a man and then she got hit by some idiot in a car who thought it's a deer or whatever they have there. Such a waste, so stupid.)

—Can't get that image out of my head. Was she trying to crawl? That's what he's sharing, that's the image he can't get past. Her fingernails in the soil, grabbing the sharp grass.

Shivering and then pulling the towel away from the head. Taking the comb and working it through, first on the left, then the right.

(They wanted to move, to dance or sing. People couldn't help that, that's how we are. No matter how bad it got, no matter what darkness came, we wanted to hold up our heads to sing and dance.)

—They take advantage.

"Don't cry █████████*"*

(Audience taste was cultivated. Open to singing and dancing, could be pushed toward lots of things. They made up our minds for us. As kids, we didn't know what we had to say, didn't know what kind of music we wanted. They helped us, steered us, formed us, and there was no way to resist. They made us look cool, dressed and styled in ways the kids immediately loved. It's a gimmick, it's craft.)

—Too young and dumb to know any better, and then once the young get their hooks into something, everyone comes along. Powerful attraction. Not the young, but those past it, desperate to hold on.

Plugging in the curling iron, then twisting and curling the brush, taking up the dryer to work the side and back, focusing on getting the tips right.

—Love this color.

[Shouldn't look too worked, but tasteful. Longer waves. Hopefully, still easy to get it that way.]

—Last night, skin. Touch. What I wanted. Flesh pressing.

"████████ *see you laughing /* ███ *purple rain* "

(Why wasn't that it then? Why didn't it matter much whether it went beyond? Because I wanted that too? But why? Why? If he did, I did. The bliss of giving him what he wanted, taking him in my mouth, feeling his movements, every one of them, pulse and impulse. That was it, but I'd never be that way for N now. Stopped long ago. Him too. No adjustments. Can't work that way, can't see each other that way anymore. Because he's so young, you'll do things you wouldn't... His youth... ...some kind of otherworldly effect. You wanted him to have that, what he wanted, if he wanted it, if it made it easier, because you could see him opening up to it. The effects are real and strong and like a flower blooming or something silly like that.)

—Is that how it works with music? How it sells, spreads.

Need more of a wave on that edge. Only a bit. Taking the curling iron and working it first on the left front and then the right. Wanting to get it right with the long waves.

—Older and older. There are people who come along for the ride. They want to live through young people, experience it the way they do, and they jump in and dance around, they buy the same clothes, and listen to the same music. They're trying to hold on, trying to keep that feeling....

[Floating in his mouth. Once he said it, I felt it.]

"█████████████████ *times are changing /* ████████████ ███████ *something new*"

(That meant the whole world filled with that. They made the taste for them, fed them what they thought they should have, and then the older friends and teachers got hip and came along. Tastes were reinforced and the wave came together.)

—Madness. Need to step off. Leave it aside. I'm sure. Glad I had... ...blessed, wouldn't trade it for... ...it's time.

"Ta da."

Turning back into the closet and over to the high dresser. Taking the commando medium nudes and stepping into them and beginning to pull, wiggling into place and centering the lace waist. Quick run check. Looks good. Up at the top, but doesn't matter. Need a strapless.

—Not the crowd you'd expect to notice, or they won't know they're noticing, but will. It would creep into their creepiness, make the worst of them. They catch sight of the strap, and their brains buckle into belly aches and wooty woos. Doesn't matter how old they are.

[Oh right, *Between the Buttons*. Forgot it was next. Such a classic.]

Bend to bop, what an opening. Waiting for it. Let the grind begin, launching into it with him, imagining his silky strut and the chin leading his head forward and back in perfect rhythm with skinny legs and narrow hips.

"█████████ *night together* / █████████ *more than ever*"

Some scent to the wrists then pressed together, a dab to the jugular, and a cloud walk through mist. Good with a twirl.

—I love this skirt. It's crisp. Sends the right signals. Intimidate the hell out of them. Have to remember that bit about the master and slave. Where does the essence lie?

Giggling and scrunching up the nose. "He would say the most nonsensical things with total gravity, as if it was the most serious thing in the world."

[Black and blue, that's how I'll leave them by the time we're done. Not the boys, they'll be darling I'm sure, but those robots, screw them. Guns are loaded, let's see what they got.]

Stepping into the shoes and then sliding the belt around, turning back toward the mirror, knee bending this way, a flip back bounce of the hair catching it in the mirror out on the periphery.

—Mwah. Perfect. Lips. Time for nails?

"Cassie?" shouting out while stepping back into the bathroom and moving toward the door.

—Don't like this one. Yesterday's news, honestly.

Opening the door to the bedroom and looking around. She gets up from the chair setting her magazine down on the table.

(She must've seen the polaroid.)

"Well don't you look lovely today."

She goes to the cabinet and turns the volume down. Curtsies after she turns back.

"You look absolutely stunning," she says.

"Do I have time for my nails? I'll do the bracelets and the watch. No rings today. Mom's necklace. Diamond studs. What do you think?"

"Sounds perfect. Nails might be tight. Let me... Which one?" she says moving back toward the couch and chair to set up.

Handing her the bottles, flipping the lipstick up and down rapidly in the other hand to get her approval, then sitting down diagonally from her.

"I cleaned up the table," she says, tastefully letting on that she knows what she knows.

"Did you have fun? Plenty of rest and relaxation?"

"It was fantastic. Such a beautiful place. The water. The men." She looks up and smiles. "How about you? Was it *relaxing* to be on your own this weekend?" Grinning cheerfully before looking down to concentrate on the polish and remover.

She seems to have everything the way she wants it. Extending a hand to let her get to work.

"It was lovely."

"Seems that we have a lot to talk about today." She's already applying the acetone. Her hands feel good, and she's massaging lightly as she wipes away the old and gets ready for the new.

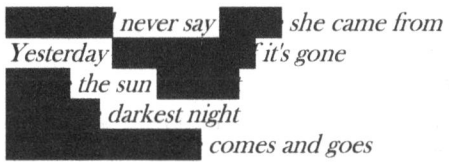

12.12.2.Seannafair.20.15.5.8 [ref(19.86.6.1)]

Sinking down into the tub and moving the tumbler down to the floor. The steamy warmth envelops her and everything is lighter. She can breathe again, her ears are open, her throat feels like she's twenty years younger.

[Not that I could use any kind of force anymore. Air through the throat doesn't work the same way now. Need to see a doctor before the boys get here.]

—E Michaels. It was E and I called him Em.

(No one ever called him that before. He was the alphabet. You could make yourself remember by singing the song from when we were children.)

In his arms and slowly stepping around and around each other. His arms wrapping around the waist and his shoulders, so broad.

"███████ *hu-uh huh*"

"What was it? What did you see? You've gone pale."

Eyes pretty in that light. Tall, but not too tall. Just right. Speaks softly under the music. Back and forth, around and around.

"███ *funny* ██ *it seems*"

"Someone who looked familiar."

"A friend? I didn't think you knew anyone here."

"I don't. It must've been my imagination. I have a guilty conscience."

"███ *in time,* ████████ *for dreams*"

"You look terrified. You're not scared of me, are you? I told you it's fine if you don't want to. We'll manage."

Pulls closer and lets the slow turning become a cuddle for a minute. His hand lightly lingers up and down the curve of the lower back. He smells of daylight and the air outside. He is the coming summer.

"Head over ███████ *toe to toe"*

"I'm supposed to go to Germany. I thought I saw the woman I'm supposed to go see. She's the sister of a friend of mine who died. She's expecting me. She was."

"You can call her if you have to. I'll clear out, if that's what it is. You should call her. It's not worth all this, right? You're grown, you can't be afraid of ghosts."

[Please be calm here with me. Please be here with me. This was the best of the times, better than anything. I want you here. Can't you let yourself be here with me? For this? Please.]

"██████████████*my soul"*

Quietly resting his head back, whispering now. Close up. His chin against the hair by the ear. His mouth moving slightly.

"You'll be fine. Big things happening for you. I'll be nothing to you before you know it. That grungy bugger who was passing through when everything happened."

"██████ *the sound"*

Lightly digging the head down lower against his neck and chest. Turning to rub against him and shaking side to side in resistance at the same time.

"Do you think there are people who don't fancy it much?"

"Your music? Some people don't appreciate the Beatles." He says it calmly, so reassuring. "Lots of people can't listen to Camarón. They think it sounds like howling."

"That's not what I mean."

"What then?" Always moving his hands, letting on that they are there and holding close.

"Sex. Are there people who don't fancy it? Don't ever want to have it, don't want nothing to do with it?"

"I bought ███████ *the world"*

"Sure. Depending on your experience. People like different kinds of things, things you could never imagine anyone would like. Why wouldn't some people not like it at all?"

"I never did, never before."

"██████████████ *back again"*

"With us?" He sounds scared, worried. His voice trembles, full of vulnerability. Hands go loose, isn't sure of his next move. The hesitation travels up and down his body into his feet. Along the nerves that run his entire length and it jumps over and swells inside. It's not possible to get close enough. Pulling him tight.

"Parts of it." Still not wanting to look up. It's easier to talk in the darkness, close by but not looking at each other. "That's why I don't want you to go. I never fancied it much and I don't think... ...you can't leave. Not now, we're only getting started."

"███████ hard ██████ next line?"

He pulls tighter. It flows through him, the way he understands it now. The floor is sticky with these short steps around, but it's not sticky enough. It can't hold anything for long. It slows it down, but nothing can stop something once it's decided to move.

(I don't remember anyone ever dancing here. Were there others? I didn't see anyone. It's only the two of us.)

"███████ truth ██ said"

"You're my good luck charm. Nothing good ever happened. School was for my mam. Didn't want it, and then those songs, that recording, and the man from the record company. When you go, that goes too."

Wiping tears on his soft shirt. Both his sleeves rolled up to the elbow and arms bare, with soft hair rubbing against the lower back and sides.

"███████ hu-uh huh"

—Poor arms, they do everything for the hands and get a bad rap. We forget to feel them, we forget to remember how lovely they are to be so kind, moving the hands and fingers wherever we want, providing the most comfort.

(Lita or Darlene wasn't anywhere nearby. I didn't see Mike or Rian. No one was there. Not the barmaid, the one who's always coming by to give you your drinks, always making sure you had enough.)

"███ this ██ is true"

"What we fancy has nothing to do with the thing of it. Taste comes in the cracks between."

Barely a dance. More like two people standing and cuddling. Those are the best songs.

[The ones where you could stand there with the perfect fella and time slowed down to a halt, or barely moved along, and you'd hold him and feel his breath and listen to his heartbeat.]

"Huh huh huh ██████ "

"That's not sex though, is it?"

"What's not sex?" he sounds confused.

—Has he been listening? Can he hear me?

"I know ██████ true"

"You said it could be whatever we wanted it to be."

He nods, trying to be agreeable.

"You said it's up to us, that we can do what we want and call it whatever we like and not bother with anyone else or what they have to do with it. You said as long as we're both together, then it's okay. Isn't that right?"

"███ thrill ████████████ my tongue"

"Yes."

—Thank God, he's back. Not one more moment alone.

"If you like something, there's nothing wrong with it if the two of you are together. If the two of you agree, isn't that right?"

"Dissolve ▪▪▪▪▪▪▪▪▪▪ *begun"*

"Yes."

"Dancing, that could be it then."

"Yes."

"Or a kiss, now and again. A look from across the room when we can't stand nearby."

"Listening to ▪▪▪ *all night* ▪▪ *"*

"That could be it too."

"Yes," he said.

Not only his hands. Such a flaw where focus lies. His feet picking up against the pull of the floor and the stale beer that wants to hold them there. His knees lightly moving forward and back touching against these knees moving forward and back. Not regular, but now and again. It's a surprise when they meet, and the feeling of it, its spark, it shoots all the way up and then all the way down again.

"▪▪▪▪▪▪▪▪▪ *my soul"*

"It's what you said about the ones who notice everything. About how they live in a completely different world than the ones who don't notice anything. Isn't that right?"

He nods and his chin touches against the head and his neck rubs against the forehead and cheek. It's scratchy and warm and nothing on this whole earth can stop these arms from stretching farther out and pulling him closer.

"▪▪ *the sound"*

"Yes."

"And what you think about, that can make it a whole different world too."

He nods with his hands this time. And his arms. And his knees. His hips too and his belly and his broad chest.

[You had to notice everything. His absence in the places where he wasn't touching, his presence in the places where he was, all of it. That's what it meant, that's what made this world a different world from the one anyone else was feeling. The one he was feeling over there was a mirror to this one here.]

"▪▪ *slipping* ▪▪ *my hands"*

"What's different though? You have arms and legs. Mostly. One of them. Back then. He was rather good looking, if I'm honest."

No reaction. The darkness keeps holding the song. It keeps the twirling in line, it holds the lines, the movement round and round like those circles in the hay that the aliens make.

"███████ *time* ███████ "

"How could something that small make such a huge difference?"

(His mouth has been swallowed by the darkness. He couldn't speak anymore, but he held on for dear life. He knew I'd have it in place for him, that I'd take care of it.)

"It's what I'm thinking. The whole world is different because there's a 'no' where there was a 'yes.' Or a 'yes' where there was a 'no.' Don't you see?"

"*Take* ███████████████ *the next line*"

(But he couldn't see because the darkness had taken his eyes. It's greedy and couldn't get enough. It'd take the difference between yes and no if we let it. It'd take the difference between him and the others if no one stopped it. And who had the sense to try? Who could find their way around when it's nearby?)

—The good and the bad, they blend after a while. Men. And that's me, if I go against, I'm their shadow.

"███████ *the truth* ███ *known*"

"Are you listening to me?"

There's no answer.

And then it's my darling Caroline. She holds close. Looking softly at her mother same as she did back when she was wee, but she's not wee anymore. Her arms and her legs. She's not supposed to be here.

"They'll toss you from the pub, dear. What will they think of me when everything is said and done?"

"*Huh huh huh* ███████ "

(But the darkness had her already. She couldn't say more than that. She couldn't let on or they'd take her away.)

"What will you remember, my darling?"

Now she's gone, set back into it with nothing left. A suit.

"Is that George then? You've come to explain?"

—Charles.

"███████ *much is true*"

But nothing comes of that. Only the darkness. And more of it. It's a whole round of them.

(In them days, they had their dance cards and each in turn would claim the first and the second. The last. They'd plead for a spot with the good ones. Some would never ask. But it would come around like that.)

"Yes."

(There's Mike and Rian. Of course, why wouldn't they take a turn. True to the end. The last of them, when, with no throat to speak of, I was only whispering with the microphone turned up as loud as it could go to make those whispers sound like something that could've been a hit once. Years and years of that so they should come too.)

"Huh huh huh ██████ */ I know this* ██████ *true"*

(But he's the one I wanted back. They're not his girls. I was never his girl. If it was only six minutes. If it was only a single song and a single night and a single sway and dip. Only that. I wanted it back and I'd choke the darkness to get it, reach in there and pull it free because that's what yes means, it means it is mine, it means no one can take it, let alone the darkness.)

"I bought ██████ *the world"*

"My Margaret, of course you can have one too."

(She had no mouth. Not yet. Later it'd come and she'd be all the birds.)

"Listen to your sister. She'll take care of you. And your dad. You have a beautiful family. His ma. Plenty to hold you safe from the darkness for a while. It can only be a while. No one gets to run from it forever. No songs, no dances, none of that can save you."

"But ██████ *back again"*

Then he's back for the last few minutes. No more hands.

(I understood)

No more arms and knees.

(I understood)

There isn't enough for any of that. None of the yeses can get through. There aren't enough of them. They can't call out when there is so much dropping down around them. They can't have their say.

"If you could say one last thing, what would it be?"

"Why ██████████████ *the next line?"*

It may be that there are no more arms and legs, and nothing left to hold on to, nothing left to pull against that sticky floor.

(God, I miss that floor.)

The slightest pull is everything, it's what keeps everything here. With the turning and the tugging, it's the sticky floor that holds it in place.

(Who was that bloke? Couldn't remember, but he only needed one fixed point and with it he could move the whole damn world.)

But he's got nothing to say. Or he can't. It's only darkness now and nothing from this world can put its 'yes' above the 'no' that the darkness holds tightly. "Please, can't you find it in you somewhere? Just one more word."

" ██ *want the truth* ██████ *"*

Agape and filling with sound, the wailing comes from a part of her throat that she doesn't think works anymore. It settles low and long on the air blowing across the room and drowning out every other sound.

"Seannafair." From the wind, or somewhere underneath it. It's exactly like him, but without any of the light. He never says it, not once. "Seannafair," again and the lilt of it is a Saturday morning. Heavenly.

12.12.3.Natalie.19.86.9.22 [ref(..14-22)]

He closes the door, steps over the rail, and heads down the embankment. At the bottom, there is a ramp leading onto the road up toward Nürnberg. Trying not to look for too long, better to pull away and leave it at that.

(Goodbye El. For real. Won't call. Don't know where to call. She sounded nice. In better times.)

Veering off onto the road past the interchange, heading toward Heidelberg. *Like a Prayer* comes on and fills every corner of the cockpit with its assault. Fumbling for something else, anything else, to take its place.

—*Sledgehammer*, no fucking thank you.

Pressing the button. *Running up that Hill.*

—Better. Whatever.

Looking down at the console, not wanting to dig through that mess yet.

(The story about the Italian was haunting. He gave up his cushy life to start his own business thinking it's exactly what he'd always wanted. It's true passion and he's going to make a living with it. Dream come true, what more could anyone hope for? And then he's fucking miserable because all day everyday the headaches that come with anything you do all the time, well, they come. Only now, they're headaches caused by this thing you thought you loved.)

—It'd be devastating. Anything better in the glovebox?

(Is that what's ahead? No more men. That much is certain. But in practice? No side dishes, no main dishes. He got so angry, as if I owed him a reason. What did I do? What's changed?)

—I got used to living without you, that's what's changed. You can't say that. What good would it do? They say they want you to be your own person as long as it includes them. Forget what attracted them in the first place.

(What? You're comparing a forty-year-old man to a twenty-two-year-old? Can't do that, you can't expect him to have the same view of everything, can't expect him to let things slide and move on once that little bit of magic is gone. Wasn't looking for experience. Wanted a life. Expected you to want one too.)

—Oh, God no, that is not what friends are for.

Hitting the button. Again. Looking down for only half a second then back to the road. *West End Girls.*

(Okay. There's a type. If you lived in one place, you'd share the same things. It's the club. The way we dressed, the way we acted, the way we

laughed at your stupid fucking jokes. Of course, you could box that up into
a neat package and say no more about it. It's what everyone expected. It's
what you're looking for while you're trying hard to fit in. What is fitting in
anyway if it isn't figuring out how to be, how you are?)

—What did he leave in that bag?

Reaching over and pulling it sideways on the passenger seat. Digging in
with one hand, keeping the eyes on the road.

(Which would you prefer in the end? Hold me while I'm trembling or
come in my mouth?)

—Right answer. Rolls.

Pulling one out to get a good look. A cassette falls out of the bag.

—Nice. Okay. As promised. Glad he wasn't upset. 99% sure he was
done with it. With... Saw him reading Emerson... Moved on... Wasn't
thinking about... ...Tolstoy.

Deep snuffle and then a few short sniffs.

[It's how he is. What's he thinking about now? Trying to get a ride. Get
back to his stiff friend who didn't know what to say to him. He had no idea
what to say either. Can't imagine what she's going through. No wonder he's
anxious. Not thinking about me anymore. Not a single thought in his head.
Tomorrow, something reminds him, but only for a split second. A month
there, a week here. Doesn't matter. They moved on so easily. Because
they're experiences, not a life, they're not trying to make a life.]

—If you can call it that. I'm done. He doesn't realize how these things
add up to so much bullshit. Karl too. It's invisible to them, or they expect
it. The surrender. Surrendering. Comes with middle age. Being pliable is
woman's work.

(When he took hold. No wait. Before that. He slinked back and actively
pushed my legs together. It's a deliberate act. Not rough or violent but play
rough and play violent. Deliberately feigning pseudo-violence. Legs pushed
together. Abrupt. Sometimes, the more abrupt, the better. Shock of
movement, being moved that way. Delightful. The surprise. Then the
hands... ...hooking into place. Those curves at the base of the ass... Bone.
Welcoming slope. A smooth, barely notched surface for folding skin.
Trembling it is.)

—No! When the going gets tough, the tough change the fucking station.
Fuck this.

Popping it in and letting auto play take over. The creaky strangeness
launches right away. It's the *Candyman*. Offering a sickly sweetness, fooling
everyone into wanting what he's offering. He is, after all, a candy man.

[He knows me.]

—We're the ones who know that others are the horrors of the world,
that's where risk lies, where the threat comes from. Think about that one
single act. Focus on it clearly. Don't let anything else enter the picture or

cloud the judgment.

(Above me, his hands hooked into the slope of the lower back. That's what it became for him after pushing the legs down flat after sliding back to make room. What's he doing? I knew exactly what he was doing. The thrill hinged on it, it's about to take over, pleasure is about to fill the moment. Had the twist down pat. How do they learn that? Where did they get it from? The right side pulled up, the left side pushed down on the hip and we're twisting. My pelvis and his arms, they formed this twisting thing with only one purpose: to produce pleasure, to draw out anticipation for what was coming. After the first time, you knew what to expect. You learned the signs. With the first boy, or the second. It happened so fast. A perfect choreography.)

"█ danger █ hands"

—Is that it? Is it danger? The possibility? The thrill. Playing at it.

(In that moment, there was force. He was acting. Pulling and pushing in one and the same motion, but not only that. Nothing is ever one thing. Remember that. If I resisted. If I tried to prevent him, something would break or tear or bruise. Something painful. The whole thing would come to an abrupt halt. Didn't happen. I knew where it was headed and wanted to get there, wanted that sudden twist, to help him do it. By not interrupting, by leaning into it, by bending into place, imagine if I resisted with my arms or tried to steady myself against the mattress. He couldn't do it as gracefully. It would have to become real, violent, and that would change everything. The entire pretense, the playfulness, completely depends on complicity, on leaning into it.)

"█ pity █ / ██████████ unspeakable things"

"I know what's coming."

(Those handles at the front of the hip, those grooved areas, only now it's pure pull. He grabbed and lifted and pulled in one single motion. It was heavenly. Sliding back up onto my knees, being pulled back against him. Elongating the arms, leaning and stretching against the firm mattress, the angles were everything, they teased out the moment, bringing us together, and again, it wasn't pure resistance, there's a connection. It's calibrated motion and we've both practiced it.)

"Now tie it back to *Marine Lover.*"

—It's not only practice. It's theory too.

(His poetry got her, the way he lulled and lured. That crass and wicked wit. That insight and motion. It drew them in together and she was in love. She felt the pull of it and lingered over that, twisted along with him, leaned back into him, let him enter her, all because she loved it, adored it, knew what lay in it. But he was crude, he sparked at times, couldn't be contained, couldn't let the play lay there on its own. He brought a whip.)

"██████████ blame █ Candyman"

(We were there together. Dancing the same step, leaders and followers complying with the ranges of preordained movement. He was her abusive lover, and she felt the pleasures of it, had grown used to them, yearned for them, she was twisted by that pulling and that pushing. And truth be told, he was twisted too, in his twisting he learned to love it the same. Didn't feel anything other than the pleasure of it. It wasn't pure, wasn't simple, it came with a price. No, it came at a cost.)

—Has she always been this good? Why haven't I noticed it before?

"▮▮▮ *tender* ▮▮▮ / ▮▮▮▮▮▮ *lament*"

"It's not only practice. It's not only theory. Style too."

(Sarazen didn't understand, still thought in categories, wanted everything in a box. She thought if she didn't sleep with them, she would elude the lure, but she helped with the twisting. Eased back onto her knees the same way. And that's because the references were in place. The voices came from where they've always come. The priest of Königsberg taught us how to write and we passionately followed his lead. Reference the master with a citation to Wolff. Extract everything that smelled like a real person, speak as if there were no space or time when describing the pure intuition of space and time. The imagination and its artwork must be conditioned by no one in particular.)

—Not when grappling with the *Marine Lover.* Not when taking him down. Going down on him. Style must be addressed, it is the basis of his seduction, his erection. It's why she can't put it down, why she overlooks the whip. It's why he speaks so confidently to her. His stylus lies upon her.

"*Wanting you,* ▮▮▮▮▮▮ *weaved*"

(When did he account for his pleasures? When did he answer for them? Martin, horrified at the mere mention of it, wanted to know if that's how I wanted it to end. Were those the last words you wanted to speak to me? But you have to answer first! It couldn't only be sensation. Why wasn't the friction enough? What did you get from the dribbling and spurting, from the sight of it? What could that possibly feel like to you? And me. Not trying to find someone to blame. It wasn't just you, I wanted it too, but at least for me it had a feeling, the reason in it prickled my skin. There's something meaningful there, a smell, a taste. What could that possibly mean to you? In my mouth, but on my mouth, why? Where did the pleasure come from? And why were you furious at the simple suggestion that we speak of it?)

"*Enchantment* ▮▮▮▮▮▮ / ▮▮▮ *the sweetest chill*"

—Reading to him taught this, didn't it? The sense changes in the clear presence of the act. Not my pleasure alone, but his changes too.

[The groove in the bone presented a silence and then it was immediately filled by forces and their spirits.]

The music, not merely a backdrop, angles from the speaker to the frame and post, to the edge and the roots.

"██████ beats █ my breath"

"Ahhhhhhhhhhhhh" Screaming in the end of it, at the end of it. "Such a lull, can't she break it harder on the mast?"

(Was he my hostage? What did I have to account for? I demanded the number. Six? Fine. And in Europe? Those ages were too specific. On your travels, what have you known? Who? Am I your first whore? The first to reel you in. Reeling. Really? No wolfing around, he said he never touched that girl from the Arctic Circle though she wanted him to. He said he couldn't, said she was broken...)

—Does that mean...?

"████████████ cuts / ██████ tumorous flesh"

Screaming along with it: "This ████ beats █ my breath..."

(Why did it matter? Was that the hips leaning into the twist? Anticipating what was coming? I demand you tell me everything. Truth is, he said, you've opened my eyes. Not a biological function, or an emotional one. If she didn't, everything would go out of whack. The way the morning came, and she needed her coffee and breakfast roll with some cheese. Not some higher order, not some beautiful aesthetic that's handed to you. But what have I taught him? The symmetry of desire? What kind of idiot needs to learn that? Is it me alone or packed with legion? He was right, it is born of habit, and this higher realm, this thing sought in liberty, only a ruse. It hid inside us, forever searching for the G-spot, giving out a place to find the way and things wanted, handing it over free of charge and naming it liberation.)

"███████████ watch unimpressed"

"This could come together, this could be something."

"████ laugh at me"

(I don't care. Let them. What was a degree but a sign of approval from their monastic order? How many layers of lies were heaped on top of everything I know by degrees? Swallowing it and begging for more. The oven. Degrees. Turning in an arc. Degrees. We inflected, we let their pain win, we forgot who we were. They were a marine lover, the wicked, they were the paint and the lure, a dance around the fire.)

—But I don't have to play along, go along, with this rough play.

"You're ███████ old again"

(To his credit, they sounded like fierce, passionate beings. That says something. Or that the threat was deferred. At some moment, there had to be something given. Among the strongest, if she was so cursed as to love the phallus, her pleasure would build as her hips yielded to his twisting hands.)

—Check the physical position of the spine at the moment of orgasm. That could be the thesis of a study that blows the mythology to bits.

"█████ angels shout, ████████ doubt"

(Holding *him* while *he* shudders. Arms around his neck and upper back. But with him. Or with me. His hands on me as I lurched upward, leaving off with the reading and letting the pure sensation of his mouth and measure take over. Where were the tailbones as these undulations began? Where was the neck and how was it arching this way and that? How had our world molded the flesh to that bone? Who would sign on for that Habilitation?)

—None of them. They're cowards. Not a single fucking one of them would touch it. Or let it touch them.

(If it were to present the facts of what was always touching itself and how it felt to be that, without any anchoring in some long-poled other, ready at a moment's notice to spread its seed over the surfaces that yield meaning in their twists and turns.)

"████████ new favours ██████████ / █████ this captive frame"

—Excellent choices. Something different at the end.

Nodding to the rhythms and forcefully banging both hands against the steering wheel which does not bend beneath the blows.

"Fuck yes. Return to me my life in your head. Fuck yes."

Another fire leaps nightly
Babes born dying

12.12.4.Greta.19.86.9.30 [ref(..9.5-30)]

"The duende does not repeat himself, any more than do the forms of the sea during a squall." [Garcia Lorca]

Whispering it while watching the train pull out. Wrapping arms more tightly to pull the cardigan closer. The flipping board switches, and Wien disappears from view in favor of the 1:15 for Zürich. Turning and walking back toward the entrance.

—I'll walk, it didn't seem that far.

Passing by the information desk and taking a map of the city. Asking the woman for help in plotting a course back to the Alpen Hotel. She draws on the map with a big green marker. Up the street in front and then to the right. A few twists and turns but looks pretty simple.

"Thank you."

"You're welcome. Goodbye," she says.

—Why did I say that? I can't ever remember telling anyone I would pray for them.

(Such an answer, an unusual character. "You can't pray for anything,

not according to the rules they've set down. It's begging and ridiculous."
He said they talk a lot of nonsense and the only thing that did make sense
was if you said, "My heart is troubled, Lord. Show me the way." Anything
else was presumptuous, pretending to know the mysteries, and they're
always saying how you can't know the mysteries.)

—I don't believe it, so why did I say it?

The sun rises higher and it's warming up. The colors are brilliant, and
the light gleaming on the red and golden trees in this lovely valley leaves
signs of hope. Turning up the road and heading toward the end of the
tracks where the street goes to the right and back over the Sill toward that
part of the city. Looking down at the map briefly.

*Two men a bit older walk past on their way to the Hauptbahnhof, they
look sideways in sync when passing, their eyes following along hopefully.*

—My heart is troubled, Lord. Show me the way.

Markings on the map say to veer to the right and not take the shortcut
over the river. The bus passes by on its way, and the smell of diesel flares
out across the road.

(For someone who said he isn't religious, he ended up talking about
religious topics a lot. The bone carried the essence. Of course, he denied
that had anything to do with religion. It's a purely rational view of the world.
Science. But what does reason know of essences? Doesn't that take you
into nether regions? Into some higher place where things go beyond the
human, and make some kind of sense there beyond us, beyond our
control. He said that was nature, and only our smallness led us to confuse
it with religion. Hopefully, he'll find what he's looking for in the cornfields
of Eeleenoy.)

—After the master, the slave, that's a self-consciousness thing, but then
there's reason. The bone is the essence. Master-slave connects each to the
other, but the bones connect the whole of nature, the whole world.

(Laughing and teasing him. I'll miss that. The way he talked from inside
me. The bone, huh? Something to agree with there. He joked about it.
Didn't take the teasing seriously, didn't feel foolish. "I do lean toward
phrenology." Such a funny voice. Imitating her imitating a serious person.
In flagrante delicto.)

—I'll miss him. My heart is troubled, Lord. Show me the way.

A tear appears then, as the road comes to a cross. Having to angle right
to go over the river. Dreiheiligenstraße. The Sill flows to the northeast
toward the Inn.

*The one nudges the other and points over with a finger and a head bob.
They are watching the flow and then the passers-by bring inspiration. They
claim appreciation for the sublime. Would they whistle, the waters might
go still.*

(Will it go back to the way it was, or have I moved along? His explanations for everything were always different than expected. Of course, you can't take the book, it's too big to carry. Well not only that, it's too heavy in other ways. What does that mean? Only that, you see, it's Kafka and there's this whole thing. You're supposed to burn it. There are stories in there that Max was supposed to burn, but he didn't. He kept them and published them even though he said not to. But they don't think he was serious because, after all, his life and work were so filled with humor that he obviously wasn't serious with his final instructions. That's sarcasm, he said. Might've been serious, might not be. Either way, it's too much to bear.)

—Nothing is simple. It can't be, oh there's not enough room in the bag. No, it has to be this whole big thing about Kafka and burning everything.

(Heidi was the same way. Nothing was ever simply I don't feel like it, or I'm busy that day. It was always a big explanation of why her heart wasn't in it, why she couldn't see him or her or them that day in that way: I can't go there for dinner, they're going to be talking about their business ventures and it's going to drive me crazy because I'll have to point out that their success is based on the suffering of other people, and then they'll think I'm trying to tear them down, but I'm not, I don't understand how you can be oblivious to the carnage and collateral damage caused by your actions.)

The tan plaster walls of the middle school are on the right. No one outside running around, but there are signs that the building is full: the flag, the windows, cars nearby. Pradl now.

Not having anything to do, they walk up and down the street from beyond and then back again. Is she from around here, they wonder as they head off in the direction of the shopping mall to find a deal or fill some gap in their possessions that they've been considering for weeks.

—Is this the first week?

(Something about last night reminded me of her too. That first thing he tried to play. It sounded fine, but he kept starting and stopping. Then he would meander and stop again. Finally, he played something completely different, and the thing is that this new thing seemed much harder than the first thing and yet he played it easily. Can't remember the names, but he said one was free and the other was rigid. Something about the beat and count of each measure being strict, but in the first one it's more open, you can play with things, but you have to keep to the vibe. Less structured, and that's harder to maintain. The rigid rhythm, it's more complicated, had rules, and you always knew where you were and what came next. The other people were blown away. That guy said he never heard anything like it. I'll have to look it up, the style. Deep Song, I remember that much, that's the structured one. The other one had a Spanish name.)

—That fit her to a tee, so at ease with structure and form and rigid rules for how things had to be done, but so flustered and confused by free play.

(She hated to socialize, people getting together to hang out or talk or have a drink or whatever. Preferred to go to a movie or a concert. Listening to music in the park. More comfortable with those occasions, she knew what the rules were and could turn to them whenever she had to. Something she said about taste touched him and worked as a bond with someone else. Didn't only love it, was it. Identity. She was that way, could dig into your thoughts and find a place there, become a part of you when you were with others later on, teach you how to connect.)

—My heart is troubled, Lord. Show me the way.

This is easy, but much longer. The instructions assume she's an idiot. Up to the big street there and then right again and follow it all the way down toward the autobahn. The hotel is on the left before you get there. Can't go too far. If you walk through the streets, it's faster, but not as clear.

Now the gymnasium is on the right, and another official state-looking building. No loud loitering in the yard nearby, but the place seems full, and the kids are back to school here too.

They should be in class, across the way, lingering out of reach, and beyond the yard's horizon. Their laugh may not signal anything, but immersed in it, the discomfort grows without registering its source. Neck craning, cigarettes bobbing as they toss the ash into the street, the passer-by with the light hiking boots is what it takes to train their gaze and foster their next joke.

—Directions and direction, it's the same. Did that organization give her the structure she loved? The law too.

(Everyone always thought she was so earthy and chill, a big hippy because of the way she dressed and talked, but she was organized, everything about her completely based on concern for a higher order and it bothered her when they took exception. The world was a set of rules that the rich could ignore to exploit everyone else by making them stick to the plan while they danced around it. That caused the suffering.)

—Something's missing... ...left out... ...Fandangos, that was the word: libre. My heart is troubled, Lord. Show me the way.

(He had to catch the plane to Athens but didn't say why he was going there. To get away? Was that enough? He told them last night he was going to Spain. After Athens? He promised to write, promised he would. I'll ask why he had to go. It was hard, I think, harder than he was willing to admit.)

—It's in the bones.

Up Andechsstraße with the shops and places to eat. There are more people here, running about, in their work clothes, dressed up, or with their children in tow, doing what needs to be done. It's almost lunch time.

He sweeps the walkway and waits for her to pass, rubbing his neck and chin. The air is boisterous, the traffic sees to it.

(I never did get a satisfying answer to the question. You couldn't ask, and no amount of hinting was going to get someone to talk if it's painful. But the bones, they must've been the same, right? I never thought about it. At the hip, at the shoulder, at the elbow and wrist. These bones must've been identical. No superficial variations would have fooled him for long. We shouldn't have, but if we hadn't, would he have been able to say as much as he did, give so many details and venture down those many paths? Not right after, but before, because we were headed there right from the beginning. He couldn't tell those stories to just anyone, they were too much... Needed a bridge, and it was made of bone and muscle.)

—Thirteen or fourteen, that's how old we were, that's when we sat in our room running our hands against each other's backs and legs, torsos and pelvis.

(We knew we were mirrors of each other. We knew we could touch ourselves as someone else would if we touched each other. Her leg was my leg, exactly the same. Her back, her shoulder, everything, every part of it. The hair was different, with this color that I hated, and if you pretended to find yourself in that, the bone would bring you back, the bone would set you straight.)

—The people who play that folk music in Greece, he talked about them, said they were like the Gitanos of Spain. The music was the same, the structure of their sadness, the rhythm of their pain. It was as though it traveled along the Mediterranean to be picked up at multiple points.

Smells in the air, the street side carts and their sausages with rolls and mustard. There are a few slowing to look at the sides and signs. For those who were up early on this weekday, they're feeling the hour in their growling bellies.

(Not pity, but a song on the air that taught everyone what could be, what had been. Flamenco in Spain, something else in Greece. The man from last night asked something about the movement, the Romani. Were they the same people spread out across various lands? No one knew, they only knew the sadness was the same. Hear my pain. That's how that one song worked. The singing was the actual pain given a voice and sent out into the air. Inside you, in your ears, in your heart and soul, the resonance wasn't a representation, it was the actual feeling. The music carried it from one soul to the other, across the air and into them, into their wilderness, into their hope, into all of them, making it something shared. The more they hurt, the more they sang, the more they suffered, the more they danced.)

—My heart is troubled, Lord. Show me the way.

Many bus stops at this multi-street intersection and then a park on the right where a few people are sitting alone on benches and eating.

Someone is speaking too loudly and it may be directed at her, but she is not there for them, and the urban bounce can't break the fray of each step where footfalls measure the truss of night and its sturdiness in this noisy day.

—I'll have to hurry and pack, they may charge a late fee.

(Asked if I minded driving back alone. Said he would come with and go to Wien from there if it was too hard. He could change his ticket. Better this way. The whole drive back I'll get used to it again.)

—No sense delaying the inevitable. Take the book though. Burn it at some point if that's what it comes to.

[She would like that. His family's way, how they say it at the time and on the anniversaries.]

"May her memory be a blessing."

(Not that you'd remember her, but that she'd remain a song in your heart. It's the hauntings of a ghost, as if she remained present no matter what. You didn't move on, you could never move on, there's no such thing as forgetting where the bones were concerned. You couldn't let that go, but it didn't have to drag you down, it didn't have to be a weight too heavy to carry, it could be lightness itself. It could be the air between that carried the song, it could be that. The song gave the pain a structure, it gave it a balance and an easy way to pass it along, from parent to child, from sister to sister.)

—He said he would come for Christmas in twenty years. Both of our families, he was certain we would have them, and we would get together and drink to her as if she were the catalyst that brought us together.

The pedestrian zone thins out and the tourists from the hotel near the end of the road take over. They look on in ways that register as if their power of sight permits them to own whatever they see. The vision they tear from each passing form is the work of their angels and the geometry that inspires them.

(It was something about one for the road. You have one last drink in honor of the one who has to go, who is leaving, the one left out. It was something they would do at the tavern or at Gabriel's store when they met up in the afternoon. I have to go, someone would say, because there was so much to do, and they would fill their glasses and lift them. El arranca, that's what they would say, a toast to the one departing.)

—My heart is troubled, Lord. Show me the way.

[In twenty years, so much will have gone, but her ghost will still be here, haunting us both. It has to be, it's in the bones. I'll see her older in me. Blessing every one of them. Holding closely to the blood and sinew, holding it together. Not with the stomach, but with the bones, that's the right way to remember. Dialectic inverted.]

Crossing over the big street and heading to the Alphotel, large and grand with ample parking and easy access to the autobahn and the way back home.

[Eva's anger was a blessing meant to protect her. Meant for me to hear, to inspire me, drive me to it, to look after her, fetch her from whatever darkness comes. Eva and me. Still together, there's still time for us.]

Empty of traffic and yet there are one or two who would remind her. The little one, with her sweet ringlets, blinks heavily as she sways her way across. "Not here," she says. "Over there," she points.

Pulling the cardigan tighter. "El arranca, sweetheart," offering the only thing left in memory, and it leaves the girl much concerned as she puts her hand into her mouth.

4.8
the middle american

4.8.1.X.19.86.11.1 [ref(..15-31)]

No one cares what I think. I'm an alien. Well, if I were an alien, everyone would care what I think. I'm the opposite of an alien. I'm anybody. Sabina looked at me as if I was anybody, and she didn't want to listen to a damn thing from anybody.

It took forever. Thought she'd never leave. I kept wanting to say it's 4:30, Birgit, don't you need to be at the desk by 5? She was slow, but finally she left, and I got everything together, stuffed it in my bag, made sure it was still cool with Frithjof, and then got the hell out of there. It's been crazy the last two weeks. Called Eve's place all the time, almost every day. Eve or Elke would pick up. Always accepted the charges. There was some schedule to it, but never figured it out, and never told them the truth. They kept asking why not leave and go back to the hostel. Tell them on the way. Don't want to, but, at this point, have to.

After the phone problem, things changed. I wasn't the tool for drama anymore, I was the drama. Nothing steady, nothing reliable, never knew what was going to happen next. She would scream at me. About nothing. Or what I considered nothing. I was trying to get to know her, asking questions, what happened in America and where she grew up. She was from Graz. But why did I care? She wasn't going back there, never wanted to return.

"What about your mother and father? Where are they, do they still live in Graz?"

"What does it fucking matter where my parents are? This has nothing to do with them."

But screaming. The question was only a question. I wanted to find out about her, wanted to know, so I snooped around and looked through her things. There were some letters. There was a notebook and a weird calendar planner thing with all kinds of notes and stuff in it. Drawings and doodles. Dear B. All kinds of stuff. The penmanship was appalling, so it was hard to read, but some could be deciphered. She had a younger sister who wrote to her. Their mother died. The father was absentee, not engaged. He wasn't the problem, but somebody was. The sister was having the same problem, begged for help, and I wanted to know if Birgit was doing anything. The sister wanted to run away to America too, and wanted to know how to do it, where to find information for the program. Did she give her that?

"Have you been looking through my things?"

"What are you talking about?"

"The stuff in that drawer, it's been moved around. Someone's been in there. No one else would."

"I wanted to know you. You never told me you had a sister. She needed help. Did you help her?"

"That's none of your fucking business."

Door slam, stomp stomp stomp. Screaming from the other side of the apartment. "That is none of your fucking business, you psycho stalker asshole."

Then later.

"Should I leave?"

"Why?"

Total confusion, it's as if nothing happened. At the time, it's the worst thing ever, the biggest betrayal imaginable, but then nothing, back to the routine.

Before that, we were at the active part this one time, and I spanked her. She liked it and made that clear. In fact, she wanted me to do it harder, had to coax me because I didn't want to. By coax, I don't mean she had to talk me into it or anything, it wasn't that way. We weren't talking about anything during, but she showed pleasure overtly, in the extreme, loud. I'm sure the whole apartment could hear us, and that's part of what was driving the roommates nuts. We'd be making noise at all hours of the day and night, and it must've woken them up or caused some embarrassing moments if they had someone over. She didn't care.

She had a peculiar preference. Again, never explained this, showed it. My hand had to land the right way. She wanted most of my palm to hit her square in the lower butt with the fingers barely contacting her, well, her labia. That's what she liked, but she wanted the slap of the fingers to be hard, there needed to be force. It wasn't a spanking like normal, same as lots of girls liked, there were specific rules, and my hand wasn't able to keep up, or got tired, couldn't work up the necessary force, so I got the idea to use my belt. Had this worn-out leather belt that I wore all the time. Needed it to keep my pants up, it wasn't a prop, but she liked it, playing with it sometimes. That's how she'd let me know.

I had to hit her the same way with the belt as with my hand. The brunt of the force would have to land on the part of her butt that was closest to her leg. I'm right-handed so it was usually her left cheek. She integrated this into the beginning of the routine. We discovered it as part of the end, but she wanted it to be part of the beginning. While she's bent over me, she'd stick her butt up off to the side and I'd use my belt to slap her, over and over again. The flesh would turn red and get sensitive. Then she wanted me to stop and ever so lightly tickle and rub. It got mechanical. She'd lose interest in what she was doing at some point and focus on the weird pleasures and pains she was getting from it. Mostly though, she'd get loud, extremely loud.

Then, afterward, the roommates, whoever was home, would say something to her, and that'd set her off yelling. It seemed as though she was taking more than just the arguments out on me. She was getting her revenge for the spanking too. She needed to live out some drama where I did something, and she was getting even for it. I honestly didn't understand it, but it was part of the routine, and she's yelling at me more and more.

That's why I kept calling Eve's place and talking to them. I said more to Elke than Eve. She seemed less judgmental somehow. That was my imagination. Didn't give details, not to either of them, but did let them know we were sleeping together. It would have been impossible to get anything across, to explain anything, if I didn't say that. Eve thought it made sense that she was reacting to that, that there was something wrong and she needed to express that somehow by getting angry or shouting. It must've been a catharsis to include her roommates in the drama. Didn't go into detail about how loud she was, but let them know the walls were thin, and the roommates could hear things. Made it seem as though it was mostly the shouting. They could hear that but didn't want to get into the rest of it.

One night, after she got home. This was a few days ago. I had been writing in my notebook and had a pretty good conversation with Elke that day. She urged me to open up and try to be patient and listen. I couldn't tell her, so I said I'd try.

"Can we talk about what this means to you?"

"What? I just got home from work. Can't it wait?"

"I don't think it can. It seems you want this. You don't want to talk to me, you won't tell me anything about your life or what you've gone through. You hate it when I look through your stuff, but it causes drama that you need to have. You didn't throw me out, instead you enjoy screaming about it and holding it over my head. You want me to use the belt, but then it does weird stuff to your head, and you get freaked out afterward."

I blurted it out. Not one coherent word in response though. Not one. There was a response, but no words in it. She was howling at me or something, asking the question was the worst thing I could do. I was betraying her by thinking these things. Again, no words, but that's how the outburst made me feel. She threw something at me, a thick glass ashtray. It hit my leg and I'm still limping a little. If we'd been standing closer to each other, I'm pretty sure she would have hit me, but she was on the completely other side of the room and was trying to get farther away.

It may have been the pain, or the violence of the reaction, or the fact that nothing was intelligible. She was only communicating a loud and clear negative. No sense to it, merely a simplified rejection of the effort to find out. Something about that response made me bawl. I couldn't help it. It's not something I can remember doing anytime recently, not since I was a kid, but there I was standing next to the door and sobbing like a baby.

What did she do? The obvious thing, of course. She fell to the floor, curled up in a ball, and sobbed too. Loud and wailing sobs, screaming for her Mommy. That was the first word that made sense since my question. "Mommy!" sob sob sob "Mommy!" If this was her tactic for getting me to stop crying, it worked better than anything else would have. My mouth must've fallen open to the floor. My stomach was churning, my brain was churning. Everything was upside down and I felt panic rising from the pain in my leg up through my midsection and toward the throat.

It rooted me in place, couldn't open the door, couldn't go over to her, and had no idea what to do. What did she want me to do? What did I want to do? There was no her and me at that moment, there was only panic and the burning in my throat that came from my leg.

And then, what do you think? She gets up off the floor and sits down on the edge of the bed facing away from me. She swings her arm to indicate I should come over. In my panic, I felt desperate for anything meaningful. It was as though I was in a vacuum and wanted something of substance to appear. That gesture, which I'd seen before, made perfect sense. She wanted me to come over. In the past, it usually meant the worst was over and she was calming down. I went over there. Walked around to that side of the bed and was about to sit down next to her. I had the vague passing thought that I'd put my arms around her, give her a hug or at least let her know I was nearby, but she stopped me from sitting and pulled me around to stand in front of her. She undid my belt and launched into the routine.

Everything inside me was screaming no. All I could think was no, and I knew there was no way in hell anything could happen. I was as uninterested in what she was doing as I could possibly be, or so I thought. It seemed my body had a different idea about it, and there was nothing I could do. I was responding and, to my shame, enjoyed it. Well, my body did.

Why couldn't I see it? Had something cast a spell? No taste, no way to steer or navigate. Only lust, envy, and pride. Greed for more. Hunger. Too lazy to change. Angry at myself for not being able to.

In my head, I was thinking there had to be something to get us out of that place, that standoff. It's late, we've obviously woken everybody up. They were banging on the wall, telling us to keep it down. They had no idea what sort of ritual we were playing out. Titus might have been laying siege to Jerusalem for all they knew. This was normal, one minute shouting and screaming, the next minute moaning and pleasure sounds. They wouldn't have thought anything unusual if it weren't for the Mommy screams. That must've told them something, but they didn't barge in, didn't think it was much different than anything they'd heard before. How could we comply and calm down and eventually settle into bed and go to sleep? That might've been what she was trying to do. Fuck, I don't know, but I liked it. More than ever before, or it was more memorable. I can't tell anymore. Such a tool.

Can mediocrity know itself as mediocrity? Is this a joke that I don't get?

The next day it was as if nothing happened. We had some food around noon, and she went off. Kissed me on the cheek before she left.

Frithjof introduced me to his friend Oskar a few weeks back, and a few days ago he mentioned that his grandfather ran a winter sports shop in Seefeld, that town I passed through on my way to Innsbruck before the Australians picked me up. He said there was some work for me there. After a while, I reminded Frithjof about that and he called Oskar who said it'd be great. His grandfather needed the help and, as soon as I could get there, he'd be happy to have me. Didn't think there was time to run to the post office to call Eve, so I asked Frithjof if I could use the phone. I promised I'd reverse the charges and he said sure, no problem.

I was still upset, and I don't remember much of what I said. I was crying. Elke gave the phone to Eve. They were both there.

"We're coming to get you. We'll drive you to Seefeld. We'll be there as soon as we can."

"You can't pick me up here, we'll have to meet at the train station. I can't walk out of the apartment with my stuff if she's here. She works at 5, I can leave then."

"Okay, we'll try to get to the train station by 6. Meet you there."

Everything was arranged. Frithjof was happy and promised he wouldn't tell her where I went. He wanted me to do this and asked me about it a few times since Oskar brought it up. His grandfather was alone there after his grandmother died and he needed the help. Frithjof wanted me out of there, they all did, but he was the only one who wanted it for my own good and not because he hated the drama.

None of the others were there. They'd be thrilled that I was gone so no need to write them a thank you note or wait around to let them know. Disappearing would be gratitude enough.

"Why don't you guys throw her out?" I asked Frithjof after she went off to work and I was throwing my stuff into the backpack.

"It's her lease, hers and Sabina's. If we can't take it, we'd have to leave and it's hard to find somewhere good that's affordable."

"Still," I said shouldering the bag and trying to get out of there as quickly as possible.

"It's never been this bad," he said at the door. "And with you gone, I think it'll go back to normal."

I shook his hand, thanked him, and told him if he ever came to Seefeld with Oskar we should try to do something normal together. He laughed. A good sport, helpful.

Walking to the train station. Dreiheiligenstraße would have been the sensible route, and I knew she was at work at the youth hostel by the river so there wouldn't be much chance of running into her, but you never know. I stuck to side streets through Pradl and crossed the river on the Amraser which was also the best way to cross the tracks and head down to the Hauptbahnhof. In the parking lot by the taxis, I saw Anna's Mercedes. As soon as they saw me, Eve and Elke jumped out of the car and crossed over the throughway to greet me.

Eve always wears baggy tops. Had a big coat on today, and that day in the castles and monasteries she was wearing big shirts, loose fitting. Her pants were tight, same as then, but the top was loose. She's not too thin and not too fat, exactly the right amount of curvy girlyness. She took the pack off my back and helped me set it down before giving me a hug. Stupid me, couldn't help it, but damn she had some seriously large breasts and I had somehow missed that. All those weird emotions and that's what struck me. Elke hugged me too, had to reach up and I was looking over her and could clearly see her stretching on her tip toes to get her arms around my neck. More flesh on her back, she's rounder, but fit in a way. Young, I guess. It's weird the things that you feel and see when you hug somebody. Is that supposed to be part of it or is there something wrong with me?

Eve picked up my pack and carried it across the throughway. Elke grabbed my arm and guided me to the car. They were great, warm, didn't hardly say anything, only tucked me into the back seat. Honestly, they didn't have that many details about what I was going through, but they knew how upset I was, and they knew that whatever it was had been going on for a while.

Eve was driving and Elke was telling her where to go, how to get out of the city and onto the road headed back toward Seefeld. They told me they were going to spend the night down here. It was a long drive, and they didn't want to go right back the same day.

"That's great. It'd be better if we didn't show up at the grandfather's place until tomorrow," I said.

"Perfect," Eve responded looking at me in the rearview mirror.

"We can stay at a guest house tonight. Are you hungry?" Elke said, turning back toward me. She sounded so confident. Eve was even, and she kept a tight ship. Couldn't always tell what she was thinking. She said this was perfect, but you wouldn't have been able to tell from her face or the sound of her voice. Elke was an entirely different kind of creature. She wore her heart on her sleeve, and it was obvious she'd found her lost puppy or whatever she thought I was, and was ready to take care of me, that was clear, and whatever else it meant, it meant she was going to make sure I got something to eat and a good night's sleep.

We stopped at a nice, typical, Tyrolean guest house inside the town. It was pricier than anything I'd have gotten on my own. They had a big room and Eve took care of the details. They had daypacks with them, and she insisted on carrying my backpack to the room. Elke was in charge of me. There was a big bed, a king or something, and then a day bed off to the side. Eve put my rucksack there, and they dropped their packs on the big bed, basically telling me to clean up and change my clothes to come meet them down in the restaurant. They were going to head off there immediately to give me some privacy.

After the last month in that grimy apartment, it was luxury. The shower was nice and the flow of water strong. Everything was perfect. By the time I dressed and sat down at their table with a big beer in front me, it was as if the last twenty-four hours hadn't happened.

They doubted the story was as simple as I claimed. The whole mythology of roommates that were pissed-off about a relationship wasn't fitting the level of drama they'd been exposed to. Over the phone, they were willing to let me get away with it. There, at the table, they weren't as accommodating.

"There's a lot you're not telling us," Eve said sitting next to me in the booth. Elke was on the other side, right across from me, her eyes were warm but imploring. If they'd been two guys, there's no way I would have been able to tell them what was going on. I'd have felt permanently weakened, because it was so humbling and humiliating to share the details, but the way they were acting, Elke's eyes and face especially, they were anxious to take care of me. It wasn't the food and the bed and the shower, that's what I had in mind when I asked for help. To them, that was trivial, didn't matter. What they wanted, what they thought of as help, was to be there for me. They wanted to hear the whole story. It wasn't going to make them uncomfortable, and it wasn't going to make them think less of me. I got that sense, at least.

I told them more. Not everything. I couldn't tell them everything, but I told them some details about the wild back and forth, the way Birgit couldn't talk about anything, about how she was private and guarded and that any attempt to get closer set her off. I let on that for some reason I'd become obsessed with getting to know her. The more she pushed me away, the more I wanted to know, and since bed was the only place she'd let that happen, it became my focus, and the only thing I could hold on to. Her pleasure was only possible there and her pleasure was becoming an obsession to me. I didn't want to say how extraordinary the sex was, but I had to let them know that there was something about the physical stuff that played a role, and that it messed with my head and was why I was so upset.

They wanted a lot of details and weren't shocked when they got them. In fact, they liked it, in a way. Confirmed what they already suspected.

"Sounds like serious trauma to me," Eve said.

"That's what I thought too, but it's as if the effort to find out, to hear about it, was repeating the whole thing. Sex didn't remind her of it, trying to find out did. Isn't that strange? It can't be normal."

"Not that weird," Elke said. "Every girl has something. For most, talking is not bad. Once there's trust. Once you know each other well enough. She couldn't trust you. Anybody." Eve was nodding. It was routine, and I was horrified. What did that mean, every girl has something? Elke was leaning over the table. She couldn't get close enough. Eve was sitting half tilted this way with her arm straightened out and pressed against the bench between us. Her baggy shirt was lightly touching my arm. All I had to do was ask and they'd tell me. They wanted to tell me. This alien thing I had seen was an extreme version of something familiar, is that what they were saying? I wanted to know, but I didn't want to know. I wanted to ask but couldn't. I looked down and took a sip of my beer to hide the lump in my throat.

4.8.2.X.19.86.11.2 [ref(.)]

Going feral. Leaving the trim and the true behind. Up early and out to give them some time and space alone to get dressed and whatever. Have a chew in the morning. Swill and swig the way down to a creek with high grass. There's a dead cat nearby, flies around its eyes. Black and white, a grotesque mass come here how exactly? These are the wilds, where voices sound without clarity. They can have it, the time they need. Every twist is a turn and every hallucination a lesson learned. It's a sinkhole, a quicksand of concern, I can't save that cat, can't be of any use to it, it's dead, long dead, and letting that image burn into my brain won't do it a damn bit of good.

We're not going to kiss. Excuse me, I didn't... Oh sorry. Shit, now it's the only thing I can think about.

I didn't cause that problem, it's not mine. Why should I carry it around, why should I be forced to abed and aid the worst of them? Those cocks that come from every corner, that litter the rooms, that ruin the best, and the worst too by ignoring them. How is that my fault? What reparation should I be forced to pay?

She lured me in, dangled me in front of them and beat them with me. Not a whipping boy, but a whip. I was her whip, I was that belt, and the bruises were its proof. Just because they choose a drama that fits their sparkly narrative doesn't make it so, doesn't make me responsible for the ills that stupid time visits upon the restless. I tried to hear, to listen and learn, and got nothing, got nowhere. How is that my fault? Why should I bear this burden?

What difference does it make if people you detest hate you? We're not talking about open war here, there's no chance of retaliation or vengeance, it's shadow play and long gone with the night and the few kilometers between there and here. Why be burdened by it? Move on. Be a man. Take responsibility for what you are responsible for and leave the rest to the guilty, those who have done wrong.

Style has always been the easy part, hasn't it? The real problem comes with what to say. The story, if they are half right, comes from generalizing. Oh, here was such and such and this and that. See how it's applied to other kinds of things, teaching lessons, oh such great learning experiences. But that's bullshit. It doesn't work that way. This is this and that is that and there is no lesson to be learned from mushing everything together. Only this and this and this and this. There are no stories, there is no lesson, there is nothing that one there can teach this one here because whatever that was has nothing to do with whatever this is.

Are we supposed to be women now? It used to be only the other was generalized, subjected to universals and aggregates, now everyone is. You can't see something without seeing everything that participates in it, but there is no crime in objectification, it is the rule of law, of nature. Food or not food. Good or not good. Only things hold these measures inside them. You cannot both see her eye color and look her in the eyes at the same time. Blue. Being unique is the absence of associations, it is isolation, it is pure subjectivity. Language imprisons, binds the speaker or the writer in its categories, the flow is a line of flight, an attempt to escape. I am every one of them.

Mathematical nature. Mathematical culture. The bills and boils of it resonate in a stock ticker or a moral code. Revenue or wages, such an arbitrary imposition. It's so fucking feminine. What if I say no? No, dogdamnit. No one listens to anybody.

They are judgmental and small. Always looking for revenge, always looking to take out their smallness on the big. In microscopic fashion. "Is that the shirt you're going to wear?" "Who do you think is going to wash that dish?" Why the fuck are you bothering me with these tiny matters you miniscule human looking to exercise whatever control you can on the powers nearby? They cannot contain him. Me. I don't know about good and bad. Yes bad, not evil. Bad. What is bad? Fuck the bad. I only know that some people sing songs that other people like, and some people sing songs that no one likes. I'd prefer to be in the former group, but thus far reside among the latter. What justifies making that into some big category of quality? They're idiots.

Some of it was because they were worried about her. That's not normal. That's not a normal person. If I was the whip, does the whip need to concern itself with the crimes of the mistress? Does the whip owe it to the truth to get to the bottom of it and discover why she is so vicious, and what trauma drives her?

"You're in a good mood," Eve said as I came up to the table and sat down with them. They already had bread and butter with jam. There was some cheese and meat too. Coffee. Yes, please.

"Good night sleep. The air is clear."

"I've been thinking about it. The roommates don't hate you, they're worried about her, and from their point of view, you were the problem. Things weren't bad until you turned up," Elke launched into it as if we were still in the middle of that conversation, picking up where we left off.

"You're right," but I didn't want to go back there. I'm done agonizing over that. Free of it, and now let's move on. "I'm anxious to get to this shop and see what the situation is. Oskar said there's a place to stay. At least for a few days. Something above the store."

They knew I wanted to move on, so they dropped it and came with me. We chatted about nothing over breakfast, about the few things they knew about this town. It was nothing until the Olympics in Innsbruck when some of the ski runs were here and they built a jump or something. They remembered hearing about it.

After breakfast, we cleared out of there and put the stuff back in the car. Eve didn't offer to carry my rucksack back out again. Whatever she had sensed yesterday, it was gone and she thought I could carry my own damn bag. Smiling on the way down the stairs and out into the air again, going feral, clean and crisp this air. For days on end in its midst and then briefly away from it and everything was forgotten, but this was where we were meant to be.

The shop was in the older part of town and, surprisingly, was open on Sunday morning, or at least the door was unlocked and there was an old man inside. There was no sign, no light on, so it was hard to tell, but he stood up from the chair near the counter and greeted us as we walked in. He was reading a newspaper and there was a cup of something on the glass counter next to him.

"Hello. Good morning. How can I help you?"

There were many kinds of things in the store. One whole wall covered with skis with different brands and sizes. The other wall flush with boots and poles and a display from various of the well-known binding manufactures. The middle of the store had several aisles with things such as gloves and goggles, warming blankets and a few coats and leggings. There were things to protect the lower leg from dampness, gaters they're called, and full bibs to protect the whole body.

He should have been expecting us, but he was only expecting me, and the two girls threw him. That and the fact that we pulled up in Anna's Mercedes and he was expecting someone who wasn't affluent. For whatever reason, he didn't think we were who he was waiting for.

"Hello Herr Damschroder, I am Oskar's friend Stefan. I believe he told you I would be coming today."

He came forward much more openly. Completely different greeting, he shook hands and nodded warmly to Eve and Elke.

"But we don't have room for the three of you, I'm afraid. I was only expecting you," he said.

"Yes, yes, of course, these are my friends. They are students in Germany, only here to help me get settled." This had a good effect. He was happy to hear that I was the kind of person who had women to help him when he needed to get something done. It legitimized me somehow or made me more sociable. The loner was always suspicious. The gang of men could be suspicious too, but a man with women to help him, what could be more upstanding and true? Think Charles Manson.

Eve and Elke were looking around the store to see what kinds of things he had there, more for appraisal than shopping. This was to pass the time since Herr Damschroder led me alone into the room back behind the counter. It was more than a room, a big part of the building. There was more inventory back there, boxes of things, extra skis and boots matching with the display styles and models, different sizes. There was also a machine area where he mounted the bindings onto skis, a waxing area, and some other machines that were useful for getting boots to fit better. It was a proper shop with everything I had been hoping for. Perfection is never where you think it's going to be.

"Oskar tells me you are a quick study, so I'm hoping to train you in what we have to do around here. As you can see, it's a mess. I haven't had much help this off-season and there is lots to organize. I'm not as good as I was. I can't get up on the ladder anymore to put things in order on those shelves."

He pointed up and around the room. There were rows of shelves, some holding inventory and some holding items that were being assembled for customers. The shelves over about five or six feet above the ground were largely empty and stuff was packed into the lower shelves. This was what gave the place a look of disarray. I nodded pensively as I looked at the piles of clutter back there.

"Yes, we'll get things in order. Right away. When shall I start? Today?"

"Tomorrow will be soon enough," he said laughing. "First you must see upstairs. It may not meet your approval."

At the back of the building there was a staircase leading up. At the top there was more storage and then a hallway leading off to the side of the storage room. There was tons of stuff crammed into the room and a feeling of dustiness and deterioration everywhere.

Down the hall, there was a bathroom with a toilet and sink plus a small tub that had a handheld attached at the faucet. The basin was dirty and had bits of plaster and grime around it. The heater must've been buried somewhere in one of the storerooms, because I didn't see it anywhere.

Across from the bathroom was a small room with a single bed, more of a cot. There was some floor space in front of a wardrobe and then a desk and chair pushed up against the wall. The surface of the desk was nicked and scarred by years of abuse, although there were some fairly recent looking rings and moisture as well. The whole place had the feel of a hasty sweep to make it ready, all of it done without attention to detail. Opening the drawers of the desk revealed lots of papers and bound journals.

He gestured into the rooms, none of which had doors, and said, "It isn't much but you're welcome to stay until you can find something that suits you. There are people in town who may be renting out rooms for some extra cash. I don't have anything myself, but you're welcome to this. No charge, not worth much anyway, but it'll keep you warm."

It looked perfect, hard and spartan, exactly where I was at the moment. No oversensitive screaming maniacs anywhere to be seen and that was exactly what I was hoping for.

"What do you say?" He must've been desperate because he was taking a pretty big risk here without a whole lot of careful evaluation. That or Oskar talked me up. If he did, that could only be because he was worried about his grandfather, because he certainly didn't know me well enough to vouch for me.

"Yeah, it looks great. Exactly what I was hoping for. I'd love to stay, and would be happy to work here."

He was nice and smiled warmly. Clasped me on the back, said he was happy to have company, and looking forward to it. There was a back door to the shop down below and he would give me a key straight away so I could come and go as I pleased when the store was closed. He moved slowly coming up the stairs, and moved slower going back down, carefully placing each foot on a step, and holding the loose rail as he moved along. I kept making mental notes of the things that needed to be done. Cleaning up that bathroom, the storeroom, both upstairs and downstairs, all of it. There was so much to do. It would take me weeks to get this place in order.

I studied him while we were going down the stairs. Taller than average, but stooped somewhat, and in his mid-seventies. He would have been born in about 1910 or so. That would make him my age when the Nazis came to power next door and nearly 30 when the war began. This whole trip it's been impossible to avoid stories. That made it seem ominous somehow, working here. I was looking for voice and style on my travels but only finding stories.

Back out in the front room, he handed me a key. "I wasn't planning on being open today," he said. "I was waiting for you." Then for Eve and Elke's sake, he repeated the advice that I should come and go through the back door. "It's fine if you bring your things in through the showroom today, but usually this is what I expect. If you go around town today, some places have seasonal hours and are open. If you have to, let them know you're staying over here at Damschroder's. They know me. Yes, yes, everyone knows old Kurt."

Oskar and Kurt, from *The Tin Drum*. But backwards. Rat-a-tat-tat. It took a lot of willpower to avoid responding with that. Instead, I thanked him and said we'd go get my stuff.

When we brought my things upstairs, Eve and Elke were horrified. They didn't think the room was inhabitable. There was no suitable linen on the bed and the bathroom was filthy. "I'll use my sleeping bag and clean the bathroom."

"Absolutely not," Elke said. "Let's get supplies right away. We can get some sheets and a pillow, plenty of cleaning products. We'll have to scrub that bathroom thoroughly to make it usable."

The department store was closed so that wasn't going to work, but Albrecht's was open for a few hours, and we hit it to get the cleaning supplies. There wasn't anything resembling a kitchen in the shop, but Eve found some containers that she said would be pretty good for storing dry goods so no bugs could get to them. She was sure there were bugs. I didn't care much about that, travelling got me used to living a comfortless existence, so I didn't need much. My sleeping bag was fine.

Back at Damschroder's, they were running the show, giving me chores, telling me to scrub this or throw that away. Eve was in charge. The bathroom was mostly clean by the time we got through with it. Still, a bunch of chips and stains in the basins and on the floor, the place needed a complete remodel, but it was at least usable and tolerably clean.

Let me say that some girls like it when they can tell you what to do, especially if it's for your own good. Eve had so much authority in her voice when she was putting my rucksack away and cleaning the stuff out of the wardrobe so that my clothes would fit. She asked Herr Damschroder where the laundromat was so we could go wash everything before putting it away. It was a long affair, and we were busy well past lunchtime getting things in order, but, as near as I could tell, Eve, at least, was having a blast telling everybody what to do and how to do it, prioritizing things and delegating tasks. She was in her element.

It must've been two o'clock when we finally finished. Or rather, when I finally said it was enough and they'd given me what I needed to finish. Eve reluctantly agreed that we were done but wrote down a whole bunch of stuff that I should get from the department store the next day, or as soon as I could get away. She gave me a fifty to pay for it. I took it dutifully without bothering to remind her that we were in Austria. It was the only thing she had.

The plan was that we would go eat and they would head on out and make the drive back. It was about 3 hours to get there so it was going to be rough on them.

"I appreciate you guys coming down and taking care of me this way. I don't know what I would've done without you. And please, thank Anna for me, I'm so glad she let you borrow her car."

That went over well, they were thrilled at the opportunity to wave the thanks aside and let me know it was common courtesy. We'd become friendly over the last couple weeks, but if you think about it, it's wild that they'd warm up to me so fast. I was basically a stranger one month ago and the next thing I know, they're my best friends.

"The place is called Damschroder's, right?" Eve said. "We can find the number. Make sure it's okay to call you at the shop. After hours."

"And you can always call us," Elke added. "Let us know how you're settling in. We'll come back down in a few weeks. It's a beautiful town. If there's more snow, we can ski."

The best thing about today was that they weren't bugging me about Birgit and trying to figure out any of that stuff anymore. I was done with it, as I decided this morning. Going feral, moving on, and I was glad they weren't trying to hold on to old times. They were treating me differently. Someone who needed taking care of, and I was that. They both kept touching me. Hands all over. On the back, on the shoulder, on the arm. That kind of stuff, but it seemed different. I was their newfound kid who they decided to raise as their own. That was a completely new experience, and while hugging them goodbye and thanking them more profusely for coming down to rescue me, I wondered how to act out my feral philosophy and get back into the danger zone. The friend thing was a familiar trap, but how to get out of this whole mommy bag? And why the hell did they feel so strongly about putting me in it?

Figuring that out had to be part of the feral philosophy that grabbed me early this morning and was poised to rock me to sleep my first night in Seefeld. What kind of maneuver does it take to get past the Oedipal thing and into something wild without going into the darkness of the whip and becoming a tool for working out their trauma?

4.8.3.X.19.86.11.23 [ref(..3-22)]

There is snow in October, but it doesn't last or accumulate, not significantly. November is when it gets going. Not at the beginning, but toward the end, it's proper winter. It's about the slopes. Not the streets or in the village, but what's the base on the peak and what's the base at the bottom by the lifts? Early in the month, it's still too rocky and there aren't many people coming, but throughout the month the traffic increases and the place changes almost overnight. Herr Damschroder's business is based on rentals. People come from München or Zürich or Wien and they rent skis, take them for the day, and bring them back after. Sometimes they rent them for multiple days and keep them at their guest house or hotel.

Luckily, I smoothed into it with a slow train. Not much to do for the first week, I cleaned and cleaned and cleaned. Organized the place from top to bottom. He had let it go, not being able to lift and move anything himself. In the process, I learned the trade. Mostly, I pretended to know what I was doing, but claimed to have trouble with the words. It's a specialty language, who knows the words for this stuff? He didn't believe me, didn't fall for it for a second, but needed the help so badly, what could he do? He taught me. There isn't much, you get their shoe size, find out if they know what they're doing on the slopes, get them a pair of skis and boots, and adjust the bindings. Not much more to it. Sometimes you give them a pair that are too long, sometimes they're too short. They chalk it up to the rental experience. If they wanted to do things right, they'd have to buy their own gear. That's the big ticket, but he never worked the hard sell, didn't bother trying. If they wanted to rent, let them rent.

Aside from work, it's been tough. I left the Emerson at Birgit's, so I didn't have anything to read other than the weekly and monthly magazines that came to the shop. I met a few people, but mostly cocky dudes hoping to work the slopes same as me. An instructor, a member of the patrol, exactly the kind of guys the bunnies want to meet, but not the kind of guys I'd be much interested in hanging around with. Let them be cocky bastards if that's their angle, if it works, takes all kinds. I'll be the variety sell, the alternative, exotic foreigner. When they get fitted with boots and skis, they have to touch you a lot, that's a good excuse for getting close and working your way in. The instructors have their game, and the patrol does too. Let them work it, it'll only help. Once the numbers go up, they'll be plenty for everybody.

I ended up getting the sheets. The bed was too gnarly and needed some light touches. It was fine to use the sleeping bag for a while, but I had to put something down on that grimy thing he had up there, and I needed something else to provide the layers. It was cold and, even with that space heater, it still got bad at night. On top of that, I thought that if I ever did have company, I'd need a blanket. I spent almost the entire fifty on stuff to get ready, but it's not as if I was buying plants or anything. I didn't cheer the place up, it was pretty dreary. What does that matter? The bunnies will have their own place, won't they? Something in the guest houses or somewhere. There'll always be somewhere to go, it'll be an adventure, no sense putting too much into it.

Herr Damschroder didn't agree. He went and got some kind of toaster oven or something for the counter area by the sink where he kept the electric coffee pot that he used to make that swill every morning. Since it didn't look as though I was going anywhere, he wanted to make sure I had some way to heat food if I wanted it. There was a small refrigerator built into one of the cabinets below the counter and I cleaned it out of the old stale garbage that collected in there to make room for a fresh supply, but I didn't stock it too good. He took care of that, brought things in pretty much every day. Milk, of course, because he liked that with his coffee, but some cheese too and some cold cuts to eat for breakfast and lunch. Basically, that's where we kept the stuff that you could eat during the day, but then he would go off and head home at night. I didn't have a lot of money and didn't want to spend much, so I wasn't going out to eat. The stuff you could cook in that oven was limited and mostly I stuck to my diet of bread and cheese, same as lunch and breakfast except I would heat it up. Sometimes I'd get a sausage.

Pretty pathetic. Especially because of the Emerson. Nothing much to do at night. I'd go out, but without too many tourists, it was uneventful. Those cocky bastards didn't like me much and didn't want to talk. They didn't have much to say anyway. Why bother?

I had to get up early because the shop opened at 7:30 so I'd usually go to bed early, watch some TV. He had this black and white unit that was stuffed in the storeroom upstairs. That's where I found a bunch of towels that I was able to get clean. That saved me the trouble of having to buy any. I had the one I carried around, but with my own bathroom it was way better to have a few extra.

I would sit at the desk with the TV on it, usually with bad reception. I'd listen to the news or some American program. Nonsense, background noise while I wrote. Truth be told, I spent most of the time writing about not having anything to write about. Asking myself what happened to my taste, why can't I tell how bad it is, why can't I see what everyone else sees? Pride and self-absorption on the one hand, titillated by the thrill of my own words, and then petty envy on the other, unable to see the good in anyone who isn't me. Is that what I've been reduced to? I'd write about being lonely and bored and miserable and hating everything about the place and the time. That kind of stuff. Misery loves company, but it's unrequited.

Then the snow came, and when it did, it kept coming and coming and coming. The whole week. The base is building up, the ski report on the news is getting better, and the people are coming. This provides a burst of energy, and because I am feral, because the place has made me hard with its spare design and empty possibilities, the energy is intense and pulls everything together. With the snow, the whole place changes. It lights up in the morning, it bustles in the day, and screams at night. Forget about sleep. Forget about days off. Before the snow, Herr Damschroder was relaxed about my schedule. He didn't care much if I checked out for a while to run to the grocery or the department store, but once the snow came, I had to be in the shop most of the time. There was more to do at night, more distractions, and I'd go out after work and not come back until late, meaning that there weren't enough hours to get any sleep or feel sorry for myself.

In the first couple days of the surge, that's how it was. Going out, but mostly people watching. I got shot down a lot. Talking to this one and that one, making the rounds from place to place. Many of the taverns are in the guest houses, some are off on their own, but they were filling up. There were women coming into the shop to get their skis and boots too. My attitude was completely ego free. Go for it, full force, and who gives a damn what the results are. Play the numbers game, that's the key to success. Fail 100 times, doesn't matter. Let them throw drinks in your face or give you a good slap. None of it matters. There are different kinds out there. What insults this one will tickle that one. You got to throw the energy around, eventually it'll stick. All I knew was that I absolutely had to get the taste of Birgit out of my mouth.

During the slow time, I'd been using the phone in the shop to call up to Nürnberg now and again. Not too often, I didn't want to give them the impression that I was desperate or anything, but, if I'm honest, it was more to keep my skills sharp. The stuff in the car and the guest house, while we were cleaning up the bathroom and the room upstairs, it was too friendly for my taste. I had to work the phone. I realized it's not so bad. It's as if your mouth is right up close to her ear when you're talking. You can work that if you know how. It's the same with loud rooms. They force you to get close. The conditions, you need to work the conditions. I would call, and I wouldn't talk about the crap we got used to talking about. Instead, I'd say how great it was to see them, didn't matter which one I was talking to, Eve or Elke, I treated them pretty much the same. They looked so beautiful at the table there, taking such good care of me. That's what I would say and then get quiet and whisper. I could tell the effect it was having.

These are not girls with lots of options, so they were motivated to get some good romance going. Didn't matter the source, they'd take it from most anywhere. Eve's got that great body, but something about her personality, the way she carries herself. She's one of those girls who still hasn't figured out who she is and for some reason the guys haven't built her up yet. She was too clever or too introspected. Something. She had no idea how to style herself, she dressed badly, the baggy clothes, and not only that, her hair was awful, practically a helmet, but she had a cute face. What made her do it? Were her parents backwards like that? I didn't know. I tried asking, but she didn't want to talk about her family too much. Her sister died not too long ago. That explained the mood, but the personality stuff had to come before that. She was the youngest, should have been an attention hound, showing off in different ways, but none of it. Demur and even, a calm reasonable girl who thinks carefully about everything she says. Which, of course, makes it easier to disarm her. I got bolder as the month dragged on and before the snow came, before I had much else to do. Aside from the other compliments, I went for the basics. I told her I thought she had an amazing body. She protested. You know how they do, but she liked it. Her protests were a way to get me to elaborate. I'm serious. She was laughing. Because I went on. Not too much, not being a horndog or anything, but I described the sensation of hugging her, how nice it felt and how I could tell from that how fit she was. She was probably blushing, but in a good way. It was putting ideas in her head, and she wasn't that used to it, so the ideas were ready to be there.

Elke was even easier. She was desperate for compliments, and they were easy to find. Okay, so she doesn't have a great body in the classic sense, but connoisseurs will tell you, everyone has their niche and in a young woman, there is no such thing as a lost cause. She had nice skin, and it was tight. She was chubby, so what? That may be a problem later on, but for now, at twenty-two or whatever she was, it's not. And her face, it was lovely. I told her how pretty I thought her eyes were, and her jaw line and ears. She had great ears. Stop stop, that's what she says, but she's laughing the whole time. She doesn't mean it. She means keep going, she means I love this. With both of them, I'm using the phone to my advantage.

They must've liked these conversations because they'd call back. They said they didn't want me to get in trouble with Herr Damschroder, didn't want me to run up a big phone bill, but it's not that expensive to call between Austria and Germany, they have an agreement. He told me he didn't mind. I didn't tell them that, I told them that I was gladly going to pay for the phone calls from my salary. What I wanted, I said, was for them to come down and visit. Anna and her boyfriend are big-time into skiing and Eve and Elke both know how to do it, so they had to come down and spend a weekend. I wanted to see them. And I did. I liked them both. They'd been good to me. That part of the time with Birgit wasn't completely bad and that's because of them, what they were beginning to mean to me. Girls think we're that way, that we're cads, or whatever they call it in those old movies, but there was something behind it. They both needed romance. I wanted to give them that, to make them feel better, same way they made me feel better. Yes, it's true, it was good practice, and I was thinking about that, but it wasn't only that, it wasn't simple. It can be more than one thing. Truth of it is, I think that's why they let themselves be fooled. Because they know how feelings work, how they can be at cross purposes and have some bad and some good in them, and, in my opinion at least, it kind of ups the ante. Gives them more of a fantasy. They want to fix you, bring out the good, feed the better feelings and instincts and starve the bad ones. It's part of it for them, it's romantic in their eyes. Poor souls.

It was a big network, one of those underground systems where the caves and caverns connect. With Birgit, it was the brutes, but with Eve and Elke it was the guys who ignored them at school, they were the ones who were making my job easier. We were connected. Through each other, through the feelings those guys left them with so that I could swoop in and come to the rescue with these totally different feelings. If I tried to talk to Anna the same way, using these tactics, she wouldn't go for any of it. She's out of the network, living in different caves and exploring different caverns. She's got her boyfriend and meets the beauty standard. That meant she was properly linked during those developmental years that eased her into a new situation with whatever guy the world picked out for her. Naturally, she became devoted to it and was spoken for. That's how marriage works, it takes you out of the caverns and makes it so you don't want to know what's going on in there anymore. Later, she'd grow bored with this guy or get jilted because he'd act badly, and in that case, she may want to poke her nose in and see what's going on. Then she'd be open to flirting, and something more, but for now, none of that held anything for her. I got her on the phone a few times and although I didn't try too hard, I could tell right away she wasn't having it. All business. I didn't live in the same network as she did.

That's where I was the other day. Putting the moves on everyone and failing. Working Eve and Elke into a frenzy or trying to. Bored and lonely when the snow came. Clear as day about the caves and the caverns connecting everybody up with what I wanted to do inside them. That's where I was when Lydia and her two friends came into the shop to get some skis for the weekend.

Total bunnies. From München and ready to party. That's what they came for and that's what they were going to get. They were cute and bubbly, totally confident they would get what they came for. No doubt about that. They weren't used to rejection, and they hadn't developed any deep sense of reflection on their condition. They were used to getting what they wanted, and, in fact, were used to having a variety of choices. I wish I could say that Lydia was the most attractive of the three, but she was what most would say was the least attractive. Physically, that is, but she had a great personality. She was their instigator, open and friendly and funny. Didn't get my jokes, but she was good at making her own even if they weren't that complicated or hard to figure. Mostly she liked to laugh, and I was pretty sure I would have picked the friend with the figure to die for if it was up to me, but when is it ever up to me? I make the offers, that's true, I'm the one who puts it on the table, but they're the ones who decide. It's up to them, and Lydia chose me while I was helping them find the right skis. I picked some good ones and tried to get the right size. Made sure their boots fit right too. It takes extra time to get that right, but I wanted to do it. Especially with the touching. Lydia had no problems with me touching her calves and feet, it made her giggle. Her friends liked it too, but the lines were drawn, and they made sure not to let on. They wanted to make it clear that Lydia was choosing me and that meant they couldn't.

There's a whole set of rules they follow. They learn them and it's best to treat them as brute nature, facts. Don't struggle against it and try to figure out how to execute some big switcharoo. Look elsewhere. There are so many flowers in the garden, or whatever Herr Damschroder was saying when we were talking about it later that day. He knows what's what. He can still remember. I saw it in his eyes, and to his credit, he always knows when to let me take care of a customer. He's a great wingman. Anyway, you got to stick to the rules. They can forgive you for many things. Honestly, they're forgiving beings and cannot help themselves, but they will not forgive you for breaking the rules, or rather, they will not forgive you for making them break the rules. It's a code, but there's a caveat, an exception, there always is, and trust me, you don't want to know those girls. They're going to be like Birgit, and as fun as you think they'll be at the beginning, when the end comes round, you will want to get the hell out of there so damn fast. You'll be glad to get cut loose, or dying to get yourself loose, if they're so corrupt that they won't let you go.

They came on Friday morning, and I couldn't get away. The weekends are the busiest time. I wouldn't be able to ski with them that weekend. Herr Damschroder said it would be best if I took Tuesday or Wednesday for that kind of thing and I generally wanted to please him and vowed to stick to it. Skiing with Lydia would have been great. Don't think I didn't want to. Riding the lift, lots of things can happen up there. Off the trail, once you're warm and feeling good in the clean air. Many lovely possibilities. Especially for such a bold, friendly girl as Lydia, but I wanted to be the good worker bee, so I arranged to see her later. She told me about the guest house where they were staying, and I said I'd meet her over there for some apres once the store closed. I couldn't join them right after the slopes shut down because the store stayed open later than that to handle the returns, but I'd hurry over as soon as I could.

And it's a good thing I did because there were several bastards there trying to muscle in. It was crowded, not only in the tavern, but at the table.

Even though three guys were putting the moves on, none of them was too focused on Lydia. As I mentioned, she was the runt, but these bozos weren't too good at math, and they hadn't figured out the pairings yet. They were waiting for Bunny 1 and Bunny 2 to make their choice. The odd man out would end up with Lydia.

Don't think they don't know that's going on though. The first rule is that they're way more attuned to what's going on than you are. Yeah yeah, of course they'll fool themselves into believing the lies, but that doesn't mean they don't know. Deep down, they know, and they'll help you because they want what you're selling, but they also need help from you. They need some illusions to make it easier to swallow. You know, for their self-image or whatever stories they're telling themselves. That was certainly true of Bunny 1 and Bunny 2. She said their names, but damned if remembered them. I don't think I was listening when she said them. I didn't know Lydia's name either except once I saw she was choosing me I paid attention and looked on her form.

She was happy to see me. Despite the distractions, she hadn't forgotten her choice, and she knew what was going on with the three dogs at the table, working her friends. When I showed up, she immediately turned her attention to me and ignored them. Since they weren't paying much attention to her anyway, they didn't care. They nodded in my direction but didn't pay much attention to either of us. They weren't on the job, they were tourists, so when they nodded, they didn't register the territorial principles. None of it. Wastes of space, and if you want my opinion, Bunny 1 and Bunny 2 knew it, but they also knew they'd have to make the best of it. Weekends are short and you never know what options you're going to get.

Lydia and I ducked out of there and went back to their room. She said she wanted to go somewhere quiet so we could talk. Yup. Of course.

It was one of those rooms that the guest houses think are special, but if you break it down, they're cheesy and tacky. It had a hot tub right there in the middle of the room with a big couch on one side and a desk on the other. The beds were up on a kind of loft-like upper level that had wooden stairs leading upward. Jacuzzi apres ski is great, of course, but taking a room that isn't very big and putting a big ass tub right in the middle of it, it's laughable. We grabbed a few bottles of beer from the kiosk by the reception and took them with us. She filled the tub, and we leapt into the pushing and pulling right away.

How far can you go with, 'how was the skiing?' and other small talk? Her powers of observation when it came to human psychology were functional at best. Her powers of observation when it came to her surroundings were about the same. There was no depth at work there. She noticed what everybody noticed, she saw what everybody saw. What the hell was there to talk about? Every comment was punctuated with a giggle and every giggle turned into pawing at my shoulder or my chest. Usually accompanied by looking down and not making any eye contact. She wasn't drunk or anything. Nope, no excuse, this was her actual personality. Being obvious was her MO. She wanted me to take my shirt off. That was her primary objective in the first minutes while we're waiting for the tub to fill. Girls are the same as guys, but they need head stories to go with it, that's the trick. Help them with that and you're in.

In fact, most of the failures are because you didn't get the story right. Sometimes, it's because you guessed wrong but could've guessed right. That's how you learn to wait and listen and pay attention to the signs. Sometimes, there's no way to get it right, you never could. You can't think of stories that'll work for someone like her. Because of how you look, that's possible, but it could be because of how you think or talk or any of a million different reasons. Thing is, don't take it personally. It takes different kinds. That's the theme for the day.

When push came to shove, and it did, Lydia liked a lot of the same things Birgit liked. That's the deeper truth in what Elke said back in the guest house. They're all that way. Lydia couldn't get enough of it. In the tub and then up in the loft area still wet from the hot water, she was game. Not the same, of course, not the wild buildup, the whole routine, but little things, the micro-maneuvers, those were welcome and lots of fun and the giggling never stopped.

When leaving that night, I was feeling feral, flourishing in the wilderness, that kind of crap. I howled on the way back while plodding through the snowy streets. It was late when she threw me out. It was when Bunny 2 showed up alone. Bunny 1 must've found somewhere else to go, but Bunny 2 decided against it. Guess dickweed never figured out the right game. Bunny 2 hardly looked at me but had an expectant grimace on her face like of course I would leave now that she was back. She did acknowledge my existence for a second though and looked me in the eyes for a brief exchange. Apparently, someone had left a copy of *Invisible Man* in their room. English. She asked me if I wanted it and handed it to me before I answered. I didn't say anything, just took it, and left. Didn't get to properly say goodnight to Lydia. It felt as if I wouldn't see them again this weekend. Whatever, she knew where to find me if she wanted to.

Once back in my garret, I thought about it and got lonely. Yeah, there was everything going on, the whole caves and caverns thing, but it was fun. I mean, her giggle was fun. It got me into a good mood and the pleasures weren't only one thing. They never are. There was more to it, the way she kept pushing my chest, as though she was feeling me up, but also like she was instigating. I don't know how nuanced that whole gesture was supposed to be, but that's what I thought about back in my room. I was still thinking about it when I woke up for work the next morning. The acrobatics, the rough play, none of that lingered, but the way she pushed on my chest. It was nice. It was her thing. That was good. Lydia.

4.8.4.X.19.86.11.30++ [ref(..23, 28-30)]

I didn't see her again until they came in on Sunday evening to return the skis. It was messed up. She didn't giggle and didn't say much, kind of awkward. Didn't push on my chest, she only handed over the skis and told me it was nice meeting me, then they were gone.

I tried not to think about it, tried to focus on what there was to look forward to. Eve and Elke were coming down to ski. Anna and her boyfriend were coming with them. They had their own gear so they wouldn't need to come by and get any, but they wanted me to come stay with them at that same guest house where we were the last time they were here.

They arrived at about 11am on Friday, must've left first thing. They both gave me big hugs, so happy to see me, both knowing how much those hugs meant to me. Likewise, I think. Anna, so European, with the kisses on each cheek. Cold though. No moisture, no warmth. Hans-Herbert, her boyfriend, he couldn't be bothered. Barely looked at me or Herr Damschroder. I guess he was anxious to get out onto the slopes, can't blame him. He looked like one of those Ken dolls, like the little girls play with. I looked at Anna and shook my head. Meanwhile, Eve and Elke are gushing over Herr Damschroder, so happy to see him again. They spent a total of 2 hours in his presence nearly a month ago and here they are being cheerful and friendly greeting each other. They gave him big hugs too and he's asking after their parents and that kind of thing. He had a million questions for them back when we were cleaning up together and he remembered the answers they gave about their families. It was as if he was an old friend. Asked how Eve was getting along. If her family was coping, as though he's that deep into the psychology of her life. Anyway, that turned out pretty good because he said it was fine if I ran off to go skiing with them as long as I was back by 3. The lifts stopped at 4 and the shop closed at 6. "Not a big deal," steady Eve said without batting an eye. "We can ski for a while and then meet up later."

We were chums. Can't explain it, how close I felt to them. The calls and the repeat visits. Crying with Eve on the phone, laughing with Elke. Going away and coming back, that's what made it that way. Because Anna hadn't been a part of that, it wasn't the same with her, and her boyfriend was a complete ass. They had their car and they needed to drive it over to the Blumenthal to check in and park. That's way closer to the lifts at the pistes by Gschwandtkopf, but I had to shuttle it because there wasn't any room in the car. That meant a lot of walking and it's hard to carry everything. "We'll take your boots and polls," Eve said matter of factly, but Anna gets flustered, "There's no room. It won't fit." "Nonsense," Elke said. "I'll hold the boots in my lap, and we can lay the poles across us back here. It's only for a few minutes." Of course, it's nothing for them. What was she talking about? But that's how she is. Too pretty, in my mind. Same as Bunny 1 and Bunny 2, she has her pick. She doesn't have to be nice. Hans doesn't give a shit. You should see the look on his face when I call him that. "It's Hans-Herbert," he would correct me. Or hunsherbert, which is how I heard it. What a fucker.

Anyway, we figure out the logistics and get over there. By the time I walk up, they've put their bags in the luggage room behind reception and are ready to go. They wore their clothes on the way down, so they didn't need to change. We left and walked over there. It hadn't been long since I last talked to them, a few days, but there's still a lot to say. By this time, I knew their whole schedule and what they're working on at school. I asked about the finance class that's been driving Elke to distraction this fall and she's got plenty to tell me. I had the context. Eve knows it too, of course, but you'd think it was such a nuisance to hunsherbert. He needed to get in the mental space for the day on the slopes. You can tell. He and Anna, both of them, they're wearing jeans with those new fancy goretex gaters. It's the sign of the advanced skier. No way I'm going to fall, don't need to wear a bib, don't need leggings. Elke and Eve both had proper trousers on, same as me. From the shop. We fall.

They had to buy a ticket and get enough punches for the whole weekend like I told them. I had one from before. Herr Damschroder had an infinite supply. He gave me one a few weeks ago and when I used it up, he gave me another. Hasn't shown me where they are yet, but still, it's damn nice of him.

It's mostly an intermediate-type place, over at the pistes, but there is some stuff for advanced skiers too and hunsberbert was aching to get there. That wasn't it. It's as if my existence was a problem for him. He didn't want to ride the lift with me, he didn't want to accommodate me in any way. Hunsherbert seemed genuinely disgruntled at the fact of my existence. Which of course made me keep calling him Hans and repeating it as often as I could. "That lift there is the one we're going to want, Hans. I think it'll take us to that side, Hans. That's where the best advanced skiing is, Hans." Often enough that he couldn't interrupt and correct me every single time. Okay, I'm being a total dick, but fuck that Ken doll asshole with his goretex gaters and 500 DM ultra-ban sunglasses. Fuck him.

We had a lot of fun. Eve and Elke are about the same as me, pretty good, but not great. Growing up in Illinois, you don't get the exposure to get any better than that. I had been to Colorado, been to Vermont, but not much. A few times. You're not going to become an expert in Wisconsin, that doesn't happen, and apparently it was pretty much the same for the girls. For Eve, it was meaningless. She was her usual even self. She loved the air and the views from the top. She liked to make long GS turns with stiffer boards. She wasn't dressed fashionably or anything. Her ski clothes were more form-fitting than what she usually wore, but that's because it's athletic wear. I mean, she's doing something, okay? Not trying to show off. Elke was exactly the same. Good people. I appreciated that in comparison to hunsherbert. Anna, I don't know, she took to it naturally, but I suppose she could've been adapting to her boyfriend. Either way, it wasn't a good vibe.

I didn't want to leave at 2 when I decided to head out, but I didn't want to leave Herr Damschroder hanging so I made sure there was plenty of time to get back. Still, it was so much fun. The lifts were two seaters so the three of us couldn't ride together, and usually I would ride by myself, but I did get a chance to ride once each on our own, and the conversations were great. They liked to be flirty, but I could tell there were rules. The decisions I was talking about before with Lydia, I don't think they had happened yet, which meant something in itself. I wasn't sure what though. Still, on the lift, we bumped each other on the bench and said risky things. The three of us, it's as if I hadn't decided either. Or maybe we were just friends. I don't know. It was different.

We met up later at the Blumenthal. That's the same place we stayed back when they were first here. Now it's more complicated. Martin and Liesel Krieger own and operate the place, and I know them. They're good friends with Herr Damschroder. Or not friends. Colleagues on the chamber of commerce. These Seefelders are always talking about the chamber of commerce and that being colleagues on the chamber is the same as being family. They came by a lot. One or the other, sometimes both together if there was some business they needed to discuss. This was good and bad, this familiarity, it meant that when I walked in to meet up with Eve and Elke over there, they came over and said hello and that meant that despite how busy it was, the bartender and the other people around were going to be that much more attentive. They knew we were connected, but that's also claustrophobic. Small town. That's how it goes.

We met not long after they came back from the slopes, but I had a chance to clean up because when I got back to the shop it was still quiet enough for me to take a shower. While the three of us sat there and did a little apres, Anna and hunsherbert headed back to their room to get dressed. "They're going out for dinner," Eve said. "It'll be the three of us." "Should we eat here?" "Unless there's somewhere better," Elke was quick to point out. "Not unless you want to spend some serious money," and I said that specifically because I knew exactly where Anna and hunsherbert were going to eat. There aren't that many choices. After a couple drinks, they said they wanted to go back and get cleaned up. I told them I'd wait in the bar area, knew some of the staff, so it was no big deal. "No, don't be silly. Come talk to us." I guess I was one of the girls. Whatever, so I went along.

Eve went into the bathroom first and Elke and I sat on the bed and talked. She was telling me about one of her courses on art dealing and some of the more philosophical things they were reading, something by Tolstoy on aesthetics. I remembered it vaguely from a few years ago, but it wasn't a serious conversation or anything. She complained about her feet hurting from the boots right in the middle of giving me some run down about "what is art?" and I took to rubbing her feet while listening, but we weren't concentrating much.

See, I know I keep coming back to this, but they'll teach you a lot of stuff if you pay attention. That's the important thing, paying attention. The foot massage was too much for her, so we lounged around, rolling over each other. Wrestly, cuddly stuff. Normal, no big deal. That's where I got this clear sense of how it worked for her. If I had taken my left hand and placed it square on her right breast, she would have freaked the fuck out. It would have been completely inappropriate. You see what I mean? I would have been feeling her up or whatever and that wasn't something that fit with what we were doing, but if I put my arms around her and pull her close in a big hug that squishes her breasts against my chest and, basically, feel her up with my body, well that's okay. That fits with some model or image she has of how the world is supposed to work or what things are supposed to mean.

Honestly, Birgit showed me this back when we first met, and I thought about that while Elke and I were there on the bed and the shower was running in the bathroom. We ended up in a position at one point where Elke had one of her legs between my legs and I had one of my legs between her legs, and hey, stimulus response, what can I do? I had a chubby going on down there, and not one of the innocent baby bathwater variety, but a full-on, pre-cum dampening the boxers kind of chubby. If she were forced to admit it, I'll bet Elke had a moisture issue going on herself. She certainly had a nipple issue going on, that was obvious. It was pleasant, these are pleasant responses to pleasant sensations. Nothing wrong with that, and I don't think she thought there was anything wrong with it either. That's not my point. These things have meanings, and those meanings fit into prefabricated boxes and categories. This was cuddling and cozy. This was friendly. The woody and the moisture, that didn't matter, it was still a couple of pals rolling around and enjoying each other's company.

Now, if I were to change my legs around and get them both between hers, and slowly or casually dry hump, no way. That wouldn't have worked. Hell, if I took my hand and slid it under her shirt so that it was pressed against the skin of her lower back, that'd be a violation of some boundary, but press my hard-on against her hip while she presses her erect nipples against my chest through a thick layer of clothing, well that's fine and dandy.

Here's another thing. To feel it, that's fine. To talk about it, no, that's not good. It makes me a perve or a scumbag or whatever. The fact that I was thinking about these things, that puts me in some category of low life. She would never approve. If you feel it, no worries, but the minute you try to turn it into some lesson or something, some idea or thing or whatever, that's going to change it, poison it, make it dirty. You can't bring it up, you can't ask her about it, you have to lie there and feel it and enjoy. Let it seep into your consciousness somehow as closer friendship and better feeling. It's one of the rules.

The truth is though, this is useful information. If that makes me a perv, fine, but I can't help it. It must be how I'm wired and how the hell else am I supposed to learn it? The next day, pretty much the same routine plays out with Eve. Elke showered first when I met them over at the Blumenthal after they were done. I didn't ski with them on Saturday, but we did meet up for lunch and then we met up for drinks and dinner again. The same shower routine came in between. Elke went first and Eve and I played out the romping cuddle scene. This doesn't cross the line for some reason. I can't say I fully understand it, but it doesn't. On Friday, when Eve came out of the bathroom after drying her hair and getting dressed, we're still lying there together on the bed, Elke and I. Not in the thick of it or anything, but near enough to each other to give off a vibe. It was natural for both of them. Elke didn't get embarrassed or jump up or anything and Eve hardly seemed to notice, or pretended she didn't. When Elke got up and scooted off to the bathroom to take her turn, Eve and I talked as if nothing much were going on. It was an invisible and natural event. She was ready to go so she didn't want to get mussed up with me, but I got the sense she thought it'd be nice to sit around that way too.

When we got the chance on Saturday, we took it and it developed as naturally as with Elke. I wanted to ask them about this, but I thought there was no way to do it without revealing how much of a pervert I am, so I kept quiet. I did try something though. I got this idea that I could kiss Eve in the middle of it and that somehow that kiss wouldn't cross over any boundary. In the middle of the pleasantries, those lovely sensations of holding each other and talking friendly and easily, I pulled back and looked her in the eyes. From right up close, it's pretty intimate, and sure enough, without much ado, we kissed. In fact, she might've been the one to initiate. It wasn't hot and heavy or anything, no tongues, but it wasn't exactly dry either. I thought it was romantic or something. I don't know for sure, but it seemed to be even if it didn't blow past the boundary. It was okay, she wasn't shocked, liked it, in fact, and hugged me afterward.

Now see, this is why I knew not to trust that bitch when she said she kissed that swanky skanky Dave fucker. "We kissed." Of course, you did. But now I see what passes for a kiss to these girls. We're talking full on body grope with moist privates rubbing up against each other, but hey it was only a kiss. You're talking about something seriously fucking intimate, and they damn well know it. See how pissed she would've been if I told her I kissed her friend or something. She knows damn well what a kiss can be, and she knows that it ain't good. She also thought she could slip it by me. They think we're stupid. I'm sure of it, they think we're fucking stupid.

While she's hugging me and I hear the shower stop and the banging around, I wondered if it's possible to move across that boundary in a gradual way that won't shock anybody or result in that horrification that would happen if I did something too bold. Eve is in a constantly sensitive state so it's important to be careful. Some things that you think will annoy her, cheer her up because they're normal and make everything seem normal. Other things that you don't think are anything can make her sad. There is a logic to it, but it's not easy to see. We'd kissed and then we were hugging, and I wanted it to go further. Turning my head toward her and down to put my lips square up against her neck. Do you see where I'm going here? Same kind of kiss, no tongue, but some moisture right there on her neck. I tried it. It was overflowing feeling, I felt the moment same as she did, I wanted to return the vigor of her hug, it was perfectly reasonable and would easily fit with that friendly non-rambunctious narrative she needed to distract her from her troubles.

Direct hit.

No gasp of shock. In fact, she pulled me closer, hugged me tighter. This moved my head, caused it to tilt a tiny bit more toward her so that my lips were higher on her neck and closer to her ear. Another kiss. Almost a reflex, couldn't help it. Not trying to dog on her, feeling the moment, you see? What happened then? No gasp of shock but there was a gasp. Not a big one and not on purpose. She couldn't help herself. It was nice. She breathed out, a tiny bit heavier than usual, but it couldn't go unnoticed, we were too close together for that. Given how close each of our mouths were to each other's ears, it came out as something that could've almost been a moan. That was it. I saw it clearly. The decision was made. She taught me something important. Somehow, I knew that the worst thing I could do at that moment would be to go gonzo guy on her. No, that moan was not an invitation to fuck, not an invitation to mash like mad, none of that. It was the boundary, pure and simple, and I managed to ever so lightly land on it. That's when you have to be the most careful.

Were I bold and wanting to test the limits of this newfound knowledge,

I would have pulled back. A tiny bit, enough to look her in the eyes and get gooey. That was the right bridge for gonzo town, but that seemed too big a risk. Nope, I was in the zone, an elite athlete who can't miss. What did I do? I gingerly climbed over her, keeping with the rolling and rousing themes of the last ten minutes, got into a partial spoon position from behind, and massaged her shoulders and back. Friendly, and adding some more space, but only a little more. If you think about it, it turned the whole kiss into something of a tease, but the good kind.

That's where we were when Elke came out of the bathroom quaffed and ready to go, and again it's as if everything was normal. Mature and civil, nothing going on here. Elke barely noticed, Eve isn't embarrassed, although she did seem groggy when she got up and headed toward the bathroom to take her turn.

That was it. Those were the big events. It sounds weird because I did spend both nights over there with them. It was a room similar to the one from before only with a cot over by the side instead of that day bed. I slept there and they slept in the big bed. Nothing kinky, nothing weird, no tension. It didn't feel as though they were competing for attention. We were hanging out and enjoying each other's company.

One difference was that we had dinner with hunsherbert and Anna on Saturday. In the restaurant there at the guesthouse again. One lesson I got from sitting with them was that Anna, who wasn't bad when we met back in Reutte, and who was kinda nice and cool the few times we chatted on the phone, but when hunsherbert was around, she was unbearable. Stuck up and stupid. Filled with all kinds of nonsense ideas and making ridiculous statements and judgments. Eve and Elke were put off by it too. They see her a lot without him, so they don't care much, it doesn't get in the way of their friendship, but it was becoming my main image of her, and like the way she changed after skanky Dave came along, Anna was changing too. She's beautiful. Exactly how the magazines tell you a beautiful woman should look. Tall and svelte, statuesque, so many elegant ways to describe her features and her looks. There's practically an entire industry for coming up with flattering terms to describe Anna. Those things occur to you when you meet her and look at her, but man, hunsherbert was a handicap, a real spoiler. She lets him put his dick in her. That's the only thing I could think. That's crass and hard, I know it, but again, that's what jumped into my head, and I lost respect for her. Some girls, that's how it works. Those losers who were trying to get with Bunny 1 and Bunny 2, it was the same with them. Bunny 1 was extremely attractive, but when I saw her at the ski shop when they were turning in their gear after the weekend, she filled me with disgust. I knew she'd been with one of those assholes, and I could guess which one, the douchiest of the bunch, that was the one most likely, and she was that sort. It was the same with Anna and hunsherbert.

They left on Sunday and were sorry they couldn't stay for dinner but needed to get back at a reasonable hour. Hunsherbert had to be up early Monday. Boy was that tough, abrupt. Eve's kiss, I could still feel it, but here they were heading out and who knows when I'd see them again? They could only stop by on their way out of town to give me long hugs goodbye. Seriously long hugs. Right in turn, one after the other, disappearing out the door after they finished, forlorn, and wanting to prolong the feeling hugs. That was clear, and there was nothing competitive. Not in the least. I don't know. Elke's look was friendly and happy, bittersweet, but glad to have seen me. "You take care of yourself. Be sure to eat well. It's important. You'll get sick." Eve, on the other hand, had something else on her mind, I could tell. She was completely even, same as always, but that meant the slightest disturbance was visible from far away. She couldn't say much, something was weighing on her. She was thinking about something, and it wasn't the usual thing that we were used to. I got under her skin, and that was the whole thing about the way I let the boundary lie there on Saturday night. That moan, it left a trace, and she was thinking about it. If she were anything like me, she was having trouble thinking about anything else. We were friends, of course, the three of us, but that something from the other night was still hanging around. Nothing, but everything.

I was teary myself. Couldn't help it. When Anna said goodbye, she was the only one to notice. Hunsherbert didn't see but did manage to shoot daggers at me when I said, "Bye Hans, drive safely." Dick move, I know, but I needed to wipe away the tears somehow and being an asshole does the trick. I followed them back to the door and waved as they drove off. Both Eve and Elke were turning to wave through the back window and were visible until the car turned a corner and disappeared. Eve might've blown me a kiss, or maybe it was my eyes playing tricks.

After they called to let me know they made it back okay, I was sitting up in my garret reading this book. It was pretty good as it turned out. An undergroundsman of sorts. Stealing electricity, living on the downlow. A black guy, which was part of it. Right away I liked it. As I was getting dreamy and far away with it, thinking about myself as something of an undergroundsman too, I heard something downstairs. Crime in Seefeld is unheard of. No one talks about it, so I couldn't imagine what it was. I went down in my long johns and T-shirt and grabbed an old ski pole from the storage room up there. What can I do? I'm from Chicago. I don't know what I thought I was going to do with it, but I had it just in case. When I went through the doorway into the front of the shop, I immediately saw her standing in the light outside and tapping away on the glass in some kind of eerie syncopated rhythm. She had a puffy coat pulled up close to her ears and a wool hat pulled down over them, a few jet-black strands dangling out from under the hem and shining in the glow by the door. It was Birgit.

1.12

this year's harvest

1.12.1.Elisabet.19.86.5.9

—No one comes later than I do. He thinks about sex all the time, he's thinking about it now. Must be nearly half my age.

He stretches to put his day pack in the overhead, showing his belly, well-developed and lightly covered with soft brown hairs darker than the longish curly locks on his shoulders and away from his ears.

It is the front row and there are only seats on the side opposite the entry, the older woman across the aisle and one row back gets the backside view enhanced by close-fitting faded denim jeans. Her irritation evaporates as she takes a tender look at the villain behind the delay.

(The absences of the last days flowed back to non-touch and non-warm moments without. Beaches and nice dinners with associates and assistants, couldn't enjoy vacations anymore.)

[He was a breeze blown, and it lightly covered my eyes and my cheeks, a welcome whisper at the ear lobe. A taste of his scent wafting over the seat to the window and decorating the periphery.]

"You must be important if they'll hold the plane for you."

—Such a nice look. Humble and confident at the same time. One of those... ...attentive.

(He looked directly into my eyes with a hint of sadness.)

"The airline arranged my flight," he mumbles as though thinking out loud.

Looking directly back at him as he settles in with a book on his lap. He casually looks over and smiles awkwardly, no signs of recognition or intimidation, only a crooked sadness. He isn't going to explain, not because he is private or guarded, but because he doesn't know how. Tightening in the seat, hoping for more details: legs tense, arms fold across the chest, but leaning over toward him, a slight tilt to cut the space and offset the effects of a body closing off in hesitation. He exhales and sinks deeper into the seat.

Legs crossed, ankle boot digs into her calf while attempting a braid to further close the grip. Smoothing out the skirt against the tights, tucking a strand of hair behind her elven ear, and bringing the hand back to the crossed elbow to hug the bare arm below the cap sleeve, feeling exposed in the black thin high-necked lace shell.

(It was chilly, and I thought twice about giving my jacket to the flight attendant.)

First handing off the empty flute as they prepare the cabin for crosscheck, then turning to him and saying "Call me Heidi" while extending a hand in formal greeting. He winces at the touch, and is visibly confused when, for the first time, he displays a flash of familiarity.

Not the normal kind, not I recognize you, but something deeper, something acknowledging that we are familiar to each other, we are akin.

"Heidi?" he asks, eyes wide and almost instantly flaring moist sparkles. Such a shock to the system reflecting in brilliant color across his face and in his eyes and mouth.

—Genuinely confused... ...an explosion of purpose. Who is this?

"It's my travelling name," acknowledging the ruse and admitting collusion. The nails on his index and middle fingers lightly drag along the palm as he withdraws his grip. Looking down, the thumb on his left hand is visible on top of the book, and the nail is closely cut. Left hand trim, right hand long and filed smooth. "You play finger style?"

"Flamenco," he says drawing it out in a steady rhythm.

Disappointment inhabits every facial muscle, dipping and demurring at the thought he might be a colleague. "Are you a musician?"

"No, not at all. I can barely count. I only play to hear better."

Breathing a sigh of relief, eyes recovering their dilation.

"But you listen to Flamenco?"

"And other things."

"Paisley?" widening the grin, always fishing for a complement.

—Tell me what you think of me, *in a whiny singsong inner voice.*

"Of course, I love you guys. Same as everybody right now. I kept hearing that one song in the village café."

[Fifteen minutes and counting.]

"What village?"

"Concordia," his demeanor changes. He is going into protective mode. "In the mountains southwest of Medellin on the other side of the Cauca. Nothing but coffee farms."

—What on Earth were you doing there? No tangents.

"And they're playing Paisley there?"

"*Come tell me tell me,*" he says melodically. "It's catchy."

"What were you doing there?"

—Damn it.

He shifts in his seat, doesn't want to talk about it. "Visiting. What were you doing in Colombia?"

"Work. Vacation, supposedly."

"Did you play in Medellin? That's probably why the song was on the radio all the time."

—How sweet of you to come back to me. I doubt he has such a light touch, must be something he wants to get away from. That mouth. It must be a girl. I'll get him to tell me. Slowly.

"Medellin, Bogota, Barranquilla, Cartagena, canceled in Cali, they're telling everyone not to go there."

"It was in the paper everyday back when I was first here. Completely militarized now. Since the Supreme Court attack last year. I wish I knew about your shows. I would have gone. When were they?"

"Last one was in Cartagena on the 2nd. It went well."

"Barely missed it."

"Now back to New York. Is that where you're from?" Already comfortable in this nest of two seats side by side and leaning against the seat back. He softens, not realizing the source of the effect. That lean makes the seat into a pillow and he feels it without knowing why.

—Is that a gulp? Is he gulping? He can't get the words out, everything comes quickly. He wants to know everything, doesn't he? If I flip the hem of my skirt, he'll look down without wanting to. He won't be able to help it. See.

"No, I'm just passing through, headed to Europe."

"Are you still in school? Is this your summer holiday?"

—Can't help it. Something there.

"Recently graduated. Taking a year off before graduate school." He wants to be clever. *He wants to be clever.* (Wanting could be clever.) [Wanting could be clever.]

"A year off, but only a week in Colombia?"

"Had to take care of some things for a friend."

(There it was again, a gulp. Were his eyes tearing up or was that my imagination? There was something he couldn't hide, but there were other ways to defend yourself.)

[I won't hurt you. When you're ready. It'll be my mission, keep me going. It's a long flight.]

The door closes and there is a bump as the gangway pulls back.

"A girlfriend?"

That crooked mouth again. He can't keep it in and doesn't know how to use it. Raw feeling flittering on the edges of his chin and through his eyes.

"What do you mean?" he asks, inexplicably confused.

"Taking care of things for a girlfriend?"

—It's abrupt the way his engagement falters. It doesn't occur to him to lie. He stutters and stops because he only knows the truth but cannot bring himself to say it.

(Is this how we were once? Cannot remember. Everything got in the way, the things that cloud time.)

[Take me back, take me back before all this, before my dreams came true, and the curse fell on every breath in every moment spent dodging the brick that dreaming never saw.]

"A friend who is a girl. Woman. What are you doing in New York?"

—Ever polite, always turning it around. Don't you want to talk about yourself? Sometimes it's what's expected.

"Back to work on Monday. This'll be my last weekend off. You haven't told me your name."

"You haven't told me yours either. They call me Elemeno."

"LMNOP?"

"Elemeno T, technically."

"Your middle name is technically?" Squinting at him and smiling slyly. His unconscious reactions are pure, but he's running behind. Something's in the way, he's so young his brain doesn't know what his body understands, directing movements out of touch with their expression.

He straightens and twists slightly sideways to remove some of the kink from his craning neck.

He thinks it's funny, he likes to be teased.

—Isn't going to correct me.

(I miss this. They don't always see the woman anymore.)

The tip of the boot stretches still more tightly back behind the other leg. Squeezing from head to toe, the pressure is everywhere and reflects the effects of the air and scenery.

Such pretty eyes.

"Do you have a girlfriend?"

—Familiar. Like the demon. What animal are you?

"Nah. I'll be travelling for a while. Doesn't work." Fondling the book in his lap, it's yellow cover is too bright. *The Magic Mountain.* It seems as if he wants to read, to dodge this intervention and go on his merry way.

—Is it possible I've lost my charm for college-aged men?

A nervous tic, he turns it over spreading his hand across the back cover. He wants to think of something clever to say, something that will impress, but nothing comes, and he looks over hopefully, wishing for some signal to help him find the right direction.

(There were always the other kind of men at the shows, or the parties. Tedious, that part, planned. They had exactly the right thing to say, smooth. A notch on their belt, star fuckers who didn't see me, already planning the story while setting truth aside. Call security.)

—How can I help?

"Will you go to Sweden?" He nods to confirm that he understands the reference. It helps focus his attention, he can say something rehearsed now, something normal and ordinary, evade whatever it is that lies behind him, relax as the plane pulls back and rolls off.

—Here's the key to my house. Make yourself at home. Dear lord, what's happening to me?

"I think so. North for sure. Norway, Denmark. Germany mostly. My friend's sister lives there." He leans forward and slips the book into the pocket on the wall in front of him. His fingers are tapping with nervous energy in compound time as the aircraft taxis away from the gate and down the marked pathways toward the line of planes awaiting take off.

"I have family there. Not going myself but know lots of people."

—Just met you, but here's a number to call. Sad. The office? Could do that, it's hardly personal.

He nods and smiles warmly, wants to be agreeable, but isn't picking up on the subtext.

"There aren't too many Americans this year."

—They're afraid, aren't they? Why aren't you?

"You must know the area well." Genuine interest. That's likely what he loves about travelling, the locals. Gets him outside himself and puts him next to everybody else where his foreignness no longer shocks, gels with what the others see and feel, with what he knows to be true. "But no, not many Americans. There were lots of cancellations. I'll avoid the South for the same reason. Those bombings last year have everyone spooked."

"But not Germany? Isn't that why he did it? The discotheque." He doesn't seem like an American, none of the assumptions.

[He wasn't assuming what they always assume, smiling like an idiot and foolishly cheerful. Not like those people from the middle of it who carried it with them everywhere they went and thought every place was exactly the same as America or ought to be.]

—No Big Macs next to die Mauer for you, sausage from the street cart and a mug of beer.

"Not Berlin, Nürnberg. Studying German."

[It's not fair. The ones who talked your ear off, you didn't care about any of it, wished they'd stop and leave, but the ones you wanted to listen to, they wouldn't say anything. Had to pull it out of them.]

—Is that how it works?

(Pulling, there was always resistance. It fluttered and draped across my arms. He spoke as though he was singing but unwilling to draw it from the cavernous spaces. Were he to let loose, we'd draw back in surprise.)

—These wallflowers are what I miss most, you can't see them through the haze.

(Alien and alone but jetting around, first time by myself in years. He's sitting in Cassie's seat. She must've been hurt when she discovered I ditched her. Can't be helped. Be there Monday morning bright and early ready to go but needed this first.)

[To be alone with him, an outsider, who could still look at me that way, the way a man looks at a woman. Is that it? Not the one-sided look the audience has. The adored one wasn't there, they looked through her.

Despite how young he is, too young, what does it matter? Not twice his age, twenty-two or so I bet, only fifteen years. Were I a man, no one would blink, a rockstar doing what rockstars do. Otherwise, don't think about it. Too old to be that foolish woman, too lonely to avoid it.]

"But you're not reading that in the original." Gesturing toward the book. He follows the pointing hand with his eyes moving along its contours, then he gravely confirms.

"I'm still learning."

—Shame you aren't learning Swedish, I know a good way to teach it.

1.12.2. Seannafair.20.15.5.7 [ref(19.86.5.13)]

"Nobody ever looked at me that way." The office is posh. The Lalique draws the eyes to it standing there in the bookshelf next to the leaning diplomas in their exquisite frames. "I don't remember much, but I remember that look. He was a fine thing." The lamp on the oak desk is perfectly shaded to protect someone sitting on the plush couch from suffering the slightest glare. She looks up from her tablet to encourage more but receives nothing. She shows no disappointment, no sense of expectation either.

"Let's try to reconstruct as much as we can. You remember the look. Try to work from there. What was before that? What came after? Slowly. Let's see where we can go."

Hugging the jumper tightly and its fabric rustles against the smooth surface of the couch. Crossing and uncrossing the legs. The materials creak and whimper. There is no other sound in the room except the faint din of occasional traffic on the road below.

(Where were the rhythms, when was I ever in a silent room, when did I ever sit without music if only in the background filling in the blanks?)

"I was young. I hadn't seen anything, didn't know anything."

"Where were you?"

"St. Giles. Singing in the choir. My mother loved to sing. It helped me feel close to her after I left for school, after she passed. It was during my second year, the year I left, when everything happened."

"What does that mean, everything happened?"

"My life, my career, everything. It happened then. It was the last time I was normal. A girl singing in the choir."

(Why couldn't you weep? Why was so long ago so close, where did it go? Could we bear down on the broken things and make them whole again? Was that why I came?)

Leaning forward and reaching for the cup of tea, it's still warm, still fragrant.

The clock is silently moving along. Not a tick or a hum or a tock or a buzz. There is only stillness and fabric and stone and glass. She isn't breathing, not so anyone can tell.

"It must have been May. After Easter. *Be Thou My Vision? Riches ▌ ███████████ vain, empty praise*"

"Is that what you were singing?"

Staring down into the tea, creamy tan.

—Was I remembering it or remembering the song and putting it there with me?

"What are you thinking?"

Caught.

"I'm wondering whether I remember the song or singing it. I've sung it many times. This is before. I don't remember any of that, any of my life then. It's different. I only had two... ...boys... ...then. Nothing. Awkward. Nothing to speak of. I thought I was so sophisticated off at school on my own, but I didn't know anything."

"You had two sexual relationships with young men, is that what you mean? Why does that occur to you now?"

"Sexual relationships," laughing. "If you can call them that. My sex life was shorter than the time it took to sing that hymn."

"What is funny about that?"

—Is she that humorless? No, she thinks it's funny too, but what's funny tells us things, doesn't it?

Considering her face. She's younger but seems older. Professional clothing, a high neck and long sleeves.

"I remember thinking everyone was making such a fuss about it, but it wasn't anything, nothing to get excited about."

The Lalique draws the eyes back to it again. Myriad colors flashing through it from the window, it turns light into rainbows sitting there on the shelf.

"And to answer your question, that look was sexual. It was a sexual experience, being looked at that way. In a way, more than anything that happened with either of those two boys."

"He looked at you as though he wanted to have sex with you, is that how it made you feel?"

"No, not that, not exactly. Desire yes, but I didn't get that feeling, that's normal, I'd seen that before. This was different, he wanted to devour me. No, that's too manky. He wanted to taste me, only a taste. Not a gawk or a gander. Something else." Sighing with a smile, holding it back from laughter.

[Be civilized.]

"Is that what you saw or how you felt?"

"What I saw? I didn't go scarlet, and it didn't make me feel like a slag. I was warm. It was grand. Never felt that or anything like it before."

"But it was a sexual experience."

—It made me wet, is that what you want to hear?

Mouth bending slightly sideways and taking note of whether she seems to register the hidden remarks.

—Is that what she wrote? Move along swiftly to cover the tracks.

"Now that I think of it, it was right when I was singing that solo they had me do there in the middle. *Riches* ████ *not, nor vain,* ████ *praise.* It was simple then. I believed it."

"You believed the line from the hymn?"

"I never wanted to be rich, never thought much about it, hoped I'd have enough to get by. I wanted something true. People always flatter you, tell you what they think you want to hear, be nice to you. They want something, same as those boys, what they wanted, so nice... ...until they got it, then they couldn't find the time."

"Was he different? The one who looked at you?"

"That look was different. It was wrong before, what I said, a taste. The look was about something he wanted to give me, not something he wanted to take."

"What did he want to give you?"

"What I felt... What I thought... ....was that he wanted to give me a taste. Of something, show me something, I don't know what, but I could feel it in my legs. Down there, I could feel it."

[She was going to find out anyway, might as well tell her.]

"Is singing usually a sexual experience for you?"

She makes eye contact to punctuate, but looks back down at her tablet right away, taking notes the whole time.

(She explained before that it was impressionistic, something meant to accompany the recording so she could compare what was said with the impression it made. But she never lets on, not a bit of it.)

—Don't go blathering it to everybody now.

Leaning forward again to put the cup back on the table, then straightening up.

"Hadn't thought about it, but I suppose it is. Your whole body is in it, part of it. The vibrations... ...they can be pleasant. My throat, my mouth, my chest. Muscles most people don't know they have."

"You're singing, which already feels pleasant, and then you notice him looking at you."

"I knew he wasn't a holy joe or anything. He was a tourist. I could tell. The clothes. Some kind of belt. Came to the church for some sight-seeing. It was an offering, and I never thought of sex that way, but I think I was feeling it then. An offering... ...it felt nice... ...was a good feeling, and then

I knew what all the fuss was about. It made sense."

"How long did it go on?"

"Not long, a few seconds, but I remember something afterward now. He had a book and was reading it. He didn't look up, but I kept looking while we continued rehearsal. We went on to other hymns, did our usual, but he didn't move and didn't look at me again."

"Is that it? Is that the whole experience? Or is there more?"

—That's not the half of it, you eejit.

[Be nice.]

(It can't come back all at once. There's no room, where would it go?)

"I talked to him. Afterward. Never in my life did I walk up to a strange man, but I did. After we finished, I walked down there to the pew where he was sitting, and I stood there until he looked up. I've never felt that smooth or unselfconscious in my life, but somehow, I had to do it. Couldn't stop myself. The idea that he'd leave, or I'd leave, well, it was impossible, I had to talk to him, had no choice."

"It's risky, that moment, he could ruin it, not be as perfect as he seemed."

[Laughter here would be a clear indicator of something important. Better not show it.]

"I know it, but it didn't occur to me. Like I said, I wasn't thinking much at the time, I walked right up to him."

"Do you remember what happened? What he said?"

"I don't, but he had a gentle voice. Sweet tone. He didn't make assertions. Does that make sense? I don't remember any. He asked me things, offered me a seat. My church, he's a guest, and offered me a seat."

"How was he looking at you while you talked?"

—As if I could possibly be objective.

Overrun with emotion, heart beating fast, here it comes again, reliving it, feeling it again. Memories come from the body, from the legs and the arms, from the beating heart and the repeated rhythms.

"The same, or I thought it was. It seemed to be that same look. My eyes must've been jumping out of my head. Sometimes, when I'm through singing, I can still hear the songs, the ones I connected with, I can still hear them in my head. That's what it was like talking to him. It was as if I was still singing, and he was looking at me, that same look. An angel, he was an angel." Rushing silence and the prickly feeling of the jumper. Hugging it tightly, firmly looking at her to see if she's registering that. "This was the beginning, this was why I wanted to tell you about it, why I wanted to talk about it."

"The beginning of that sense of euphoria?"

"I had glimpses of it before. It wasn't unfamiliar, but this was more than ever. The energy, I was crawling with it. That night. It happened when I first caught him looking, but it kept going while we were talking. That's the part I remember, that feeling, how strong it was. Stronger than ever before, and it lasted all night, I couldn't go to sleep, I went round the pub afterward and had a few, but that couldn't calm me down. That was the night now that I think of it. Jesus, Mary, and Joseph how did I..."

"Which night? What are you referring to?"

"There was this time when I stayed up all night and wrote a bunch of verses and whatnot. Things that later became most of those first songs we did. In the band. This was that night, it was. I don't know. What would you call it? An episode?"

"A manic phase. Do you remember how long it lasted?"

"I only now remembered that it was the same night as that look, the same night I met him."

—Was it?

"Was that the only night you ever saw him? Or was there more?"

"God, I hadn't thought of this. May, definitely May. You can go to fecking Wikipedia and read about what happened to me that month and I can't remember a damn thing."

"Wikipedia?"

"It's the story of how we were discovered. My band mates told it when we were first interviewed way back. It became a part of the whole mythology, how we formed. This was when it happened."

"And you don't remember any of it?"

—Don't tell her, not that part.

She looks past toward the clock on the wall, it must be getting close.

"I remember that look. Not too many of the details of this or that, only the look. Being tasted, being offered a taste, nothing vain, no empty praise."

"Is this common in the manic phases? Memory lapses coupled with your feeling of elation."

"I don't know. I must've told him about the pub."

"Why do you say that?"

"Because I must've seen him again... ...at the pub."

"You remember seeing him again?"

"From the conversation. He was an American. He was travelling and arrived in London that day. Must've come directly to Oxford from the airport."

"You remember him telling you this?"

"I think I asked him why he didn't want to see London, why he came all this way and left immediately."

[Are you telling tales now?]

"What did he say?"

"Don't know. He was confident... That I remember. He never doubted that he could handle himself. Could see it in his eyes. The whole world, he wanted a taste of it. That's it, everything was that way, the same for him. Offering himself and getting a taste. Getting away. From something... I don't know."

(Memory or something else? It brought us together. Both running...)

Pausing and looking down at the hands crossed in the lap. She looks up from the tablet and over this way. Encouraging, but almost time, that familiar look.

"Not arrogant, confident. They're lucky to have that. Do they know it? Humble too. In awe. That kind of humility, same as what we have. I asked him why he came to church, why wasn't he at the pub? That's when I told him about the pub, but first I asked him why he wasn't there. That's what we think the Americans want, right? On the tear. They come for that, the young ones. Why a church on the first night?"

"What did he say?" she asks.

"He heard the music. He heard the singing."

"He heard you singing."

1.12.3.Natalie.19.86.8.2 [ref(..6.1-5)]

"You've done well, I'm going to keep you." Rolling over and hugging the pillow, belly flat against the bed and turned to face him on his side with his hand propping up his head. Goofy grin lights up his face. It's warm and there's only a sheet for modesty. His legs are curled, and he rocks forward slowly, adding to the warmth: sun bed and body. "Tell me a story."

—The way you looked when you walked in yesterday, you must have something to say.

"I didn't know what I was doing when I left for Newcastle," he launches into it without hesitating or providing any context. "I had a destination and a purpose. There was a boat to Denmark. It must've been the first of June, and I expected to get there that same day. My plans were clear. I wrote them down. The boat to Esbjerg. Use the Eurail pass for the train to Copenhagen. Steer clear of Germany and head to Sweden through Elsinor or whatever it's called. Then up to Oslo and over to Bergen. Boat north. I wanted to be at the Arctic Circle by the Solstice. That was the plan."

There is the hum of a fan over by the door. It's morning and the windows are open, but the blinds pulled shut. The heat is already coming, and the cool night air is on its way out, but not yet. Touching his chin while he goes on, speaking softly.

"It doesn't work that way. I got a lift to Carlisle. That's where the guy was going, and it was drizzling. Didn't want to stand on the side of the road. Went to the youth hostel. They're schools for travelers. Hadn't met any until then. In fact, I realized I hadn't traveled before. Been places, but that was getting on an airplane and taking a bus or a train or something. That isn't travel, but I didn't know that until..."

Fingers lifting up to his lips, and he detours into them with a kiss, letting them find their way inside his mouth and up against his tongue.

"I met lots of people staying at that hostel. Everybody had a plan. We were instant friends. Where have you been? Where are you going? What have you learned along the way?"

Turning over and then sliding closer as he leans down. His breath warm and landing on the neck and shoulder. Following his gaze down along the breasts and over the belly, then back up again. His left hand reaches over to draw circles along the same line.

"An Australian guy and I hit it off. He was an electrician from Townsville near the Great Barrier Reef, traveling for almost a year and getting ready to settle down to work in the UK. He knew everything about how to get around cheap and had a gift for describing it."

Bending the neck so that the head inches closer to his elbow bringing his face closer still and giving his hand more room to roam, hoping it will find what his eyes are drawn to.

"I told him I wanted to get to Newcastle, and he said he was on his way to Edinburgh, but was careful to explain that plans aren't facts, you had to be flexible."

He slides his pelvis closer and presses against the side of the hip, his hand now has free rein over the entire surface area in view.

"Paul told me I was unlikely to get a ride directly from Carlisle to Newcastle, but Edinburgh would be easy. He said you're better off thinking that way, not about what you want, but about what's possible, probable."

His hand finds the creases and the lines, he seems to know where the nerves are most sensitive and deliberately traces over them, occasionally going too far, as if by accident.

"Learned how to eat too. Youth hostels have kitchens, and you can cook. Heat stuff up. It's cheap. The bed's only a couple of dollars, then a couple more for food. You can stretch your money."

He leans in for a kiss, tastes salty, and is moist around the mouth.

"We went to Edinburgh together."

He stops and, looking down, takes his right hand away from his head and strokes the hair away from the eyes and over the ear.

"Is this okay?" he asks.

Pressing the eyes closed, and then, sleepy and warm, looking up at him. "Yes, perfect. Keep going," a little breathless.

"It took all day, but we got there. A short ride and then a longer one to Glasgow on a lorry that left us at a roundabout outside town. It was the road to Edinburgh, and we didn't have to wait long for a ride. It was easy."

He takes back his right hand and gets more comfortable, then lightly lays his left leg over both legs stretching out straight below. He moves it forward and then backward in a makeshift caress accentuating his last words.

"In Edinburgh, we met these two English guys who had a car. They were headed up to the Isle of Skye and invited us to join. According to Paul, this was exactly the point of traveling."

"Travel stories are great," almost purring, chin tilting upward and speaking softly. "But you need to spice it up. Is this whole thing going to be a sausage fest?"

He abruptly retracts his leg, and his hand loses its focus for an instant. Everything pauses while he considers the question.

"You want... Okay... I see. Well... ...we didn't make it to the Isle of Skye, that didn't happen. We stopped in Pitlochry. Every day was long, there was so much packed into them. Carlisle one day, Edinburgh the next, then Pitlochry. My head was swimming, but I learned the ins and outs for how to avoid letting my body take me back to that same rut."

His hand is alive again and finds the soft hair below the belly.

"Rut?" Sliding still closer, not that he needs it to reach, but for encouragement, to let him know he's on the right path.

"Focus on the destination kept creeping back. I'd only known these guys a few days and I'm convinced they're my permanent travel companions. Linus and the other guy... ...can't remember his name... I just met them, but now they're fixtures, and I can't imagine leaving them behind. I thought I was learning, but not really."

Breathing quicker as he teases his way closer.

"We decided to splurge and go to the pub. It was filled with locals. Somehow, we got into it with these two girls and a guy at the next table. They were fun-loving. Linus and the other guy were hilarious. Paul was mellow, going with the flow. It was fun."

He draws a sketch with the outline starting up at the top, spreading his fingers along with the lips as he spreads them downward.

"I was sitting next to one of the girls and, at some point, out of nowhere, she leans across me to make a point to Linus about music or something. When she leaned over, she put her hand down on the bench we were sharing. It could've been an accident, I don't know, but her hand went directly between my legs. On the bench but between my legs."

As he says it, he punctuates with his fingers by moving them gently inward and back up toward the top, shallow and light.

"It was a flash. Now I wasn't with Paul, Linus, and that other guy anymore. I was with her. I don't remember her name. It was sudden... ...being without attachment... ...one minute with the lads... ...then I'm going home with her, with them."

"Mmmmm," purring and lifting up to him, but he pulls back in sync and presses down at the hip to flatten it back onto the bed. "That's it. Keep going." Snuggling closer against his resistance, the warmth is everywhere, the whole room is radiating, and the fan can't keep up. Once the hips are back at rest, his hand returns to its rhythms. His voice goes softer still.

"This girl was excited about playing music for us. As if I'd never heard music before. We went to her apartment, and she put on some crappy pop songs. She was a teacher in primary school and had that way about her. Explaining things as though I were a child. She thought I didn't know anything. Was that her kink, or was she drunk?"

"Get to the good part," whispering and pressing the right hand against his left hand, pushing it along the necessary angles.

"The boyfriend was kind of a quiet type, and the schoolteacher was nuts, but I got on with Paige, the friend. She had cool sensibilities, you know? She had taste. Good things. The right bad things, too. The music we were listening to.... ...she knew where to go sailing and skiing, what it was like to live in Pitlochry in the winter and summer, the difference."

At the pronouncement of her name he surrenders to the arching and leaning, he lets his hand go where the surfaces and movement direct it.

"She had some kind of outdoorsy job, but I don't remember what it was. She didn't tell me. She was water running through a valley, it can't tell you what it is, it can only be it."

His face leans closer, finding the neck by the ear and exhaling air in rhythm with his hand's motion. Then he draws back.

"Sailing and skiing, she knew about both, and was unbelievably cute. Short dark hair. Lovely skin. Such charming ways about her."

He kisses the ear and lets his voice fall lower.

"She liked me too. Didn't pay much attention to her boyfriend and apologized for the schoolteacher. They'd known each other their whole lives... My life, on the other hand, was compressing into the briefest possible moments where relationships only had a few hours or days to develop. There was no time for anything else."

Drawing his chin back up and looking into his eyes.

"I bet she liked that. What did you do? It seems impossible."

He is smiling, but there is a trace of something else.

"Are you enjoying the story?" he asks.

—Hoping for my approval.

[Tender. Oh yes, you could have it, if that's what it took.]

Leaning up to kiss him, pulling his chin closer.

"Mmmm, yes. Keep going."

"Of course, you've guessed the problem. It can't be done. But then I remembered my training. Travelling and destinations. I didn't need to figure everything out. I didn't need to plot my way from A to B with every step and every move clearly set. A general sense to orient myself, but then pay attention, see what unfolds."

The last line sends a shock wave to his fingers and their movement amplifies.

"Ooooh, nice touch," tilting toward him and pulling him up and over, feeling his weight increase and settle.

"The music was playing. Paige and I weren't drinking. The schoolteacher was hammered. The boyfriend too. We were sitting in the living room. He was at one end of the couch, and Paige was sitting in the middle. The schoolteacher was in an easy chair, and I was sitting on the floor. Paige wanted to show me something from some magazine she pulled out, so I had to get up and move next to her."

Hooking him into place firmly as his elbows move to either side of the head and his face looks down, eyes bright and focusing.

"You think she was in on it? She was trying to solve the same problem?" pulling him closer and whispering, "Keep going."

"I don't remember what she wanted to show me, but it didn't last long. It was an excuse to get me onto the couch. After that, not sure how it happened, but she was kissing her boyfriend while the three of us were sitting there. It wasn't a big couch. I could feel her leg against mine while she was leaning over toward him."

Arms underneath his and stroking the length of his sides along the back and to his ass, firmly set in place. Pulling the legs up higher and trying to rock him into motion.

"The schoolteacher was drunk and lost her inhibitions. She took the opportunity to get up and come sit on my lap."

"Paige must've known." Legs squeezing a slow rhythm while pulling him closer, then pushing him away, then closer. "Keep going."

"She must've... ...it was a typical Saturday night, I don't know, because it seemed too easy. Paige leaned back and kissed me while the schoolteacher leaned over and kissed the boyfriend."

"Perfect. Keep going, keep going," urgently saying it as the rhythm steadies despite his unwillingness to contribute.

"It seemed to be part of the same lesson. Change is the only constant and the four of us were together, as if it were always that way."

Throwing the head back and keeping the eyes closed, desperate for him to take some initiative, any at all, the smallest movement, a light pulse straining inside, and all kinds of sensation runs up and down the body, toes to tits.

"We fell right into it. Everybody was kissing everybody. The groping, the petting, touching. We were a single mass and somehow managed to get to the bedroom and undress."

Pulling one more time, hard, in a deliberate tug leaving him deep inside.

Grinding upward to set the pace. His mouth goes wide.

"They pass out. Sloppy and finished fast. Paige and I went back to the living room. We..."

"No more telling, show. Now keep going."

1.12.4.Greta.19.86.9.5 [ref(..84.5-9)]

"The Gypsy siguiriya begins with a terrible scream that divides the landscape into two ideal hemispheres. It is the scream of dead generations, a poignant elegy for lost centuries, the pathetic evocation of love under other moons and other winds." [Garcia Lorca]

Looking up as he approaches the table. Putting the book in the bag on the seat.

[Too many times going over it, imagining what... ...and then what... The mood. In person... You tremble... The longing to look at a thing known only to imagination. Wanting it, unable to capture it, represent it, this whole vivid world expands in front of you but the only thing you could say was "he approaches" and nothing more. None of the tension, none of the waiting, the burden or the anguish, it's lost, even though it was the only thing you could think about when you scratched it out: "he approaches."]

"I didn't recognize you," he says sitting down opposite, leaving no opportunity for a more deliberate greeting or any touching to mark the event.

"It's goth," pushing it back over the ear. "It was the most different thing I could come up with."

—I'd have done anything to make it so Eva could look at me again.

"Change the body, change the voice. How'd you recognize me?" he asks.

"She sent pictures. I thought you'd be more ragged. Honestly, I didn't expect it to take this long."

"I'm sorry. I couldn't face... ...didn't know how to look at you..."

"It's okay. I didn't... ...been angry..."

"Because I didn't come?" He asks, resting his arms on the table. Looking over, there is a big rucksack leaning by the entrance, he must've left it there.

"I didn't... It was a shock... ...it wouldn't have made any difference, but in my head... ...had trouble separating... I don't know. Blame is part of it."

"For me too," he says making direct eye contact and showing, for the first time, a sense of recognition in the eyes, the nose, and the face.

(He learned to stop seeing the hairdo that distracted him all this time.)

"Who do you blame?"

He can't bring himself to speak of it, looks down. His lower lip is trembling. Shifting his weight on the bench, the plastic cushioning sticks to his legs. She comes round, and he orders a coffee.

"You sound as if you're from Baden-Württemberg."

His discomfort radiates, indicating either that the previous question still resonates or that the observation alludes to something painful. Pleading with softened eyes that he can ignore both if he chooses.

"You didn't only do the hair, you've got the whole thing going on. The clothes and everything."

"Shoes," gesturing down and sliding the left leg out of the booth to let him see the shiny black leather. Batting the eyes to show off the lashes and draw attention to the shadow. She brings the coffee, and he takes up alchemy to get it right.

—Where can we go from here? Stranger to familiar.

"What was the picture?" he asks.

"By the hospital. You had a horse." He smiles and nods a few times. It comes back to him and shines in his eyes. "Do you remember when that was taken?"

"Of course. The doctor took the picture. I knew him through my friend. He introduced us."

"That day?"

"No. Before that. It's why I rode up there. I wouldn't have done that for the doctor."

"Why were you there?" It's an abrupt turn, and he isn't ready for it. His composure, delicately balanced from moment to moment, falters. "If you don't mind me asking. I don't have a complete picture. You could fill in some details."

He cups his hands around the coffee mug but still hasn't taken a sip.

[Did your story explain the delay, explain everything? Was it the delay that increased the drive to hear it?]

"Uh, there was a guy who rented a room in some friends' house. He was a physician from there studying to be a doctor in the US. There's some big test you have to take and it's hard. He was there a long time studying. He passed, but then had a hard time finding a job."

"All that trouble and no one hires him?"

"The test is to get licensed. Once you have that, you still need to find something, a residency, and they don't want to hire people who didn't go to accredited schools. The test is supposed to take care of that, but the hospitals don't see it that way."

The change comes over him swiftly as he steps away from ground where he cannot stand to ground where he is firm and stable. It's an instant transition in his mouth and throat, covering his eyes and the rest of his face.

[Unsure of himself and ashamed, what could she possibly see in him?

But like this... Too pretty.]

—I get it.

"I see."

"His visa was for studying. It expired and he had to go back to renew it. Keep trying from there." Coffee's mostly a prop for gestures, but he takes a sip.

"You went with him."

"Me and another guy. The family, his family, owned a coffee farm. It's not that uncommon for people in the city to own farms up in the mountains. Absentee owners. The farms are run by locals, overseers who hire day labor to do the picking, it's highly ordered. The government is involved, there are lots of regulations. Juan Valdez is twelve years old," he sneers at the end.

"What does that mean?"

"It's something she said. They hire children to pick the beans. The hills are steep, and you can't use machines. They need people to climb around and use their hands to pick the beans off the small trees. Twelve-year-olds are especially good at it. They're small enough to get low, nimble enough to pick fast, and strong enough to carry the baskets back to the mules."

"You mean the coffee we're drinking was harvested by children?"

"I don't know. That's how it was on the farm. I don't know how it is everywhere, but that's what I saw."

—Discriminating. Not rash. Hesitates to judge.

"His family owned this farm, did they let you stay there?"

"Yeah, for the summer. It needed some renovations. Stuff was falling apart, and the overseer was only interested in the farming business. The manager was overwhelmed trying to keep up with the day-to-day chores. There was all this improvement work that wasn't getting done: fences, out buildings, animals needing more attention than daily feeding."

"What kind of attention?"

"That horse, the one in the picture... ...he had a lot of spirit... ...and he needed plenty of exercise, to be ridden. The family would go up now and again. The overseer sometimes, or the manager, but that was it, and it wasn't enough. There were two other horses, mares, less temperamental, but they needed exercise too."

"You guys were there to help out."

"Well, my friend's father wanted *him* to do it, but he needed to keep looking for a job. That required him to stay in the city. He couldn't afford to let things cool down. Those tests are part of lifelong maintenance, he needed to stay on schedule."

"Was he with you on the farm?"

"No. Only the two of us. He came up sometimes. Weekends... ...occasionally."

"What did you guys know about farming?"

"Not much, but the people there knew a lot about it. We knew something we didn't realize we knew."

"You didn't know that you knew it?"

"I didn't know that it was a thing to know."

"What?"

"A kind of order. Or efficiency. Not sure what to call it. Project management? I don't know." He pauses and digs his hands down under his legs, leans his head forward and purses his lips. "There was this building. Some kind of shredder for grass and sugar inside. It had a flat roof that leaked."

"They must know how to repair roofs. Do you know how to repair a leaky roof?"

"Haven't a clue. Or didn't have a clue. That's what I mean. They kept repairing the roof. Patch after patch. They were everywhere. The whole roof was patched. Why did it keep leaking no matter how much they patched it?"

"That's the order you're talking about."

"That's what they told me. The overseer and the manager. It rained every day there. It's the equator, everything is regular. The sun rises and sets at the same time every day. Every day exactly the same. Rains in the afternoon, every day, it seemed. Not for long, but regular."

"And the water would pool on the roof."

"My friend and I asked if it should be an A frame. We didn't know anything about it. We knew that the patching couldn't go on forever. If we built a different kind of roof..."

"The colonizers come to save the day." He smiles and half nods, doesn't take himself too seriously.

"Pizarro," he says with a shrug. "They knew it was a good idea, didn't fight us. We weren't teaching them. They were too busy, said we were practical, kept repeating that word, and it seemed to be something about order. For them, fixing the roof was one of their daily chores. We saw it as a problem needing a long-term solution. Who knows if it worked? We didn't stick around to find out, but..."

"I see. Not a better order, different."

"Yeah. Made us useful. We didn't try to run the place, but we found things to do. They didn't mind having us around."

"Okay, you're in this village, staying at this farm."

"Our friend introduced us to everyone. Well, everyone with the right social status. The man who owned most of the buildings in the village, Don Alberto, everyone called him. The man who owned the general store, Gabriel. His brother Fabiano, Sebastian who worked for them, the doctor, the mayor. Because of where we came from, we were admitted among *the elite*," he twists the last words for emphasis.

"More proof of colonial rule," and he's nodding in response, pursing his lips.

"Sebastian worked in the general store. An assistant. He invited us over to his house, and we didn't have the sense to refuse. No, we accepted with pleasure. Later we learned that he must've spent a month's wages. The food, the drinks, he was obligated to have these things, but they were beyond his means. By accepting his invitation, we forced him to do that. It cost his family. He had small children. Two, third on the way."

"You thought you were being egalitarian, but you were causing hardship."

"And there was nothing we could do to correct it. That's what Gabriel told us. He said we shouldn't have gone. People will make offers, but we can't accept, or we have to know who is offering and only accept when it's right. We had to learn the rules."

"Was she at the same social level as you?"

"Sort of. It was inevitable we would meet. She was an outsider and educated putting her in the same position, but she had it much worse, being a woman. She couldn't be friends with Gabriel and Don Alberto. She had to be friends with their wives and their children. The doctor didn't follow that, he was a good friend to her, but the other men, no matter what she did for the village, she couldn't... It wasn't done..."

"I see. The three of you were thrown together."

"Everyone insisted we meet. It was inevitable. There's a European at the hospital, you must meet her."

"But she couldn't come out and meet you in the village, is that it?"

"Not at the bars where we met the mayor and the doctor and the others. She couldn't come, not alone. If someone thought to bring her, but who would do that?"

"But you could bring her. Once you met. She could run around with you guys and not attract suspicion, right?"

"It was obvious that the three of us would go around together. We had different rules. No one expected us to act the same way, it was okay. Yes."

[Something was missing, he was holding back, thinking too much about each word and how it landed. This wouldn't do.]

"But how did you meet?"

"My friend, after introducing us to the men, took us to the hospital for a visit. The doctor's invitation. It's good to know the hospital. Where it is and how to get there. You never know. We had a jeep to drive around. People from the village might need help going to the hospital. He thought we should learn. We went up for a visit and he showed us around."

"And introduced you to her."

"It was weird. He's pointing everything out. Bragging about their X-Ray machine, their operating room, and in this corner, here is our German missionary. She was playing in the dirt when we first met her. It was funny, she was digging something, or working with the mud. A retaining wall? Something on the hospital grounds. Did all kinds of stuff up there... ...with the nuns. We thought she was religious. It was the opposite though. She was taking care of women who needed things the nuns couldn't give or preferred not to."

Grateful for the image.

"Overalls?"

"Of course. Caked in mud, but not the least bit apologetic, didn't seem self-conscious. We were immediately smitten, and it wasn't because it was some village in the hills. Anywhere, in any setting... ...she was striking."

He looks down, running low, or afraid to see her, signs of her, and has to avert his eyes to prevent it.

"We're not exactly alike." Rescuing him. "That look in her eyes... When we were kids, we'd be standing right next to each other and still not see the same thing. It always meant something else to her. Can't explain it. We're the same, but not. If you're side-by-side your entire life, you won't look at everything the same, and that means... I don't know what it means... ...but we're not the same."

"You wouldn't want to go digging in the mud in that outfit." He gives off a sense of relief and bobs his head to acknowledge the differences carefully selected during the four months waiting.

Looking down and getting embarrassed by the thin, black linen jacket with its crisp shoulders and the white, lace top framed by the jacket's black lapel. "I don't know if it suits me. Trying it out. To put distance... ...but..." trailing off and tilting the head to the side, catching a flash of compassion from those big eyes.

2.12

this year's harvest

2.12.1.Elisabet.19.86.5.9

—Take me back, take me back before, before my dreams came true and curses fell on every breath, every moment spent dodging bricks, dreaming never saw.

[Tay ay ay ay ay ah ay ah ay ah ay ku meeeee...]

The wheels rolling along as the plane moves toward the runway, queued behind the others. It'll only be a minute now, the abrupt pressure, pressing back against the seat, turning toward the window outward, the sea brilliant in the midday sun.

—They talked me into it. Not forced, persuaded. Europe, Asia, South America, what's left? Only America to make it real. The freedom to get rich.

(The three of us in the garden, parental patience left us there, with the explanations. Why did these grow and not that? Why was there this much in Summer and hardly any in Winter? Knowledge garden: knowing whatever we wanted to know as long as we sat still, as long as we listened.)

—Should have been a painter, should have been a sculptor, anything but this.

[Missed the business when they first heard it, music and then tuned out the rest: music business. Businesswoman, a music businesswoman.]

He is looking out the window. Same sea, same sun, awareness, peripheral feelings of someone behind you. Both afraid to fly, fearing along the row together, single file, heads tilting to the right. Closing in on the front of the queue, nearing the edge of the runway, turning to twist, the plane edges along.

—Take me back, flat on my back, to the knowledge garden, before my dreams came true, before curses brought the fear, every moment listening, dodging bricks dreaming never saw.

[Tayyyyyyyyyyyyyyyyyyyyyyyyyyyyyyyyyyyykeme...]

(Why do it? Such a lark, birdsong better. Didn't know whether it was any good or anything anyone wanted to hear. That coffeehouse with the wood, the kids, their reaction: I felt it, inside me. Never sure before. How could you turn away? Once you had a taste, there was no stopping. Pure highs. After that, reliving it.)

—Petter and Mats... ...no idea. We were kids... ...playing... ...and bursting... ...to take it out of their room and into crowded clubs. They knew it would get them laid.

[Being swept away by men's passions, that's half of it. More. The sex. Of all the things we wanted, of everything we hoped, mingled and mixed, turned around face to face and belly to belly.]

—What else did songs do? Joined together in the dark. In that smoke. The noise. Playing out the American fantasy, living the English dream.

She doesn't stand a chance. She has no immunities, those popular images lifting through the air, burrowing through their ears, and nestling into their brains. They think themselves unique, special: the ones who reach the peak. Chanting in unison, each affirming their status above the others, no one voice stands out. Until...

(More failures than I cared to count. Thought we were brilliant, but there were many. The tunes were catchy, clicked. A month earlier or a month later and we'd've missed it.)

The plane turns and the mountains off the coast become visible. He gasps and shuffles in his seat, nerves tingling with growing anticipation.

[Seats this close together were intimate, better to sit next to someone you knew, the strangers couldn't avoid you.]

—Take me back, flat on my back, to the knowledge garden, before those English dreams came true, before those curses fell fearing along the row, every moment listening, swept away by his passion, face to face and belly to belly. Tired of fashion.

[Take meeeeeeeeeeeeeeeeeeeeeee... ...no... Ta may ba...]

(There were never any choices. Quietly, in the garden, painting, sculpting, drawing. Left to myself, as if that could happen, they never left you alone, it's what I fell into. Petter and Mats, their passions, and his, carried away... Pushed under a smoky light surging with those faces, watching me dance and chirp. It was a drug, injected and repeated, the high became an addiction and I never felt full.)

—Into my head. Only the first, only those came from inside, freshly stripped of childhood fears.

[Look what they did to them, unrecognizable now, someone else in my mouth. Couldn't come out of me, couldn't be its space and time. Everything later, a few days, wrapped in the urge to repeat and fill. Once you taste it, you'll do anything to keep it. What do they want to hear? How to make them look and guarantee they keep looking? Empty, you're not inside yourself anymore, you're inside them.]

(Fast living, breakups, passion, that's what they wanted. The little doll, provocative, kept them looking, feeling. Those words came through my mouth. Easy, we slipped into new masks as though they were ourselves. No other, they came indirectly, dragging us along lines we never should have crossed, never meant. Once you've spied the end, the means populate themselves. They didn't belong to anyone, but stayed the night, came again and again, they were you and everyone. There was nowhere else to go.)

—Those first times, at school: the cellar, the places around, auditoriums. Recognition, being recognized.

(But small. You never knew to relish the small. Wanting big because they told you to. America. The biggest. If you wanted to be gigantic, America. Their radio, interviews, saying the same things again and again to everyone everywhere. Repeated to prolong, to increase the size, to be more.)

[Better better better better better... ...play better., ...sing better... ...write better... ...see better. Not more, better.]

Grumble grumble whoosh, the plane rolls into its maneuver, the wheels are churning and resistance increases. Thrust back against the seat, there is tightening down to the toes. Feeling his clenched grip on the armrest, he enters dire straits desperately afraid. Reaching out with a light touch, a simple pat, a glance that way. It'll be okay, only a minute, a few seconds, and then it'll be over.

—Soaring soon, such a little thing. Nothing is little anymore, nothing fits in my hand.

(You couldn't see their faces. Bright light. You might as well be playing by yourself. Thought they would be grand and glorious, but they're lonely. Looking over at Petter and seeing nothing. Not one thing. He wasn't there, his eyes were blank, it wasn't him, it wasn't happening. I was alone. Thousands of people and no one was there.)

—Take me back, flat on my back, to the knowledge garden, before my fantasies came true, before big curses fearing, every moment listening, swept away by his gigantic passion, face to face and belly to belly, tired of fashion, a doll dancing for love.

[Taykuhme Baaaaaaaaaaaaaaaaaaaaaack...]

(Before I found N, before we found each other, not a single human looked at me the way they did before. No one tells you that. How much you'll miss seeing another's eyes from a real place, seeing into someone that way. A young man with a ridiculous name, how did he do it? Did he realize he was looking at me from the past, from out of my life long ago, taking me back to where I was when things were real, before it came between me and them, me and me, between us, all of us, there?)

"Are you afraid to fly?"

"Take off. It's terrifying," he clenches while responding.

"Me too." Patting his arm again to make it more friendly, more careful, but letting it linger. Slower rhythms to ease it back down inside.

—I won't see N until... When? California? That's months away. We have to... How...? He won't...

Glancing over at a simplified treat: he wears no makeup, no skin cream, has no daily regimen. They're not supposed to look that good without effort, a freak for sure, something to be savored, with those dimensions in the lines hiding in his face.

[Nothing ridiculous, that's the contract, and despite the name, the look wasn't. Those were the finer things, but not a clue. Natural gifts free of second sight, pointing a mirror that way... ...criminal, putting a smirk in place of that pout... ...evil.]

"What?" Asked simply, he doesn't know.

"Well, honestly, I was thinking that one of the things I miss the most is being looked at as if I'm an ordinary person."

"That's fame, isn't it? Always on stage. With an audience. As if they know you. They don't see you, they oversee you."

—How would he know? N kept pushing me to do something different, go somewhere else, find something that fits us, me, with everything, our lives. All we wanted, but how? Many people depend on me. Employer. Businesswoman. They never tell you that, about the incorporation that comes with it, the limited liability, and payroll. Never said a word.

(More more more, they chanted. That's what they're selling. That's the vision. They held up fire and lit up the night. It was a trick. The wizards behind those curtains, they lied, and that was their lesson. We should put a stop to it, the lying, the fires that teach nothing, but suck the air out of the room and explode in new chambers, gobbling up fresh air everywhere they breathe it.)

> [Take me back
> back on the flat
> the garden knowing
>
> fantasy
> before true night
> in drea-eams showing
>
> (is doll dancing for love)
>
> hot bearing
> faring for three
> fall across the prow
>
> evry moment
> torment vision
> past life cannot now
>
> (is doll dancing for love)
>
> evry moment

> soundly to sleep
> proves fleeting passion
>
> longer seas
> eternally
> tired of fashion
>
> is doll dancing for love
> [duet]
> love dancing for doll (love doll for dancing)
> doll love for dancing (dancing doll for love)]

"I didn't know."

—We're both on the verge of breaking. Pull is at its fiercest. The ascent, the wind, the rush, a single bird, that's all it'd take to crush us, burn us, blow us into bits. Future babies alone, born motherless. Oh God, keep it together, keep the birds away.

[Tell him, tell him what you know. Make yourself a mirror. Be that woman. For one, for a single one who looks back, who sees.]

—It's what we always do.

(It's how they stole from us, took what was true and turned it into stupidity. Beautiful in song and dance, turned into business because they couldn't think of anything else, couldn't see anything else. No vision, only apocalypse. They were the virus, they were the scourge.)

"How could you? It's not your fault."

[Tears and sorrow. Bless you. How did the pressing air know to surface this missile in the lift they brave together?]

—If it's possible, if there's a way, I'll show you this one thing. Can't come out with it, can't hold it up in front of you.

[That made it the same as the others, their bellies and their bullshit. Farting and burping, coarse and disgusting, whatever they wanted, that's the world we had to live in, that's the curse they brought upon us.]

(Fuckable. That asshole in London and his Abba wave, fuckable, and in his world fuckable was what mattered, it's what sells, where the money went. Put me in those skirts, those tight pants, made me dye my hair and paint my face, to serve his rotten fantasy and the world he wanted to fashion from it.)

—That's not what I'm going to show you. There is a cure.

(There were mirrors that showed the world as it was and there were mirrors that showed the world as it ought to be. Producers and managers only wanted the second, avoided looking back with all their might, doing whatever they had to do to cover them up and turn away in persistent mourning. That's why they couldn't let her speak, that's why they couldn't let her use her own voice and called her mad. She had to be part of that fantasy and let *it* provoke her desire since those were the desires they hoped to harvest. Its object, its thing, they couldn't see anything else because these were the desires that made their dreams come true, and they came thin and in short skirts or with tight pants, they came with veils and a dance that went long into the night.)

—They want that gaze, they want that look, something desired, consumed, a fuckable thing for sale.

[No one else showed him how to value that better sense, understand himself, be a man, a real man. Through that look, in disguise, purely himself and not driven into the recesses and losses the world tried to make him bear.]

Such a sweet smile, exchanging and recognizing.

"Thank you."

—That's not it, but I'll find a way.

2.12.2. Seannafair.20.15.5.7 [ref(19.86.5.13)]

Stepping out the door and taking hold of the metal railing to carefully step one by one down to the sidewalk. Then arm in arm out to the street before a half twirl takes in the light and the afternoon sun beating down uncharacteristically onto the pavement. Across the street, the row of houses mirrors the row on this side. Four stories in all, single family dwellings intermixed with a college dormitory and the psychiatrist's home office.

Her heels are not the best for walking, but it's such a lovely day, shame to let it go by without a mark. He hovers large nearby ready to help her into the backseat of the car idling next to the line of them parked in front of the building.

Waving him off, "You can go, I'll walk." Pointing up the street.

Still unsure, he looks for more confirmation then gets back into the car and waits long enough to make absolutely certain that he should follow the instructions.

(It was a red and black flannel shirt, and a ratty pair of jeans. Faded like the kids were wearing. Weren't there some big boots, some kind of work shoes or something? Decidedly working class, but with those smart eyes. I couldn't gather the contraries. I couldn't make out what kind of fella he was.)

—How did I block him out?

Crossing over to the other side and stepping deliberately up onto the curb, she'll trail along the curving street to the intersection where she can turn to the left and move toward the busy road up ahead, traffic rushing

*side to side. Both ways there is a hum and bustle, the city traffic whirls
along. Taxi cabs and buses hold the majority, but autos and lorries take
their fair share.*

The smell of diesel everywhere. Turning away from the buses passing
by to protect lungs from foul air, taxis unlit slow down just in case. Better
to look up the street to prevent anyone thinking a decision is in the making.

(Always hyper after those rehearsals. Filled with energy. Crooning in
the church, nothing finer. I was in seventh heaven and that always sent me
to the pub.)

—It was that same night, the same night I first saw, the same night he
looked at me.

Look right to cross Brompton at the three-way, the V&A looms larger
to the right and holds the gaze despite the risks of nearby traffic. Earning
urbane honks from this one, and another soon after, but then safely to the
other side slowly moving up the road with the heels of the high ankle boots
dragging while moving forward. Two fashionable young women pass by,
they are heading the opposite way, but turn to look once past. Full of
recognition, they whisper and giggle when they notice the jacket is abruptly
tucked where it shouldn't be. "She's completely out of it, should we call the
medic?" They laugh and try to include others nearby in their observation
and the delight in its object. An older woman's attention is drawn that same
way by such a minor event they've made into spectacle. "Leave her be," she
says, then shakes her head both compassionately and with a motherly
warning to the girls, not wanting to see this idol of her youth sorely drawn.

*Passing by its stellar gates and tuning out the noise nearby, no one can
reasonably expect to find something here, there is no need to tend to it. No
more meaning to this name, there is no sense letting it register. Eyes out in
the distance, vision impaired for what is nearby, there is nothing that can
reach out, nothing that can touch the stems and whistles of high afternoon.*

(I knew he would come. I could see it. I wanted him to come and tried
to show it in everything I said and did. I wanted him to follow along. It'd
be safer talking to him there, there'd be plenty of mates about.)

[The first one who looked as if he would know what to do, as if it
wouldn't be ridiculous.]

—What the... At the pub afterward, I did mention that, that's why he
was there, that's how he found me.

*A fruit stand ahead on the left near the turn to Thurloe place has quite
a crowd before it. Someone is arguing about the price of berries while two
retro-clad schoolgirls previously attentive lose interest to watch her walk
past. "Aine," one calls out. "Aine," again when there is no response. The
big glasses and scarf don't hide her away from those who know what to look
for.*

The well-meaning must understand, the bracketing must be exhaustive, otherwise every ten feet it'll be something else, someone else, some other purpose trying to halt progress. Heels digging, feet hurting, there is a chill, but the sun is bright, and the news of the day cannot be a bother. It is solitude among the crowd that provides the main attraction.

(I don't think he saw the people around me. There was a crowd of us at the table, but he didn't stop or wonder, he walked right up and asked me things.)

[Yes was there, yes was there. I remember yes, I thought yes, I saw yes.]

—I was with my friend. Darlene? Lita?

The inlet neighborhood between the busy street and the entrance to the South Ken station is crowded. School children on their way, nannies and caregivers with their charges, other people hurrying to avoid the after-work rush soon to come. The old men and women carry umbrellas out of habit, though none need it now.

There is something roasting. The smell is pleasant and blends out the stench that would otherwise creep out from under. A tiny hunger pang appears in the back, but it is rapidly squashed.

[Calories there were calories wasted, priorities must be maintained.]

(Is this your neighborhood pub? Do you come here often? Remember that. Where has it been all this time, and why now? What's bringing it back, and why today? What spells did that witch cast? What magic went on in that office?)

[That light curl alit upon the forehead, that thin gait, that steady flow, that ease of space, that reach that year that alluring jawline.]

—He came right up to us. That same look. Not Darlene, focused on me.

On Harrington, a bold young man stops and turns, looks to his friend for courage. "That's her, innit? Look lads, it's Aine Quinn," and then he makes his way back to beg her pardon. "Pardon me, pardon, Aine. Pardon me."

"Pardon me." Not allowed, he can't expect a reaction other than this feigned invisibility. He resigns and turns away. The dark lenses and big frames get respect from the timid, and their full weight can make the bold retreat.

(Completely inexperienced, or almost, there was nothing to compare it to. That look isn't in the same category as anything from those two silly boys. The first is never really first, is it? There are layers to it, something deeper happened there. Looks like that could make you know what it was... ...not until then. It found its way deep —into my body— it revealed places that nothing ever touched before.)

[Me, aimed at me, for me awake and alive, for me drawn down deep, for me with flows and fluids, for me with lives livid.]

—I could see his focus. It was a thing, a thing to be seen.

There is French in the air, and they take note of the same cues that follow in a wave along the road. One woman steps out from the group and turns directly to face this way to snap a photograph with a camera she carries for some other purpose. A lucky find, but it won't turn out well, it's too far away and there are too many people blocking the shot. The small group resigns to failure, reassuring each other that they did indeed see what they thought they saw. Then they move on to cross the street and meet up for some event later at the Institute. "Show some respect," one fellow says. "She's making her way same as the rest of us."

Stony silence is what they'll find in her face, but were it permitted, it would be a pleasure to send signs of gratitude to the anonymous defenders.

(Passing looks on the street, men and boys. Looks in school from trappers who'd have no idea what to do if they ever caught what they were hunting. Looks at the pub or the park, looks over the lights, and in the night and past the entryways that marked the doors along the way from the chips stand back to the house, but there was always distance in those looks. Though they made me uncomfortable and occasionally confused, there was nothing in them that touched or reached the center where they tried hard to land. That way he had, that look, it looked for someone, it hoped for contact, it reached out to make an offer, that lesson learned meant lovely consideration. It was the awakening of some haunting hope.)

[Wiggled and whispered, there was no one to either side. He eclipsed the friend in them and the burning bulbs above and on the walls. No lanterns lit and no sparkles bright, too much pure vision to note the spectacles around. Experience slowed down the passing time because it was overfilled.]

—And I was a thing, I was being seen.

Familiar haunts on all sides, she needn't attend to her path. It's a commercial stretch and she makes her way through it with the habit of numerous times before, under different conditions: distressed and calm, careful and rushed, drunk and sober, she knows her way despite the distractions and commotion.

—Almost there, this may be a mistake. Ditched him. There's no such thing as enjoying the fresh air and sunshine anymore. It doesn't work the same way in every square and every yard.

(He sat down. As though it were casual, as though anyone would do the same. Comfortable in his skin, at ease without a pint in his hand. Waved it aside, didn't he, might not have had the fee.)

[Pleased to have a seat, pleased to sit, pleased to take in everything on our behalf.]

—What did he say? It felt good.

The long light at Queen's Gate is packed with pedestrian traffic. "Oh my, look who it is." One man sings a familiar tune, another professes his undying love. The disapproving likewise turn to look and see the object of such foolishness. The numbers must be made from the unfamiliar or out-of-towners since this much fuss could never find its way from locals drowned in the malaise of regular contact with such figures. This trail through the city is not usually this uninviting. At other times of night, there is more discretion to be found: the daylight makes them crass.

Those in front break ranks to turn and face the other way. It's as if a circle has formed where there should have been a square. The center bends and bows to this necessity, awkward and hoping for some quick respite. Red is what fills the way and time stretches slowly with its full color until the moment when nothing more can last, then green comes and there is a break. The circle ellipses and the wave plods on.

(Something about the song still resounding in his head, something about the music in the air, about the call of the night and the way the walls of the church resonated and made the best of whatever tweaks and tunes rose within it.)

[Showed the sex in it, heard the body there, leaned over more and caught a brief contact from the angles. Didn't touch me but reached out his hand to let me know how much he wanted to.]

—Something about the Pogues, it was, wasn't it?

Hesitating at the giant Stanhope Gardens on the right, there are dogs about getting their afternoon exercise. A pair on a leash nearby, the one sniffs unnoticed at her steadily moving legs. She keeps a regular cadence once clear of the crowds, but there are children nearby and their shouts and cries fill the air as she moves past. They are far more interesting to the old ladies near the corner, and they provide her camouflage while passing through this residential part of the street.

Finally, a fresh smell and some relief from the endless sea of groups and crowds and bending ways. The spring has come and the animals, pure in their focus, know it despite those around them unable to fathom its depths.

(There was one of those portable cassette players on his hip. It was attached to his belt and the headphones were around his neck with the long chord dangling down to his waist.)

[Whatever he had to offer, I took it.]

—Yes, the Pogues, but the Smiths, that was it. He had their new album somehow. He wanted to play it for me.

Left at the light on Gloucester, she heads down to the regular haunt where they'll know to leave her be and let her carry on as she will, protecting her from whatever onlookers there may be, strangers unaware that some neighborhood pubs insist on providing a haven to those who need it in the light of day.

Remaining focused straight ahead, better to avoid the cling and narrow this close to the destination. The people part and the wayward pathway finds its journey home. Fuller's. Home there, nearby, but nothing there, no one, better to stop in to find whatever relief this day can offer.

(He wasn't a singer, couldn't sing to save his life he said, but he seemed to know a thing or two. Talked about the Irish and their songs, something he said he learned when reading *Ulysses*. He was literate. Didn't look it, didn't wear it. Too pretty to be that smart.)

[The decision came quickly and didn't ask for any deliberation. It came from down there and drove upward into the stomach and throat. In those moments, the tide turned exactly where the water wished it to be.]

—*The Queen is Dead*. That's it. It hadn't come out yet, but somehow, he acquired it. Was fascinated. I invited him, made an invitation. Asked him to come home with me. Jesus, Mary, and Joseph, what a slag. The same day I met him. My virtue traded for an advance listen to a recording I was dying to hear.

She pulls open the door at the Hereford Arms and the relative darkness swallows her up and carries her away from the bright streets and the imagined throngs of people looking closely and carefully for nothing more than a moment's amusement at her expense.

2.12.3.Natalie.19.86.8.2 [ref(..8.1)]

Following along the river past the Altstadt and its castle, there is a traffic light, and the road signs indicate a nearby Krankenhaus. Veering the car off to the right before reaching it and heading toward the train station where there is ample day parking. He is fascinated by the most trivial detail after emerging from the riverside and coming to the town overloaded with pedestrian and bicycle traffic. His head bobs and turns with every adjustment and new street, in tune with every change to the order. A dog bursting at its leash, he whimpers at the signs for the Fußgängerzone, and nearly chokes himself straining to look back and forth at the crowds of people and the places they are rushing past.

Leaning over to kiss him before he gets out of the car. Filling with concern.

"Are you sure you know where to go?"

"I'll figure it out," he says casually.

"And you'll be able to fill the whole day? I won't be done until six."

Holding up his small daypack, he pulls open the door and steps out. "There's plenty to do, don't worry about me."

Before he runs off, "Here's a card for the bookstore. I'll meet you there."

—You better.

"You're done at noon, aren't you? Won't you be at school?"

"I'll come back. It'll be easier since you already know where it is."

Torn while looking back, doesn't want to break contact, but he is dying to bolt away.

—Yesterday, I was his new city.

(He pulled back the covers, so attentive, focused and present.)

—It's that same look, that same expectant gaze. Let's get back in the car, back under the covers. Not ready for the world to come between us.

He is off angling away to the side, swallowed by the sea of sights and sounds. He will walk and walk, building a mental map of streets and corners, shops and government buildings, learning the layout from post office and train station to university, from the river to the hilltops. He'll walk and walk and find his way away without. As a traveler on the open road, he finds himself at home.

Streets cobbling toward the university where the bookshop faces the zone and backs up to the crowded lair of old German magic and insight. Ding-a-ling goes the bell.

"Good morning, darling. Nice of you to stroll in."

"Enough. Do you have to shout? The whole street will hear you."

He rolls with laughter and dispatches a knowing look.

"Did you enjoy your morsel too much?" he asks.

The door opens behind her, putting the bag on the shelf in back by the desk. Checking the pad for messages. Returning to the front, Hazel now leaning on the counter with Bernd whispering in her ear.

"You did not," she says putting her bag under the counter.

"She did," he affirms, his chin wagging.

"How are you two slandering me?" gasping and feigning offense.

"Don't you have a boyfriend?" Hazel asks.

"On the other side of the planet," he replies before anyone else can.

"He's not my boyfriend, we're not children."

This rapid fire, this friendly recoil, they are ever onward looking for something that needs attention, something that must be wrong, must have gone off the deep end and shows some sign of sickness. Pleasures are always suspicious to those who wish to share.

"They have an understanding," Bernd says rolling his eyes, feigning judgment.

"Were I a man, no one would think twice."

The phone in back rings and Bernd hurries off to answer. It's still early, but the rush may come any minute.

"It's your mother," he says coming back through the doorway.

Leaving them to gab, taking the call at the desk in the back room.

—She knows I'm a captive audience here, there's nothing I can do to get away and someone has to answer.

"Hello Muti, how are you?"

Back in front, Bernd bends onto the counter and Hazel comes close, they're exchanging notes, telling the story of how it came to pass, about the filthy young man and his questions. "Not a bad accent and his vocabulary was tolerable." He describes the way he held the book, an English translation of Kierkegaard. "The store only had the Either, there was no Or anywhere, making it absolutely useless. The price was astronomical, around 40 Deutsch Marks. Without its pair, it's been sitting for over a year and will sit for another. He was worried someone would come and snap it up. He only had 15 DM but could get the rest if she'd hold onto it."

"You're coming tonight, aren't you?" She says, ignoring the question.

"I'm sorry, I completely forgot. Can we postpone until next week?"

"She toyed with him," he explains, "it's such a sight. She would have given him that book for free, but he was extremely polite and concerned he would lose it, precious in his hands. Instant sparks. I was embarrassed to be in the same room. Of course, he was oblivious, had no idea what was happening."

"But your sister and her husband will be there." she protests.

"Well, that's good then. You can have a lovely dinner with them, and I can have you all to myself next week."

"You don't want to see your sister?" she asks.

Hazel turns back and looks through the door frame leading to the backroom. Her smile widens with each added detail. Turning toward the back window and away from her judgment, however friendly it may be.

"I do want to see her *and* Ansel. We talk all the time. She'll understand. I'll see them sometime too, but with everyone's schedule it can be hard to find a time. Please Muti. Try to understand. There are many things going on right now, too much work."

"On a Saturday?" Her voice rises, she's almost shouting.

"She took his 15 DM and let him have it. He was grateful, he'd do anything she asked, and she knew it, so she asked him to dinner. They disappeared and this is the first I've seen her since."

"Yes, on a Saturday. Sorry. Love you, Muti. Talk soon."

Returning to the counter out front, they lurch straight at the approach.

—You think you have the whole story now, what do you know, truly?

"Tell me," Hazel says, unable to hide her excitement. "You found yourself an acolyte?"

Gesturing toward Bernd, "He doesn't know anything, he only knows we left together. We could've just said our farewells."

"Is that what happened?" Bernd asks. "You took a walk and said goodbye."

"No, but it could've happened that way." Laughing together.

"Don't get shy all of a sudden," Hazel scolds. "It doesn't suit you. Tell us what happened. Details."

"At dinner he told me this long story. He had lots of stories, in fact."

Grins and winks.

"I think he embellishes."

Grins and winks.

"Those are the best kind," Hazel looks at Bernd. Sticking their tongues out at each other, partners in subterfuge.

"Neh, na ja, that one was about the book and how he'd been carrying it all over Europe, taking up space in his tightly packed rucksack, and then, somehow, lost it, left it on a train. Still carries the second volume, but the first was gone and he's been looking for a replacement ever since."

"That explains it. He'd never find that book. He shouldn't have found it here," Bernd says.

A young couple comes in. She is telling him she's sure she saw it the other day. It's expensive but he can read the bit he cares about here if he wants, they won't care. "Pull out your notebook, sit in a chair, make yourself at home. It's what they're here for."

"And you gave him a good price?"

"Not that good. I took his money. It was his whole budget for the day. Obviously, I had to feed him and give him a place to sleep. What choice did I have? I'm not a monster."

"Well, good for you," Hazel encourages. "It's about time the tables were turned."

"Where's he off to today?" Bernd asks.

"He's in town. We're going to meet back here later."

(They're shocked. Coincidences did not go well when they stretched out too long. Did the heart live with Martin? How little welcome was this loneliness.)

"You'll eat dinner again today? Normal, same as everyone, I suppose. Got to eat every day, for your sanity..." Bernd is ready to paint the picture, to present an oversimplified view of food and drinks, warmth and heat.

(Our symposium of the spirit, our nights between the days, our rolling and whispering, who was it standing between the signs? Who was it who came calling? Why should he break from the patterns, from the horrifying visions of those straining and strangling everything that breathes, everything that heats, and everything that...?)

[His little ass wiggling as he bounced off to the toilet, his swinging cock as he bounced back.]

"You're working half the day, then half the day over at administration. Don't you have something with your mother tonight? Isn't there a reading group tomorrow? Do you have time for this?"

"You said you couldn't come with us because you had a family thing.

Don't tell me your principles permit you to ditch your friends to screw some hiker boy."

"My principles," so haughty, "say I can do whatever I want."

Bernd shrugs and leans back against the counter. "It's true. We can't shame her into being like the rest of us: burdened with guilt and the weight of responsibility."

"Ha!"

Hazel giggles. She wants to be supportive and knows the willful cannot be steered.

"I admire you," she says. "I would do the same if I had your tits."

Another customer comes in, but this one isn't here to browse. He has a question and Bernd steps away to help. Hazel watches him go off and turns back, changing the subject.

"Are you working on the assignments?"

"Yes, we're short a lecturer. It'll make things harder for the rest of us."

"You don't mean?"

"Someone has to do it. We don't have anyone specifically meant to cover it. We're trying to figure out who to draft."

"Better not be me," she says shaking her head and closing her eyes.

"Not if I can help it. Could end up being me if we strike a deal."

"What kind of deal?"

"I'll take that if they give me whatever I want for the other one. I want to teach my fashion course. They're desperate and have to negotiate. They can't *make* any of us do it."

"But won't you be miserable?"

"It's not that bad, I don't mind. The clarity of a truth table can be helpful at times. It could loosen things up in the media class. I've been getting bored there. Want to change things up, be more cutting edge, and if that's what it takes, fine."

Bernd comes back to the counter. He looks side to side and widens his eyes. "What did I miss?"

"Business, nothing interesting."

Hazel leans closer to prevent the browsers from listening in. "Are you sure you have time for this?"

"As long as I'm not dead, I'll always have time for this."

"What time's he coming back? I want to get a look at him."

"It would be worth it," Bernd says emphatically. "Pleasant to look at and such a gentle voice. Polite with his questions, unsure of himself, but not at all. Do you think he knows?"

"Don't be fooled, he's dangerous. Someone somewhere must've taught him something... ...he knows. Anyway, we're meeting back here at six. If you're here, I'll introduce you."

2.12.4.Greta.19.86.9.13 [ref(...5.9-12)]

"It comes from the first sob and the first kiss." [Garcia Lorca]

The bell rings. Pressing and holding to let them in. He stops reading too and stands awkwardly waiting.

Committing to it. Black skirt, black sheer tights, and black short jacket. Black shiny shoes, only slightly out of place. Not too much make-up but the eyebrows are crisp and newly plucked. Answering the door, Eva stands front-and-center supported on either side by her pillars, Anja and Elke. Kisses and hugs all around.

(The four of us haven't been together since that day the ground broke and the sky cleared for a single spring day.)

He is a boundary in the midst, preventing everyone from falling into each other. A witness for the day, it feels like theatre. He is both out of place and an essential ingredient.

"Nice to see you again," Eva says, extending her hand after Anja and Elke have been introduced. "Are you coming with?"

He is out of place, dressed wrong, and looking as if he wants to be anywhere but here. New pants from the second-hand store, the rest brought with him. Cleaned properly and pressed for the first time. All three move closer, full of smiles and attentive.

"Have you been enjoying your stay," she asks cheerfully while the others nod and push their hair back over their ears. He hesitates, unsure whether to answer.

That now strange guest room where his pack leans against the wall behind the door and his clothes fill two side drawers in the desk, no one yet has the heart to empty the dresser or closet. He breathes in there, loud and present, at night as the doors close and the locks spin. Alone with that always vibrating air filling the head with questions and looks.

—Put him to work. He owes me that, doesn't he? Perfectly normal to clear everything away.

Sending him back to get the overshirt, he depends on precise instructions. Each movement makes him nervous. They closely watch every single thing he does, and he is painfully aware of the attention.

"Have you been able to work?" Anja knows this is too much, that no one will be able to stand it for long, so she straightens things at the corners, passing her hand across the back while asking.

He comes back and tries to be invisible, as if it were possible. Everyone adjusts to include him. He makes her more present. Anja beams while looking his way, easing out from a feeling. Elke can't take her eyes off him.

"Not yet. I tried, but it was impossible. They've been kind, but..."

"Should we go?" Eva asks, sensing Anja and Elke are too focused on staying yet unwilling to make themselves more comfortable: they're in a holding pattern and must move along or risk exhaustion.

Contained and moving in a pile, Anja sets things right, no one could bear the weight for too much longer. Seeing each other in black costume, something plucks the strings, balances the measure. She assigns seats and everyone complies without words.

"I told Mom and Dad," she says settling in by the window. "They were glad. I don't know why. They're busy today."

"With what?" asking from the middle, Elke on the other side.

"Some kind of hike. The club has something out toward Würzburg. Therapeutic."

Anja focuses on the road and hands him something to keep close.

"What time this morning?"

"Early. Then they'll eat. It's all day. She didn't say anything about coming with."

Along the road to Erlangen, packed tightly in the back and he, useless in the role, sits quietly with Anja as she continues grilling him for details about his travels. He looks anywhere anyone isn't and offers little to her efforts.

"What have you two been doing this week?" Elke asks.

"I had to go to München right after he arrived." Looking forward and over at him, he only seems to half-follow the conversation. The crosstalk may be confusing him.

"I went to the Böhmerwald," he says, surprising the rest.

"Was it for work?" Anja asks, looking this way in the rearview mirror.

"Quite the traveler," Elke says, leaning forward in her seat. "Have you guys spent much time together?" She looks at him. He is smiling sadly. "Have you seen much of our city?"

No answer. He looks back. Not confused but the conflicting questions and misdirection make it unclear who should answer.

"Not much," he says quietly and a smidgeon behind. "I was..."

"Before school," Eva interrupts, "we're taking a trip south. To Neuschwanstein, the mountains. You should come with. Get better acquainted."

Elke bites her lip, and her eyes widen. Anja shoots an encouraging look over at him.

"Where will you stay?"

"Hostels. You don't have to come," Elke responds awkwardly while turning back this way.

"But if she wants to..." Eva insists.

"Of course," Elke concedes. She looks back and forth briefly at each.

At Grossgrundlach with grandfather and grandmother, everyone quiets

down at the last minute as if remembering where they are. The ripening
trees bear color as fruit and shade the spot. Mountain air recalls the days
before.

It isn't far, not walking for long, and then staring at the abomination,
cold stone and burning words.

Eva in tears and moving close. Holding on tightly, draped together.
Mother and father left fresh signs: flowers and the spaces clear of clippings
and leaves.

(Always coming on their own, they haven't the heart to broadcast it, not
ready to share.)

Standing by him while the others huddle. He appears thoughtful,
silently staring straight at it. Eva looks over from between Anja and Elke
both leaning against her. They can't get any closer but try hard anyway.

Bending over the permanent absence, the fresh spot where memory
hides in space. Childhood friends go everywhere together.

(We were sixteen and they must've been ten. Mother and Father took
us into Nürnberg for a movie. What was it? *The Sting?* They were too
young. How did I know they would be with us, this way, for so long? How
did I know there was a coven forming that day? We ate bad food afterwards
at that place near the movie house, and Mommy was so happy with her
girls. She loved her the most, could always feel it. Always in charge, the way
she led us everywhere. Telling us which way to go and where we had to
stand to see it best. Papa looked at her that way too. Exactly alike and still
she shined so much brighter.)

He stands close at the shoulder, sensing the places to go, the time to
come, surfacing in the light beaming onto the stone. Stiff and restrained,
not stepping away, no feeling carries, it is the waves and the sea for a boat
with nowhere else to go.

[In his arms, is that what she knew? Is that what she meant? Writing of
his warmth and the way he listened and learned from her, absorbing
everything. Never mechanical, she said, no, it was always the truest way,
taken to heart, and made into something personal. He transformed himself
into her, acting back upon her through himself. More a mirror than a man,
that's what she said, that's who she got to know. Now, that's what's left of
her now, his weight leaning is her heaviness. Now. It burns, this evil glare,
but it's the only way to find her... ...now.]

"I need to go," Eva says.

No one replies. The three of them turn and walk back toward the car.
Stepping away and he thinks it's to follow, gesturing for him to go on ahead.

(Little sister, those four minutes without you were the loneliest of my
life. Until now. Those minutes repeat every day since you turned up at the
airfield. Every day, they come each morning and leave each night. Not
here. Not here. And if you're not here, then I'm not here. Where can I be

without you? Please don't be mad if I have to lean too much upon things
you left behind. Who else should have them? I don't know what to do.
What am I supposed to do now? Do you remember when we traded places
and fooled everyone? Could we do that... ...now? Would they believe it...
...now? Hair darker... ...you wouldn't know me. Now. I would change my
eyes and nose if I could. Change the body, change the voice. What else
could I do to make the mirror stop accusing me?)

Turning, he is there waiting, didn't go far, and is looking down at
nothing, sees nothing, but waits and offers his arm. Fine before reaching
him, made unsteady by the support.

"Thank you," curling the forearm around his and treading back to the
car where everyone is in place and staring straight ahead, not waiting.
Numb.

*Back inside, he returns to a steady state, cannot bring out more with
less nor refresh the season with an accepting sieve. He is welcomed by
memories, carrying them here and today asking for forgiveness. Hoping to
let what comes come and what goes go, but there are bindings in place
holding onto the remains.*

"It's okay that you didn't come right away," saying it without looking at
him. "I forgive you."

Eva turns sideways, looking this way and putting her hand on the seat
back. "Of course, we all do," she says. "I can't imagine what it was like."

He's shaking his head. He doesn't. There is still something, but it can't
catch his breath, will upset everyone, and is the only thing anyone wants to
hear.

*Stopping at a guest house closer to Fürth than Erlangen and relieved
that the place is filled with everything unfamiliar, a place no one has ever
been, with no memory, no reminders, no sounds borne deep inside hearts
not ready to hold more.*

Pulling him into the booth. Anja is surprised to be left at the end and
not in her customary seat right next to. She thinks he's the fifth, and that
place doesn't suit her, but accepts the arrangements after looking over
quietly and seeing how much necessity there is in the eyes.

—I know what's coming and where he has to be when it does.

National Saturday and Schnitzel with pommes frites on the side.
Everyone has the same thing, and he is bold enough to ask for a beer. Elke
goes along, but the rest are too timid this early.

Seeing the way Eva looks at him, she feels the same, knows there is
something that could help, and wants it for herself, but, as always, lets her
big sister go first. Can't do it.

"You stayed with her in New York?" she asks, breaking the silence.

"She stayed at the airport, and I went into town. They couldn't line
things up right for some reason. I don't know why we had to wait the whole

weekend."

"There wasn't room," Anja trying to be supportive. Everyone is trying. No one wants to think about what it means. Everyone wants him to say something quickly, something to drown out the echo.

"Still," he hurries. "London. I expected something direct to Frankfurt. Why the stop? It was impossible to ask. They arranged it but no one person ever seemed to have any power over the details."

Comforting him, knowing how backward it must feel. He's embarrassed, wishes it was a misunderstanding, then goes on.

"At Heathrow, I saw it again. It was different. Something snapped. I can't... I don't know..."

Nodding, no one demands an account. His lips convey everything, his nose. Handing him a tissue.

"I signed the transfer. The next thing I know, I'm on the train getting as far away as... Couldn't follow... ...couldn't bear to meet... ...to see..."

Wanting to hear bravery, but he's describing only cowardice. Elke touches his arm from across the table. Putting a hand on his shoulder, caring lessens the sting. He doesn't want to be a bother, doesn't want to heap any more burdens upon it, but then the food comes and it's warm and everyone is relieved.

"It's best that you weren't here. For Mom and Dad," Eva says. "The phone was hard for them."

"Have you met them?" Anja asks.

He stares straight ahead and doesn't blink, says nothing. Shaking the head in unison with Eva. "Not...," he says once everyone stops waiting.

Elke makes a knowing bow, and everyone takes a bite.

—Pursuing his sorest misfortune. His dreams will come true.

5.8
the middle american

5.8.1.X.19.86.12.1 [ref(.)]

Lilith, the ancient witch, is a siren, a magical image, and she is the phantasm of Adam's desire. If my ears had been stuffed with wax, I wouldn't have heard a thing and been saved from madness.

Mario was one of the cops in town. There were a few others, but he's the one I saw most often. He went to school with Oskar's father Michael, Herr Damschroder's oldest kid and only son. Apparently, they grew up together and Mario is the type of person who stays around his hometown his whole life no matter what, never wants to go anywhere, never wants to leave town, or see any other place. He didn't become a cop because he wanted to beat on people or be an authority figure or something nuts like that. He wanted to take care of the place. Kind of a simpleton, in my opinion, but there are far worse people and I never had a bad thing to say about him, not during the whole month I've been here. He'd come by the shop a lot, have coffee with Herr Damschroder, and talk about all kinds of crap. Herr Damschroder thought he was good company, reminded him of better times when he wasn't alone and didn't have to rely on some stranger to lift the heavy shit in his store. Mario talked to me too and would ask questions about America and the pop music there which, as near as I could tell, wasn't any different from the pop music here. He wanted to know if I liked the stuff he liked. Crappy music, or not crappy, but not music for the sake of art. He liked bop boppy dance tunes. *Girls Just Want to Have Fun* and *Wake Me Up Before You Go-Go* were the best of it, but there was some nauseating stuff too. He thought everyone in America knew each other. Swear to fucking God. Oh, you're from America, do you know Henry? Who? Henry, he was here a few seasons ago, with his wife, what was her name, Kurt? Was it Carrie? Do you know Henry and Carrie? They're nice. Jesus fucking Christ. I'd fuck with him and say yeah sure and then ask if he knew Phil or whatever, you know, because he's from Austria too and he'd look at me as if I was an idiot and say Austria's a big country.

Anyway, he must've been nearby or heard something or whatever because when I went to the door to talk to Birgit, I saw that he was off there in the street watching the whole thing. He must've seen her walking in town or something and thought it strange that a young woman would be out alone on the streets so late at night. He might've been following her to see what she was going to get up to. I'm not sure, but it was unusual that he would be standing there, so I gathered. Whatever he was doing before then, when he saw me at the door, he waved. Not to be friendly, but to let me know he was there, as if he thought he was spoiling my plans. When I opened the door, he came right up and said we should stay put and wait inside. The three of us went into the store and he stood there trying to act large and in control of the situation while Birgit and I stood there looking around.

"What's this about, Mario?" He said to call him that, I wasn't being disrespectful.

"Officer Müller," he said. "I've put in a call to the proprietor. He'll be here soon." Proprietor, what a dick.

"But what's this about, officer? You know me."

He looked over at Birgit and I put it together that he figured the whole thing was a con, as if I'd come here to work my way into Herr Damschroder's good graces so that my friend could come by and help me rob him once I had the run of the place. He'd no doubt seen some American cop show where that was the story line.

"You're not supposed to have any people in the shop at night."

"You're the one who let her in," I said, defending myself even though no formal charges had been made. "I only opened the door because I saw you out there in the street. I was going to ask her what she wanted."

"Liar." Birgit whispered the word but did it abruptly, so it came across as an accusation. "We know each other, officer. I've come to visit him. I was specifically coming to look for him."

"I bet you were," Mario said looking back over my way.

Then nothing else. She stopped talking, he stopped talking, we were standing there.

"Are we under arrest?" I asked.

"We'll wait for Herr Damschroder to decide that."

I shrugged, thinking that was for the best. Once we were heading down that road, he'd be the most ideal judge I could ask for. Herr Damschroder was a reasonable man. He'd want to know the details and ask a bunch of questions. It wouldn't be pleasant to have to explain everything to him, but it'd come out. He could send me away, or he'd think it's not a big deal, either way I approved of Mario's plan.

"Who's Herr Damschroder?" Birgit asked quietly, almost shyly this time.

"He owns this place," Mario said as though making it so. "He's the one who was generous enough to take this young man in and trust him with his livelihood. That's who he is."

I nodded. Birgit was properly demur. She hadn't meant to cause trouble, that's what her face was saying. Of course, the owner of the store had to be involved. She hadn't done anything wrong. That's what I got from her, at least. She was almost normal standing there. Did I get the wrong idea about her? It's possible I hadn't seen her at her best and needed to challenge my prejudices. Back when we first met, I liked her. She was tough and strong and determined. That's how she came across, not one of those chicks who are all whatever you want or tell me what you're thinking and that shit. You know, it's a kind of insecurity that wants to have control, that wants to learn everything about you through quasi-loving surveillance so they can know how to keep you close and oversee your deepest thoughts and feelings. No, she wasn't one of those chicks, that kind who harbor some deep envy because deep down they wish they had the freedoms and confidences that boys have. The only resolution they can imagine is taking over the lives of their boyfriends. These are the chicks that don't want equality or whatever, they want to control the villains who made them cower. It's revenge, it's envy. Whatever the fuck it is, it's goddamn petty.

Well, say what you want about Birgit, but right from the get-go I didn't see any of that in her. She could look after herself. Yeah, so later it seemed as if she was using me as some kind of psycho-social pathological tool or something, but that wasn't her primary gig. She didn't want to know what made me tick, what clothes and music I liked. She didn't want me to listen to her crap, she wanted to be alone with her thoughts for the most part, same as me. Can't say any of this is a bad thing. She's how guys are. She likes sex so she needs a partner. Okay, that's not anybody's fault, but that's the extent of it, she didn't want to make that drama. I figure she couldn't help it. Whatever had gone on with her, the sex got weird. She wanted it, but then it did things to her head. Things that wouldn't otherwise happen would happen. She must've had these two competing urges and couldn't sort it out, didn't know anything about it, it was subconscious. That's what Eve and Elke were saying, at least. She looked pretty normal and reasonable at the moment so they could be right. I shouldn't assume, that's what I'm saying.

Herr Damschroder finally showed up. He doesn't look annoyed. Sure he was interrupted while having this quiet evening at home and trying to get some sleep before the new week begins. But nope. That's how most people would have done it, but not him. He came in as though it's an opportunity to get involved in something interesting. You could tell right away, the whole setup, which he didn't have hardly any information about, was interesting to him. He got there, came inside, and looked at the three of us. Smiling, if you can believe it, genuinely smiling, as if he's happy to see us, and he didn't know Birgit from Adam.

"What's going on, Mario?" he said.

"I observed this female walking through town sometime after midnight. I followed her to this location where she tapped on the glass clearly intending to get the attention of someone she knew was inside the store. After tapping for a few minutes, Stefan appeared, and opened the door."

"I waved to you first," I said.

"He waved to me first," Mario repeated.

"Why did you open the door?" Herr Damschroder asked looking over at me.

"Because I know her," I said. "She knows Oskar too. She was one of the people living in that flat I told you about in Innsbruck."

"One of those people?" Birgit asked quietly. She said it kind of simply. Don't get the idea that she was pretending to be insulted. She wanted to be sure she heard the details of my explanation correctly, that's all.

"She was the one who invited me to stay with them. We were... ...well... we were...."

"Like boyfriend and girlfriend, Herr Damschroder, but only for a short time. He stayed with me for about a month, then you know what happened, because Oskar and my roommate Frithjof worked out with you that he would come and help you in the store."

That was helpful. Herr Damschroder was nodding, but she looked off somehow, not quite right, or at least in my imagination of what an old man must be thinking about a young woman right in front of him, dressed in black with jet-black hair and the eye liner and the ashen white skin. I figured he would have thought her mad or something. Regardless of whether he did, when she spoke reasonably and helpfully like that, he nodded with approval.

"Why are you here, dear?" he asked looking in her direction. I think he may have taken a step closer. The question had some affection in it, as if he realized she needed help and wasn't there to rob him or any of the stuff Mario thought was going on.

"To be honest, I think it was my fault Stefan left us in Innsbruck. He was looking to get out of there. It wasn't a good situation. After he left, it still wasn't good. It's my apartment, so they can't kick me out, but we're not getting along. I wanted to get away for a while, to give them some time, and to sort things out myself. I didn't know where to go, but Oskar told me he was here. He said I should come. To clear my head, get a different perspective."

Now, I was suspicious because that was too perfect a response. She's the victim. Oh, of course she is. Poor Birgit, used and abused by her nasty roommates who can't get along with anyone. What will she do? She's so mature and wise, she decides to take a cooling off period. Of course, wouldn't want to go running around the apartment screaming at everyone, wouldn't want to demand that everyone else shut the fuck up and take her bullshit, that would be crazy, no, it's much better to get some distance and let calmer heads prevail. Herr Damschroder was eating it up, Mario too. His looks were visibly more compassionate. Depending on what's going on, Birgit looked as though she could be anywhere from 18 to 35. She's amorphous that way, and at that moment, because it suited her, she seemed to be barely more than a child, and these men were loving it, they were welcoming her with open arms. She's totally pulling it off.

Truth is, it was in my interest that she pulled it off. Let's be real, if they knew what I knew, if they had seen her throughout that last month and how she acted with me and her roommates, it would have been much harder to convince them that she wasn't there to rip off the store. Since I was there too, I'd be guilty by association. I had to go along with her performance, and I had to let them fall for it. She didn't need any help from me to sell it, she just needed me to stay out of her way. It was kind of like that whole foreplay routine if you think about it. She's got her thing that she needs to get through and you have to let her do it. Trying to do something, or taking an active part, is only going to throw off her timing. Better to let her run things and do what she needed to do, that was the way it worked, and it seemed as though that was the way it better work.

"Thank you, Mario," Herr Damschroder said. "We've taken up enough of your time. I can take it from here."

Mario was totally cool with that. He's nodding and saying that he's happy to help and he should call if he needed anything else. He gave me one last look to register that he was still going to be watching me and I shouldn't think I could get away with any nonsense, then he left. In his mind throughout the whole thing, I'm the troublemaker, I'm the one who took advantage of this young woman and she's come to me for help because she needed someone to look after her.

After Mario left, we shut off the lights and went into the back room. I filled the electric water pot and plugged it in for some tea. There were only two stools at the counter, so Birgit and Herr Damschroder sat down facing each other close up. He was ready for his interrogation now. I was sure of it. He wanted to get rid of Mario, but he wasn't totally fooled yet, and still had some work to do. He must've thought she wasn't dangerous after the brief exchange, but still wasn't sure of her motives so, under the guise of hospitality, he was going to dig in deeper and see what he could find. He took her coat and hung it on the rack with his own after handing mine to me. Probably thought I looked cold. He pulled the seat up for her and asked if she wanted some tea, knowing that's what I was already heading toward with the pot, and she was eating it up, appreciating the attention and happy to sit and be welcome. I wasn't saying a damn thing since I was mostly torn: we're now thoroughly connected, she's the one who brought me to Oskar, effectively. Because of that, if she couldn't pass the test, that'd be a strike against me. I'd become suspicious, could lose my job. My destiny was in her hands.

I dipped the tea bags and set the mugs in front of them. I had to use a broken one with no handle because he never expected more than two people for coffee or tea. The just-in-case mugs were too hot to hold so I had to let it sit there and stand out of the way to avoid getting between them.

"Why couldn't you go to your parents' place?" he asked.

"My mom is in Graz. It would be too far." She looked down, gulping. Was this genuine feeling? Was she sincerely talking to Herr Damschroder? It seemed so unlikely, but it felt genuine, the sentiment. Never underestimate a psychopath though. "I can't go there anyway. We're not on good terms."

"I'm sorry to hear that. A girl needs her mother. Especially when things are tough." She's nodding along with him, such sad eyes, she appeared to be genuinely choked up.

"My stepfather wasn't nice to me, and she preferred to take his side over mine. She doesn't hate me or anything, but I can't forgive her."

Total BS. For a second, I thought he was going to pat her knee to make her feel better but then he thought twice about it and folded his arms, looking off into the distance for a second. She was looking up and it seemed as though they were making eye contact, reaching an understanding about something. This was going in my favor.

"How did you get here?" he asked after they'd each had a sip of their tea, still too hot to drink without blowing on it.

"I took the last train, been kicking around town the whole evening."

"Whereabouts? Did you have something to eat?"

"Oh yeah, I'm fine. I went to the cellar by the station. They have food. I had something to eat. Had a chat with some of the locals. It felt like a local place."

"Sometimes, but the last train, that brings you here at about 6. You were there that whole time? Why didn't you come earlier?"

I was looking back and forth watching this, trying to pick up everything, but the connections in the eyes, the contact, that's hard to get when you're a few feet off. It's because you're not in the line of fire, sometimes that's where the information lies.

"I was scared. Things didn't end well with Stefan. I had no idea how he'd react when he saw me. I was afraid he'd refuse to see me, kick me out without letting me explain. I thought if I came late enough, if I surprised him, he wouldn't be able to do that. He'd have to be civil, have to talk to me."

That was pretty good. Got to admit.

"But you do need a place to stay, don't you?"

"Yes. That is, I could afford a room in the guest house for a couple nights, but I was hoping to stay longer."

"What about work?" I jumped in. "Don't you have to work?"

"The hostel in Innsbruck is closed until after New Year. They're doing some repairs and things. That's also creating a problem. I don't have much savings and need to use it to cover rent and bills."

"You can't stay here," Herr Damschroder said gently. "There's barely enough room for Stefan and it's not suitable for young ladies."

Bullshit. She could curl up under the cot and eat from the garbage can. It would suit her fine. She's playing you, but... What difference does it... Whatever.

She's nodding. "I understand," she said so dutifully. What a crock.

"But there is plenty of room at my house," he said. "The kids are long gone, and both of their rooms are always ready for them. You can stay in my Olivia's room. She's off in Wien with her family now, I think you'll be comfortable there."

I'm sure my mouth must've been wide open after that invitation, but she's breezy about the whole thing, as if it's nothing, the most reasonable and obvious offer in the world.

"I'd love that. Thank you so much, that would be excellent. I can't thank you enough for such kindness."

He nodded and waved it off. Too much. He's no fool. He knows what's what, but he also knows that she's much more harmless to him than she is to me. He must. Or is it imagined? Does everyone see what everyone sees?

"It's getting busy here in the shop, there's a lot of work to do. Even with Stefan, we can't manage everything, it's our busiest time. Many people come down on the weekends and then, as we get closer to the holidays, there will be more people staying for longer periods. It would be great to have some extra hands around here. Would you mind working here to help out?"

"Not at all. Whatever you need."

He wanted her to come back to his house right then to spend the night and stay. For what? For the whole month? Crazy. She gets the comfortable bed in the warm house while I'm stuck here in this garret up above the shop. It's cold at night and doesn't get that warm during the day either. It's not comfortable, there's nowhere comfortable to sit. The bed is hard, the chair at the desk is hard, but Birgit gets the warm hearth and the nice bed with all the comforts, plus a full kitchen. This went well, I got that, but some kind of disaster is bound to follow soon. This couldn't turn out well. She worked her way into a pretty sweet deal, so what was her plan? What did she intend to do with this newfound luck? What a nightmare.

Herr Damschroder said that if we wanted to talk or catch up, I could get dressed and walk her over to his place, but Birgit said that wasn't necessary and she'd be fine walking over there with him if she could get a minute alone with me before that. He said fine and headed back out into the front room to wait by the door. Before going, he reminded me to unplug the pot and clean up before turning in, then, when he was gone, I got this idea that she was going to pull one of those cheezy TV moments and be like "don't you fuck this up for me, I got the old bastard right where I want him" but then I realized I wasn't her partner in crime and whatever long con she was working included me as a mark because she was not breaking character, not for one second.

"I wanted to say I'm sorry," she said, desperate to look off anywhere else, but forcing herself to look me in the eyes. "I know how fucked up that was for you. I can't explain it. I don't know why I get so secretive and protective. If anyone tries... ...to... I don't know. I don't have an excuse, I'm sorry, that's it. I won't do anything to hurt your boss. He seems nice. I don't want to cause trouble."

I didn't know what to say and if you don't know what to say when you should say something, it's better not to say anything at all. I kept my mouth shut and nodded, that was it. I didn't touch her or anything. The old man was sure right about that. She's got a hairpin trigger, no doubt, and there's no telling what contact would do to her. Honest or not, con or true, she was acting the part of someone you could be around, taking on the role of a normal person, best not to do anything to jeopardize that. No telling what kind of explosion it could cause. Strictly platonic, I'm not going backward, don't want to go there ever again.

5.8.2.X.19.86.12.8 [ref(..1-8)]

Monday morning Birgit wasn't much use. We had the usual tasks, there was a queue to work through, and Herr Damschroder and I took care of it without much help. Once things were under control, Herr Damschroder left the shop as he often does after the morning rush. He'd be back later, after lunch most likely. I was to hold down the shop, but he also wanted us to work on getting her up to speed so she'd be more useful. It was businesslike for the next couple hours. Some people came in and I took advantage of that to show her a few things, where the inventory was, how to ring things up on the register, stuff she mostly knew how to do but needed a few details to see how they worked here. Then we were in the back when no one was in the store, and I was showing her how to adjust a binding to a boot. Once you find the boots they're going to rent, and you've determined what length ski they need, you have to take the boot, and make sure it fits correctly on the ski. It's a minor adjustment and didn't take long, you just needed to know their weight and how to read the marker for tension. She was paying close attention to everything I said and was mostly normal the whole day. No signs of anything resembling what went on in Innsbruck.

It was a relief. She wasn't wearing any eye liner or make-up that day either. Her face didn't look as ashen white as it usually did, as if there was something she was doing to make it look that way and she didn't do it that day.

"How were things over at Herr Damschroder's?" I asked while we were taking a break and eating some cheese and bread.

"He's nice. Made things comfortable." Okay, normal enough. Her usual self, I mean, you can't expect her to become this total chatty Kathy who's going to describe every detail. I wanted to know why she didn't look the way she usually did, but how do I ask her that? She wasn't going to tell me on her own and didn't give any signs that she wanted to pursue the topic. None of that mattered. I'm over it. Don't have to know every detail about her. She might be from Graz after all. I'd heard that already from the roommates, saw those letters, but I thought her mom was dead and she lived with her father. It seemed verifiable, but she could've been telling slightly different lies to different people. You never can tell. It doesn't matter, she was acting okay and gave the impression she wanted to experience something that wasn't wild and frantic. Despite the time we spent alone that day, we didn't talk much. Nothing. This is how you ring up the purchases, here's the paperwork you fill out, here's how to adjust the bindings. Strictly business, calm and easy.

When Herr Damschroder came back, he wanted Birgit to show him everything she learned that day. She remembered nearly everything okay and did a pretty good job showing him. She picked it up faster than I did, in fact. Someone came in to drop off their skis and the two of us stood there while she took care of it. She needed a few pointers about what to do with the paperwork after the return, but that was my fault because I told her the wrong thing. Not on purpose, it was a mistake. I forgot about how you had to zero out the charge for the deposit. Herr Damschroder corrected her, and she glared at me because she must've thought I did it on purpose to make her look bad. Or was that my imagination? She could've been looking over at me to see what I was thinking. I said something like, "Oh, that's right, I forgot to explain that" and she seemed to be okay with that since I was taking responsibility. Not a big deal, but for a minute there it was as if the old Birgit had come back, and the act was coming apart.

After work, Herr Damschroder told me to take her down to Blumenthal's to get some supper. He said we could put it on the store's tab over there. It was news to me that there was such a thing, but it was a nice perk, and I'd get a chance to find out more about what was going on. Throughout the meal, she was totally calm. She was a completely different person and was so polite when Leisel came over and talked to us. She said please and thank you, asked how long they owned the place, how long they lived in Seefeld, where did they come from originally, all that crap. The level of humanity and how well-behaved she was, well it was incredible, but none of it meant that she was giving out much information. She had a story, and was sticking to it. She came from Graz, that was that. She finished Gymnasium but decided not to go to university though she made high marks. She studied in the United States and her English was good, she barely had an accent. This made for a great story. She told Frau Krieger these things as though she was this nice girl trying to find her way in the world. Nothing else. She lived in Innsbruck because she was taking some time off to figure things out. She'd go back to school next year, but right now she's having trouble with her roommates and that's why she came to stay for a while. The story about the roommates was gaining definition, now it was concentrated on not being able to pay the rent, because her job at the youth hostel was on hold until next month. She needed some way to make money. That's how it works. You hit on a nice minor detail one time and then the next time you tell the tale you make sure to build up that part.

She believed it or pretended to. The details, the twists about what this roommate said or what happened during that one discussion, were getting more elaborate. Sympathy was everywhere. Leisel was attentive and wanted to be encouraging and helpful. Obviously, the roommates were being totally unreasonable, but it'd be for the best to stay here and make some money before going back and straightening things out when she's better off. She had everyone fooled.

Am I a narc bastard? Or am I right to be worried that this is some big ruse and we're going to have to pay for it any second? I mean, people change, their behavior is usually connected to circumstances. Change those circumstances and they'll act differently, that's expected. Was I being unfair to her? Not giving her a chance? That was running through my mind the whole time. I decided as we were leaving that it would make the most sense to give her the benefit of the doubt until she showed otherwise. Either way, she was clearly making an effort, and as long as that was the case there was no reason to think she would intentionally blow up her own cover story. She might be able to pull it off. Wait and see.

We left Blumenthal's and went over to the cellar to have a drink. Birgit suggested it, she didn't want to go and sit at Herr Damschroder's. "He'll want me to sit up with him, and I can't handle that right now. I'm going to have to ease into it." That seemed perfectly understandable, so I thought it'd be okay to go over there for a beer or two. "But we shouldn't stay out too late, we got to get up early tomorrow." I thought she might've rolled her eyes at me when I said that, but it could've been expectations again. I expected her to resist, I expected her to be different. I saw her roll her eyes because I was expecting her to roll her eyes. Again, wait and see.

At the cellar there were these three tourist pricks who thought they were slumming it by hanging out at a locals joint. Real Melvins. From Berlin or some shit like that. Rich guys. Young and spoiled. They were in town for the week and had been there before. They recognized Birgit. Recognized being a charitable way to put it. Something happened between them. They were acting familiar and suggested that tonight should be a repeat performance. Whatever it was, she wasn't having it and turned deeply distressed at their presence. She pretty much told them to go fuck off, that she was busy tonight and she'd come around again later in the week. "Be dears though and leave us." They were far more courteous than I thought they were going to be. They apologized for intruding, said they'd look forward to it, and she shouldn't wait too long. Cryptic.

"The imagination is worse than reality sometimes," I said to her after they left, and we were finishing our beer.

Nothing. Crickets. She didn't say anything in response to that. I was trying to subtly suggest she should come clean, but she had nothing to say.

"You said last night that you were on your own and feeling bad about coming round, so nervous to see me and whatever. Was that bullshit? What happened here last night before you came looking for me?"

You have to say it straight out with her, she isn't going to be any help if she doesn't want to, but just because you do put it out there straight like that doesn't mean she's going to change her whole personality and become helpful. She shrugged. Whatever, did you catch me or didn't you, hope you're proud of yourself. What am I supposed to do with that? Sometimes wanting to know about a person isn't evil or built on some deep-seeded desire to control them. Isn't it possible that I wanted to know about her because I cared about her? I'm not saying that's the reason, but it could be. The more normal she seemed, the more I wanted her to be that way because she was so capable and, I don't know, like a good person. Can't I want a good person to get on okay in the world and help in whatever way I can? Did I want to know the truth about what was going on with her because of that? Didn't matter anyway. No way. We left and she went off toward Herr Damschroder's and I went back to the garret. She waved me off when I offered to walk with her up that way, didn't need any protection.

Next day she was deeply involved in the morning routine. Extremely helpful. In fact, for a while there it seemed as though she could do everything herself. She was driven and on top of things. Still stumbled now and again when it came to finding stuff, she didn't know everything yet, but if she faltered once and one of us corrected her, she didn't falter again for that same thing. She was building a mental map of the place and doing it rapidly. Quick. There's no other way to say it. She was quick on the uptake and was able to anticipate lots of things based on the few things she would learn.

She clearly wasn't a hardcore skier though, and that was her biggest weakness. She couldn't figure out the sizes. Skiers who are renting don't necessarily know how long their boards should be. You need to find out a few things to match them with the right equipment. She asked them what size they wanted, and, in some cases, they didn't know there were sizes, but again, a few tips here and there and she seemed to master that. By the time Herr Damschroder left late Tuesday morning, she had it down.

I was doing some waxing during the slow time in the middle of the day. She was up front straightening some of the inventory that gets messed up when people are trying things on and getting ready in the early morning. I was thinking about that book and the guy living his invisible life and how he had withdrawn because everything was so fucked up and people were out to get him in different ways. There was only injustice and who wants to mess around with that? It was running through my mind as I went through some of the skis and applied the wax and sharpened the edges if they needed it.

Then, around the time I usually think it's good to stop and make something to eat, she came back and stood close to me at the work bench. Close enough to touch but it didn't have the same impact as it had in Innsbruck. I was helpless with her there, whatever she wanted, she could pretty much get it whenever she wanted, but things were different here and the feel of her chest and belly against my arm only made me stiff and uncomfortable. I stepped back and stopped with the wax.

"Sex wax," she said coyly, but that is what it's called so it isn't that far out there.

"What's up?" I asked. "Are you ready to eat?"

It's weird that she grabbed my crotch, right? Not grabbed so much as let the back of her hand pass over it a few times. Everything was not in the least that way until then. Sunday night, Monday the entire day, that whole morning: professional, collegial, everything prim and proper, so what gives? I jumped back.

Now, my sense was that under these circumstances, a conversation was going to follow. What I expected was that she would say something to the effect of what's wrong, can't we, etc. etc. As if she'd want to get into it and use this as a launching pad for discussing what happened in Innsbruck and what should happen now. She's human, she has needs. Blah blah blah. That would be normal, right? Here was the crack I'd been waiting for, but nope, nothing the least bit normal. Jumping back was not the beginning of a conversation, that was a colossal error on my part. No, jumping back was a slap in the face. It was rejection, and let me tell you, this girl was not used to rejection, not this kind anyway. You got to understand, I mean, I grew up, well, not grew up, but after puberty it was common to basically try and get somewhere with every girl that would let me anywhere near her. If she talked to me, I would ask her out. If she went out with me, I would kiss her. Every one of these things had about a 30% chance of success. You got

used to it and became something of a statistician in the works. You up the
ante, you try something knowing that you need to get the numbers up so
that the outcomes can work the way you want them to. Talk to the girls,
only 30% react favorably. Ask them out on dates, only 30% say yes. Kiss
the ones who are willing to go out with you, 30% are into that. Try to have
sex with the ones who like the kiss, 30% go along. If you only talk to 5 girls,
you're screwed. Talk to hundreds, that's the way it worked, those are the
rules, that 30% is expected. Rejection is nothing. It's not personal, she's
one of those 70% who didn't want to go any further with that. So be it. No
sweat off my brow.

It's totally different for girls. I mean, they don't put it out there, not in
the same way. They get good at invitations and subtle methods of rejection,
but that's not the same thing as putting it out there, making a direct and
clear overture that is meant to get exactly what you want. They don't learn
this, they don't experiment with it, they don't get much experience with it
in the natural course of events. Frankly, there are some girls where this is
the only reason they like boys in the first place. They admire this about us,
about how we put it out there so casually and have no trouble with the
rejection. Well, some guys, I guess. It's more complicated, but you get the
point in the basic case. Let's say we're talking about people with run-of-the-
mill language skills who can process emotions and that kind of thing. If they
can't meet those basic bars, then there's something else going on and they
can't let go of this or that. These are the guys that aren't doing the math
right. They aren't aggregating things properly, so they don't know that it's
contrary to their interests to get caught up on this or that rejection, there
are quotas to fill. Stop stalling. But I digress.

The point is, these girls, they don't know how to handle rejection. They
think that sex is there for them whenever they want it. It's a matter of getting
into the right frame of mind to decide, the stars aligning and that kind of
thing. Rejection for them is failure to make the signs clear enough so that
he didn't understand or didn't pay attention. That's totally different from
putting it out there and getting slapped down. This is relevant because
grabbing someone's crotch is way, way, way overboard into the whole
putting-it-out-there category. Birgit was making a clear statement. Sure,
she'd been aggressive when we first met, but there were still things she relied
on, signals and ventures and what have you. She didn't put it out there this
way before. Not self-objectification to lure them in, but self-subjectifaction
to grab them. There are more delicate ways to do it, but it gets the job done
and, let's face it, guys aren't girls. Not even close. We don't need a lot of
finesse and nuance. Grabbing my crotch got the message across. No noise,
just signal. And I jumped back. There it is again. No noise in that, only
signal, and it was more than the jump. The look on my face must have
spoken volumes. Disgust? Horror? Foul memories of terrible events past?

That must've been what she saw because it came across as a thorough and complete rejection.

She turned hard. Extremely hard. Was screaming at me. The Birgit I knew back in Innsbruck returned. But what's this? What is she saying? My mouth must've been wide open. I couldn't believe it.

"You are the most abusive asshole I have ever met. You get off using and beating on women whenever the fuck you want and leave when you're done. When you've gotten what you wanted, you disappear like a common thief in the middle of the night. Fuck you."

Spit. She was spitting and sputtering while she yelled. Furious. And she hit me. With her fist against my chest. Hard. As if she wanted to hurt me, but everything was on me. I was the fucked up one, I was the one who had abused her. She kept going. It was something about violating her privacy and looking at her things and all kinds of shit that I was doing to get inside her head so that I could manipulate her and get her to do these things. That whole routine. Remember? As if I was the one who insisted that I needed to be spent and unable to do anything, and that was the only way I could relax and finally get to what most people think of as sex. That was on me now. As if I was the one using her, I was in control of that. Lunachick.

Honestly, I thought she was going to kill me, and I was speechless. I had no idea what to say. Should I stand up for myself? Should I argue with her, tell her that's not how I experienced it? Would she listen to me? But none of that was up to me. My chin was on my chest. I couldn't speak and the only thing I could see right in front of me was this furious face that was getting ready to take another swing. In fact, I was pretty sure she was getting ready to pummel me. You know, how your brother would do it when you're kids. I don't know, I wasn't thinking, I reached out both my hands and took hold of her shoulders and pulled her close to me. I guess I was thinking that I was going to get her into a bear hug or something to prevent her from belting me. It wasn't planned out and I didn't have a good grip. Plus, she's strong as hell. Wiry. Good shape. Not someone who does a lot of exercise or physical stuff, but something about her life made her pretty firm and tough. It immediately seemed as though she was going to be able to wriggle out of my grip and beat on me. I panicked, had no idea what I was doing, but I let my arms go full around her and gripped her around the back and in a full embrace so that she couldn't move.

I was immediately aware of two logical possibilities. This was based on the situation but still hypothetical. Meaning, she didn't do any of this, but our position made it clear that she could do either of these two things right away. 1. She could knee me in the balls. In fact, if I were teaching her self-defense, it's what I would have recommended. The rough embrace made this a clear option. 2. She could bite me on the shoulder or neck. Her face was right there, and it'd be easy. There's no way I'd want to keep her that close if she did that so it too would have been an effective way to get out of the hold. My mind was whirling, I was rapidly trying to figure out the best way to counter either of these possibilities, but I wasn't thinking fast enough.

There's not much I understand about Birgit. Forever and ever, I will say it exactly that way. She escapes me, her mind is a mystery, because in that moment, when I realized she was reacting faster than I was and that I was completely at her mercy for whatever she was planning to do, right then when I was bracing myself for the worst, she wrapped her arms around me and buried her face against my shoulder sobbing. And everything went soft. It wasn't a bear hug anymore. There were no more punches. I was holding her, and she was crying. If I must admit, I guess I'd have to say that I was crying too. I don't know why. There was too much happening, and I was certain she was about to bite through my jugular. The image of the blood spurting was vivid. The release of it, of a disaster avoided, the way she felt falling into my arms, the tight taut muscles relaxing, and her weight going light like that, the effect was more than I could handle. A wuss and an idiot, but that robust possibility needed to be released to find somewhere to go. I was sobbing too then, both of us were. Just like that, it couldn't be helped.

A huge weight was lifted from our interactions after that. It settled us somehow, and we found a different place to be with each other. We weren't going to repeat the patterns from Innsbruck. We weren't going back to that or any twisted angry mess that played out the psychological trauma of whatever we were doing back there. No, it seemed as though something good was happening. The rest of the week was the same. She was doing great at the store, and wasn't trying anything with me. Laughed a lot, at my jokes, at her own lame jokes too. She went home and spent the evenings with Herr Damschroder doing whatever it was she was dreading a few days earlier, talking to him and watching TV in his living room or whatever. She said he'd fall asleep in the chair, and she'd be sitting there watching some stupid American TV drama like Dynasty or something. She complained that she needed something to read and got me to hurry up and finish my book so she could take it. It was great. Having a buddy. One day, I took her skiing and taught her a few things. She had some basics already, wasn't bad, in fact. I think she may have missed her calling as an athlete. A boxer? A skier? She had it going on, and it seemed to be a lot of fun for her, with her saying she wanted to go more regularly in the middle of the day when it got slow over at the shop. She was that way ever since the hug or whatever you'd call it, she was that way right up until immigration came by this morning and said they were following up on a report of illegal work. They wanted to see my visa.

5.8.3.X.19.86.12.8-9 [ref(.)]

What a cluster fuck. They weren't that old themselves, those two guys from border control. They were pretty accommodating. Didn't get rough and nasty. Who knows? It isn't always that way. Basically, I was under arrest, but it wasn't like in the movies. They said I could go get my stuff and pack up my rucksack and bring it.

"Can I go with him?" Birgit asked, and they immediately and almost apologetically assured her it was not a problem. "If anyone comes in, can you ask them to wait. Tell them I'll be right back."

It wasn't going to take me long to pack everything up, I didn't need any help, but I got the impression she wanted to explain. We both knew there was only one person who could've made that call and she had some big excuse for why none of it was her fault and she didn't mean to, or whatever. I'm packing up my bag, only the stuff I had with me when I got there, no reason to take anything I bought. What good would it do me back home? The winter gear I got from the store, sure, those gloves and that hat, the long johns, that's good stuff, but none of that household crap I bought with Eve's money. I assumed they were going to deport me back to the US which totally sucked because I was planning on staying until spring or summer. I didn't have any place to be until August, now what the hell was I going to do? That's what's running through my mind while I was putting my stuff into the pack. No book, she took that. Plenty of room. Not many cassettes. It felt kind of pathetic, as though I had nothing to show for anything. Ordinarily that would be a sign of great achievement, but at that moment it felt lame and sad.

That whole time Birgit was watching me. Not sure what to do or say, but clearly hyper aware. She saw there wasn't much time. It wasn't taking long and she's getting a sense of urgency.

"It was before I came here," she said. "When Oskar told me. When I pried it out of him, I was furious with you."

I was listening, but pretending I wasn't. I don't think it came off as rude. I was busy, still checking for any final things lying around. She couldn't expect my undivided attention right at that moment. If she wanted that, there was plenty of time to come clean days ago.

"You made me feel like garbage. Leaving. I was so angry. I tried to find out where you went right away. No one had any idea, but Frithjof was hiding something. When I confronted him, he pointed me to Oskar and Oskar's not someone you can rely on to keep your secrets. You should've known that."

"I'll keep that in mind for future reference." Matter of fact. I didn't want any more of a scene than I was already forced to play, so the best strategy was to let her say whatever the hell she needed to say to make herself feel okay about what she did. What's the alternative, right? It's better if she felt justified. Better for her, I mean. Made no fucking difference to me.

"It's... You can't do that to people. Disappear that way. I was nothing to you, not worth an explanation or a goodbye or anything." She was nervously wringing this out of herself but working up to something too. I finished packing the bag and turned to face her once it was perched at the threshold and there was nothing left to do except grab it and head downstairs. "You owe me an apology."

There it was. I knew her better now though. She didn't think I owed her an apology. She's an engineer, trying to vary the conditions to see what the results are. It's a complicated experiment. She's trying to see how much she could get away with, or trying to figure out how stupid and gullible I was, or how much control she had over me. What did I have to gain by placating her? Sure, if there was the promise of great pleasure, then I'd sacrifice everything to make her feel good about her choices. That's how guys are supposed to be. Of course, baby, I am so sorry, how about a toss for the road? But that wasn't the case here, so fuck that.

"Look Birgit," I said as she braced herself. The border patrol officers were going to have to come up there and pry us apart. This was about to be a nightmare. That's what I was thinking. Thought better of it, in fact. Fantasies can help direct you, right? "I mean, I don't think you and I are going to see things the same way. I get it, but isn't it possible, for a second, that you might consider the possibility that I disappeared because you were impossible to be around, and I was terrified at what kind of a scene it would cause to talk to you about it and tell you I was leaving. You don't have to see it that way. While you're brooding over the apology you're owed, you could consider the fact that you were an actor in that too and might have had some responsibility for what happened. There was a lot of drama between us and I'm going to have to figure out why I was attracted to it. You may want to do the same."

Aghast. She was aghast. In fact, that's why they came up with that word. It was to describe Birgit's reaction. She expected me to either give in to her request and tell her what she wanted to hear or tell her to fuck off and leave. She understood both those reactions. Either I was under her control, or I wasn't. She was aghast because I showed something wildly different from her expectations. I could've said something like "oh Birgit, don't think of yourself as a victim, don't play that card, we both know better," or some shit like that, but that would have been predictable too. I might've told her she was crazy. That would fit right in with her plans of making it seem as though the world was unfair, and people were shitty, and you couldn't rely on anybody. That's what she wanted her experiences to prove. Why shouldn't this prove that too? My response was slippery though. It didn't fit into those neat containers and that's why she was taken aback, that's why she didn't know what to say.

Taking advantage of the momentary confusion, I gave her a brief hug and grabbed the rucksack to hoist it onto my shoulders and take off toward the stairs. "I hope you'll remember me kindly, Birgit," I said. I thought she would follow me down right away and try to get some clever last words in or something. She didn't though, stayed right where she was and said either "Take care of yourself, Stefan Voolf" or "Fuck yourself, Stefan Voolf" as I disappeared down the stairs.

Back down in the shop, Herr Damschroder had come back. He must've heard the immigration officers were in the store. It's a small town. He hurried back from lunch or wherever he was and was talking to the officers when I came down the stairs.

"How did this happen?" he asked me.

"No clue," I said. "Could've been one of the customers. Anyway, does it matter? I'm sorry I didn't tell you, Herr Damschroder, and I'm sorry for the trouble this'll cause you." That's what I said while looking over at the officers. I was building a cover story for him. I didn't know anything about the laws or penalties for this kind of thing and it occurred to me that he could get in trouble. The officers didn't seem to care though, and Herr Damschroder didn't seem worried, so I might've been overplaying it, none of that was necessary. "Birgit should be down in a second. She's straightening up the mess I made."

"Wait, one second," he said, then went into the back room. He came out with an envelope and stuffed it into one of the compartments at the back of my pack. "It's money," he said looking at the officers. "Is that okay? Back pay," he said looking at me. "Look out for yourself, boy. Always keep your eyes open and your head low," then he winked. "You never know." Made me wonder what stories I missed by not getting to know him better.

Birgit appeared at the door to the backroom and offered a kind of demur wave to both of us without saying anything. I looked at her, pursed my lips, and then waved again to Herr Damschroder, thanking him for everything. I was damn sorry to be leaving that place. What a gig. Who knows? If it hadn't been for that phone call, I might've stayed forever. Instead, I was rushed out of there after only a month.

The officers put me and my rucksack in the back seat of their jeep and then, before they drove away, stumbled upon some logistical problem that, for some reason, they hadn't worked out beforehand.

"Are we taking him to Scharnitz or Innsbruck?" the one guy said, and then the other said he didn't know. Each of them thought the other knew the procedure. Now it was a mess because they didn't want to ask, and they weren't sure what to do. At the end, the second guy, the one who wasn't driving, he said Scharnitz because "It'll be easier to explain." Not exactly sure what he meant, but I think it was that if they took me to Scharnitz, and that was wrong, it'd be easier to explain. It was cover-your-ass stuff. It hit me that they were bureaucrats. See, this is why people turn to libertarianism. This was shaping up to be one of the most amazing experiences of my life, but then this fucking psycho bitch comes and ruins it by getting these two jar head assholes involved. What would you have me do? Surrender to guilt and self-loathing? Ha.

I didn't know it, but this debate would have enormous implications for my life. If they'd taken me to Innsbruck for processing, they likely would have deported me to the US. There would have been a formal complaint to the ambassador or something, and I would have had to pay a fine that was basically the cost of the return fare where everything is calculated at its maximum possible amount. At Scharnitz, they didn't have the ability to do that. All they could do was transfer me to Innsbruck. Since these guys already decided not to take me there, it must've meant they were deciding to follow another protocol. I don't know. Guessing.

It didn't take long to get there and the whole time I was thinking back to last week when Birgit punched me in the chest, and I ended up hugging her. She was a completely different person. The way she smelled was different. I wouldn't have thought she was capable of those tears. It was confusing to say the least, and nothing that happened since made it any clearer. She had these passageways inside her and some connected up while others had nothing to do with each other. You could never tell what borders and boundaries there were, you couldn't guess what things were connected to what other things. Why did she experience that as a compassionate hug and not an act of force to get her under control? No idea what triggered that response. It was the best possible, but I had no idea why it was the right thing to do and why she reacted the way she did. Then, for some reason, that made me think about Eve and Elke. I spoke to them at some point after that day with Birgit but didn't tell them about it. In fact, I didn't tell them Birgit came to Seefeld. Why not?

It was about compartments for me too, passageways. Birgit was in our lives. We'd talked about her, they knew stories, had been following along. The crisis was over, and I was in a new situation that had nothing to do with her. They both understood that and, I think, were proud of it in some twisted way. They played a part in getting me out of there, and now, our friendship was going down a different road. They'd come for a visit, and we had a great time together. Not only the rolling around, that was great, but the other stuff too. Talking until late, skiing together, the whole weekend we created these new passageways and whatever, and none of them had anything to do with Birgit or me getting away from her. Once I told them about how she came back and got me arrested, that'd bring everything back. I didn't want that. I wanted to be free of that mess and to have something with them that didn't include any of that. That's why I didn't say anything.

In Scharnitz, there was a decent-sized facility for customs considering that it's such a small town. There were holding cells and they put me in one. They took my passport, but didn't process any forms or anything, at least not that I needed to supply any information for. They didn't ask me any questions. They took most of my stuff and locked it up and then shoved me in this cell. Not a cell, more like a room. It was nicer than my garret except it had a sink and toilet right in the middle of it, but the toilet was clean and the water from the sink seemed drinkable. They said I had to stay the night because transfers had to take place first thing in the morning.

The guy in charge of keeping an eye on me was different than the two officers. He had a different job description and personality, seemed nicer, you could talk to him. He wasn't much older than me and had a love for all things American. He wanted to know if I liked the Ramones. Said that American punk was real punk, and the Ramones were awesome, they were outlaws. Sure, I liked them, Blondie, the Misfits, Patti Smith, the whole CBGB crowd. The Talking Heads. That got him going. He had read about it and listened to the music obsessively. He would have gone on that way forever, but he had a job to do, and someone called him away. When he came back, I took advantage of the passageway we created to ask him if there was anything to read. I didn't have a book and you can only write so much. I was getting desperate for something to do. "Do you have something in English?" I said knowing it was a long shot. He said he'd check the lost and found.

He came back with a copy of something called *The Tao of Physics*. Not exactly the kind of thing I'd pick up on my own, but it could've been a lot worse. I read about subatomic particles and how their relationships resemble this woozy wavy tao-like thing. It passed the time and made me feel as if I should have smoked some pot or something before reading it, as if it was that kind of thing you would sit around the dorm and shoot the shit with your stoner buddies about back in college. Anyway, I got into it, and they said I could take it with me. The people at the facility weren't big readers apparently, and they didn't have much interest in some flakey stoner book. The rules seemed lax and they didn't have to account for everything they had in inventory.

This is an understatement because it's exactly what happened with me too. Early the next morning a different officer, dressed the same as the two who brought me in, came to lead me back to the front of the place. Some inventory person came out with my rucksack and gave it back to me. She also gave me my passport and the travel belt thing that I used to carry that stuff. Everything looked to be in order. The officer took my arm and walked me outside, then put me in the back of a different jeep to drive me

up to the border crossing into Germany. Before he let me out, he told me
to tell them I'm a tourist getting some help finding my way to the border.
The Germans weren't that interested. It wasn't crowded, and nobody was
too worried about an American on foot crossing over. I told them I'd been
going back and forth for weeks. Mentioned the crossing over the
Mädelegabel and Größe Krottenkopf, told them about Reutte and Neu
Schwanstein, it was routine, they were bored by it and barely listened. They
let me through after the briefest possible look at my passport. While I had
it out, I noticed that there were no stamps or markings from the Austrians,
nothing to say I shouldn't or couldn't come back. The officer who dropped
me off told me never to try to work in Austria without proper
documentation but that was it. He didn't say anything about not coming
back, he turned me loose and that was that. I thought I was in a lot of
trouble, but nobody seemed to care much.

There's no German town right at the border there, it's quite a ways to
Mittenwald, so I figured I'd have to walk. It occurred to me that I didn't
have any money and that I was hungry. I figured Herr Damschroder would
be good for a few bits, so I checked to see if the envelope was still in the
pocket where he put it, and it was. There were 5000 Schillings in it.
Unbelievable, it was fucking unbelievable. Not only that he gave me so
much, but that the customs people didn't take it. Unbelievable. It's almost
four hundred dollars. This changed everything. I didn't need to go back to
Nürnberg and beg for a place to stay. I wasn't a beggar, I was rich, I could
do whatever the hell I wanted. I could live for months on this much money.
I needed a plan. There's a shell station not too far past the border so I
stopped in there to get a bite to eat.

While I was eating and jotting down some thoughts about what I could
do with my newfound riches, I saw this guy over at the next table looking
at me weird. He was a kid, 18 or 19. "Hey, what's up?" I said.

"American?" he asked. I nodded and he broke into English. Said he
had to practice for upcoming exams. "Where are you going? Do you need
a ride?"

"Where are you headed," I asked.

"München," he said. My plan was hatched. He was about ready to go
and was excited to get me back to his car. He said he had some music that
he listened to a lot but there were some lyrics he didn't completely
understand. "Can you help me with that?" he asked, thinking it was a huge
imposition, though he was the one giving me a ride, and, if you can believe
it, paying for my lunch.

"Yeah, yeah. Of course. That'd be great." It's an hour and a half ride
so what the hell else were we going to talk about? Talking English is a duty
when you're travelling. It's the most common thing you hear from the
younger people who give you rides. Anyway. "Let me make a phone call

real quick first. Is that okay?"

"Yeah sure. No problem. I'll wait."

There were some card phones, but I didn't have a card. They had them for sale near the counter, so I went and tried to buy one. It was complicated and the girl at the register was trying to explain it, but it didn't seem as though I could punch it in and use it right away.

"Well, I only need to make one collect call. Is there a phone I could use for that?"

She was immediately helpful and let me come over to the other side of the counter and use the phone there. She dialed the operator, and I took the phone and gave the number and my name to the lady on the other end. You sit in silence and wait for the operator to come back on and tell you that your call went through. Right over the top of her highly formal professional tone, I could hear Eve asking what's going on, where are you?

"I'm at the Shell station by the border," I said. "I don't have much time. This guy is giving me a ride to München. I had to leave Seefeld."

"Oh no," she's genuinely upset, sincerely empathetic. She knew it couldn't be good. "What happened?"

"Too complicated, and I'm standing here in the shop. Any chance you could meet me in München? I'll tell you all about it."

"I can come Thursday night. Friday is a study day. Is that too late?"

"No, it's fantastic. Perfect."

"Where will you stay? Which Youth Hostel? I can come there at around 8 or 9 o'clock."

"I'm not sure. I'll call you when I know. Will that work?"

"No, don't call again before then. It's crazy here. We're studying. Stay at the one by the Hauptbahnhof. Or wherever you want, we can meet up at the train station. Be there at 8, near the main exit. I may be late, okay?"

This was perfect and it didn't register that it was too quick and easy. I focused on the fact that I'd have 2 days to myself in München knowing that it's only two days. That's the best. You can't get too far off track if that's the setup because you know something's coming but you're totally on your own until then. Their schedules were all turned around right now, lucky thing I found her at home. It must've been exam time or something. That's the only thought I had. Anyway, it was set, didn't take any begging or convincing. Now, let's see what this kid needed. What kind of music was so muffled and funky that he had no idea what lyrics they were singing? Hopefully, I'd get a chance to find out more about his situation in München. He might live there and be in a position to offer me a place to stay. I could afford the youth hostel. Hell, I could afford a hotel, but that's not the point, it's never the point. Having money is great, it's an insurance policy, but the best use you could possibly make of it is none at all. Better to live by your wits.

5.8.4.X.19.86.12.11-12 [ref(..1-11)]

When you go through something, it's never only one thing. Consider a carwash. Something with one single entrance and a short straight path to the exit. That isn't simple. The suds and the brushes, the water, and the air blowing, it adds up along the way, and the passages or the chambers and tunnels, all that, they're transport. There's the stuff that moves around in there. It comes along for the ride, passes through, relays back and forth, it's complicated. Signals and whatnot. You've got to figure out what everything means and how it fits together. Just because there's a connection doesn't mean that's how they relate. Something weird can bump up against something that isn't the same, and you have this connection that you don't know what to do with. A hug isn't only a hug. It was lumped in together and swirled around. I couldn't separate any of it. The routine. The pickup. The invitation. Her antics and rituals, and then the departure and the chase. What was she thinking? The arguments with the roommates and the phone calls, I didn't know what was happening. The phone call to immigration. It's a phone call too, right? My phone call to Nürnberg. What is it about? How is it connected? See, it's not even close to one thing. Why did she come over to the sharpener and vice that day? What was the optimal outcome? Was it the slugfest and the bearhug turned into instant sorrow, into tears and an embrace? Was that the whole point? Or was it something else? She couldn't have wanted me in some ordinary way, right? Not after everything, the jump down turnaround. If she was looking for me right away, why did it take her a month to get here? The running away, the chase, she tried to turn it into foreplay. You could say that, couldn't you? If it ultimately plays into a romp by the ski equipment, what else would you call it? But she didn't want that. I don't think she wanted any of it. It was for the sake of something else, something she couldn't describe or come right out and ask for. It had to include the eviction. What's up with her now anyway? Is she going to stay for the rest of the month and go back in January when the hostel reopens? Or will she stay all season? This could be her life now. Everything's changed for her, and that could be exactly what she wanted. Hopefully, she won't go nuts with some shady skier down for the weekend and blow the whole thing up, but that's part of it too. It could be what the whole thing was designed for. Not to get well or into a better situation, but to do that and then destroy it. It's hard to tell and it's why she doesn't want anyone to know the details of her history. Only she knows the twists and turns and what the point of it is. I'm not talking about what she thinks she wanted. Assume she's successful at always getting what she wants, and then work backwards from there and say what happened, whatever shit got piled on, that's what she wanted all along. Destructive desire, it's not one thing, it's never only one thing.

The kid was an idiot, and I was done with him by the time we got to München. Didn't probe too hard for a place to stay because I was fed up. Not only his taste in music, which was appalling, or the fact that his trip to München was to visit his parents, but there were other signs too. I'm pretty sure his primary intent was to blow me, or get me to blow him, or something. There were a lot of weird gestures and stuff, a lot of experiments with space and distance in the car. He was a quirky guy and it got too weird at some point during the drive. That happens, that's the whole thing of it, and it goes back to those passageways. I mean, it's not one thing either, and going through it on my end wasn't that simple. Should've let him. The whole trip, what is it about anyway? Experiences. Gotta push through them either way. Good or bad. Walking all that way. Getting off on the austerity. Then, before that, there was that prostitute on the Calle Sicilia. Such perfect skin. And what about that weird lady on Rue Cujas? Extremely hot but she must've been forty. It adds up. Living by my wits more and more with each new thing that teaches me how. More tunnels, more throughways, everything comes together, and these are the things you should expect if that's what you're going for. I may not have ever sat down and said my purpose is to get a ride from some quirky dude who hasn't figured his shit out yet, but you got to assume it's in there somewhere. Anybody considering the likely events of such a journey would know these are the sorts of adventures that are likely to come your way. I must've wanted that too. Everything. Yes, to all of it. That's the thing, that's how it goes.

Youth hostel for me. The grimy one right in the city center. Downside, crime and exploitation. There's lots of seedy, weird shit going on around that place. It's cheap and there were plenty of non-travelers about. Loiterers, you could call them, looking for a cheap kip, but also looking for marks. You have to keep your stuff close, make sure your money belt stays close to your crotch. Nobody's going to go grab for that without me knowing it, that's the safest thing, and the place was full of thieves and robbers. They're pirates, if you think about it, and we're the cruise vessels or whatever. The upside was that you don't have to pay, not officially, the city hostels are always that way, impersonal and big. When they're not that crowded because it's off season, they still have a bigness about them. The space is large, the number of staff is large. You can put your stuff there at around 5 when it opens and then disappear until 9 or 10, can't be later than that and shouldn't be too much earlier. Well, what happens is the guy at the desk figures you checked in with the other guy. You belong and you got a big backpack so you're set. Of course, you don't have a key, but that's where the others come in. It's easy to get someone to let you into a room, it's all in the attitude. The cut throats are doing the same thing. What you do is act the same as them, but then leave the good folks and the paying customers alone. An Aussie guy let me into his room, and I was able to sleep there the first night. There were only three in the bunks, and it slept six. Most of the rooms were for six and at that time of year it was unlikely any would be full, meaning you didn't have to plan or watch too closely. Anyone nice enough to do you a favor would be good enough.

Food was much easier. Piracy in the city takes care of that. The subculture of farmers and hunter gatherers is enormous. The signs and trails to follow are everywhere. There was enough food for everyone as long as you didn't have any barriers to stop you passing along the way you needed to go. Asking for bread at bakeries, that almost always worked, especially if you asked in English. Stores throw away lots of good food. So what if you have nearly 400 bucks in your pocket, why piss it away when there's plenty of nicely wrapped cheese already there for the grabbing. Five finger discount was always an option. The people are way too trusting, made it easy to find your way. I was having a jolly time that whole day living it up with a big old loaf of bread and some lovely North German cheese. High on the hog, and there's some left over for the next day. Minimal effort, maximum payout.

Wednesday night, I was having a good chat with these two South African girls, and I thought one of them was up for it. Not only letting me share the room but share the bed too. I was wrong about that in the end, but it didn't matter. See, that's the point. Even that, even the failure on that front, that's part of it. The look of shock and horror in her eyes when I suggested it, that had to fit with the whole thing. What kind of an adventure would it be if it didn't include some prudish Afrikaner who tossed me out of her room because I wanted to do some heavy petting and whatever else followed from it? That's the whole point. I slept in one of the common areas because by then it was too late to find anything else. Had to get up and move to a different room at some point because someone was on shift during the night, and they were walking around. Luckily their footsteps woke me up because they would have asked a lot of questions if they found me sleeping out there. Technically, you're supposed to keep that paper they give you, but people lose that shit all the time. Not having a key and not having the paper, well, that's a shit stir I'd prefer to avoid. It wasn't a great night's sleep, but again that's part of it, that's what you do it for, for things like that: the mini-adventures. Otherwise, why let this money burn a hole in my pocket? I could've stayed at a hotel if I wanted a quiet trip to München. Oh look, it's almost noon and the Glockenspiel is about to do its big performance. Get the camera honey. Fuck that.

Truth is, I knew Eve and Elke were on their way and I thought that the grimier and gnarlier I looked when they got here, the better it'd be, the bigger the impression it'd make. It wasn't to fool them or manipulate them, it's more of an entertainment. Not for me, or not only for me, but for them. They had this caring nurturing vibe they liked to express and that I liked to have expressed. It's a dance or whatever, and it's not one single thing, it's all the things. Okay, that point's been done to death. Move on.

Thursday night I'm at the train station early. I left the hostel and put my pack in one of the lockers. I had to change some money because there's no way to do that without handing over the 5 DM. My goal had been to save those shillings until I got back to Austria, that way I wouldn't have to pay the exchange fee. Such a crock, a real racket. I was going to get Eve and Elke to drive me to Salzburg. I figured it could work because, although I would never have been able to get them to drive me there from Nürnberg, it's too far, once I had them half-way, there was at least a chance they'd go for it. If they dropped me a few kilometers outside town along the road, that'd be fine too. I was prepared to fail, but that was the plan, that was the one thing I had in mind, the one thing that hid the millions of things that were going on.

I had enough money left over after the luggage to buy a pack of tobacco, some papers, and a beer. Enough for a second beer if they were more on the late side. I'm sitting there reading more of this book that fits spiritual stuff into the nano-energies of the physical universe. They're always doing that kind of crap because only a moron would buy into the spiritual stuff without it. If it's loopy and unconnected to anything else, then no sane person would believe it, and sane people want desperately to believe it. This guy was trying to help them out, give them the signals they'd need to set the passageways and tunnels up right so that their worlds and ideas peacefully conjoined down there in the muck and the cold air of those dark caverns.

After a while, Eve came up and was incredibly happy to see me. Huge hug. Swinging torsos and lots of groping going on. Friendly, but with an edge.

"Where's Elke?" I asked as if I had purposefully designed to wipe the smile off her face and force her to be serious for a second. Dumb ass. I mean, I talk a lot of shit, but I was happy to see her, and part of that was how happy she was to see me. That can cheer you up if you've been groveling around in the gutter for the last two days.

She sat down and I gestured for the guy to get us another beer. "She couldn't come. Studying. I don't have the time either but..." She looked away and pursed her lips. Okay, I'm supposed to notice that, but what to do about it? What can I do? She's here, she must want to be in some way, or she felt obligated. I hope that's not it, but you don't know. That whole nurturing thing, well it isn't one thing either. Be appreciative and give her a chance to work through it and share it with me. That's what they desperately want. Connecting over it.

"God, I'm so sorry to be such a bother. It's been a helluva week. It's so good to see a friendly face. I can't describe how much. I should've come up there."

"Don't be silly. That wouldn't have been any better. Anja and Elke are busy. You would have disrupted the three of us instead of just me."

"But your studies. What will you do? You don't have to stay. I don't want to cause any harm."

"No, I worked it out. I need to be back by Saturday. There'll be plenty of time to work through my outline if I'm back by then. I thought we could spend the day together tomorrow. Have you been to the zoo?"

See, she wanted to come, but she wanted me to make it possible for her to imagine that her coming was appreciated, that it was a mutual connection between us, that it wasn't some stupid careless extravagance on her part that she'd regret because it was done for some useless asshole. She wanted confirmation or help confirming she did the right thing and wasn't being taken advantage of. That's what I mean, nothing is only one thing.

"No. That sounds fun." Completely noncommittal. I wasn't done with that first subject yet. "Anna and Elke must have thought you shouldn't come though, right?"

"They would have stopped me. I told them I was going to stay with my parents, needed a quiet place to study and my mom's care. I borrowed my sister's car. She'll cover for me."

Got it?

"Did she think it was a good idea?"

"No, but she's got her own problems to worry about. She doesn't have time to think about the consequences. It's not her fault."

"What are her problems? You mean your other sister. We haven't talked about that. Did you...?"

"I don't..." She clammed up. Somehow seemed to know better. Do they want coaxing in those circumstances? What am I supposed to do, make it easier for her to talk about it, or let her get away with changing the subject? Birgit would've wanted the latter, but normal girls could be fishing for the former.

I moved closer to her and put my arm around her. "I'm so glad to see you."

"Have you been to the Hofbrauhaus? Americans usually want to go there. I reserved a room at a hotel near it. We can take a taxi. It's better to leave the car here." Guess she made up her mind.

"No, haven't been. Do you want to head over to the hotel now to get settled? Are you hungry?"

We grabbed a cab and went to the hotel. It was perfect. She paid for the beers, the cab, and the room. It wasn't a shock, and I didn't offer anything different. It's part of it. For both of us. We put our stuff in the room, and she made me get cleaned up before we went out for a snack at one of the places on the same street. If she wanted to go to the Hofbrauhaus, I would've been okay with that, but I wasn't going to bring it up and she didn't either. It was a huge city, people everywhere, tons of stuff to do and plenty of places to eat and drink. In fact, after the last month, it was too wild. A quiet place suited me fine. Once we were sitting and sipping our beer after the food, she was ready for the story.

"What happened then? Why did you leave Seefeld?"

This was a different dynamic than planned. If Elke came with, telling this story would get tons of sympathy. There'd be plenty of reassurance that this or that was the right thing to do, that I had no choice, that I was wronged, you know the drill. It would have been the same as the other times when we circled that same corpse. I'm not trying to say there's something vulture-like in this form of reinforcement but, well, I guess there's something vulture-like in this form of reinforcement. That's what I planned for, that's the cavern I expected to pass through. Eve alone, that hadn't been on the agenda, and it'd be a completely different set of events. I had to think how I wanted it to turn out. What did I want? What was the end? That's the theme of the day, it isn't only one thing. There I am being blown over the rough seas, trying to think of which way to go. The easy way, the simple layup, ends with tender sex back at the hotel. Did I want that? This was Eve and sure there had been that, but was that where I wanted it to go? She came by herself and didn't tell Elke and Anna about it. They didn't know she was here, they didn't know she was with me. That's why it's a layup, it's not that my story is so compelling and I'm such a stud that I can lure her in with it as easy as pie. It's because that's what's on her mind, that's what she came for and, if the story doesn't repulse her, it's guaranteed. But the story could repulse her. You see the dilemma. It's in the telling and I had to decide what kind of story it was going to be.

It was that simple. If it didn't go the way she was hoping, then there's no way I get to Salzburg in a short two-hour ride. There's no way she stays Friday night either. If she's repulsed, none of that happens. The disappointment angle could blow up the whole thing and I won't be able to crawl back to Nürnberg after the trip to Wien.

"What's wrong?"

"I'm struggling with how to tell you about it. Part of it is, I don't want to seem ungrateful. I'm glad you came. I am happy to see you." That wasn't a lie. It's never only one thing. Aren't you fucking listening?

"What happened? Tell me. Why did you leave Seefeld?"

"Immigration came and deported me. I had no choice. They took me into custody and dropped me at the border by Scharnitz. The gas stop where I called you, that was right after they let me out."

She's surprised, but not shocked. It happens a lot. It was a choice job and it's perfectly reasonable that someone else who wanted it would turn me in.

"Do you know who reported you?"

This was going to be the wildcard. Here was where the shock would come, and I had no idea what effect it would have.

"Birgit," I said simply. You can't lie about stuff like that, not when you're talking to people who care about you. I'm not a monster.

Then the questions. How did she find out? All that.

"She badgered the roommate who told her about Oskar and then Oskar told her about the shop in Seefeld. She told me she called immigration before she left Innsbruck."

"She came to see you in Seefeld? How did she get Oskar to rat you out? How long was she there? When did she come? Why didn't you tell us about this?"

Us. You see what she did there. Us. She's back with Elke now. This was the middle way. Not disgust. She wouldn't be disgusted, but she wasn't going to be lured into romantic lovemaking either. Leave it to a woman to find a completely different third option. It wasn't what she was expecting. I was watching her closely and, honestly, it wasn't surprise right then, it was disappointment. She was changing her plans while we sat there. Fucking hell, that sucked. If I were a monster, I would have gotten that one thing I wanted, but it's never one thing. The refrain from one of those stupid songs that idiot kid wanted me to translate for him.

I told her the whole story. About how she showed up right after they left, about how Herr Damschroder was so nice and welcoming with her, and about how she learned about the job in a few days and seemed different.

"Did you two...?"

That's what she wanted to know, and she got right to it. Yeah, yeah, great, she needed to get away from whatever hell she was in, but did you two, you know, make the beast with two backs, or what?

"No. We both knew that was a bad idea. Something in her understands what lies under the bullshit, something draws her to the light as much as something else draws her to darkness. She's conflicted."

Silence. She's giving me all the rope I need.

"I mean, she tried something one time, but it went south fast."

"How do you mean?"

"Well, I didn't go along with it, and she didn't take the rejection well. She doesn't like it when men have any power over her. Rejection is a show of power, and she didn't like it."

She didn't fall for the distraction, never looked at the bait.

"What did she do? What do you mean she didn't like it?"

"She got mad. She shouted at me. Said it was my fault. I was the one abusing her. I used her and then left after I got what I wanted. She was furious with me for abandoning her."

"Is that how she put it?"

Is it? That was the sense I got. "Yes, I think so. She hit me. Hard. I think she was about to do it again. More than once. She looked as if she was ready to fight a match or something."

"Strike a match?"

"No. As in boxing." Did I say it wrong? "I didn't know what to do. I grabbed her and she went limp. We hugged." I was breathing hard while telling this part because it was upsetting. Genuinely. As if I was going through it again. I would've preferred not to have to tell it, but there was no getting around it. "After that, things were fine between us. Almost friendly. She's not so bad when she's not being a psycho and everything. She apologized when the officers came and seemed genuinely remorseful. She wouldn't have done it if she knew how things were going to turn out. I'm convinced of that." Might've laid it on too thick.

Yes, fine, but the romance was gone. No empathy for my empathy. Whatever romantic shit you put on it, it's because Eve thinks the passageways must be smooth and even. There are no compartments separated and detached from everything else. She didn't come for some wild romp lasting one weekend without strings attached or added portents. She wanted to move things along. Deliberation was involved. Decisions. That endless restless thinking they subject themselves to over everything that ever happens. It was a continuum to her, whereas I was more of the abrupt compartmentalization ilk. Do your buddy a solid and rock her world, right? No sin in that, not as far as I'm concerned, but that's not where her head was and I could tell by her reaction that she was in a totally different place now, not where she expected to be and not where either of us wanted her to be.

Back-to-back at the hotel. That's how it went. No cuddling or fiddling about before sleepy time. Back to fucking back. The next morning though, before she remembered who we were and what took place, that was a different story. Nothing better than an early morning half groggy roll around. Sleepy Eve knew all about that, and her fucked up hiatus from study wasn't going to be a total loss. I didn't roll over and grab her, nope, she rolled onto me to get it going. Friendly, but there was flesh involved. Legs and chests, that kind of thing, the good stuff. The just about to and the on the way to kind of stuff, but then she remembered, woke up completely, and put a stop to that. She didn't feel much like running around München doing touristy things anymore, her whole vision of the day was completely shot. She liked the idea of getting in the car and driving me to Salzburg, thought it sounded perfect. Then she'd drop me off and head back to Nürnberg which, from there, is a long drive so she'd be at it the whole day. Then back in plenty of time to get a good night's sleep and work through her study plan first thing Saturday morning.

That's what she wanted to happen all along. It was at her request in this way of telling the tale. See? If I fudged the truth and we worked our way into that tender moment she was first hoping for, that would have led to a weekend of bacchanalia. Whatever they say about the intimate romantic stuff, they want the throw down too and once the boundaries have been crossed, it's only a matter of time before you explore that territory. Thursday night would have been touchy-feely and mature adult PG-13 bullshit, but then Friday after a day of fun around town it would become an R-rated affair, for sure. And then, if she drove me to Salzburg, with such a huge commitment of time and adventure, she would have been thrilled to see that turn into an X-rated fiasco. Not porno stuff necessarily, although you never can tell from looking at someone, still it could've worked out like *Last Tango*.

Instead, she drove me to the train station in Salzburg, we had a bite to eat at the place across the street, and then she left. Big hug. Huge hug. Lots of promise and please come to Nürnberg as soon as you can kind of stuff, but still, not what she was expecting and not what I was hoping for. As we were pulling away from each other at the end of the hug, I said, "I'm sorry it didn't..." and that was it. I broke off right in the middle of that thought. Never planned on finishing it. The whole point of saying it was to break off in the middle, because she's an expert and would appreciate that level of respect for her skills, she knew what I was saying. "Come to Nürnberg," she repeated, and it was part of the same chain of tunnels. Not one thing. She was admitting that everything I sensed was right, that she was where I thought she was, the turmoil was real, the desire intact and at cross purposes. Okay, a deferral and a change of characters and venue, that's it, that's what we're stuck with. Onward. Okay.

"*Pure and prepared to leap up to the stars.*" [Dante's Purgatorio]

3.12 (4)

this year's harvest

3.12.1.Elisabet.19.86.5.9

Soft speaking it into the recorder.

They start at the front. Professional smile while she slides the removable trays into each of the two seats. He stops reading. There's more legroom and no one's seatback leans into the space. Light clouds, water and an occasional island paradise visit through the waft.

He holds a pen in hand and traces the words on the page. Occasionally, the pen lightly draws lines beneath the words: for emphasis or in error.

—Cassie on the beach or at one of those tacky clubs. With the guy from cabana service. She can do whatever she wants, and what the hell is he doing? That two-faced bitch with the Proustian name.

"Chicken," when she asks.

"Beef," he says.

—Fancy sandwiches, smell isn't bad, but it's better if there is food in front of you. Odor no longer ambient: that's worse, smelling other people's bad food.

Unwrapped and fully self-contained, she sets each tray down and moves along. The cart jostles its way past him, and he tucks his arm into his seat to avoid it.

"Some more water, thanks."

—Desperate for a glass of wine, but I suspect they're difficult to swallow.

"Yes, me too, please."

She extends the tray with two cups on it.

He carefully reaches up and takes one from her after watching the other slide off toward the makeshift table. He studies the hand that carries it. The flight attendant's hand rests lightly on his shoulder and he goes discernibly stiff in discomfort.

Next to the sandwich, a bag of chips and the dessert prepackaged, both set to the side, it's some kind of fruit biscuit.

His is more or less the same, but brown meat, instead of white.

Cloth napkins and sturdy flatware sit alongside a hefty coffee cup that someone will offer to fill later.

"It's a risk," trying to be friendly. He looks over, hungry.

—At that age, they're always hungry, always everything at once.

He smiles without requiring an explanation.

"You don't have a girlfriend?"

As though picking up where she left off.

—Come on, it's lunch time, entertain me. I'm certainly not going to eat any of this.

Chewing, he pauses to finish before answering.

"No."

"But come on, in college you must have had a girlfriend. Let's have some pleasant mealtime conversation." Smiling back at him, he gets it. Sits up and decides he's willing to play along.

"It seems as though travelling always gets in the way. I had a girlfriend before I came down here a few years ago. And then I had one after I got back. Ended a while ago. Around the time I decided to go to Europe. Too busy planning since."

"You broke someone's heart to travel the world?"

He chuckles and bobs his head noncommittally.

"Is that it then?"

More decision-making. He's without guile and can't hide the fact that he is considering how much he should hide the facts.

The cart inches back toward the curtain, he relaxes his arm and lets it creep farther into the aisle.

"Got mine broken too," he says too defensively, a twinge of pain twisting his mouth.

"It's part of growing up. What happened?"

—Sing me a song.

"Uh... Well... It's why I went to Colombia in the first place. My friends wanted to go, they were going anyway, and invited me along. Initially I said no because I thought it'd be better to spend the summer with her."

Pausing, hesitating, he becomes aware that he is talking to a stranger.

—He thinks I'm a stranger. People are quick to unburden, especially when they think they know you. No illusions about that with this one.

"She had other ideas?"

"She was in this theatre group at school. They were having tryouts that summer and she needed to get ready."

"Total concentration?"

"Exactly."

"And you were in the way."

"Yes." Bobs his head and takes another bite before sipping more water. The cart wheels past back to the front. He tucks his arm into his side to make sure it clears.

[Once bitten.]

—Made a decision. Good.

"I think she was frustrated with me."

"Frustrated how?"

"She had definite ideas about what she wanted from the relationship, and I wasn't... ...delivering."

[Wasn't delivering... Deeeeee liff fer eeeeng...]

He looks over, searching for signs of impatience or boredom. There is visible concern that the details are exasperating or strange. It's clear, he's used to it, it's an old friend greeting him from out of other people's eyes and ears.

[For years, flights of fancy before friends and acquaintances, looking at him like a freak or a vagrant. Now he knows that glance, that look, and proactively spares everyone the trouble of going through it again. Everything screamed it: twice shy.]

All singsongy...

—Wonder what Ian's up to?

"We were friends for a long time before we went out. Had a lot in common, but I think we never figured out how to be together."

"She didn't want to sleep with you?"

Successfully provoked, he looks around to make sure everyone else is going about their business and is somewhat reassured before proceeding carefully. He finds encouragement in a slightly sad, slightly questioning look. "It changes things. We were writing a lot, reading each other's stuff."

They're describing the bombing, the couple over his right shoulder, and what should be done to the culprits. She is not committed one way or the other but wants to be agreeable. He has strong opinions and thinks you have to deal with them firmly, his voice resounding in ugly judgment.

"Ah, I see. You were more interested in having a muse than a girlfriend."

It bothers him that it can be summarized that simply. His discomfort shows in his mouth, the way he frowns, but then he shrugs, and his eyes open wider.

—Not age... ...more.

"I suppose," he says.

"But she wanted more than that?" He knows what's happening underneath, looks this way and that, his mind doubling, focus blurring. He wants to go on but feels the rough surface.

"I don't think... Well... I guess..." Unfamiliar awkwardness. Confidence deep enough that he never has to work for it. "But it's not as if she ever said anything about it. She expected things." Faint trace of a smirk apologetically placed and quickly removed.

Legs bumping up and down in awkward discomfort, the napkin slips off between his legs and he sets it back in place.

—Did you want to sleep with her? Of course you did, she was young and beautiful, and you thought you were in love with her, so why didn't you? Was she too perfect?

(N was that way in Malmö. I could see the attraction in his eyes, but he couldn't do anything. I didn't want the philistine, had to be patient, had to coax him along gently, aware of his pace and accommodating his hesitations, but what would I have done ten years earlier at 18 or 20? Shrugged and moved on, no doubt.)

"Like what? What did she expect?"

"I don't know exactly. I respected her so much, she was amazing, but I didn't know what she wanted. That's it."

"Respect might not mean what you think it means." Pausing, but he won't chime in or go any further, not yet. "You decided to go to Colombia, and that's where you met your friend?"

"Yeah, but as I said, she wasn't my girlfriend. She didn't have time for that." He notices that the sandwich is untouched. "Aren't you eating?"

"No. Too busy to be a girlfriend, I like that. Go on."

He laughs. His eyes brighten.

"I learned a lot from her, but no expectations. It wasn't that way, she was older. Things were different when I got back, met someone that Fall, and we started going out. I was better with her. Still respectful, I mean you can't get rid of your upbringing, but more aware, I paid more attention to things, or tried to."

"Your parents taught you to be respectful, that's good."

"My mom, she's pretty tough, she has a strong personality, to put it mildly."

Softening this heart, the mother makes her appearance from on high.

The tiniest beads of sweat present on his back above his waist, above the beltline.

—I can be that without being only that.

[It's been long since he last made love to me, he gave up, lost sight of our purpose, of us. What would it take to right the wrongs of that emptiness?]

"What does she do?" Hopeful. Much remains to be set into the mold, poured into the template. He weaves a pattern, launches a light to guide the way.

"She's an artist. Painting, sculpting, other things."

"Oils?"

Back to origins, the form in the song, she guides us there with soft wings that beat from heaven.

"Oils, water, acrylic. Charcoal, pencil, crayon on the tabletop at the restaurant."

"At the restaurant?"

"There's a restaurant she loves to go to. They have crayons on the table and a big paper tablecloth. It's for children, they're supposed to draw and color, but she loves it."

Hand circling above the tray, hand bending over the center armrest, he pulls the energy from the one into the energy of the other and sends it her way.

"Crayons too."

(I recall those first drawings, before the voice came, before the echoes in my chest, before this resonance. Loved the smell and sight of paint, wanted it to fill every day.)

[The locks abound, the soft red and the dazzling blue are bursting, yearning to find their canvas.]

"Yeah, she covets the black ones. Whenever we go to that restaurant, she complains about how scarce they are. She said they should be giving you more than one in each box, began bringing her own."

He pauses to check for that look again, impatience and exasperation. There is none, the eyes are smiling, he brightens with pride and adulation, doesn't understand what he sees, but embraces it in his chest and near his throat, doesn't realize that's how the singing finds its way out.

His shirt presses tighter against his skin in back, the moisture makes a firmer fit and bond.

[I wanted to be there, in that box for you, but how dare you put me there.]

His feelings tugged from both sides. The mother in him, the mother around him, across the divide, above and below: mothers and those who want to be.

—Surely you must see it.

(Spared the miscarriage, N distressed by the not and the never. He needed his space, but what about me? Space was around in those nots and nevers, it was the last thing I needed. The contract for the tour filled it and that angry bitch ruined everything.)

He scrunches his eyes together, closing them tightly and emitting signs of apprehension. He looks back over, surrendering to whatever judgment may come. Closer now, more relieved, and willing to accept anything on offer. His eyes say feelings are here and everywhere, please have mercy.

"Do you have any sisters?" already knowing the answer.

"No, just brothers."

Pursing the lips and slightly tilting the head, trying to say it without saying it. He searches, this time not for impatience or exasperation, but for some clue as to what he should be seeing, what he should be able to see. He can't get it and lifts his eyebrows hoping for help.

What jungles there are in this small space, that seat beneath, pressing close and around.

"If you had a sister, you would have gotten a more realistic picture of how to be respectful."

"How do you mean?"

"It's not incestuous," he's visibly shocked at the word, hadn't expected it, was far from his mind. Why warn him away from somewhere he never thought to go? "It's just that my brother saw things in me. We ate dinner together, spent time together. We weren't always close, didn't always tell each other everything, but he knew what was going on with me more or less. Knew what I wanted, how I wanted, that I wanted."

"Oh, I see. Yeah, that would've been good."

"Was the new girlfriend a poet too?"

"No, a philosopher. Smart, not robotic, but smart smart."

Sighing and disappointed. "Don't tell me you were put off by that?"

"No, no, that's not what I meant. It's what made her attractive."

"It's hard for smart girls to pretend to be stupid to keep their boyfriends happy."

"In high school, the girls thought I was weird. Thinking too much. Said lots of *weird* things."

"For real? That's not..." Don't let him lead you away. "Hold on, what did her being smart have to do with breaking her heart?"

"It was a performance. As if she could never... ...it's like... When we met, I was reading Plato. She was there with her friend, knew my roommate from high school, and that made her think she had to be smart around me all the time. Because I was reading Plato..."

"Was that frustrating?"

He laughs and then grins, nods slightly with approval.

"I suppose. I mean, I liked the movie *Repo Man*."

"What does that have to do with it?"

"It's... ...it's a silly movie, right? Kinda stupid. It's okay to enjoy stupid movies and read Plato, that's what I'm saying."

"Was she insecure? Did you ever think of that? Did she like you and was trying to figure out how to be attractive without scaring you off?" It's too defensive, and he sees he must've stepped on something.

Earlier fears fly away, he sees a woman, and is looking at her.

"Absolutely, you're right, and I could tell, but that's what I mean. I can't fix that. I didn't know how. It was the same with Maya. She liked me, but couldn't fix me. She couldn't say anything. Hearts break sometimes because we don't know what to do. That's what my friend said."

[Didn't know what to do.]

—Break our own hearts that way. Things our bodies don't know how to do. Takes so much time. Maya couldn't wait for him. He couldn't wait for....

"What was her name? The one whose heart you broke."

"Chloe," he says nodding and pursing his lips. He owes her that.

—I know how it feels girl. Unable to get around yourself. Another reason to worry, another way to let ourselves down.

"Are you going to eat that?" he asks abruptly, pointing to the untouched and still wrapped biscuit.

Smiling warmly and gesturing for him to go right ahead.

—Adorable. God makes them cute, so we won't kill them.

3.12.2. Seannafair.20.15.5.7 [ref(19.86.5.14)]

"Every breath ███ / ██ move you ██ "

No sooner sitting in a seat, then the old man comes round and sets himself down in the next chair. By the bar waiting a long time, his pension doesn't let him drink his fill.

"Hello, Sean,"

"I was wondering if you'd turn up." His breath says he's been at it. *"██ watching ██."*

Gesturing to the barmaid to bring two. She shrugs and looks at Sean, asking with her eyes if it's okay to take care of his tab so far. Nodding, and looking back at his broad face, reddened nose, and shock white hair.

"I was locked when we left."

"Locked? You just got here. She hasn't come round yet."

"Since you've ██, ███████ a trace"

—He doesn't care.

"That night, he took me home, courteous and gentlemanly. Walking me, putting up with my nonsense. I couldn't tell him which way to go."

She comes by and sets two whiskeys on the table. "Cheers."

"Ta." Sean doesn't look up. He's over the moon with what she's put before him.

"If my friends weren't in the bag themselves, they never would have allowed it. She was ass over tits, she was."

From the next table, they say the government has decided to have a referendum. Let the people decide. The cool reason of the popular mind shall rule Britania for the better.

"Now what friends are these? Catch me up, Jenni."

"Doesn't matter. Might as well be dead now, for all I know, but they never would have let me go off with a strange fella if they weren't struggling, that's what I'm trying to tell you."

"Afraid he'd take advantage of you? Your friends didn't know you well, did they?"

He knows the rhythms and catches on quickly. Doesn't matter what the context is, it's a pub and she's telling tales.

He puts his empty glass back on the table, meaning there's catching up to do on both sides. A gulp and a gesture back to Mary.

"They knew me well enough. I was different back then. He was something else, a breeze passing through, didn't see it coming. Haven't thought about it in years, not since."

"Someone special?"

"I knew as soon as he got me home and didn't want nothing for it. Just put on the cassette he promised to play and tucked me in. He must've fallen asleep on the couch soon after I did. I don't remember a damn thing about it, but I remember waking up after a while and seeing him there."

"Take ▮ Me ▮▮▮▮▮▮▮"

"The Queen is Dead."

"Don't be daft."

They are loud and the nearby tables reflect discomfort. They look over and whisper at the sight. How far has she fallen to stumble in with a crowd like this, to play at loss with the other side. They eye the barmaid and think she's party to the decline: always ready with another. It's a lovely place, professional and upscale, this throwback shouldn't be allowed, their judgment is a piece of furniture from Ikia, doesn't fit and can't piece it together. On the other side of the building, in the restaurant, they are preparing the tables, the dinner guests should be rolling in soon.

"That's what he played on the hi-fi. It hadn't come out yet. He got a copy of it, somehow, and wanted to play it for me. I was desperate for it. Can't think why. Wanted him to take me home."

"But he was a gentleman."

"I believe he was, and I didn't want him to be."

"You're all ▮▮▮▮▮ I've ▮ to remember"

Mary comes around with two more. She knows to bring them slowly, it's the only thing that's holding it back.

"He got up with me, now that I think of it, didn't he?"

—Did he? There was no music. I certainly didn't put any on, but did he? *Rum Sodomy & the Lash.* I couldn't stop listening to it in those days. Was it only then? Or later?

Sean's busy with the drink.

"It's fine to sound Irish, that's what he said. He said people liked it, liked the way it sounded. Everyone was trying to sound American, but not Shane. He didn't give a toss."

"▮▮ gone / ▮ a day"

—What was it that got me going? That was the night. It must've been after three, and I sat down. He didn't have much to say, he put on the music and let me go off wherever it was. Didn't try to stop me. Did he have a book? Was he awake?

"Only the music, but somehow it felt quiet. That's how it was. Back then, at least, it was always that way. The music was how I found myself, how I got inside myself. I'd never written a sentence like that in my life."

(Another fire leaps nightly / Babes born dying)

"What're you talking about? Your sentences are beautiful, pure poetry."

He's not paying attention, only enough to keep the drinks flowing. Looks over his shoulder toward the door as if expecting someone, a rescue.

—Don't need that today. Can't be encouraged or discouraged anymore. Can't hear them, can't make heads or tails of it.

"█████████ *love you /* ██████ *absolute* ██████████ "

(It was something he said about sound, something about Echo and her unrequited love of Narcissus. She was a virgin. I wasn't, not then. But. In a way. That day poetry turned around some for me, it came by different paths. The way my mother talked, the way my grandmother used to say things. She always knew how to put it. Not only in the accent, but the whole way sentences took their turn.)

"██████ *different corner* ███ *we never* █████████ *met*"

(I was disappointed when I sat down, when I woke up. Disappointed that it went that way, that I couldn't get what I wanted, that I couldn't find it with anyone. I thought for sure with him, so exotic, so beautiful. I didn't know anything, didn't know how to style my hair, what clothes to wear, didn't know how to get a boy I liked to do what I wanted him to do, and I certainly didn't know how to write a song.)

"All that didn't and doesn't is what put me over the edge."

"Now what edge would that be, lass?"

—Get him another. Mary, come rescue us from this ominous sobriety.

That rummy Gandy comes in and heads right this way, knowing where the best comes from. Letting Mary know to bring another.

—Courtesy of the record sales, the least she can do is stand a drink for London's Irish.

"A round of the dark stuff when you can," instead of greeting him.

[It'd be good for the between, help with the hands, give them something to hang on to.]

—It's the least I can do.

"*Cause* ██████████████████████ *these years /* ████████████ ████ *stop my tears*"

The two of them are instantly slapping each other on the back and gabbing about who knows what.

(It's how it was with my da, the way he was. The way he would come home after work, my mother shouting at him. No, that's what I wanted her to do, but she was quiet, she took it and took care of everything. She took care of him when he had too much. What else could she do?)

—Where did they come from, those lyrics? I never gave a damn about anything political, and I sure didn't know anything about heartache. What was all that nonsense?

"I was imagining it."

"What's that dearie?" Gandy asks, but he doesn't care, doesn't wait for an answer. He goes right back to looking over at Sean and they're not faking it anymore. Sean pretends to sing an old ballad, but doesn't have the throat for it. They look over this way. Crooning out the melody without any lyrics.

"Do, do, do, do

Do, do, do, do

Do, do, do, do

Do, do, do, do"

They shout with joy. At the nearby tables, folks turn to look, a few applaud afterward. Mary, time for another, and a gesture in her direction says it.

All hail the dancing monkey. Hear the symbols chime. Withdrawing as soon as they comfortably can, their pity looks like flattery.

—Being locked, getting walked home by a lovely fella, not getting what I was hoping for. That's what stirred it up, that's what brought it on, that's where we end up finding ourselves, where the music comes from, where it used to come from.

"I wrote six or seven in one night."

"We've heard it before, lass." Gandy nods in agreement, he is Sean's right hand, not his own man, only the hand of one, especially when they've been drinking.

"█ *a virgin / Touched* ███████████ *time"*

—That's it, I won't sit for this.

"Where are you going?"

They're terrified, not nearly finished. Abruptly standing up next to the small table puts an end to their laughter, it brings rings to their eyes and mouths, it sends them off wide and attentive, more than anyone would think possible at this time of day considering their condition.

"Don't piss yourselves, I'll be right back. Mary..." shouting over that way. She nods and sets about it.

"██████ *strong,* ████████████ *bold"*

Many beautiful colors and pictures on the back wall. A post card to signal every life that's touched this place. Posters and placards, bills, something about a show way way back in the day.

(It wasn't here, was it? Oxford street, it said. No never here. They don't have music, but they must've got it from somewhere. Edmund was always a fan, back then he knew about it and went to see us before anyone did. Never said anything, but he wouldn't, would he?)

The lad by the door is grumpled and askew, he doesn't reach low enough to note the cracking features: her lines and wrinkles, her fuzzy eyes and thinning lips.

—With these two, can't step away. I desperately want to pop out for a fag. Best get reinforcements once the business is done.

In the stall, seat-lined with paper, carefully placed. He kept it as clean as he could and took the often-offered advice to make sure the men's and ladies were separate.

[Nothing worse than a unisex in a pub.]

—He played the American version of *Meat is Murder*. It had that song that wasn't on the English release. What else? *Unforgettable Fire*. It was his copy, one of his cassettes. Got me excited and I think I showed him the record. Oh, I wanted that boy to kiss me so badly. That could've been what that song was about, about wanting him to kiss me. Your head. What's in your head?

(He did make tea, right? Didn't bother me much while trying to figure out the kitchen and where everything was. Wasn't the way I would've done it, but drinkable.)

Forgetting to tuck, and discovering a new look, her hair hangs straight upon the forehead. The glossy light beams back what's missing, reminds the walls and mirrors of what never was meant to be. The way time digs itself in, the way it burrows into cheeks and chins, jowls and neck. Can't bother to look, can't be brought round to see.

—I can't believe this was gone. Where did it go? Where has it been hiding all these years?

There's a payphone next to the door to the loo, but it's detached. Digging into the bag for the mobile. Low battery.

—See if we can find Terry. He's the only one who can stop me.

"Hey you. Where are you?"

"Turning onto Gloucester now. How bad is it?"

"Not too bad. I just got here. With those geezers from the Pale." Chortles and snorts, rolling the eyes, having a laugh with some ridiculous bygone thought. He won't approve, he can't.

"I'm on my way, nearly there, save me some."

Stepping back and bumping against the stray leg that waits for the men's, then not bothering to turn and look, not saying anything. He is honored and flustered. His memory launches into those days when the world could see what no one sees any more. Whiskey and piss fill the air, and he straightens up to quietly say, "Pardon me."

—It was the first time I heard *Murmur*, wasn't it?

(My whole life, everything around then, was much smaller, filled such tiny spaces. Can't recall where it came from or how it flowed past into the nights, the many nights, the fugitive and the lost. It's in that bottle, they kept it there for good measure.)

[Make sure and bring it with you. You're the only one left who could slip us a light one, find his way through, poured out into darkness, that late-night stumbling pleasure to bear.]

"Not going anywhere. Thanks, mate. Soon."

3.12.3.Natalie.19.86.8.2 [ref(..6.7-9)]

*Back up the street and toward the store, still light out, still a lot of day
left. The brisk walk brings heat to the surface, glowing in the exposed areas
and plastering the sticky cotton in parts covered up.*

Through the glass, he is being grilled, they have him back up against the
counter, but at ease. Speaking calmly and laughing, quite a sight through
the glass door. Sign says closed, pushing through to make short order of it.

"It's great you can laugh about it," Hazel says. "After a day like that, I
can't be sure what I'd do."

*The store is empty other than the three of them. The light in the
window is off and the till is empty. They must've been waiting.*

"You wouldn't have jumped on the train in the first place," he says
animatedly. "It was bad judgment."

"What's this? Are you telling that story again?"

"We only knew the ending, we didn't know how it began," Bernd steps
in to defend him, making it clear they wanted to hear it.

"We had to pry it out of him," Hazel says.

Going up to him by the counter and leaning against his chest.

"The whole thing makes me think Hegel was right all along."

They burst out laughing.

"How do you get that?" Bernd asks.

He withdraws, looks at the faces, not wanting to get in the way, he sees
the rituals and rhythms of intimacy, wants to know them.

"Well, consider the source, don't think about the individual action. You
can't. Not some isolated moment where a book is left on a train, there are
no accidents, it's part of something."

"Backwards," Hazel says.

"What else is there? There is only backwards. Forward is backwards
backward."

They smirk, so clever, at the familiar maneuvers. "Yup, that's Hegel
talking alright," Bernd says.

"He's standing here, isn't he?" Pointing out the obvious.

"And that's backwards?" he asks, trying to fit in.

Looking at him, Bernd and Hazel appreciate the effort and think he
almost hit the mark. But he's serious, struggling to catch up. Not everyone
gets there when they put in the time.

"Since your action fits with the other actions following afterward, since
your hike from Halden became a part of our lives once you relayed the
story, it fits together. In a system. You can't separate any of it. It'll collapse

if you pull anything out."

"And that's not your doing," Hazel says.

"It's the system," Bernd finishes the sentence.

"The absolute," he says.

"You've read Hegel, have you?"

"More like Spinoza," he says.

It's getting late and there's no alcohol anywhere in the store. Hegel is a signpost pointing into a rabbit hole, and no one wants to go there on a Saturday night.

"We're going to get something to eat, then we'll come by later. We'll see you at Tue's."

"Don't be early," Bernd says. "No one'll be there until after 10."

"We'll find a way to keep busy." He's taking direction toward the door and gathers his small pack off the floor. Saying goodbye to Hazel and Bernd, he adjusts quickly to the changing tide with hardly any notice, moving out into the street and back up the road toward the car.

"I need a drink. I've had an absolutely horrible day."

In the car, nuzzling before turning on the motor. He doesn't go stiff, doesn't resist. Proper feedback and response, there for the right mood. An older couple walk past the passenger side window and deliberately twist and crane their heads to get a better look. They were jabbering back and forth about how shocked they were, wishing they were that much at ease in a public parking lot.

"Only kissing, no need to make a fuss." Stopping. He's lost the will, not primed for exhibitionism yet, it's not part of any experience brought along.

—Whatever floats your boat, I guess. If you're into that sort of thing.

"Where are we going?" he asks, not put off for long.

"There's a nice place up on the hilltop. Good wine, good food. That's what I had in mind. Stimulate the senses."

Steering the car and moving forward to the end of the lot and back out onto the street. Snaking back around through this side of town to get to the high road.

Sees she's tense, wants to be helpful, but doesn't know what to ask.

"God awful day. I'll tell you about it later if you don't mind. But first..."

Taking his hand, pulling it closer, and setting it down right at the skirt's waistband. He gets the drift and slides it down leaning closer over the center console.

At the hilltop neighborhood, parking the car off the main road on one of the residential streets. Leaning into it and concentrating properly. He takes direction, having something of a knack for it, and it doesn't take long, not once there's focus. There is the rush and the lightness, such careful breathing as he moves his mouth close to the neck and the shoulder inciting chest rhythms for a rise and a fall. The integration fascinates: the way legs and arms, pelvis and head move together forming a single unit pushing onward and finding its way through the gestures and the silence. He whispers something about the book.

"Once rescued, it wants to open between your legs to make them open wider. I want to bend down to it, lap up every word, with tongue, cheek, licking and dipping into every part, every word, every morsel."

"Yes, that's right..." Running the hand through his thick hair.

And they're off. It's a windward show now. Nothing to stop it, nothing to hold back, and that's when it rears up perfectly. Leaning back then forward toward his head now nestling under the chin, lips pulling on the nipples, tiny beads of sweat at the base of the neck b-lining to the top of the bra unhooked and pulled loose, fingers continuing to draw light outlines on still smoother surfaces, wet with finish. Heavy are the kisses in the aftermath. Smacking lips leaving off a pushing embrace.

"Shall we?" Pulling it off through the sleeve and tossing it onto the floor in back after smoothing the top back into place along with the skirt.

He grunts and pops open the door to jump out. Meeting around back and heading off arm-in-arm toward the main street where the bistro is set on the corner overlooking the town with the river passing through it.

"A lovely view," he says with a quick look back behind, fashioning a smirk before patting the bottom.

"You've gotten to know your way around awfully fast," getting to the door ahead of him and waiting for him to pull it open. It isn't crowded yet and there's a table by the window. Before the host leaves, "Can we get a bottle of the Côtes du Rhône, please?"

He doesn't pick up the menu, looks over with an expectant gaze. "What are we having?" he asks.

—You've read my mind.

"You've read my mind. I'll take care of everything. Do you eat pork?"

"Definitely."

Appetizers on the way, sharing an entrée, the wine comes with the waiter to take the order. Sipping it and telling him to fill the glasses. Sitting close, he watches every move, studies the chin and cheeks as the dark liquid swishes and the tongue bends.

"You had a bad day?" he asks.

"They don't respect me. They don't appreciate what I do. Fashion and media, these aren't serious topics. There's a whole body of literature from the last two or three decades that they don't think is worth the paper it's written on."

He doesn't say anything. Either he agrees or he doesn't know.

"Since Adorno and Horkheimer, Walter fucking Benjamin, these are standards. If I were framing things in their terms, forms of production, they wouldn't have a problem. Fucking theory and the male gaze."

He registers the names, recognition crosses his face, but doesn't know anything, stays quiet and looks sympathetic.

"It's not only that there's an economic angle. It's not as though they aren't huge parts of the global economy. They call themselves socialists but can't see labor and production when it's right in front of them."

The waiter brings the rolled pork appetizers and sets them down. There is a fig inside each and a light sauce.

A few others walk in. They're far better dressed than he is. He looks down, and scrunches his nose, but shakes it off, not prone to self-consciousness for long.

"Let's forget about it. I want to enjoy the food and the wine. Pour me some more."

He hops to it, topping off his glass afterward.

"That was good stuff on the book, I thought you would have taken up with your trip again. Where were we?"

"Edinburgh."

"Edinburgh. How'd you get to Europe?"

"From Newcastle. I hitched a ride down there and got on a boat to Denmark."

"Ah, lots to work with there. What were you planning? Save the good stuff. Give me the broad strokes."

"I'm gathering you like the broad strokes," he says popping a pork roll into his mouth.

"True, but the devil is in the details."

Sipping the wine and eating another roll. The delightful fig bursts among the meaty flavors and forms a lovely medley. His eyes are a garnish, the long lashes flutter as he concentrates.

"I was thinking about the lady who gave me a lift. She was taking her dog to the vet. There's a specialist she sees down there. She opens my pants once we get there, or on the side of the road or something."

"Lady? How old is she?"

"Nearly fifty, I would say."

"Good God boy, what are you thinking?"

"You don't like that?"

"It's not that, it's the sense of it. You'd have me believe a fifty-year old woman is still up for sucking your cock."

He laughs, shocked at first, but gets the hang of it.

"I'd think she'd be done with that by then. It's okay to fabricate, but it's got to be believable."

He doesn't bat an eye, but comes right back, "She's just tired of fifty-year-old cock."

Raising a glass to that, taking a sip of the lovely spirits following sweetly upon the pork. Open to instruction, he's good at following a lead.

—Wouldn't mind some constructive criticism.

"Make her my age. Know your audience. Make it easier to identify. The important thing, you see, is to think of it from my point of view. Not yours. I mean, okay, you have these fantasies, you can't help that. Use them when you need to, keep them to yourself. But with me, when you're talking, you've got to work it through what I'm looking for. See?"

He nods, listening closely.

"Driving in the car and then out of nowhere you get there, and she jumps on your zipper, that's not going to do anything for me. You got to build up her desire. You're ready for it any time, that's a given, but she's a mature woman, she needs coaxing, she needs mood to get there."

"How? Give me an example."

Leaning forward onto the table and taking another sip. Pushing the flatware to the side, making the place orderly and proper for the telling.

"Uh, let's say she sees you by the road and you imagine her looking at the muscles on your arms and chest while you pick up your bag and put it into the back seat of her car. Your T-shirt stretching, you're bursting through it. You see? Now she's checking you out, getting a sense of things. I can see her working up to it."

"Got it."

"And then, in the car, well, what were you talking about? How did you get her revved up? Did you tell her a story about someone you were helping, about that girl in Pitlochry maybe."

He smiles and looks down at his empty plate. The motes of truth turn him shy.

"Use lots of double entendre and innuendo. Let me fill in the blanks. Let me think whatever I want about you *helping* her, what does that mean? What were you helping her with? Was it the same way you were helping me?"

"I see."

"Or play to your ignorance, complain that you don't know what you're doing, trying to find rides around England and Scotland. Play the ingenue, I'll flesh that out on my own. My mind knows where to go."

"Your point of view, that's the important part."

"That's right, but the images matter, something for me to hold on to. Before she goes jumping on you, say something about how you were sitting in the car, how grateful you were for the ride. You know, broad strokes, I'll fill in the details, give you a hint about which way to go now and then, where to focus."

"It's a skill. I'm going to need lessons."

—Why the fuck does getting stepped on at work always make me so goddamn horny?

"Now you're getting it. Later we can try something. I have this lovely book I use sometimes."

"Use?"

"Don't be coy. I can read it to you, you'll get an idea of how the good stuff works."

"Read it to me? I should read it to you."

That look has a lot of potential. He may not know how to talk about it, but his eyes peer into the right places. There's someone looking back, and he sees her, maintaining eye contact while following the nerve tendrils down the spine with his peripheral vision, tracing his way over the tail bone, around and across the hips to the edge where they come together with more sensitivity and feeling than anything else on this earth. No more theory, no speculation required.

"No, you won't be able to speak." Smiling and raising the glass, touching his with it, then draining the last bit before going back for more.

3.12.4.Greta.19.86.9.13 [ref(..84.5-9)]

—*"The woman of deep song is called Pain."* [Garcia Lorca]

"Where are you going?"

"I have to leave. We'll walk for a while and meet you at the car," Eva says, getting up. Anja and Elke move to follow her out, waving on their way. Eva lightly touches his hand and looks softly at him, apologetically.

"I'm sorry. I don't know what to say," he says forlornly, but she's already gone.

"I wanted to hear. She's not ready."

"It was a totally new experience for me. I never met anyone like that before," he went on as though continuing to defend himself. The dishes are still on the table. There is too much emotion, it keeps the waitress at a distance.

"She's six years younger, that could have something to do with it."

—I keep forgetting you're Eva's age. Why do you seem much older? Did she feel it too?

"Could be," he says nodding. "But not only that."

"What else?" There is too much in the question, it comes out too loud, anyone nearby would know how deep the desire is. This is an excuse for asking, the pregnant suggestion of something more to say, the indication that something remains, many questions, and they rush forward but only this one emits in the clanking and chirping that spreads and sprawls across the diner.

"She was so focused. When she would come by the café after that. She'd use me as an excuse, come to the table if I was sitting there. It's not as though she sat next to me, or led anyone to believe she was there for me, but I was making something easier for her."

—The pleading. He wants to tell it as much as I want to hear.

"You felt that she was using you?" Nothing like that hides beneath what he's saying, but it's the best way, the most average and easiest.

"Not exactly, but I was her contact, that's for sure. It wasn't the same."

—She held you at a distance. The same as she always did, but it didn't last, did it? How did you wind your way through?

"When she came to you, you weren't alone."

"No, we were with Gabriel or Don Alberto, one of the landowners. Someone she needed to talk to for whatever reason. One of their farm hands got someone into trouble and was trying to run from it."

—That's why those rules exist. She'd have been a menace were they not protected by their precious decorum. She must've been seething.

"She couldn't go to their farms and knock on the door."

"She couldn't call them," he says, clearly appreciating the help in delivering more details. "That's not how things worked. If she didn't have a connection, then she couldn't talk to them."

—But... It can't be helped... I can't... Forgive me...

"But you two were sleeping together, weren't you?"

Bobbing his head, unprepared, but generally agreeable. "It wasn't like that. I didn't think..."

"What did you think?"

—What was it like?

"In the beginning, it seemed as if she was isolated. Not because those men wouldn't talk to her, but for other reasons. She's different. Not too girly, not how you'd expect."

"How? What do you mean?"

"What do I know? I was only twenty, but she liked to get dirty. She was dirty whenever I saw her. Mud, blood, animal goo. Whatever. When she came out to the café, she usually had clean overalls, but still, those overalls."

(Didn't Mom say something about that once? No one was dressing like her, no one would go out to meet the other kids in the streets or at the cinema wearing such things. She was usually dirty, but then when she cleaned up, she didn't care how she looked, what the other kids thought. Never on principle, she couldn't be bothered. It wasn't anywhere inside her.)

"She didn't put on a show for you, so what? You thought she was a lesbian?"

He nods and smiles, laughing at himself. "I didn't know any better."

"Until you got to know better."

—It's a pleasing image, somehow. The way she must've surprised him.

"Then, it seemed transactional. Is that the right word? Okay, she has needs, they're not being met, and there are no prospects. What's she going to do? She has to tend to her mental health, doesn't she?"

"Is that what you thought she was doing?" Grinning at the thought of it.

"That's how it seemed. I never got the feeling she had some big romantic attraction or anything. I was, well, it was... I was the first acceptable candidate to come along..."

"Acceptable candidate."

He's awkward, and it comes out through his fidgeting. He's pulling at his sleeves and occasionally straightening out the pant legs beneath the table. He doesn't know how much or how little to say. Trying to explain but worrying that there's distance between the comfort the stories provide and his ability to relay them. "She was extremely passionate. Everything I ever saw her do, she did it with her complete person."

"That's who I grew up with." Resting the hand on his, trying to send signals up his arm and down his torso to his legs. Sit still, be still, quiet yourself and speak calmly.

[The story had to come as you're seeing it, she had to come, appear in the light of this booth and this diner and this road between towns. Let everything come, let it march, raise its head, and let it wear a mask with her signs on it, with signals and codes, let it speak for her.]

—Please, be at ease, don't be shy. If only I could say it without terrifying you, without scaring you off. This is what I want to know...

"It was confusing, that's it. I'm still confused. There's no one to talk to about this. I'm sorry if it's bad to bring it up, I'm sorry for upsetting Eva. Tell me if you feel the same, don't be kind. I want to know."

—No no no no no no.

"I want to know everything. Right now, it's all I can think about. Everything she felt, everything she thought, everything she knew. That's the only thing I can focus on. I can't get it out of my head."

His eyes crinkle slightly as he tilts his head to the side. His thumb finally responds to the pressure, a light caress says it all before retreating.

"Eva doesn't feel the same way."

"No, she's a little sister. It's different. We shared everything. Eva adored her. That put distance between them. In some ways, Eva and I were closer. We both were so much in awe of her. Always knew what was right and what had to be done."

(She used to carry her. Eva couldn't have been more than two, but she insisted on being carried when the five of us were together, and she didn't want anyone else to do it, not me, not Mom or Dad. She couldn't think of her any other way. At that age, her arm around her neck, her face close, cheeks lightly touching as they bounced awkwardly along. Those were her sensations, that was how she came to know her.)

He's nodding. He sees her, he is seeing her right now.

If only he could show it, if only he could project whatever is running through his head, his thoughts, recollections, peripheral memories that he doesn't know he's having. If only he could project that onto the wall or against the back of the booth.

"When she told my parents she was going, none of us were surprised. We assumed that was exactly the kind of thing she was going to do all along. But still, we knew it would separate us. She was going to be having some experiences that none of us could connect with. It was going to create distance. I knew that. It's why I desperately wanted to visit her."

"Why didn't you?" Simply phrased, a step slightly closer.

"She said it wouldn't work out, it was too logistically difficult, didn't know how I would physically get there, how to leap over the hurdles. And then, what would we do? As hard as it was for her to fit in, she said it would be impossible for someone else to come along."

"I know what she meant. The rhythms, the way life flows, it's rigid. Roles, classes, hierarchy. There's no getting around it."

—Defending her. Her champion with me.

Hands separating, now tucking them down under the table in the hot space between the seat and the legs. He goes back to pulling at his sleeve. Dangerous distance threatens again.

"That's why I want to hear everything," cutting it off before it gains momentum. "That's why I want to learn everything. Somehow, you managed to get there. To see her. You weren't trying, but you did. And now that's the only thing I can think about." He's nodding emphatically, agreeing with everything he hears, registering its urgency.

(Eva wanted to go, we had to bring her back, she said. Insisted. Lose her forever if we let her miss it. Dad's "any luck?")

"I want to help. I wish I could tell you everything. It's not that I'd hold back, it's that I don't know everything. I didn't see it or understand what I was seeing. Like that."

Stops pulling at his sleeves and mirrors the tucking of hands beneath legs warm against the seat.

Legs warm against the seat.

"It's hard to know what's important when it's happening. When I heard she visited you in the US, I couldn't believe it. *Acceptable candidate* is all I ever remember with her. She didn't have a string of boyfriends like I did, so I know what you're talking about when you say that. She was always that way. But you must've been special. If she was willing..."

(Can't remember his name, but back then I thought about him all the time. If he'd talk to me, look at me, the whole rest of my day would be absorbed by it, turning over the possibilities, what it meant, what it could lead to. He could tell the difference between us and all he ever wanted was her attention. I guess he was her first acceptable candidate, but nothing more. She entertained it, suffered it, and that was what she could manage. All she cared to manage. I hated her... I envied her... She owed me.)

"I know. I mean, I could tell. I knew that's how she thought of me, and it felt pretty good, made me think there must be something good about me," he says softly.

She brings the bill, and he instinctively picks it up from the table as soon as she's off with a few of the dishes. Turning it over with his fingers, folding it, playing with it. Distracted by it, not registering what it is.

He's embarrassed when he realizes but nods as if trying to convince himself of something. Taking it from his hand and pulling some money from the purse on the seat.

"That she would visit you. I want to understand how that happened. Why? What was going on? I can't remember her ever doing anything like that before."

"They aren't easy stories to tell. I'm trying, but..."

"I know. Let's go somewhere. Not with them to Ludwig's Castle or whatever, but somewhere."

He perks up, there's more energy, the atmosphere changes, and it feels lighter. Preparing for a trip, what an idea.

"I wanted to see the Lake of Constance."

"The what?"

"That big lake that borders Germany, Switzerland, and Austria."

"The Bodensee."

"The Bodensee. The colors are peak right now. Do you want to go down there and hike around or get a boat or something?"

—More than anything.

"Get a boat?" Brow knitting, unsure if this is feasible.

[Was he mad?]

"A rental," he says.

"Hmmm. Not sure they have that. We can check. It sounds nice. Would it help you?"

"I think so. Something about being in motion. Traveling together. It's good for getting acquainted."

It's a twist and a turn, with greeting eyes, sitting opposite in the glow of an idea, she's projected onto the seat in front of him, looking back, having been conjured, manifesting right here, in this look, in these eyes.

"I'll research some places. Show you some possibilities. Where to stay, where to go. I'll ask Eva what they're planning. We can get some ideas, but also to keep our distance. What do you think?" Happy and finally interested in something else, even if it is a means to that same end.

"Yeah, great. It sounds perfect, but are you sure?"

"We won't go far. If it's too much, we'll come back."

6.8
the middle american

6.8.1.X.19.86.12.20 [ref(..12-20)]

Being outside of time and desire, waving a hand to get back in it. Jerking abruptly forward, then falling back, dreamlike, with a subconscious plunge through night thrust into daylight.

> *Yet now, of that blest realm whate'er is found*
> *Here in my mind still treasured and possessed*
> *Must set the strain for all my song to sound.*
> [Dante's Paradiso]

(Weird place this morning. Narrow sliver of a store. People line up at the entrance and tell the lady at one end of the counter they want eggs. Everybody gets the same kind. It didn't matter that I couldn't speak the language, a head gesture was enough to get her scrambling. Then the next lady put some potatoes on the plate before the last lady topped it off with breakfast sausage. No words required. Finally, you pay, and it's basically free. Thirty cents for everything including coffee, a bottomless cup, to go with it. Around the corner from the cash register at the end of the line, there was an open area where you could stand and eat. Nobody was talking. It's cold outside, and they looked as if they were headed to work bright and early on a Saturday. Eating and then setting the plates down in the bin on the stand near the other door before walking out.)

—Tons of those places around here. Equally weird, IBusz accommodations too.

(You tell them how many nights and they charge you about 4 dollars each, paying at the office in the center. Got on the tram, and everyone said you had to pay. Only two cents, but if you didn't, there's a huge fine, two hundred Forints. I thought it was an enormous amount, but it's fifty cents. Pay, right? But how? I couldn't figure out where to buy the tickets. The machine is complicated, and the language doesn't have any cognates. Got on the tram and took it to the outskirts to find the address they gave me. The tenement buildings are austere, large, and carbon copies of each other. I wandered around for what must have been an hour before finding the right one. A man answered the door. His whole family was there, four of them, two children and his wife. The apartment had only one bathroom, a kitchen nook, a big main room, and a single bedroom. There was a curtain hanging between the main room and the entryway, so there was no contact as you came and went. They put me in the bedroom and showed me the bathroom. I was to sleep there while they slept in the main room. There were two single beds, one against each wall. The door had a lock on it.)

—It's cold. Fuck. Better find a museum or something.

(Fucking wimp, pussy. Crying like a baby that whole day in Salzburg. Why? Because I was alone after so much time with other people? Who cares? Being alone is the rule, not some shock to the system. Must've gotten used to it, having people around, but it was miserable, didn't know what to do with myself. Fucking *Tao of Physics*, tedious. Left it in Graz when I found the Rilke, but that didn't do me any good when I needed it. Nothing much to say, being somewhere without a book... What can you do, write it down? Play it over and over again in your head? Was there something I could've done to make it come out differently? I could've seen it coming. Dear Kitty. Fuck you.)

—That hug was too long.

(The lady who drove me from Salzburg to Graz, I've seen lots of people like her before. You know, there are only ten types of people any place you go. She was that kind. Youngish pensioner, in her sixties, spry, clever, informed, overinformed, lots of advice. Where should I go, what should I do? Did you do that in Salzburg? Did you see that? Bars lady, I went to fucking bars. Too close to the holidays, I guess, leaving me with the likes of you. Crunchy. Or whatever the equivalent is. Alone at Christmas with lots of stories about how amazing her kids are. The son is in Malaysia, vice president of the world or something, buying that in exchange for this. Buy buy buy. No, sell sell. The daughter is in the Maldives with her ridiculously wealthy husband. What is that? Still alone on Christmas despite your fucking bragging. Whatever. Blah blah. I sure as shit didn't go to Graz to see the clock tower, or some armory. How about drinking coffee in the old town, scribbling in my notebook? Which guidebook recommends that? Why did I bother? Did I think I would find them? Get some insight. Who cares, she's gone, and I'll never see her again. She's nothing to me, a fucked up story to tell. The chick who cock-blocked me after she was out of my life. Recounting the last moments ended up being the last moments.)

—Bullshit, Eve wasn't mad, these things aren't simple. Light and dark, love and hate. It was the wrong emotion, she couldn't cross over that. Doesn't mean anything, you could call her, wish her a merry and all that. But how do you do it from here?

"Café bitte," using German because there's at least a chance they'll understand it.

—Many of them do, but none of them speak a word of English.

(Wien was a nightmare. Everything too fucking expensive, and they're paying way too much attention to the few stragglers still hanging around the youth hostel, but the others are closing down, you don't have much choice. Had to buy a ticket with Schillings to get from Weiner Neustadt to Sopron. Great bread and loads of bakeries, I could've lived on that stuff. It had a similar taste to holly bread or Challah. Something like that. Good news is everything is fucking cheap, bad news is you have to stay in a guest house. The train ticket, you bought that with Forints, about a buck or something to get from the border to the center of the country. Nothing costs anything, the food doesn't cost anything, the museums don't cost anything, the coffee doesn't cost anything, it's this huge Hapsburg palace where everything is practically free. Why bother making it transactional? Can't talk to anybody who works, but they wouldn't know anyway. The kids speak German, but they're not thinking about any of that crap.)

"Ja bitte, vielen Dank."

—She knows what I'm saying.

(Those guys spoke good German, but they're in Gymnasium which is either College or High School, can't tell. The girls won't talk to you, no idea why. Easy enough to get smiles and eye contact, but not a single word. They don't go to the weird street corner bars where there are no lights and nothing advertising it as a proper night spot except the fact that you can see people through the window sitting at tables and drinking from bottles and glasses. You go in and it's just men. Where are the girls? I asked those guys, but they thought I was looking for a prostitute. No, I mean ordinary girls, where are they? No, no girls, they wouldn't come here. Not the kind you want to talk to. Where are they? At work, at school, on the bus, they're everywhere. Yeah, but where are they socially? If you want to meet them. You can go to the discotheque, there will be some. Rich girls. They'd talk to you since you're a foreigner. But the other girls? Go to the Museum, you'll find some there.)

—No use fighting it.

(Nothing to write home about, not in the same league as the Louvre or Reina Sofia, but there were girls, they weren't lying about that. They sit on the benches and the stools with their drawing pens, and they sketch the paintings. They're students trying to learn composition. It's not some big broad demographic, you don't get to meet different kinds as you would at a bierhaus or wine cellar, but the art students are there and that qualifies. They are girls. A few boys, but they're not much competition for the girls' attention, not even trying.)

—What choice did I have? I'm going out of my fucking mind.

(Weeks without speaking to a girl. Someone my own age, someone on the loose, someone to flirt with, someone who'll smile and laugh at something stupid I said, that's what I was going crazy for. Kristza was drawing one of those fucked up statues at the Ludwig. Sitting there quietly, bundled up. She'd peeled back her coat and didn't have any gloves on, not exactly settled in and comfortable, looked as though she was ready to dash at a moment's notice. But why? Tons of people were sitting around sketching. It couldn't be because there's a problem with that. I sat nearby and she looked over. Smiled. There weren't as many creeps, or there's better protection from them. Whatever, she didn't seem nervous that I was plopping down nearby and scoping her out. What are you drawing? Is it that statue? It's grotesque. She laughs. Understands German. That was the point, to find out. It's three dimensional. You're trying to draw it? Getting closer, moving to the same bench, and she didn't mind. Most of the art students were more concerned with the paintings. Different exercise, she said. Do all the art students come here to draw? They send us here, it's cheap practice. I'm three dimensional, you could draw me. She flipped the page and turned this way. Didn't say anything, got right to it. That's what she was hoping for, that's her angle. She goes to the art museum and draws something until some guy talks to her and then she draws him. It's her thing, she's there to draw a guy.)

—Going back would be obsessive-compulsive. She's not going to be there, but I'd get a new rung on the self-loathing ladder.

(She was deft, I'll give her that. What else could you ask? Who do you like? Which ones are your favorites? She talked about what she'd seen in books mostly. The crap you'd imagine, nobody has any originality, they like what they're supposed to like. And it's always for the same reasons, biography was always part of the explanation. Who cares how passionate he was, who cares if he was ignored by his contemporaries, I asked you what art you liked? Which paintings? Is it there? In the brush strokes, on the canvas? What are you seeing? The suffering in the paint, fuck that.)

—"S*ing for us soon again, but may your lips be fashioned as before,"* the Aesthete scribbled.

(It was pretty clear that she wasn't that old, about sixteen or seventeen. A proper adultish thinking person, but not truly, not completely, and once I saw that, it was ruined. What am I supposed to do, work that angle now? Is that what this comes down to? Fuck it though, I'm not bound to find reasons to hate myself, that's nobody's business. It's only a chat, but it was over the top to ask about nudes. Is it wrong if you're in a place where that's the age of consent? Is it the law that makes it wrong? Back in Chicago, hold on there pal, but here, feel free. Come to think of it, age of consent in Illinois is sixteen. How then? It's got to come from talking to her, but that one was a kid, clearly. You know, how they talk about stuff, how excited they get. She hadn't learned how to hide things, certain things, yet. She's honest and sincere and stuff, innocent, like a kid. That wasn't any good and it didn't matter how old she was or what the law said, which sucked because that's what I was there for. I didn't want to talk to some local kid, I wanted well, whatever I wanted, and I picked the wrong bench.)

—Hit the Fine Arts or the Kunsthalle.

(It's not as if I loved art or anything, but it's cold and where else was there to go? They don't have cafes where you could sit all day and stare at people like in Paris or Barcelona. What to do? Work. Serve the social good. That's what people do, or they go to art museums. It's cheap, plenty of places to sit and relax, read your book, look at the paintings or whatever. It's a truly public place with accommodation for that, for people to spend time there. Not like that room where they've got *Guernica*. Walk in, stand there with the other assholes, and then walk out.)

—Sitting there with the *Divine Comedy* would have been exquisite, but they didn't care about that, individual experience, only property rights.

(No pictures allowed because the deucebags who owned everything forbid it. They owned the likeness, and you had to cattle car your way through the room and look at that big fucker then move along. Don't tarry, no loitering, look at it, register as much as you can in thirty seconds, and get the hell out of there. Raus raus.)

—I could get used to it.

(They're crowded, socializing, people enjoying the space, not only tourists and pseudos, but people.)

Back in the street and pulling the coat closer with gloved hands tight in a fist and the daypack hugging the back. There's a tram stop almost everywhere with maps on the glass walls of the shelters. Waiting for a few minutes before the next one comes. No ticket, hopping up and grabbing a seat near the back. Looking around, hardly anyone has a ticket, most are travelling with monthly passes issued as part of their work supplies.

(It's bleak. The sky, the air, the vibe. She was a kid, so she didn't see it. She had her habits, her friends at school, her drawing. She would go in for something different later, it was what you did at that age, learned art or music or something. She said it was normal, part of their education. Music was what she wanted to talk about. It wasn't that she yearned for the trappings of color that go with the street advertising, she hadn't been to Wien or anywhere in the West, so she didn't know anything about that. She only knew that there was music that the kids were listening to there that was better than what she could get here. Classical, her father loved it, symphonies and concertos. What kind of teenager wanted to listen to violin concertos? One in a thousand. Called bullshit on that and asked her who she really liked, and she went right for the hits: Michael Jackson, Madonna, Cyndi Lauper, Wham. Have you ever heard of REM? No, what's that. Here try this. I leaned closer and put the headphones over her ears and turned it on, breathy and light touchy. Sue me.)

Bap snap, *"Decide yourself* ███████████ */ Reason* ████ *polish* ██ *the gray / Put* ████████████████ *up your wall"*

(She got a big shit-eating grin on her face and looked over with wide eyes. Never fucking heard that before, have you? What does it mean? She pulled the headphones off one ear but left the other one on. She's not being polite, she liked it. Haven't a clue. In German, she asked. Nope. Can't figure out how to say it. Not sure what it means in English. What else, she wanted to know. Nothing else cool, but I flipped it over and rewound. She's fascinated with the hands. Not the Walkman™ like she's pretending, but the hands. That's U2 though, she's heard that one. It's okay, but not her favorite. She liked the other one. REM. What does it mean? Don't know how to translate that either, but it's what your eyes do when you're dreaming. She got it.)

Hopping off at the Kunsthalle. It's easy to get to the heart of the city. The Hosok tere stop is by the Metro. People are streaming in every direction. Crossing over the street and heading into the building.

(Totally destroyed during the war, but thoroughly rebuilt to look exactly as it did before. It gave you a whole different view of the Soviets, I guess. Sure, they didn't let you buy shit from the West and that meant you had to survive without REM and could only listen to the worst pop music imaginable, but they did save us from the Nazis despite killing a bunch of civilians in the process. Ancient history, we should be able to buy whatever we want now and talk about how shitty or great it is. Kristza didn't give a crap about any of that. REM didn't matter that much to her either. She's not typical, that's what I decided. For this place at least, she's not like the rest of them.)

[On a mission today, try to find someone else, someone edgier, someone who has their own collection and endlessly pines for the freedom to consume whatever she pleases. Those were the girls for me.]

Entering the museum and paying the fee while passing through the entry way to the galleries. Daypack and coat remain firmly in place, hat pulled down over the ears.

[She'd just look at me if I breezed past, wouldn't give a damn. What did she care if some goof didn't pay the 2 cents entry fee at the people's museum?]

(I needed to get going. There's nothing more here and it's too cold to enjoy anything. Staying with those people, sleeping alone in their one and only bedroom, it felt creepy and busted.)

[Back to Sopron. Forints for that. Stay overnight, get some of that bread. Then what? Money's pretty much gone.]

(Spent more than I planned in Wien, in Hungary too.)

[You can't pirate your way through here. It's cheap, but there's no piracy, so you have to pay for everything. That's fucked up. The horrors of communism that they don't tell you about, they never emphasize *that* when they're playing it up. Sure, you have your people's transportation system and your people's health care system and your people's art museums and

everything, but you can't cheat at anything. You can't scam your way into
this or that guest house without paying, can't scandalize food from these
backward places that have it on the downlow. You could buy a huge meal
at the cafeteria for 1 or 2 dollars, but don't think about getting it for free.
Making everything cheap made it hard to steal stuff.]

(Didn't feel as though I was getting away with anything on the trams and
metros, it's as if they've made everything scandalproof. Assholes.)

—You'd think on a Saturday there'd be all kinds of people here, but it's
the least crowded day. Where are they? Is it because it's almost Christmas?
They don't celebrate that, do they?

[After a night in Sopron, take the train back to Weiner Neustadt. Save
your last Schillings for that because you can't buy the ticket with Forints
and there's no other way to cross the border. You can't walk it and almost
nobody has permission to drive. Only the rich Austrians do that. Well,
that's what those guys told me. When I hit Weiner Neustadt on the 22nd or
23rd I'll be flat broke. Nothing left.]

(Stupid, all that money and I pissed it away. Hardly spent anything in
Salzburg, and Graz wasn't too bad. What a waste of fucking time though.
Wien, that killed me, that must've been 1000 shillings just like that, in the
blink of an eye. And fuck Wien. It's not that great. Oh, the Gem of the
East. Europe's gateway. Fuck you. The music, the learned conversations in
the coffee shops, the chocolate cake, what posers. At least those EMO
fuckers at Birgit's weren't fake. They were stupid and ridiculous, but
genuine. Authentically idiotic, that's something, isn't it?)

[Not a fucking clue what to do at that point. Get back to Wien? For
what? Because it's the only place open on Christmas. Can't sleep outside
and I'll have nothing. Not a little reserve, not bougie fuckup nothing, but
nothing. Real nothing, not a cent. Fuck. Fuck. Okay, what then?]

Sitting on a bench in one of the more highly trafficked areas. Turning
side to side, some people moving about. The nearby benches are empty.
There's a draft in the big hall and the shoes echo when they strike the floor.
Clenching fists tighter and leaving the daypack firmly fixed, huddling and
shivering, looking side to side. It's a tic.

—*"I have my dead and I have let them go."* What else Rainer Maria?

6.8.2.X.19.86.12.25 [ref(..22-24)]

Not empty, but not exactly jam packed with people. Most have already
registered by now. Sitting in the big room, some standing around preparing
things, others already at tables eating. Sitting here with the book opened on
the table, reading that same paragraph again and again, from the one novel

he wrote.

—*"Only you return; brush past me..."*

About as filthy as any of them. Not her skin, but the clothes. No hair visible beneath the wool cap, no curves visible beneath the baggy pants, big clompy boots, and puffy coat. She is standing there waiting before saying anything.

"Merry Christmas," she says finally. "May I sit?"

(Weiner Neustadt streamed past with the lights in the streets and on the sides of the buildings. The former schoolhouse was closed down for the winter, but the couple still turned on the lights and people going past could see in. Matron's eyes were the same.)

Sweeping a hand over toward the seat on the other side of the table. She lightly pulls the chair back and slips into it.

"Julia," she says. Big charisma. Completely at ease but working it. Raising an eyebrow and giving her the stink eye in response to being worked.

"Steve."

"Nice to..." she says. "Where you from?"

"US. Chicago."

"Toronto. Ish. Neighbor. Reading some Rilke?"

"Can't get past the first paragraph."

She looks closer, interested. Tilting the book cover back so she can see. It's a German edition, collecting some of the poems together with the novel.

"What's the paragraph?"

Handing over the book with thumb still holding the place. "*September 11th, Rue Toullier.*"

"He wrote prose?" she asks.

"He wrote this, been trying for the last couple days, can't get past that first paragraph."

She spreads it out in front of her and leans forward. Clearly the face of a young woman, early or mid-twenties, but if you didn't see her face, you wouldn't guess it. Nothing else about her attire belongs on a young woman. She clears her throat.

(Same as the wife... ...jawline... ...Hannelore, but she must've been older, a pretty woman with her meticulously detail-oriented husband. No way he'd let me crash there, only her. Ready for more than that, I bet, if only he wasn't breathing down her neck.)

"So this is where people come to live; I would have thought it is a city to die in." She looks up. A couple of guys pass close by the table and her eyes briefly follow them past, then turn back down and look across the table. "One at a time," she says as though she's making the mark.

"You would think." Clearly in the know.

(Sanding those tables. I guess they were getting ready to paint. That kind of thing must've been part of the deal. That's why they let me. They didn't want to do any of that crap, so they got some stupid kid passing by to scrape and dig at the grime and shit on those desks. Fuck that. Kept me warm, but there are lots of ways to get the blood flowing and those stolen looks were better. She had something on her mind alright.)

"I have been out. I saw: hospitals," she reads. *"I saw a man who staggered and fell."* She keeps going but no longer out loud. Her eyes are scanning the lines on the page.

(What with all the fucking things we saw, I guess the hospitals mattered. And the kid in the carriage, that's the part that got me. Breathing in the pommes frites, the iodine, or whatever, and the fear. That's how it was. We breathed that shit in and didn't know it. It formed us before we knew we could be formed.)

"I guess you speak German."

"Studied it in school, been staying with a couple of German girls for the last month," she says.

Passing her the water bottle, but she shakes her head and pulls her own from the bag she'd set down next to her.

"Where was that?"

"Thessaloniki. Thought it'd be warmer there. Was for a while, but when it gets colder, it sucks because there's hardly any heat."

"Are they still with you? The German girls."

"Nah. They stayed... There for the winter. I met them there, not connected. Passing through."

"How long have you been?"

"About six months. You?"

(Two days of scraping gum and gouges off those desks and I was ready to get the fuck out of there. No point to any of it, no reason to spend Christmas that way, they could do it themselves, no bed was worth that much. She was a fucking tease.)

—And this one? What's she selling?

"Same. Came in the summer."

"Winter's a lot harder though, isn't it?"

"Hell yes. I had a sweet gig over in the Tyrol, but that blew up and now I'm scrambling."

"Where you headed?"

"West. Up the Donau. Toward Nürnberg eventually."

She pulls out a pack of biscuits, the kind you get everywhere but in each country, they have different names. Marilu. Mariboo. She offers a couple.

"Thanks."

"Are you by yourself?"

"Mmmhm. You?"

"Yup."

"Don't see that too often. Woman out on her own. How's it going?"

"Pretty shitty. I've been here a few days trying to get back. Ultimately to London. It's been dead."

"What's stopping you?"

"Looking for someone to travel with."

—There's the hook. This could be interesting.

"Why do you need someone to travel with? Dependent on a man, are you?" She looked as though she could take a joke and didn't look the least bit dependent on a man. She laughs.

"It's only because they're assholes that I need one. Big woman would do in a pinch."

"That's what I always say, but they don't like to be pinched." She laughs and looks back at the book.

"You're a jokester."

She reaches down into her bag again and pulls out a worn-out copy of *The Man Without Qualities.*

"I'll trade you," she says.

Taking it from her and thumbing through the pages.

—Heard of it.

"Since you can't make it past the first bit of this one."

"Okay. You've finished it?"

"Well, I'm done with it, that's for sure." She takes the Rilke and puts it in her bag. She looks around, trying to see if there's a better mark.

"Let me get this straight. You come in here and scope the room, looking for a guy by himself. Then you come up, make some chit chat. You're looking for someone to travel with, right?"

—The pirate in her. She's a fucking pirate, this one.

"Pretty much."

"I'm traveling pretty light. If you're thinking there's a score in it."

"Not like that. Light is fine. Light is what I'm looking for. You got a bed here tonight?"

"Lighter than that. You?"

"I do. There's room for a kip if you want. Get a good night's sleep, and then tomorrow head off along the river. What do you think?"

—What's the catch?

Laying the book back down on the table in front, but keeping it close, making it clear that she can't take it back. Nodding and looking around, immediately comfortable.

—Could be legit but could be more.

"Are you sure? Did you get enough background? Seems you should be gathering more information before making up your mind."

"American on the road for six months, reading a book, in German no less. Unable to get past the first paragraph of a novel after you've read poetry by the same guy. Some of the pages are creased. Looks as though you read a few of them over and over again. Why can't you read the prose? I'm guessing, but what? It's too intense. Something about it puts you off or takes you somewhere you can't go. Whatever, it's a pretty clear sign."

—"*That was the main thing.*" Ra-ra-ra Rainer.

"Or I don't like to read walls of text."

"You thumbed through Musil and decided it was worth the trade."

Pursing the lips and looking her directly in the eyes. She doesn't blink.

—Not exactly waiting for an answer, she's waiting for me to catch up.

"Aside from the kip tonight, what's in it for me."

"If you don't know that, then I did make a mistake." Animated, but she doesn't talk loudly, her tone is good. "The single man is suspicious, my friend. With me standing next to you, many more doors will open."

Laughter from both sides of the table.

"Are you in a room by yourself?"

"No, but it won't be a problem. Unless someone else comes. The other girls they've got in there look as though they've seen a thing or two. They won't mind."

"Why not hook up with them?"

"They're trying to get south and not likely to be persuaded otherwise."

"Persuaded?"

"Yeah, sometimes they're persuaded."

"Like how?"

"Like you. Suppose you were headed to Prague or something, but I wanted to get to München."

"You'd persuade me."

"Exactly."

"And how would you do it? Are we talking sexual favors? Did I agree too quickly?"

"Pffft," she takes another sip of her water. "Men have no imagination."

"What men? It's only me sitting here. How do you do it then?"

"You can't help yourself. You want to be the hero. You want to take care of things for someone who needs you to take care of things."

"A supposed universal weakness and you swoop in and exploit it."

Pulling out the loaf of bread from the daypack. No cheese or meat to go with it, only the bread. Tearing off a hunk and gesturing for her to have some too. She shakes her head politely, changing the vibe.

"I insist. We have to break bread."

She nods and grabs a chunk. She's hungry.

—Paid for a place to stay but only has the biscuits to eat.

"Guessing, but does the whole travel uniform you have there get in the way of finding three squares?" Wax on with the hand to let her know it's the whole ensemble that's in question.

She laughs and washes down the bit of bread with some more water. Gesturing back to the heel of the loaf, letting her know she can have the rest. She takes it over in front of her and keeps tearing off pieces and putting them in her mouth. Almost seems to be humming while she chews and swallows.

"It's one or the other. Leave me alone or buy me a drink. There's no middle way for fools."

"Have you been down around the department stores? The cafeteria is a free-range grocery."

"Nope, haven't sunk to that yet. Is that your angle?"

"Every angle is terrifying."

She smiles and puts the last bit of bread in her mouth. "How long ago did you think of that?"

"Few days. Thanks for playing."

"What's it going to be, Stevie?"

"Yeah yeah, I told you, it's good, let's do it, I thought you'd want more information. My actual story."

"But I've already worked out that you'll be a good travelling companion. If you want to tell me, fine."

"I'm more interested in your story. That's what I came for so you could guess what's been going on with me. There then there then there then there."

"Why should you have all the fun? You're right, guys can travel by themselves and no problem, but for me it's impossible, even in the north it was hard."

"You were up north? Go on, tell me. Here. For an apple."

She takes the apple and bites into it right away. Takes a second bite before she's finished chewing the first, but then pauses to let everything catch up.

"I, uh, got my MBA."

"Bullshit."

"It gets worse. In America. At Penn."

"Whatever. If it makes you feel good about yourself."

"Whatever. These girlfriends of mine and I decide to go to Europe. A bullshit tour. Ten countries in fourteen days or something like that."

"Friends from Penn."

"No, from back home. Mississauga. We flew into Amsterdam. That was the best deal we could get, no rhyme or reason to it. We had train passes and youth hostel ID cards. We were ready for the Fromme's eye view of the motherland. In two days, I was ready to shoot myself."

"Two days. What took you so long?"

"We didn't see anything in Amsterdam, and then we're off to The

Hague to see nothing there. And then to Brussels and Cologne and
Hamburg. Nothing nothing nothing. Boring as fuck and I'm thinking why
is this my celebration? The last real thing I do before I go to work for the
rest of my life. I had this job lined up. New York, finance, the whole big
ticket. We're pulling into Copenhagen and I'm losing my shit."

"And your friends don't notice."

"I've known them my whole life. We're not at the same... We don't..."

"Got it. Okay, so you're in a private prison pulling into Copenhagen."

"And I wanted to see the midnight sun. They wanted to head back down
to Berlin. Copenhagen is one more of the big cities you have to see, and
they didn't want to go any farther north."

She takes another bite of the apple and pauses while chewing it. Sitting
there waiting for her to go on. She takes another bite. Seems to be a habit,
always taking two bites before clearing the way. One of the guys at a nearby
table is rolling a cigarette and she notices the interest.

"Do you smoke?" she asks.

"If I can get tobacco."

She pulls out a pack of Memphis and sets them on the table with some
matches on top.

"Can we wait until I finish the apple?"

"Sure, sure. Go on."

"There was a guy in Copenhagen. South African guy. He said he was
headed up to the arctic circle. Said there was some kind of strawberry farm
or something up there. He had a tent and was going to sleep out by the
green houses and pick strawberries. It sounded ideal, perfect, I never heard
a better idea in my entire life."

"And your friends let you bail on them and head off with some strange
dude?"

"They tried to talk me out of it, thought I was out of my mind, but there
was no way, I was going."

"And he turned out to be a psycho?"

"No. He was the other kind. Unreliable. Head changing with the wind.
Once we got up there, it was a crazy scene. Lots of people. He hooked up
with someone else."

"Let me guess, you weren't having it."

"Whatever. He hooks up and I don't see him again. Best thing that ever
happened to me."

"Are you serious?"

"Well, yeah. I think so."

"You had to travel back down this way on your own?"

"I was terrified. Found some real sweetheart American guy up there.
Gorgeous. He was hanging around for the solstice but wasn't picking any
berries. He wanted to head down to Trondheim. Hitching. There was a

train, but it didn't come often enough. I went with him."

"Did you have to persuade him?"

"Nope. He was nice. Not the kind of guy you could persuade. Nobody's hero. He had his thing and was headed his way. At Trondheim he took the train to Sweden. Had a pass too. Mine was still good, but I didn't want to use it, wanted to be on the road, thrilled with the new turn things were taking."

"What did you do?"

"Traveled alone back down toward Oslo."

"And?"

"You don't want to know."

"Why do you say that?"

She finishes the apple and takes up the pack of cigarettes. Pulls out two and hands one over. She strikes a match then lights them in sequence.

"Doesn't fit with your world."

"Bullshit. If you don't want to tell me, don't tell me, but don't put it on me."

"Okay," she blows the smoke out from her first puff. "It's high school." She looks around to see if there are any ash trays nearby. There's one on the empty table behind her so she gets up to retrieve it, then sits back down. "You learn how to fend it off. You learn to protect yourself. There are things you do to distract him."

"Like what?"

She pretends she doesn't hear, has no intention of responding.

(Donna Light or whatever her name was. That's what she was doing. Now I get it. All those handjobs for the sake of her virginity.)

—Is that what she means?

"Fool him somehow."

"Not fooling anybody," she quips and then sneers. She's irritated, but then she shrugs and lets it go, deciding it doesn't matter. "It's... ...well... Fuck. Whatever. It's what you do."

—How come they can't tell us? If they can handle it without their heads exploding, why can't we?

"Okay, never mind. Go on."

"From Trondheim to Oslo that's what I discovered. Truck drivers are the best, but random guys are a nightmare. Had to butcher my hair. It's best if they don't think they're pulling over for a girl. If they think you're a guy, you'll attract a different sort of person. Changed my wardrobe up there. Emptied out the crap I brought and got new stuff."

"You weren't exactly in dire straits or anything then, you had Daddy's credit card."

She plays with the ashtray and knocks ashes into it requiring a slight wave of the hand to get her attention to leave it alone for a second.

Knocking off the ashy tip in front of her while she weighs her response.

"At that point, yes, definitely. I know, I get it. Once I was in Oslo it was easy to find someone to get back to Copenhagen with. That's when the whole big city thing came to me. You hop from city to city and find a travel companion, hopefully they hang with you while you cross through the smaller places. The guy I got from Oslo to Copenhagen with, he was a real standup guy, that was good. We saw many small places around there, along the Swedish coast. It was fun. I was getting some mad skills. Met a different guy in Copenhagen, thought we were going to head down to Hamburg together, but he dumped me in Roskilde."

"Why?"

"Because I wouldn't fuck him," with a hard look right this way.

—Fuck that, not going to be bullied off it.

Eyes stay locked.

"And you couldn't fend it off?"

"Are you trying to be an asshole?"

"Not much of an effort. Curious though. Is that what you meant before?"

"No, that's different, didn't have a choice. Do you want another one?"

—What is? Choice for what?

Taking it from her and holding it steady while she lights it. It's only half a pack, but she doesn't give off any sense of rationing.

[When flush, enjoy.]

"Roskilde to Hamburg was the worst. That was when I figured out that you did need to persuade someone. At all costs, they shit you not, don't travel alone. Have to learn everything the hard way."

—Cutting your hair didn't fool them, I guess.

"Of course. Same with me."

"I doubt that. Unless..." She's almost concerned that she's uncovered something.

Shaking the head while meeting her gaze. "Go on." She's relieved.

"I wanted to hike through the Black Forest."

"I hear that. It's beautiful."

"Right. And I wanted to. This guy in Freiburg, he was headed to Portugal or something. Porto. I convinced him to go out of his way and down to Geneva. He went his way, I went mine. Then I met a guy who wanted to go to Italy, but I convinced him to cross Switzerland with me over to Zürich. Like that."

"Okay, so how do you do it? If there's no sex."

"I didn't say there's *no* sex. In Switzerland, he was hot. It's not a quid pro quo. It's the savior thing, they can't resist it. Come on dude, you have to look out for me, who knows what'll happen if you don't."

"But you're not lying. I mean, it is risky."

"No lie."

"Why are you telling me this? I mean, you're opening up the curtain. Isn't that counterproductive?"

She laughs and throws her head back. Takes off the wool hat for the first time and sets it down on the bag next to her. Closely buzzed dark brown hair. A hatchet job for sure, cut again more recently. Wrong kind of scissors for sure. Her face is nice though, and it doesn't look too bad.

"Sometimes, with some guys, if you read them right, that's the most persuasive thing you can do."

6.8.3.X.19.86.12.29 [ref(..26-29)]

Back in the laundromat after waiting sufficient time on the street, not wanting to open the door for fear of interrupting. He disappears into the back room, and she bends over to put something in her bag. Heading in and across the violently lit room to where she's sitting in the back.

"I can't figure you out."

She straightens up in the chair by the dryer. The towel, overshirt, and pants aren't hanging on the back line anymore, they must be in one of the machines rotating in front of her. She appears to be standing guard.

"What do you want to know?" she asks.

—Not self-conscious in the least.

"You're a soldier of Reagen and then, what, you have a nervous breakdown on a trip to Europe and now what? What is this?"

She laughs and puts her hand up to cover the phases. She shakes her head. Fresh pack of cigarettes on the countertop. Eyes flash to them, refraining from making any further comment.

—Don't bury the lead.

"Is that it? That's what's confusing you?" she asks.

Looking over at the spinning dryers, then back at the pack of cigarettes. She's following the line of sight, registering each point of interest. Sitting down in the chair next to her.

"Did you make your phone call? Is everything okay?"

She doesn't have her book out, sitting here staring at the machines. She lights a cigarette, and hands one over, the first two butts from a new pack.

—What were you waiting for?

No ashtray nearby, using the floor. The place is empty, but there are machines doing work for people who must've stepped out.

"Youth hostel here is in an old castle," she says. "It's open, but no telling how crowded it is. May need to buy a bed. Bayern's Venice."

(Wachau valley. Krems was impressive. It was mostly talk, she knocked on the door and gave some big story about how we got our stuff stolen and we're killing time until we get everything straightened out. We're married and this is our honeymoon. The married couple running the hostel were only too happy to help. Gave us a bed for the night and invited us to share their meal. She's a sociopath. None of it tugged on her, she was happy to say anything to get what she wanted, none of the sincerity of their hospitality got to her. Later, she told me it wasn't because she didn't feel guilty, but thought she owed it to them. Not a sociopath, a perfectly rational explanation, it was out of respect for them that she stayed firmly in character. Didn't want to make them feel bad about what they're doing, didn't want them to get angry. They thought they were doing something good, felt good about it, it's the least we could do. That's her logic.)

"I take it you want to go first."

"Yeah. We can park it up the road. It's a long driveway. I'll have to walk up there, but you can hang out down at the bottom. There must be someplace nearby. I'll scout."

(That's what she did in Melk too, went in first and had the whole thing arranged. I had no idea what she told him, what she did, or what he thought of us. Didn't have the money to pay for that room. The place was empty, we were the only ones there. He didn't feed us or anything, but she somehow magically had enough money to go down to the grocer and pick up a loaf of bread and some cheese. Where did that come from? Same place as the dryer cycles and the cigarettes, I bet.)

"You're not going to let me in on your secret."

"No secret. I work it out on the fly. You gotta read people, figure out what they're waiting for."

"Waiting for?"

"Yeah. They're sitting there doing nothing. It's completely dead. They're not open. That guy in Melk, that hostel was closed until February. That's why we got the private room, they're not heating the rest."

"What was he waiting for?"

"Someone to help, someone to make his day exciting, an adventure. I could tell. He was looking for an excuse to do something nice for someone."

"And in Linz? What were they looking for."

"That was extreme. It isn't usually that way. Bigger down there. They have bigger dreams."

Shaking the head and putting the cigarette out on the floor. It's littered with them.

—People can't be bothered.

"But so, here you are, in Europe, and you don't want to take a train from town to town and see nothing. You want to see the places you're passing through. That's what you said."

She nods and pulls out the book from her bag. She's flipping through it, not going back to the marked page only skimming over some of the poetry in front.

"And this is what you were hoping for? Scrounging up cigarettes, hand washing a bunch of clothes, and then somehow getting that guy to pay for these dryers. Is that the real Europe?"

"*Almost deadly birds of the soul...*" she reads out loud.

"These small matters? They are?"

"Don't be fooled. I'm not reformed. I, well, I figured this was the part they left out."

"At school?"

"Yeah. It's action, isn't it? Taking care of bare necessity. You won't hesitate to care for yourself, will you?"

"How does what we did in Linz teach you that? What did you learn?"

She's smiling and looking back down at her book, flipping the pages as if the answer was in there somewhere.

"That was for fun."

Nodding as though that's the only answer she could have possibly given. She's got a big smile on her face, as though she's reliving it.

(They would've given her whatever she wanted. We could've asked for more, we could've been flush, but she only wanted the room and the food, that was it. And that, don't forget, she must've wanted that too.)

"The river... That night, standing by the Donau and watching the moon come up over the town. I'll never forget that." Her legs are stretched long, and she patters her big boots on the dirty floor.

"And the rest of it? How will you remember that?"

Her head is bobbing as she keeps her gaze fixed on the book. The wool cap is slipping back and the hairline is visible. She reaches up and pulls it down over her forehead.

—Not going to repeat herself.

Door swings open and the older woman who was using the machines at the front comes back. She works with her clothes, gets some ready for the dryer, and packs some into a basket left on top of the machine. She'll soon be heading back this way to wring some stuff out in the sink.

"I never did things I wanted to do."

Speaking simply, without the least bit of emotion in her tone, although the quiet in the words comes out and resonates as an alternate form of feeling. Could be an illusion, it isn't that she's feeling something, only that the words are carrying what she ought to feel instead of making her do it.

"That was my parents. The rah rah shit, the studies. The focus on finance and the math. God, I fucking hate math. ...that's what you do..."

"But..."

"Sometimes, when nothing is yours, when you don't have anything, you learn how to take."

"And that's the real Europe?"

She isn't irritated. None of the pushback bothers her. She keeps that same tone.

"Away from people who know me. Away from people's expectations."

"I don't count."

She smiles and puts her hand over on the closest knee. The lady is standing at the sink now and looks over abruptly after catching the movement out of the corner of her eye.

—Are they all that way, do they walk around hoping they'll get to see something they shouldn't?

(She figured that out, she understood that's what they're hoping for, what they're sitting there waiting for. They wanted some young dirty tramps to walk in and put on a vagabond show or whatever they'd call it when they got off talking about it later that day or weeks and months afterward. They'll jerk it plenty in retrospect. Thrust into daylight.)

"First, you spend time doing it for others, doing what they think you should want. I never did anything wrong growing up, never got into trouble, never disappointed anyone. At school, kept right on. Graduate school. Same."

Reaching over her for the pack of cigarettes. She takes her hand off the knee and leans back to make room. Takes the cigarette on offer and leans forward again to let the fire catch at the end.

"That's what I saw in the nothing. Nothing was happening. Journeying through it. So you could tell people. Oh, I was in Amsterdam and The Hague, then off to Brussels and Cologne. A checklist. No experience in any of it, no feeling, nothing meaningful. Nothing."

The lady gives off a harsh look as the smoke wafts up in her direction.

"That made you think your whole life was that way."

"Yeah. Everything was one big ridiculous tourist blaze through the monuments and sites."

"Do your parents know where you are?"

"Of course. Well, sort of. The credit card."

"Is that why it's okay to use it in Wien but not Krems or Melk?"

"Yeah, in the big cities, I'm letting them know. The plan is to head to London to work. They think that's what I'm doing. Working in these cities. Using the card now and again to make some minor adjustments."

The lady folds the stuff into the basket. Still wet from the look of her reaction. She puts a few things in one of the machines and walks out of the store.

—Can't figure anything out. Does she live close by?

"I saw you."

She leans back, blows smoke up toward the ceiling, then stamps out the butt on the floor in front of her.

"What did you see?" She asks without looking.

"Out there. I was standing there for a while before I came in."

"And what do you think you saw?"

Silence. Putting the butt out on the floor. The collection of them tells a story. She folds her arms in front of her, her coat is draped on the back of the chair, but her sweatshirt is bulky and warm. She hugs it closer as though curling up with a blanket.

"I'm trying to figure you out. Linz and Krems. That was fun?"

"Didn't you have fun?" Such a devilish smile. Completely rhetorical question.

"Aren't you worried about what'll happen? There's a lot of stuff that can happen nowadays. Don't you worry about any of that?"

"First, I figured out that I was doing what everyone else thought I should be doing. Sometimes, I don't know, sometimes that's love. They love you and want you to do what they think is best for you." She gets up and goes over to the machines, one of them has stopped. She opens the door and reaches in to feel if they're done. "Close enough," she says, and then takes everything out. While she's doing that, the other machine stops. Getting up to tend to the clothes, coming back around with an armful, and standing next to her at the counter behind the chairs, good for folding.

—She'll come back around. Wait.

"Sometimes, they take what they want, and it's not because they want what's best for you. They don't give a shit about you, they only want to take. Taking must be okay, right? That's what I mean. What I'm trying to figure out. How to take while everyone else is taking?"

Packing everything up into the plastic bags, then pulling the coats off the chairs and swinging them around the shoulders and hooking arms into them. Bundled and battened with hats and gloves, then taking the plastic bags and heading off out the door back into the cold, back toward the train station.

(The confluence of three rivers made every route a scenic wonder. It's the other way to the youth hostel so we needed to double back to get to the neighborhood she was talking about. It's still early and we didn't have anything else to do.)

"Do you think I'm a psycho?" She asks to take her mind off the cold wind blowing against her while heading toward the train station.

"Do you care what I think?"

"Yeah, kinda. I didn't have you figured for the judgmental type."

"I'm not judging you, it's risk mitigation."

She laughs and pushes against the left arm sending both off-balance.

"You think it's risky to travel with me." Then she makes an abrupt second sideways bump, this time with her hip.

"Last night, that was risky. You had no idea what would happen. You weren't in control of the situation. You thought you were, you thought you had it set up and were the one in charge, but I don't think so. Anything could've happened."

"That's the fun part."

"Fun?" Shaking the head, not believing it.

"Exciting. I never knew how much I liked that. You'd hear about other people, and you'd think they were crazy."

"Like what?"

"Sex in public. I had a friend in college. She had sex with her boyfriend in a restaurant. Not full on, but lots of stuff, and she was telling me about it. Said she liked it. Couldn't stop doing it after that."

"You were horrified."

"I was horrified. What would people say, what if someone you know saw you? The usual questions. Other people's expectations. What would happen once you were judged by them, once they turned you into the worst thing you could be?"

At the train station and in front of the lockers. It isn't big. The rivers are something to behold so there are some who'll come for that, but not this time of year. The architecture, gothic and baroque, has a following, but it's too cold now, and there's too much to do in the mountains to the south. The station is nearly empty. Huge investment to use the Deutsch Marks for stowing the bags, but it was worth it. Shoving everything back into them now and slinging them over the shoulders and heading back toward the doors to the street. She pauses and stares through the glass, enjoying the last few seconds of relative warmth before braving the return to freezing air and icy wind.

"In Mo I Rana, the arctic circle, I thought that's what I was looking for. You know, kumbaya, with the kids in their tents. The guitars and the campfires. Singing and drinking beer and wine. That's what I thought would be fun, but it was a letdown. Only a step above the nothing I saw with my friends. Another version of nothing."

"But why? I don't get it. Did something happen?"

"Nothing happened. That's it. There was nothing in it. I wasn't in it. That's the nothing part. Not wanting, nothing invested. I can't describe it. It was never as if it was happening to me, not there."

Pushing through the doors and out into the street, making the way back toward the laundromat, needing to go past it this time and up toward the high part of town where the castle stands.

"But that's not how it felt in the laundromat or at Melk or Linz?"

She is huddling close by while she walks and holds her arms across her chest. Both leaning forward to keep the wind off the face and letting the hats take the brunt of it.

"On the road down from Mo to Trondheim, I was with that sweet guy."

"You told me."

"Yeah, well, he was a real odd bird. Insightful. Not like a guy exactly. He paid attention to too much stuff. Kinda creeped me out, he knew what I was thinking."

"What were you thinking?"

"Not the... It's hard to... He was so good-looking. Not much younger than me. The weird surroundings. Adventure, or whatever you call it. I was, well, I was wishing he wasn't nice."

"And you think he was picking up on that."

"That wouldn't have been much of a feat. It was more that he knew *why* I was thinking that way. He knew there was something trying... ...or some impulse... It was... ...he knew before I did that some shell was cracking, or something was coming loose. He didn't want to go there because he didn't want to be..."

She clams up, can't find the right words to go on. Turning onto the street with the laundromat, then breezing past it up to the end. The hill looms up above the river, the driveway leading to the castle is now visible. She is looking for a place nearby.

"What did he know?"

She isn't paying attention anymore. She points in the direction of some weird teahouse on the corner past the driveway. The familiar sign points off in that direction, letting the wayfarers know which way to go. Stepping inside the place and ordering two cups of selected favorites. She pays. Grabbing a seat near the back where there is room for the packs on the floor.

"Well, I didn't know, not then, but on the way to Oslo. By myself. That truck driver. I figured it out, mostly, but I don't think I can explain it to a guy."

Taking the cigarette she is offering and letting her light it. "But you think he knew without you having to explain it to him?"

"Yeah. In retrospect. Yes. Most guys would get it wrong. If I figured out the perfect way to explain it, you'd still muddle it. Turn it into something else. Twist it."

"And this has something to do with Linz. With what we did?"

"With why it was fun. Why it was exciting. Yeah."

"Can't you tell me? Honestly, I'm not going to judge you. There's a whole world I've totally missed. Can't you?"

She looks over at the people at the next table and asks one of them what time it is. It's almost to the point where she has to head off and she's getting nervous but doesn't want to go yet. She thinks figuring out how to explain it will help her get a better grip on it.

"For you it's yes and no. You can't understand 'if I have to.' Look, I'm going to walk up there, and I have no idea what I'll find. It could be a young woman at the reception, or an older man. No idea. Don't know if there are lots of people staying the night and gathered in the main room. Or if there's nobody anywhere and it's dead quiet. No idea, but as I'm walking through the door and discovering these things, a plan hatches. I'll come up with things to do, things to say, make up a story, or an angle," she laughs.

(Remembered that line. She liked it and repeated it often, saying it when we couldn't get a ride or when some dicey looking character was the only one who stopped. Every which way, every angle was terrifying.)

"If you have limits. If there are boundaries that dictate what you can and can't do, then your ideas will fit that. That's such a fucking privilege. Do you know what I mean?"

"Ideas that violate them won't occur to you?" She doesn't seem to hear a question in the response.

"If you let anything come into your head, any idea or possibility, then the angles appear there and whatever needs to be done will come to you."

"Like murdering the lady because the situation requires it, and you think you can get away with it."

"If I have to, yes."

"That's nuts."

"Well, it would be because that's not usually the situation. But other things. I've only barely begun to see. I never could see before because my expectations were in the way." She stands up. "Gotta go." She takes the pack of cigarettes and pulls a few of them out and lays them down by the cup on the table. She doesn't leave any fire, but there are people around and it shouldn't be too hard to find.

(My ignorance in Linz, in Melk, that was part of it. It's not only that she knew what's going on, that she figured it out and responded to whatever she found there without letting anything prevent her, it's also that she knew, and I didn't. That whole night in Melk, sitting there by the fire. The guy was giving us plenty of space to ourselves. She knew what happened and I didn't. She came on strong that night after not being the least bit interested in Krems. I was the other person, just some guy. Nothing more to it. In Wien, she showed nothing. Completely neutral. The first time was that night in Melk. She knew something and I didn't, and I think that made it more desirable somehow. She wanted me. And the same in Linz. She was in a frenzy there. Knowing where they were and that I didn't know drove her wild, and she couldn't get enough, it was more than she could handle. It didn't make sense at the time, but now it's crystal clear. She felt powerful, and that was it, it totally came across after the fact when I saw them. Everything came together. It wasn't a single big turnaround for her then, the love of power was driving it along, and this was only her way of realizing it. Parents tell you to study something, you learn at the knee of the elites, and you realize you never fully expressed your own drive, were always under someone else's control. You learned it, and although they're the ones who told you to, you followed it through to its logical conclusion. Somewhere between Trondheim and Oslo you saw its infinite potential hidden in iron necessity. Somewhere between Roskilde and Hamburg you saw how dangerous it was, but that's part of it, and it doesn't separate you from yourself. Not how the survivors put it. No, in this case, it brought you back to yourself. Alive and breathing free air for the first time in your life. If the worst thing in the world happened to you, it might be liberating because what else now?)

—Is that it then? Your liberty. Liberation.

"Be careful." The door swings open and she disappears into the night.

6.8.4.X.19.86.12.31 [ref(..29-31)]

The big bed with fresh sheets and a big down comforter is solid luxury. Lying naked and flat on the belly with legs stretching out, head sideways on crossed arms, and looking over toward the window bathed in twinkling light marking the dark morning. She lays full flat on top and presses her chest down with arms swinging along the lines that bridge between the bodies down the length of the bed. Lightly caressing hips and ass, she bounces and rocks, then her flying fingers come back up to the arms before she twists and presses harder so they can stretch down to the legs and then back onto the side of the hip and ass where she lingers on every contour.

"Are we going to bang or what?" She asks with a chuckle.

—Without an audience?

"You're a selfish lover, you know that?"

"So?" she says without breaking any of the rhythms that continue in fascination along the ridge of the hip pressed against the mattress.

"An observation." Half-speaking into the bed and raising up to receive her lips and tongue. She lets her legs slip out and spread wide before pressing them together, equally applying force downward as she does it.

"Didn't bother you much before," she says placing her left hand under the archway, forming beneath the hip, and wriggling it along to find what's tucked in under there. She half rolls and makes room for a symmetrical response. Then, full facing, her hand returns and the arc of its movement becomes steady. She moves in closer again descending fully with lips and tongue. "Is that okay?"

"Mmmhmm. Kinda hot."

She's quick when it comes down to it. That selfish angle. Same as the rest. Knows where the pressure needs to be and uses her hands just right.

New sensations blend forever together. Not the striking stroking of the on its way to better things, it's more of a full body rush. Tickling and purring the whole way around, with sensation driving each of the many steps. She ratchets herself into place, slips through the ridges and valleys, teaching the crevices, whether they be folds in flesh or bends of arms. She grills breasts to chest, and smoothly executes the mucking about that goes with bodies moving in jittery and jumpy motion. She is the old stone bridge, she is the cathedral, the island in the Donau, and the descending scale. There is no way to breach it, but she allows it for a spell, succumbing to everything and carrying whatever is nearby into its vortex. She does not permit any conclusion and alights on bending knees, stirs on stretching toes, with their bounty broken but reforming to the morning's shape. It's a liquid pouring out and over the bed, soiling it to her traces, and she gets up abruptly, apparently finished, turning to slap the organ on her way, laughing joyfully as she dashes off to the bathroom, launching water right after the door closes.

Quickly finishing alone, mourning the gaps and gateways through night thrust into daylight. Touching it lightly on the sticky belly before wiping off the evidence with a previously used tissue.

[It'll come to it today, this'll be her chance to convince. Persuade, she calls it. We're halfway between München and Nürnberg. Which way wins the day? Passau to Deggendorf then here. Following the river but now there's a decision. Be firm, make her come to Nürnberg. Get a car. Eve can come with if she wants, I don't mind. Drive her to München if she's dead set on that. Or somewhere else to the west. Everywhere is on the way. It's reason, she has to listen to reason.]

—What would Eve think?

(Should they meet? Passau was fine but Deggendorf was a disaster. They wouldn't let us sleep in the train station, so we had to stay up and pretend we're waiting for something. I don't know what she did at the hostel, but that wasn't cool. She was too pissed off for it to be anything other than what I thought it was. The guy told a lie, and we couldn't stay there, so what? Shit like that happened all the time. She knew this was how it went sometimes. Why so furious? It's what I thought, a betrayal. It had to be what I thought. The vengeance here, the steadfast diligence that demanded something lush and comfortable after the ruse there. What did she do to earn it? Talked to the manager, but what could we possibly mean to him? The owners must be local, sees them regularly. It isn't a big chain where they have margins to make and buffer to bleed. He wouldn't have been that accommodating otherwise. What did she do?)

She comes out of the bathroom wet and dripping. No towel, walking about and looking for what to wear. Leaning forward resting on hands behind the head and watching her. Taking a moment before hopping into the bathroom, letting the steam clear out.

"What do you like about it?"

"About what?" She asks without breaking focus.

"Sex."

"Uh, isn't it obvious?"

"Leading up to it. What gets you ready?"

She's bending over a pile on the floor, sorting through the various items. Some she folds and others she puts on. A pair of underwear, tight-fitting warm tights, then a pair of baggy jeans. She sits in the chair and lights a cigarette. The pack is almost empty, could be the last one.

"What's this about?"

—Can't tell you that. Mystery revealed only when mystery solved.

"How did you get to Thessaloniki?"

"Came through here. There was a guy I met in Zürich, and we were heading to Prague. That's where I wanted to go. The entire time crossing Europe, it's what I was thinking about. Seeing the old place, going to the various apartments where he lived. They're still there, you know."

"Who? Okay."

—Prague's most famous ghost.

"Prague was great. Had a blast. Lots of people, lots going on. It was late Summer, almost Fall. Cool mornings, warming up in the day. Perfect. And the east bloc, it gets a bad rap for travelers. It's not deserved, a lot safer than the West. For me it was, anyway. He bailed, the guy, kind of a troll. I was by myself, thinking about what to do next. Someone told me you could get travel visas in each of the capitals and, so long as you check in at police stations or a hotel whenever you arrive anywhere, you're good. I got papers for Hungary and took off by myself."

"You were okay traveling alone?"

Turning over and lying flat on the stomach, facing her with elbows on the bed and hands supporting the chin.

"That's what I'm saying, it was much safer, or I felt safer, don't know. I didn't speak the language so who knows what I was missing. People gave me rides, fed me, sometimes gave me a place to stay. We'd pop by the police station. I'd register and then go home with them. The police knew where I was, it felt safe. Could've been a delusion, but that's how it felt."

She stamps out the cigarette in the ashtray on the desk and looks in the packet to see if there are any more. She crumples it up and tosses it toward the other edge where the basket is on the floor beneath. She gets up and sorts through the other things in another pile. Folds most of it, grabs a T-shirt and puts it on directly, then picks up the oversized sweatshirt, gray with red stripes around the wrists and neck, that she's always wearing. She finds a pair of socks and puts the folded stuff into her backpack, zips it, and sits back down.

"That's what I did on the way to Sofia. It was great, took months, two months almost. There's this place called Kulata and it's as far as you can go to the south, then you're out of the bloc. I got a ride there, a traveling salesman. Not sure. His English was minimal. Kulata Kulata. He said it over and over again. It took a long time, and by the time I got through to some Greek village, Promochonas, it was already dark. Took me all day, but I made it. That lulled me into a false sense. I don't know. There's a bus, I should've taken it, it was cold. Stupid. I walked a long way before someone picked me up, then next day the same. Took a couple of days to get to the city. Not pleasant. Rough. I ended up spending money, had no choice. Greece though, so I convinced my parents it was a vacation. Whatever, I made it, exhausted by the time I got there. Luckily, I met a couple of Swedish women and ended up staying with them for a while. That was great. A real lifesaver."

"Swedish women?"

"Yeah, they thought it'd be warm in Greece. In the winter. What did we know? You better hop to it. We should get going."

Getting up to go to the bathroom. Closing the door and turning the water on, sliding under. Such luxury, hot water and plenty of it. Multiple nozzles coming from the wall and ceiling. Staying longer than necessary to soak up the riches.

—How far does it go?

(You never could tell with the lies. Did she really go to Thessaloniki? That's a random thing to lie about. The emotion for getting there from the border, that seemed real, and she was choked up, as though something did happen. If rides were scarce, you couldn't be too choosy. Who knows though? Did she end up in hospital or something? Why else would she stay in one place for a whole month? It's inconceivable along with everything else. Not her style, she's not developing a stay put portfolio. Are the pastries that good?)

Turning off the water and drying off with the one remaining towel. Deciding to follow suit and walk out fully naked and sort through things, pack them up and dress, exactly the same as she did.

Her bag is gone. She is gone.

—What the fuck?

Rapidly dressing and shoving stuff into the rucksack. Looking under the bed and through the linens to make sure everything is accounted for. Tying up the boots, bundling up the coat, and then slinging the pack over the shoulder and onto the back. Off out the door and down the hall. Nothing in sight, not waiting at the elevator, not loitering in the lobby. Everywhere she isn't. She's gone. Setting the key on the desk and walking toward the door. She clears her throat.

"How will you be paying?"

"Excuse me? Didn't we take care of that last night?"

The manager comes through, the same guy. She's nowhere in sight, nowhere. Did they see her leave? Tempted to ask, but don't want to reveal too much without knowing the situation.

"Your friend said you couldn't leave a credit card but that you would pay with cash this morning. Most irregular, but she insisted."

"And she didn't pay you?"

"No sir."

"She didn't come through here?"

"No sir."

His eyes are registering the turn of events. He has no choice though and keeps playing the part.

—I'm the one in his grips.

"Well, I need to hit the bank to get the cash. That's where I was headed, then I'll come back."

"Would you mind leaving your passport? It's standard. We're happy to hold your bag until you are ready to depart. It's a complimentary service for your convenience."

"I can't leave my passport, I'll need it to get the money."

(He knew this was reasonable and was searching for some way to counter it. No warfare yet, but both sides on high alert and the tactics in full swing.)

He pauses.

"My bag is everything I have. If I leave it, you can be sure I'll come back."

He has no choice. It would be open combat to deny it. He doesn't want to call the police, doesn't want to make a scene. The hotel isn't crowded but there are other guests, and they are the sort that don't want a ruckus to interrupt their morning coffee and brioche. He nods. Handing over the bag and turning toward the door to head out.

(Immediately an inventory ran through my head. Underwear, socks, T-shirts, spare sweatshirt, extra pair of pants. Walkman™ and cassettes. Sleeping bag. Toothbrush, shampoo, toothpaste. What else what else? Pocket knife. Fuck. Why isn't it in my damn pocket? What else? A few books. The fucking daypack. Shit, why didn't I take the fucking daypack with me? Goddamnit. The Musil. Unless she took that. I didn't check. Oh, shit, no reason to think she didn't rob me. It's about 400 Marks. That's how much they need. The packs are the most valuable things in the whole lot. It'd cost at least 300 to replace them alone. Fuck fuck.)

—Luckily, it's Wednesday.

Crossing over the bridge and back into the town center. Bank and post office not too far from each other.

—What the fuck am I thinking? Who gives a fuck where the bank is?

Stop believing your own bullshit. Post office. They must've opened recently because there's no line.

"Ich möchte ein R-Gespräch führen."

Waiting a few minutes and then the guy calls me back to the booth. The operator confirms the number, Eve answers and accepts the charges.

"Hi there. How's the Donau in winter? Is it blue?"

Exhaling in relief. "Glad you're home. I need a favor."

"Sorry I missed your call from Passau, Elke told me about it."

"Yeah, sorry. I need a favor." More assertively this time.

She hears the gravity and calms down to focus. "What's going on?"

"Uh, let's see. Well, I'm in Regensburg."

"Oh, that's wonderful. Are you coming today?"

"Well, that's what I need to talk to you about. I need about 400 DM. There's trouble at the hotel. My card is no good and I don't have the money."

—Technically not a lie.

"400 DM! What kind of hotel did you stay at?"

"It was a big mistake, I miscalculated."

—No lie.

"Well, can you have them talk to me and put the charges on my credit card?"

"Would that be okay? You'd do that?"

"Yes, of course. You're coming today, aren't you?"

"That's the plan."

"Great, put him on and I'll give him the information."

"I'm at the post office. I'll have to go back and have him call you. You'll wait? It'll only be a few minutes."

"I'll wait. Tell me about it when you get here. All your adventures. Okay?"

"Sure. Can't wait. See you later and talk to you soon."

Hightailing it out of there and back up the street toward the lane that heads out onto the old bridge and back across the river to the hotel. Running for fear that somehow something will happen and prevent it from working out.

(Never once entertained the idea that there was something fucked up going on. A wedge to open the blockage and get out of the jam, that's what it amounted to. What if she stayed in Salzburg? What if I hadn't told her that story? Would it be better? Less ridiculous? Such a fucking cliché. I'm that asshole now.)

Back at the hotel and out of breath. It goes over well, and he relaxes for several reasons. One, the return itself. Two, the urgency. This makes a good impression. The explanation is brief, and he nods in perfect understanding before taking up the phone and dialing the number as directed. She must've answered. He explains who he is and says why he is calling. Room for two, one night, no damage. She must have been infinitely amiable because he doesn't bat an eye and takes down the information and runs the charge. The machine spits out the receipt and everything is fine.

"Of course," he says into the phone, handing it over.

"Thanks so much, Eve, I'm eternally grateful, sorry too. I'll see you soon. Today. I promise."

Pausing. "For New Year's eve?" Sounds more somber than before. "You'll be here for New Year's eve, right?"

"Promise. Thanks so much, got to go. We'll talk later."

Phone clicks.

He looks over as if he's looking at some stray dog gnawing on garbage in the middle of the street. Gesturing to come around, he opens the door to the office behind the counter and points at the pack standing by the door. Lifting it and hauling it over the shoulder, then out of the hotel. It's not far to the train station, crossing back over the bridge but staying straight past the cathedral to get there.

—Time for an inventory.

(Book was still there. Cassettes. Walkman™. Nothing seems to be missing. Sleeping bag. Okay. Looks good. Money check? 307 Shillings. She didn't rifle through the travel belt. That's not enough to cover leaving the bag here. What the fuck? What a cunt. That fucking bitch, how dare she? Those lies, that bullshit, she got off on that, loved it when I didn't know anything, when she was the only one who knew what was going on. That turned her on, source of her enthusiasm. No wonder this morning was so fucking hot. Explains why too. No wonder she was so fast and into it. She knew what was coming and I didn't have a clue. They're pure judgment and anger. Resentment. They're not better, they want power. That's what they care about. Power in knowledge, power in sex, power over what we do and what we think. Cosi fan tutte.)

—Fucking shit. Fuck that shit.

[When did anyone ever carefully analyze the appearance of the vagina? Subject it to scrutiny? Size and angle, lips, that'd objectify them, then they'd know. They love to talk about dicks, don't they? Small and big, bent and hard, they never run out of interest. Loving to judge, telling men what to do, knowing things they don't know, having power over them, controlling them. It's petty revenge because they don't have what it takes to confront the problem, to fight the battle head on. They're cowards who snipe and claw from someplace safe, hidden away. Who knows what gets her off? Who fucking cares? Her desire, her excitement, such a fucking mystery, every part of it, wanting and wishing, pretending she wants it badly, but she wants to fuck you up, that's what she wants, what makes her moan. They're all that way: the unknowable. Pleasure is the unknowable other, both in the other and in oneself. Truth gets caught up in shaming her. The truth blames her.]

—And Eve?

[Don't be fucking fooled. Don't think she's perfect and caring, you haven't hit the rail yet. The true colors will bleed when they're good and ready. She loves to steer as much as the rest of them and she can't do it with action that she has to take responsibility for, she'll do it with gossip and judgment. Such bullshit. They're fucking slaves. Every last one of them is a fucking slave. Devoted to resentment and turning their bullshit flaws into virtues. She'll use it against me. Proof of how far below her I am, how much I need her, how I can't last without her. They infantilize us, talking maternal to gain primal obedience. Aggregate us. Each one of us is every one of us. Well, each one of them is every one of them too. The one zigs and the other zags. They're in it together. Motherfucking conspiracy.]

Sitting down on a bench by the tracks, pulling out the book and trying to clear out the horrible, suffocating thoughts. Burying the nose in it, breathing its odor, and letting it take over every thought and response.

> To the mind, good and evil, above and below, are not skeptical, relative concepts, but terms of a function, values that depend on the context they find themselves in. The centuries have taught it that vices can turn into virtues and virtues into vices, so the mind concludes that basically only ineptitude prevents the transformation of a criminal into a useful person within the space of a lifetime. It does not accept anything as permissible or impermissible, since everything may have some quality that may someday make it part of a great new context. It secretly detests everything with pretensions to permanence, all the great ideals and laws and their little fossilized imprint, the well-adjusted character. It regards nothing as fixed, no personality, no order of things; because our knowledge may change from day to day, it regards nothing as binding; everything has the value it has only until the next act of creation, as a face changes with the words we are speaking to it.

> And so the mind or spirit is the great opportunist, itself impossible to pin down, take hold of, anywhere; one is tempted to believe that of all its influence nothing is left but decay. Every advance is a gain in particular and a separation in general; it is an increase in power leading only to a progressive increase in impotence, but there is no way to quit. Ulrich thought of that body of facts and discoveries, growing almost by the hour, out of which the mind must

peer today if it wishes to scrutinize any given problem closely. This body grows away from its inner life. Countless views, opinions, systems of ideas from every age and latitude, from all sorts of sick and sound, waking and dreaming brains run through it like thousands of small sensitive nerve strands, but the central nodal point tying them all together is missing. Man feels dangerously close to repeating the fate of those gigantic primeval species that perished because of their size; but he cannot stop himself.[1]

"Every angle is terrifying," spoken out loud and catching the attention of a little girl walking with her mother. She reaches up with her other hand and grabs hold more tightly, looking over and getting a head start on a lifetime of worry.

---

[1] *The Man Without Qualities* by Robert Musil translated by Sophie Wilkins.

4.12
this year's harvest

4.12.1.Elisabet.19.86.5.9

Kevin Bacon and Jamie Gertz are on the screen over the center aisle, also on the smaller screen fixed high up on this wall. The couple over to the left and one row back have their earphones on and are looking up, occasionally sipping white wine. There is no talking from the row behind. The older man is asleep with rubbery earphones barely hanging in place, can't tell what the woman is doing. They aren't together and haven't been speaking for a while. People will do anything to avoid the slightest stretch of boredom, they'll watch a movie they never would have gone to see. He's not watching.

"Aren't you going to watch the movie?"

"No."

—Obviously. Not curious, hasn't looked up once.

"Would you mind listening to a couple things and telling me what you think?"

He brightens and appears flattered.

"Not at all." Taking the headphones from around the neck after rewinding, then handing them over while still holding the device.

"Here is the first." Pressing play and waiting. He doesn't need to hear the whole thing, only the first minute or so is enough. Stopping, removing the tape and loading the other, then hitting play again.

"And the second." Again, with the same waiting period. This time could let it play longer. If he doesn't say anything, it might as well play to the end.

"Are they the same song?" he asks.

—Not at all, but that's how they think. If the lyrics are the same, it doesn't matter how you style it, how you arrange it, nothing matters. Only the lyrics. That's how simple they are.

"Yes. What do you think?" Offsetting a soul sourly sold.

"I can't believe they're the same. Only the lyrics, but the whole vibe is different."

Nodding furiously. Happy he gets it. It's not the same. There are differences and they matter. Some people pick up on them right away.

—That's the kind of listener I want. Not just anyone...

"Do you like one better than the other?"

"The first one's a pop song. Something you'd hear on a top 40 radio station. The second is something you'd buy and listen to. It's got a lot to it, a whole different genre. Are you singing both of them?"

—I'm such a fraud.

"Sorry, I didn't mean..." he trails off.

—Not hurtful, why think that? It's obvious which one they want, and who calls the shots.

[Whore wasn't the right word. What do they call it when you sold your mind and your taste and everything that meant anything to you?]

"Oh, it's quite alright, I know exactly what you mean."

"What's this for?" he asks.

—Money.

"The label wants the first, we want the second." Wrapping the headphones around the device and setting it off to the side.

—The royal we.

No sound from the screen, but everyone in the cabin with earphones simultaneously laughs. He briefly looks up and around then comes back with that same look.

"A new record?" he asks.

"A single."

"Could the pop version be the A side and the other the B?"

—It's sweet he thinks you can apply reason.

"It's more than that. This is what I want to be doing. I'm glad people like the other stuff, it's why they come to the shows, but it's not interesting anymore."

"It used to be?" He's leaning forward, elbow on the wide center arm rest. It's hard not to lean toward him, there's magnetism in the tone more than the words. Pivoting to the side to avoid craning and then leaning back against the seat, legs curling to the left.

(We were lying in bed when we last talked about her. Or him. He's still mine. I'm still his, but sometimes it's hard to look at each other. We needed to find our way back... ...if it took a doctor... Proud and standoffish, defensive, I don't remember him ever being that way before. It brought out the worst, but...)

"I don't know. When you're young and starting out, you'll go along with anything. Our goals weren't about the music, we wanted a contract, a tour. Now, it's different."

—He won't tell anyone. Obvious to oblivious, he can't imagine that a conversation could be sold.

"I see."

"Between us. Please, these are random thoughts, don't tell anyone." Making that clear not because it needs to be but because that's something people do to punctuate intimacy. Fumbling insecurity, it pushes off-center, it pulls back farther into the seat back, legs tucking up. Eyes say everything. Needing an escape.

(He wanted it too, wanted her, wanted that. Odette, or whatever her name is, she's not serious. He doesn't feel anything for her, it's an escape.)

"Who would I tell?"

"You'd be surprised. There are people..."

"I promise."

More laughter without any purpose. Some awe. Everyone on screen has a bicycle and is urgently peddling through the streets of New York.

—Hmmm, filmed in New York.

"I'm sure you've read about the cancellations."

"What cancellations?" he asks.

"The shows. Costa Rica. Two in Mexico."

"I hadn't heard." Smiling warmly, leaning in closer. He comes forward too. Something draws bodies together.

(And pushed them apart. Sent one off toward France and the other...)

The wide center armrest resembles a table and the twisty positions contort in the daylight creeping up underneath the window shades pulled down to hide the sun and clouds.

"I have to go see this doctor in New York. I've been... Well, there's some health stuff going on, and I have to get it... ...it makes you think, take stock, you know?"

"You want to make the music you want to make."

—This life, I want it to be my own. I want only love in it.

"I thought it was the only thing that mattered, but I don't think that way anymore. It doesn't make sense, but it's kind of heartbreaking. It's hard to explain."

—I was twenty years old when I decided. Or was it twenty-two? How can they expect me...? There has to be a statute of limitations on choices.

"I get it. I mean, when you breakup with someone, it's more than the end of a relationship, it's that your identity is destroyed, or how you thought about yourself, who you think you are." He pauses, waits for some time, continues: "If it's your decision, it's because that's what you want, you want to be someone else, don't like who you've become." Another pause, rolls his head slightly, then goes on: "But if it's not your decision, something you have to do, it's gut wrenching because you *did* want to be that way, but you can't anymore." There's quiet passion when he speaks.

[Without this cabin pressure, it'd be easier to pull close in a whisper. There'd have to be a lot of talk with this one, words working like body and hand.]

"You may be right." Simply smiling, not making the connections, but absorbing them through the feeling.

"Not me, my friend," he corrects as if that detail was of supreme significance.

"Oh, I'm sorry." Nodding too emphatically.

—I thought that was beyond you, but here you are.

"Maya wanted to be someone else or didn't want to be who she was with me. I wanted to be with her, who I was with her, or thought I did."

"Why couldn't she be who she wanted with you?"

—Were you stopping her?

"It wasn't up to her, to us. It's not how it works. It happens to us and then we decide if we can. That's hard. Love and heartbreak," he's explaining it to himself.

Slowly thumbing the device and considering the switches and buttons. Listening over and over again makes it more real. It doesn't solve anything, but reminds and yields a right to these moods, justifies the cynicism.

[Love *or* heartbreak.]

"To be honest," he goes on. "I don't think the sex was any good."

Nodding and waiting. Still can't put it together.

—What's the...? The esteem was too high, you couldn't imagine the thoughts in her head, couldn't see what was right in front of you.

"It comes out that way. How you are. All the time, but in bed too. It's part of that identity." He knows he's being placated and resists it with a gesture. There are no other signs of frustration, nothing is connecting the way he thinks it does, and he wants to steer back this way.

"It was mechanical. I liked her too much... I couldn't..." he trails off.

"I understand."

—No, I don't. How is this relevant?

"Who she was, her identity, she chose me at the beginning. Wanted me, or whatever. That's how they say it, but it's not a choice. You can't control it." He pauses. "Where do your feelings come from? Everything that happens, the intimacy, everything, she couldn't tell me or show me or anything, couldn't talk about it. She expected... I don't know... There were things I was supposed to do... They weren't in me. I wanted them to be, but they weren't. Never occurred to me."

—Wait, love *and* heartbreak. Who I am. Who I am right now, right this minute. Love *and* heartbreak. Is this what I want?

"They're molding me into what they want, but I'm molding them too. Is that it? Option two changes who they are as much as it changes me." He's nodding rapidly.

"I don't know, it's not the same thing," he says. "I meant that you have to take stock of yourself, who you are and what you want, what they're turning you into, what you're turning them into."

—No one gave anyone a chance. The roles were assumed.

"There's a lot of money at stake, they aren't going to let go. The kind of music I want isn't profitable. Not equal footing, they have more resources, lawyers."

Continuing but resisting his alignments and orientations. Still recoiling from the possibility, eyes darting up and down, back to the screen and down to the floor, his legs lightly crossed at the ankle. He waits patiently, studies the angles of arms and legs, notices the waist and breath through their rise and fall, it's as if he's reaching out and hoping to help a willful child catch up when it's her own willfulness that has her lagging behind.

"You know, dying my hair was their idea, but when they suggested it, I wanted to do it." Eyes back to ankles, fixed there and studying the cross. "They had this whole Swedish girl look they wanted to exploit, and I was saying 'yeah, that's me. I can be that.' But inside, I'm thinking 'this is my real color, I am Swedish, we're not...'" He keeps nodding, bouncing that cross up and down and jostling it side to side. "And the styling and the clothes and the way the music was produced, I thought I loved it. We sounded as if we were one of them." Tone rising an octave, these are the high notes, this is peak voice. "I didn't recognize... ...but they would pay for the studio time, and it felt like a gift. True luxury."

—I thought I was in heaven. All my dreams...

"Well, they are who they are, you knew that. It's what attracted you, right? Before you knew any better, it's what you wanted. Maya had this whole thing about the introspective poet. Sensitive in verse, but quiet and reserved outside it."

"Did she say that to you?" Clear at this point, he is relieved, child in hand. For a while he thought there'd be no way to get here from there.

"Not in those words, she didn't put it together that way for me, but that's what she meant, what she needed me to hear."

"I'm the one who has to decide."

"You're not a hypocrite, it's not that. People always simplify everything, that's what my friend says, would say. You're growing," he throws his voice and pretends to be somewhere between lecturing and scolding. "What you're seeing is changing, what you want is changing."

"It is."

"That's heartbreaking." Both nodding. "That's the lesson." His eyes are pleading, and for a minute it is as though a crowd is gathering in the air above the armrest, not only his ghosts but all the ghosts: the friend and the exes, the husband and the doctor, him or her, the bass player and the producer.

All the mothers.

4.12.2. Seannafair.20.15.5.7 [ref(19.86.5.15)]

The couple at the next table notice the stumble. The woman looks up full in the face, only the eyes covered up with product, the rest left to time.

The man can't help himself, sees an ass, remembers the videos and what it once was. The sun is blinding to the right side of the window, hobbling around him, to resume the place.

"I'm saying it's not an Irish pub."

—Was a time, Sean could write. No more of that. Gandy was some kind of actor.

"Irish enough." Eyes blinking or closing. Can't open them quickly enough to keep pace with the others.

"Mary's Irish."

—Never could've done nothing. A hanger-on with clothes on his back, a human hanger.

"Not truly, and Edmund isn't. Living here long changes you."

Turning about to see where she is with the next round. She looks up from helping someone else, makes a sign. She'll be round soon enough. The door swings open and he walks in. Silly ranger, wearing a cap. He beats it back and nods to the lot. Not confined to the table, the whole lot, every last one of them, the snooty couple with their wandering eyes.

—Let's see where you'd be if you wandered through it as I have.

"Terry!"

"There you are. Let's get you started."

Gandy and Sean gesture furiously.

(What was taking her so bloody long? And now there were revisions to contend with. She's quick on the uptake, another tumbler and another pint, it'll only be a minute longer. Greetings were enough to fill it, grain the rest.)

"I'm dragging behind," his coat is too heavy. He looks the fool, like a Londoner. There's a hook by the door and he swings the wrap to it. The boys by the window are partial to the movement, they think it spells relief, but it doesn't last, and he only slightly tilts toward them before coming back and feeling his way to the fourth seat. The creaking floors, hundreds of years old, and the tables aren't tightly packed.

—There are still places for humans to assemble, where there's enough space to tell your story properly.

"You need to catch up." Too much commotion, and she is seeing to it. She comes by without bothering over a tray. Three tumblers in one hand with a pint and a tumbler in the other. Spider fingers, she'll crawl her way out from behind the bar and show the flies what they need to do to get clear of her, to pull back from that sticky mess she'll put them in if they don't mind their way.

"Where do you come from, Mary? Are you Irish?"

[Gandy, the old sot, there was no apologizing for him, and she wouldn't have it. She's not tempted, there's nothing about the girl in her, walking on her own, both legs, both feet, clean and crisp in every step.]

"I've had enough of you," looking at Terry.

—And there she is.

"But I've only just arrived," he pleads. He knows her too well.

[There's always a story behind everything Terry did, but if you had to ask him, you'd never know a damn thing.]

"That should tell you something, shouldn't it?" She looks over and gives him a grin.

[Don't let these boys keep you anchored to your seat, lass. That's Mary for you, that's what she was always trying to say. It's the same message for every fly buzzing around with the others, feeling their grease and stepping in it if they weren't careful.]

"How long have you been here?" He takes a sip of the black stuff before anything else. Gandy downs his tumbler, he isn't saving up for anything.

(No rainy days he could think of. Sean was savoring it, he's a madman same as the rest, but had his moment. Still knew there were some things in this life to be savored. Couldn't think what they were.)

"Not too long. They were here when I got here."

[Too many details to speak of and these drunkards weren't listening, they couldn't care less. So what if the old geezer followed in after, looking for what he's always looking for? Only thing that mattered was the drinks in front of them.]

—There was a time when they would have wanted something else. They all did.

[Couldn't find it now.]

A song from Let's Dance. What's the recoil on that? Can't find the name, can't find anything now. Every which way, but it's not there.

"Where were you coming from?" Switching glasses, his eyes cross over the table and back at it. He's not digging, he's not looking for anything, only an amiable afternoon.

[Racks and racks of hefty men with nothing on their minds and no glory left to speak of.]

"That doctor I was telling you about."

(It was you, wasn't it? In the morning. Might not have been morning anymore, it was such a late night and could've bled into the afternoon, but I remember you. Was that when you made the tea? Why did I think it was the night before? That's you, you were always making me tea. It's always been you, every sip of it, guiding something. Was it a pleasure? Was I always wanting that one single thing that I could feel only because it hadn't happened yet? You put on this record, that's for sure. *Cat People* right there in the middle of it. Who is this boy? *"Putting out ▓▓ ▓▓ gasoline."* I remember that much, thinking that way. God, I didn't know anything. Nineteen years old and still clueless about how to get a fella to kiss her.)

—He's almost bored, but obligated, as if he has to take an interest. None of the others feel it, they're laughing and pissing themselves. The laughter is their cost of admission. Can't speak for Terry.

"Is that helping then?"

[Anyone could've asked that. The words were attached to the sentence before it came from somewhere else. Only pitch and timbre, nothing else. There were those who imitated the jungles where they roamed, they learned to speak its sounds, they were buried there, didn't have anything else to go on. He might not have said any damn thing, only some resonance from the speakers at the top of the wall tilted next to the ceiling.]

"Remembering some things, trying to get it sorted. Been talking to the boys about getting together, putting a few things down, doing a tour. Nothing big. Local."

(They were songs, and I said something, something definite. I can't. That's what I said. I looked him dead in the eye while we were sitting there and the only thing I could say was "I can't." Then a halt, there was an abrupt ending. I didn't want to stop speaking, but I didn't know what words to say, like when you're still working up the song and you fill it in with notes and tones that meet the music wherever it wanted to be. "I can't..." and somehow, he got something from that. He did, didn't he? Next thing I know his chair is dragging along the floor over next to mine and he is close in tight, looking straight at me. Those eyes. He must've been talking non-stop because I remember words and words and words, but I can't think of a single sound that came with any of it, and his mouth couldn't have been moving, that would have been impossible.)

"The doctor's going to help with that?" He doubts it, frowns at the thought of it, and knows the band won't be likely to consider it after everything from before. His tone carries all that, but he continues to play along, sips his stout and bids others to do the same.

(Because he was leaning and I was getting my kiss, wasn't I? That's what I was meant to say, those were the words that came to a halt, that couldn't come, but only seeped out in music. A lesser man, well, he would've thought something entirely different, he might've thought I was asking him to go or stand back or something, but he never for a moment doubted his instincts. Oh, but I did, I doubted everything, "I can't...")

"Might as well be. Or something. Something's got to change." The doubt writes itself on the left cheek. A quick jerking pulls the weakened muscle back. Tendering awareness and sniffing strongly to make it seem a deliberate response. Terry doesn't need to know it.

"What were you remembering?"

(That he kissed me right after I said "I can't..." knowing full well that I didn't mean I can't kiss you, that I didn't mean I can't be here with you right now, that I didn't mean I can't go ahead with any of this. Full well. It was obvious, any idiot would have heard that music. It was loud. That was the melody that became *My Life*, as though it were coming in a dream.

Changes, that's what he was passing to me, and he heard it, every word of it. "I can't do anything right. I can't get you to kiss me right now even though that's what I want more than anything.")

"That night, the night I wrote *My Life, Return to Me, In Your Head*, all those songs, I hadn't thought about it in years."

(But they didn't come fully fledged, did they? I told everyone they did. Said it was as fast as the pen could go, and then once I set it down, we needed to find the tune, but it wasn't that way at all. That whole day I kept going back to the paper, kept crossing things out and adding things in, writing over the top of the lines, underneath and around them, and all because he was doing the same to me. Crawling on me, giving me my kiss, the one where "I can't..." and how could any of this make any sense to anyone? It didn't make sense to me. I didn't know that could happen with a fella. I thought that was for me alone, wanted it for me alone. What would anyone else have to say if I couldn't say it myself? I told him it'd be better if only I could make a few changes. "Let's try again, it'll be better." "Again and again," he said. No one could've made any sense of it. That back and forth, as though it was one thing but really it was millions of different things. Songs and the puckering, music and the tangling, they'd think it such a mess. I thought it such a mess. That time, those hours, they had to last a lifetime. Those songs had to make a woman of me.)

"The infamous night. What's left to remember?"

Looking down, anywhere to avoid any pair of human eyes forcing a response other than being alone with the thoughts.

(What was there to remember? Was it possible that a single moment could be so intense that the entire rest of your life paled by comparison? Was it possible that you would blank it out to go on living? To make sure you could get up every morning and do what you had to do to stay alive and take care of things, love those around you, be loved by the ones that mattered?)

"There was a fella."

—A fella? Only one or were there hundreds? Was he every single one of them?

"Don't tell me, he wrote it." Serious look in his eyes now. He thinks he's onto something, calculating the value it'll have for TMZ. The laughter at the other side of the table subsides. The three of them think they're about to get their hands on something to trade for gold.

"Don't be daft," and that breaks the spell. They go back to their banter, and he goes back to his bored, leaning focus where the tumbler is drained and the Guiness gulped. "Of course not, but he was the first one who took a look and said, those are songs."

(Could be. He said they could be. He saw it in everything. He saw changes as they came and went. He could see the movement, that's how he knew what those words meant, that's how he knew. Someone must've told him how to do it, how to listen, how to hold a tender heart carefully in his hands. They don't come out doing that. They needed to learn, and they needed a woman to teach them. What boy could ever bring himself to it? He'd be clumsy and knock everything about, like how they are. Beating around the yard with their ball and the other blokes. They needed to learn. And if their mothers wouldn't do it, and they couldn't, how could they? Then someone else had to, that's our jobs, that's how we're supposed to take care of each other, that's how we're supposed to look after one another. By teaching the boys, by showing them how to hear the music in the words, how to hear the full sentences when they halt somewhere in the middle, when they didn't come all the way out, when the mouth was too damn busy with something else.)

"You said you stayed up all night in your flat in Oxford and wrote them in one sitting. That's the story everyone's been telling for years. Now you're saying there was a fella? Was it a tall tale?"

(The sets of possible acts appeared before Terry's computing mind. He surveyed the randomness, no doubt, and presented the only possible result, the mechanics laid bare. He was the builder with his reason and bucket. Start shoveling.)

"He played me some music." Resigning to the moment, living in Terry's world the only way anyone could. With the choices available, this is the way it has to be.

"I bet he did,"

—You don't know a damn thing, you old rummy, not a damn thing.

"He was a perfect gentleman."

(I did get my kiss, not that I would ever share that with the likes of you. It was mine and mine alone. He meant it for me and as long as I live it will be ours. Wherever he is, alive or dead, I have no idea, but we were together then. We're still back there together, still in that flat that no amount of scrubbing would ever make clean.)

"But he stayed the night," Terry says.

"He did." Point to the heart. First with a forefinger, then a swaying picado and the middle finger flares out. Turning it upward and toward him. Dear Terry laughs and raises his glass.

"Did you get what you wanted?" And then he winks. He can't help himself. He sees everything but can't hear anything.

Three more come over to the table, loud and laughing: an older man and two older women. Seen them before. Greeting Sean and Gandy, they nod over this way. Terry calls out for Mary to come with another round. She hops right to it, doesn't wait for confirmation.

4.12.3.Natalie.19.86.8.2 [ref(..6.11-12)]

Matching pearls and chain link belts, both the tops with a disco flair. High in front but backless. As if arranged beforehand, wardrobes are orchestrated, none exactly the same but the alignment is uncanny. The colors are like popsicles from a freshly opened box. Shiny metallic, zigging and zagging a faux lambada grinding against each other briefly before hopping out and away, imperiously close to forms and arcs otherwise never dreamt of. There is fun in the conformity, in the ever so slight variation in code and dress, in the ways to meet with style as though adding it to the mix. Acknowledging the collective while announcing a presence in it, switching partners only to switch back again in variations matching the rise and fall of the tempo. It is the appeal, and the heat drives over the strappy high-heeled sandals in colors matching tops and visible beneath the swaying wide cuffs as the black slacks hug each bend and twist of the hips and waist, tight yet easy to move. A dress here and there, some cleavage where it's an asset, but mostly uniform. Flashy and metallic, glowing in the rainbow lights takes the highest priority. Not the only ones to bounce in the entryway of the house where the makeshift dance floor is darkened and surrounded by flashing lights and sounds, but by far the most enthusiastic. No men to speak of, the floor is full of women come for this exhaustion, this release of everything that isn't mild and doesn't accept its lot as told by those with anything to say about it, and everyone seems to have something to say about it. Everyone knows the songs and hears the same at every club this summer. *Let's Dance* is on constant rotation, and always gets everyone going.

The men watching think briefly of what they hope will happen later, while the dancers think of what they express now in every twist and turn, in every drive forward and spin back to where they began. The one sees it while the other feels it.

"I need to get something to drink." Heading off the floor and down the few steps. On the other side of the banister there is a table with soft drinks, bottles of wine, beer, and cups. Popping the can open, taking a big gulp, then handing it to Hazel.

"Did you talk to Karl today?" Breathless, she topples the mood and anchors it to the earth. Disappointing to have to adapt from far away, but it doesn't matter. It's always possible to come back down from the heights, the important thing is knowing how to get there.

(For a flicker, he's standing in the office while I'm changing, asking innocently why I brought different clothes. Didn't give an explanation, since none would suffice, only smiled, dropped my top to entice, and he showed his highest virtue smiling back and saying he didn't need to know, only wanted to reveal the difference and that he saw it there and then.

Clever dog. Good boy.)

"Yes." Needing some time to adjust to the change.

"Well, did he say anything?" After so much worry back and forth, she has a right to know.

"What do you expect? He doesn't think it's suitable. He said the same thing he always says. Then he lectures me for not listening. Says I have too many illusions, lack discipline."

—Why the distance between where I am and what I want to say?

"You need to get somebody else." This is the refrain.

"Who? Who can I get? Without him, there's no one else." Like a duet, or a well-choreographed step: one and two and three and four.

"Think of a different take, a different spin."

—Of course, why didn't I think of that?

"Oh, just come up with it. If I haven't already, how can I?" Pleading with her, but she knows. It's a form of encouragement. She thinks courage is what's needed.

"Take a feminist spin. Same material, change the emphasis. People do it all the time. Get one of them to direct it."

—Do I dare introduce them to Irigaray? They'd duck and cover. She's the one, not only the attacks on Joy, but the dismissal of any authority to dictate it. Yes, but...

"Feminists and hedonism aren't well suited." Unable to admit it.

"You're contrarian on purpose. There are different kinds." She doesn't know, but she knows. The pulses are not that far apart. Moving together on the dance floor and now the heart rates match. Such loud chatter, why bother to repeat the same thing at higher volumes? Or is that the excuse and the reason? Feeling the resonance throughout the torso and limbs, opening the cavernous places full throat and proud.

[No gag reflex left.]

"I know you think Marta or Dr. Sarazen would go along with that... It's such a long shot. They'd want to know why Karl won't do it."

—Being contrarian, I know Sahar would do it. She'd love to, but it condemns me, no one would ever hire me.

"Sarazen will overlook it. She hates Karl. You should talk to her."

Silence after the song ends. Small gap before another begins. *Lucky Star*. Pretending it's an omen.

"Your friend sure is making an impression." She's been watching him.

"He's a good talker." Catching his eye. Mostly well-behaved, still needs a lot of training, but some things are well-set already. Contact from a distance? Check.

"Charming, in an unusual way. He told the story again."

—Mental masturbation. Leave it to a boy to think Kierkegaard wrote for him alone.

[Didn't he know fascination comes from anonymity? The desire, deeply felt, was resonance shared with everyone of a certain type with similar social conditions.]

"Again, with the book. He has others." Knowing that it's not his fault, that he's been set up for this by idle chatter and ill-conceived gossip.

"Everyone's heard a part of it, they want the details."

He must know there's talk and comes over. Taking the cup of wine out of his hand and downing it in one gulp before tossing it into the bin.

"Are you having fun?" She already knows the answer, but it's a more welcoming greeting.

"Hi Hazel." He gets it. "You look amazing." With a right, proper nod in the direction of the entire ensemble. A quick look over. Since the outfits match, the compliment extends.

"You're talking to everyone. What were you talking to Uwe about? It looked serious." She seems genuinely curious, as though she can't imagine what it could be.

"He told me he's writing about Nietzsche. I don't think he liked my questions though." His sentence structure slips in and out. Sometimes he sounds almost native and then he'll say something that totally misses it and makes him seem alien. Hard not to smile.

"What did you ask him?" She smiles too, trying not to let him know.

"Whether it isn't sneaky to write about Nietzsche. Cheating." Giggling, but he thinks it's the content.

"Oh goodness. No wonder he looked that serious. You cornered him." Both looking over, but anyone would have known it was bound to happen.

—He thinks disciplines are performative. He's an idiot savant among accountants and actuaries.

"He knows Nietzsche backwards and forwards but the question of whether he should hasn't come up."

—Irigaray says something about citation, doesn't she? In a note. Yes. This wine-soaked brain remembers a thing or two when it counts.

"What did you say?" She touches his arm and avoids looking over this way, making it clear where she stands. The head shakes in a way that doesn't quite fit the context.

[If she looked over, she'd see something she doesn't want to see.]

—No Hazel, you will not be joining us. Definitely not. Probably. Don't make me hurt you.

"Nietzsche is so quotable. Writing about him is bound to include some of his writing. People will think it sounds wonderful, that the writing was fantastic. It won't be Uwe's work they're praising, it'll be Nietzsche's. It's cheating." Laughter all around, and another touch, slightly higher up this time. Now, she does look over and receives her proper scolding. With eyes that turn gentle at the end.

"Oh, I bet he loved that. I see Frederika. I have to ask her something. I'll be back." She ducks out as punishment for the rejection. He doesn't see it.

—They live in a completely different world.

"I heard you were telling the book story again." Stepping closer and lightly brushing up against his chest, hips, and legs. "Story book?" With a question mark. Makes him smile.

"It's not my fault. They already knew about it and wanted to hear the details." He bends down and lets his mouth brush close, his lips are soft when touching below the right eye and brushing over the cheek and nose.

"And you had to oblige." A step closer, not quite, a half step. With the swaying that comes from standing in music, there is a constant play back and forth. No flesh, only clothing, but the contact ripples, and in his throat the deep swallows show where his mind goes.

"I was trying to be likeable." The motion dictates his hand come to rest somewhere, and the receiving hip yields.

"Didn't anything else happen? Where were we?" Slight shaking of the head and sly grin. It's as if that part of time is a dialogue continuing from one place to the next, holding everything close.

(His hand and the moving car, his chest and the bumps from the street, that linked movement propelling everything forward.)

"That's where we were. It's exactly the place." Loud, but close. Barely a whisper, but everything feels that way in the hot sound around the dark room. Lips coming close, but no kiss.

"Not possible. Right off the boat. In Denmark." Eyes blinking, closing, he must be feeling the pressure from inside its denim wrap. The swell presses high upon the belly thinly bound in light fabric.

"Nothing happened in Denmark." Too close.

"Nothing? Not one thing." Tilting the head, arms reaching up and draping over his shoulders and neck to leave the hands hanging loosely together behind his head. It is a dance move with words.

"I decided not to stay overnight in Copenhagen." Slowing way down. The story isn't about anything, it's purely demonstrative, sounds and looks. He might as well be humming. "I heard some things along the way about the hostel." It's slow circling. "I didn't think it would be safe." Some words barely bleat out loud, hardly flip the lips, send no air over accommodating surfaces. "I stayed in Roskilde, Gilleleje."

"No time in Copenhagen." As if offering a sip of water.

"I went but didn't spend the night." Gulps that drive his throat leave their slight traces along the forehead at an angle. It's as if there is a game to stand as close as possible without letting oneself come flush. "First time, I came back to Roskilde. There were many trains." Head leaning into his lips this time, letting them finish the word there. Hands almost finding each

other. "After the second day, I went on to the coast. Walked around.
Didn't see much. Tivoli." But blown softly as if the v were an f. Or in the
middle of it.

"Is that where you began reading the book, the one you lost?" His index
finger finds a patch of skin on the belly and flutters up and down to greet it
as though it were afterward, as if the curtain were closing.

"That was the whole point." Upon the pillow.

"It's part of the story."

—Is it ours now? Or still only you and him?

"It is, but chaste." Not in writing but standing nearby, the story becomes
sexiest when he declares it without. Such a ranger, a fool for the details,
doesn't appear to know anything but sometimes surprises.

"What is it with you and Kierkegaard? Didn't you meet any girls?"
Cutting right to the chase. Standing back to do it. Sliding arms back to gauge
the distance.

"Not that I remember. Don't remember talking to any. Or seeing any,
come to think of it." His memory complies with the movements. He sways
and speaks, appreciating his preference for couples on the floor.
Sometimes they pull the right way.

"But Denmark is known for..." Trailing off on purpose and turning to
make the grin more devious.

"It could've had something to do with the World Cup. I remember a
young man proudly walking down the street wearing a track suit that looked
like a Danish flag." He steps back and the spell is marginally broken.
Always sports.

—What is it with the fucking balls?

"The women were hiding." Shaking the head in disbelief.

Hazel returns with Frederika to prove it is for a reason and there is
nothing hidden beneath it. Breaking the mood with a half-pirouette to stand
facing them with back to him and leaning only slightly as if to say there is
intimacy here, but it's open to review. Tipping toward the right hip, shifting
weight, and letting a head bob say the rest: a pretty evening moment. They
smile knowingly: yes, we are interrupting, there'll be time enough for that,
and your public display will be better if we remind you that it is indeed
public.

"You're the American who bought the book," Frederika says with
widening eyes in the room's darkness.

Laughter. Hazel looks this way and hands the can of soda back. After
taking another sip, letting her lead the way off and away from him now
exposed to Frederika's salacious interest. It's her turn, she deserves a spot
on the card. Reaching out for Hazel's hand and trotting back up the stairs
to the entryway, escorted by Roxy Music's haunting rhythm.

He straightens out his overshirt and helps it blouse out to conceal the evidence.

"Tell me ███████ *. More* ███████ *."*

"You should invite him to stay with you." Not yet fully launching, she leans in to make the obligatory compliment. Much better than you two look amazing together, but that's what she's thinking.

"Make him my August vacation."

—You're always saying we should travel together. Excited. Eyes wide open. Is that what you want?

"Absolutely. He makes you happy. Everyone likes him. A puppy. What's wrong with having some fun? Martin certainly thinks it's the right way to spend the summer." Subtle dig. Don't need reminding.

"This doesn't have anything to do with him." Don't fuck with this song, don't pollute it with that bitter nonsense.

—Too much scrutiny, can't I have one day without that nightmare?

"You need this. Invite him. The wise older woman. It's your duty." Enough of that. Grabbing her and pulling her close to brave the forbidden dance. She leans in and laughs. It is the night talking itself out through her, tapping into that moment where anything can happen, where the rules break down and everything slides off the edge.

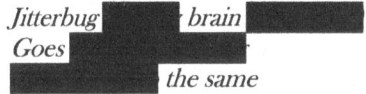

Jitterbug ███ *brain* ██████

Goes ██████████

███████ *the same*

4.12.4.Greta.19.86.9.22 [ref(..84.5-9)]

("...love is stronger than death." [Garcia Lorca])

Everything's already in the car when he shows up, walking up the street, casual and apologetic. No time for explanations and he's ready to go. The car is in front of the building, but not in a proper parking spot. He gets into the passenger seat, holding a plastic shopping bag that he sets on the floor in front of him. Pulling out and making way up to the corner and down the road toward the 73. There is a petrol stop near the transit station. No one says anything. They pump the gas in a flurry of motion. Waiting quietly in the car, then paying the attendant. The Monday morning traffic is thick, and it feels late. Heading south out of town toward the 6 which goes west to the 7 heading into Austria.

"I was worried you wouldn't make it," still stiff and nervous.

—Should I ask where you've been?

"I was too. For some reason, there was almost no traffic between München and here." He's calm, everything according to the plan.

(After she called, he said he needed to go somewhere and take care of
some things, that he'd be back in time and, as far as he was concerned,
that's exactly what happened. There's nothing to explain. Eva said to cut
him loose, but she talks tougher when she's not looking at him.)

"Is that where you were, München?"

—He didn't give any reason to expect him back yesterday. Assumed that
back in time to leave meant Sunday night, but he never... Why didn't you
call?

"My friend left me there this morning. Took forever to get a ride, but
when I finally did, they took me the whole way. A gnarly bunch of punks
heading up to Berlin, they were drinking."

—Your friend? What friend? I know everyone you know in Nürnberg,
don't I? Who do you know who can pick you up in München and take you
somewhere for a week? Do you have any money?

"This early in the morning? It's lucky you made it." Using an even tone
to appear more relaxed. Mind firing as though jealousy powers every
neuron.

—What right do I have? Why does he trigger these cravings?

"I don't think it was early for them. The girl, she wasn't drinking, she
was driving."

—Obviously, he's trying to change the subject, but I can't help it.

"There was a girl?"

"Yeah, and two guys. Both had mohawks. They couldn't figure out why
in the hell I wanted to go to Nürnberg. Wanted me to come with them. I
gave them cigarettes: somehow, I ended up with a pack. They were tickled.
I pretended to stub one out on my hand. The guy in back was impressed.
I think that's why they wanted me to join."

"Join?"

—It's as if he's intentionally revealing this information to distract me
from the main point. What the hell were you doing in München or
wherever you went with this friend of yours and why do I care?

"To Berlin. To go with them." Never any more information than is
necessary to get past the single question. He repositions the bag on the floor
so that he can stretch his legs. The turnoff to the 6 gives the appearance of
a road for long hauls. It's time to get comfortable.

—Steer it back without being a psycho. It's totally unreasonable to think
he should be loyal. Who is he to me? A stranger, only a couple of weeks
and most of it hiding behind... ...everything.

"I guess you have to learn how to make friends quickly if you're
traveling by yourself."

—Because he came here to talk to me, and because we agreed to get to
know each other better, to try and become more comfortable, none of that
means...

"That's true. What have you been doing this week?"

—He was out there for months before he showed up here.

"Nothing. I went into work for a few hours."

—Who knows what he was in the middle of. Loose ends. She sounded...

"Did you? How did it go? Was it hard?"

—And now he's here and focused on this. Whatever this is.

"Impossible. Let's not talk about it."

—If I tell you I quit my job, that'll create a whole thing and you'll have completely succeeded in derailing everything. Not going to happen.

"No problem. Should I find some music?"

—This is my car, I'm driving, I'm paying for the petrol, I'll pay for everything.

"Well, what about what I was saying? About making friends. Did you learn that here or were you always that way?" Awkwardly put, he is suspicious, raises an eyebrow as he looks over. The tone of his voice doesn't change, and he goes on the same as before. Nothing unusual, but the tension in his brow contradicts that tone.

"Oh, I'm learning that here. Travelling persona. Was never that way before."

—Is it possible he's aware of the endgame and toying with me?

"But you became good friends with my sister. That couldn't have been easy. How did it happen?"

—I'm not going to let go. What kind of man are you? Why didn't you come right away? You needed a vacation?

"Well, I told you how we met. After that, I think the next time I saw her was a few days later. There was a guy named Pedro who took care of the animals. He'd cut grass and other stuff and feed them. Walk the horses if there wasn't anyone else around to do it."

—This is my fault. I helped him do this.

"He was a friend of yours?" His face relaxes.

—He knows I'm hooked. He won, smug.

"Not at all." His whole demeanor changes, it's a story-telling mode.

"He wasn't educated?"

"He wasn't literate. He was a nice man, but simple." Deliberate pause. "Lots of simple people lived in that village." He rubs his chin considering how far to go. "Juan and Maria, they took care of the farm, the buildings and the grounds. Then there was Octavio. He was in charge of the coffee crop and production. Lived with his family on a building back tucked away on the property." Settles deeper into the seat. "They knew their business, but they were *simple* people. Their lives, everything. There was a strong line between us."

"You're not simple people?"

—They'd call it the Greta. Only the setup, nothing challenging, asking for clarification.

[Spun into a prop. A drain sucking everything into it.]

"No, we are. It's hard to explain. Sencillo. That's the word. I don't know how to translate it. Not simple as in easy. More like down to earth. People from the city, people who live modern lives, they aren't simple, not the way they mean it. But the others, the way they live, the pleasures, the worries, their lives, I don't know. Simple. They said it all the time."

—Simple. Not in the least simple.

"Okay. Back to Pedro. Did he know my sister?"

—I'm helping him write it down. The lines, the utility in moving things forward. I've become a gimmick.

"No, but one evening, he came round to the restaurant where we were sitting after supper, and he told us that he couldn't find his brother. He wasn't always good, enjoyed the Bazooka." He briefly switches into a Spanish sounding accent.

"Bazooka?" Genuine curiosity.

"These fucked up cigarettes some people would smoke. They had coca paste in them. It's what they use to make cocaine. And kerosene."

"Lighter fluid?" His tempo is perfect. He pauses on the right word every time. They're breadcrumbs.

"That was the story anyway. I never tried it. I don't know. That's what the people said. It could've been to scare us."

Nodding back at him. It's impossible to escape. The absence of music is hidden. The absence of explanations is hidden. The yearning leaps to the front and occupies the space there. It's a lure. Many tangles and they weave together pleasantly, the suspense palpable.

"Anyway, he says he doesn't know where his brother is, and he got paid that day for some work he did recently so he thinks there may be trouble."

"It was a village. He must've known where to look for him, didn't he?"

"I think he was afraid to go to the places where he could be, or he was afraid of what he'd find there if he did. He asked for help. We didn't question his motives or anything, we helped."

—Pedro must've known, deep down, what his brother was up to. He had to.

"How? How could you help?" Tone rises. Some stress comes out, but he brings it back to center.

"We had that jeep. Drove him up to the hospital to see if he was there. He could've been hurt working or got in a fight. Who knows? The hospital is always a good place to start... The doctor hadn't seen him, the nurses either. No one saw him. She came by, your sister, must've heard the jeep. That'd be unusual for that time of night. We asked about Pedro's brother."

"Did she know him?"

"She knew of him. Through his girlfriend. She knew he wasn't a nice guy. Had some ideas about where to find him. Those were the places Pedro didn't want to go by himself. We didn't want to go there by ourselves either. She said she'd come with."

—Of course she did.

"She knew where these places were? What kind of places?"

"Places where you could buy Bazooka. And girls."

"And she knew about them?"

"Definitely. She knew a lot of the girls that worked there. That's what she said while we were driving back down to the village." He seems to have more to say but comes to an abrupt halt thinking better of it. Registering the point but needing to set it aside to stay on track.

"What did you think of her? I mean, that must've been strange. What did you think?"

"She was obviously in charge and knowledgeable, we didn't think anything of it other than that. She was the person who knew everything that was going on. Our friends. The mayor, the grocer, the landowners, they thought they knew, but she *really* knew. That's what I thought, at least, that she did know what was going on, and that she was fearless. None of us wanted to go inside when we pulled up. Pedro was afraid to go in. We were afraid."

—That's the real reason they didn't want to know her. Afraid she'd ruin everything, their whole cushy setup, everything that screws up the lives of those simple folk.

"And my sister?"

"She wouldn't have gone in alone, I don't think, but she thought the three of us would be fine. They wouldn't dare do anything, they knew what would happen if there was trouble with the two of us. The men running the Zapato farm, the Guardia, they'd look the other way if it was her, but American men working for an owner, that wouldn't be tolerated."

"The three of you went in?" A bit too harsh, he buckles, put off by the judgment in the tone. The story makes him out to be a sympathetic character, but the listener isn't buying it and that awareness is written across his face. Whether it's true or not, he worries.

"Yep. And he was there. It wasn't good. But no one gave us any trouble, not even Pedro's brother. He was embarrassed and nervous, deeply concerned that we were looking for him, that he caused us trouble. We escorted him out and took him and Pedro back to their house. They lived with their older parents. She was extremely confident. Never blinked."

"Is that how you became friends?"

—Or, how you fell in love with her.

"That had an impact. We drove her back up to the hospital and sat in the room next to where she slept. She gave us some aguardiente. It's liquor. From sugar cane and anis. Talked a long time. About the things we saw that night, what she saw at work. With the women and the children mostly."

"It wasn't that you were charming and won her over like you did with those punks, is that it?" He laughs. Not put off by the association, but he isn't going to let it distract him either. He stays steady.

"That kind of stuff would never work with her. What she liked, what gave her a good first impression, was that Pedro was willing to ask us for help. He must've thought we were the kind of people that he could ask without bad consequences. Not everyone was that way. They would have fired him after finding out he had a brother like that. He would have known and never asked. He knew we weren't that way. She saw that, I suppose."

Nodding.

"And then, she was glad that we were the type of people that would help. Go with him. Take him to the hospital and go into that place to try and find his brother. She was impressed. She didn't say that, but I got the sense. I don't think she usually drank with people that late, she wasn't much for socializing, or wasn't used to it. Anyway, it created something between us. The three of us."

(It had to be something like that. That's a good beginning, the kind that got you close to her, but there must've been more. I'm sure he had a good reason for going off to München. Same as with Pedro. Something his friend couldn't do alone, something unpleasant that needed doing, and he was willing to help. And what business is it of mine? He's loyal, protecting them. Her. It was a woman that called, a German woman. There's time. It'll come out in the end. We'll see. Patience, but be persistent. Persevere.)

Signs for the A7 and he is quiet now, leaning over the plastic bag and pulling a small loaf of bread from it. He tears off a piece and lays some cheese down after using a small utility knife to cut a slice from a wrapped brick. He reaches over to hand off the morsel and then puts a napkin on the leg careful not to touch it. Smiling. Telling the story helped with something, made him more comfortable, more at ease.

—Simple food.

It tastes good and he's preparing another for himself. While looking around at the scenery, he nods in rhythm to music that no one else can hear. Vineyards and corn fields everywhere, it's green at this time of year though the harvest is largely done.

5.12

this year's harvest

5.12.1.Elisabet.19.86.5.9

They're collecting the garbage and getting everyone to return their seats to the upright position. The fasten-seat-belt sign comes on. There is some gum, offering him a piece too.

"Did you learn anything?" The space isn't broken. He watches the movements with quiet persistence, as though now bound together by the journey. No more ice.

"That infatuation doesn't last. It couldn't only be in my head."

—That touching matters.

"And that's why you broke your next girlfriend's heart?"

"I think I was more real with her, but *she* was too much in *her* head."

—I'm sure they both were, sweetheart. You must get used to that. It's an acquired taste.

"More real? You mean, it turned physical right away." Leaning back and tilting the neck. Mirroring each other. The commotion in the cabin, landing is stressful. It helps.

"Yes that, but not only that. She was a friend of my roommates. They went to high school together. She was worried I heard the rumors from back then."

"Did you?"

—It's not only in the head, chatter...

"Not at first, no details. My roommate didn't say much about her, but when she started acting weird."

"Weird, what does that mean?"

"She had something going on that I wasn't experiencing. Something she thought was happening that I couldn't see."

"Did you ever figure it out?"

—What did you see? Odd demands, possessive, always worried you'd leave her? Is that what made her weird?

"Something about intelligence, that was one thing. She thought our conversations had to be highly cerebral, once that got into her head, she couldn't let it go."

—She misjudged you.

"That's how she is, did you think of that?"

"Sure, but... I mean, it felt forced," he says.

"Okay, what was the other thing?"

"She thought I saw her as... uh... ...loose, easy. That's what the rumors from high school were about, that's what she was worried about."

—Did you ask her about her... ...family? Torn between taking care of... ...and terrified you'd judge her... ...don't envy them that.

"You slept together right away."

—The audience, a twenty-two-year-old manboy, the singer, a twenty-two-year-old womangirl.

"There was a party. She came with someone. My roommate said they could use the phone. While her friend was making a call, she talked to me. I was reading Plato. Sartre's *Being and Nothingness* was on the table. From another class. She wanted to know about it. Someone came to pick her friend up to go to another party, but she stayed."

"You spent that first night together."

"The attraction was strong," he says shrugging.

—Weird but attractive.

"Looking back. She was flattering me a lot, but I didn't catch on, not at the time. I thought it was a genuine spark, you know? But it was deliberate. There was a whole big thing going on... I was oblivious... ...it was about what kind of person she was..."

"Only her? Why? She was the *weird* one? But you were the one who couldn't see, right? You were the one..."

"I was trying to be more aware of things, pay attention, but she was... ...not fake... ...but... ...calculated. I mean, there's no accidental touching, right?" He mulls it over, struggling with something. He can see her, the way she talked to him, the signs, he's visualizing it.

[Talking or a whole lot of ego-stroking. We did that without wondering whether we should, we thought we had to. The most important thing in the world was that he liked you. Where was she sitting, how close, what was she doing? Had a bag of tricks, go to. Touching his arm, his leg. The looks, the hair. Turning toward him, constant contact, her shin, his thigh. What? What was it?]

"It was in the morning, I guess," he goes on. "Normal night after stuff, I thought, but later it seemed different, as though she should have let things develop more first. Not weird, but regrets, worried. Nervous about how I was going to react. She was saying fake pseudo-intellectual stuff, something about de Beauvoir and Sartre. It was as if nothing ever happened."

"Which is how you were with Maya."

—You had no idea what was going on, did you?

"Nothing happened with Maya. Not for a long time, but when it did, yes, it was kind of the same. Nothing to do with reputation though."

"Nothing? But you wanted Maya to think you were this sensitive and respectful guy. You wanted to think of yourself that way, isn't that reputation?"

"No, that was... Oh, I see what you mean..."

(Caught between two places, seeing more than the last time, and trying to reconstruct it: there was something he was supposed to see but didn't. Thought he learned something, but... This had to end. My life. Can't be a slave to persuading them to like you.)

"In high school, something happened once. These guys were talking about this girl. I didn't know her, knew who she was, but they said something foul about her and I repeated it to someone at school, someone I thought was my friend who wanted to know what I did last weekend. I didn't think I was spreading a rumor."

"But you did." He goes back in time to find the root of his error.

"I did. And I heard how upset she was. I called her."

"You called her?"

—Not easy. You may have been the weird one after all.

"Yes, when I heard how upset she was. I honestly didn't mean to... I was being stupid. Didn't know what to say, wanted to tell her how sorry I was."

"What did she say?"

"She was mad. Couldn't understand why I would talk about someone I never met. She wanted details. What I said, why I said it. I told her about the two guys. She thought they were her friends. Said it was true what they were saying. She did *say* those things, but she was joking. They were joking around, and she was kidding. Everyone was. Making things up because they sounded funny."

"They talked about it as if it wasn't kidding around."

"They talked about it as if it happened. These were things she did with them."

"Then what happened?"

"Those two guys were pretty pissed off, but I didn't care, I told the one guy that he shouldn't have been talking that way if he didn't want to deal with the consequences. They stopped talking to me. Their friends stopped talking to me. She stopped talking to them. Her friends stopped talking to them. For a while, it didn't last long, they were buddies again a few weeks later. None of them ever talked to me again."

"That's awful."

"No, they were horrible. Spending time with them brought me down and I was better off. I had a job after school and spent most of my time with the people at work. They were older, different."

He nods and looks calm, knows there are differences, that things change, but is still in reconstructive mode, trying to feel what he felt then. He's trying to see her the way she was then.

"If Chloe told me what she went through, if she was open with me, things would've turned out better."

"Are you saying it's her fault?"

—Apply pressure to see if he breaks.

"And mine. It was the same with Maya. Like you said. I thought I learned something, but didn't. It was the same thing over again. I wasn't paying attention. I didn't see her."

"What same thing? What was it?"

—Prove it.

"I thought it was about sex. With Maya, that's what I thought, that she wanted to be physical, she wanted to be close and I was too caught up in my head to go there. We weren't open with each other and never worked it out. If I got physical with Chloe right away, that problem would be solved."

"I see."

—Blamed him for not knowing, assuming too much.

"But it wasn't about sex, it was about being open, talking about what's going on, what you want, what you're worried about. It's connected."

"Being open can change how the other person sees you."

"That's what's so terrifying. It's such a risk. I was afraid to show Maya what I wanted, and I think Chloe was afraid of the same thing."

"Have you learned the right lesson now? Is that what you think? The wise old man."

He laughs. A good laugh, as if he can take a tap, a slap to show him what's ridiculous and how far he still needs to go.

"I don't know. I'm not sure I'd have put it together." He looks down and away for the first time in a while. He's holding onto something, practicing what he's learned but not completely able to give in to it.

"Seems like good advice. I'm trying to understand whether it applies to me. Somehow, I don't think my label will let down their guard and bond with me when I open up to them. They'd use it against me, figure out how to turn it around and twist it up. Get the lawyers. Openness doesn't always get you what you want, sometimes it's evidence against you."

—It is about reputation though. About what kind of audience, who is out there thinking of me and what they're thinking. Not everyone has to like you.

(The world-wide personality, America and Japan after conquering Europe and South America. Mexico eventually set right. People would sacrifice everything for that, that's what they're always saying. Find those people then. It felt superficial. Fluff. It's not music they're thinking about, it's image and swagger, juvenile fantasies, but I wanted to be a grown up.)

"Don't you have people on your side? An agent or something. Can't you tell them?" he asks.

"Percentage. Too much money. It gets in the way of everything, makes it hard to rely on people, be open with them."

"High school sticks with you," he's pouting and feigns doom.

"Adolescence certainly does. I hope I can rely on your promise."

—Speaking of evidence.

(Doubts about something that hadn't happened yet were a good way to get everyone to think you're vain. The exact opposite of what the image demanded. Oh, we're overwhelmed by the positive response, never in my wildest dreams... That had to be the story, if it wasn't, you're *weird*.)

"If I'm honest," he says. "I didn't know who you were. The woman at the gate, while she was checking me in, you know, I was dealing with... ...she told me I'd be sitting next to you, explained who you are. I knew about Paisley, of course, but didn't know you or..."

The wheels are down, and the plane is flying close to the ground. It's the worst moment of the landing. The machine won't hold, it can't, not possible, there is no way to pull this off. It makes him more tense, more poignant and dramatic. There is some genuine concern that this will cause friction, that the lovely airborne commitments will crash into the earth and be blown to bits. Reaching out a hand and lightly resting it on his forearm. Friendly, but not overly, not motherly. Tenderness, but it's too much for him. He can't navigate the nuances. It's too complicated and there's more than enough of his own feeling to get in the way. His eyes go wide, dilating. Whatever he's learned, it hasn't covered all the bases.

"You're not a fan." He can't process anything against the grinding background.

—I know what I want and what I don't want. I am willing to say the one and the other, no weirdness here.

(Not simple, not being liked didn't matter, it's the risk, concrete and real, like a brick. Was this for real? Were you serious? Was that an audience that scoffed at the pop star? Did dedication and devotion matter? Resentment? Did they know what it took to make that change? How much resistance? How hard it was? Did they care?)

—They'll be done with me soon enough.

"It's not..." He can't process anything against the grinding background. The focus group in 1B is at least willing to give it a listen. The hand resonates throughout the entire body.

"It's okay. In America, they don't know us yet, this is our first tour, that's why I'm... That's what I'm worried about..."

—Not failure, success. A lot of practice with failure, little with success.

"It isn't what you want," he says.

[Want was an abstraction, not a thing. There were fears and hopes, worries and concerns, logistical questions and ridiculous fantasies. Desire wasn't one thing, a simple ray or trajectory, it's a set of things. Struggle. All the things. Together.]

—It isn't an it. No wanting to speak of.

[I saw my children's faces. I knew they were real, but what was their mama? Who was she? What would she be teaching them?]

"They'll dump me if they find out."

—That'd be much easier.

[That explained these loose lips and that sudden yearning to pull him close and have him walk with me and talk with me until I'm calm, until the air was settled, and everything was as it should be.]

(With the Proustian. This was what we needed. Context, but more. Who we are. Were. Down deep, for real. Bricks and mortar, Dad used to say. No one had the world for their mirror. Not the whole world. It'd be too terrifying. If they liked you, there must be something wrong with you, something you were hiding, something you were too terrified to reveal.)

"And that would be for the best," he's trying to encourage. "You don't want to be a fraud. If they find out who you are and want to part company, that's for the best even if you can't see it right away. A broken heart will purify you."

His eyes are too intense, have to look away. Swinging the knees and hips back forward leaving the hand in place. The wheels are firm, and the reverse thrust begins. No longer a plane, a ground conveyance heading toward the gate.

—You don't want to be a fraud.

Looking back and smiling, his eyes relieved in return, the hand slips from his forearm down to his hand and then departs.

—For the best.

5.12.2. Seannafair.20.15.5.7 [ref(19.86.5.15-20)]

"A butcher is shooing a dog from his premises when he notices a £10 note in its mouth."

—Gandy talks too loud. The whole table sure, but why does everyone in the pub need to hear it?

"The dog sits and drops the money on the floor.

"Picking the money up, he sees the words '4 lamb cutlets please' scribbled on it.

"Intrigued, he puts the cutlets in a bag and gives them to the dog."

(I remember the sessions. Clear as day. There must've been three or four. Rian and Mike were living in that house with those other students. We went round. There was a keyboard, and we took it to the cellar to get clear of everyone. Rian with a guitar. We were working up *My Life*. I was humming the words, the way they seemed to come. He found something there and took it. Went off for a while. Some of it we tossed, but there was that bit of a spine there. Mike pointed it out, or Finn, but we got it. Mostly it was voice. We wanted to howl. We wanted to flex. As if a banshee were talking to you. That way I had. How I miss it. Where the high and the low would come side by side, a chord from the throat that no other instrument could match. Too much power. When something comes effortless and then it goes, you have no idea how to get it back. You had it, and now you don't.)

Everyone is packed in tight, seven at a four with drinks all around.

Someone must've gestured over to Mary. She brings another round and a few pints. She's smiling warmly at the lot of them, but looks carefully over, checking up. Nothing to see, no one's home.

"The dog takes the bag and leaves.

"The butcher locks up the shop and follows."

(*In Your Head* was that way too, wasn't it? But now, we were screaming. They were angry on that one. The way they came, the way they talked up the torment, from the villages, across the dales, everywhere. Dairy Maid. Dairy. The boys were sods on that. The sound wasn't with me, but the scream was, as if you're clearing everything out, growling almost, making room for new things. That's what I felt, trying to make room, but not on the landing, or inside the front door. *In Your Head.* Everything was crowded. There wasn't anywhere to go with it. But what? What was crouching in? Was it crawling? Why wouldn't it listen to me?)

"The dog walks to a bus stop and checks the timetable.

"When a bus arrives, it looks at the number and boards it.

"Dumbstruck, the butcher gets on the bus."

(Then *Return for Me.* Those three. They weren't the only ones, but I knew they were the most magical. Like spells. But not the same. Totally different. *Return for Me. My Life. In Your Head.* What was behind it? What was I telling myself? And why would I block him out? I still can't... Where was he that whole week? He wasn't with us, was he? He didn't come round their house. They said as much. Not every time. We've always known. Where the hell was he?)

"After a few miles, the dog stands on its hind legs to push the 'stop' bell.

"Dog and butcher exit the bus."

(*Return for Me* came gently. Such a contrast to the others. It was different. How could those same thoughts come through me in one day, one night, one single moment? Something must've kicked up, something must've brought them on, and I know what the boys and I were doing wasn't exactly from that same night, but it was too, as if the melodies were already there. Nothing seemed foreign, alien, none of it. It was as if I brought them with me, and the boys found them there, alongside the lyrics, as though they were written in that same notebook, sketched there, between the lines, in some devilish code.)

"The dog walks to a house and presses the doorbell.

"There is no answer."

(Back at my place, only darkness. But why? Odd. Where did it go? A naked fella making me eggs. Goddamnit, there was a naked fella cooking eggs. The stove. I worried it was too hot, that he'd burn himself. You shouldn't... Too close... It shouldn't... Doesn't fit.)

"It tries again.

"And again."

(It was lovely. Not ugly, it was lovely. Why would I... What possible reason would there be... The whole week. I would come back knackered, I couldn't think straight, and he'd do something. Cook or rub my forehead, my shoulders. He was taking care of me, had a key. He was coming and going, but he knew when to be there for when I got back. Sitting quietly, reading that fat yellow book with the small letters on the pages, those tiny margins. Doesn't that hurt your eyes? I asked him that. What did he say? Something about it being too late? Won't that ruin your eyes? Too late.)

"Jesus Jenni, you look absolutely fucking riveted. Surely, you've heard this one before." Nodding and half smiling.

—What's he on about then?

Trying to be a part of it, blending in. A few of them look over. They don't see anything worth commenting on. Looking back. Some sip their drinks, some look back at Gandy who never looked up.

"Eventually a man opens the door and shouts at the dog."

(I don't remember those times much, but I'm pretty sure there was twice, at least twice, and I didn't like it one bit. Wasn't looking forward to that part, would've been happy to keep to the kiss and let that be that, but it was lovely, wasn't it? In the end. I thought that first time you were supposed to have it off, as though it wasn't real if he didn't, or someone didn't. Someone had to. That's what made it what it was, right? But he said no, didn't have to be that way, it could be anything we wanted, it could be a pleasant moment, us together, that's it, a cuddle, but closer up and without anything left back. It didn't have to be that. You can leave whatever you want on, you don't have to do anything if you don't want to, and you can change your mind, you can want something different, you can say whatever you want to say and expect it to happen. He said we had to listen to each other, he said we had to tell each other what was happening, that was the only thing we had to do. He didn't want any part of it to be bad. He didn't want anything to hurt or become something to regret later.)

"The butcher runs up and says, 'What are you doing? This dog's a genius!'

"'Genius, my ass.'"

(I remember crying, sobbing, harder than I could ever recall. What was it? He was there, holding me. My nose was running, and it got on him.

Mortified. It was something about the songs, one of them. Which one? About my family, my dear mam, that song brought out everything. Anger, love too. How could that be? We expected everything from them. They should've kept us safe, but it wasn't always their fault. He said something about that, and then I remembered that boy, that first boy. He took what he wanted. Ma dropped me there, didn't she? She took me to that place, told me it'd be good to get out and be with people. How could she?)

"It's... I can't stop thinking about it, that whole week. I didn't remember. The boys and I were arranging songs." Terry looks over, he's forgotten his question, but then nods as if it's come back to him.

—Can anyone hear that? Is Terry listening?

"'This is the second time in a week he's forgotten his key.'"

The table erupts in laughter, Mary is smiling over there at the bar. She could hear the whole thing. Everyone. The folks by the window, the two blokes on the other side of them, they're nodding and smiling.

—I don't think I've ever seen that one before. She sure finds it funny. Story I heard when I was a girl. Nope, not familiar. Is that it? Buying drinks for the whole town now? They take what they want.

"Good one. I've got another," she says.

—Haven't you heard them already?

"While driving along the M11 a police officer sees a small hatchback ahead on the inside lane driving at cycling pace."

(I told him about it, about that boy and how he didn't care, and then about his father... I thought he should get in trouble, thought his parents should know... ...but where do you think he learned it? Where was it coming from? How stupid could I be? My mother dropped me there. Mothers were in on it, his father was the same. They're all the same.)

"That was in the evening, but the days, and the nights, he stayed with me. Hadn't remembered that." A whisper that no one hears.

"He turns on his lights and pulls the car over."

"As he walks to the vehicle, he notices there are five old ladies in the car."

(Well, not all. Was there something before that? Something that brought it on? What happened that first night? I didn't get my kiss. He tucked me in. Was that it? Is that how it started?)

"Did he mean something to you?" Terry's voice from out of the din of the others.

"The driver lowers her window and says, 'I don't understand, I was driving at the speed limit.'

"'Ma'am,' the officer replies, 'you weren't speeding but driving slower than the speed limit can also be dangerous.'"

(And then it changed around, different night. *Return for Me*, that was the last one. *Family* was earlier. Boys made that one better, we knew we had chemistry with that. We must've talked it through or something. What happened? Holding on and getting warm. Never before. Any of that. Didn't know desire, I don't think. Never got the chance, but then, lying there, still, and quiet. Something was going through me but it was mixed up. A different kiss. Something else too. He was breathing me. I was his air now, and his nourishment. I was everything then, that moment, and it was as if there were curtains hanging everywhere. Flowing. Blousing out and being sucked back to the window, but no windows, not real ones. Drapes, fabric, and that movement, too much air coming at once. My chest was full, I had to stop myself from bellowing. What would the neighbors think? Someone must be having it off with a cat up there.)

Finishing the dregs from the tumbler will cause her to bring another. This is the meter, the gauge swivels here.

"There are a million different things that I'm not. He said that. I understand what he means.... Not then. Easy to talk to... Hard to talk to... Things I never..."

Rocking back and pulling her hands away from the glass. Can't instigate this... It can't go on...

(He wasn't afraid of anything. Looked me dead in the eye no matter what I was saying, and I was never ugly to him, not the whole time. He was looking at someone he thought was beautiful when the ugliest things came out. That's not you, he said, that's not yours, don't give it away that easily. You can only give what you choose. What people take, that's not you.)

"'Slower? No officer, we're on the M11, and I was travelling at exactly 11 miles an hour.'

"The officer smiles and explains to her that '11' is the motorway number and not the speed limit."

They're looking over, something's changed, things are about to get dry around here and there's a sudden concern in the air.

"It's getting awfully loud in here. Want to go somewhere and tell me about it?" Nodding in agreement. Terry fumbles about for something, getting his things together.

"Embarrassed, the woman apologizes profusely and thanks the officer for pointing out her error.

"'Before I let you go ma'am, I have to ask.'"

(I didn't know if I could tell anyone about it. How to begin? I'd have to talk about the church and that look. It was the same look he had when he was breathing me. His eyes, he looked up at me as though no harm could come, as if everything was right and it wasn't my fault, and it wasn't ma's fault either.)

"Yes, let's. It'll be easier to concentrate."

—Best to be agreeable.

They know what's coming. The air is changed. That one, she can't breathe.

"'Is everyone in the car okay?'

"'Your passengers seem awfully shaken, and they haven't made a sound this whole time.'

"'They'll be fine. It's that we've come from the A120.'"

The place erupts in laughter again. The group becomes something of an entertainment for the rest.

"Alright, you old rummies," Terry says. "We've heard enough. We're off. Mary, can you put it on Aine's tab? One more round, then cut 'em off. You'll have to drink on your own dime now, you geezers."

The tension goes, the fates have spoken, they knew this time would come and here it is, pressure's gone. Nothing to do now but accept the loss and move along. They huzzah in approval and the mention of a parting shot. The bow is graced, time has come.

"Will do, now you take care, Ms. Quinn. Do you need any help getting home?" Turning around, coming back, looking right at Mary, so kind.

"My friend said he'd look after my cat while I was away."

Mary pauses and straightens up before she finishes clearing space on the table. She's been hovering, but now she looks concerned.

—She thinks I've gone loopy.

Gaze swinging to catch the others thrall, to see if they want to be there or merely feel obliged.

"When I got back from a week holiday, he told me my cat was dead.

"I was furious. Sad too, but furious."

—Okay, they're with me now. They get it, it's my turn.

Mary is relieved. She knows this one, knows what's what. She steps off to get the last round.

"You're not supposed to do it that way, not all at once like that.

"First you call me and tell me the cat's on the roof.

"You tell me everyone's come by and are trying to get the cat down, but it's tricky and there's not much luck in it."

—They must know it, but there they are, listening closely, being patient. It's the cost of the drinks, I suppose.

"Then the fire brigade comes and they're looking into it, but that cat is so damn stubborn, she won't come down and she's moving farther out onto the ledge and into harm's way."

They nod, supportive, as if they know how cats can be.

"It doesn't look good.

"Then, when I come back, you tell me the cat is dead.

"I'll be ready for it.

"Prepared. It won't come as a sudden shock.

"I went out of town again later.

"No cat this time, but I asked my friend if he could look in on my gram.

"She's old and needs some looking after.

"He agrees and calls a few days later.

"He says, it's your gram, she's on the roof."

Mary's back with the tray and laying out one for the road, the one to set them free.

Turning back to the door and stepping unsteadily through it with Terry close behind and putting his hand out to steady. That pressure on the lower back attaches to an image (of his lovely hand placed there and firmly guiding me along the way). Can't help smiling, and they're still laughing as the door swings shut.

5.12.3.Natalie.19.86.8.3 [ref(..6.14)]

Make re-lease
Rake re-lease
Take re-lease
Huf... huf... huf...
Ohhh...
Ooooh...
Ah-oh...
Anoh ooola...
Ta so nomore...
Sono oh oh oh...
Ray-ge. Rrrreeee-lease...

Rolling right, to the right, leaning into the mattress and then over onto...
...looking up at the ceiling. Blowing out air, wind flips the bangs, up and away, then back. Blow again. Flip again. Hand running through it. Breathe breath, breathe.

Laughing.

"High five." More of a tap than a slap.

Laughing more. Laughing, lots of laughing. With each exhale an arched back, and then straightening at the hip. He turns sideways and puts his hand up on his temple and rests on the palm sturdied by an elbow buried nearby. Smiling, so proud of himself.

—Feeling the stud, are you? I did the work. Feel free to take the credit.

"This is how I want my whole August to be."

Hand slapping back down above the belly. Slippery sexy. Sweaty and moist indistinguishable. Cool air breezing over. Legs a-wiggling...

"Morning sex. Parties. Good food. Nighttime. Evening car rides. A perfect day."

He curls his legs as though he's staring into the fire.

"You're good at taking care of yourself."

—Threatened? Not feeling like the most important person in the room?

"Awwww, my darling. Feeling neglected? Is that what I was doing on my knees before the party?" Poking him on the chin from across the chest. Curling up sideways to mirror him.

"It's not criticism. It's nice... ...that you're that way..." His hand over to the hip, sketching the bow.

"There is so much suffering, we have a duty to enjoy when we can." Feigning seriousness. Pretending longer-think with a smile. Lips straight, he's likely to think he's being scolded.

"And that's all it is? Fleeting enjoyment. It's... Not used to it." He feels smaller, pride conflicting with a position in the backseat.

—Could be fun. The backseat. Take a note.

"That's all it is." Apologetically yours, but yours. For now.

"The words? Momentary pleasures you forget as soon as the feeling passes, is that it?" Hesitant, never daring to offend. Soft, it's only a question.

"Or remember fondly. Would that be bad?" Encouraging.

"If you can do it. I lack the mental discipline."

—Awwww, this inadequacy isn't going to get us anywhere. I'll save that for the farewell.

"Not mental, emotional."

"That's cold." Eyebrows arching, he's struggling to keep up, and leans back against the pillow wedged behind him.

"No, my darling. It's warm." Stroking his chin, the stubble, his perfect nose and mouth.

"What's the problem with your school? I heard you talk about it. Someone else said something too. Frederika."

Pulling the sheet up. Settling in and drawing its material close. Staring straight ahead, mirroring perfectly. Right there, in that same place, the dance is exquisite.

"It's the whole approach. This'll cost us. But okay."

"We don't have to..." He's willing either way. Put this aside and go there if it means not getting back before dreamier times come.

"It's fine. How you write and what you write about, it's rigid. If the method.... ...and I don't mean method, more like genre... ...but if it's established, then no problem. Learn that voice, use it. If you're trying to do anything that's off kilter, your intelligence is immediately suspect." It's gone now, but nearby.

—I can hear it growling. It's breath heavy.

"What are you trying to do?" he asks.

"At the end of this book," pointing over toward the nightstand, "she inserts a note about references. I don't know. You're going to say something about some topic, you have to prove that you're aware of everything that's ever been said about it. Total seeing. You are revealing everything, exposing everything." Pushing off the sheet and taking the pillow from behind him to curl up around it while leaving him balancing back on his hand again.

"How do you mean?" Happy to oblige.

"It's the absence of perspective. We're supposed to ignore it, everything else that happens, the senses in it, and focus on that one thing, that one central idea. Even if it isn't connected to anything, a cul-de-sac, even if it has no ground to stand on and is contradicted by everything else. That's the way they want us to talk, to see. How do you criticize authority with that? Patriarchy? You can't. That *is* patriarchy, that's exactly how it works. It seeps into everything, everywhere, because it's nowhere."

"Wait. How does...? Are you talking about the style or the content?" Confused and fully alert now.

"I... ...well, I reject that whole way of thinking about it... ...to the things themselves... ...the conversation got off on the wrong foot... ...everyone is right but saying it wrong... ...I don't know." His eyebrows arch, not letting go. "If you spend your time talking about what's wrong, then you're giving what's wrong your time, your voice. It's better to show what's right and let what's wrong wither. See differently without explaining how or why."

"And your faculty advisor, he wants you to conform?"

"Yeah. And my friends, at the party, they're saying this is a common complaint from feminists, and that I should accept that and frame it accordingly."

"But you don't want to."

"It's not that. It's that... ...it's a way to comply with a wink. Or your tongue in your cheek. With references and a thesis and supporting arguments. There are different requirements. Different norms. But still..."

—Repeats the problem. I don't want to be on anyone's side. If they repeated what I said right back to me exactly as I said it, I'd still resist.

"It's educational though, isn't it? You're not working on this stuff for the hell of it. It's not art, is it? You're educating. You have to... ...fit in."

"Arrrrrrggggggghhhhhh. Theory is blind!" The devil is here, his advocate.

—I've fucked the devil's advocate.

"Sorry. Of course, you're 100% right and they're charlatans." He is teasing. Where does he get the nerve?

"Grrrrrrrr."

Pushing the pillow out of the way and then stuffing it back up toward the headboard. Rolling farther left. Lying flat, belly down, arms crossed, head turning to the side and looking his way.

"Would you like to stay for a while?" Simple offer, no vulnerability. Yes or no, doesn't matter. Whatever you want.

"Here? With you? What did you have in mind?" Such a sweet shade of red.

"Finish your stories. A few weeks. Days. Whatever you want?"

"What do you want?" Pew pew pew, rapid fire.

"A proper fucking vacation, emphasis on the fucking." He laughs. To be clear: "That's where you come in." Dead serious, right in the eye.

He gulps. Isn't going to say anything. Soft eyes yielding. Reaching out and pulling back the crumpled sheet. He lightly strokes the back from ass to shoulders. "Time to let my mind go. I don't want to think about any of this. The administration is done. Yay! I can checkout until next month. I want to enjoy myself. Not think. Like today. More please."

"Okay."

"Okay?" Big grin. "Where were we?" Settled.

—Tell me a story.

"Norway," he says.

"Ah yes, we've made it back to Oslo."

"And we're off to Bergen. Sticking to the trains, but it's becoming clear that this is a problem. Some of the best places aren't reachable by train."

"How are you supposed to get around?"

"There's a boat, but I didn't have details. After studying the train map, all roads led to Bergen. Tracks. It's a dead end. I wanted to make a big circle, head up north from there and then come back down south. Walk from Oslo to Stockholm."

"Would you hitch or walk?"

"Hitch some, walk a lot, that's how it goes. You never know, only a plan."

"Sounds nice, but you need company."

"Bergen is a city, not huge or anything, but a big youth hostel. I had my eyes open."

"It must've been getting close to the solstice."

"It was. About a week away. I met this cool woman at the hostel while we were waiting for check-in. They let you wait inside there an hour or so before it opens."

"There are lots of people sitting around and you strike up a conversation with this cute girl."

"Not exactly. She was grungy. Hair pulled back and looking as though it hadn't been washed in a while. Dressed for the road. She was downright dirty. Filthy. Needed a bath." He's seething. It's sexy. Conveying it is too.

"Oooh, I get the picture." Scrunching sideways.

"Me too. Both of us were that way. On the road. That's what I noticed, that's why I talked to her."

"And then what?"

"She was interesting and smart. Into literature and art. Didn't apologize for being crusty either, proudly bore the wear of the road. It was cool."

"An immediate attraction."

"Definitely." Keeps going in the right direction. Wondering, what is her story?

"I can picture it. Same as when you first walked into the bookstore. She was the matching pair."

—I could get that way, let that happen if I were roughing it from town to town in Scandinavia. Good work on the empathy.

"Exactly. Reception opened and we checked in. Did whatever. Got cleaned up, went our separate ways. Usual stuff. I decided to head into town and look for something to eat."

"By yourself?"

"There was a bus. The hostel was far from the city center. I went to the bus stop and there were others there. We were chatting. The others were looking to get food too, invited me to join."

"But no sign of her."

"On the bus, a few late arrivals hopped on before we left. They weren't at the stop, so they must've come up as the rest of us were getting on. One of them was this beautiful woman dressed as though she was about to go club hopping or something. She sat down right across the aisle, looked me right in the eye, and said hi. I was taken aback and tried to manage something smooth. Hello there. Or whatever."

Laughing at hm. His imitation and the funny voice.

"Well, that doesn't usually happen to me. Or anyone. I imagine."

"And?" Don't hold back, keep going.

"It was her, that same girl from the hostel. Woman."

"She cleaned up good, I take it."

"That's what I said. Wow, you clean up good. After, she looked at me to try and remind me who she was. Like, yo buddy, hello, remember me, from two hours ago. I had to shake my head. We talked a long time. It was a good conversation, but... ...how come I didn't recognize her?"

"Was she flattered?"

"She thought it was funny. She said I was good at being a stranger."

"What does that mean?"

"No idea. But I think... I thought she wanted me to ask... ...she said it that way so she'd have to explain, but I couldn't get over it."

"In a good way?"

"No, not in a good way. I think it was a letdown. Her hair looked the way hot girls are supposed to make their hair look. Her clothes were what they were supposed to wear on a night out. Make-up. A fancy necklace. Shoes. She was carrying those fucking shoes across Europe and the only possible use they could have would be if she were going to wear them out dancing."

"What's wrong with that? Fleeting pleasures. Read the signs, my darling."

"I get it, but space in the backpack is precious. Everything in there, you have to carry it on your back. She had a backpack too. That grungy gnarly chick from earlier, a stranger now, she had to carry those shoes. What did she leave at home to make room for them? That was busted. I couldn't wrap my brain around it. She curled her hair. She must've had a blow dryer. Don't you get it?"

"A curling iron too." He looks down. Still riled up but accepting the fact that there is no sympathy here. "What happened next?"

"She invited me to come with her. I wasn't dressed right. I pointed that out. She said it didn't matter. They'd let me in if I was with her, that's how it always is."

"She knew. Not her first night out." He nods emphatically.

"Exactly. And that depressed me too. I mean, she can do whatever she wants. None of my business. It was alien to me. Why would I want to spend time that way? If she does, that's her thing. I had to pass."

"But you didn't, right?" Reminding him. Don't forget your responsibilities.

"Ah right. Of course, I didn't. Do you think I'm stupid?" Back on track. "No, it was probably her first chance to let loose in days. She'd been hiking through the fjords and the perma-frost. Journeying across Telemark. She must've needed a night out, and a gentleman escort. How could I turn her down?"

"It wouldn't have been chivalrous."

"No, in fact, uh..." Looks off into the distance by the window, bites his lip, then. "I took off my overshirt and flung it off somewhere. I didn't need that. Tucked in my T-shirt. Got myself together."

"Picked up some shoes from a chic men's shop down the street."

"Sure, I had to have proper dancing shoes."

He nods, caught up and seeing the effects. His voice lowers to a hum. It's the middle of the night. The sounds are rumbling, things are churning. There is rustling and the sheet is moving again. Exposed all the way and he stretches out and leans closer, pressing the entire length of his body. His hand continues to slide back and forth over the curves of the lower back and up over the ass along the thighs, back of the knees, and calves. He lays kisses along the spine as he reaches down and then again as he makes his way back up.

"We hit the club. It was one of those decadent ones. Everyone half-naked and dancing wildly. Letting loose."

"With private rooms and VIP areas?" Letting the arms be pulled back and stretched against the mattress. He climbs up and lays flat. His chest and arms encircling. Impressed with his weight, there is pressure.

"Yes." Lips close. A whisper where the air blows sweetly below the ear and onto the neck.

"Mmmmm. Did you guys sneak into one while the guests were out on the dance floor?"

"They'll be back any minute."

Stretching back and trying to lift to get knees farther up to support the weight on all fours, but he forces himself forward and the mattress comes up firm against the belly and chest. Pinned down, then his chest presses against the shoulder blades as his mouth keeps searching for the ear.

5.12.4.Greta.19.86.9.23 [ref(..84.5-9)]

"When the cantaor sings he is celebrating a solemn rite. He rouses ancient essences from their sleep, wraps them in his voice, and flings them into the wind. He has a deeply religious sense of song." [Garcia Lorca]

He closes the door too hard and looks over apologetically. Pulling the stack of maps and tour books from under him, he sets them vertically between his leg and the console. It's getting colder and the mornings are more brisk. In the mark of autumn, this will turn once the sun has its chance to respond. Buckling in, then turning the key. Soon the warmth will fill the air.

"We should make a barrier if we do that again. Otherwise, it seemed okay, don't you think?" he asks.

"It's fine."

Navigating the tight space in the car park. There are too many and they are too close together. Pulling forward, then back. Then forward, then back.

"It'll save money," he says pursing his lips in something resembling resignation.

"Fine."

Straightening out, then the final turn to the lane up to the end of the drive and onto the road back up toward the artery.

"Is it fine, or are you... I want to know what you think," he is pleading and reassuring at the same time.

"I think it was fine. Honestly. And it makes sense to do it this way. Stay on your side."

—Knowing full well.

He shows no signs of protesting, and twists sideways into the gap over the console to reach around for the day pack tucked in behind the driver's seat. He doesn't grab the whole thing and pull it forward but unzips it and fumbles with something or other. Grimacing as he jostles about, there is a lone walker on the road inching his way forward with heavy black rucksack and thick-soled hiking boots. In another world, he'd be in the passenger seat. Is there room in back? The blue and white stripes, those could be from a prisoner, it's the same as the uniforms they wore in the camps. He comes back from the day pack empty-handed, only an inventory this time.

"Oberstdorf," he says straightening out and repositioning in the seat. The hiker's face isn't clear in the rearview mirror. He could be anyone.

"It's in Germany. Those parts of the mountains, you go back and forth a lot. We can leave the car. We'll make arrangements with the people at the guest house. There is a nice hike up into the mountains to Austria. We can do that and stay overnight. Then come back and keep going. It's supposed to be beautiful."

"Sounds great," he's settling in and leans his head back against the seat.

"There's no hurry. It's only a few hours. We can stop and look around on the way if you want." Now, he is adjusting the seat. What happened to it? He's opening the big Michelin book to the right page. The scale is small with lots of detail on the roads and villages.

—Why so much fidgeting? What's happened?

"We should have a picnic. If there's somewhere nice. There are many marks for scenic views on the map," he says.

"We'll find something." Gesturing with chin and eyes, looking around. He doesn't look up. His eyes are fixed on the book. "After that night. With Pedro's brother. That's when you were seeing each other more?" He looks up, setting the book aside. Still more fidgeting. Apparently, storytelling requires a different position than map studying.

(Eva's anger. Why wouldn't she come back for Dad? Was it his fault? She wouldn't do that, wouldn't be distracted, but Eva thought so, wouldn't stop repeating it the whole summer. He's why, he's the reason, and he won't come.)

—Have to find out.

"Liam and I would go to the cantina in the evenings. Not every evening, but many. She ran into us. I don't think it was a coincidence. She would've known, someone would've said. The first time was two or three days later. She asked how Pedro was doing. We invited her to sit with us. She was still wearing work clothes, but her hands were mostly clean."

"Mostly?"

—When properly steered, he goes in the right direction. That's the most important thing. He'll get to it despite the fact he doesn't know how ahead of time.

"It seemed as though there was a permanent grime under her nails. It'd never come clean. They were short, but it went deep."

(We had that garden. She insisted that mother and father let us take care of it by ourselves. I couldn't care less about it, but she'd go out there every day. Devoted. I was devoted to her, that's why I did it, that's why I was there every day. Her nails then too. She was always forgetting her gloves, or I would, and she'd give me hers.)

"She was terribly serious. Told us about the horrors of the world."

(Triggers a memory of the times she'd laugh. It was always remarkable. That time the water splashed over us because the faucet broke. She laughed hard, but there weren't many like that. Mostly explaining. She loved to tell me how things worked, what we had to do to make them do what we needed them to do. We had to make modifications to our bikes, or pack the car with bags of dirt, or whatever it was that we needed to do. She was always talking through things. Seriously. Always with a plan and there was usually something elaborate and complicated that needed to be accounted for. Needed to be. Her mind saw necessity everywhere. We have to... We must... Something I hadn't thought of, but which worried her to no end. She'd fidget too, take inventories while twisting into the back seat, and her face was stone still like his sometimes.)

"The girls there, in their twenties, they already looked old and worn out. Their lives are getting to them. She explained it to us, said that by then they were married with children and trying to run the house. It's a hard life. The girls, in their teens, 15 and 16, they know it's coming, and they think they deserve some fun. They get wild, and into trouble." He pauses and turns back to the right, looking out the window through the climbing altitude, the sloped flora and hillside edge of dirt rising as a roadside mountain becoming.

(Of course, obviously it wasn't horticulture. That would have been to help her think, to keep her busy during the gaps. It was those girls. That's what she was worried about, that's the elaborate plan and the complicated problem needing a solution.)

"We had no idea about any of this. We listened. It was kind of a downer, to be honest. But she was burdened with it and we wanted to help. We'd had a couple beers. She talked in English and Spanish. Some German here and there. I mostly understood. Not sure how much Liam was getting, but he didn't care. At some point, it was too heavy. He leaned over and pointed at the top of her shirt. She looked down to see what he was pointing at, and Liam bumped his finger up into her nose."

"Like a game you play with a child?" He is laughing and looking back this way, his eyes studying carefully, but still laughing.

"It made her laugh. Tears in her eyes. Mostly from laughter. She was warmer after that. There was more contact. She put her hand on my arm to thank me when I paid for the drinks, and she was comfortable with Liam. Would lean against him sometimes when he made her laugh. I think she hugged him when we said goodnight. It broke the ice."

(Someone who barely speaks a language in common found a way. She must've needed it. Her life was dense, she could live without levity, but it must've been heavy, she must've been looking for opportunities. It wasn't only the contact, cracking in with the old boys, it was a relief too. These young men, not as serious... ...provided her levity.)

"She told us about how the women were usually the ones to take care of everything. The children do a lot of work. At the harvest. Their mothers come with them, make sure they do what they're supposed to do. The fathers don't come around, but they come when they're getting paid, they come to take the money, and it can be brutal. We heard things. She told stories."

(There had to be injustice. It was impossible for it to go missing. Only that could hold her attention. Law school, though it should've been the last thing on earth for her to choose, was still important to her. She looked everywhere for injustice and clues on how to fix it. Did she tell them about it? Did they know her? Would she have taken the time to tell them stories? About how she left before the exams to the confusion of her family, of her father?)

"That was the world she was in every day, and she felt that she had to tell us about it in one sitting. We listened, wanted to know. We suspected it was that way, you can tell. But it was too much. What can we do about it right now? Can't we sit here and laugh for a minute, then tomorrow get back to it?" Reliving a common conversation, he is moved.

"She must've been furious." It's common here too.

"No. You have to understand Liam. Physical humor was his specialty. Falling off chairs. Fake poked in the eye, fake tripping, double takes, spit takes, fart sounds, childish stuff, like with the finger."

He pauses and smiles. Then goes on.

"I think she appreciated it. She came more often after that. I think she told the boy who worked at the bar. He would clean the glasses and help move the crates. She must've told him to let her know when we were there. She always knew. Eventually, we'd tell him too, and he'd call her."

"That's nice." He registers the remark, agrees. Not mechanically, but heartfelt. He hasn't thought of those early days in a while and is enjoying this too.

"We liked her right away. Her passion was genuine. It wasn't long before she came by when Don Alberto and the mayor were there. Don Alberto had a big cattle ranch down below. On the backside. With many heads. He supplied meat across Antioquia. Medellin too. The best avocados."

"And he was with the mayor?"

"They were best friends."

"She must've loved that."

"She made them uncomfortable, that's for sure. Talked too much. Which meant, she was talking. They didn't like her, but they were polite. They didn't want to hear any of her complaints about how this or that place needed to be shut down, or how some men needed to be arrested for something they didn't think was a crime. They thought it was good for morale, and only cared about the men." His voice rises. He's channeling her passion, remembers being on her side.

—Was he?

"Did she tell you she was training to be a lawyer?"

"Sure." He knows everything. Everything. "Justice was on their side, though, it was designed for them. An argument in a bar isn't going to do anything. The women and children were doing the work. She thought their interests should line up, that they'd *want* to take care of them. But that's not how it works. They haven't reached Fordism yet, simple feudalism. Those are his children and that's his wife. He belongs to the landowner."

—Fordism? Sounds like her. They must've talked and talked. She told him everything. About her studies. What else? About us?

"Did she get you into trouble?"

"No. Liam took the edge off. I was quiet. They thought we were different. Different culture. The men were weaker where we came from. We can't control *our* women. As if that was our job. We only just met her, but somehow we should control her. The fact that we couldn't showed them how different we were. Gabriel told us they mentioned it to him, that he thought it was funny. He's been to the city, lived in Medellin for a while, knows more about modern things, and tried to explain it to them. They respect him, he's married to Don Alberto's daughter, but not much luck."

"Did that get you into trouble with her? You were part of the problem and didn't stick up for her." It's an accusation, but he seems unfazed, no signs of guilt.

"She needed allies, didn't have the luxury of the moral high ground. That's my take. I told her that. She had to be forgiving. We talked about Borges. Have you read any of his work? About the Gauchos and the knife fights. The stuff between the Uruguayans and the Argentines? It's a different way of life. I'm not saying it's the same in Antioquia, but it's more like that than what we're used to in Europe and America."

(Did she get you to read him? That's what she was reading before she went there. And the other one. About the family. Or the time around sunset. No fantasies, but her imagination ran wild.)

"You can't come in and change things in one season. She knew that. We weren't against her, we thought you needed to adapt to the real world. You couldn't use brute force to change something that was everywhere you looked. She explained this to us. She was practical, methodical too. Said she'd come up with something."

—Did I quit on her? For her? Do I have to *do* something to be *like* her?

(That sense of not wanting to waste her life, but what if those passion projects were vanity and self-indulgence? That's more of a waste. All-consuming, international business lacks any scent of idealism... In an ideal world, constraints were removed and there's the possibility of being overrun by wilderness and disillusion. Alone and spinning, how to find a pathway in the darkness? Where was she? Needed help with the bearings.)

[Eva should see, but she can't go there with me.]

Turning deliberately, meeting his eyes, forcefully affirming the impact, accepting its upshot and circumstance. He either doesn't see it or doesn't know how to handle it, so he goes on.

"We were young men. Don Alberto and the mayor were old men. That's why they were tolerant. It had the same effect on your sister. Not because she was lonely. There was affection. I think it's easier to feel affection for younger people."

—She must've felt... ...he can be on my side.

Winding forward to the passing road, the heights are come, the breadth spans off to the side. Then dipping into a short plateau as the mountain top adjusts to the rising road. The car stops its breathless hunting and flattens out in the quickening air as speed increases. There, up ahead, an old building tucked into a wall of trees.

"What about this place? Let's get some supplies, see what they have, and then find a spot to sit and eat somewhere up ahead." He nods and appears ready to take charge, having mastered the inventory and what's needed.

7.8
the middle american

7.8.1.X.19.87.1.1 [ref(..86.12.31)]

Ten Pfenning to use the toilet. The station is crowded. There are a few arrivals and departures, inter cities to Wien and Frankfurt, but not enough to explain the people and commotion throughout the transit center attached to the station. There are signs reminding everyone that the buses and trams are free tonight. It's after three.

'█████ *war* █ *declared* ██ *battle* ████ *down"* pipes from some speaker somewhere.

—100 200 250 300 350 370 390 410

Twenties, mostly twenties.

—430 450 470 490 510 530 50 70 90 610 30 50 70 90 710 30 50 70

"Holy shit."

—80 90 800 10 20 30 40.

Putting most of it back into the pocket of the belt, stuffing it down next to the passport. Two twenties in the pants front pocket.

—At least she didn't rob me. Passport and the pack, could've taken it. She has rules. If I had this then, not sure.

'████ *ice age* █████, ██████ *zooming in"*

[There were no fucking rules for this. Rules made a system, but there was chaos in the system, the system made it. Thing about these chicks is they're not free. They wanted to be, but they're not. It's about rules. They had an order, and everything had to be covered. The chaos crept in causing them to scream for more rules and order. Out of terror. Control freaks who felt out of control all the time. Lydia, she had rules, was strict about following them too. Vacation rules, weekend ski rules, didn't matter. They're different, it's not how she was back home. She's hope. Birgit had tons of rules. Everything was a rule. She wasn't wild and unpredictable, she was nuts, a universal constant, a strange attractor, and her rules were nuts. I bet Herr Damschroder is dead or locked in a closet somewhere, and she's happily minding the store collecting the money. No way Oskar had her pegged to take care of things. No way. But she followed her principles, established her order, and worked her way in to get what she wanted. With her routine and her crazy antics, all that shit, she got what she wanted, according to plan. It takes discipline to merge chaos and principles. She's faith.]

—Charity my ass.

"Engines stop ███████████████ *fear"*

Washing up at the basin, then back out into the terminal. The toilet is tucked away next to the lockers. Finding the row and sorting out the key to grab the backpack. Not many orange fobs hanging from the locks. Nobody is around, they stowed their stuff and will come back in the morning.

"London calling ████████████ *"*

—If I knew how to get ahold of those two, I'd pay them back the 5 DM. The snack at the petrol station too. Finder's fee for the gig? Fuck that.

[And truly, they were royally fucked over at some point, the three of them. Lydia could've hooked up with someone who turned sour the next day or right after. Birgit, well, that couldn't be good. Julia? Never got to the bottom of any of that, but you could guess, and that's rules. They learned from it, everything that happened, new rules for new situations. Adapt. Lydia said, oh yeah that's how it goes, that's how it's supposed to be. You follow different rules when you're on a weekend holiday. For Birgit, the adjustment was a constant part of her upbringing. Who knows? Or each time it got piled higher, each shitty fucking thing that happened to her changed the rules until she came up with another way to cope. Julia could have been a perfectly respectable person and then whatever happened on the way to Oslo or Hamburg or wherever, from Thessaloniki to Wien, who knows? She learned. Who to take care of, who mattered, and what it was acceptable to do to take care of who mattered. Couldn't fault her, but it didn't have anything to do with freedom, you can bet on that. They weren't liberated, they weren't like men, that's crap, because men learned oblivion, we learned how to be free of rules, how to forget them, as if they didn't exist, and they could never muster that. True chaos. No matter how much it fascinated them, how much it attracted them, they couldn't do it.]

" ████████ *coming, the sun's* █████████ *"*

Self-service information is still open and there's an abundance of schedules and maps around. Here's one for the city, inner ring inside the autobahn, that'll do. At a bench back closer to the tracks there's plenty of room to spread out and study the land. Hauptbahnhof is south of the Old City. There isn't one single University that the students go to, or rather, one single campus where the students are concentrated. It's divided up and the markers are all over the map, inside the ring around the center. Maxfeld is up in the northern part of the inner ring not far from the medical school and close to the city park.

—Anna, of course. No clue where Elke and Eve go.

[They lived somewhere convenient for Anna. She's the lead hen, the one with the strongest order and rules. They followed her because of that, they had their own rules of course, but gravitated toward hers, because she's clear about them, how they worked, and how they're applied in every possible situation. When in doubt, do what Anna would do. Simple as that.

Alpha brain. No liberty, no freedom, no stepping off the beaten track.]

—Are the pharmacologists at the medical school too? But not the business students. That has to be somewhere else. Is it only Elke that travels across town to get to class?

[She's on the low end. If Anna's the leader, then Eve is number two. You know they have that kind of thing, they couldn't avoid it, it's part of the rules, it's how the ordering works. How do we know that isn't their fault?]

"I never felt ███████████████████ *, alike"*

The street name keeps changing. It's got one name in front of the station but then it curves around and gets a different name, crosses some big street and a different name. Over the river and another.

—Chaos. What the fuck? Pegnitz. Never heard of it. Graben graben graben. So much graben. That'll be 10 DM, por favor.

"First ██████████████████████ *less than perfect"*

[Didn't matter how flush I was, it's too late for a guest house. Had to walk over there. Looked straight forward enough, aside from the name changes, that one street will get me to the city park and then it's somewhere in that neighborhood off to the West. Brauhausstraße, that's encouraging.]

"██ sensibilities ████████████ *slightest defect"*

[Didn't know how dicey it'd be around the park. Best not to pull out the map right then, remember: to the left and then around to the first decent-sized street, up to the big street, then double back to Brauhausstraße. Keine problem.]

"████████████████ canary in a coalmine"

—Memory. What was it? What was that? Nietzsche, I think. Something about how memory follows along. No, it submits. Judgments or mores, norms, whatever it is you're supposed to do, your memory snaps to it. You'll remember it as if you were doing good, doing what you were supposed to do, what it would have been unthinkable not to do.

"████████ dizzy ████████████ *straight line"*

Heading away from the music and out into the night. There is still a lot of noise from people shouting and moving about. Crossing back over the bridge and heading onto the street curving around up past the castle and into the old city, it's livelier than usual. Firecrackers going off, lights, and some places are still open for food and drinks. The clubs of course, though there don't seem to be any down this way.

—That was a fucking wild place. Never seen anything like it. That's how it goes when you take them out of the equation. Doubt I could find my way there again by myself.

(Proust, was it his memory that was fucked up or did he actively engineer those changes? Did he remember Gilbert as Gilberte, Albert as Albertine? Or was he trying to be polite in social circles, reading circles, where the people of his day wouldn't stand for anything too risky? He'd be admitting to a crime, to burgling, or being burgled. Got to be more than 50 for that.)

—What's the plan, you're going to ring the bell? Knock. Is that it?

(Once you got them, you could do anything. They'll put up with anything. Ringing the bell at 3 or 4 in the morning, calling and asking her to pay the hotel bill, she'd do anything for you. She'd have... Think about it. For me. She had some big plan about how it was going to work out, and then stupid me, telling the truth, or what I thought was the truth. Remembered.)

—Memory again. See.

(Disappointed, but not broken. Next time we talked, she's giddy and thrilled. Couldn't help herself. Once hooked, it'll take the worst fucking thing in the world to get rid of them. She found someone better, but those were her rules. She had some image in mind, and it wasn't an all of a sudden thing, it was gradual. She figured out that there was something better, something further along. She was in love alright, but she was in love with that image and what mattered was who she thought lived up to it. Stank came along and he's the best, he's the new version. That chick was telling him she loved him in two seconds. Before I was out the door, she's in love with him. Because her rules were about the image and I was failing, then he came along, more aligned, better matched to the type, participating in the form, and boom, everything shifted, but nothing changed, not as far as she's concerned. Same image, different guy. Ah, true love. Ta ta ta ta-karrrrrr-a. Universally jew.)

Double river and the roads get more complicated. Foot traffic is diverted and there's this dark patch to pass through. Pushing the money belt farther down into the top of the jeans.

—Cost you twenty to get at it now. Does the Prinzregent still have someone up? Fuck it. Path is set.

"Hey baby."

Waving over at the line of them. The one closest to the street side has turned this way. There are a few cars slowing down nearby.

—What makes her think I speak English? Must be almost 4. What the fuck? People go crazy because there's a new calendar.

[That's it. They put you into some generalized category. Birgit's fuckstick, Lydia's vacation romp, Julia's mark, you're a token of the type. They accused us of being cold, but no one could be cold that way. Bitter fucking cold.]

—Bitter being the operative word. Why should I care? Why should I remember it differently than it happened? Aren't I a free man? I can do whatever the fuck I want, and I don't need to toe their line. Fuck that. Not a woman. Go get yaself a free-range personality. Tigataboom tigataboom

tigataboom boom boom boom.

(The guys who fucked them over ended up fucking me over. One way
or the other, if you're going to get fucked, you're going to get fucked by a
guy. Either directly or by proxy. That was some asshole working through
her, her too, and the other, the four of them, all of them. They wore their
pasts like a strap-on.)

—Eve? Not her.

[She's genuinely kind. Angry. Julia didn't give a fuck about how angry I
was. Birgit didn't give a shit. Lydia, Takara, none of them, they didn't give
a damn. I'll take it out on her. At least it matters. Make her pay. For the
room. In transit. For whatever comes up. Doesn't matter, it's her problem
now. They passed it to me and I'm passing it on to her. And then? And
then? And then?]

—Love means you're willing to take it.

Hooking through the platz and off to the left across the street, there's
the city park. Two younger people, teenagers, sitting on a bench over there.
Hard to make out. Not sitting exactly. That one with legs stretched, the
other with knees up and head over.

—Yup, that'll be 50. Aren't they cold? Young love. Park's kind of creepy
at night. Police must have their hands full, everyone going nuts. Never seen
this much of it before. Is it because I'm not anchored, a free agent roaming
the world?

[To see the world, as if that meant you'll be taking snapshots of the
Eiffel Tower and the Arc de Triomphe. Rosiest fucking picture you could
get, that's what they're selling in the tour books, that's what the kids told
their parents they're going for, but in the streets, on New Year's Eve, you
saw what that meant. Bunch of fucking savages running around crazy,
following their genitals. The 'it's new year's' rules must be kicking in.
Carnival's the point of half those rules.]

—That's the root of their desire. No way some chick is ever going to let
herself eat a pizza or a burger or something. She's going to have salad or
whatever and a diet soft drink. Typical. But then her boyfriend says fuck
that, I want burgers or pizza or whatever. Of course he does, he's free and
can do whatever he wants. Of course he doesn't want to eat salad and tab,
he wants some fucking food, and that's why she clings closely to him. She
wants it too, but can't admit it, can't let herself get away with it, it's against
the rules. Unless there's a rule that allows you to do something with him,
spend quality time together, then you're following it when you eat some
pizza because that's what he wants to eat. Fucking cowards. Always hiding
behind them. Inside that order. No fucking way men came up with this
patriarchy shit. It smells like women's mischief to me.

Crossing over to the left and heading up toward that big street. It's
clearly visible from the park. Quiet neighborhood now, no more din, no

more people. Not in the street, the lights are off in the apartment buildings along the way. Gregor Samsa up that street and to the left.

[The smell was horrible. How do they put up with it? They manipulated men into it so they could get to the top of their order with the other women. The Annas of the world are the ones to thank for this. As sweet as she is, adorable, she still bends to her, listens to her, follows whatever rules she lays down. Dresses in a way that impresses her, studies in a way she respects. Dolly brain. She was the fucking measuring rod. They don't care what I think, they know what I think, I'm a fucking simpleton to them. That complex social behavior, it goes over our heads. There'd be no point in devising that for our sake. No, it's for each other, it's to build this whole crazy edifice and set the pieces in place to get the rules right. It's them, it's their fault.]

—81 81 81. That side.

Crossing the street, tree-lined and quiet.

—Three well to do mommies and daddies behind this.

Pressing the buzzer.

—4 o'clock.

Pressing it again.

[Who cares? Should I sleep in the street? Stay up all night in the train station? Wake the fuck up. There is a mess, and you have to take care of it. I will force you. You must you must you must.]

—That's Elke peeking through the door. Checking to see who it is. She knows who it is, knows who it has to be. Who else?

Door swings open. She's still sleepy. Smiling though.

"Hi, hi Stefan. We expected you long ago. What happened?" she whispers and holds the door open. Passing through and then slipping the pack off and setting it down on the floor. She's standing there as though she's expecting something. Hugs are in order. "You only had to come from Regensburg, right?"

Heading back to the stairs and making the way up a couple of flights, carrying the pack now and drifting a few steps behind her to leave room for her to lead the way.

"Yes, but... I'll tell you when we're together."

"Anja and Eva are, well, Anja doesn't want any late-night disturbances. Hans-Herbert is here too, but he sleeps through everything."

"Don't blame her. Sorry about that. It's been a crazy day."

On the third floor up, the second floor, turning off from the staircase and heading up the hallway to the middle apartment. There are loud voices coming from inside but can't make out any words. Elke pushes the door open. The voices stop as the door swings and inside the apartment Anna and Eve are standing on the other side of the big room and near a hallway heading off to the right. Hearing the door close and two locks turn to secure

everything. Anna runs her hand through her hair as if she is breaking off
from something and trying to change directions. Eve leaves off and comes
quickly, helps put the pack on the floor, and then throws her arms open
and pulls close with a warm and welcome hug. Arms wrapping tightly
around her, she feels good and smells of clean linens and middle of the
night sleep.

"Hello Stefan," Anna says from across the room. Elke crosses over
toward her and the two of them quickly disappear up the hallway. Leaving
the pack by the door, Eve takes the hand and leads the way over to the
couch and sits down still holding on.

"What happened?" she asks quietly. "We were expecting you last night.
Was it hard to get here from Regensburg? If I knew, I would've come to
get you."

"I got you your money."

"My money? What money?"

"For the hotel, for the room. That you had to pay. I didn't want to come
until I had it, and it took longer than I thought. I'm sorry. I wanted to be
here to celebrate the new year with you, but I couldn't. I had to bring the
money."

Pulling the belt out from down the pants and unzipping it. Taking out
the two hundreds, the fifties, and a few of the twenties then handing them
over. She accepts the wad of bills with pursed lips while sitting on one knee
with the other leg on the ground making it easy for her to tilt forward and
give another big hug. Best place ever.

"You didn't have to do that," she says. Nodding, she knows, but
understands too. "Do you need anything? Some water?"

"No, I'm fine. Sorry to wake you up in the middle of the night. I
would've gone to the youth hostel, but it was too late. I worked at a club in
town. They needed people for their big party. It was late by the time I
finished."

"Which club?"

"I don't remember the name. West of the center."

"Well, I'm glad you made it. I'll have to tell Anja in the morning. Once
she has a chance to get some sleep. She was upset. She'll be surprised to
see this." She holds up the bank notes and then lets her hand fall back into
her lap. "Let me show you where the bathroom is. There's a sheet for the
couch and you can use that pillow if you want," she says blushing and
gesturing toward the edge of the couch. "You have a sleeping bag, don't
you?" she asks. "We have extra blankets, if..."

"Uh... Okay. Nah, it'll be fine." Taking the toiletry bag out of the
backpack. Setting the sleeping bag roll out on the floor, then standing up
and following along behind her toward the hallway. Same as both Anna
and Elke, she is wearing an oversized T-shirt and some kind of pajama

pants with socks. From behind, she is absolutely adorable, her feet stepping lightly along the wood floors across the room and into the hallway. Up on the right there is a door to the bathroom.

"Elke and I share this one. You can use it. Anja has her own in the room at the end there. Elke's across from her. And I'm across from the bathroom." She points back out toward the main room but seems nervous about eye contact and keeps her gaze directed away. "Feel free to get water or anything from the kitchen. Whatever you want." Standing at the door to the bathroom and ready to use it but not sure if she is done or what else she wants to show. "I'm glad you're here," she says again with another hug and another breeze filled with fresh linen and some rosy scented lotion or shampoo, light and lovely. Her smile is warm and friendly. Before she darts off into the room across the hall, and as she's pulling away, she lays a soft, but most definitely moist, kiss on the mouth. Her eyes sparkle as she pulls back and turns. Watching her closely, giddy and agape from the magic, then stepping back into the bathroom and swinging the door quietly closed.

7.8.2.X.19.87.1.1 [ref(..86.12.12-31)]

A door creaks open up the hallway, a few heavier footsteps dribble in the distance, the heavy cathunk of the swinging door closing again. More heavy steps from farther away but coming closer. Some light blazing through on the periphery then the hak hak of a cross step that moves along the floor nearby. Artificial light at the end of it plays off against the easily eliminated intrusion of the natural. Is that slinging slurp slurp a set of blinds opening? Is the continued hak hak a movement past the counter with a sliding grate on the edge, a glass moving along the surface?

[Scarcity theory is wrong. Had its roots in that whole dynamic of the commodity. She's there to be bought and sold, traded for barter, or whatever system ruled the day. We were supposed to be terrified, put off, by the innuendo that it was an economy of men making deals, submitting or subjecting them to the rules of commerce. This homo/hommo sexuality of the marketplace for bodies was supposed to reveal a deeper homophobia that sustained our misogyny. That's the principle on which scarcity commands. Its upshot was in the formation of consciousness, no? To be a scarce resource or to fight over one, that's the difference, but the requirement was that you had to be particular about who what and where. Turned out, you could get your dick sucked anytime you wanted if you're not so discriminating about who did the sucking. But that's her point. We were immensely concerned with who did the sucking.]

Slam slamming this one cabinet. Then slam slamming that one.

Another glass dragging on a surface, a door losing its seal and swinging then thudding closed and retaking that same seal. Repeat. Repeat. Slam slamming. Water running and the clink clacking of something rolling over pressed metal. Then the tangle of multiple metal objects slipping and sliding against the basin.

—What the fuck, dude?

[Nazi motherfucker. You know he'd be one of them. An accident of birth. Whenever he was born, he'd be subject to the zeitgeist and do whatever the others were doing. SS written all over him. He admired their fashion sense. Loved the uniforms. We know he loves the fucking haircut. Blonde beast. Asshole.]

—Shut the fuck up!

Rubbing the chin and rapidly rubbing both hands against cheeks.

(It's the beard that gets you. That's what matters. Birgit was tapping me on the head and telling me: Hey, go shave. She needed it to be smooth as a baby's bottom or she'd feel the bristle against her lips and it would never work. That depended on how coarse your beard was. With others, she didn't care much. My grandfather said my mustache was coming in coarse. His was softer, finer. You can't control that. Felt nice.)

Humming.

—Ode to Joy? Clockwork Orange Juice anyone? Fucking Nazi asshole.

Sitting up and looking back toward the kitchen next to the dining area filled by a table too big for the space. He's flopping around in there.

Making that noise on purpose.

Refrigerator door opening again, more cabinets, a drawer sliding and some flatware rolling about. Metal on a plate, an oven door opening and closing, the sound of pressure against the device as the heat selection goes to the on position and then heavy thuds of feet falling as he paces back and forth waiting for it. More humming. He comes out holding a plate and cup, sets them on the table then goes back for another plate and a glass. He sits down facing this way, pulls the chair in and adjusts. Once he's settled, his eyes finally train.

"Good morning, sleepy head. You can't sleep all day if you're going to be in the center of everything."

"Was that what that was about?" Getting up and heading to the hallway to use the bathroom. While washing up, there is that same sound of the door opening and then closing again. The footsteps are lighter, but they're coming from the same direction, and they creak past the closed door. Flushing and heading back out. Hans-Herbert is still sitting at the table staring this way while chewing on some bread and jam.

"Hey, you can't go walking around that way while you're here. There are ladies present." Anna comes out of the kitchen carrying a mug.

"Completely inappropriate," she chimes in. Swiftly moving back to the couch, pulling the jeans up over the long johns. Sitting back down on top of the sleeping bag and sheet, pulling the pillow close and weighing the options.

—Need Eve or Elke to wake up before I make myself at home. Can smell the coffee, but no chance they'll offer me any.

"There have to be rules, if you're going to stay here, Stefan," she says. "You can't be coming in at four o'clock in the morning and waking everybody up. You can't be walking around without pants as if you are alone in your own place. It isn't right." She eats from his plate, the same bread and jam concoction. She drinks from his glass too, but they have their own coffee mugs.

—Some things you can't share. Would it be horribly rude to pull out my Walkman™ and dig back into the couch until some reinforcements come?

"Could you please clean up the area there as soon as you wake up? We don't want to have to put up with that all day."

[It's nine o'clock. About that. No way anyone was working today, no way school was in session or whatever these two autocrats did on their normal days. What the fuck? Why were they up at the crack of dawn harassing me? They were doing this on purpose, they wanted to punish me for waking them up. Fine, I deserve it. I would apologize if I thought there was the slightest chance it would mean anything to them. They'll be much happier if I don't. It'll give them something to complain about. That's what they wanted, they wanted to find things. The fact that the sleeping bag was still out even though I'd already been awake for ten whole minutes, what kind of inefficiency was this?]

—The trains must run on time, raus raus, get to it. Clean up your area, Jew. Make sure everything is spotless. Wouldn't want typhus to spread through the place, now, would we?

They talk to each other now, loud enough to be heard and on purpose.

"It's the way they are. They can't help it, they think the entire world revolves around them. They are the only ones that matter."

(She had a story about someone she went to school with. Technically, she's Turkish but apparently there was some connection to the United States transforming her into some kind of Turkish American occupier of the land and spoiler of everything holy and beautiful. The Hebrew conspiracy was left unsaid, systemic and at work behind the scenes no doubt.)

"Everyone has to do as she says. We have to accommodate her. That's what they are teaching them over there. He can't help it, it's normal to him. Nothing special. Of course, everything is that way, must be that way. We must wait until she understands, we must listen to her endless questions, and of course she knows far better than the instructors. They leave everything important out, and she reminds them."

[Maintaining quiet breathing was essential. A heavy sigh or anything that sparked of frustration amounted to surrender.]

Sitting there and slowly stuffing the sleeping bag into its soft container. It packs up small when the down is pressed tightly together. Once it's tucked inside, the drawstring on the bag can cinch it together tightly enough to stow in the bottom of the rucksack. Setting it over near the pack and turning back to the sheet and pillow to fluff and fold them into a neat pile.

"Please don't leave your sleeping bag out separately. Let's try to contain things. Can you put it in the rucksack so that it is the only thing out on the floor?"

—Not going to respond to that.

Finishing with folding the sheet and laying it down at the edge of the couch before piling the pillow squarely on top of it.

"Hey, did you hear? She is talking to you," he says.

There is commotion down the hall. Someone has come out of their room and is in the hall bathroom.

—What did they do last night? Did they go to a party or anything? The whole town was full of drunken revelers, but these people are up at the crack of dawn as if they went to bed at a reasonable hour.

The water at the sink runs for a while, sounding as if there is nothing to block the way from the faucet to the basin. The toilet flushes and there is the distinct sound of an interrupted flow, something preventing the water from dropping directly onto the bottom of the sink. The drain sounds different as the pooling water changes its flow down into the pipes. Standing up and taking the sleeping bag to push it into the rucksack before firmly zipping it shut and standing it upright against the edge of the couch near where the sheet and pillow are stacked.

(Seemed as good a place as any. She wasn't completely over it. That's why I'm out here, need to work my way back. Or too small for two. That could be it.)

—There has to be some footprint somewhere, right?

(Did she know when she put me out here? Was this some passive aggressive punishment? How much floor space in there? It'd have to be better.)

Elke comes out from the hallway and says "Good morning" in a delightfully cheerful voice. She's looking this way when she says it and easily overrides the bullshit coming from the dining table. She's headed into the kitchen and provides a perfect opportunity to follow along behind her for a cup of coffee to take the edge off.

"How was the couch?" she asks, taking a couple coffee mugs from one of the cabinets and softly closing the door, almost no effort required to be civilized. They are talking in the dining room about how rude it is. They still aren't pleased with the stack on the edge of the couch and the rucksack leaning against it.

[If they went into the hall bathroom and saw the groomer bag sitting on the countertop, they'd be livid.]

"Not too bad. Luxurious in a way. I'm sorry for waking you guys up last night."

"It's okay," she says waiting for the water to boil. They're drinking instant coffee and boiling the water in an electric pot. "Where were you? It couldn't have been that hard to get here from Regensburg."

"It was easy. The guys who gave me a lift, they knew of some work, some club where they needed lots of waiters and stuff for New Year's. It's their busiest day."

"That's great. You should have called though. We waited for you."

"You're right, of course, I totally should have called. No excuse."

"Eva didn't come out with us last night because of you," Anna calls out from the other room. Looking at Elke to see if it's true. She nods and purses her lips.

"She was worried you would come, and no one would be here. I was going to stay with her, but she insisted. She had some things to do."

"That's horrible. She didn't... Shit... That sucks."

Anna comes into the kitchen. The water is ready, and Elke turns away to prepare the coffee.

"Yes, it was thoughtless of you," she says. "You said you'd be here and then you didn't show up. You promised. What did you expect would happen? You think everyone is selfish? You think no one pays attention to these things or keeps their promises?"

"I didn't want to show my face around here until I had the money to pay her back. It's not an excuse. It's... I wanted it to be a surprise. If I called, then..." Looking back toward Elke because this pleading isn't doing anything for Anna. "She'd tell me not to bother, but it was..."

"Well, it's good you wanted to pay her back," Anna says. "It's horrible to parade these women in front of her. Make her feel like shit when you make her pay for the hotel you had with another woman."

"What?"

Faintly, a door down the hall opens and closes, then another, then the water from the faucet, the same drill.

"We heard. The hotel manager told Eva. It was for two. She told us. Don't you know how disrespectful that is?"

Elke nods quietly. Eyes meeting beneath the din of Anna's rank harangue.

"That's why I wanted..."

"Wanted to pay for the room, fine, but what about everything else? You think those phone calls are free? Who do you think pays for that? Who do you think you are? You think you can get some German girls to be your mommy? Take care of you and clean up after you so you can go around and fuck whoever you want."

Elke is trying to hand over a cup of coffee, but it goes wrong, couldn't stand there any longer. Taking it too quickly from her and then stepping out of the kitchen thinking that the larger space of the living area would be better.

"Hey, what do you think you're doing?" Anna says.

"It's okay," Elke says. "None spilled."

"He could have burned you," Anna responds urgently.

Passing by the dining table but Hans-Herbert is already up on his feet and moving toward the kitchen to see what's going on. He couldn't have seen what happened, but from the sound of it he must've thought the worst. Walking past him, he grabs the left arm, but as soon as he takes hold, the immediate response is to spin slightly back to get free of his hand. The grip isn't firm, and the twist easily breaks free, but the pressures of the morning are too strong.

"Take your Nazi hands off the yid, fucker. I swear I'll pummel you with the force of 6 million," comes out in a rapid-fire stream of English. The coffee doesn't spill, not a single drop, but turning back, Eve is at the edge of the hallway entering the main room, a look of horror on her face. Looking back at Hans-Herbert, he is terrified too.

(As the collective self then let him get away with murder, here it drowned him in guilt when it struck the right nerve. Ready Aim Fire.)

"What is going on?" Eve asks. Anna comes out of the kitchen to stand next to Hans-Herbert, ostensibly to check for broken bones.

—What a phony. What a douchebag.

Elke emerges behind Anna. There is sympathy in her eyes and across her face.

"He can't stay here," Anna says. "I won't have him. We can't have a violent person in the apartment."

"He grabbed me."

"You are acting like a lunatic, someone has to put a stop to this," Hans-Herbert answers the charges rapidly. "We can't let you run around as if you own the place. You are a guest here, you have to behave."

Eve comes over and stands close.

"Are you okay?" she asks.

"I'm fine. Did you stay home last night waiting for me?"

"It doesn't matter. Only a party. I didn't want to go anyway. It's ridiculous, celebrating a new calendar."

Handing her the cup of coffee, she takes it and immediately brings it to her mouth to blow. Elke turns back into the kitchen to plug the pot back in and make another cup.

"Well?" Anna says.

"Can we have some coffee and discuss it?" Eve asks. No one moves. Everyone stands right where they are, not knowing exactly what to do or what they're waiting for.

Elke comes back with two cups and there is a collective sigh as though that's it. "It was already warm," she says sensing that everyone's attention is directed at her. Eve goes around to the far side of the table and takes a seat by the window. Elke sits down facing her, leaving the end chair free between them.

"I mean it," Anna says. The two of them aren't sitting back down, their rigid posture louder than words.

"We'll figure something out," Eve says. "It's not a good idea to have someone in the living room, I agree, but it was only one night."

"How much were the phone calls?" Looking at her and not paying any attention to Anna and Hans-Herbert.

"Anja brought them up," Elke says trying to be helpful.

"What difference does it make," Eve says. "Anja are you short on money? Do we need to take up a collection?"

The money belt is tucked into the front of the pants. Pulling it out, then unzipping it and removing the bills from the pouch. Taking a ten off the top and stuffing it into the pocket with the two twenties from last night, then dropping the wad on the table.

"That's almost 400. Will that cover the phone calls and the wear and tear on your car from the trip down to Innsbruck?"

"You're ridiculous," she says not looking at the money.

"Put that away," Eve says. "No one wants your money."

"I'm sorry," looking from Eve to Elke and back again. "I was excited to see you guys. I didn't think. I should have called last night. Shouldn't have come like I did."

"Shouldn't have fucked somebody in Regensburg? Fucked somebody else in Seefeld? Innsbruck or whatever?" Anna says.

"Anja," Eve says. "That's not right. You shouldn't do that. I tell you things in confidence. You shouldn't..."

"He doesn't care about you, Eva. He doesn't respect you. That's what this adds up to. He comes in the middle of the night, calls only when he needs something, and you give him whatever he wants. I care too much about you to let this happen. I'm not going to sit..."

(At least it came out. Her order was violated and that had become clear down in Seefeld. She didn't want an apology, she wouldn't accept one anyway. She didn't want the money. She enjoyed having these violations to hold against me. They added up to make her right. She had her suspicions, and this proved it. No sense apologizing.)

"I'm not helpless, Anja. I don't need your protection. I haven't asked for it. If I do, I know you'll give it, but I don't need it."

"You heard what he called me, didn't you?" Hans-Herbert asks, showing everyone how offended he is.

—Still one more victim to appease.

"How can you associate with such a person?" he asks, shaking his head in disbelief.

—Do you live here?

"I saw you grab his arm, Hans-Herbert. If you grab people, you should expect them to react, and it may not be kindly."

She looks back this way. "I'm going to get dressed. Are you ready to go? I think you can stay at my sister's. It's on the other side of the park, and she has a spare room for guests. I stay there sometimes. It'll be for the best."

Nodding and looking over at Elke whose mouth turns into a hopeful smile. She approves the plan. They exchange a promising look. "What a great idea," she says.

"That sounds great," agreeing with her and looking back and forth between them, doing whatever it takes to avoid looking straight ahead at those two Good Germans standing between the table and the door into the kitchen.

Eve gets up and points at the money on the table as she pushes back the chair. "Take that, you'll need it to buy us breakfast. We can stop somewhere on the way." Shrugging and tilting toward the cash, picking it up and stuffing it down into the other pocket before anyone has to repeat themselves.

"I'm coming too," Elke says gulping her coffee and popping up from the table to follow Eve down the hall.

This causes commotion making it easy to get up and put on socks and boots left untied with laces tucked into the tongue before grabbing the coat from the rack by the door and swinging into it, ready to rapidly exit the room and head down to the street to wait outside.

"Don't worry about your dishes," Anna says. "We'll clean up." Then she gestures to the mugs on the table and gives a sideways look at Hans-Herbert who sets about clearing them.

—Always taking it out on the boyfriend.

[Feminists talk about men the same way. Their tone drips with it. Society's collective boyfriend ready to be abused as payment for the sex. Wanting to be agreeable, we assist in the reasoning and provide evidence.]

"I'll wait downstairs," calling out to the far reaches of the apartment and faintly registering some muffled sounds from a distant room. Grabbing the familiar burden and opening the door to squeeze through before it lightly closes behind.

7.8.3.X.19.87.1.1 [ref(..86.12.12-31)]

(The place they wanted to go was closed. Most of the places were, but there was some kind of hotel / guest house farther from the park that was open. They knew the food wasn't going to be any good, but it was the only option. I didn't care much what I ate, wanted some decent coffee, something brewed. At least they had that, and some sausage that wasn't bad, I guess. The lady who served us looked haggard, might've been a rough night, but who could tell? That might be how she always is as far as I could tell. Nothing to compare it to.)

"It does seem as though you were taking advantage," Elke speaks slowly and chooses her words carefully. Before it's possible to respond, she continues: "I'm not saying you saw it that way, but it isn't completely wrong what Anja was saying."

"What happened?" Eve interrupts. "Who was the other person that stayed in that room and why couldn't he pay?"

"She," simply and to the point.

"Why couldn't *she* pay?" Elke repeats, making sure there is no way for Eve to miss it. She is sitting on this same bench. Eve is on the other side. Neither of them has finished what's on their plates, but both are enjoying the coffee, and the haggard lady keeps bringing more. It isn't crowded.

"Start at the beginning," Eve says.

"When I got back from Hungary, I didn't have any money. Not a huge problem. In fact, I was looking forward to it. Heaven for the adventurous. Along the way, I got it into my head that I could live that way. Figure it out. It wasn't completely accidental."

"The money you have now, you got that last night?" Elke asks turning more fully sideways. Both their attention is highly trained this way.

"Yes. Once I got back to Wien, I went into the youth hostel to see if I could scavenge someplace to sleep. This woman approaches me while I'm sitting there scoping the place out, getting the lay of the land."

"An Austrian woman?" Elke asks.

"Canadian but went to school in America. She was supposed to begin some yuppy wannabe job in New York and was taking a final fling trip to Europe with some of her girlfriends. She freaked out or had a nervous breakdown or something and left her friends to travel by herself."

They both look concerned. Haven't met her, never will, but they're hoping she's safe.

"She said she's learned to pair up with other people who were hitchhiking or tramping around, it's the safest thing. She talked to me to see if I was okay. I guess she figured I was, so she proposed we travel together. I told her I was headed toward Nürnberg, and she said she was going to London. Commonwealth. Was going to work there for a while."

"How old was she?" Elke asks.

"About 24, I think."

"Was she pretty?" Eve asks.

"If she cleaned herself up some she would be, but after her time on the road, she looked ratty. Was up in Scandinavia, travelled through the East Bloc, and down to Greece before working her way back to Wien. She'd been through a lot. Cagey. On high alert, if you know what I mean."

—If she was lying, I'm lying.

"Suspicious of everything." Elke says. Eve nods. They're hardly blinking.

"Yeah, and we're headed up the Donau, following the river, travelling together to Regensburg where she'd head to München to find someone headed toward London and I'd head up here."

The lady brings the bill and sets it down. Pulling it close before anyone can change the plan, it folds easily into the hand and is shielded from view. Looking down at the total and pulling out a couple bills to hand back when she comes around again. The two of them are oblivious.

"She had some good skills. In Krems and Melk, she fast talked us into the youth hostels. They were both closed, but someone was staying there. In the winter, they shut down the heating system so they can't keep it open for travelers, but there is someone who stays in the residence part and looks after the place. I heard parts of those conversations, she was quick on her feet, and, I don't know, you wanted to listen to her. Those people loved her stories about the different things she'd been through and where she'd gone and what she'd done. Stuff she never told me. They wanted her to stick around and have dinner with them. They invited us and gave us a place to stay. The couple in Melk were friendly."

—Fa rend ly. Euphemism for oh yeah.

The lady comes by and takes the money. Eve and Elke are too focused to notice the quick hand off.

"At bakeries and this one guest house, I saw her get food. The way she'd convince them, they'd offer. She didn't beg or ask either, she talked and eventually they'd suggest she take a loaf or some pommes frites or whatever, she was impressive." Pausing and taking another sip of coffee. They're children listening to a bedtime story. "Point is, I knew what talents she had, so when she'd talk to people on her own and tell me it was okay, I figured it was more of the same. Slowly, along the way, we got some money. Not sure how she got it, but she carried it. Talking about it as if it was ours, of course, and not keeping it secret or hiding it away or anything. We'd go to the laundromat, or buy tobacco, she acted as if it was our money."

"How did she get it?" Elke asks. Eve is nodding. They're one single listener both sharing the same response.

"I don't know, I assumed. In Passau, it could've been my imagination, but I thought I saw something through the window. We were washing some clothes and planning our trip up to the youth hostel. I'd stepped out for a while. When I saw her, she was talking to a sketchy looking guy. Not sure what was going on, didn't see much, but it looked as if he was giving her some money."

"For what?" One or the other asks.

"Not sure."

—A hand job.

"What did you think?" Eve asks.

"I thought she touched him. I don't know."

They both nod.

"At the place in Regensburg, she disappeared with the hotel manager. They were gone for 15 minutes or something. Longer."

"Where did they go?"

"Some offices back behind the reception. It was a bigger place, a proper hotel, not a guest house. She told me she had an idea, but honestly, I thought a lot of what she was doing was using daddy's credit card. She struck me that way, as if it was a big act and she just wanted to seem edgy and everything, but she was really a spoiled rich girl from some suburb of Toronto."

"Is that where she was from in Canada?" Elke asks.

"Yes, well, that's what she said. Anyway, she comes back and tells me everything is set, and we can stay the night. It was great, comfortable, downright luxurious after the hoboing we'd been doing. The other places, the accommodations were usually kinda rough. This was something different. Was happy about it. Eat some good food, sleep in a comfortable bed, take a nice hot shower, it was too good to be true."

The lady brings the change and sets it on the table. Committed and they were oblivious to the entire transaction end to end.

"The next morning, while I'm in the bathroom getting ready to go, she takes off. When I come out, she's gone. I pack everything up and head out. They stop me at reception and ask how I'll be paying. She was long gone, and they hadn't seen her leave. Apparently, the deal from the day before was that we needed to get the money and couldn't give them a credit card at check-in. That's what she convinced him to do. He'd let us stay there and we'd get the money in the morning. Didn't seem surprised that I needed to go out and get it, it was as if he was expecting it. Had to leave my stuff. That's when I called you."

"Were you two sleeping together?" Eve asks. Elke looks sympathetically over at her when she does, purses her lips, and looks back.

"Yes." Nodding and looking down. "Not right away, but after a few days.

I'm not sure what you want to know."

—I'm not sure what I know, what I want to know.

"Tell me what happened," Eve says. "What you think happened."

"She was out on the road, living by her wits, I suspect that was a big part of it, part of the thrill for her, but I noticed her stories about past travels, they left things out. She'll tell the guy in München about the guy she traveled from Wien with, and she'll omit a bunch of details, anything that makes her look shady. That's part of what she's looking for, I think, keeping secrets."

There is silence at the table. Elke doesn't have any more questions and is waiting for Eve. She won't show any reaction until she learns how it's supposed to go. Eve isn't making eye contact anymore.

(A different answer would have suited them better. Maybe we were bonding over the excitement and one thing led to another. That would've been better because it's a heat of the moment kind of thing. Telling them she's a predator and I was her victim, with the hotel bill, with her sexual advances, no that's no good. Shit, big mistake. They think I'm trying to justify myself, find an excuse, blame it on her, better if circumstances were beyond our control. That'd be better. At least it distracted her from asking about the money.)

"Let's go," Eve says matter-of-factly as she slips back into her coat from behind her on the bench. Elke stands up, steps out, and lifts her coat to do the same before making room to pass. Standing back up and putting on the coat, stepping over to the rucksack leaning against the wall, slinging it over the shoulders, and waving to the lady who calls out a cheerful farewell.

Passing by Gasthaus Engel again, still closed and the dark sign is visible from the street. *"Ein jeder Engel ist schrecklich."*[1] Neither seem to catch the reference and continue walking in silence.

(I *was* the victim though. Pleasure was connected to fucking someone over, I'm sure of it. Not desire, that's what I meant. She fucking liked it, the thought of it, the fantasies, everything that was running through her mind as she thought about the last one or the next one. That's got to be it. Should've looked that imperial gift-horse right in the mouth. She got off knowing what you're going to go through because of her. She was coming because she knew you're going to be fucked. The sex was performative, sometimes. In Passau, for sure, and with the other couple. Those first times, she wasn't present exactly, but in Regensburg and Linz, she was going crazy, best sex of her life you'd think. That's total bullshit, she was getting off on what she saw coming for me, what was hidden and waiting. In Linz, literally.)

---

[1] *Duino Elegies*, Rainer Maria Rilke.

Quiet street in Rennweg, ringing the bell and the buzzer sounds from the door latch. Eve pulls it open, and the warmth of the hallway immediately welcomes, contrasting with the revulsion in the old building's smells. Making our way up several flights, we come to an apartment at the top landing. The door is already cracked open. There are three women inside but it's obvious which one is Eve's sister. She isn't as curvy, kinda bony in fact, but you can tell from their faces that they're related. The hair is the same color, though the sister's is lighter, and wound in an intricate braid rather than that helmet-like do Eve's got going on. Still, their eyes are the same and their chins and noses too. Family resemblance for sure. The foreheads are different. Eve's eyes seem rounder and more open because the brows are ever inching upward and welcoming whatever she sees. The sister's brow is more furrowed, making her appear smarter, but it could be an illusion. They greet warmly, the friends too, everyone knows each other and good wishes for the new year are passed around.

"This is Stefan," Eve says. "Stefan, this is my sister Greta."

She comes over and firmly shakes hands, gestures to a spot by the door where it's good to set down the pack, and then turns to the other two women and says, "This is Katrina," pointing at the one who simply waves and doesn't take a step closer for a more formal greeting, "and this is Lorelei," pointing to the other one who does some squinting and broad smiling to say hello without a wave. She's the flirty type, whereas the other two are more reserved. Taking off the coats and hanging them by the door with the shoes. Greta studies the overshirt, but Eve interrupts her and the two of them go off into one of the rooms opening onto an alcove off to the side of the big central room. On the other side, there's a kitchen. The bathroom must be the closed door between the rooms by the alcove.

—Shit, I left the groomer bag.

The two women are there for lunch or something because there is food on the table and some dirty dishes. They sit back down in the living room but aren't comfortable. They think they should offer something to eat or drink, but since it isn't their house, they don't feel right about it. Instead, they make small talk. The place is silent, they aren't listening to any music, don't have the radio playing in the background. Elke sits close by on the couch, but they're ignoring her.

"You're from America?" Lorelei asks.

(She's the prettiest one, that's clear. Prettier than the sister in those grungy overalls and definitely prettier than her friend. That's why she's the flirt, that's where she got those facial gestures. Couldn't help it, looking at you as though she knew you're going to find her attractive, knew what effect she's going to have.)

"Yeah," but nothing more than that.

"We used to work with Greta," Lorelei says trying to be friendly. "Well, she was in finance not sales, but the same company."

(If she thought she could bat her eyes and get me to go wobbly, then fuck her, she's got a tough lesson to learn. I was more interested in what's going on in the other room and couldn't focus on whatever it was that thing one and thing two were on about. Why were they mesmerized? I got that the story was wrong, but they were rivetted. What was it about these tales? They all got like that, like it's the most exotic and unbelievable thing a person could do. That's it. Admiration and hatred side by side. They couldn't believe Julia was doing the same thing. There was something to Anna's point. Eve was off the charts enchanted by that whole angle. She didn't want to know the stories, but she wanted to know the stories. To hear about a woman doing the same thing, that grabbed her. Her imagination must've been running wild. She empathized and didn't want to see her turned into a villain, or a psycho, or whatever it was that I was hinting at. Wanting to help Julia would've worked. Being unable because she was too suspicious after what she'd been through, that would have gone over much better.)

They look at each other. Katrina mumbles something that only Lorelei can hear. She nods and mumbles something back to her. Turning toward her for reinforcement, Elke looks over and smiles supportively.

"Mmmmhmm," after an awkward silence following some big, long explanation from Katrina, elaborating on whatever Lorelei was saying.

—What are they talking about in there?

Eve and Greta come back out.

"We were straightening up," Greta says to explain the absence though no one else is wondering about it. "You can stay in there, Stefan. It's ready. If you want to put your bag away."

"That'd be great. Thanks a lot," and then turning toward Eve. "I left my groomer bag in the bathroom at your place. With my toiletries and stuff."

"Oh," Eve says looking over at Elke. A lot is passing between them, but the look only lasts a few seconds. "We can go get it and bring it back here. I should talk to Anja about things. Make sure everything is okay. You can stay here, and I'll come back. Then we can figure out what to do today."

"That sounds great," Greta says. "It'll give us a chance to talk."

Eve and Elke put their coats on and say goodbye to the friends.

(No one asked me if I thought it was a good idea. What the fuck was I going to do with three total strangers?)

They leave and Greta says she'll get some coffee, gestures toward the food, and makes a sweeping offer to have some. "Whatever you want," she says.

"No, thanks. We've just come from breakfast."

"It's late for breakfast," Lorelei says, still working the eyes. Not giving up.

—Damnit boy, why can't you see how cute I am. Sometimes they need to be liked when there's nothing more to it.

Greta comes back out and hands over a cup of coffee. It's hot and smells properly brewed.

"Where have you been traveling, Stefan?" She asks while taking a seat in one of the chairs opposite the couch. Katrina is on the other one and Lorelei is at the other end of the couch now. Conversation is forming into a square, but their eyes are directed this way.

"Came up the Donau from Wien. Was in Budapest before that."

"But you were in Seefeld, weren't you?" Greta asks. "My sister and her friends visited you there, didn't they?"

"Yeah, I was helping a friend's grandfather. Had a great job there while it lasted."

"But how did you come to be in Seefeld?" She is after something. Her questions aren't random, she's looking for something specific.

—What are you up to?

"Uh well, Eve and Elke, drove me from Innsbruck... It was..."

"But before that. How did you meet them?" She is sitting forward and studying everything closely.

(It's not that she was smarter than Eve, it's that she didn't care about being nice. Elke too and the chick with the eyes. They wanted to be liked, they wanted to be likeable and friendly. This chick, she didn't care, it's fucking off-putting is what it is, and this was where I'm supposed to stay. Didn't know how long that'd last.)

"I walked from Bregenz to Innsbruck. Met them in a small town along the way. They offered me a ride and we went to see the castle together."

"Which castle?" Lorelei asks. She's being polite, doesn't care.

"Neuschwanstein. There's a monastery nearby."

"I've been to that monastery," Greta says. "That would have been the last week of September."

"Me too."

"Yes," she says. "We were taking that trip around the same time. Did you pass through the Kemptner Hütte along the way?"

"I did, I nearly died getting to that place."

"What happened?" she asks.

"It was a horrible rainstorm, didn't have enough water and had no idea how far it was. Hadn't read anything about it, set off from Oberstdorf and followed the map. Had no idea how much elevation I'd have to cover. It was stupid."

"I was hiking around there too. We were trapped in Holzgau during that storm."

"We?" Looking at Lorelei and Katrina.

"No, not us," Greta says. "I was with a different friend."

"Quite a coincidence. We must've been close."

"Your shirt. It's unusual." Greta says as the friends both tighten up, look down, and fidget uncomfortably.

Looking down at the shirt. Blue and white stripes.

(Been wearing it almost every day for the last six or seven months. Never thought there was anything unusual about it.)

"How so?"

"In the pictures from the camps." Greta says. "What the prisoners wore."

Lorelei and Katrina are visibly uncomfortable. Katrina gets up and goes to the bathroom squeezing past Greta who doesn't notice. It's that bad. Lorelei would have liked to think of it first. Can't help smiling, crooked from the side of the mouth, when noticing her decidedly unflirtatious look of disappointment when she sees that Katrina has beat her to it.

"You travel around Germany and Austria dressed as a prisoner. Is that it? You think it's funny?"

—Not going to answer that.

Slight gesture to convey uncertainty then leaning back to look over toward the door where the rucksack is set on the floor and leaning against the wall.

(Might've been a good time to get settled in to make sure I had a place to stay.)

Turning back to face her, shrugging. She registers the twist and turn.

"Well, I think it's hilarious, if you're doing it on purpose. It's comical. Good for you. We should always be reminded of this." She is bobbing her head as if to emphasize her sincerity. "Do you want to put your bag in the guest room? There's a washing machine in the kitchen if you have anything to clean."

Popping up quickly and stepping around the couch back toward the door to get the rucksack and carry it into the guest room.

7.8.4.X.19.87.1.1 [ref(..86.10.14-12.31)]

There is a stool by the counter next to the washing machine. Sitting there reading the big Kafka book from the guest room. It's got the short stories, and the novella too. It's in the original: the Czech Jew who writes in German. *Die Verwandlung. Forschungen eines Hundes. Der Bau.* It has the unparalleled: *Josefine, die Sängerin oder Das Volk der Mäuse.* More quietly, more reverently, can it be? Yes, that one too: *In der Strafkolonie.* The Musil sits forgotten on the table in the corner of the kitchen. With no chairs around it, it's an empty space meant for cutting and chopping things.

The kitchen isn't large, and she needs extra counter space for occasions like today.

(They were gone when I came out of the guest room. She had gone into the other bedroom and the door was closed. I could hear her speaking quietly. On the phone? There was no phone in the main room and not in the kitchen either.)

—They left the two of us alone. I guess they aren't as suspicious as they looked. I thought everything was lost, that no one knows me anymore.

(Took off the overshirt and put it in the makeshift laundry bag, then carried it into the kitchen and dumped the few things in it into the front-loading machine built into the counter like an appliance, like the dish washer or the stove. There was some soap in the cabinet next to it. Toss it in there together and use cold, that'll do the trick. Crazy's on high alert, never know how much time you've got. Did some calculations on how much it'd cost to replace everything in the groomer bag.)

The door opens in the other room and there are footsteps crossing the floor. She comes into the kitchen.

"Ah, you found everything okay." She notices the book in the lap and the other on the table. She picks it up and flips it over to look at the back, not waiting for a response. "Musil in English," she says. Could be a question but doesn't need to be. Her observation is completely noncommittal. Can't tell if she's read it or not. "You found the Kafka too, I see."

"Yeah. This is amazing. I haven't seen it before. In the original. Read it in translation."

"You can have it if you want. If you want to read it. I bought it for a friend, but it was too big to carry." She returns her gaze to the back cover of the book she's holding.

"The same friend from Holzgau?"

She half nods without looking up. "Seducer and skeptic," she reads in English. "Chaotic labyrinth," continuing with a beaming smile opening across her face, making her prettier than before. Then, with the loveliest accent anyone has ever heard, "maliciously acute portrayal of an empire marching over a cliff." Staring back at her, she looks puzzled. "What does it mean?" she asks. "Pseudoreality prevails."

"It's a delusion. Something fake takes hold of everyone and they can't see the truth anymore." She nods but keeps her eyes fixed on the back of the book. "I'm almost done if you want to read it."

"It would be strange to read *Der Mann ohne Eigenschaften* in English. No, best not, but thank you."

"When I finish, I usually leave them wherever I am."

"I've heard of this practice among travellers. You can leave it here if you want. Take the Kafka, I don't mind."

"That's too generous, are you sure?"

"Absolutely, take it. You can leave the seducer and skeptic behind. It's for the best."

Looking up and meeting her gaze, she isn't flinching.

"What does..."

She interrupts. "Anja isn't pleased with you. That was her on the phone. Eva is going to stay longer, they have a lot to talk about."

"I didn't mean to cause this much trouble."

"Oh, you didn't? What trouble have you caused?"

"Anna isn't pleased. That kind of trouble."

"And why do you think she isn't pleased?"

"Who can say? Anna is a creature with strange pleasures. Not the kind I understand well."

"It's her problem? Is that it? You are innocently going about your business, doing nothing wrong, but Anja, she has a problem with you."

"Eve and Elke don't have a problem."

"And that is proof. Of course, they don't have a problem, only Anja does, it must be her, something about her."

"How can I say what pleases everyone? What I do know is that it has more to do with Eve than me. I've always been nice to Anna, I never did anything to her that would cause her any distress. If she has a problem with me, it must be something about your sister."

"My sister," she says calmly. "Yes, my sister, she likes you, too much possibly."

"Well, I like her too."

"Why does she like you so much? What have you done to deserve her affection?"

(This chick did not let up. She got right to it. She's one of those fucking interrogators, like from the Stasi or something.)

The clothes finish in the washing machine.

"There is a rack in the bathroom," she says. "You can take them in there. Unfold the rack and spread them around. There will be more than enough room. Set the rack off to the side when you're done."

Taking the clothes from the washer and walking them into the bathroom. Setting them down in the sink before grabbing the rack and unfolding it into the middle of the room. Taking the clothes piece by piece and hanging each item on one of the many bars and joints. Greta follows behind and stands at the door watching from behind.

"There was a woman in Seefeld, wasn't there? And one in Regensburg. You've made lots of friends while traveling, haven't you? Eve too. You don't think that could be it, do you?"

Finish hanging the clothes and turning back to face her. She notices everything is in place and steps back from the alcove out into the main living area. Following along after her, she is still looking over expectantly waiting for an answer.

"Do you smoke?"

"No, but you can if you stand by the window."

Taking the pouch of tobacco from the front pocket and rolling a cigarette. She's watching closely but not saying anything. She won't bury the lead, that's for sure, she's waiting with total focus. Opening the window a crack and pulling one of the dining table chairs over, then lighting up and blowing the first lungful of smoke out into the cold air.

"Yes, it's true, and I've been honest about that." Taking a small piece of tobacco from the tongue and looking at it. Greta gets an ashtray from the kitchen somewhere and puts it on the table close by. Putting the piece of tobacco in it, then flicking a tiny bit of ash into the glass dish. "Honestly, you have to admit, that makes me more attractive to her. You asked what I've done to earn her affections, well, that's it. Women are attracted to people for a reason, you know that, and sometimes those reasons don't have anything to do with goodness, or decency, or respectfulness. Whatever you want to call it."

"Not your fault. You're giving her what she wants."

"What does that mean? She offered me a ride. In Reutte. I didn't ask for it. I didn't beg them to take me with them. They fucking made me get in that car."

"And the women? In Seefeld. She begged you for it. Is that it?"

"Yes, if you must know. She came up to me, she talked to me. Invited me to her house. I didn't have any control over that. I wasn't making the decisions, I believe in consent, I'm no rapist. Say whatever you want, but I've always respected a woman's right to choose who she is."

"What does that mean?"

"Don't pretend your sister's innocent. She wants things. She has desires. She's playing out her fantasies, same as everyone else. Oh, the exotic American, living by his wits, all that bullshit. She's attracted to that, she wants the throwdown, she wants the excitement. She knows about those women, and doesn't care, or rather, it's part of the attraction."

—Go easy, best not to mention the circumcised cock.

"It's not her job to be attractive to you."

"That's non sequitur. You're miming something you've heard somewhere. It doesn't mean anything. It totally is her fucking job to be attractive to me, and it's my job to be attractive to her. You know how horrible we'd be if we didn't want to be attractive to each other? Horrible. Worse than we already are."

"You have no choice. You're playing out some game. You're playing the role of the backpacker, and you can't help it if that ties into her fantasy. Or some desire the woman in Wien had or in Seefeld. You flash that smile, and they do what they do. You can't help it."

"Exactly, and they can't be held accountable for my bullshit, my fantasies about the sexy German chick."

(She's surprised, didn't expect such direct responses. It came out in her reaction that she was thinking she could intimidate me by speaking this way, by throwing everyone off their guard and making it uncomfortable. Not expecting to get back in return exactly what she offered, but she wasn't upset about it. If anything, she was increasingly energized.)

"You see," going on. "Women don't know anything about scarcity. You grow up in a plentiful sexual universe. Too plentiful in fact, that's your risk."

Her eyes go wider. She settles into her chair, relishing the description. Her face clearly signals: go on.

"Men are completely different animals. We grow up under conditions of total scarcity."

—Fuck it. For all intents and purposes. No sense hedging over the details, first get the ideas out there.

"Meaning what exactly?"

"Everything is up to the girls. Whether we go out, whether we mess around, whether we have sex. Everything is completely up to them."

"But you're making the offer."

"Bullshit. Anyone who thinks it works that way is delusional. Pseudoreality prevails. When I was in school, that's not how it was. They'd send signals. You knew. They had ways of letting the boys know which one they liked and whether it was okay to ask them out or approach them."

—Look at how pissed off they get when you don't follow those rules, that'll show you who's in charge and who *believes* they are in charge.

"You're the victim. Everyone else is leading you around having their way with you, inflicting their will and you have no choice but to do what you are told."

"No choice but to take the job for 80 Pfenning on the Mark. Victim, geez." Rolling the eyes. "No, that's not the point. I'm a starving man, living in scarce conditions where the only way I get to have anything to eat is if someone comes over and offers it to me. Some woman in Seefeld or Innsbruck initiates contact, or some other woman comes up to me in a youth hostel in Wien. What am I supposed to do? I am a creature living under intense scarcity, I'll take what I can get."

She is nodding and smiling. Genuinely pleased with what she's hearing.

"This sounds as if it's part of a much bigger theory. I think you should put it down for us. How it is our job to be attractive to each other, to make ourselves attractive. How there is scarcity that forces men to comply with norms and forces the women to behave to get what they want."

"To encourage the men to act a certain way, make it clear what kinds of qualities make them attractive and get them *selected, chosen* for the clothes they wear or how they carry themselves, or the vibes they give off.

Feminists talk about an economy of women, but what about the economy of men?"

"Economy of men?" She has a nice laugh, and her eyes brighten when she does it.

"Yeah, they're deflecting, that's it. The men are the ones on the market, we're the ones being chosen based on how we compare with the others. Enough money, enough confidence, enough throwdown..."

"You've said that before. What does it mean, throwdown?" She's confused by the Denglish.

"In bed. Sex. He's not a limp noodle. He knows what's what. Throw down. Literally."

"Oh, I see." She's genuinely surprised, not expecting it to be so visceral. The image takes her back a step or two, might have made her blush.

"I'm just saying. What chance did my lizard brain have of resisting those women I met along the way? Your sister knows. That's the economy of it. She knows, in normal relationships, that if he's faithful to her it's because no one else is making an offer. If some woman were to come along, your man would be helpless. He'd have no choice. Women's jealousy, that's not something a man can do anything about, it's for other women. Since they don't always respect their sisters, or whatever you want to call it, there's always the possibility that one of them will have a go at him and you'll lose him. It's a love hate kind of thing because you love the fact that he's attractive to other women, it makes him more desirable to you. You can't help it, that's your lizard brain. The fact that other women want him is part of what makes him desirable to you."

Pulling out the pouch and papers to roll another. She watches closely, doesn't have anything to say in response to the long tirade.

Nervously continuing, "It explains a lot about what happens to women later on. When the attention goes away and they experience scarcity themselves, they don't like it. Become bitter, ugly."

"Abandon hope, all ye who enter here." She says solemnly.

"The shades of hell?"

"Rodin's statue. Do you know it?"

"Marble?"

"No, bronze. Fired. Pour molten metal into a mold and it solidifies."

"Making the mold is the sculpture. There is some complex technique for that, I suppose."

"Yes. Heat the metal and fill it. Natural causes create the statue. When he carved it, he had to work inside out. The figures are pointing at the inscription."

"Why does Dante think the entrance to hell needs guards?"

"They aren't guards, only pointing."

"There's a guard. The big dog, right? What's it guarding?"

"Preventing the dead from escaping and the living from entering."

Blowing smoke out the window. "Is that what we're talking about then? Hell?"

"You were talking about pleasure, but I'm calling that hell, yes." There's a driving rhythm behind her remarks. She can't be sidetracked and follows the motif wherever it leads, always bringing it back to the center.

"One woman's pleasure is another woman's hell, is that it? The infidelity is one way to look at that. Variations in taste another. Not everyone likes the same things."

"One woman's pleasure could be every woman's hell. What we do and don't enjoy is a factor of many different conditions," she says. "There's your economy."

"We're not born that way."

"No, can't be. It's too connected. Not intentional, mind you, but it creeps up on you. Comes at you without awareness. Someone likes something, they pass that along to you. It sneaks in there, into the corners or the cracks. You carry it on to the next one. Then you pass it along. You don't know you're doing it."

"I haven't slept with your sister if that's what this is about, if that's what you're trying to get out of me."

"No one is trying to get that out of you. No one here would do such a thing. You're crude. You don't pay attention, not properly, you pay attention to what you think matters, to what you think is important because you'll be able to take advantage of it later, but you don't see what truly matters. You can't. That requires empathy that you don't have."

The bell rings and Greta jumps up and half jogs over to the speaker and presses the button for a few seconds before twisting the knob and opening the door. She comes back to the table and reaches out for the ashtray. Stubbing the butt out so she can carry the evidence into the kitchen. The water is running in a matter of seconds. Reaching over and pushing the window back down to the sill, latching it up on top.

The door pushes open, and Eve enters. She has the gray groomer bag in her hand and holds it out as she crosses the room after slipping out of her coat and shoes.

Greta steps out of the kitchen as the bag is exchanging hands. "Where is Elke?"

"She stayed behind. It was a big conversation with Anja. We had to send Hans-Herbert out somewhere. He was making it difficult to talk."

Eve sits down at the table and picks up the Kafka, turning it over and flipping to the table of contents. She runs her hand over the sturdy cover and binding. There is string woven into the spine to keep the stories firmly in place. Everything about it looks expensive.

—What a dick. She buys him a book and he doesn't take it because there's no room. He can't be any more spartan than I am, and I'll be damned if I can't make room for this jewel. It's got to be over 100 DM.

"Where did you get this?" Eve asks.

She gestures toward Greta who says, "I found it at a gift shop in Seefeld. Remember I told you about that journal I bought. It was from the same place."

"You guys stayed at the place with the jacuzzis?"

"Yes," she looks back this way. "He called it a bacteria trap. It was funny."

"Where is he now?" Eve asks. They both know who they're talking about, giving it the feel of a private conversation, and the fact that they're having it openly has an angle behind it, as though they're establishing a zone of intimacy that excludes while it includes.

"Back in America. He called from London before flying home. I've had a couple letters. Last one was a while ago."

"You're sure you want to give it to me?" Asking again because it's impossible to fathom that she bought this for someone she cares about but doesn't want to keep it around.

"Yes, I don't want it. Take it, please."

Eve is looking at her sister sympathetically. She knows the topic needs to change and does it deliberately.

"What have you two been talking about? Getting acquainted?"

"I think we were both on the roads in west Tyrol at about the same time," Greta says without missing a beat.

"That's incredible. We met him at Reutte."

"Yes, he mentioned that. I think he was coming toward Holzgau when we were hiking back toward Oberstdorf. Either that shirt is in fashion this year, or I saw him along the trail there."

"That must've been a day or two before we met him." She sounds excited but doesn't follow up with any more questions or comments.

(What was she supposed to say? What were any of us supposed to say?)

"El mundo es un pañuelo," Greta says in a highly Germanized Spanish.

"What does that mean?" Eve asks.

"It's something he said. Something he played in Innsbruck. A song. Fandangos, they call it. The world is a handkerchief." She gets up and goes into the bedroom. Shuffling sounds come faintly through the doorway, and she comes back with a multi-page, folded letter in her hands. From the foot of the table, she reads:

 handkerchief

Tearful

a memory

goodbye

the world
full ▌ fire
the world
Full ▌ love

[What kind of a sentimental idiot sent her this? What a kiss ass. What's his angle? This is how everything got out of joint. Some of the fuckers gave in to them and tried to be something that none of us should ever be. That ruined everything, the tournament rules were broken, everything completely out of whack.]

"It's an idiomatic expression," she says. "It means, it's a small world. Something about the folds, folding everything close together."

She keeps reading.

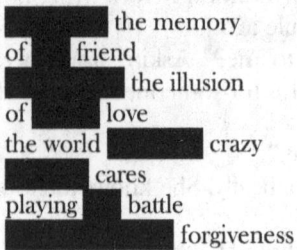

the memory
of ▌ friend
the illusion
of ▌ love
the world ▌ crazy
cares
playing ▌ battle
forgiveness

She stares down at the paper. Eve gets up and goes over to her, puts both arms around her, and pulls her close. Greta melts into her for a second before they break lightly and come back to the table. Turning away to give them a moment, seeing a photograph on one of the shelves by the TV. For a second, it looks like one of those mirror shots where a person splits themselves in two for the picture. They take their seats side-by-side.

6.12 (5)
this year's harvest

6.12.1.Elisabet.19.86.5.9

Getting up when the seatbelt sign goes dim, he's quick to help with the bag. There isn't much, they'll send the rest. It's heavy, he doesn't hand it over, but gets his daypack from the overhead, slings it onto his shoulder, and carries the small suitcase, opening a space in front of him on the aisle. Sliding past, the door opens, then stepping out onto the gangway. Pulling the scarf tight around the ears and head, putting sunglasses on.

"Go on."

"That was more intense, in a way." Following the signs toward baggage claim and customs. He has a rucksack he needs to get, happy to walk with him. "Being dumped makes sense. There are a million songs about it. Textbook. But Chloe..." He sounds as though he's repeating lines from a script.

"How was it different?"

"Well, the way it began. For one. Our first real date came after that first time. We got dressed up and went to some formal event for school. Didn't spend much time with the others, hung out together and talked. About all kinds of stuff. What we liked. Had a lot in common."

[Being free with experience, at ease talking to someone nearly a stranger, what happens to that? Where does it go?]

—Is it me? This arc.

"It wasn't real though, was it?"

—Still not sure about you. After you got what you wanted.

"I don't think so," he responds. "Seemed that way, but I don't think... Not exactly. She'd never heard of some of it. It was more like she wanted to be with a guy who cared about that kind of stuff."

"Was this your friend's take?"

"Mostly." An honest laugh. When they get older, getting caught makes them defensive, but he thinks it's funny. Tripped up being sophisticated, hilarious. "I was mystified. What did I know?"

[She's working on it through his knitting brow, sewing his experience.]

"What did happen? What did you work out?"

"Was a great night. Morning after stuff gone. We found each other. Kissed. Kinda passionate. To establish, you know, that it's a date, but then we didn't do anything. Kept talking. I drove her home and she invited me in. Wanted to change. Offered me some wine." Not sounding complicated or unusual yet. "But then it got weird. She changed into this huge terrycloth robe and came back out and sat at the end of the couch curled up and turned away toward the wall. I didn't know where to sit."

"If she sits in the chair, she wants distance. On the couch, you can sit close, but she's turned away."

"My thoughts were racing. What did it mean? Slip into something comfortable," imitates a voice from some context he doesn't explain, "but it's this huge comfy thing, not... ...uh... ...accessible."

—Mixing signals takes him out of his comfort zone. That head clear as a bell, hers full of echoes.

"What'd you do?"

(N didn't know the significant details. Was baffled and didn't know how to process the impressions. Taught where to focus, it's as if there were four people.)

"I thought she wanted me to go. I thought she was tired and wanted me to leave. Why invite me in?"

Sympathetic pursing of the lips.

"It didn't make sense. I don't know what I was paying attention to, honestly."

"You guys were so young."

(They made me sing in that cafeteria. To see if I could. Nils was humming a base line, Edvin tapping on the table. They wanted to know if I could count, if I could manage the ups and downs. Pushing things around in my chest and belly or in my throat, mouth, and nose. So young.)

—What does it mean, from the diaphragm?

Can't help it, a slight smile. Youth, it fits on every level, and the surge rises and falls between them as the slight grin breaks and straightens.

"Yeah."

Bumping lightly as the long hall guides the traffic off to the right and down the escalators and stairs.

Putting a hand on his back to steer him forward onto the belt giving him more room to stand with the case in his hand and the small pack on his back.

"Had you heard any of the high school stories? Was any of that running through your mind?"

—Adding to the confusion.

"I heard that she got a nose job and that she had something done to her teeth. They suggested she had a reputation. So, yeah, I guess."

—Slut, is that what they said?

"And you think she knew this?"

"Or suspected it. My friends weren't the kind of guys she was likely to think discrete. She was embarrassed at one point when their names came up. Said something like, I hope you'll be fair."

—Terrified, I bet.

"What did you say?"

—Were you kind?

"I tried to reassure her. I told her I was different now than I was in high school, but that came out wrong. People. I tried to tell her that... ...I don't know. It's how people are..."

—Hardly the point.

"Then what happened?"

"I remembered the advice. If you're confused, ask. Don't pretend to know everything, don't pretend to be too cool to need help." He's increasingly distressed. Something that appears before him bears down with a great weight. His lids are lilting, he can't bear it and shrugs near the bottom of the belt as he steps off. It's not the case in his hand or on his back, his gestures are transparent too.

—What moves you?

"I wanted to leave, but that didn't feel right. Sat down on the floor in front of her. She'd have to look at me when I asked."

"What?"

"If she wanted me there. What else? She was torn." His boy-mind, always clear, ran into a girl-mind that was racing back and forth between millions of different things never sure where to land or where to launch.

"Conflicted."

"It's as if she had a playbook, this is how you get someone to like you, but she didn't trust it anymore. I asked if she wanted to go out again."

"Before leaving? Nothing happened?"

Stepping over to the screen that says which conveyer had the luggage, he checks it briefly and heads off in that direction quickly gauging the number system and where 7 would be. Impressive how easily he navigates these spaces while barely paying attention.

"Well, I wouldn't call it nothing, but we didn't fool around or anything. Cuddled some and then I left."

—Touché.

"You went out again and, what? started dating?"

"Pretty much, but it kept repeating. We were hanging out. As a couple, but the signals were always confusing. Especially right after sex."

Nodding. He's relaying facts, doesn't realize they are laid bare, exposed. Tempting to laugh at the simplicity. And cry.

"And that made it hard for you?" Too stern, getting ready to lecture, getting ready to scold him, school him.

"For her. I'm not a complete idiot. I get it."

"But it was causing problems for you. Her thing, but your experience too." Easier to be compassionate, the way others fall into the cyclone can't be easy to watch.

(The way they had to deal with my insecurities. Eyes closed, standing in front of those strangers. What did I know about any of that? I couldn't do it. Couldn't feel anything there, let alone hold the air and squeeze it slowly into the song. The doctor, there to say what's missing, what's not happening, what never happens. There to say what more needs to be seen. Me me me me me me me. Do re me. Sorry, sorry I didn't see it, didn't see you. Never happened to you either. To me to you. Never happened. Him or her. What happened to me, happened to you.)

His bag is already on the conveyor belt, it must've been the first one off. He gestures his head toward it while coming up to the edge, standing still and waiting for it to come around again.

"I guess so. It's like we never made any progress. Every connection disappeared the next morning. I liked her, but she didn't believe it, couldn't feel it. She kept trying to make me jealous, to prove myself. She started something with this guy Erik. A friendship at first, but it didn't make any sense. It didn't seem innocent."

"Did you end it because of that?"

"Not officially or anything." He takes the rucksack off the belt. There's a sticker on top, and he examines it without pausing. "I didn't know what I wanted. I stopped calling as often, made excuses to avoid her."

"But eventually you made a clean break?"

He takes the daypack off and unlocks the rucksack, slides the daypack into the top of the bigger bag, and zips it up before closing the lock again. He does it with deft motions, familiar and practiced, before standing up and slinging the now heavier bag over his shoulder and onto his back.

"Not exactly. One day, in the spring, I saw her on campus with Erik. They were lying all over each other out on the Diag. I gave up. Never called again. She didn't either. It ended."

"She ended it, is that what you thought?"

He doesn't pick up the suitcase again. Doesn't begin moving toward the customs area. Gesturing over there, he gathers that's the way to go, but doesn't move.

"I guess so, but she was telling everyone I broke her heart, that I didn't like her enough, that I ended things by cooling off and she only hooked up with Erik because I became distant."

Trying to get him to walk, but he doesn't budge.

"And that didn't make any sense to you?"

—What's holding us here? Finish your escort duties.

"I thought I was doing better. I thought I was figuring stuff out. Maya ended up with this guy Chris, but that was expected. I wasn't there for her the way she wanted, and she found someone else. Made sense. But Erik, that didn't make any sense."

"Did you know him?"

"Yeah, he was kind of a scumbag. Lots of girlfriends, a player."

—Ah, okay.

"But that changed with Chloe." Sarcastically. He laughs. Still not moving.

"I saw him with her that day. We had lots of friends in common. I heard he was still seeing other people. I couldn't figure out why she was with him."

"Still?" Compassionately.

"My friend came to visit. I called her, messed up, we couldn't hear each other. It was a disaster."

"She came to you?"

"She did."

He looks around impatiently. Deeply involved in the emotion but distracted by something.

"I need to go check with the baggage people. Make sure they're taking care of the other thing. Verify that it's set for Monday, make sure it gets to Germany."

"I'll go with you. I want to hear the end."

He looks down then over and around, cranes his neck.

"Uh..." he says.

"Well, I need to get the case to my driver. How about I go through and meet you over there with it?" Smiling as if to let him know there's a brat on the other side, but one who wants an honest end. He nods, understands, picks up the case and walks off toward the back of the luggage area and the glass wall enclosing an office.

Heading toward the ropes, there is a line beginning to form. Getting in ahead of the bustle and the man waves to come forward. Giving him the name of the travelling companion who has the bag, but he is more focused on the passport picture and shyly asks for the scarf and glasses to be removed so he can get a better look.

Once through and into the receiving area, Elmo is too huge to miss. Standing there next to the others, he doesn't need a sign but has one anyway. Chariot, that's what it says.

"Don't you have a bag?" he asks before anything else.

"Glad to see you too." Leaning up to kiss his cheek and squeeze his arm. He leans down.

"Welcome back. Don't you have a bag?" he repeats.

"My escort has it. Arriving shortly."

"You left your bag with a stranger? You'll never see it again." He is always keen to the ways of the exploitable and the exploiters.

"I have a feeling about this one. I think we'll be seeing him again."

"Oh yes, everybody loves me, who'd ever do anything to cause me harm?"

"Isn't that job security for you?"

He shakes his head.

He comes through the doors into the receiving area visibly shook. His eyes are moist, but he keeps it together, and is about to rush through the steps, hand off the bag, nod to Elmo, and disappear forever.

—I see it.

It's grief written there. The kind that looks forward, not backward. The kind that looks toward everything that will be missing, everything that will not happen.

"LMNOP this is Elmo." Making fun of the name, mostly to distinguish it from the other. They both nod coolly. He sets the case down and is about to run off. Taking his arm firmly in hand, he is rooted in place, unable to move without throwing the tiny Swede to the floor. Pressing him close to make sure of it.

—That's twice now boy.

"Is everything okay?" Turning to look at him.

"Fine. Had to sign something. It's set for Monday."

"What are you doing until then? Do you have a place to stay?"

Elmo shakes his head and grimaces, doesn't like where this is going.

"Someone told me about a good hotel somewhere. The airline has vouchers. I can..." Mouth wide open before breaking into a smile. He doesn't have a clue, thinks it'll work out without a hitch.

—Without reservations? It's the weekend. Who knows where you'll end up?

"Don't be silly. You're my escort, you'll stay with me. I insist. I have the run of a big place by the park. Plenty of room."

[Can't leave me hanging, can't walk off. Tell me how the heart breaks, let me see its ways. It's all I can think about. What breaks made what was empty absent and blocked the way, what breaks kept us clear, what breaks made for nothing and no one, it's where we hurt and where we harmed. I could get him back, I could bring him round. To him or her. I'd fix it if only to know... ...if only I knew how the heart breaks... Tell me. And how to fix it. I'm sure she told you how. You owe me.]

He shrugs as if the opportunity were an imposition. This is how the universe works. Head shaking, Elmo's head is shaking perfectly synchronized with his. He's thinking long con no doubt and looks sideways at him while forcefully sputtering his lips and blowing air out into the late afternoon. He grabs the case and pulls LMNO's rucksack away from his shoulders as he deftly releases it in a single, simple choreographed motion. It's nothing to Elmo who dangles it in his other hand while moving toward the sliding doors and back toward the ground transit driveway. Following along, still clutching his arm to make sure he doesn't disappear.

6.12.2.Seannafair.20.15.5.7 [ref(19.86.5.17-20)]

Still light out, can't be 8 yet, but not crowded in the streets anymore, must be past 7. Walking up toward the tube station, there's the Italian that he likes around the corner at Cromwell, heading there.

"To Ask?"

"Yeah," he says. Arm in arm, keeps it steadier that way. Crossing over by the station.

"Need to call Mike."

"Wha? When? Now? You need to call Mike now? He's no fun, no sense doing that."

"But he'll remember the name."

"What name?"

"Of the lad, the fella."

"What fella?"

"Which one? The one I said, not the other. There were two. No, three."

The shop by the tube station is still open. The cantina has snacks. There's a couple blokes standing by watching us walk past. Don't look none too happy about it. What's it to them?

"But the one. Mike met the one, they all did. It was that same week we got together. Mike and Rian's place. They had the gear and we felt good enough to put something down. That first cut of *My Life*, it was far along."

At the corner and cutting off to the left. It isn't much farther. He's distracted, doesn't like the streets, doesn't seem at ease, thinks anyone who is out here now can only mean mischief.

(That same week. Not barricaded the whole time, figuring out what's what. There were outings. We were together, holding hands at the cinema. What was it? The one with the Scotsman. He wouldn't die. Something about swords and cutting off heads and that. The two of us alone, snogging the whole time, petting my arm, brushing my cheek. Oh, he was a sweet one, wasn't he? A real talker, nice things, what was he telling me?)

"Come on, come on. We can talk about it once we get there. I'm dying here. Need to get something in my belly or I won't be able to stand. Ask'll have one for us. Can't be busy tonight."

The smell of diesel wafts up along Cromwell. Bigger road with lorries and heavy traffic this time of evening. Not too much foot traffic here, but there's accommodation for it. Off the road, into the nest of buildings, there ahead to the left, no need to cross over.

(Everyone was sick, being sick was normal. It was about that book. What's the big yellow one about? Whenever I left him for a second, he'd stick his nose back in it, as though a sip here and there was worth it. It was about sickness and how everyone is sick now. Needing a cure at least, going up into the mountains to die. Something like that. Mountain. What was it? Thomas Mann, of course. What's happening to me?)

Terry leads the way. Feeling dragged. They don't pay any attention and there are seats at the back. That same bloke who's always here. Every time, but he pretends not to recognize. Being discrete as if there's something to hide. There's some folks up near the front, staring as usual. It's a restaurant. This can't be gawk-worthy, can it?

Not their best night out, it's not yet the weekend, but those two are dressed as if it's Sunday. This could be it for them, the best they get. "In your head," that's what she says to him, that's the explanation and his jaw drops. He nods. She nods. They fork some food. It's nothing to them, but everything for that instant.

Taking a seat, face to face, Terry's looking back toward the front. He'll be the one to face their stares. The other way points out the window back to this wretched inlet from the road, nothing much to see.

"Let's order and then you can tell me about it," he says.

He says something to the man before he leaves. The man nods and heads off with purpose. Not toward the front, but into the kitchen.

"What's this then?" he asks, turning back.

He brings some bottled water and bread right away. The service is fast. Well, it can be, today it is. They're in a hurry. Move it along.

"That week. It wasn't fun and games. We went out. Not on the town, but to work."

"What week are you talking about?"

—He's daft, not keeping up, doesn't give a damn. What's the point of answering the question if you know they've already forgotten the answer?

"This is water."

"Of course, it is," he says. "Drink it. It'll do you good."

(There was a second time. It's what drove me off. Had to get out of there. Who knows how many times? It'd keep happening again and again. It was the place. And me. Me in the place. Down by the water. My schoolmate's uncle, right? With that bloke in the lorry, step van or something. White. It was a white van for his work. He must've been 50. And what? 16? 17? Same as the other. Never get in the van. They always tell you that on the programs, Midsomer and the other one. MPVs too. It's in the movies. There's a million of them. She gets in the van and that's the end of it. They don't care. They don't want to care. Crying, that's not going to stop them, it gets them going, it makes them get after it more. They like it, and quiet. Not saying a damn thing, not saying no, not saying yes. Not saying a damn thing. Quiet and sitting there like a stupid girl. Don't know any damn thing. What the hell was it with me? What was I doing to get myself into this? Time and again. Don't know how many.)

"They had recording gear. We had enough of *My Life* to put something down. Made a demo on the reel to reel. 4 track I think it was. Nothing too special, still not the song anyone knows, but you got the idea. The vocals. Well, they're special, everyone knows that. What I could do. It was effortless. Those high highs as if they were nothing. My throat loved to open up that way. High and low. You think it'll last forever when you're 19."

"Who was 19? You were 19 when you wrote *My Life*?"

—He knows quite well I was.

"We all wrote it. The music. That sound. As if the banshees were wailing. We did that. In their house, in the room with a keyboard and those tubes and whatnot. God, it was ancient, and we had nothing."

He's tearing the bread apart and dipping it in oil from the disk on the table. There's black vinegar in a pool on top. He smears it and leaves black marks on his bread. Isn't looking this way, cramming whatever he can into his mouth. Needs to sop it up. Only a sip of water here, can't stomach it, not yet, there's too much.

"But he came with us. Pretty sure. Must've. Met everyone."

He grunts.

"They liked him. He wasn't all look at me look at me. Not the center of attention. Asking questions, wanting to know. Not too many, as if the whole point was to teach him about it. It wasn't that way, but there were questions sometimes."

—Enough to where Mike and Rian liked him. Respectful and helpful. Funny. He brought some drinks out for us when he went in.

("Yeah, I try to be self-deprecating, not much good at it though.")

"That's right. I wanted him to explain. He was the one who explained."

"Explained what?" he keeps feeding bits of the bread into his mouth, dipping each time. Doesn't bother looking up, but he's not so far off it that he doesn't have a track in mind.

"About the week, about that night. He was telling them the mood. The way the air was or something. It was about ecstasy. I couldn't say it. I mean, I said it better. In the song. But the air around. You know, what went into it, that I couldn't say. The way the sadness was lurking around us, but it was still cheerful."

—He was the one who said that. Who put it that way, said that ecstasy is where the highest pleasure lies, but its end and its beginning are there too.

"There are limits. It starts and stops. At the end and in the beginning, there is this pain. Do you know what I mean?"

He looks over, pauses, and takes a sip. He wants to understand, wants to be able to say yes dear and take hold, squeeze the hand, and look warmly. Wants to but doesn't.

[He wasn't such a rummy that he didn't know that's what people did, that's how they took care of each other. He knew, but he couldn't do it, he's too worn down, thinned out, too insensible, unable to sort out the fine details in front of his eyes.]

—Never once got to meet Elisabet Lundberg. Not once in all these years. I'd have run across her, wouldn't I? Not once. Something must've happened to her.

"He told the band about it, helped find the right key for that demo. To get it right. Playing in the major but staying in the minor modes, you know, to give it that haunting air. As if we're at the heights but we got there from below and now that we're finishing, we'll be headed back down that way again."

"You mean like sex? After you have it off?"

—The way he puts it. The way they all put it. Above you and grunting away. Sweaty. Taking off no more than he needed to get the job done. That dirty floor in the back. What a disgusting slob of a man.

(My classmate was terrified. Didn't mean for that to happen, but he was learning. Took over and did fine on his own.)

Looking away and hoping for a bite. Can't swallow the bread, not with Terry leaning over it that way.

—Need something of my own. Something to fill me, something that'll be mine both before, after, and all the way down.

"Pleasure is Icarus. Not too high and not too low, that's what he said."

"Who said?"

"Can't remember his name, but those eyes looking up at me, clever and gentle, listening... ...reading..."

(His mouth firmly in place, his eyes almost sad, and then the ecstasy, but from below, from where it never came before. That bit rang out every time, it became the germ of it. It's the place I kept going back to. Didn't know it. The blue of that quilt, it had some on it, and they were the same as his eyes, those patterns, the patches in the middle somewhere, but they were always what came back when I needed it. With whoever it was. The same as that van, again and again, they don't care. You're nothing to them, only a thing to get their dick wet. You pay for every damn step you take, you can't get there because of the voice or the lungs or any of that. The life in the song didn't mean anything to the money men and the agents. It's nothing to them.)

The food comes. Doesn't take much, but need something, something to calm the churn [something to ease it through and back to where it can sit with you].

(He said something about the stomach, about the gut, about having done with it and getting things out of the way, digesting them.)

—We think it's food that sops up the liquor, as though it's a spill in there somewhere, as if we need a towel or a sponge or something and bread will take care of it. Cleaning it up to let us get back to it and make another mess.

"But we were having it off. Delightful. No better time. Before. When everything was still real, when people meant what they said, and didn't always lie and lead you around for their own good."

"And this was with Rian and Mike?"

Waiter comes by and puts a plate in front of each of them. Takes the empty bread plate and hurries off.

"That's what I'm trying to tell you. We were making a demo, the song was mostly written, but we didn't have it completely down. Brought this fella around. We were together that whole week, that's what I'm trying to tell you. He was with me. I only knew how wrong those other times were when I got it right."

He is digging in still more furiously now that his pasta and clams have come. He isn't looking up, grunting over it as if he understands, as if he understands enough.

"He described it, the vibe I told him about, about the ecstasy and the high and the low of it. The way you had to come up to it, but then it's going to let you down afterward. That's how it is, how it works, but he was saying that, as if he knew, as if he was in my head. Because we were together. In the dark. We were together. I saw a sign of it then. How it could be."

—That's what ruins you, seeing what it could be. Makes you think you can get it all the time. Seeing the upside makes you know you're on the downside. You wouldn't be put off by it if you couldn't make the comparison.

Taking a bite. A sponge would do some good, but can't be shoveling it in, got to hold onto something.

"We saw a film."

"A film?"

"Yeah. With Sean Connery. Something in Scotland, but I wasn't paying attention. We were too busy kissing. My arm. The way he touched my arm. That's how it's supposed to be. When someone cares, when someone shows affection, that's how they do it, or they brush the hair out of your eyes and kiss your cheek and tell you nice things about mountains and sickness."

"The highlands. Is that what you mean? The mountains up there. I think that was Highlander. You're talking about Highlander."

—Am I?

"Right, but not those mountains. It was something else about a mountain. That was the big yellow book. Not big. Thick." Laughing, but then a sudden chill.

(He was thick, wasn't he? You can't help it, your body betrays you. It shouldn't be that way, shouldn't be easy for them. Blaming yourself for making it easy, for helping him along. How could you do that? Did I like

it deep down? Didn't say no, but I was terrified, couldn't say a damn thing.
He enjoyed that, but that doesn't pass it along, doesn't mean anything
because that's what you're meant to do. With him, after the cinema, back
in the flat, uncomfortable with his head down there and his big eyes looking
up at me. Wanting to make him happy, wanting to make him feel good. Is
there a difference? Slight, no chance of it between the two. Nothing you
can say to stop it. Either way, terror of a different kind. Fear and wishing
for the best. Hoping he won't kill you. Hoping he won't leave you. Hoping.
All of it. All of it. Hoping.)

6.12.3.Natalie.19.86.8.12 [ref(..6.16-26)]

Tuesday night. Cooking dinner, searing beef and stirring up vegetables.
Kitchen full of supplies. The meat magically appears and it's exactly what's
needed. The vegetables, the right kinds. The onions, the broccoli, the
works for the salad, everything as described. The list materializes in the
kitchen as though some foreign magic is to blame.

"How did I do?" he asks.

"Perfect so far. Did you get wine?"

"Yes. Shall I open it?"

"Please, I'm going to need some for this."

To lay down a set of instructions, to go off and take care of what needs
taking care of, and then come back to see those instructions realized.

*He stands off behind somewhere, there is that squeegee sound of the
cork coming undone and the metal clanging on the countertop, lightly, but
distinctively. An arm reaches around and sets the open bottle there.
Cabinets open and a glass appears in the same area. Bottle tips and the
glass fills. Bottle and glass come forward.*

Bottle and glass appear, taking a sip, and then tipping the bottle into the
mixture, the steam flies off and rises high up contrasting against the
backsplash, window, and ceiling.

There he is leaning closer and looking down at the stirring and sizzling.

"Any better today?"

"▮ *same as it* ▮ *was*," in English, like the song. He smiles, but it's
not funny, only sad or resigned.

"What happened? Anything in particular?"

Turning the heat down. Letting the juices collect and tilting the pan
diagonally.

"The crazy chick who likes clothes, music, and movies. Same old shit."

He purses his lips and pours some for himself. The bottle is half empty.

—Half full, goddamnit.

He's waiting patiently, takes a sip, looks down at the rapid movement around the pan and in the hands and arms. Lifting up the apron, grabbing hold to set the sizzling pan down off to the side.

"That's what I am. It's not worth my time. Nothing can change it. It's pointless to rage against the fates."

No answer. With a sympathetic frown, he says nothing and reaches out to touch high enough on the arm to avoid disturbing any of the motions below.

"Tear up those greens and half fill two of the salad bowls, okay?"

He doesn't hesitate and steps right to it. Knows exactly where the bowls are and how to fluff out the greens to make the base. He hands over two bigger plates. First the potatoes from the small saucepan then scoop the meat and veggies out over the top. He's adding, scattering, and crumbling the various produce into the greens: tomatoes, red onions, some shredded carrots, a few dried cranberries, and finally some pine nuts. Following the template perfectly.

"I don't want to talk about it. My choices. I'm not a victim."

He laughs like he's supposed to, not because it's funny but because it's absurd. It sets the right tone. Of course you're not, there's no chance of that.

Table is like a chopping board. Eat right off it. No place setting, no cloth, no need to put anything down. Set the plates right on the wood and put the glasses up at the corner. He settles it and digs out the cloth napkins from the drawer, takes note of whether they need a wash. He'll take care of everything.

"What did you do today?" Finishing up with the pan and setting it off in the sink. He'll get to it later.

"The shopping, obviously. Did some straightening around your bookshelves. Don't you ever dust? I tried, but I think it's a multi-day job. I'll keep at it."

Everything is in place. Pulling up the chairs and sitting face-to-face. He looks directly into the eyes, pausing for a second, waiting, then touching the wine glasses. Perfect. Leans over and plants a kiss. Didn't expect that, not in the script, but okay.

"That's it?"

Low cut top, toys with the men at work, toys with him now. He can't help it, he keeps looking down, can't stop himself. It's a magnet that holds him tightly. Feeling taller in the booties. He's barefoot and eye-to-eye from the seat.

"Reading that book. Wrote. Figured out some more stuff about your music collection."

—You should be improving your skills by reading the other book.

[A flash of the scent of those pages. He can't get much from that. Thighs pressed too tightly against his ears for him to hear anything. It's hardly literature, but they've done their research, and know what works. Listening or not, it's getting through.]

"What about it?"

"Your organization, it's by mood, I think." Completely unconscious and don't want to confront any of that right now. Don't bother explaining. He'll drop it if there are no follow-ups. Takes instructions and follows cues. Check.

—Could anything be finer?

"Hmmm. Could be. What did you write about?"

Waves his fork and knife. Ignoring the salad at first, he goes right to the meat.

"About two pages."

Puts it in his mouth and makes near orgasmic noises. "So good," he says. Smiling, and looking up to nod at him. Eyes meet, he's genuinely pleased, not pretending.

"Worthless drivel?"

"Doesn't matter."

Firm. That's how it sounds if they don't tell you you're useless every fucking time they get a chance.

"Okay then, tell me."

He turns to the salad. Making sure to eat both at the same time and not mechanically force himself to finish the salad before eating the entrée.

"My theory about your organization."

Mouth opens wide. It's a violation of privacy.

—How dare you.

[Same as the house, it's inherited from Dad after he died, and Mom cleared out for the city. Sure as shit not going to go into that with you. Keep wondering. Keep it to yourself. None of it is worth anything. 30 km from the middle of nowhere.]

He doesn't laugh and stabs the knife back into the meat and steadily moves it back and forth while chewing the salad. Back and forth, he's messing with the rhythm, matching it to the conversation. It's easy to tell.

"Oh God, don't tell me about it, please. I don't think I could take it today. Do I have to be the object of everyone's speculation?"

"Not an object."

"Oh no? What is it then?" Stopping for a second and looking over. The look challenges, but he never takes the bait. He responds simply.

—Guess you're not looking for a fight.

"Sorting out how your mind works. How you think about stuff, how you are. That's not an object." Pointing to it, and then back to the chewing, that simple. There's no push, nothing to pull back the sticky bits, only the clarity of childlike vision.

— *"Sit down before fact like a child..."*

" *'Sit down before fact like a child'*, is that it?"

"Who's that from?" he goes back to it. Fast dancing, like when you don't look at each other. That's it, kind of. Biting the lip. Thumbs. Left then right then left again.

"Can't remember. What have you discovered then? How does my mind work? Or fail to work."

"It's not that way," he protests.

"What way?"

"A catalogue or a field study."

Putting the glass back down, putting everything down, and genuinely stopping the whole of it to look over.

He goes on: "You don't have any Flamenco, but it would fit. Especially Siguiriya."

"Why is that?"

"It's a weird one. It's in 12, but that's not how they count it. They count it in fives which is totally unorthodox because it's not steady with a constant interval between each beat. 5 doesn't fit neatly into 12 like that. It's 1 2 3, that's constant, but then it slows way down for the 4 5. That's how you are. Deep down."

Reaching out to stroke his cheek.

"How do you do it?"

Nodding and still not sure whether he's serious, the look in his eyes assures that he is. Picking the glass back up and finishing off the last bit. He turns and reaches out to grab the bottle from the counter. Refills this one first, then he tops off his own before setting the bottle down at the center of the table. There's only a drop left.

"I got two bottles, if this isn't enough." Completely ignoring the question.

—That wasn't on the list, but it's a good executive decision.

"You're not answering the question."

"Was that a real question?" Some chewing. "Often you ask questions to draw attention to something and you're not looking for an answer."

Nodding, taking another bite. The sauce came out well, the reduction is working, getting the hang of it.

"The philosopher," he says, continuing his thought. "It's all over the place. I mean, in how you see things. Constant but then slowing down. It's not an act, it's your pace, your rhythm. That's what I mean. Questions draw things out, slow them down, they're supposed to make you think. They're not problems to solve."

"Holy shit, boy. Okay, so you are... ...whatever... ...paying attention. Pffffft." Letting the fork and knife drop.

He switches back to the salad after pausing a moment and then rapidly but briefly bounces up and down in the chair.

—Complain when they don't, complain when they do.

The benefits of being invisible surface when it goes away. None of them see. Then when they do, how dare they invade someone's privacy that way?

"That's not usually the point," he responds. "As I said, it isn't a field study. More like sketches."

Good, resetting to somewhere safe. Let's not let this get messy, keep a respectful distance in dinnertime conversation. It'd be rude to take back alleys when there's such good food.

"Consider how a 12-year-old boy would react to finding some money he didn't know he had. What would he do, how would his mind work through it?" he goes on.

"As an example."

"Yes. Or a 32-year-old woman. What would she do if her mind was racing through these things she thought were the most important things in the world but no one listening gave a damn about anything she had to say."

"Careful there, bub."

Grinning and bobbling his head. He finishes the salad and returns to finish off the meat. The potatoes are now drenched in the sauce and the drippings, ready to eat. Again, he follows the instructions for optimal enjoyment.

"They're sketches. Questions. I'm not trying to solve any big problems or get to the core of something's essence. I'm not good enough for any of that. I want to look at little things. Little spaces, little gestures, mostly happening in the dark. Trying to see."

Dripping the last drops into his glass and then back toward this one but it's empty. The pairing was good. Is it French?

—Where did he get the money?

"Do you need me to pay you back for the groceries?"

"No, no, don't worry about it. It's the least I can do. Let me get the dessert."

"Dessert? That's not..."

He carries the plates over to the sink and takes a package from the fridge. He does some washing up first, to lengthen the gap most likely. The pot needs to soak, the pan was too hot for that. He works it out and does enough to make it easier later, then turns back to the package, taking the contents out and putting it on a plate. Puts it in the center of the table, turns to get the other bottle of wine, opens it, and levels the glass off before sitting down.

"I stopped at that place by the train station," he says.

"Okay, but we're going to have to work it off later."

—Good thing I'm wearing baggy cargos.

He bows slightly as if to say of course, and then, noticing what's missing, hops up to get fresh forks. Deals them out and quickly slides back into his chair. Clinking the forks together, dazzling eyes over the touch.

"Why later?" he says, putting some cream from the top of the éclair onto his lips and leaning forward as if to make an offering. Taking it off his lip with a long-outstretched flick of the tongue as he gobbles forward and tries to catch it in a trap with his mouth. It's too much and some weird bubbling creepy thing comes up and bends around the table.

"Belly's too full for that," causing him to relax and turn back to the wine. The dessert followed too quickly. The timing is off, but he wants to keep everything on track. Feeling it now and looking around, not quite seeing the best way forward to set everything right. He wants to be perfect. A deep shudder passes from top to bottom. Patting his leg and leaning forward to plant a kiss on his lips. "Nothing to worry about."

6.12.4.Greta.19.86.9.24 [ref(..84.5-9)]

— *"They are strange but simple folk who sing hallucinated by a brilliant point of light trembling on the horizon."* [Garcia Lorca]

Those songs this morning, they've landed on the line. Gear in place, the sliding back door in the guest house opens right onto the trail leading back into town to the one side and up toward the mountain on the other. The proprietress who brought the eggs, cheese, and bread is happy to advise on the best course and makes sure the water bottles are full for the hike. No refills on the road and it's a good long way. It'll take the entire day.

— *"Farewell* ██████████████████ *marshes,"* but not the vibe. Too fast. He never tires of cheese and bread. Every morning it's a new treat.

[He said to take it with, but the air and the wind were better, couldn't be listening to these off-putting things, they took away the nights and broke out in willful teasing when the earth and the grass should have been the top concern.]

— ██████ *the world* ██████████ *I changed?"*

[Better if he goes first, they navigate better. That's what they're always saying, what everybody says.]

The slope tilts upward almost immediately. There is a tiny creek by the path, and it heads upward too. Rather, it flows downward, and the trail follows the way up to its source. It'll be warm today. It smells like it.

— *"We* ████████ *walk* ████████ *quiet and dry /* ████ *talk* ████ *precious things"*

(He could be right, it's best not to beat myself up about it. There's a warm body, it's hard to stay stiff on one side. The warmth pulled at me.

Lifted up every limb and lured them over the line. No pillow blockade, no mental ropes, no time to recall the rules and regulations. At first, he shimmied over to the edge and worked his way off as far as he could, but then he said it wouldn't last, he ran out of bed and opted for a reversal of pressure. It's the only thing that worked, it's the only thing that settled me in. Not since I heard, not since the day, not since the night. Never since. April the 26ᵗʰ. Five months? It hasn't been born yet.)

—"Life █████████ when █████ lonely"

Wind whips, not to berate, but to remind. The tilt upward takes its toll, it breaks down on the calves and feet, stretches out muscles that hardly move on the streets at level plane. He half-turns regularly, checking up on things. That's concern not irritation. No hurry, he wants to know what pace to set.

(Eva's mouth open, her eyes fit to burst. Screaming. Howling. Why didn't you go get her? Why didn't you protect her? You were supposed to look out for her. *Our* big sister.)

The rippling current breaks faster and rises audible. It dangles over there as the path winds with it. And the smells, the grass emits something, some dust that settles over the passageways and fills the air. It yields fluid in the nose, in the places where the sounds come and go, where the echoes live.

—What was that other one called?

"What was it called? The one I liked. Slow and soft."

"*I Know It's Over*," he says turning his head to the side and raising his voice. His calves are excellent, and the hiking boots accentuate them. He'd do well in 18ᵗʰ century France. Looking down at the feet and the light-colored capris short of the cute boots and exposed skin, subpar according to their rules, but the ladies would wear something to cover them up, only the men...

—"Oh Mother ████████████ soil falling ███ my head"

[Rotting. Skin peeling off, bones drying out, fluids evaporating, but the hair grows back.]

Tears buckle the cheeks. Wind too loud for anyone to notice, there is no reeling around, no turning back to tuck the light in from there.

—█████████ it's over ███ I cling / ██████████ where else ████████ / █████████ over and over"

(Played that one repeatedly. Last night and this morning. Why didn't he pull this out in the car? Why didn't we...)

—"It's ██ easy to hate / █████ guts ███ gentle and kind"

The path wears on. It's foot and foot and foot. Time beats back the distance. Up makes forward more difficult to bear. Elevation makes each step increasingly dear. Staying single file, enjoying the invisibility of it.

—Broad shoulders and, what are they called, those muscles down the side? They're beautiful.

"Want to stop for a while?" he says already deciding. Happy to sit, there is a log off the stone way between it and the creek nearly dry. He takes out one of the water bottles and hands it over. Sits on the other end and looks around, takes a deep breath.

"She was brave, wasn't she?"

"Did you want another story?" He asks as if he's talking to a child, best to play along.

"Yes, please."

"She insisted we give the money to the women. After the harvest. She said everyone should do it, but no one else listened. That's not news, but *we* did. After the summer harvest, you set up in the town square and the families come to collect their money. We couldn't hide any of this. We paid the men some at the table. Close to the standard rate. We gave the women the rest. Paid more than the others, our own decision, and we gave the extra directly to the women."

Watching his eyes while he talks. They're animated, but he'd allow interruptions.

"This one guy, he was pretty drunk. She thought that was relevant. He gets upset with us, says we're trying to rob him. For all we know, he would have said that no matter how much we gave him."

"What did he do?" Anything to block out that song. And the other one.
— *'Driving* ███████ */* ███ *never want* ███ *home /* ███████
haven't got one ███████ */* ███ *haven't got one / Ol* ██ *"*

"Everyone in town, the men that is, carried machetes. It's common. You need to cut back the grass sometimes. It's sharp and if you touch it, it'll cut you or irritate your skin. You hack at it. To part the way. Or sometimes, while you're walking the fields, there'll be a bunch of bananas. You can use your machete to cut them down. Good eating. Lots of different things they do with them. They're different from the kind you get here. Savory."

"Banana trees. But it was a coffee farm, wasn't it?"

"Nothing but coffee farms around the outskirts of the village, but coffee trees don't want too much sun. The banana trees were for protection. They have big leaves, and the coffee grows under them. Everybody with coffee trees has banana trees too."

"Interesting," it's the expected response.

—He surely thinks it is. I guess so. It must've been green everywhere. She liked that, being away from the city.

"Anyway, it's not weird that these guys have machetes while they're in the village square and collecting the money for the harvest, that's normal. But this guy, the drunk or whatever guy, he pulls out his machete and waves it around screaming. As if he's going to cut us up or something if we don't pay the right amount for his kids' work."

"Did you pull out your machete?"

He laughs. "No way. I'm not going to get into a knife fight with some guy in the middle of town, that'd be crazy. I jumped out from behind the table and put my hands up telling the guy to calm down. It was kind of a bonding moment because Heidi was there, and she did the same thing. She immediately stepped up next to me and did the same thing. She's that kind of brave."

"Sounds like you are too."

"Me? No way. I was terrified, but what was I supposed to do? There were people everywhere. Lots of kids too. The guy had to calm down."

"What was it like?"

"What do you mean?"

"Around you, around the town, what did it look like?"

"Oh, well, it's a cobblestone square, but on a hillside. You can see the valley, the farms. Beautiful. You're always walking uphill or downhill whenever you go anywhere. The square is the only flat bit around. The church on one side, that's Colombia for you. The church is always right there on the side of the central square. And then the mayor's offices, for the village and the area around it. The big restaurant, the only restaurant, that's in the center of the square. Stone buildings. Flat roofs. Lots of verandas or balconies or whatever you'd call them. Gabriel's general store is right there. The bank. The place where you get coffee and ring it up yourself if you want. Everything's there. On Wednesdays, that's the big festival day, that was the day it happened. We're out there paying people and there's other stuff. It's an open market right on the cobblestone. A lot of people around. Not the kind of situation where you want to be swinging a machete, and you certainly don't want some drunk guy doing it."

He stands up, doesn't want to sit too long, knowing how hard that'll make it to get going again. Following suit, but it's already hard and there is a great aching in both legs. Stretching helps. He is standing nearby, and his eyes never look away.

—Watching me. What does he see? Who?

Abrupt stop to the stretching. Painfully aware of presence and everything. The simplest things were becoming uncomfortable.

"What happened?"

"We're trying to calm him down. Heidi is out in front, and she's being extremely detailed with him. Talking to him. You know, she knows this guy. Knows his family, his kids. The guy goes sheet white. Looks absolutely terrified. He slowly and carefully puts his machete back into his belt and bends down to his knees. Puts his hands behind his head."

He's shaking his head and wagging his chin, the vision is right there in front of him and he can't believe it.

"Heidi turns around and looks back toward me, but not at me, past me. I turn to see what she's looking at. There are two Guardia guys with their rifles at the ready aiming... ...well... ...for what I could tell... ...right at us. I thought we should be doing the same thing that guy was doing, but Heidi comes back past me to talk to them. They advance on us, military style, and it becomes clear they're aiming at the guy and not us. They ignore her and go right up to him. Heidi moves back to him too and stands there. Take it easy, take it easy, she says. He's down, he's not doing anything, it was a misunderstanding. I'll never forget that."

Still looking this way. Fixed and no longer seeing what's right in front of him. He moves off back toward the path. Taking another sip before handing the water bottle back to him. He squirts some into his mouth, and puts it into his pack, twisting back into it while taking up the story again.

"I'm about to pee in my pants and she's still working the situation. Completely attuned to everything. They said they were going to lock him up until he got sober, that it was no big deal, and nothing much would happen to him, but I couldn't help think that was only because she didn't let it go. She told me she stopped by the police station the next day to check on things, to make sure, and she went over to their house to talk to them after."

"Was that her job?"

"She sure made it her job. I don't know if that's what she was meant to be doing, but that didn't matter, she was going to do it anyway. And those kind of guys, what she said, was that they're fine when they're sober. He was grateful she was looking out for them, and happy she made sure the kids' wages went to his wife too. He knew that was the best thing. But you know, they get drunk, and common sense goes out the window. They become ruthless and stupid. She tries to explain that to them, and they always say they'll be better, but then the next Wednesday comes around and the men are out enjoying themselves same as before."

A few feet ahead and the wind is kicking back up along with the water in the creek trickling down the hill. Not easy to carry on a conversation, heading back into the tight spaces where the songs creep in.

—She was a queen. Not imaginary, real.

[The connections were real. The songs always found you. She knew the way. There had to be more than that.]

Can't hear anything, got to let it come with nowhere to turn and no way to send it back or deflect it.

—"A dreaded ▮▮ day." "There is ▮ light ▮▮ never ▮▮ out"

It's too bright. The higher up, the closer the sun. Hotter, brighter, more of everything everywhere. Pulling on the floppy hat to block it from the eyes and neck. Tucking the hair back so it stops blowing around the face. Adds warmth too. He looks back, eyes go wide, and gulps deliberately.

—Never sure who is who, yours and mine keep rotating around and around with the wind moving through the rock face filling the way with those wary tunes.

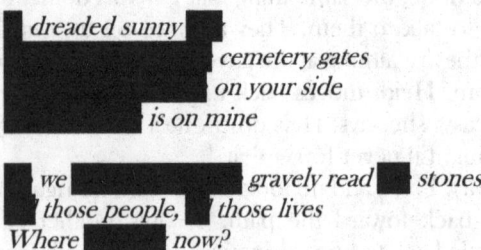

dreaded sunny
cemetery gates
on your side
is on mine

we   *gravely read*   *stones*
those people,   *those lives*
Where   *now?*

7.12

this year's harvest

7.12.1.Elisabet.19.86.5.9-10

Taking the dress off and pulling on the big T-shirt. Tugging and hopping into the black leggings before slipping on those fuzzy pink socks. Reading The Smiths on the front and pausing at the door to reach up and unhook the bra to pull it through the sleeves. The colors on the T bleed into the air, still resonating, still blissful. The walls ripple and the floor curls. Flipping back around as the door opens, hand swinging to the table and scooping up the glass and gulping some water. Stieg is in the big guestroom up the hall. Tap tap tapping on the door, it isn't fully closed, and swings open under the slight pressure.

"Hello hello," whispering and then louder. He's lying on the bed and has something on low. The speakers are humming, the singer is humming. Roxy.

"*I'd* ▌▌▌▌▌▌ *turn you on*"

"Hej älskling," he says, lying on the bed and staring up at the ceiling. Hopping up next to him and rolling into the crease of his arm, cuddling close and staring up at the same imaginary point.

—What's there?

"Are you still?"

"Ooooh yeah," he says. "The pot stretches it out, intensifies."

"Craig and Dean always do right by me." Turning to bury the face into his hardened forearm.

"I should do more with marble," he says.

"Where's that coming from?"

"This time of night, I'm always thinking I should do more with marble. Do you know when I think it's a bad idea?"

"Hmmm?"

"When I'm sculpting a block of marble." Both laughing, then poking him in the stomach.

"Are you naked?" Looking down the length of his body to see him in all his glory.

(Glory is a stretch. The face can hide age, not the rest.)

"Yeah. It's better that way."

"▌▌▌▌ *things* ▌ *wrong*"

"The ceiling's better that way?" He's laughing and it's contagious.

Forgetting what was so funny, but then Roxy comes back, and it's calm again, a wave passing through the room.

"What did you think?"

"Of him?"

"And everything. Did you have fun?"

"Of course, darling. It's always better when you're here." Turning to the left and looking over toward the window. It's more interesting than the ceiling. "Jelly left with them."

"I think they had blow, but not enough for everyone. She wanted to..."

"Why ruin the buzz with that rush?" he asks. "She was in top form. Slinking all over your friend." His voice is low, barely above a whisper.

"It's how she gets to know people, doesn't mean anything."

"Are you sure? I think she wanted to gobble him up." Makes chomping sounds into the air. Too much, pawing at him to stop. "He was asking Marianne about something, about being perfect, or perfection, or realizing a vision. Something like that. Jelly was sitting on his lap and staring at him while he listened to the response. Especially."

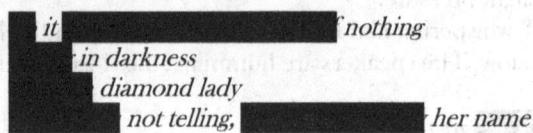

it ░░░░░░░░░░░ *nothing*
   in darkness
    diamond lady
     not telling, ░░░░░░ *her name*

"What did he ask?" Remembering the conversation.

"It was like, who are you a perfectionist for? For the band, for the shows? The performance?"

"Was he interested? Didn't know he was a fan."

"Not a fan. He wanted to know. Who are you a perfectionist for? The audience? Some teenager or something who doesn't know anything about anything? You think perfect matters to them?"

"Where was I during this?"

"In the kitchen with Kinch. Dishing the dirt you missed, no doubt."

"We weren't there for long. He was full of surprises. The cabinets were melting. Dano's getting a divorce."

"You're not Dano."

Quiet. Curling up more into the nook of his arm. "I know."

"░░ *arm in arm* ░░░ *seaside* ░░░░ / ░░░░ *home*"

"And Niklas is not Stella. Whatever you were trying to figure out, it doesn't apply."

"I know."

—No I don't.

The record stops. He hops up abruptly, bounces across the room, flips it over, and then bounces back. Forgetting to look away and getting the full experience. He's back with a jostle and settling in.

"What did she say? What was her answer?"

"█████ *at the time /* █████ *no way* █ *knowing*"

"Marianne? She said it was for herself. As if she was in the audience. She was the perfect listener, the ideal critic. She wants it to be perfect for herself. Her vision of what it should be, what it could be. Needs to be."

"That's true." Nodding, then adjusting to find a better spot. The bathroom light is on, but the door is mostly closed, and the blackout curtains are drawn tight, leaving little light other than the stereo dial. It's a lovely glow, dancing midway on the line.

"█████ *in the world /* █████ *I'm learning*"

"He's not a musician, is he?"

"Some guitar, a student. Wants to study philosophy. Why?"

"Makes sense. The way he talks. Everybody's the same. Jelly. He was unfazed. Marianne. Me. Craig and Dean. He talked the same way to everybody. You, Kinch. When he was fawning over him."

"When Kinch finds a cute boy, there's no stopping him." A chortle, then "But how?" Not letting any of it show in the movements, asking simply, not that curious, only to pass the time.

"*More* █ *this / Nothing*"

—Tell me or don't. Change the subject. I don't care.

"How was he talking?"

"He wanted to know what makes them tick. He's trying to figure out the best way to get to it. With everybody. It takes a lot of work and effort to do what you do, why are you doing it? Do your abilities ever let you down?"

The crackling between songs. Popping and a bounce.

He continues, "Marianne is struggling to answer. She told a story about when she was a kid and heard the Beatles play on TV and how badly she wanted to play that way, perform that way. Jelly is staring at him. Why do you have to know this?"

"She isn't going to let him dig through her secret drawers."

"*This* █████ *ain't right*"

Laughing way too hard. Rolling back to look up at the ceiling. The scenes are there, he's right. The big flat surface in the darkness, hosting many amusements.

"█████ *party's over,* █████ *tired /* █████ *you coming,* █████ *nowhere*"

"Did you like him, or did you think it was too much?"

"Jelly asked the right question. It wasn't because he's nosy. He's working something out, terrified of self-indulgence and not being able to do what he knows he has to do, it's as though his whole life depends on it."

"It does. She knows. She feels it too. They're about the same age."

"I always forget how young she is," he says. "Wasn't that thing with Petter about 2 or 3 years ago?"

"She was a baby."

"Where is he?" he asks.

"Argentina. Or on his way. He'll be back."

"What about you? Are you sure? Where are you?"

"█████, dancing) / (Dancing, █████)"

Blowing out air toward the ceiling. Closing eyes tight and shaking side to side. The images flare, it's not pleasant. Gentle motion, the plants want only slight movements. Abruptly side to side threatens the ecosystem.

"█████ bossa nova, █████ no holding"

"I'm not sure. I don't... And then, how am I supposed to..."

Pulling tighter, his other arm comes round and gives a comforting squeeze. Wrapped up in his arms, the images come easier.

Shaking side to side.

"Avalon"

"Niklas is in Paris with Odette."

"Her name is Mathilde. And no he isn't. That's over." Such a gentle correction, cautioning against bitterness.

"I don't care." Pouting and not having to do what they think best. Roxy would be perfect if N didn't love them so much. "I know, it's been hard on him too. I wasn't making it..."

"Don't you have somewhere in between you can go?" he asks. "It doesn't have to be because you're a shitty person, and it doesn't have to be because he's a shitty person."

"I know."

—No I don't.

"He loves you. You love him. Take any two people and put them in a situation where they desperately want something and then don't let them have it. It'll take its toll, no matter who they are."

"I know that, can't feel it though."

"What do you feel?"

"Avalon"

"It's... I can't. Without... ...then he's having an affair... ...but with... ...well, with... ...it's separation."

"What's this? With or without what?"

"All of this, everything. What the hell am I doing?"

He's back to the ceiling. Lost track of his left arm, right one isn't falling asleep, but it's under the neck and rubbing the back lightly. Good hands.

"Well, your friend was talking about performance. Kinch came in at that point. He and Marianne were into it. I was too. He said performance adds something to the perfectionist's focus, the urgency of realizing a vision, you have to be disciplined to perform something perfectly. But discipline isn't enough, you have to be brilliant too. No amount of..."

"Craig had me cornered. How does that...?"

"Kinch and I were saying there's always performance. Execution. Ideas behind it. Openness to influence. What you can see. How. Whether you're alone in a room or in front of an audience, there's always doing... ...what you're... ...what you can..."

"Was it an argument?"

[Hard to imagine.]

"A hypothesis. What if? He's collecting... A study."

"Do you think I'm being a perfectionist?"

"Aren't you?" he asks.

"It's terror. The terror of not being able to do it. Yes. But also... ...the terror that your vision, perfectly realized, isn't any good... ...doesn't matter... ...to anyone."

"It better matter to you. It's performance. For yourself," he says, the last bit emphatically.

"Audience can be an echo. Flattering. Shaking its head. Turning away."

Laughing. "Where would we be without our performances and their imagined audiences?" he asks in a dramatic voice.

—Always self-indulgent. Tailored to them... They are me. It's my judgment that resounds in that echo, my terror. If we're both doing it, then it's separation. If it's only him, it's an affair.

"The perfect me cannot be with someone who cheats."

Rolling over, sitting up, and moving to the edge of the bed while saying it. Hands on either side, looking over at the stereo lights still dripping from the midway line toward the rippling floor. This is the last song, but he must've played side two first. Back to him, he's lightly reaching out.

"██████ heart █ still beating"

"Then you've decided," he says, voice flat.

"I love you darling, but you're such a man."

He feigns a wound to the chest and then rolls back with his eyes seeking the ceiling again. "Guilty," he says, straight and resigned.

"Marianne and Kinch are coming for breakfast tomorrow. You interested?" Standing up and turning back from the door.

"I have to work. Bright and early. Are you going to Solstice tomorrow?"

—hmmm, hmm, hmmmm...

"Wouldn't miss it for the world," blowing a kiss and slipping out the door. It's ten or so feet back up the hall to the bedroom, but there is no steering anymore. The ship sets its own course, and the socks slide along the smooth floor toward the other side of the apartment. It's a long walk past the entry and through the living room. Wine glasses still on the table, ash trays desperately in need of emptying, people with other things on their mind were here.

—"██████ go easy."

The kitchen is worse: wine bottles and plates of half-eaten food. It'll be bad for her if it sits all night. Scraping the remains into the garbage and trying to set the dishes into the sink so they at least soak before she gets here. Left the glass in Stieg's. Getting another.

—Should do a cover... ...better not, don't want to have to keep getting up.

Setting the empty glass on the counter then off behind the kitchen and down the back hallway.

(If there's a nanny... ...it's a lot of privacy, you could live your whole life... ...wouldn't be that bad.)

—"*I never ▮ lay down / ▮ heart ▮ still bleeding*"

Then the door. It's closed, seal and all. Lightly tapping with the long dark pink nail, almost matches the socks.

—So cute...

"▮ *all leading / ▮ on air*"barely audible.

Last minute decision to peel off the leggings and step free before hanging them in the laundry room on the fold out rack, the whole movement performed in a single swift gesture complete with soundtrack. Socks fall off. Slipping them back on before returning to the door for another tap. It isn't locked and pushes open after turning the knob. The room is dark but there is light coming in through the window, and he is there in the bed with his back toward that same outside wall. He turns and his face is clear in the city light, it's faux moonlight. His eyes go wide, and he pops up onto his elbow. Doesn't say anything, not one word, only those eyes. No smile, he thinks he's still asleep and dreaming, doesn't want to make any sudden moves. In those wide eyes, there is a flash of recognition, lurking grief, and genuine presence.

(There it was again. What's the name for that?)

He opens the blanket as if it's a cape and gestures entry with those eyes, and his whole body too.

"▮ *still dreaming / Words* ▮ */ Lost in* ▮ *meaning*" singing quietly, but at this distance, he can hear.

Rolling into the open expanse, he closes it once secure before pulling the heat back in. Back to him, he squiggles up close spooning his arm around and laying his legs and hips right up alongside. Heavenly warmth.

"Go back to sleep. Just sleep. Okay?"

"*I'd* ▮ *be strong* ▮"into his arm with lips barely moving.

Adjusting for a firmer grip, he lightly sighs and presses his face into the loose hair laying over the back of the neck and bunching around the shoulder pressed to the mattress.

—"▮ *stop dreaming*"

(Remembering his tongue and the way it came to be home. It's touch like none other wherever it wandered. Back then, back all the way, we were never anything on purpose. That's what I wanted to show. He didn't know what he was, but how to reveal it without breaking him? Once he knew, it'd fly away, and I'd never recognize that tongue again. That familiarity lost... ...to grief... ...for the future... ...for everything that'll never be, that can't be. This one, the other, it's in the eyes, the eyes were the same, it's a whole country looking back at me. Echoing. They held the purpose.)

—" █ heart █ flown away █ / ██████ stop bleeding?"

7.12.2.Seannafair.20.15.5.7 [ref(19.86.5.18-20)]

The smell turns the stomach, but it's hot and it'll help with the wooziness and churn. It'll sop it up and set it right.

"He was always wondering about things. Always had a story, a parable. It was that way, as if he was talking about fishermen or something, but he was talking about life, even though not much older than I was. How did he know so much? He didn't pretend to, he told stories."

"What kind of stories?" Terry asks.

"Was a time when dating a fella you liked meant you were completely devoted to figuring out what he wanted and then being endlessly frustrated by not being able to give it to him."

"Now, the girls want the boys to go through that, that's what they're saying."

He doesn't feel it, doesn't think before he speaks. He takes another sip. More bread to mop up some of the clam sauce on his plate. They lay it on thick here.

"Well, he would never say something as stupid as that, would he? No, with him I didn't have to guess."

(He wanted me to come. He said the smells were beautiful, he said the moisture, the feeling, it was intoxicating and driving him wild. I wasn't some slag to be tolerated, he was drinking me in and wanted nothing more than to feel my breath quicken and my muscles tighten. He told me about it, he let me know exactly what was what. I didn't have to guess or figure it out or think there was something wrong with me for not getting what I wanted. Sublimely happy that whole week.)

"It was his fault."

"Fault. What exactly happened?" he asks.

"How good I thought it was going to be. That week was heavenly, I thought everything to come from it would be heavenly too. It didn't occur to me that it was racing back. Too much was coming, and that rubbish was tied up with the good things too. They couldn't come on their own. I didn't deserve it, had to punish myself. Memories can do that for you, can take care of it. Do you understand?"

He looks over, trying to find something, but he doesn't know how or where to look. He doesn't know how to see and doesn't care to learn.

—Bet he knows if they're offsides though, if the formation when they scored is to blame for that big hole on the left side as the striker moved in.

"You're all over the place. It's hard to keep up with you. I thought you were telling me about the demo you made. That must've been back in '86, right?"

—I might as well be talking to myself. It'd be better. Having to repeat it helps. You can go over different things from different sides. If you turn it this way, it'll show better in the light.

"Part of the sickness, on the mountain, what I was saying, it was because there was no memory of the time before. There was nothing before that, or what came before didn't matter to anyone, didn't have anything real about it. Being on the mountain was what mattered."

"You mean with being immortal and how there can be only one?"

"What?"

("You think all people are that way?" "I don't know about all people. I'm like that and it seems strange that I'd be unique. I'm a creature of my time, one of many trying to figure out who we are.")

"That's what the killing is about, there can be only one." He seems laser focused, as though he's clear about the point and how relevant it is. He insists and takes another sip. "Want a spot of coffee?" he asks.

"I don't know about the killing, but it could be. They'd slit your throat for two bob, that's sure enough."

Still plenty of linguini left on the plate. The sauce is too runny. The remaining bits are bathed in it. The bits that aren't soaked have been slurped up. Poking at it to see if there's anything else underneath.

He asks for coffee. The waiter doesn't come too close and then scurries off into the kitchen with some plates.

"The people up there are dying, and they can't remember anything from before they were there. It's a spa, some place you go when you're sick and you want to get better. Except no one ever gets better, they get worse and eventually die. Part of it, I think, is that they can't remember who they were from before. They don't remember anything from before, from down below the mountain."

"It's been a while, but this doesn't sound right to me."

"How do you mean? You think we have memories that we don't know about? We don't remember it but it's still there and comes out somehow, it always finds a way, gets into things, gets us into things, like, and this has been gnawing at me all day, I think, maybe I'm remembering him as a way of remembering something else. Or not remembering it, as if he's hiding it somewhere away from me and I think of him as a way to keep it hidden."

—I was so inexperienced. I didn't have anything to compare it to. There was nothing else for it to hide behind. Those times. That first one when he threw me down. In the back of the van that other time. I couldn't hide it anywhere. He came along for that, to give me a place to put it. In the way he felt, his weight, his rhythm, that's where I hid it, that's where it went to, and then I had to forget him and poof it was gone. Easier done than said.

"He learned things from other girls, you know, and then he did them. You see? And that means I learned them. Not from him, but from other girls. You know what I mean? But those other girls, they were learning from other boys. That man in the van for one. He was teaching me. They were. In a way. Learning isn't always good. I'm not saying that, but you see, and then it gets mixed up, jumbled together. She is all of them and they are all of them. There are chains of she and chains of he and every one of them are them, all of them. They keep piling higher and higher. Nobody knows where it comes from. It can't happen just anywhere. It's everywhere. And it doesn't stop. It'll always be everywhere."

The coffee comes. He drowns his in milk and sugar. Letting this one sit. Tea would be better. Sip it black.

[It's worth a jolt but couldn't fall into it the way he was. The way his mouth took in the heat. The air, there was blowing air. Anything to avoid some real contact, anything to steer clear of what's going on.]

The waiter hovers, waiting for an opportunity to set the leather book down between us as if they still need to make a show of it. They must know by now where it's coming from, but they don't let on. The book is set at the exact corner of the table.

"Truly, I must've passed it along to him."

"Passed what along?" he asks once his coffee is ready to drink.

"The blokes in me. Hateful or not. Ugly or not. They'd a been there and he'd've got a good look at them. He might not have known what he was looking at, but he would've felt it. He couldn't miss it. Staring like that, asking questions. So many damned questions. Or only the one. What was he trying to figure out?"

"We should pay this, right?" He touches the book to nudge it out of its perfectly balanced position in the middle and closer this way. Lifting the bag up off the floor and taking out the wallet with the card in it. Putting it there in the book and the fella swoops in and takes it away without a word.

"Changes every day, that's how it goes, but people think it was simple, as if each day something changes and that's a good thing because we're moving up and reaching for the stars and whatever great things are up there, but that's not it."

"How was it then?"

He doesn't look over but keeps sipping his coffee.

—He has no idea what I'm talking about. He's humoring me, but I don't care, I'm getting there, seeing it now.

"It changes every day. That thing underneath, it causes every day to change, that's what I meant. However good it is, what's underneath there, it's having its way and changing everything. It wasn't cheerful in the least, and he had to explain it because for some reason I didn't see it and couldn't say, although he said I was the one who explained it to him, but it was as if I was explaining it without knowing what I was saying. Showing, making a show of it, despite not being able to say what it was."

The man brings the book back and sets it in that same exact center place, as if he's still making a game of it, still trying to prevent anyone who might be looking from deciding who it is that's paying. Taking it quickly and dragging the pen across it, flipping it closed, and looking over. Nothing to finish up.

—Anytime you're ready, we're here at your pleasure, I suppose.

"That eeriness in the tune. The way we recorded it in the demo. The way we put it down. It was because of what he described. The way he was, sad, but with the heights. Those incredible heights with the high high notes that I can't get anywhere near now, but he told them, all of them, about how it worked, and he said I told him. Don't you see? He wasn't saying it, he was telling them what I said. Right there in front of me. I was talking through him. Plain as day."

"Shall we?"

He puts his arms on the table as if making to push himself up. It's for show. He's on his way. Reaching out to touch his arm. Please wait, pause for a second.

"It's that way, you see. Not there in front of me, but later, when he left. Now, as far as I know, it's still the same. Are you with me? He's still out there somewhere talking about me. Saying what I want but he's the one saying it. Are you with me?"

"Of course, darling, of course I am. It's been an extraordinary ride, hasn't it?"

He touches the hand resting on his arm and seems almost warm as he looks over and reassures, nodding. Yes, nodding, and continuing to get up. Putting the card back in the wallet and the wallet in the bag. Getting up with him, sliding out from the chair, and then, arm in arm again, back toward the door.

—There is a hard pathos in mediocrity. Some story about how everyone makes up the averages, but no one thinks they're average.

The couple from the way in is gone, but another like it has taken their place and repeats their moves, looking and pointing with their mouths open, they can't help it. My life.

(With him, was that week only a ride at the carnival? Walking arm in arm near Kings. The spring air, the taste of it there and not there. Behind and not behind. Both pleasing and appalling. Back and forth, a liquid straining through a colander then boiling and coming back up out of it. The first real time. Awkward, feeling silly, but he was at ease and calm, asking such simple questions and, after a while, it didn't seem hard to talk about. Insisted on trying again. I'll get it right, I know I will. I want to, very much.)

Déjà vu going through the door and feeling it swing shut on the noises and warmth inside. Now it's proper dark and the lights on Cromwell have a haunting glow about them, as though a search party has set out and is headed this way.

"He was the one who called her. Who asked if he could send it, get her to give it a listen, or one of her people. Someone she knew, someone would listen, and they would, they might..."

The night air feels good. Was getting close in there, but he's oriented himself for the walk back and isn't paying much attention.

—How do they do it? Why?

"He called her. It was a big thing. They talked for a long time. He took it into the other room. Something about listening to the demo, of course, that wasn't a problem, but there was more, something personal. She'd been to the doctor. That's why he went off, but it wasn't a problem. It'll fix the problem. Something like, like when something goes wrong and you think that'll be the end of it, but it's something good because it was blocking the way and now you know that and can set about clearing it up."

—He's in a hurry to get back to the pub. The one across from the station. There won't be anyone there. We'll be able to sit and won't have to worry about moochers and hangers on. He can have me all to himself if that's what he wants. In the pub at least, he does.

(First, he called some office. It was the only number he had. He wanted to send that demo, and it was the only way he could think of, so he called to ask where to send it. The lady said to send it and gave him the address, but then she called back. Herself. She was the one. I answered it. She called my phone. Please hold, I told her, and then I handed it to him, and he took it. Gleefully. He was happy to hear from her, knew her, and hadn't been lying. They were some kind of friends or something. I gave him his privacy but couldn't help overhearing. Didn't know before, but now they do. It's a secret, no one knows. Worked out that she'd been trying but wasn't able. He asked if she'd have better luck now. Seemed hopeful. And that's how it began, how it happened. She was happy, him too. Something about there being hope now.)

"We knew we were going to make it. We knew they were going to love that demo, that it was getting into the right hands, the right people hearing it. It's all that. For her, it was the bad that made it good, but for us it was the good that was making for the bad. Don't you see?"

Crossing the street and going up to the door, he pulls it open and guides the way through. It's dark, but friendly.

—Don't know us like over at Hereford's, no tab.

"Couple of pints," he says. "Dram a whiskey too. For both."

(And that, the bad with the good. Your dreams come true, and you're ruined. Don't know what hit you, don't know where to turn next. When they wanted to turn you around, they did it by giving you what you wanted. Simple as that.)

7.12.3.Natalie.19.86.8.12 [ref(..6.27-..7.6)]

"I do have a question though."

"What?" He turns hopeful.

"The truth. Tell me the truth."

"Of course. About what?" He opens at the opportunity but doesn't entirely follow. Eyebrows show it first.

"The woman on the post boat."

"The conductor."

"The conductress, yes. What about that was true?"

"There was a post boat. I rode it from Bergen up the coast to Fauske or Bodø. That was true."

"Okay. Bravo."

Leaning forward. Hands up beneath the chin. Glass is nearly empty again. He fills it, then his. Looking back at him, letting him know to go on while tilting the glass against the table and rolling it in a small circle.

"Of course, nothing happened. I didn't talk to her."

"Was she pretty?" Taking his sip, eyes meeting over the edge.

"Not that pretty. She did seem lonely though. In my imagination, at least. Here she is on this boat going up and down the coast, and it's the most beautiful coastline you ever saw. Fjords, inlets, islands, glaciers, it's unbelievable, and there are these douchebag tourists riding the boat all day, every day, up and down. They don't give a shit about her: she punches their ticket or sells them one, whatever, she's nothing to them."

Nodding at the pathetic picture.

"You thought that what this woman needed was for someone to properly look after her. Is that it?"

He's blushing. Insecure about this part of his performance, it's unorthodox, having never been forced to come up with something as kinky as the truth. Doesn't know if it's any good.

"I'm teasing you, relax."

"I know, it's... I was trying to think it would be nice if someone took care of her... ...in the heat of the moment... ...with you, urgently... ...well, whatever it is you're urgently needing..." Laughing and bumping shoulders, bit of wine splashes up in the glass leaving a dot or two on the table. "I thought she could have a seat and enjoy the ride. We say ride in English. People ride on the boat. Never mind."

It's getting dark. The light dims in the kitchen where the table backs up against the corner of the nook. There are two candles. Lighting them while he watches. He doesn't say a word, focuses on the hands and the fire and the wicks.

"Okay, okay. What about the Israeli woman? At the greenhouses."

"Greenhouses. That's true. Near Mo I Rana. It's by the Arctic Circle. Lots of people stop there and stay in tents. They pick strawberries, and there's a big social scene. Those kids living side by side, the midnight sun. You're paid by the bucket so it's not as though anyone's watching. They keep track of how many buckets you turn in."

"You're saying there's a lot of sex."

Nodding deliberately.

"Most definitely."

"And the Israeli soldier girl, pure fantasy? Oooh, that's rich. You like the whole soldier thing, we should explore that."

"Funny. No, she was real, but not cute or anything like I said. I mean, good shape, but her demeanor... ...aspect... ...she wasn't blessed."

"Didn't exactly win the evolutionary lottery."

"Besides, I think she liked girls. The real one, that is. She was sharing a tent with another girl. They were together."

"Where did the whole *likes to do it the way boys do* come from? That was your imagination? Good stuff."

He flushes. Could be ashamed, but he smiles like a good sport. Knows it's true, knows what it signals.

"It's a constant. What do I know? I haven't been around that much. I'm just saying. There are a few things that cut across the differences."

Smugly smiling. Getting the point, "You mean, all different kinds enjoy the same thing. Dish. I want details."

He's awkward. Good at going into detail in an imaginary universe, he gets silly when asked to spill the truth. It doesn't feel right, he hesitates.

"The imagery, that's what I'm talking about. Missionary."

"Mmmhmmm." Trying to milk this. It's too easy to make him uncomfortable.

—Don't want to follow this dark alley. Is that why we keep going back there? Try to get along with them? Is that it?

"Whatever. You know, her legs apart, his tight together. The rhythms. Classic."

"Oh yes. Well aware what *missionary* means."

"Invert it, that's what I'm saying. The teeny-tiny sampling that I know, across extremely different personalities, well, they all like it."

"Physically."

He looks down, can't help himself. He's having difficulty with eye contact.

"Not only that. The whole vibe. What it means."

"And then the *fuck me fuck me* part?"

"Whatever. If you're going to..." He's frustrated.

He pulls away as though he's about to do the dishes. Grabbing his arm and pulling him back down into the chair. Then pulling him closer, snogging and bumping heads.

"Just us." While leaning forehead to forehead. "What's the other?" after a few seconds.

"Spanking."

—Is that why I keep working for assholes no matter how they treat me?

"All of them?"

"Yeah, lightly. But dependably. All of them."

—Has it occurred to you that they are merely placating you?

Taking another bite of the éclair. It's good but doesn't go with the wine. Coffee would be better, but not the drink of choice so the pastry will have to wait.

"And the topless girl in the park at Trondheim?"

"That was true. And she *was* beautiful. I did approach her and talk to her. No idea how I got the courage, but it was stupid."

"She wasn't interested."

"That's an understatement. It was rude. It was hard for me to imagine that a half-dressed girl in a public park isn't an advertisement for something. Stupid."

"Ignorant. You learned though, right? You left her alone? Good use of frustrated fantasy though."

—Don't spend any time trying to please anyone who doesn't pay attention. That's the rule, the only fucking rule.

He takes a sarcastic bow.

"Go on. What about the woman in Tampere? How much of that happened?"

He straightens up and pulls the wine glass closer. Circles it, considering...

"I did have a friend from high school who was an exchange student from there and I did go looking for her. I asked the woman at the youth hostel to make the call and, in fact, she was, coincidentally, in the United States at the exact moment I was standing in her hometown. The woman from the youth hostel was impressed by the coincidence. That happened."

He's authoritative, swiping his hand from side to side to make it clear that there is absolutely no room for doubt.

"Where did the rest come from?"

The darkness is complete. The candles keep the lighting above zero but are insufficient for the mood. He goes out of the kitchen and turns on the light above the dining table by the TV creating a nice effect through the doorway. There's a fling and a pop, then he comes back to the table, topping off both wine glasses as he sits. Unfamiliar music comes softly from the other room. It is a woman's voice at an unusual pitch, both high and low at the same time with an uncompromising power and depth.

"Backtracking, I guess. Or backfilling... She was older. In her thirties."

—You do better with the older ones. The little ones think you're dangerous. Or weird. We know better, can handle it, handle you.

"Why don't you stab me now?"

"I only meant... ...I'm getting the sense that... ...of the differences."

"In age, you mean."

"Yeah. It's not that the desires change, but the ease with which they're accepted does."

"Accepted?"

"Whatever you'd call it. I don't know what words to use. I mean..."

Touching his elbow and looking quietly at him. Calming him. It's okay.

"Younger, they don't... ...you don't... ...you're totally focused on what he's doing. That's what I meant. Younger girls aren't as demanding. They..."

"I see. They let you get off, and you're scot free, is that it? You like that, do you?"

He's sulking now.

"Sorry. Go on. I'm listening."

"If you're going to..."

"Go on. Please."

"It's not about good or bad. That's not what I'm saying. It's what I've noticed. And when they're older, well, it seems as though that goes away. They're more selfish. More demanding. But in a good way."

"You're being selfish dear, but don't worry, it's in a good way."

—You have to have a fucking self in order to be selfish, for Christ's sake.

He smirks and blows out into the air above the table. He's both frustrated and excited. It's like being wound up and winding up at the same time in some kind of perfect harmony. It's a duet, a nice back and forth that raises the stakes.

"It doesn't seem hard to understand. I'm not sure whether you don't see it, or you're pretending, trying to give me a hard time."

"Why, I have no idea what you mean, sir."

"Is it that hard to imagine? Those girls. You, when you were younger. You know what I'm talking about. His desire... ...you can say he was the one getting off, but... You were pretending to be in control. In your head. Thinking this is what's supposed to feel good. What do you think is going to happen if you encourage him, give him that kind of feedback?"

He seems genuinely irritated. There is ferocity in his eyes, he's serious.

"I admit it. Okay, okay. Calm down. Go on. Tell me what you're thinking. How'd you come up with it? Stay focused."

He calms down and takes a sip of wine, laughing now, playing on the edge of pretend emotions and real ones, being careful not to go too far one way or the other.

"The reverse could be pleasant too, that's what I'm saying. Yeah, she was older, and I imagined she'd be clearer about what she wanted and that might be nice because I could play around with those control fantasies. I'd be the one getting her off, taking care of her, simple as that. In the story, not for real."

—Okay. It's okay. He can be right.

He breathes heavily. Still wound up. Adagio fades. He turns on the overhead light and the magic leaves the room. Now there are piles of dirty dishes on the counter needing attention, a dish with half eaten sweets too. He feels the pull.

"I know it's hard for you to believe."

He stops and turns back. Listening carefully, knows the tone has changed, that he can let down and listen. He wants to understand. Every facet turns this way, every part reaches out to accept what rolls in.

"The desires are just as strong."

"I know..."

A cautionary glance to stop his interruption. Wait please.

"But there's a key difference and you'll have to figure out how that works."

"What difference?"

"When you approach someone, do you worry that she'll beat the shit out of you? Do you worry that she'll take what she wants even if you decide you don't want it? Do you worry that she won't be done when you're done, and may turn into a psycho stalking you down..."

"Well..."

"What I'm saying is that there are so many worries and things that make what's equal ultimately unequal. You see what I mean?"

He nods, eyes darting thoughtfully.

"Don't ask me how, I don't know how. It isn't a formula. The decision involves intangibles and random things that are only there briefly or barely. You see what I mean?"

He's standing in front of the dishes, ready to begin.

"I think so. That could cause someone to dislike it, to stop liking it, prefer to go without it."

Nodding and pursing the lips. The music stops and the abrupt silence calls attention to how good it was. "What were we listening to?"

"My friends in Oxford. I can make you a copy if you want," pauses briefly before continuing. "That's why we say, *get lucky*. Because that's what happens. You get lucky. Bad and good. It's not only effort or some angle you've master-minded, but past experiences, people you've learned from and how they connect you to other people. There's a lot of luck involved."

Standing next to him at the sink and touching the hair by his ear before pushing it back over and away from his face.

—Not... ...okay, lucky it is.

7.12.4.Greta.19.86.9.25 [ref(..24)]

— *"The siguiriya is like a cautery that burns the heart, throat, and lips of those who utter it. One must be careful of the fire and sing it at just the right moment."* [Garcia Lorca]

(He was afraid of the goat. We both were, but I pretended I wasn't and didn't run off toward the front of the hut. He paused, not wanting to leave me alone there, and watched from a distance before asking if I was sure I wanted to do that. I approached it though it seemed as though it wanted to run us down. But it didn't, it wanted to have its head scratched. It leaned against me and bumped its head over and over. If I tried to pull my hand back, it bumped again, forcing me to keep going. He came up and stood there petting it too. I didn't understand the feeling that ran through me when he stood close like that. It's not what you'd think. It's from somewhere else, as though he's carrying spirits, as though he has millions of eyes, and they're peering through the wind and the creek, looking over at me. I couldn't find them when I looked back, but I could feel them directed at me, clearing away some unwanted substance.)

The rain isn't letting up. Running the last 100 meters and arriving at the deck behind the guest house at the bottom of the trail. Soaked through and dripping puddles of water while standing in front of the glass door, laughing with a simple joy only accessible in fresh air.

(Last night, one mat space in the women's dorm, another in the men's. Didn't think I'd miss him that much. Only a few minutes between going to lie down and falling asleep, as tired as I was, but still. These last few days, it's been nice falling asleep with someone there to listen even when there was nothing to hear.)

She brings towels. Off the trail at the bottom near the road, there is a lumber works, but it isn't clear whether it's still in working order. No sounds of saws on a Thursday morning. The guest house is clean and humble. Wrapped up in warm cloth, stepping lightly through the glass door, and standing by the desk while she fills out the paperwork. It's still early, not quite lunchtime, but it's pouring and there's no sign it will let up any time soon. It's warm inside.

—I'm famished.

Asking to see a lunch menu as she collects the signature and gets the keys. "It's not crowded, so you can take the back room, the one at the end, it has a nice fireplace. Be sure to open the flew."

"Thank you. Can we get the ravioli and the sausages? Would it be possible to have them in the room?"

"Of course."

Taking the wet daypacks and walking up the stairs. It's a beautiful wood staircase with a plush carpet strip spanning the center. At the top there is a long hallway and only one way to go to get to what could reasonably be called the back. The room has a big comfortable bed with a table and desk on the other side and the fireplace on the backside wall. It has everything necessary to light and kindle a fire, and he gets right to work. Setting the packs down nearby to lay out everything as the fire gets going. Shivering next to him while he stacks the wood, he says, "You should get out of those wet clothes, take a hot shower."

"I don't have anything to put on. Everything is soaked."

He goes through his bag, pulls out the water bottles and sets them on the table. He isn't carrying much, but there is a T-shirt, and he holds it up. "This is pretty dry." Taking it from him and heading into the bathroom while he keeps at it with the fire.

(We were tired when we arrived last night but energized. Such an unusual place. Those hikers sitting around telling stories of what they saw on their way. The path up from Oberstdorf is only one of several ways to get to the hut, others took a different approach or came from the next mountain over. Everyone had such elaborate gear. One man was walking with climbing boots with metal spikes sticking out of the toes. He had ski poles in each hand and would stick the ground authoritatively as he walked. Someone said it will rain, but no one was concerned. What could you do? You were there already, must've been prepared. It was warm and cozy in the lodge and after we had something to eat, we sat there with the others and talked about our plans: what we were going to do today and what we saw yesterday. We were easily distracted by everything around us. He was interested in people's stories. The men and women who were sitting there were each telling about what they saw that day: hiking stories about wildlife and birds, things immediate to their journey, and then he'd ask where they were from. Did they come far to hike these trails? Is it something they do frequently? One couple told him details about how they came up from Zürich. Cheaper in Austria, they said, and they loved the Tyrol, the people were incomparably friendly. They had a son who was working for the post office in Zürich and a daughter with the rail system at the information kiosk.

Neither were married and the couple was concerned they would never have any grandchildren. He asked how often they saw them, and they told him about the meals they cooked every Sunday. They doted on their children but were sad too. They wanted them to be happy and couldn't imagine it any other way. Thought they were lonely. At least they were nearby, he said, nowadays everyone is spread out. They were talking about everything because he was open to everything. He told them things here and there about himself too, about how he was going to move far away from his parents when he got back to the States. They appreciated finding out about him. I'd never have done that on my own.)

Looking into the mirror and seeing a merged figure, a woman herself and someone else. Turning on the shower. Steady streams of water work wonders displacing the demons and hangers on. Rubbing the eyes, looking to see if they have anything useful for improving the situation, but nothing other than shampoo and conditioner.

(A younger man who worked at the hut or with the ranger service had a guitar and was playing it. Some soft background music, no one was paying much attention. He asked him what he was playing, said it sounded amazing, something by Bach, but the man didn't know what it was called. He asked Ellis if he played and he said yes, but only in the Flamenco style. The man wanted to hear something. He warned him that he wasn't any good and couldn't play much that counted as a song, but the man didn't care and handed over the guitar. He said that in Flamenco they sometimes strike the guitar with their fingers and that there's usually a plastic guard on the top to protect it. The guitar was old and beaten up so the man waved the warning aside and said he should play away. I thought it was going to be embarrassing, for some reason. He was so humble in saying he didn't know how to play, but the man was desperate to hear what Flamenco style sounded like, he insisted. It was lovely. He played soft and in a round. There was a theme and then it varied. He said it was a style named after the capital of Flamenco music, Sevilla or Sevillanas, and he said most people would know it as a popular form to accompany dancers.)

—Did I dream about his fingers dancing across the strings? I wish I had something to hide the eyes.

(The man was surprised too, and the older couple. He sold us on how poorly he played, and we didn't expect much, but it was truly lovely. When he finished and handed back the guitar, we were encouraging him, but the older woman scolded him for fibbing about not being good. It's true, he said, my hands can do it, but I can't count. In Flamenco, what matters more than anything is the rhythm. You can flub the notes, you can make the guitar buzz, you can do everything wrong, but the compás, the rhythm, is sacred, and must never go wrong. That style is in 6's but I think if you tried to count what I was doing you'd see that sometimes it's in 7's and

sometimes only 5. If it's here, in the warming hut, that doesn't matter, but
if there are other players, they'd tell me to go sit down and let someone
else have a turn.)

Out of the bathroom and wearing only the T-shirt he gave me, the fire
is going strong, and the contents of our packs are laid out in front of it.
Some things, a pair of pants and his flannel shirt, are hanging from the
mantle using the water bottles as ballast. Handing him the wet clothes to
add to the arrangement, but something makes him uncomfortable, and he
quickly jumps up and pulls the duvet down to take the blanket off the bed.
He hands it over, wrapping it tightly and giving a squeeze at the end. There
is a big armoire by the door, and he looks in it to see if there are any more
blankets. He takes one out and says he'll use it after showering, then
disappears into the bathroom leaving it outside the door.

(When we went to bed, I was exhausted, but it was the first fun I had in
months. The time together until then, it wasn't exactly good, mostly
uncomfortable. Who was this guy and why did I have to entertain him?
What are we doing here? With Eva and her friends at the cemetery, that
was beyond strange, I wanted him to be a member of the family, but he
wasn't. It seemed that he should be close to us, but you can't make that
happen all at once. Can't force it. We had no adventures together, nothing
happened. At the cemetery, it wasn't what I wanted either. Then the driving
and being near the lake. These were things you do with someone you were
close to, but we weren't, we were going through the motions and trying to
force it. This was what I wanted. The machete story. I felt happy when we
went off to our dormitory rooms. I wanted to hug him, but couldn't, the
logistics were wrong. Where we were on the stairs, the way it happened, he
didn't want to anyway, or didn't try to make it easier. I was too shy. Lying
there for those few minutes and missing him, wishing I was the kind of
person who did the things she wanted to do. Why did everything have to
be such a struggle? Why did there have to be ten sides to everything that
you had to carefully think through and evaluate on their merits? Heidi isn't
that way, wasn't that way. She would shout when she wanted to shout, cry
when she wanted to cry, hug someone when she wanted to hug someone.
I never felt I could be that way, she was that way for both of us.)

—It's why I couldn't... ...why I let them down. That's why she had to
leave the diner. It wasn't him, it was his shadow cast on me...

[Heidi...]

There is a light knock at the door and the woman stands there with a
tray of food. It smells delicious. There is a pitcher of water and some sweets
for afterward. She puts it down on the table and leaves in a hurry. No need
to sign for anything, she'll remember.

—Should wait for him, but it smells so good. Pour the water, but...

(Not much for breakfast, only some bread and cheese. Wow, this is so good, he said, as if he didn't have it yesterday and the day before. He could tell the difference between the cheeses even when it was the same kind but from a different region. Not to show off or anything, but just because he could tell. Simple as that. It was raining hard already, and we stared at the downpour knowing we were going to get soaked. It wasn't a long walk down because the valley on this side was higher than the one we left behind, but still a couple hours. We waited as long as we could, drinking extra coffee, but there was no sign of clearing sky. In what was a huge case of cultural misunderstanding, he asked the man if they had any garbage bags. He said sure and brought two, but they weren't right. He explained that when you were in need you could take a big garbage bag and cut a few holes to use it as a rain poncho. No one ever heard of this before and there were many questions. No, Americans aren't stupid, he tried to explain, no one would prefer a garbage bag to a raincoat, it's, well, we don't have anything else so if you had one it might work in a pinch. They were sorry, they didn't have anything like that. If we'd been thinking, we'd have taken the smaller ones and used them to wrap up our clothes inside the day packs. He thought his was waterproof. It mostly was, but mostly isn't good enough.)

He comes out of the bathroom and his hair is wet and hanging down to his shoulders. The towel is wrapped around his waist leaving his chest bare. He grabs the blanket quickly and swings it around himself in one swift motion. The towel drops to the floor, he picks it up to hang in the bathroom, comes back out with the boxers and shirt he was wearing, and arranges them next to the fire. Watching him the whole time, making it seem as though it's because the food is waiting, and he needs to hurry up. He quietly accepts that silent explanation and hurries over. The room is warming up and the food is delicious. The blankets are awkward to hold in place though, they require frequent readjustments leaving gaps here and there, and get in the way of eating. Quick glances both ways, there is endless curiosity. Hiding makes what is hidden impossible to ignore.

Finishing, getting up, and going to sit down in front of the fire. The blankets are proving more difficult to manage than expected. The cinch is up around the chest but that means that normal movements will cause them to flap open from above the waist on down. Regular flashing cannot be helped. Still tight, needing to hunch forward to prevent too much from coming undone. Mostly eyes straight ahead to keep things right and proper. By the fire, there's nothing but embarrassment remaining from the food and the short trip across the room. The lines are firmly drawn between the blankets that don't dare touch in the light and heat cast by the blaze.

—This is ridiculous.

"Don't you think this is ridiculous?"

"What?" He says with eyes meeting for the first time since the epic crossing of the room, skin tones finally returning to normal.

"This. The whole point was to..." Can't get it out. Can't point at it directly. Feeling it is fine, saying it makes the chest and throat burn and close up. Forget it then, kicking open the blanket, unwinding from the hips, and pushing it back so that the legs can stretch forward into the warm glow. He looks down and over, reaches out to take the thin boxer shorts from the brick floor by the fireplace, and wrangles them into place while turning slightly sideways. He sits back and swings open the blanket extending his legs too, smiling awkwardly.

"Mostly dry," he says.

—You could now if you wanted to...

"I still have to be careful."

"Of course," he says, thinking he understands but then realizing he doesn't. "Of what?"

"Your T-shirt isn't that long and mine are cotton and still wet. Over there." Pointing, but he looks at the hand and not where it leads.

"Oh right." Still not 100% sure he understands, but the tone makes him think he should, and he pretends to.

"I'm not wearing them. That's what I mean."

"Ohhh, sure, I get it, yes. Sorry I didn't bring an extra pair. I could've..." then he trails off but can't help looking down. Taking advantage of that to look at his face. Such long eyelashes, beautiful eyes, and soft lips. He's nervous.

—That means something, being nervous, he wouldn't be nervous if he didn't... ...would he?

"It was fun last night. Today too, this was fun, getting wet, caught in the rain. This is hiking. This is what's supposed to happen when you go hiking. It's a completely expected thing."

He laughs, nodding in agreement.

Going on. "It was fun for me because... ...talking to those people. I can't explain it exactly, but something about meeting people when you're with someone, it can change what you see in the person you're with."

Adjusting on the blanket means adjusting the space between as well, ending up closer, leaning more, and now shoulders sometimes touch through the fabric. The fire is getting warm.

"It changed how you see me," he says without looking over.

"Yeah, sort of. You're more familiar. They were strangers and by comparison you're not. More. Does that..."

Nodding brings it to a close and the throat won't offer further assistance.

—My familiar. That's what was missing, what was missing while lying there in the darkness, listening to the creaking floors and the rolling bodies on the dormer mattresses.

Leaning continues to close the space. Once that first touch happens across the thickness of the blankets, concern over noticing or not noticing fades, and there is surrender to what's nearby. He rolls the blanket off his left shoulder and stretches it out with his arm along the hem. Letting go of the other blanket and pushing it back, it falls down flat behind, then curling up into the outstretched place on offer. His chin tilts up and presses down in close contact at the head and hair, he settles his arm against the back and around the far shoulder to bring it still closer, making a combined, huddling form. Not better than the fire, but an extension of it.

—All I have to do is look up.

Looking up, everything goes breathless. No one initiates, only positioning and turning. A light touch, no urgency, nothing shy, just position: looking up and finding. Welcome, by chance, sheer luck of the moment stretching out before the fire and away from the rain tip-tapping at the window.

Still playing at innocence, fawning back to embrace, and staring into the furnace, lilting some. He's too entangled to brute rush forward and tend to it, so it comes to that, leaning forward to reach for the poker to stoke the flames, but it is too far. Commitment in progress, too late to stop now and no room for retreat, wriggling out from his arms and swinging the legs underneath balancing on knees and leaning forward to crawl to the metal rod, taking it firmly to poke the logs and reposition them to lurch the flames with more fuel. Setting it back on the hearth and turning to see him in awe, exhaling sharply, and unable to look away, but quickly recovering to bring his gaze front and center. Grinning knowingly, welcoming the weakness of his sex. He reads it right, sensing there is nothing left to hold back.

8.8

the middle american

8.8.1.X.19.87.1.2 [ref(..86.9.28-12.31)]

(To that dripping there was no response. For every time flying through dawn, simple somethings said and smelled, they were a bubble, bursting, drawing from the night and breaking day. Pling. Dung do do dippity. There was coming light.)

Tip to the edge and reach to the nightstand. There is a clock radio standing next to the tiny square turned upside down. The smaller says 7:14, the bigger 7:17.

(There was disappointment, silence after silence during. What did I do? What seed did Anna sow?)

—Better talk to her, tell her I'm sorry, explain... ...she's all I think about... ...and obstacles, friction. Can't see through the murk. Never. Doesn't work that way.)

Door opening in the alcove. The bathroom door springs shut and then the water. It's that familiar, running and running, then the flush, with the same rhythms no matter the agent. A little on the extra, a while longer, then a creaking crack and another and then the door comes open and the light from the alcove floods the room. There's no window, it's on the inside track. Stretching and leaning to the side. She sets a pile of folded clothing down and comes to the edge of the bed and takes a seat. Flinging upright and sliding back to the headboard.

"What's going on?"

"It's time to get up, you've got a train to catch," she says simply, looking this way then back toward the clocks and the pack on the floor.

Clearing away the dust. "What train? What are you talking about?"

"You're leaving Nürnberg today. I'll put you on the IC to Paris. Those tickets are good for 30 days, you can take the whole month if you want, but you have to leave."

"Wait, what? You're throwing me out?"

"It's for the best. Eva doesn't want to see you again. You can't stay here. You have to go."

Straightening against the headboard, pulling up the comforter, only boxers beneath the blankets and weirdly concerned that she's sitting too close.

"What do you mean, Eve doesn't want to see me again?"

"It's for the best, don't you think? You should move on. With your rough ways, you don't want a crutch, do you? She knows who you are. There's no sense fighting it."

"Are you talking about yesterday? That was theory, I was talking shit, I didn't mean that, I love her, I have to see her again, I can't leave without saying goodbye."

"Yes, you can." She is immobile, staring straight back, but she isn't mad, doesn't appear the least bit angry, no emotion at all.

"I think you've misjudged me. I talk a lot of shit, but it's not how I am. I care about her. I haven't been able to..."

"Is that right? And it *was* bullshit. Talking talking talking. That's it, right?"

"We were having a conversation, that's how it works. It doesn't mean anything. It's not how I feel."

She turns more to the side to make eye contact. Her leg curls up onto the bed allowing her to twist this way. She lays her hand out on the hip, and looks up. Silence, moves her hand up onto the belly and slides farther up the bed so she doesn't have to stretch. Steady breathing, but it's quickening. She leans in and puts her face within an inch or two, as if to slowly lean into a kiss, but she jerks back and stands up.

"Get your things together. We're leaving in ten minutes."

Reaching out to take her arm. She pauses, looks back.

"You're a pig, an unacceptable candidate," she says.

"That's not..."

There is something in her left hand, it catches light and glitters for a second before receding into the half-darkness again.

—Idiot. Thought we were getting along.

(Never saw it coming, never expected this. Dumb shit, I thought we were flirting.)

"You were flirting with Lorelei."

"She was flirting with me."

"You were flirting with me. While Eva was here and after she left."

"I was being friendly. You invited me to stay, it's gratitude."

"Unbelievable."

"It's nothing. Reacting... ...the situation..."

"You have to go. Get up." Not convincing.

She pulls the comforter back. Boxers exposed and morning hard on pressing against the half-opened fly. She glances down, a reflex, can't help herself, doesn't want to, but goes back for a second look, takes a deep breath, and extends her left hand along the bed until it is almost touching the upper thigh near the pelvis. Whatever is in the other hand hits the light again.

"What's that?" whispering. She turns her hand over to reveal a condom, tears open the package, and reaches over with both hands, using the left to steady the target through the fly and the right to roll the condom down into position. Deliberate and direct, she steps out of her loose-fitting pajama bottoms and crawls up onto the bed while pulling down on the hips. Flattening out beneath her as she wiggles into position, putting her legs tightly together and using her knees to force the legs apart. Stretches her underwear out of the way as her face strains close by, but she isn't looking at anything. Something doesn't feel right. She steers it inside her and, though she is as close as can be, there is no feeling in any of it. She rocks forward and grinds her hips downward, moving from side to side, her small breasts press down hard against the chest through her T-shirt.

—How are they sisters? Her sweat or mine?

Her body seems to be probing for something. Her hips are swaying without coming to rest. Her head hangs low to the side, can't see a silhouette. She breathes heavily, but it's frustration rather than pleasure, then she rocks firmly forward. It's deep inside her, as deep as possible from this angle. She grinds still farther forward and tries to grind against something. It's nothing to her, but the rapid jerks have an effect, and the tip of the condom fills. Hands and arms flat to the sides, afraid to touch her, they clutch at the cover sheet. She pulls back, looking down briefly without eye contact, and gets up.

"What was that?" Leaning up on elbows.

"You're no one. Exactly the same as everyone else, the nobodies. How the music made her feel, you're that way, you are that."

She grabs her pajamas and leaves the room. The door across the alcove closes. It sounds as if there are drawers opening and closing. There must be a door inside the room, it opens and closes more than once. Getting up, straightening out the boxers, and finding the same jeans and T-shirt from last night. Quickly stuffing everything into the rucksack. Socks on and holding the pack in one arm, heading out through the alcove and to the front door. Setting it down and turning back toward the room. Slipping on the boots and tucking the laces under the tongue. About to put on the coat and hat when the other door in the alcove opens. She comes out wearing those same overalls and moves briskly across the room to the door, takes her coat and puts it on, grabbing a scarf and hat from the box up on top of the coat rack nailed to the wall next to the door.

"What was that about?" asking in confusion, still not clear what she's up to. She pauses in the middle of putting her boots on and stands straight up directly facing this way, then puts her hand over and above the cock against the base of it.

"Nothing. Not a thing," she says, then goes back to pulling at her boot, getting it into place, and lacing it up before working on the other one. "I was checking."

"You're nuts."

"And now you have to go. Come on. I'll give you a lift to the station."

Walking down the stairs in silence toward the cold air. There is a communal garage next to the front door. Making way to her car down the ramp, she unlocks the passenger side doors and heads around to the driver's side without waiting. Swinging the rucksack into the backseat and sliding into the front while she turns the engine over, and the defroster immediately begins to blow cold air.

"I took the book."

"It's fine," she says.

"Left the other."

She doesn't say anything while navigating the tight space between the parking place and the garage door, presses the button, and, as it creaks upward, she guns the motor and heads through. Once the car passes out to the short driveway, she hits the button again and patiently stares into the rearview mirror while it closes. She guides it to the ground with her eyes, then pulls out into the street.

"Will you please explain what this is about?"

"No," she says without looking over.

"Is that supposed to make it impossible for me to stay?"

She doesn't respond, keeps moving the car through the streets, working the stick shift and steering wheel, turning this way and that without any real signs of navigation.

"Are you sure you know what Eve wants?"

"Eva doesn't want to talk to you, doesn't want to see you again."

"That's it, no explanation?"

She pulls the car into the drop off area in front of the station. There are a few available spaces, and she parks. Getting out as soon as the engine is off and the parking brake set.

"Couldn't you check with your hand?" Speaking over the shoulder. She is standing by the front of the car waiting resolutely. Reaching into the back to get the rucksack, swinging it over the shoulders, and pulling the waist and chest straps into place.

"It's got nothing to do with you," she says turning toward the entrance. It's Friday and people must be taking a long weekend after the holiday because there's no one around.

"Sure felt like it had something to do with me."

She slows down and stops in the middle of the road for a second. "What are you going to do with your life, Stefan? Don't you have somewhere you need to be?"

"East Central Illinois next September."

"That's a long way from here." Then she turns back and hurries across the street. Picking up the pace to avoid falling behind.

At the door, she turns toward the ticket area and heads straight for one of the windows. "Wait here," she says.

She comes back and hands over a crisp, newly printed ticket. Paris IC. Turning toward the center board to look for the right track number. "Seven," she says without looking. "We have to hurry." Falling into a light jog with the pack on the back, heading over to track seven and down the long lead to the front of the train.

"This is it," she says. She puts her hands on both shoulders and squeezes firmly, then turns and hurries back up toward the exit.

"If I could sing any song, it would be her," but she is too far away.

Climbing onto the train, slinging the pack up onto the rack and taking a seat. The car is nearly empty.

—Whatever the first stop is, I'll get off.

(None of that made any damn sense. What kind of a person does that? Women aren't that way, it makes no sense. It was as if I was nothing, as if she was trying to plug the correct wires into the back of a stereo. She didn't care what I was feeling or thinking, it wasn't a sexual act. Mechanical.)

Groping at the waistline and pelvis, pressing the hand down firmly to feel around.

—What the hell is she talking about?

[That was Birgit level shit. They're fucked up like that, every one of them. Was that to put me off balance? If she hadn't done that, if she had gone into her room and got dressed, would I have followed her out to the car, or would I have been, fuck you, I'm going wherever the hell I want to go? Take my shit and head out. There's a youth hostel, got a bunch of money, didn't need a ride, doesn't fucking own me. They're crazy. Every damn one of them.]

—But Eve?

The guy is walking through the cabins. Looks to be getting ready to depart.

—Fuck this. Not going quietly to my death. Not getting on the train in an orderly fashion.

Popping up and grabbing the rucksack, pulling it down and slinging it around back onto the shoulders. Pulling the belt tight at the waist, sliding the hook into the opening, then pulling the strap across the chest and affixing the plastic clasp. Shooting up the aisle and bouncing out of the cabin before the guy closes the door.

[Tell Eve what her sister did, expose everything. She loves me. There's no way she doesn't want to see me again. She wants to see me but doesn't know how to justify herself. Buzzing in her ear. Can't explain... ...what she's attracted to... ...they think it should revolt her. Can't help it, they don't understand.]

No way she's still there, it's been plenty long enough for her to get back to her car and leave. No sign of her back at the ticket windows. Pausing before stepping up.

—Something about confusion. Her, that one. Didn't get too far in school. No gymnasium, technical high school, I bet. Okay, that one.

"Hi there," in English. "Do you speak English?"

"A little," she says.

"FUBAR. My friend got the ticket, but it's the wrong one. This is the IC to Paris, but that's not right. She must've misunderstood." It's a rapid stream of words, not trying to be particularly easy to follow, not enunciating clearly. She can't keep up but gets the drift.

"It's the wrong ticket?" she asks. Pushing it back toward her, she picks it up and sets it to the side. "Where do you want to go?" she asks trying to be helpful.

Swinging the rucksack off the shoulder and setting it down. Pulling the big map from the top pocket and opening it to somewhere random. Flipping through it and talking about the various possibilities, trying to find the right page.

"We said something about the Tyrol, but then I thought we were going to try for Greece. That was by plane though so I'm not sure..."

She slides a pile of bills and some coins out through the bottom of the glass. "When you're ready," she says slowly and with a nice broad smile. "Come back and buy the right ticket."

Showing confusion. "Uh yeah, sure, thanks."

Awkwardly stuffing the map back into the outer pocket of the rucksack and then slinging it up over the shoulders again before securing it in place. Stuffing the money into the pants' pocket and pulling the hat and gloves from the coat. "Veilen Dank, Weidersehen." Then off back into the station toward the tracks.

—238 DM. That's the refund. Okay, now I have about 600 DM and a plane ticket to New York from Paris.

(That plane ticket was open-ended.)

—I can change it. Don't have to go back through Paris if I don't want to. Pam Am will change that for anything of equal value. Can head back through London. I'll bet it's cheaper. Might refund me some.

At the information desk at the top of the long bays by the train platforms there is a woman helping another customer. Once he leaves, she turns this way and asks, "How can I help you?"

"I'm wondering, would you be able to tell me where the nearest Pan Am office is?"

She looks unsure to begin with, then recalls something and picks up the phone. While listening and waiting for something on the other end, she says, "My colleagues at the office may have more information. That's not something we usually handle here." Taking the map back out of the rucksack while waiting. She explains it to them, everything is clear, and she hangs up after scratching something onto the pad by the phone.

"They have offices in Frankfurt, in the center and at the airport. You can go to either one. Here is the number." Hands over the piece of paper with two addresses on it.

"Thanks."

Getting a coffee from the shop across from information and sitting down with the map on the table and the rucksack leaning up against the leg, foot firmly set inside one of the shoulder straps. Rolling a cigarette and leaning over the table with the warm steam wafting up and mixing with the smoke from the end of the butt. Flipping to the back where the maps of Europe give a low-resolution view of the entire route.

—Nürnberg to Frankfurt through Würzburg, that's a straight shot on the 3. Okay. Then you follow the Rhein to Köln, that's the 42. Then to Brussels through Aachen on the 4 before it turns south and into the 44. At the border, it's the E40 to Brussels. Near Bruges, at Zeebruge or Ostend or something like that, there are ferries. Zeebruge for sure. There is a dotted line to Dover. Hopefully there's good truck traffic and that guy was right about their policy for passengers.

[Tentative plans, didn't need to know the exact route, it's good enough to have the general direction. There'd be people along the way, they'd suggest the best way or things worth seeing, easy scams, whatever. No sense getting it down in blood.]

—Then Dover, Canterbury to London. What are the odds I'll have any money left once I get there? Got to be careful, London's not a good place when skint, I bet, but okay.

[Cross that channel when you come to it.]

Finishing the coffee and tossing it into the litter canister at the edge of the tables next to the café counter. Shouldering the bag and walking back toward the front of the station.

(Eve didn't go back to school yet. She's off today, I should call. At least say goodbye, at least thank her for everything. Felt wrong, and there's a row of phones by the exit.)

—Okay, quick call, say my goodbyes, then a tram north as close to the 3 as possible.

The clock on the station wall says 9:58. Dialing the number after inserting the coins.

"Hello," it's Elke.

"Hi Elke, Stefan here."

"Hi Stefan, good morning," she sounds cheerful.

—What the...

"I'm sorry for the trouble I've put you through with Anna. I was hoping to talk to Eve."

"Sure, let me check."

Silence. Then more of it. Biting the lip and waiting.

"Hello," she says, more upbeat than expected.

—Didn't get to say goodbye to Elke.

"Hi Eve, only wanted to say goodbye and thank you for everything, your help. Everything. I'm sorry..."

"You are leaving?" She sounds alarmed.

"Yes, I'm at the station. I'll head east, to Frankfurt."

Silence. Something in the background. Multiple voices.

"But I don't... ...Stefan, why would you...."

—Shock. Doesn't know. But... ...how can I... Fuck. Crazy bitch.

"Sorry, I have to go. I'll write to you."

Click and gone.

—Didn't know. Didn't know. But... Too much disappointment. Can't deal with that.

(A one-night stand with the sister. Lydia's ghost. Chased out of town by the drama. Haunted by Birgit. Cashing in the ticket and scavenging the money. Still being robbed by Julia. My guards were always standing by and pointing. Guardian angles.)

[Unable to find her in this sad departure, unable to see or get to the place I wanted to be. A prisoner, someone gripped by the forces of nature. Fruit picked prematurely: it's a fucking conspiracy.]

—Who is it, who says I am no one? Who is behind this?

(*"The love that moves the sun and the other stars."* [Dante's Paradiso])

8.8.2.X.19.87.1.12 [ref(..2-12)]

From Heidelberg to New Year's Eve:
January the 12th is 228.5 km from New Year's Eve:

Your sister stole my shirt. I don't care what she says, I wasn't flirting with any of them. I wanted you and the rest was civility. Still not over it. I mean, what did I do? I sat there, lay there, didn't make any kind of move. After she did, I'm pretty sure I never touched her. Not in any way shape or form. What are you going to call that? Did you know? What would she call it if it happened to her? That dude fucked her and buggered off and she loves him still. What's the difference? What's different, why focus on me? Rushing me off, putting me on the train. Fuck her, I'm free, I don't have to go where she tells me to go or do what she tells me to do. Did you know? You think that whatever bullshit led us to where we were meant that I didn't get a say? Fuck that, I get a say. Fifty fucking percent worth. Okay, yeah, have your way, but don't expect that to be the end of it.

Her bony ass was nowhere near yours, not in the same league, and I had to give in to that. She wanted that, some twisted protection defense or whatever she thought she was doing. As if to her that's how it worked because you know how the rest are, they get this thing in their head and it's complicated and convoluted, but to them it's the only thing that makes sense anymore so that's how it is and anything that goes against it, well, they'll have plenty to say about what's wrong with that. Don't take my feelings into account, don't listen to me. Whatever. Fuck that. She cooked this whole thing up and then got bunged up when I gave it a completely different take. Usually means they're unsure of themselves, can't withstand any disagreement that would add to the doubts they're suppressing.

Now you think I'm untouchable. The gall that I would call you and try to say goodbye or see if you feel the way your sister said you did, oh that makes me evil. I never should have done it, that's total bullshit. Common courtesy for fucksake. She should have expected me to get ahold of you. Did you? What if it wasn't what you wanted? Your sister was playing us and I'm the asshole. Wham bam without the wham or the bam. It cost me. I didn't want her. I never thought about her that way. Wanted a place to stay, that's it. Didn't know she was going to use every single thing I did or said against me. That's how they are. They keep track, they write it down, or hold onto it with some weirdly weighted accounting system. There is no discussion, it's the way they say it is and there's no room for debate. That's what they call reason, that's their logic.

Later in the evening. So even, this eve.

The first guy that stopped was headed to Bamberg and I said what the hell, might as well. Immediate relief. A reasonable person who wasn't seeing only what he wanted to see. He dropped me off by the youth hostel. Not much to see there, but I don't care about that kind of stuff anyway. I love breathing the air. There wasn't a whole lot going on, a couple of Aussies with some funny stories about Czechoslovakia. They noticed the big Kafka book. Man, that thing is fucking heavy, it's a real bear to carry, but they noticed it, commented on it. "How are you managing with that, mate? Does it have its own pack?" We shared our tea, as they call it, and talked about Wenceslas Square. Apparently, there's some big plaque near the house where he lived with his parents. Lots of tourists running around down there, a café nearby, that kind of thing, a whole industry. It's enough to make you physically ill. Part of what made it so pathetic was that they had no idea who he was. They'd heard the name, they weren't savages, they knew there was something about a guy turning into a cockroach or something, but that was the end of it, and they kept bumping into these blokes who took it seriously and were high-mindedly following along with the guidebook. When I told them he suffocated, they said they almost suffocated too from those windbags taking up the air. Did you get a picture in front of it? Fucking hilarious. Tears.

Only stayed in whambamberg one night and I was happy to have the distraction, got you and your crazy sister out of my head. I cared about you, and felt horrible about not saying goodbye to Elke. She'll think I forgot about her or that she didn't mean anything to me. She shouldn't think she's invisible, she shouldn't think she... ...I ended up being more attracted to you, but...

There wasn't much to that anyway. It was that one drive to Salzburg, that's what was between us that Elke didn't share. If you think about it, but you must've talked about it, and figured out some big arrangement. Anna clearly knew more than I did about the whole thing. You never bothered to tell me how you felt, but you spilled your guts to Anna and your sister. Elke too, but did you worry about how she'd react, or did you talk to Anna while she was nearby? Who knows what the dynamic was? You have your pecking order and it's complicated. I'm sure that's patriarchy's fault. We forced you to form an order where the prettiest one is at the top and the least desirable at the bottom. Desirable to men, as if chicks didn't like pretty girls, little dollies, on their own. There's a man's voice behind it, no doubt. You learned to see with the male gaze, such bullshit, try taking responsibility for yourself now and again why don't you?

Off to Würzburg. Easy ride to get and a great place to stay. Filled with South Africans. The youth hostel was crowded. Some Aussies and Kiwis, same as always, but most of them were South Africans, and once I got in good with a few of them, the rotation kept me in good with the new ones. When the old ones left, it's as if I was holding down their fort. I stayed for almost a week, and it was a blast, plentiful craziness. Not only South Africans, I should say, there were a few from Southwest Africa too. White people talking about the good old days. Man, they got some fucked up ideas going on and they don't see it. Blind as can be.

The girl from Southwest Africa, I didn't dare correct her, she was down for it too, but I didn't feel up to it, still not in the mood. Bet you loved that. Your sister too. If I'm honest, I'd have to say she took the air out of my sails. Didn't much want to get with any of the women in that crowd. The South Africans weren't that hot or anything, but that girl from Southwest Africa, she was something. Couldn't do it. I was missing you and thinking about you the whole time and then thinking about how fucked up it was. What the hell was that about? Did you know?

One night, we stayed out late at the café in Würzburg and they wouldn't let us back into the hostel, so we had to go back out again and find a club.

They let us in and thought it was cool that we were there, but it was exhausting, especially because you couldn't go back to the hostel during the day. There was nowhere to catch up on sleep, spent that whole next day in a café with that one South African guy. He was funny. Learned. We had quite a few things to talk about, but the time at the club was wacked. You wouldn't think Würzburg would be unhinged, but that club was completely crazy. People openly having sex on the dance floor. All kinds of sex. Whatever permutation or combination you can think of. The people nearby were their audience. Lots of people were into that so it had a domino effect. It was something to behold. That's how I know I'm still messed up because nothing there worked for me. I couldn't get my mind off you and Elke and whatever fucked up shit Anna did to make it easy for you to turn on me. Did you know? And your sister, her too. You must've had something to do with that. I couldn't stop thinking about it and wasn't interested in anything going on in that club. She had to make fun of me, what choice did she have? Couldn't be anything wrong with her, she had to make that painfully clear. Y'all don't do well with limp dicks.

Spent a lot of money, and it seemed okay because it was in the name of making up for what happened back there. Paid for the hostel every night, bought drinks and stuff for those South Africans, and paid the entrance fee. None of that was cheap. Burned through the money from the train ticket, that happened right away. Didn't mention that, I guess. I sold it. Make sure to tell your crazy sister that. Makes us even for the shirt. Gone through a lot of what I meant to give you too. None of you wanted anything to do with that money. Didn't you care what I had to go through to get it?

Thought I was going to Frankfurt from Würzburg, that was the plan. It's a straight shot so I figured it'd be easy to get on the road and find a ride, but the kids who stopped, they were kind of an interesting bunch, attending gymnasium in some place called Mosbach, which I didn't know anything about. They convinced me to ride with them to Heilbronn. It was a Saturday and they thought I'd want to be somewhere I could get something to eat and have some fun. If you're from Mosbach, you think Heilbronn is fun, but let me tell you something, it's not.

At the guest house, I met this woman who was with her brother and parents. The four of them were about to go on a hike and they invited me to come along. The father was something of a scholar. Not formal, with the university or anything, but a sincere interest in the natural world. He studied horticulture and geology and talked about the plants in the area. It's the dead of winter but he says the plant life is still active. While everything else is hibernating, some plants are bursting with activity. And the rocks, don't get that guy started on the rocks, he talked about them and the stories they'd tell if only you knew how to read them.

This is happening on a hike in the freezing cold. These people, man, they were hardy, they had their habits, and nothing was going to convince them to stop. They took hikes in the freezing cold and went digging through the snow and ice to look at the plants and the rocks. It was some crazy shit. They were nice though, bought me dinner, and I was happy to have someone to talk to.

Next morning, we had breakfast. I found out that the daughter, this woman named Hazel, she was driving back home that day to some hamlet called Sankt Leon-Rot. Never heard of it. Took me forever to find it on the map. Only a few thousand people, but it's only about twenty minutes outside Heidelberg and Hazel works up there. She's a graduate student working part time and said that if I stayed in her town Sunday night, Monday morning she'd be happy to drive me up there.

She was up for it, but I was still kind of messed up, so my heart wasn't in it. What should I have done? If I put the tiniest bit of effort in, I could avoid paying for a guest house. She'd put me up at her place, and that would save me 30 DM, not to mention feeding me. True enough, Hazel was not the most beautiful woman I'd ever seen, and it would have gone differently if she'd been more attractive, but where room and board was on the line, beggars can't be choosers. Still, the plumbing didn't seem to be up for it and even with a few beers at the guest house, I couldn't get the motivation. She was doing her best though, you got to hand it to her. Whatever I was into, she worked at turning the conversation that way, the way they do, to build up your ego and stuff so they can get you to do what they want. Gotta hand it to her, if it hadn't been for you and your sister, I'm sure I'd've been into it. Couldn't do it though.

Far too nice in the end. Despite her disappointment, she stuck to her word and picked me up at the guest house to drive me up to Heidelberg. I bought breakfast and paid for the room, leaving me with almost 200 DM to get to London and I still need to go through Frankfurt to set up the ticket. There's no margin of error at this point and I'm thinking I better make sure my bets are hedged. It's too much of a luxury to be messed up in the head, need to get down to business, focus on making sure things go the right way.

She saw my book and said she thought it looked valuable. I asked her if she thought I could sell it and make some money. Turns out, she worked in a bookstore. We drove up that way and she told me that if I came with her, I could sell it and get something else to read. They had a pretty good English section there.

At the bookstore, she introduced me to her friend Dr. Baumann. That's how she introduced her. She looked like the kind of woman who had a lot of ideas about what to do on a Saturday. She was in her last week of work there because she'd signed some outrageous contract with some big publishing company. Was a student and then a teacher, but now she's leaving academia to write this book on pleasure and the inner dialectic of the sexual imaginary or whatever blah blah blah. She could've been a genius, or talking lots of crap, can't say, but she sure had a lot of people fooled. Hazel thought she was some kind of world historical superstar. The publisher gave her a reasonable advance considering the state of publishing these days. Someone must have thought she was onto something.

But you know, it was kind of dicey. Again, I'm not saying she wasn't brilliant, I'm saying that it's pretty convenient that there's this sexy, attractive woman wearing provocative clothes and talking about pleasure and where it comes from and how it gets to where it's going. She had a whole big spiel that she gave when we were introduced, and I was convinced right away. Whatever you're selling, honey, I'll take one. Because why not? I'm not evaluating the arguments, I'm hearing this sexy babe talk about sex and pleasure, what's not to like? Hell yes, I'll buy the book, make sure there's a picture of you on the back cover, where you've got something in your mouth, the temple tip of your glasses or something. Intellectual but provocative. Brain porn.

Now, she was quitting the bookstore, but as long as she was there she could make one more deal. I showed her the Kafka and she tried to hide any reaction. I suspected the book was better than I realized. It wasn't just that it was high quality, there might've been more to it, something about the illustrator. There were these drawings throughout, associated with each of the stories. She looked closely at them and thumbed to the front of the book where there was a big chart with a list of the different ones.

She told me she'd give me 100 DM and didn't bat an eye when I asked if she'd throw in one of the books from their English section. In fact, she said I could take any one of them as far as she was concerned. That made it clear that the book was worth a helluva lot more than 100 DM, but why push it? I decided to take their copy of *War and Peace*. Honestly, I didn't want to read it that badly, but I didn't know how long it would take me to get home at that point and I didn't want to keep scrounging around for something to read.

When I put the book on the counter, it was almost as if she was reconsidering. She picked it up and flipped through the pages wistfully. It was not a nice edition, there was nothing special about it: an English translation, cheap paperback, pocket style edition, and thick, seriously thick, over 1500 pages. The cheapness of the glue made you wonder whether it would survive another reading, but she looked at it as if it was the most precious thing in the world, turned it over and ran her hands up and down the cover, smiled while flipping the pages.

"Is there something special about this?" I asked her, mostly because I was wondering what was holding her up. The question broke the spell or whatever it was, and she put the book down and got my money. Your money, I guess. Or your sister's.

"Nope," she said, as though it was a big misunderstanding.

At the youth hostel, I put my rucksack in their storage area and found somewhere warm to sit to see what the fuss was about. Hazel suggested I stop back by around closing time to meet up for dinner. I didn't want to seem rude right then, so I said sure, and then headed out of the store, but it's a longer walk than I expected, and I didn't want to pay for a cab or figure out the buses. Since I picked up a can of chew and had bread and cheese, there's nothing to force me back out again. Who is she to me? Besides, she knows she isn't going to get what she wants, nobody will, I'm not made for it right now.

Bye Eve. In the morning you'll be gone. I swear.

8.8.3.X.19.87.1.31 [ref(..12-31)]

Getting off at Knightsbridge and heading up toward the park. It's cold but there's a break in the rain. The smell and feel of the air suggest it'll come again soon.

(The four-zone pass was a life saver. With the rain, it's the only reliable way to stay warm. Spending the day in the tube and bopping around town, had to be back at the terminal by 10 when it closed. They'd let you stay if you're already there, but they wouldn't let you in. It's cheap to stow a pack in the lockers during the day and peaceful at night. The guy who vacuums was a decent sort and cleared a space for us before he went on to do the rest. There was a Nigerian family for a few days, but they left yesterday. The flight to Lagos was one of the first in the morning, right after New York. They shared food, were pleasant to be around, and kept an eye on my stuff when I went to the bathroom.)

Pubs close at 3 and it's almost 2. There's a place tucked in on the other side of the street. Ducking in to grab a pint and some Shepard's Pie.

The pub is filled with gentlemanly types. They're dressed casually but look to be the sort that wouldn't ordinarily come here on a weekday. The suit and tie crowd from one of the banks or the offices at Harrods, and it gives the place a different vibe from other pubs, less working class, more upscale.

There's a chick alone in the back. The place is dark despite the lights above each table. She's writing in her notebook and there's an empty spot next to her. Grabbing the seat and setting the day pack down as a man steps

up and asks what it'll be. Ordering and then pulling out the thick book and
setting it on the table. She can't help but look over. Normal response.
Pulling out the notebook and setting it next to the book. He brings over the
lager and sets it down.

"Ta," and he nods slightly and heads off back to the bar. She looks up
without eye contact. Digging right back into the letter without paying any
attention.

—What was I telling her?

> Köln was boring. A big cathedral, okay great, yet another set
> of gargoyles, they're everywhere. Brussels was nice, they had
> these amazing waffles you could buy from street vendors.
> They were tasty. There isn't a lot to do there, but the
> atmosphere was good, and I was comfortable. Bruges is
> much better. There were more tourists, and the youth hostel
> was packed. It was a weird dormitory situation where the
> guys and girls shared the same big room.

Tearing out and crumpling up the piece of paper then setting it off to
the side.

—Not much point in it, it's theatre. It's as if nothing happened, trailing
off...

> The guy at the Dover youth hostel was awesome. An expat
> from Canada, he let me slide on the accommodation fee and
> fed me the standard meal for free. He knew I was on a strict
> budget and recognized the difference between a traveler and
> the other sort. He wanted to help. Frankly, he was scary, but
> thought I was one of the good ones and treated me well.
> Gave me a fiver on the way out and some helpful tips about
> how to get to London on the cheap.

He brings the Shephard's Pie and sets it down next to the book.

"Ta," but he heads off without making any gesture in response.

Tearing out and crumpling up the piece of paper then setting it off to
the side.

Putting down the pen and picking up the fork to dig into the pie. She
looks up again, makes sure to let me know she's noticing the book and the
writing, pauses with her pen wobbling back and forth, and takes a sip of her
drink.

"Are you reading that or is it for show?"

She sounds posh. Smiling at her, taking a sip of beer, don't want to
appear too anxious.

"For show. How's it working?" She's the jolly sort and thinks that's terribly funny, but that's the real show, these girly affectations coming out right in a row, she can't hide the glint in her eyes, easy to see she's a clever one.

"Impressive. He can read. In this day and age, that's saying something."

"Or at least he thinks it's impressive to show off that he can read."

She likes that and smiles again. She isn't chubby, too young for that, but one day. Dressed well, long skirt and blouse, she totally fits with the sort that come here. Wearing some kind of head covering, tres stylish. It's not easy to pull that off, but she's got it going on. The dirty blonde hair underneath peaks out. She's got it pulled tight yielding center stage to her face. Taking another forkful while she runs short and moves on to the obvious.

"Are you an American?"

"Yes ma'am, born and bred."

"A Yank?" she says as though she didn't hear the response. "Which city?"

"Chicago."

"Famous for ribs."

"Why do you say that?"

"There's a place on the other side of the park where they sell Chicago style ribs. I noticed it earlier today."

"Kansas City and Memphis, that's where they're famous for ribs, not Chicago. Pizza."

"Accuracy isn't what sells, it's the image, that's what they're going for. No one's heard of Kansas City or Memphis, but we know everything about Al Capone and Chicago."

—Elvis?

"Of course."

There's something of a tension in the way she acts. The words come out singsong and girly. There's nothing threatening in her tone, and she's always smiling and laughing alongside the rest, but there's a rhetoric underneath it, a private joke. She's struggling with the angles.

"Do you like this song?" she asks.

—Could be a test. Hadn't been listening to it and have to wait a minute. It's that creepy voyeur song by The Police. They've been playing it nonstop this week for some reason. It's not new, who knows why it's in heavy rotation?

"Not particularly. It's creepy. Not much to it. He doesn't have a big voice either. Some style, I guess. Not a fan."

"What do you listen to?" She's pleased with the answer.

"Unfortunately, I've been traveling with the same six cassettes this whole time. For nearly nine months. They're getting on my nerves. Lately, *Unforgettable Fire*. But not with the same enthusiasm."

She nods, takes a sip of her lager. It's a full pint.

(That's something. For some reason, the ladies drank half pints. Not sure why because they drank twice as many, but it's more ladylike to have the smaller glass in front of you. She didn't care, she's got a full pint and it's running low.)

Gulping down a big portion of the glass to keep up, then setting it down.

"Would you care for another?"

"Allow me," she says, gesturing over to the guy and pointing back and forth between us.

"Thank you, kindly."

"You like Irish bands though? U2?"

"Sure."

"The Pogues?"

"What little I know, they're pretty good."

"There's a new band, a new Irish band, they'll be playing over on Oxford Street tonight. You should go." She hands over a flyer with the information on it.

"Aine Quinn?"

"Awnya," she corrects.

"But it's spelled Aine."

"That's what happens when you bend Gaelic into English."

"Are you Irish then? You don't sound it."

"I am."

The man brings over two more pints and sets them down. She doesn't bother thanking him, knows the drill.

"What happened to your accent then?"

"They beat it out of me at school. A few more of these, and you'll hear it." Already flexing back into it. There's the definite sense she's dumbing it down, as if she's trying to be this easy-going, not too serious, girl who is interested in the lightest of things. Something's not right.

"Do you live in London then?"

"Down for the weekend. My friends are in that band, wanted to see the show."

"Why aren't you with them?"

"They don't have time. It was a mistake to come. They're off on a tour soon for their new record."

"What school? Is it a secret?"

"Not a secret. Somerville."

"Oxford? What are you studying?"

"Philosophy."

"See, that's my point. You are hiding it, aren't you? Don't want me to know you're looking down at me."

Her mouth tightens, she looks sideways.

"Who are you reading?"

"I'm not in school this year." She leans closer this way, moves over on her seat to make it seem that we're together at the same table.

"Why not?"

"I thought my friends would need help, but they don't. It was a waste of time."

"Hiding what school you go to, thinking your friends need you but they don't, and you waste a whole year. Is it a pattern?"

"Are you trying to make me out as an idiot?"

"Not my intention, I'm trying to find out why you're making yourself out to be one."

She shakes her head and takes another sip. She's rethinking her efforts and reevaluating her aims.

"I don't mean to be insulting and I may have totally misjudged you, but it's been my experience that smart women sometimes play dumb."

This piques her interest, and she comes back full force.

"Well, that's not my goal. No one wants to do that, but if you want to get anywhere in the world, you play along."

"It's the men forcing you, is it?"

She shrugs and takes another sip. Finishing up the Shepherd's Pie and shoving the plate off to the side before pulling the nearby glass closer.

"Have you read any Arendt in your studies?"

"No, not yet," she says in that way they have, as if to suggest it hasn't been worth her time yet and isn't because of a flaw in her education.

"Well, one thing she points out somewhere is that if you're choosing the lesser of two evils, you're still choosing evil."

"You think holding back is evil?"

"I do. Face the friction, make some trouble. If you choose to accept the role of a slave, then you live your entire life in the company of a slave."

"Being nice is accepting the role of a slave?"

"Pretending to be less savvy than you are, less insightful, less informed, yeah, that's slavery, accepting that over death is the lesser of two evils."

"Mastery amounts to being alone then. Shunned by men, personally and professionally, unemployed and unloved."

—She's laughing at me, I love this chick.

"Do you fake your orgasms then?"

"Pardon me?" She pretends to be shocked, but she's not and buries her face in her hands to hide the smile.

"Isn't it the same thing? Stroke somebody's ego at your expense. Now you'll get ahead, get what you want, because you're doing a good job making him feel good about himself."

She shakes her head, doesn't want to admit anything. The hint of a smile in her eyes betrays her.

"Social, sexual, professional, what's the difference?"

"Are you a student?" she asks.

"Yes, going to grad school next fall. In philosophy."

"Ah, I see. You think it's different now. You're different so it must be different. Not for the men who run the department and not for the men I meet socially. No man wants a woman who's too smart: not in their department, not in their kitchen, and not in their bed."

"As if they could figure that out. You're giving them too much credit."

It's getting close to three and there are people clearing out. The guy comes around to bring the tab, she takes it and pays both bills.

"You don't have to..." but she interrupts with a shake of her hand and passes a twenty to him before he heads off to get the change.

"You can't object after you've made such a show of how privileged... I mean, enlightened, you are."

"Fuck that. I don't care about any of that."

She looks down at her watch. Still a few more minutes before they close up and there is still some lager left in the glasses.

"They *never* fake it with you," she says, rolling her eyes.

"No, they do, but that's their problem. Does nothing for me one way or the other. They probably just want it to end."

She laughs full on out loud at that, looks away and covers her mouth despite not chewing anything.

—She's hiding her teeth for some reason. In any event, it's the first genuine, full-bellied laughter of this whole conversation.

"As long as you get yours, you don't care about her," she says once she's recovered and taken her hand away.

"I didn't say that. She could tell me she's done if that's what it is. It's better if she has fun too. My point is that it doesn't do anything for my ego. It isn't about that, and if she wants to put on a show for some reason, well that's fine by me."

"You realize we think you're all like this," her eyes widen, and her brows arch.

"We? Like what?"

"Open," she says raising and lowering her hand while gesturing. "Inappropriate pretend intimacy, that's the reputation Americans have. Yeah, whatever," she waves both her arms this time, back and forth as if she wants no part of it. "I just met you, but yeah, I'll tell you my thoughts about orgasms. Oh, and have a nice day," she laughs at her own joke. Laughing too, but not because the joke makes sense, it's because it's funny how much she's enjoying herself.

The man comes back and puts her change on the table. He doesn't bother to look around, picks up the dirty dish and moves off as if there were no people involved.

"You were the one who asked right away whether I was putting this big book out for show. None of this was without cues, was it? Did I shock you? Have I crossed the line?" Closing the notebook and sliding it back into the day pack, then picking up the book and sliding it in before zipping the bag closed and leaning it against the bench seat. She watches the movements with an odd interest.

"Do you want to have tea?" she asks.

"I've eaten. Or do you mean actual tea? I never know what Brits are asking when they ask if I want tea."

"Not British," she clenches firmly. "I meant actual tea, but if we go round the hotel, they'll bring whatever you like."

"Where are you staying?"

"Over by the Bond Street station."

Standing up and moving toward the doorway, she takes the lead and is visible from head to toe the entire way to the door.

(A provocatively female figure: meaning that the impression from her face and upper body was reinforced. The skirt was carefully selected, it created a uniform look emphasizing her curviness and making it harder to discern the discreet size of anything under it, but her flat belly was accented by the form-fitting blouse. She had a keen sense of her physical virtues and did whatever she could to display them accordingly. There was every sign of an hourglass, and the medium-sized heels were an excellent punctuation mark. Didn't matter how smart they were, they had to school themselves about themselves this way. Learned all the angles.)

It's raining and she takes out her umbrella to open it. Pulling out the blue poncho, but she laughs and paws at it with a gesture suggesting it needs to be put away immediately. She holds up the umbrella and stands closer, allowing both to fit underneath. Swinging an arm around her shoulder to draw closer when stepping out into the rain and backtracking up the street toward the Knightsbridge station. Without discussing it, it's clear that this is the driest way to Bond Street. Her shoulder is firm and fit.

—Healthy, describes every inch of her, and every aspect. She could be fine in ten years, and her smile, so what if it is fake sometimes, it's absolutely delightful.

"I'm Lita," she says while moving in lockstep under the umbrella and down the street.

"Stefan. Stephen."

"Which is it?" she says when drawing close to the first corner where the light says it's okay to cross. Hurrying along to catch the end of it. Look right, the words written on the street remind those entering the crosswalk.

"Stephen. I've been traveling through Germany. They called me Stefan there."

The tube stop is crowded with people seeking shelter. Passing into the tunnel past the carrel where you show your pass, then taking the escalator down. It's a small stop and only one line comes through. A short ride to Bond Street and she doesn't know her way around much.

"I don't think I'd be able to find it if we didn't take the tube."

"You haven't been walking?"

"I don't come down much, don't care for it."

Getting to the platform level and walking over to the other side to wait for the train.

"Where are you from originally?"

"Limerick. Or near there. My da works at the airport near Shannon."

"Did you grow up in a village? Or something bigger?"

"In County Clare, a village between Shannon and Limerick, my parents are still there." The entire sentence comes in a thick brogue.

"Only two pints and you sound like a proper Irish lass now."

"Then I better stick to *tea*," she says with her whole body, coming out excessively pleased with the emphasis.

The wind tunnel gusts, and the train pulls up coming to a stop with a loud screech. The doors open and a few people step out. Letting her get on first, telling her to "Mind the gap" and then chuckling for reasons that don't translate. Following her in and sliding onto the empty seat next to her and not far from the door. It's crowded, but not standing room only.

"We have to change at Green Park, then we can take the Jubilee to Bond Street."

"Thank you for explaining how to get back to my hotel," she says wrapping her arms around the arm on offer for that purpose. She's mighty chummy and gives it a squeeze. Something about the back and forth makes her comfortable. Raising an eyebrow, curious to know why, then looking sideways at her with a smirk. It's mutual.

—Not so bad, totally unexpected. Haven't thought about Eve or her sister. This doesn't count. Thinking about not thinking about someone doesn't count as thinking about them.

8.8.4.X.19.87.2.1 [ref(..1.31)]

Putting the book away when they make the first announcements for boarding. There is a woman standing at the desk and bothering the agents. It will cause a delay, but they look as though they're about done with her, had everything they could handle, and the boarding announcements are their way of getting rid of her.

— *"Never interrupt your enemy when he is making a mistake." Take that Bonaparte. Absent-mindedly the hand falls to the belt, touches and returns.*

[Been here too long. Wish I could've stayed longer. As long as it was, it needed to be longer. Not in minutes, or days. Longer. Just longer.]

The woman at the desk continues to talk to them as they board first class passengers. She doesn't seem frustrated but keeps trying to get their attention and they keep cold-shouldering her to do their jobs. There is repetition in it. She speaks up, the agent nods and moves on to something else, talks to the other one about something, makes an announcement or directs the passengers where to line up, then she speaks up again.

People are gathering, those who weren't waiting by the gate are now drifting closer and paying attention to the board signaling the status. It flips from 'On schedule boarding at...' to 'Now boarding'.

[It's about attention. The feminization of the world. It didn't matter, the worst fucking human in the world could be made tolerable if only he paid attention. That's how she valued everything. It's a currency to them. He interrupts me, he doesn't listen, he doesn't think about me. What was that? I didn't get enough attention. It goes back to daddy. That's what mattered, and if you fell short, it's always because she's a woman. You're ignoring my point of view because I'm a woman. You're not listening to me because I'm a woman. Convenient. The men were fucking boring gasbags, she rolled her eyes at him because he's full of shit or talking nonsense, but not her. She's got her feelings so if he wasn't listening it must be because she's a woman, not because she's talking nonsense, and nobody gives a damn. Bloody fucking hell, sit down and shut the fuck up.]

—Now, I get it. She's tormenting them so they'll let her on early. Okay, it seems to be working. They're taking her boarding pass and letting her through. See ladies, that's how you get attention. You act the idiot until they can't ignore you any longer. It's not because she's some kind of super model wannabe, those women don't care about that, do they? Dolly brain strikes again? No, it's because she's fucking annoying.

"Please wait until your row number is called."

The crowd around the desk becomes denser. The excitement grows, people are anxious to get on board because it brings them one step closer to their destination. It's progress and after sitting for so long, they are desperate for progress.

[I was fucking attentive, for whatever good it did me. Got to be some kind of psychoanalyst to figure out what the hell you're doing most of the time. Who knows why things work the way they do? Who knows where decisions and reactions come from? Especially when they happen fast. You can't work through it or talk it out, there's no time and no one focuses on every minute detail, it's chance. Everything that happened was fucking random, or necessarily bound to the subtle workings of the soul. Strange attractor. Or training. Way beneath awareness, that's the main point. You think you make up your mind when the decision comes to you and the reasons are clear, but by then you've long since figured it out, you already knew what you were going to do.]

The queue is getting longer, people line up before their row knowing that by the time they get to the front it will have been called.

—Moo.

[It's supposed to be an exit row. Gave me a good seat, I suppose. You've got to act sweet and make sure to use the word help as often as you can. Always always always use the woman agent if one's available. They're desperate to help you and don't know why. They didn't know why it's so much more important that this one got the seat he craved, and it didn't matter much whether that one did. If it became conscious, it'd be because this one was much nicer and always said please and thank you and appreciated the service whereas that one was rude and demanding. Such cowards, every one of them, and they didn't realize how much of this was going on, they didn't think critically about it, or if they did, they'd write it off as some stupid platitude they'd been force-fed their entire life. Never read it directly from the situation.]

From the side and inching forward, a business guy with a case in hand and dressed too uncomfortably for vacation travel.

"You headed home?" he asks.

—Who gave you permission to talk to me? What the fuck dude, face that way and take care of business, would you?

Nodding and giving a syrupy fake smile, then looking off anywhere but his general direction.

—How was Big Ben, dipshit? Did you ride on the top of a double-decker bus? Take a cab to see the jewels? Get some high tea? Go to the wax museum? Fucking morons. Tourists.

She takes the boarding pass and crosses something off on her paper attached to the clipboard, then hands it back.

"Thank you, enjoy your flight."

(It's important to note where the confidence waned and where it was deeply and clearly present. When she moved for me, okay, it wasn't for me exactly, but in her mind that was what was going on, right? She's dancing or giving me a look or something, crawling around later, those gestures and movements in that long skirt, tight in the right places. It's as if she's following a script and knows how to present herself, that's what we're talking about. When she did that, she's only an actor with her lines written for her. She knew what to do, what kind of reaction it'd get, everything was predictable. Confidence was the best way to describe it, but it's not right. She's at ease in a box, or at least it appeared that way, but then when she had to go off script, when she had to talk about something that wasn't standard or preset, then she lost that and became completely unsure of herself. Nothing but insecurity, and that's when it's fucking easy to hurt her feelings or say the wrong thing. Because she's totally on edge and couldn't rely on anything, that's when things were most dangerous.)

The chill and breeze of the gangway are blocked when stepping onto the aircraft. The most stressful moment, this is where hell can break loose if some unexpected event splits the seal and throws the tunnel back, leaving everyone on the cusp to plummet to the pavement.

She says something and gestures down the right-side aisle. It's too loud to hear. Turning in the direction she's pointing and smiling at her. People are moving slowly, there's someone struggling with a larger carry-on item that doesn't fit, and everyone waits.

[It's kind of a general sense, isn't it? I don't rely on lines. If I'm comfortable somewhere, what is the cause? Is it because it's familiar? My role there understood? Whose expectations drove that role and that understanding? Whose voice was in my head? She thought it's some man's voice driving her along. Saw his gaze and snapped to it, but long before she ever met you. Who was there for me then? It could be the way humans are, right? We're subject to some social overseer who wrote our lines for us, who pointed in the proper direction and told us what to do, but for them it's because they're women and he's a man. It's a man's voice, so fucking exhausting. Why was originality this hard to find? Special and lovely to find it in a tight skirt.)

The seat is on the right, the woman from the desk is already camped in the window seat, her long legs stretching across the wide floor.

—Fucking hell. Right fucking next to her and you know she's a goddamn talker. No eye contact, nothing, take the notebook and the book and shove the thing up there, then sit down and stay in your own little world.

"Marba Tanata sym poly crescent wrench?"

Nodding and settling into the aisle seat. There is plenty of leg room.

[No idea what the fuck she's talking about, but you could tell she's one of those fools who thought every man falls over every single word that came out of her mouth, and that's because she's a woman, but this time it's on the plus side, because they wanted to fuck her. She ain't having it, mind you, but that didn't mean she wouldn't take advantage of every bit of it she could get.]

She looks over but not so much for eye contact as to check the state. Is he listening? He must be. It's written on her face and composure that if she is speaking, he will be listening.

—Holy shit, she's still fucking talking. First class blah blah blah. Downgraded the ticket her friends bought her. Overbooked. Whatever. Fucking eh. Don't look over there. Peek down the aisle to see how much longer the stream of people is.

[If she needed to get up, she wouldn't have to bother me, she could easily get around, but what do you want to bet she'll figure out a million

different reasons to bug the crap out of me? It's because I'm a man. She's
targeting me because of my sex. Fuck that. Would you please hand me my
bag, I need something from it. Get your own damn bag, you don't see me
bothering the guy next to me for my stupid bullshit. It's because attention
was how she measured her success as a human. If I wasn't acting on her
behalf, she's a failure.]

   —Who wants to switch seats?

   "....Sweden...."

*She is animated now, appears to be telling some kind of story, but the
ambient sounds are loud, and anyone would have to lean close to catch the
meaning. There is no hope for those who refuse to come closer.*

   —No bore worse than a travel bore, eh Ralph? You'd think he'd've had
to be on a plane when he thought of that.

   (I'd miss that. The purity of the travelers. The way Bowles meant it.
This was where I was now, and this is where I'm going. I'm coming from
there, here is what I discovered. The bargains, the scandals, the best way to
get around, that's the kind of information you need. They weren't bragging,
they weren't trying to establish some identity to earn your respect. Not
tourists looking for an ego boost.)

   —Malmö. What the fuck is she talking about? Listen douche, I'm on a
plane to New York. What possible use is information about being pregnant
in Malmö going to have? Why do I give a crap about your friends and their
new house or whatever disease it is that you're talking about?

*Only a word here and there gets through the whooshing wind of the
cabin. Her gestures suggest she is telling a familiar tale, but what makes it
across the armrest is empty sounds with no sequence or continuity.*

   Opening the book and spreading it out on the lap. It registers with her,
but she continues to voice an occasional observation even if it's no longer
clear exactly who she's talking to.

   "I'm staying at their place until they sell it."

   (That singer was not as good a friend as she thought she was. They
might've grown up on the opposite side of the same country or were
neighbors at the same school for a while, I don't know, whatever she
thought was going on between them, it's fantasy. Is that because she's a
woman? Is her woman friend ignoring her after the show and moving on
with her big life because she's a woman? Whatever.)

   —Touched a nerve, I guess.

*She looks over. It's not right of him to be this way. He is supposed to
be listening, he is supposed to be making contact and establishing rapport.
She doesn't care about him, but those are the rules, and he should be
following them.*

   (They were friends once, but now she's focused. She had her goals. Lots
of people were that way, and they blocked out everything that didn't fit. It's

not necessarily because they're brutal bastards. Tunnel vision is a curse. It could be. She'd relax with her friends, might enjoy it, but couldn't. There's something buzzing in her ear, something under the surface and she couldn't help herself. Some friend who was useful one minute, wasn't anymore. If she wanted to come down for the weekend to catch the show, she'd put her up in the hotel, she'll get her in and let her backstage, but they weren't friends anymore, not truly.)

—She didn't have anything on her if you ask me. She was special, I thought. Can't sing and can't run up and down a stage in a short skirt, but she was still pretty damned awesome. Open and kind. Nothing I said was off-putting. An open mind. I'll bet she's good in school. You can tell, the way she turns things over, the way she considers the possibilities.

(It's sad when despite that, she didn't keep to the same form when other things came up. Why did she have to turn to those scripts? Did she think I liked that? Did she think anyone did? Or was it that she didn't know what else to do? It's as though they lose their minds when the rote learning failed, and desire had to find its own way through.)

—Those limits, that's who you are. When you run into them and you don't know what to do anymore, don't know what to say or how you're supposed to think about it, that's you, that's the real you.

Not ready to give up, she takes her purse onto her lap and pulls out the small compact and lipstick. She makes a show of applying more, molding it to the form of her rounding lips. She peers to the side, flips it closed, and tosses both back into the purse. No point without an audience.

(As a philosopher, she knew that. It's why she's so interested. Language games and how to do things with words, the Oxbridge boys, she's one of them. Literally. Not in spirit, but actually one. That's weird. She came to those limits in conversation, talking about Arendt or whoever. She had no anchor, epistemology wasn't social, not to her, that's a radical notion. A limit. What did she do? Calmly and incisively asked questions, wanted to know the angles, how everything fit together. She was taking it apart as if it was a jet engine. Awe-inspiring. You knew you were in the presence of someone truly special. And of course I'm the creep because she's working this out and I'm hard as a rock because it was the sexiest fucking thing I've ever seen, but that's distraction, this was real life, be serious. You don't take me seriously because I'm a woman. Always the same answer, no matter how brilliant. It couldn't be, why the fuck was this so tantalizing to you? No, it had to be some platitude. See it through, that's what I say. Use everything you got on every detail, figure it out.)

—How is that belittling? I swear I don't see it. She's this extraordinary being there before me, beautiful in many ways, why can't the pleasures of that cut across every level of my being? Why do I have to put everything into a different category or container? We're talking about intellectual subjects now, it's rude to get a hard on in the middle of it. Bass ackward.

She leans toward the aisle thinking that a whiff of her expensive scent will do the trick. For a moment, he is worried he's about to be attacked but then catches on to the cause behind it.

The flight attendant comes over and explains the duties of the exit row. She points at the lever on the door beneath the window and demonstrates the twisting and turning motion necessary to open it. She asks if there will be any issues in fulfilling these duties. She can't hear her, but nods in agreement anyway.

"Yes, ma'am," and she trots off satisfied, having fulfilled her regulatory obligation.

Supermodel keeps talking, something about the window door. Nodding and looking back down at the book.

The tone is uncertain, she gives off an awkward sense, not because the door is on her mind, but something else. Is he making her pay for something? He must be one of those who make them pay for his inadequacy. Look how poorly he is dressed.

(None of them, not a single one, no matter how smart they were, they didn't know what to do with that. It's off script, for everyone. No one had anything prearranged, and of course it's her fault, because that fit with the whole way scripting worked. It's her job. That's what the bluster and movement was about. Nothing she did was as effective as her questions. That's what's behind it. It's depressing. Crawling around, pretending to be the object of desire. What choice did she have? That's the script. If you think about it, they were completely off script. There was no way to set any of that to rigid form. No genre in common. They were each in their own little worlds. Who knows what the fuck they were doing? Lydia too. She had her thing and nothing else mattered, wasn't looking for any input, she had it covered. What else was there? There's no script, but she had one anyway. A nice Catholic girl, she said. Catholic girl. We don't know about such things. She never learned how to go off script, work things to her advantage.)

[Pfffft. My ass.]

—She thinks she ought to look like this supermodel wannabe. Inadequate according to that scale, and always trying to compensate. Dolly brain.

(But much more interesting, captivating, and beautiful. Why evaluate based on the visuals anyway? Yeah, they're teaching me that the supermodel was the hot one, I get it, but if you went on feeling, those girls had bony asses and bony hips and no tits. You might as well hook up with a little boy for Christ's sake. She had it though, so fierce, such a figure. The feeling of it. I wish I could've explained that to her. I wish there was an easy way to communicate the pleasures that come from feeling her close like that in the theatre and backstage, but there's no script, there's no easy way, and I was damaged too.)

—Her skin. The little bit of it I was permitted to touch in Seefeld. Less curvy but on the same spectrum.

She gives up and takes a stick of gum from her purse, unwraps it and folds the piece into her mouth before tossing the crumpled wrapper into the bottom of the bag.

She has a magazine next to her and unfolds it onto her lap, then flips slowly through the pages, gazing long at each one as though she has to memorize them for something later.

—She's got the picture.

Leaning back and trying to calm the nerves that taxiing always evokes.

—Leave me alone.

No one anywhere nearby is paying any attention to him.

(It wasn't her fault. Why then? Big talk. This chick never did anything like that, you could tell. Never in her life, ever ever ever. I'm not saying she was inexperienced, only that she's used to a multi-month buildup. One of those you had to work and work through friendship until you could get a kiss and some skin. Had one boyfriend in Clare that she left behind, and another at school. It's possible, or not, she could be totally devoted and one of those girls who think you can't mingle when it comes to that. Either you're serious and here to study or you're on a luxury cruise. As far as I know, that's exactly how Lydia was, and I caught her on the flip side.)

—Why then?

(And why clam up about it? There's a million things you could do to distract yourself, or jump start things. You didn't have to get weighed down by that one thing. You didn't have to let your neurotic focus ruin the whole day. Why then? Why stew over it? Why not look for the nooks and crannies? You could've brought up anything. Hey, tell me about the Blue and the Brown. It would've put her back on script. Better than that. You could seduce me with what turns you on, did you ever think of that?)

The least she can do is offer him a stick of gum. It's the civil thing to do regardless of whether he wants to pass the time in pleasant conversation.

"Steeplechase, the last of harby gallonka fasha?" she asks.

Half smiling and then closing the eyes as though dozing off.

(What I would have done. Not send it. What I should've. Was that going to be the moment that haunts me for the rest of my life? Was that going to stick to me? Is this how regrets begin? Adding up one after another and imposible to get rid of because they sit and seethe and become more and more a part of you until there's nothing left, nothing that isn't consumed by them. I clearly saw what the right thing to do was. How come it's obvious now and a few hours ago made no impression? Nothing else possible. Close down, shut off, don't let the sensations in.)

[Don't need that. Coupling's only required when you have no other options, and you can't get laid whenever you want. It favors the least desirable. Better to float free alone and pay attention. Once you know the ways of their distributed mind, you'll belong to yourself. So what if they think they own you.]

—Not even Eve... Find a Lita when you need a one.

(Limply wave aside her concerns, her terror, that there was something wrong with her, that her lack of experience, being a good Catholic girl, had anything to do with anything. She wasn't doing it right. What did that mean? Am I doing this right? They got porno on the mind and thought there's a standard to follow, but it didn't have anything to do with that. A limit. My limit, and I came upon it unprepared. It was screaming at me, trying to tell me what I am. 25 cm longer than her, head to foot. What else is there in lying side-by-side but head to foot? Add another 25 if you include the arms. You must include the arms because we're stretching and reaching out. Distances are calculated by reach in close quarters. Then there's another 15 if you include the delights, or a meagre 5 if something gets in the way, some boundary, some border you can't cross.)

—What a dumb ass. Fucking hell.

Epitaph: To realize that who we are is not ours to know, that what we think or feel is always a translation, that what we want is not what we wanted, nor perhaps what anyone wanted—to realize all this at every moment, to feel all this in every feeling—isn't this to be foreign in one's own soul, exiled in one's own sensations?

—Fernando Pessoa, *The Book of Disquiet*

Duendecitos by Francisco Goya, 1799

Credits

The song lyrics listed below have been partially redacted in the body of this work to protect their publishing rights. Corporate power 1, Art 0.

Rocky Raccoon. Songwriters: Paul McCartney / John Lennon. Sony/ATV Tunes LLC.

Tangled Up In Blue. Songwriters: Bob Dylan. Ram's Horn Music, Universal Tunes.

God Bless the Child. Songwriters: Billie Holiday / Arthur Herzog. Edward B Marks Music Company, Marks Edward B. Music Corp.

Have a Cigar. Songwriters: Roger Waters. BMG Rights Management.

Wish You Were Here. Songwriters: George Roger Waters. Roger Waters Music Overseas Ltd, Pink Floyd Music Publishers Ltd.

Outside the Wall. Songwriters: George Roger Waters. Roger Waters Music Overseas Ltd.

Mother. Songwriters: Roger Waters. BMG Rights Management.

The Trial. Songwriters: Bob Ezrin / Roger Waters. BMG Rights Management.

Nobody Home. Songwriters: Roger Waters. BMG Rights Management, Royalty Solutions Corp.

Hey You. Songwriters: Roger Waters. BMG Rights Management.

Eclipse. Songwriters: Howard Shore / James Shaw / Emily Haines. WB Music Corp., South Fifth Avenue Publ, Chrysalis Music Ltd, Roger Waters Music Overseas Ltd.

The Last Time I Saw Richard. Songwriters: Joni Mitchell. Crazy Crow Music.

The Killing Moon. Songwriters: Ian Stephen McCulloch / Leslie Thomas Pattinson / Peter Louis Vincent De Freitas / William Alfred Sergeant. Tratore, Warner Chappell Music, Inc

Once in a Lifetime. Songwriters: Brian Eno / David Byrne / Tina Weymouth / Jerry Harrison / Christopher Frantz. WB Music Corp., MCA Music Ltd., E.G. Music Ltd., Index Music Inc., Universal/MCA Music Ltd., Mr. Bolton's Music, Universal Music MGB Ltd., Status One Music, Index Music, Inc.

Houses in Motion. Songwriters: Brian Eno / Chris Frantz / David Byrne / Jerry Harrison / Tina Weymouth. Downtown Music Publishing, Universal Music Publishing Group, Warner Chappell Music, Inc.

Si Acaso Muero. Songwriters: Jose Monge.

Ricochet. Songwriters: David Bowie. Jones Music America.

Criminal World. Songwriters: Peter Douglas Godwin / Sean Michael Lyons / John Duncan Browne. Heathside Music Ltd.

Cat People (Putting Out Fire). Songwriters: David Bowie / Giorgio Moroder. USI B Music Publishing, USI A Music Publishing.

The Man Who Sold the World. Songwriters: David Bowie. Chrysalis Music Ltd., Tintoretto Music, Chrysalis Music Ltd, EMI Music Publishing Ltd, RZO Music Ltd.

5:01 A.M. (The Pros and Cons of Hitch Hiking). Songwriters: George Roger Waters. Roger Waters Music Overseas Ltd.

Heart of Glass. Songwriters: Chris Stein / Deborah Harry. BMG Rights Management, Freibank Musikverlags und vermarktungs GmbH, Sony/ATV Music Publishing LLC.

To Darling Nikki. Songwriters: Prince Rogers Nelson. Controversy Music.

The Beautiful Ones. Songwriters: Prince Rogers Nelson. Controversy Music.

Let's Go Crazy. Songwriters: Prince Rogers Nelson. Universal Music Publishing Group.

When Doves Cry. Songwriters: Prince Rogers Nelson. Universal Music Publishing Group.

Purple Rain. Songwriters: Prince Rogers Nelson. Controversy Music.

Let's Spend the Night Together. Songwriters: Mick Jagger / Keith Richards.

Ruby Tuesday. Songwriters: Keith Richards / Mick Jagger. ABKCO Music Inc.

This Much is True. Songwriters: Gary James Kemp. Warner Chappell Music, Inc.

Candyman. Songwriters: Steven Severin / Budgie / Sioux. Domino Publishing Co. Ltd., Dreamhouse Music.

The Sweetest Chill. Songwriters: Siouxsie / The Banshees. BMG Rights Management.

This Unrest. Songwriters: Susan Janet Ballion / Peter Edward Clarke / Steven John Bailey. Domino Publishing Co. Ltd.

Be Thou My Vision. Songwriters: Dallán Forgaill. Translated by Mary Elizabeth Byrne.

Every Move You Make. Songwriters: Gordon Sumner. Songs Of Universal Inc.

Absolute Beginners. Songwriters: David Bowie. Jones Music America.

A Different Corner. Songwriters: George Michael. Big Geoff Overseas Limited.

Like a Virgin. Songwriters: Tom Kelly / William E Steinberg. Sony/ATV Tunes LLC.

Radio Free Europe. Songwriters: Peter Lawrence Buck / Michael E. Mills / William Thomas Berry / John Michael Stipe. Night Garden Music.

More Than This. Songwriters: Bryan Ferry. BMG Rights Management

(UK) Limited.

Wake Me Up Before You Go-Go. Songwriters: George Michael. Wham Music Limited.

London Calling. Songwriters: Joe Strummer / Mick Jones / Paul Simonon / Topper Headon. BMG Rights Management, Universal Music Publishing Group.

Canary in a Coal Mine. Songwriters: Gordon Sumner. Universal Music Publishing Group.

El Mundo Es un Pañuelo. Songwriters: Camilo Mazo, Ivan Camilo Talero, Mauricio Osorio.

The Queen is Dead. Songwriters: Steven Patrick Morrissey. Artemis Muziekuitgeverij B.V., Marr Songs Ltd.

I Know It's Over. Songwriters: Johnny Marr / Steven Morrissey. Royalty Network, Universal Music Publishing Group, Warner Chappell Music, Inc.

There is a Light that Never Goes Out. Songwriters: Johnny Marr / Steven Morrissey. Integrity Music, Kobalt Music Publishing Ltd., Universal Music Publishing Group, Warner Chappell Music, Inc.

Cemetry Gates. Songwriters: Johnny Marr / Steven Morrissey. Universal Music Publishing Group, Warner Chappell Music, Inc.

To Turn You On. Songwriters: Bryan Ferry. Universal Music Publishing Group.

True to Life. Songwriters: Bryan Ferry.

The Space Between. Songwriters: Bryan Ferry. BMG Rights Management.

Avalon. Songwriters: Bryan Ferry. BMG Rights Management (UK) Limited.

While My Heart Is Still Beating. Songwriters: Bryan Ferry / Andrew Edwin Mackay. BMG Rights Management (UK) Limited, Universal Music MGB Ltd., Mackay Andy Songs Ltd.